Out of the Shadows

The Saga of Caroline York:
Her Days Among the Cayugas

A Work of Fiction

by

David J. Fogarty

ARPress
45 Dan Road Suite 5
Canton MA 02021

Hotline: 1(888) 821-0229
Fax: 1(508) 545-7580

Ordering Information:
Quantity sales. Special discounts are available on quantity purchases by corporations, associations, and others. For details, contact the publisher at the address above.

Printed in the United States of America.

ISBN-13:   Softcover   979-8-89389-150-8
            Hardcover   979-8-89389-161-4
            eBook   979-8-89389-149-2

Library of Congress Control Number: 2024914536

FOREWORD

For the purposes of this story the narrative represents extrapolations from Suzanne York's diary, a compilation of notes gathered with the cooperation of the leading characters of the story. Thus, Suzanne, enthralled by events on the frontier, committed her observations into text. Physically present during most engagements and encounters, she provides the single most universal source of the narrative Where she did not interview directly, she drew conclusions from third parties and hearsay. Keep in mind that this is a work of fiction and that, with few exceptions, the leading characters did not in reality exist.

Suzanne spent a major portion of her life on the frontier among the Cayugas and interviewed the Bear Chief at length during the course of her family's association with him and his family. She also interviewed Lt. Simmons from his prison cell. He agreed to speak with her after he became a witness for the prosecution in the trial of Captain Worthy.

She accompanied her mother on Caroline's ground-breaking activities at Albany and beyond. The story is a culmination of the events of Caroline's rise from obscurity and privation to a position of renowned stature in the community. It builds upon her preoccupation with the attainment of human justice, especially for the disenfranchised peoples whose paths she crossed in the Lake Country.

DEDICATION

B ack in the early 1960's I took Freshman English at Auburn Community College, in Auburn, NY. One of my instructors was Mr. Brunell, a learned man and stem task-master. Among his students' many assignments, he demanded a term paper of their own choosing. I thought mine a work of art, but when I received a 'C' I sat crushed. It was more a case of following instructions, he averred.

In the 1990's I again met Mr. Brunell, in this instance in Technical Writing at Cayuga Community College(formerly ACC), in reality an English class, I made certain to follow instructions and to write an appealing report as well. This time I received an 'A', something that Mr. Brunell rarely gave out.

Mr. Brunell subscribed to the rules of grammar implicitly and demanded the same of his students. In short, he demanded that the finished product make sense in grammatical, if not in literary terms. He may not have taught me how to write, but I knew that as I continued I would want to create a work worthy of his approval. Unfortunately for myself he passed away before I completed this novel. Nevertheless I dedicate this work to him, for I know that he is somewhere up there looking over my shoulder, frowning relentlessly on his legions of 'peons' here on earth.

AUTHOR'S NOTE

For a work of historical fiction, the question arises concerning authorship. Who, frankly, is the true author of the work? Shall it be myself, who painstakingly wrote and edited these pages over a lengthy period, or shall it be the characters in the work itself, set in the mid 18th century?

In the text are passing references to Suzanne York and her journal in which she penned accounts of her life on the frontier. She was physically present alongside the major player, her mother, during her rise from obscurity to celebrity. For purposes of story development, I have attempted to solve the question of authorship:

Suzanne wanted to memorialize her mother's ascension within the 18th century colonial New York community. It is a story of success over failure, of good over evil, a story of a prescient and determined woman who longed to open opportunities for those who may never be able to scratch out a better way of life on their own, given the tenor of the times.

Suzanne drew from sources from within the milieu in which she found herself. Principally she interviewed the major players with whom she and her mother commiserated. All contributed either directly or indirectly by word-of-mouth. After compiling all relevant findings, Suzanne secured the assistance of a publisher, most likely in Albany, who published her journal to coincide with her mother's 55th birthday in 1791, the year in which the family settled in what eventually evolved into Auburn, NY.

In keeping with the story's development, I gathered up Suzanne's accounts and turned them into a story of historical fiction: that which may have happened in another place at another time, a story which redirected the authentic narrative of the period, encompassing the work assigning heroes and villains throughout. With my guidance, the major players speak. I have put into final form that which they individually contributed to the life and times of Caroline York, the overall leading character of the novel.

D.J.F. 05-05-13

" . . . Brothers . . .

We must unite all our tribes into one band of brothers. In that
way we shall be able to keep our enemies from our land . . . And you.
Cayugas, whose habitation is the 'Dark Forest' and whose home is
everywhere, shall be the fourth nation, because of your superior cunning
in hunting. You five great and powerful nations must unite and have but
one common interest and no foe shall be able to disturb or molest you.
If we unite, the Great Spirit will smile upon us. Brothers, these are the
words of Hiawatha; let them sink deep into your hearts. Admit no other
nations and you will always be free, numerous and happy. Remember
these words. They are the last you will hear from Hiawatha."

S.C..Kimm:
The Iroquois: A History of the Six
Nations of New York(1900).
Press of St. Pierre W. Danforth,
Middleburgh, NY, pgs: 14-15

PART ONE
RUDE AWAKENINGS

CHAPTER ONE

When Strangers Meet
The War Chief of the Oscos.
Summer Rains.
An Angry Lord.
Forging Friendships.

Pffffffft!! The slender, reeded missile sliced silently through the early morning mist rising from the cool, clear stream. Arching ever-slightly, it crested, then bore down on its unsuspecting target with deadly accuracy. In an instant, the bottom-feeding wood duck emitted a muffled gasp and disappeared briefly below the surface of the water, only to rise up feet first, bobbing in the wake set off by its final, frantic attempt at flight.

The Bear Chief, sachem of the Osco village nearby, known by several appellations, yet to a chosen few as Sans Sourire—the one who does not smile—came forward to retrieve his quarry. Methodically he parted the camouflage of fern boughs surrounding him and stepped out into the radiant morning. Gliding effortlessly over the forest floor, he bent quickly, snatched up his inert prize, and, placing it in a pouch made of deer intestine, traced his footsteps back into the dense, verdant undergrowth from whence he issued. Pausing to press a wood grouse freshly taken into his pouch, he muttered indiscernibly and continued northward along a moccasin-worn footpath.

Approaching a meadow thick with tall grasses, the Bear Chief assumed a steady pace, undeterred by yearling deer gathering to graze. Knowingly beyond the reach of his arrow, they nonetheless cast a wary eye in his direction as they tested the wind for signs of danger. He bristled under the warmth of the sun on his uncovered shoulders. Before he reached home, the sun would bear down upon him unmercifully, this day in the middle of the 'Season of the Growing Corn'. Pausing, he covered his neck and shoulders with a cloth, knotting it under his chin, then resumed his gait. He looked for the familiar ash tree, a sign that he neared home, the ash tree upon which he carved the symbol of his clan, The Bear, in his youth. Finding it, he stopped long enough to trace the ageless etching with his index finger, knowing that two leagues separated him from his family on the shore of Lake Osco. Ever-conscious of his surroundings, he remained vigilant.

Ahead on the footpath, something luminescent caught his eye. The sun's piercing brightness danced from the shiny object, blinding him. His curiosity aroused, he halted and knelt, creeping furtively forward. Embedded in the folds of leafy grasses, he discerned not one, but two iridescent tiny spheres, so vivid that they seemed to beckon to him. Creeping still, he reached out tentatively to fasten upon two small stones, gleaming: the color of the sun itself. He half-expected to receive a solid burn, but found himself gingerly holding them. To his astonishment, they did not burn. They retained their luster. He dropped them and picked them up playfully, rolling them in the hollow of his hand, blowing upon them softly, finally dropping them into the pouch at his waist. Securing his catch about the waist, he rummaged through the bag at intervals to ensure himself that the two treasures remained undisturbed. Resuming his walk, he believed the brilliant stones a gift from the Lord of the Forest, a reward for his having cared for the land, the forest, and its creatures since becoming War Chief of the Oscos.

Walking with confidence, the Bear Chief took note that the stream he followed rose up from a valley cut through the low-lying hills many ages ago. Communing with Nature in this manner refreshed him. Narrow from where he stood at its inlet, the stream gradually flowed into a crystal blue lake of some six leagues in length. The lake ran north and south in a ribbon-like pattern and at its northern terminus rolled to a stop against a sandy beach bestrewn with fine white sand. A stream, serving as the lake's outlet, wound briskly to the north-west through richly-populated woodlands, a stronger and deeper version of its grass-choked southern counterpart or inlet.

This vibrant outlet he named Osco. Lush vegetation lined its banks, home to many species, many of which regularly graced his dinner table. At the height of the summer season the outlet became a river and inevitably overflowed its banks, the waters flooding lowlands. This outpouring of the outlet he attributed to the intercession of a vengeful Lord of the Forest, who longed to punish His subjects for waging war upon each other over many centuries. Moreover, the Lord left behind a permanent sign of his ire, the Bear Chief believed, for He carved Lake Osco in the shape of a sinuous serpent which became apparent when viewing the lake from a great height. It is the early People's lust for blood that brought the Lord to trace the serpent with His finger into the fertile soil that formed the lake bed. Once the lake bed filled with rainwater, the ominous form of the serpent rose and took shape. It remained manifest forever, a perpetual stain upon the People for having decimated entire villages over the years. Try as they may to redeem themselves with good deeds, the Lord of the Forest did not allow the People to forget their insidious past. Hence the serpentine lake with its slippery shores retained its sinuous form for all to see forever. The Lord wished to teach the People that Good and Evil are not strangers to each other—that out of one may spring the other. In the lore of the People, man is forever in a struggle with Nature to win the Lord's forgiveness. In thought and action he tries to lead a worthy life, his sole tool in placating a vengeful Lord, and he, the Bear Chief, had been chosen to model the good life for his People, lest great misfortune befall them. For the few occasions in which the Lord of the Forest rewarded good deeds, the satisfaction of having gained His good grace is worth the effort in attaining it, according to the lore of the People— the People of Osco— the People of the Swamp—the Cayuga. For the Bear Chief, the brilliant stones represented one of the few occasions in which the Lord of the Forest recognized the attainments of his subjects, the People, in an otherwise imperfect universe.

Cresting a small hill, the Bear Chief sprinted down its opposite flank to enter yet another verdant meadow on the final leg of his journey. The fortress-like palisades of his village rose up to greet him, their spires protruding boldly to rival the height of the surrounding forest oaks. Soon the gates of Osco would sweep open to welcome him and his day's catch. Colombe Blanche would roast his grouse and duck for their evening's supper, a ritual he looked forward to with great anticipation, in as much as supper represented that part of the day when all family members came together in a cohesive unit.

Osco itself rose from the forest floor, the creation of hardy laborers, well-adapted in the art of converting the wilderness into a village fit for habitation. With stone implements, they transformed lofty pines and maples into dwellings. Pitched rooftops prevented precipitation from dampening both the hearth and human spirit. The women of Osco made certain to keep the home fires perpetually burning, sheltering coals by day and breathing new life into them by night. In his lodge, this task fell to his adored wife, Colombe Blanche, the White Dove. At her call their two young sons, Raven and Little Bear bounded eagerly to her side to assist her with affairs of the hearth.

At Osco the lodges encircled the central or great campfire, an oval-shaped pit formed from smooth stones placed in concentric layers. He and his family inhabited the lodge closest to the great campfire, for he held an exalted position within the Confederation. Initially, laborers carried the stones from the banks of the Osco, the robust stream, flowing nearby. Its banks furnished not only the stones, but the sand with which to buttress the stones. From the waters fishermen pulled out perch, pike, trout, clams, oysters, and the occasional frog. Geese and duck frolicked in the deeper water and deer came down from the hills to drink. A self-sufficient community, Osco drew its sustenance from the surrounding river and woodlands, giving the Bear Chief a sense of fierce independence in this pristine and wild land.

Upon entering the village, the Bear Chief greeted several women laboring beside the campfire near his lodge. They carried water over the shoulder in casks made of woven rushes. With a ladle they transferred hot stones from the campfire to the water in the casks until the water heated sufficiently. Next, they carried the casks to the stream to pour over garments to be washed, drawing them tightly over the smooth stones. They pounded and kneaded the garments, scoured them with the hot water and rubbed unwanted particles out of them. Upon rinsing the garments in the cool, clear waters of the stream, they allowed them to dry in the warm sun on racks made of saplings.

Coming to a halt beside his lodge, the Bear Chief called boldly: "Venez mes enfants!"–Come my children!"

The sound of rushing footfalls, combined with children's laughter, emanated from his lodge. Two raven-haired young boys dashed into the bright afternoon to take up places at their father's side. Tugging gently at his buckskin leggings, they gazed imploringly upward into the stern countenance of the man who rarely smiled, who conversed little, yet one whose stamp bore the hopes and aspirations of his People. His sons gripping him tightly about the waist, the Bear Chief afforded them a thin, crisp smile, a gesture which brought joy to the cherubic faces, a prelude to an attempt to abscond with his catch, he well knew. Uncomfortable in the role of shielding the family's supper from preying hands, the Bear Chief jostled for position, shifting to left and right. Suddenly the boys bolted for the familiar wood pile, bent over in laughter. Confused, yet alarmed, the Bear Chief searched his pouch in vain, knowing implicitly that once again he fell victim to his sons' chicanery. Tauntingly the boys held out the grouse to him from a safe distance. A defeated Bear Chief complimented the boys for their guile, abiding by the rules of their self-serving game. Approaching them, he exuded confidence that his wood duck remained secure, strapped tightly to his girdle. He held it aloft to them, calling in defiance: "Have you forgotten something, my children?"

Their total victory aborted, the boys turned to consoling each other, after which they took turns scolding each other in mock derision for having failed to purloin their father's secreted catch. Abandoning these tactics, they playfully exchanged blows, yet when the blows grew menacing, the boys broke into antics: Little Bear imitated a wounded duck in retreat and Raven called out in his version of a duck in distress. Growing weary of these maneuvers, the boys broke out in laughter and ran back to their father. Hugging the Bear Chief, they attempted to fracture his stern countenance with their laughter. Maintaining his composure, the Bear Chief ceremoniously dropped his duck into Little Bear's outstretched hand, the customary ending for all such encounters. Turning briskly, he headed back toward his lodge.

"Never fear, father. I will give this one a good send-off," the boy called, scampering off with his prize. Raven followed in hot pursuit and the Bear Chief tossed him the grouse. Together the boys ran off to the stream to wash the catch, the final segment of an act played out with regularity.

From within her lodge Colombe Blanche anticipated the laughter and commotion of her two sons, knowing that their arrival at her table lay moments away. She glowed with pride whenever she conjured up memories of her sons. Stepping out into the brilliant sunshine, she paid them a fond greeting, accented by her broad smile. Bursting with enthusiasm, the boys bounded to their mother's side, thrusting their prizes to her breast, while showering her with hugs of affection. Presently the Bear Chief appeared. Colombe Blanche entwined her hand in his and together they stood apart from the boys, admiring them from a distance, while gazing into each other's eyes. With every summer season, Colombe Blanche and her husband made note of their sons' eagerness to partake of all the benefits which Nature held in reserve for them, in a sense reliving their own youth through the eyes of their children. The boys' vivacity, they believed, kept them youthful in mind and body, one of the incontrovertible benefits to raising children. They stood together savoring the moment, fixing it in their memory. Changing course, the boys scampered off to engage in a new adventure before supper commenced.

A full head below her husband in height, Colombe Blanche rested her head against the Bear Chief's chest: she, the supple willow to him: the mighty oak. She exuded a bubbling warmth which drew all to her, even the most irascible. On the surface she struck a bold contrast to her taciturn, yet noble mate. Silently the Bear Chief pressed the two golden orbs into her hand. She blushed scarlet, recognizing the gesture as a sign of her husband's true affection. Touching the stones to her ears, she smiled in appreciation, eliciting a terse, yet touching commentary from the man she loved:

"Your smile makes the stones shine ever-deeper."

Holding each other in firm embrace they dispelled all thoughts of supper, thinking only of each other. Joining hands, they departed the lodge and walked slowly side by side along the path leading away from the village toward the stream where the boys often frolicked. En route the fully-developed trees effectively blocked the sun's rays and cast dark shadows upon the luxuriant, verdant landscape at all hours of the day. Man and wife relished these stolen moments together, during which their conjoined physical and sensual presence conveyed that loving sentiment which mere words failed to communicate. Colombe Blanche broke the silence between them:

"Oh, to be young again," she murmured.

"In my eyes you are forever young. Do not forget."

"Ahh! You speak too late my husband, but I welcome the thought," she laughed lightly.

Squeezing her hand, he gazed at the heavens, and, in that instant the skies turned gray and the towering branches along the path creaked and swayed menacingly. He announced concern for the boys and leaving Colombe Blanche behind him, set out boldly over the path. Slowing, he allowed her to overtake him.

"So much for small surprises," she heard herself say, running to him.

Suddenly, squalls started up, blowing sheets of rain headlong, bringing visibility to a minimum. The gray skies turned darker. The warmth of the day turned to coolness. The once refreshing vapors grew harsh and combative. Standing fast, the Bear Chief and Colombe Blanche called out for the boys to no avail. Mounting an eroding bank of the swollen Osco, they strained to peer through the turbulence of driving rain and wind. At length they concluded that the boys abandoned the region in order to seek shelter further ahead. The familiar path, cleansed of all human traces, bore no signs of the boys' footfalls. The pair struggled past fallen trees, the carcasses of which began to accumulate around them.

"The cave! They fled to the cave!" Colombe Blanche shouted, thoroughly frightened.

Quickening the pace, the pair joined hands in order to gain stability before the driving rain. Forging ahead, they straddled obstacles, finally abandoning the path altogether. They sought the large earthen mound or cave which the boys regularly visited during the summer season. Structurally it provided a suitable refuge for those seeking shelter, Colombe Blanche recalled. It lay hidden from view a few lengths beyond the bank of the Osco, standing in a grove of trees and surrounded by tall bushes. Open to the elements, the mouth of the cave stood agape: a source of temptation for the novel explorer. The region itself lay populated by mounds, the Bear Chief recalled, approaching the cave. He remembered that further downstream giant mounds rose like sentinels in a region where, according to legend, an ancient race lived. Stories from his youth told of people living within the mounds. Certainly they once lived *upon* the mounds, he concluded, for they constructed them into cone-shaped towers or abutments from which to observe distant points of interest. When very young, his father brought him to the mounds where he marveled at the symmetry of the structures and imagined himself carrying on intercourse with the ancient people. From that point on, he developed a strong attraction for the region in which he lived. This cave before him, carved into the swollen earth by a mysterious hand, bore an uncanny relationship to the mounds of his youth, most of which he committed to memory, when he dreamed of them far into the night, probing their mysteries from deep within the warm confines of his bearskin blanket.

Colombe Blanche urged him and he shouted into the mouth of the cave, his deep voice leaving no doubt that someone of stature stood at the entrance. There followed an eerie silence, after which he released yet another report: "Raven! Little Bear! It is all right, children. We are here," Colombe Blanche called plaintively.

Treading cautiously, the Bear Chief stepped through a stand of saplings sprouting rakishly about the cave's mouth. He startled a fawn seeking shelter from the storm. It withdrew deeper into the grotto, rather than dash out into the blinding rain. The Bear Chief noted the path taken by the fawn and summoned Colombe Blanche. Side by side they set forth, calling the boys' names, while conjuring up macabre images of the cave's interior. Expecting the unexpected, they crept through tight passages, the dampness and musty odors invading the senses. Groping slippery walls and side-stepping obstacles, they plodded ahead where little light befriended them. More than once immutable objects refused to yield to the touch. The way proved harrowing and, receiving no response to appeals, the pair believed themselves at the mercy of forces more durable than they were able to muster. Forging ahead of her husband, Colombe Blanche stopped abruptly and gave a start:

"Ah, there you are, my children." She gave an audible sigh of relief.

"Est-ce que tout va bien, mes enfants?"–Is everything all right, my children?" the Bear Chief called, coming forward. He came up quickly before his sons, finding them huddled in a corner of the cave, sobbing, small hands covering frightened faces. Swiftly, he swung the boys around to face him, waiting until they captured his eyes boring in on them. They appeared at once elated and frightened. A sobbing Raven peered out from between his fingers:

"I am so sorry, father." Beside him Little Bear sat motionless, eyes fixed upon his father.

The Bear Chief thumped Raven vigorously about the shoulders and the boy ceased sobbing. (Later, under Colombe Blanche's counsel, he understood the manner of his son's vulnerability and his own willingness to demonstrate aggressively). Colombe Blanche came to stand between her husband and the boys, at which point the Bear Chief swept Raven up to his chest and rocked him gently from side to side, an exercise he resurrected since the days of the boys' infancy. Raven calmed appreciably and his father spoke soothing words to him. Colombe Blanche reached for Little Bear's hand and, together with her husband, gently rocked the boys back and forth between them. At length Colombe Blanche gave a sign to her husband who guided his sons to the orifice of the cave from whence, bridging the threshold, the beleaguered party dashed out into the incessant and driving maelstrom.

Everyone breathed more easily, now that the dank restrictions of the cave lay well at their backs. The change of venue allowed Colombe Blanche a moment to recall her innermost thoughts during the rescue. She shivered, not so much from the coldness, but from the fear of losing her sons. Now challenging the elements, the Bear Chief stooped to swing the boys up to his bosom. In a single maneuver he secreted Raven and Little Bear beneath the ample folds of his buckskin trail jacket. The taut hide of the jacket repelled water and its soft lining provided warmth, two qualities essential to a garment destined for wear out-of-doors. The boys calmed down, secure within their father's mantle of protection, emitting little squeals of contentment, confident of reaching home soon. Infrequently they peered out from their haven of safety to test the surroundings, ever-mindful of their father's stern glance.

Bent upon reaching Osco, the Bear Chief advanced his pace. He struck out parallel to the stream, formerly a thin, placid ribbon, now a torrent of rushing waters. He took note of the waterway's new depth and the strength of the swift-flowing waters. Swollen to the extreme, the Osco sought its own pathway, pushing lesser bodies aside, and carving small islands out of once sturdy banks. The little party passed several such islands of various sizes, large and small. One bloc in particular impressed the Bear Chief because of its great size, a mass of earth torn from its bank and deposited with upheaval in the middle of the waterway. It brought with it branches and small trees, even sizable rocks, which wedged themselves firmly against it.

The little party paused in order to contemplate the practicality of taking temporary shelter in the face of the driving rains. Huddled together for warmth, the Bear Chief and Colombe Blanche gazed upon the dark skies for signs of an abatement of conditions. Disappointed, they pressed on, determined to reach home before complete darkness overtook them. Shaking from the cold, they trod on, heads bent into the wind and blinding rain. Husband and wife confessed concerns about the ultimate safety of the boys and themselves, indeed their family structure as they had come to love and cherish it. To this extent the Bear Chief kept watch for the slightest vestige of relief along the way.

Again he called a halt. His eyes rarely departing from the raging waterway, he came to a full stop in mid-stride. There, in the midst of the tempestuous stream, hemmed in by floating blocs of earth, a figure, a form driven by its own strength, rose into view. Amorphous for the most part, the form clung to one of the large rocks stemming from the giant bloc he spied moments earlier. Parts of the form moved, indeed, waved appendages toward him and uttered strange guttural sounds. Twisting and writhing on the bloc, the form began to assume the outline of a human, a man waving arms frantically at him, a man staring wide-eyed through the thick mist which hung suspended before them. Leaving his family on the muddy shore, the Bear Chief struck out over the bank in search of stable footing from which he may better observe the pitiful creature that met his gaze. In the next instant a voice called to him in French, a voice forlorn, yet pleading:

"Attention! Aidez-moi! Suivez!"–Hello! Help me! Come on!"

The Bear Chief responded: Stripping off his jacket he gave it to Colombe Blanche, instructing her to wrap the boys in it. Beneath he wore a deerskin tunic, tight-against the chest, water-resistant. He must save this man, he shouted to Colombe Blanche, plunging into the chilling waters. Strong strokes propelled him toward the victim, who tore apart from the rock to which he precariously clung, and groped the waters in an attempt to reach his rescuer. Pausing, the man divested himself of his tunic, whereupon he slipped beneath the waters. Emerging, he fastened upon a stout log in his path. It rolled beneath his weight, however, leaving the chilling waters to swallow him whole.

Once again the man emerged from beneath the surface. Splashing through the waters, he came upon what the Bear Chief determined to be an underwater shoal. He attempted to mount it and lunge himself forward to the more shallow waters near the shore. More than once he failed to secure solid footing, slipping from the shoal into the waters, growing increasingly more weak and desperate. The Bear

Chief meanwhile, well-possessed of the man's plight, reversed course, retreating to the shore, from which he launched a plan:

He called to Colombe Blanche to secure a strong sapling, one from among the many which succumbed to the fierce winds. Diving into the waters, he relied on his keen sense of touch to ferret out the man. He found him floundering on the shoal, which showed signs of washing away. Quickly he unfastened the rawhide belt about his waist and brought out the fishing line he always carried deep within the pouch at his waist. Treading the waters, he tied the two together, making of the whole a line of considerable length. Breathing deeply, he dived beneath the surface where he fashioned a noose in the rawhide belt, the better to fling over the man's shoulders, a maneuver which he employed with ample dexterity upon surfacing. The man, desperate, yet willing, drew the noose around his waist and allowed the Bear Chief to pull him to shore with a series of well-executed back-strokes. The unrelenting rains devastated the shore, however, sending a great portion of it into the churning waters, leaving behind thick mud, a viscous, intractable layer of saturated earth that repelled solid footing. With a second calamity looming before his eyes, the Bear Chief summoned another plan:

Following her husband's instructions, Colombe Blanche gathered the boys about her. The trio, always eager to meet a challenge, set off to gather stones of medium size—a great many stones. They came from an exposed hillside, having been torn apart by high winds and rising waters. Many stones collected freely at the base of the hillside, a development which did not escape the keen eyes of the Bear Chief during his flight through the devastated region. He formed a detail. Heading it, he, along with Colombe Blanche and his sons, carried stones of various shapes and sizes to the muddy river bank. They constructed a bridge of sorts, placing the stones tightly together in the mud, spreading them into a walkway, one beside the other, each stone edging yet closer to the stricken victim. At length the Bear Chief beckoned the man to fall upon the stones, whereupon he pulled him over the sleek surfaces by means of the rescue line which the man secured about his shoulders. Raven and Little Bear came to their father's aid, for the mud had reached the level of the man's thighs. The three, in applying the sum of their combined strength, slowly pulled the man free from the certain death trap into which he had descended. The man ended by sliding over the stones, coming to rest on them face-up, trimmed with mud, shaken and unrecognizable, yet alive.

Colombe Blanche knelt beside the prostrate form. She rejoiced when finding a heart-beat. Backing away, she yielded to her husband who inspected the man's limbs, mouth, and eyes. Save for the man's general appearance, he appeared in good form, the Bear Chief noted to his family. Regarding the man with interest, the Bear Chief spoke:

"You indeed enjoy the Good Life. You have no injuries."

The mud-caked victim solemnly responded: "Thank you, Fearless One."

The little party gasped, for only close allies of the Bear Chief knew him by this name. The Bear Chief stooped to inspect the man more closely, who sat up to accommodate him.

"My old friend, Chien Aboyant," the Bear Chief exclaimed. He allowed himself to partake of a bit of humor:

"Good afternoon, Monsieur. What brings you out on such a fine afternoon?"

"I wanted to catch my dinner in the stream, Fearless One. By the way, I lost my fishing pole."

The Bear Chief tossed him the fishing line he employed in his friend's rescue: "Is this satisfactory, Monsieur? Are you all right, my old friend? This is not the place for you. The Lord of the Forest is angry this day, but has chosen to spare us his wrath."

"He may have chosen a better way to show His kindness," the little man quipped, sarcastically.

The object of the Bear Chief's concern, Le Chien Aboyant, bore the label of The Barking Dog. Although he came into the world bearing the appellation Great Bear, only a few knew him by that name. The name of Barking Dog took precedence among his fellow villagers, stemming from an observation which Colombe Blanche made one afternoon years earlier. Apparently a bear wandered into the village in search of food. Chien Aboyant confronted the beast. Setting up a commotion, he terrified the animal, causing it to abandon all attempts at securing a ready meal. According to Colombe Blanche, Aboyant approached the animal, barking wildly, much in the manner of a wolf. He gesticulated wildly. Intermittently he made bird-like calls and rolled his head forcefully from side to side. His bizarre conduct succeeded in driving the bear from the village, never to return, whereupon the little man danced a two-step at the beast's departure and broke out in peals of laughter. Colombe Blanche sought to give a single label to Aboyant's conduct. Discarding several choices, she settled upon 'Chien Aboyant' and communicated her choice to her husband. In the days which followed, the little man invoked parts of his repertoire at unannounced intervals, much to the entertainment of those around him. It became a part of his 'uniform,' she believed, and she and others looked forward to his ostentatiousness whenever he appeared in crowded places. He did not disappoint them.

In preference to walking heel-to-toe, the man himself tended to bounce along, occasionally swinging his arms from side to side across the mid-section, his neck bobbing to and fro. To the uninitiated he appeared bewildering, an unknown entity, someone to be feared and subsequently avoided. 'Small wonder that the bear fled,' Colombe Blanche recalled. Suspicions of his mental state traveled through the village, but no one judged him dangerous and children grew accustomed to his erratic posturing and eventually such black rumors dissipated, leaving Aboyant unencumbered and free to carry on with his gyrations.

Short and lean, but with a massive head and chest, Aboyant sported a bulbous nose which turned red when he became excited. He maintained a broad, some say, voluptuous smile, and shoulder-length hair, shaggy, yet clean. He piled his hair into a bun on top of his head, fastening it together with a strand of sinew. Fond of wearing headpieces or hats, he often made several changes in them during the course of any day.

* * *

Aboyant rose tentatively. Supporting his diminutive form against a tree, he extracted a crumpled piece of cloth-material from the girdle at his waist. He passed his hands over the surface in an effort to smooth it before pulling up the sides to reveal its true form: a hat. A rather tall head piece, he shook it and gently shaped the crown before placing it on his head. Drawing the hat over his temples, he wedged it against his ears and smiled at his audience who uttered not a word, lest they disturb the chain of events which the little man brought to bear on them. He followed with a quick two-step, keeping within the bounds of a circle which he inscribed on the soggy river bank. While he danced, Colombe Blanche confided to her husband that Aboyant reminded her of a bag of mixed nuts, for pulling them from a sack, you find a different one with each attempt. Despite his eccentricities, Aboyant stood as one of the Bear Chief's staunchest allies in the village. He performed the roles of confidante, spy, and guardian of the boys with such ease that husband and wife tolerated his infrequent displays and outbursts without rancor.

Aboyant terminated dancing in order to attend to matters of grooming. He plucked extraneous matter from his hair and wiped away seemingly layers of drying mud. All the while his temperament diminished from frivolity to that of stoic seriousness. His rapt audience prepared themselves by exchanging glances with each other, whereupon Aboyant delivered a series of orations which simultaneously startled them and piqued their curiosity:

"The river has claimed two victims, Fearless One." Without waiting for a reaction, he started off along the shore. "There are two humans caught in the river. They are holding fast to floating islands."

"They are of les peaus blancs,—white skins—of whom we have heard stories, Fearless One."

Stepping lively along the river bank, Aboyant gestured out upon the waters, a mere shade their former ferocity.

He shouted to the Bear Chief to follow and ran to secure a vantage point from which to support his claim. Presently he halted abruptly, turned to the river and pointed: "Follow my arm and look closely, Fearless One."

The Bear Chief peered into the river. With the sun having chased away the gray clouds of the morning, he discerned a man and a woman clinging precariously to a log, which sat upon a bloc of earth ripped from its foundations and tossed into the waters. A boulder rendered the bloc immobile, hence preventing it from moving into the current, itself a factor of considerable force. Clearly the lives of the man and woman lay in peril and once again the Bear Chief struggled to devise an effective plan of rescue.

He judged that sheer fright, coupled with stubborn resolve, combined to keep the couple alive in a rapidly-deteriorating situation. He knew that he must intervene in this, another test thrust upon him by the Being who held tight reins over all of His children. He questioned merely the quick succession of incidents in which he was called upon to serve. In his mind's eye the Supreme Master trusted in his prowess to assist the less fortunate and he intended to become worthy of His trust. He began to ponder a decision, choosing from several which raced through his thoughts on that foreboding day.

The desperate victims clung fast to the pitching log, which lay wedged against the boulder. The man, upon glimpsing the Bear Chief, tried without success to reach shore under his own power. The woman, young and distraught, called out to him in French, whereupon the Bear Chief put a plan into motion: Turning to Aboyant, he instructed him to select a tall and supple sapling from among the many which fell during the storm. To his relief, Aboyant produced two small knives from his girdle, and both men began stripping away excess branches. Soon, only a naked spar remained, some ten meters in length, capable of supporting great weight. The men cradled the heavy piece between them, half-dragging it to the river bank where, standing it on end, they toppled it into the river, taking care to secure one end hard against the bank with their feet. A wall of white water leaped upward dousing both victims who, overcome with elation, burst forth in joyous acclamation.

The Bear Chief and Aboyant mounted the sapling fore and aft. Lying face down, they set their arms to paddling the spar forward, much in the manner of canoeists. Intercepting the strong current, they reached the stricken man without incident. Entering the waters, the Bear Chief instructed the man in French to latch onto the spar. Behind him the young woman translated for the man, who, at that point, became infused with the will to live. Sitting astride the spar, he allowed Aboyant to paddle him to the safety of the shallows. Meanwhile, the Bear Chief swam to the young woman's side. They struck up a brief conversation which ended with the Bear Chief placing her on her back, grasping her apparel and swimming steadfastly back to shore, cargo in tow. The man, upon reaching shore, collapsed and lay motionless. Soon the young woman joined him. She sat on the bank, stiffened and shaking, while Colombe Blanche covered her with some of her garments.

At a word from their mother, Raven and Little Bear scampered off to find comestibles for the stricken pair. In their absence Aboyant carried water to them, his hat a suitable receptacle. Weakened, the man and young woman sat still, inured to their surroundings, save for swallowing handfuls of berries and imbibing water lightly. The members of the little party made no effort to disturb them, although the daylight grew dimmer under the gray skies of the early afternoon. The man began to cough incessantly, his flesh a pale blue. Colombe

Blanche urged her husband to act quickly: He moved behind the man, and instructing Aboyant to hold him upright, began to compress the man's chest, coming down firmly across the ribs with fists clenched. The man coughed all the more, whereas the Bear Chief pulled him to his feet, doubled him over at the waist, and approaching him from the rear, compressed the victim's chest in a series of rapid strokes. He released him to Aboyant who sat him on the bank and proceeded to buffet him about the cheeks and jaw with open hand. The man's flesh took on a rosy hue and he struggled to rise. Standing, the Bear Chief instructed him to breathe deeply and to cough and heave in a single motion. This the victim did without fail, once the young woman rendered her translation from the original French.

The Bear Chief, betraying no emotions, walked his charge back and forth over the bank. At intervals he administered well-placed blows with open hand across the shoulders, and through translation, ordered the man to walk in short steps, lifting the knees near the chest. The round of applications proved successful, for the man exhibited renewed strength. However, both he and the young woman shivered from exposure to the cold waters, a condition which set the little party to collecting firewood. They found it in the form of dried, bleached shreds of wood, long lying dormant in rushes apart from the beaten path. Light and porous, the remnants burned easily, the warmth of the fire most pleasing to the man and his companion. Aboyant placed the pieces in a four-tiered rectangle over the bank and everyone gathered around to luxuriate in a bit of calmness and tranquility. With the fire emitting a robust glow, Colombe Blanche awaited an opportunity to open discourse with the pair.

The immediate crisis having ended, the Bear Chief lay exhausted upon the bank beside the fire. The boys scrambled to his side to comfort him and to their surprise the young woman accompanied them.

"Est-ce qu'il va bien?"—Is he all right? She asked, in French.

Her response struck the little party with astonishment, for they did not expect such concern to be offered by a stranger, much less a peau blanc. Aboyant applied his nimble fingers to the Bear Chief's neck and shoulders, whereupon the young woman joined him. Together they soothed the Bear Chief with firm manipulations, a maneuver which brought him to sit upright to voice appreciation. He spoke somewhat languidly:

"L'homme. Est-ce qu'il va bien?"—The man. Is he all right?

Colombe Blanche beamed with satisfaction and the boys tousled each other, leaving Aboyant to maintain a stern profile. The stricken man, however, although breathing steadily, slumped backward upon the bank. Aboyant alternated between breathing into his throat and manipulating his cold hands and feet. Laboring diligently, he watched for the sickening blue pallor to leave his extremities. The sun began to shine and light vapors graced the little party, making of Aboyant's task a renewal, not a chore. The young woman came to face the prostrate man and, throwing herself upon him, shouted: "Papa! Reveilles-toi.! Je t'en prie!" —Father! Wake up! I beg of you!

Aboyant brought the man to his feet and, gripping him from behind, applied a powerful scissors-like compression to the abdominal region. In response the man doubled over at the waist, coughed, and released heaps of foreign particles mixed with bile, into the river. He continued at will, giving Colombe Blanche and the boy the occasion to look away, lest they become ill. A blow applied to the shoulders brought the man upward. Turning about he faced the little party head on, a robustness flooding his cheeks. He muttered unintelligibly, sufficient for the young woman to burst forward to his side, exclaiming:

"Il est sauvé. Mon Dieu! Merci à tout le monde!"—He is saved! Good Heavens! Thank you everyone!

The little party repaired to the shelter of a stand of giant maples, a lone stand which withstood the summer storm. There, the Bear Chief made a visual inspection of the scene about them. The customary path along the river lay strewn with fallen trees, interspersed with pools of wind-driven water. There lay no retreat along that route, he reasoned and he began to select alternatives from among a narrow list of choices. Raven and Little Bear huddled with their mother. Unknown to their father, they asked Colombe Blanche to bring the man and young woman home with them. She conferred with her husband who agreed with the boys' wishes with one exception: the man appeared too lame to support his own weight. Aboyant proposed supporting the man between himself and the Bear Chief at the shoulder, half-walking and half-pulling him. To Aboyant's delight the Bear Chief adopted the plan and no sooner did they wedge the man between them but the full body started forward, bound for Osco. The Bear Chief fixed his gaze upon the land, looking for a clear patch over which he may launch a sustained march back to Osco. For the most part the land rose in gentle drumlins along the river. Residue piled up from the summer rains lay in profusion at their base. He decided to skirt the drumlins altogether and began a wide and circuitous path around them, a route leading through thickets and brambles. In retrospect, the storm disrupted not only his family's daily intercourse, but that of other endemic residents of the region: Before him a fox scurried with her kits in search of shelter. Deer, losing much forest cover, congregated in a broad meadow ahead. The little party spoke not at all, the crunching of footwear in the underbrush the sole testimony to their presence. Passing in front of a small, innocuous cave common to the region, the party disturbed a family of wolf cubs. The little creatures howled in fright for their mother. Scrambling inside the orifice, they glared suspiciously at the advancing party. Little Bear reported that the land beneath his feet writhed with snakes. He shrank back from them, leaving Colombe Blanche to explain that they held something in common with the snakes: fleeing the wild river. She gripped her son's hand and spoke to Raven, who in turn grasped the young woman by the hand and the march resumed.

The journey led to smaller drumlins, less statuesque than their larger neighbors, yet objects of concern nonetheless, for one never knew what lay on the opposite side of a drumlin. Where the waters pooled, flooding occurred and small marshes sprung into being. Insects, idle throughout much of the spring season, rose from the murky bottoms to leap and fly before the faces of the travelers, the mosquito among them. Perhaps to escape the winged pests, the little party hastened down the far side of a lesser drumlin. Clumped together at the base stood a growth of low-cropped blackberry bushes. A mother bear and her two cubs occupied themselves sampling the treats, unaware of intruders. The travelers stumbled upon them after pausing to gather their bearings. The mother bear charged the troupe, knocking the once-stricken man to the ground. She may have slaughtered him save for the intervention of Aboyant. The little man struck up a dance before the bear, all the while shouting at the top of his voice and putting on and removing his hat in rapid fashion. The bear stopped short of making a kill and, rising to full height, swayed back and forth, nose sniffing vigorously, seemingly captivated by the gyrations of the creature before her. With the troupe frozen in step to his rear, Aboyant tossed the headpiece to the animal who swooped it between her giant paws. Driving it between her jaws, the mother bear gnashed at the hat, rending it mercilessly, before stomping off to share the scraps with her cubs. Cautiously the travelers retreated to the far side of the drumlin, where pausing, they collected their thoughts before pushing on.

Another drumlin brought yet another adventure: At its base a rather innocuous opening invited the curious among the little troupe. Raven and Little Bear eagerly dashed forward to explore it. Squatting on all fours, they peered inside: defying warnings from their mother. When Raven skimmed the inner surface with a hand, he recoiled in fright, for a nest of bats flew out in wild abandon, screeching as they sought to escape the intruder. Finding his footing, the startled Raven retreated behind his brother who laughingly pushed him aside. Both boys ran to their father. Hands on hips, the Bear Chief uttered not a word, his stern countenance carrying a message of its own.

"Look! I still have the stones," Colombe Blanche announced, seeking to mitigate the boys' fears.

The young woman approached Colombe Blanche. She remarked that les pierres d'or—the golden stones—held great value in the hearts and minds of some men, avaricious men, who have fought wars over such pieces. She ended by cautioning her benefactor to keep knowledge of the stones well within the confines of her family. Colombe Blanche regarded her with interest. Saying nothing in reply, she dropped the stones into her pocket, but the words of the young woman carved a path into her memory. Her husband, meanwhile, spent a quiet period of meditation in which he thanked the Supreme Being for sparing his family and staunch ally, Aboyant, the vagaries of Nature. He lingered momentarily on the man and young woman, asking for the wisdom to set them on a straight course during their stay with him. To him the young woman appeared willing to embrace a new chapter in her life and he hoped to be able to assist her in fulfilling her ambition.

The weary party pressed on doggedly. Presently the Bear Chief called a halt. Turning to address his adherents, he spoke in French, out of deference to the young woman. She in turn came forward to serve as translator for the once-stricken man who stood beside her.

"We seek higher ground. Our usual paths of retreat are flooded. The marsh lands will rise up to consume us. We will mount the hill which rises up before us. Let us rest for a while. We have not long to travel." He sat cross-legged before the little troupe, eyes straining ahead, leaving the others to form seating arrangements.

The young woman approached him, her pleasant countenance depicting concern. She spoke in French: "Thank you, Sir, for what you have done for us. Let me speak for my father. His name is James . . . James York. I am his daughter, Suzanne. We have journeyed a long distance through this country, but we know little about where we came from and nothing of where we are now." The Bear Chief listened intently to the tall, thin young woman of perhaps sixteen seasons with the hair of corn silk and a splash of "des mouches"—freckles— beneath her blue eyes. Her words drew the others around her. She moved to her father's side, and, stroking his hair, asked:

"Is he going to be all right?" She studied her father's face and tears formed in her eyes.

"He is the only one I have left in the world. My mother is gone. My brother is far away. I am not able to go on."

Colombe Blanche dwelt on Suzanne's every word and the boys exchanged glances. The Bear Chief rose. Approaching James York, he inspected him briefly, touching the man's forehead and listening to his heartbeat. He located James's pulse and turned to Suzanne to speak:

"He is shaken from his encounters. His signs of life are good. With food and rest he will recover fully."

Raven and Little Bear surrounded their father: "We have something to give to the man." They brought forth a handful of grouse's eggs purloined from the mother hen who squawked loudly nearby. They placed the eggs into James York's hand, retiring under a mischievous smile. Aboyant, ever-prepared to challenge new frontiers, snatched an egg, and cracking it, drank its contents outright, smacking loudly in satisfaction. The young woman broke out in laughter, her genuine mirth serving to dispel the austerity of the moment. Reaching beyond Aboyant, she opened an egg for her father who consumed its contents before holding one out for his benefactor, the Bear Chief. With deference the Bear Chief refused to deny the man a well-deserved meal. He walked apart from the little troupe. Studying the landscape, he turned to face everyone, poised to speak:

"We are not far from home, but the way may be wrought with danger. You newcomers among us are with friends. We will guide you as matters dictate and see to your well-being as long as you stay among us." James York's demeanor remained unchanged, yet with the young woman, Suzanne, his words resonated full of hope and she allowed a tear of joy to drop to her cheek.

During this brief respite Suzanne explored her thoughts on the adventure which befell her in light of the people with whom she found herself. She bore a true attraction to these denizens of the forest. She rendered them a gregarious and generous folk, bound by a strong sense of family and community. The term 'stranger' is not germane to their lexicon, she mused, and she found herself safe and secure with them, long-lost relatives who longed to introduce her to their ways on the frontier. She welcomed an opportunity to live with them, communing with them as one does with a friendly neighbor, she, the eager student, always probing, always learning. Perhaps the storm generated a new beginning or sense of direction marking the next stage of her life. She hoped it to be one of wonderment.

The Bear Chief introduced his family and Aboyant to Suzanne and her father, James. He described Osco to them and disclosed his host of appellations, reserving the name of 'Bear Chief' until the end. He explained that he bore several names, alluding that people of her race maintained the same practice. Upon hearing his name, the quixotic Aboyant launched himself into a series of somersaults, bringing a round of applause from Suzanne and heroic shouts from the boys. Aboyant offered Suzanne his hand in greeting. She marveled at the soft touch. It exceeded her expectations for one who stripped saplings barehanded. His voice, a soft baritone, unnerved her. She anticipated a gruff, guttural bass to counter balance the small, lithe body. Dancing in an imaginary circle, Aboyant repeated her name, drawing out the syllables slowly, until he achieved the desired effect of causing everyone to break out in laughter, the silent James notwithstanding. At the height of Aboyant's hilarity, Suzanne broke away from her new companions to study her father. She reported that he was hungry and that she was about to swoon from hunger.

Colombe Blanche turned her full attention to the thin, pale young woman before her. In French she offered her words of comfort while bathing her brow with cool water and giving her morsels from the boys' catch. At length the young woman rose of her own volition and announced her willingness to proceed. The Bear Chief and Aboyant aligned the man, James, between strong shoulders and, with the boys trudging behind, the little troupe recommenced the journey to Osco. Colombe Blanche longed to learn more about the young woman, but refrained from pressing her for details during this stressful juncture. She believed that the young woman displayed admirable traits thus far: a lively spirit, an inborn inquisitiveness, and a genuine curiosity for all things new and foreign. In recalling the days of her own youth, she remembered when the village elders spoke of her in a similar manner. She discerned a bit of herself in this young woman, this newcomer, with whom she may one day share her thoughts and aspirations. For this reason she sought to keep the young woman Suzanne, close to her, at least in her thoughts.

The Bear Chief maintained communication with his flock as a means to buoy up everyone's confidence. Cresting one more drumlin, he announced that Osco lay over the next hill. They must go by a circuitous route, he admitted, in order to avoid marshy and water-logged grounds where snakes and snapping turtles congregated. He broke into a description of Osco for the newcomers' benefit and waxed prodigiously for one customarily so taciturn: He spoke about the arc-en-ciel—rainbow—which always appeared in the western sky following a summer storm. He urged the travelers to cast their eyes to the heavens once they climaxed the final hill, a mighty promontory, where he expected the rainbow to greet them in full splendor.

"When very young I came to the hill to hunt for small animals, but most of all to see the Grand Bow when it came due to appear. Today is such a day. Knowing the strength of the storm, the Great Bow will burn long and bright for you. It rises from parts unknown to shed its beams over the land. It lingers of its own accord before vanishing. Such is the mystery of the Great Bow. It tells the tale of life itself: Arriving-Lying-Dying-and- Rising again. In watching the Great Bow, the burdens that humans carry seem small and meaningless. Indeed, they become more bearable. The Great Bow is a sign of hope, hope in a better tomorrow. Believe me. Tomorrow will bring a better day for us. You, Mademoiselle, and your father, will reap the benefits attributed to the Great Bow as long as you remain our guests."

Suzanne imbibed the Bear Chief's every word. Fighting pangs of hunger, she chose a word to describe the Bear Chief's delivery: Eloquent. 'Here stood a man of the forest', she mused, 'gifted with the tools of writers whom she read when back home. Incredible!!' She turned to find the boys beside her. With teasing glances, they prompted her to blind her eyes and open her hand. She complied without reluctance, trusting in the boys' apparent sincerity of purpose. Giggling, they deposited a handful of blackberries into her outstretched palm, delicacies she read about but never tasted. Smiling appreciatively, she tousled their hair, sending them scampering back to their mother.

Undaunted, the little troupe pressed ahead. The hill of which the Bear Chief spoke rose up to meet them. The broad, denuded summit stood proud and tall, terms that Suzanne assigned to the Bear Chief and his family. He explained that the summit stood bare because strong winds stole away seedlings that otherwise may have produced high grasses. The hill served the villagers in two ways, the Bear Chief offered: First, it restrained strong winds from bearing down upon Osco during late summer and early fall. Second, it served as a point of observation from which one may study the land over great distances. A stream began somewhere near the hill,* the Bear Chief stated. Where it coursed past the village, residents bathed in it and washed clothing, even mixing the waters with sand and mud to make a paste with which to fortify strained palisades and lodges. He told of following the stream during his youth, finding new hunting grounds and fields to plant with corn along the way. He never found the stream's source, he confessed with dismay, nor did any of his trusted comrades, yet the stream meandered off to the northwest through open fields and marshes, master of its own destiny, bold and determined and independent like so many of his People.

The Bear Chief related another story, one that until the present he kept secret from Colombe Blanche and the boys: When a young man he often ventured to hunt small animals in the region where Osco presently stood. He found the tracks of an animal larger than the fox, yet smaller than the wolf along the soft soil of the river Osco. Remnants of its kill lay strewn beside the river, chiefly small animals. He decided to lie in wait for the animal, but it never crossed his field of vision. He waited by day and night over several seasons and the creature failed to come to stand before him. All the while the creature kept to its strict hunting practice along the river, signs of its spoils readily apparent to the most prosaic of observers. He never found the creature or its lair and decided that it was such a master of its surroundings that it was able to choose when to surface to strike at prey and keep him at bay en route. The creature, he posed, kept him in its sights along with its prey. That is why he *never* caught a glimpse of it. Though it relied on strength and swiftness, its greatest weapon was: *stealth*. From that period *stealth* became important for him.

The travelers began to ascend the great hill. Its sleek surfaces proved trying to the little party after the abundant rains. Beneath, the rock-hard earth rose up to punish those unprepared for it. The Bear Chief recalled to his guests accounts of sledding with his sons over the sheer face of the hill. A light snowfall made the surfaces very fast and the boys needed no encouragement from their father as they pushed their wooden craft at breakneck speeds from top to bottom. He gifted both Raven and Little Bear with a sled of their own, outfitting it with reins and a rudimentary rudder to guide their flight. They longed for winter to arrive each year when they were able to plunge down the hill with the swiftness of the falcon. Often Aboyant accompanied them and the boys stayed on the hill until pangs of hunger compelled them to return home to dinner, for, next to sledding, they enjoyed Colombe Blanche's preparations.

The Bear Chief, the first to reach the summit, ** allowed the little troupe to close around him. Below lay Osco's lodges, mere dots on a cartographer's map. Suzanne pushed ahead to glimpse the scene beneath her feet. Beyond the village facing east, the land ran flat and grassy-covered beside the expansive beach of Lake Osco: a deep azure blue. The white sands of the beach sparkled under a burst of sunshine, and she sighed in comfort. The trees and greenery lining the lake shore cast corresponding images into the clear, blue waters where gentle vapors scattered them before bringing them together again. Tiny, diaphanous clouds rose over the lake and, where they pooled together, the images of the trees and fall foliage on the waters seemed to move and toss about, enthralling the senses. The splendid panorama excited Suzanne, leaving her to step about lightly, casually colliding with her comrades.

The Bear Chief extended an arm overhead: "Look closely and you will see Le Grand Arc-En-Ciel"—The Great Rainbow. Joining her fellow travelers, Suzanne spied a great bow of many colors arching over the summit. Coming from an unknown origin, it climbed mightily before descending far afield into Lake Osco. Suzanne counted on her fingers at least five bands of primary colors, each separated by gossamer wisps of vapor churning lazily. The Arc hovered overhead. It absorbed all available sunlight, bathing the colorful bands, leaving them saturated in a deep iridescence. Some of the colorful bands hurled strands downward to earth where they intermingled with the forest images on the lake's surface, making of the whole ensemble a garish tableau of rich hues shimmering beneath soft vapors. This latter discovery sent Suzanne skipping over the summit and when the Bear Chief announced that the spectacle represented the creative hand of the Supreme Being, she choked back tears of joy.

Her heart racing, Suzanne stood weak about the knees in wonderment. She noted the calmness and tranquility of her surroundings. A stillness pervaded the summit and its environs where no one or nothing moved. She likened this transformation to one who set foot in heaven— this heaven on earth. Closing her eyes, she prayed that this miracle of the rainbow may shine upon her in order that she may know peace and tranquility forever. Looking upward, she stood firm that man lacked the means and power to explain such breathtaking majesty. With head low, she genuflected, convinced that she stood in the palm of the Creator.

She utterly dismissed a scientific explanation for the rainbow. She recalled that back home in Ireland her professor, a stodgy, overstuffed gentleman, went to great lengths to provide one for his students. Therefore, in layman's terms, sunlight, or white light, broke down into its several component rays in the presence of a rapid cooling of the earth, chiefly following rainstorms. Hence to her professor, no heavenly intercession took place to form rainbows. Until this very moment she accepted his view, but looking up once again, she harbored new thoughts which she placed into an encapsulated refrain, the likes of which her priests and nuns in Sunday school often reiterated: "There are simply some things which man is unable to fathom." Preoccupied with the matter of religiosity and science in general, she caught herself stumbling once the Bear Chief began to lead the way down from the summit.

She drifted to the rear of the processional. Again faltering, she stumbled over Colombe Blanche's feet. Her benefactor stepped to her side where she recognized the young woman's weakened condition. She summoned Raven and Little Bear who brought out edibles from a cache at their waist. Aboyant gave her a drink from a skin of cool water and Colombe Blanche spoke assurances to her and allowed the boys to tug her to her feet. Her father, no longer suffering from tremors, guided her about the waist and, tentatively, the little band made its way down the great hill. Once arrived on the grassy plateau, the gateway to Osco, Suzanne slipped back into her father's arms. The boys ran headlong into the village where they retrieved a litter. A curious retinue of onlookers followed the boys to the plateau where Suzanne lay in her father's arms.

Many gazed in wonder at the new-arrivals, yet several came forward to assist Raven and Little Bear with their delicate charge.

"She needs food and rest," Colombe Blanche addressed the congregation. She looked down upon Suzanne:

"You will survive, young one. I will make certain of it, for you are a young woman of consequence." She patted Suzanne's brow. Several villagers, tenderly raised Suzanne. Descending the plateau, they made straight for the village. James York looked about. The village* lay straight away. It stood before the great hill, now rising to the rear. At his feet the land rolled out into a plain lush with green grasses. It ran much in the same manner to the north and then south where it debouched against the sparkling sands of the beach. To the west the plain narrowed before the mighty hill. It flanked the hill to left and right, beginning a gradual ascent. Before the village itself the plain crested into a low mound or plateau which served as the point of entrance to the village. A narrow spit of land spun out from the plateau directly opposite a similar extension on the grassy plain. Through the gap a stream flowed unobstructed. Clever laborers had placed planking over the gap above the stream, in effect constructing a footbridge which may accommodate pedestrians and small conveyances. On command the planking may be easily removed, thus prohibiting direct passage to the village proper. Palisades rose up to greet the eye. Dropping far back on either flank, they came to rest against the great hill to the rear, the lower stretches of which stood bedecked in thickets and forest greenery.

James walked beside his daughter who lay couched among several bearers. Upon crossing a footbridge, the village's portals swung open to admit the exhausted troupe. The Bear Chief and Aboyant vacated the processional to disappear within the village. Within, servants and bearers dashed about the village hearth where he and Aboyant assumed positions of command. The bearers placed the reclining Suzanne atop a bench and when she sat up she beheld the makings of a banquet in the process of unfolding. Placed about the great camp fire, trays of mouth-watering foods stood out in bold relief. Villagers coming forward beckoned to Suzanne and her fellow-travelers to join them. Colombe Blanche obtained Suzanne's permission to place her upright on the bench, after which she summoned her husband. The Bear Chief came to stand beside Suzanne and her father, Colombe Blanche at his right hand. All signs pointed to a forthcoming introduction of the guests, yet the Bear Chief plunged into a stirring delivery. He began by telling of the courageous battle his two guests fought with the raging Osco. Following, he commanded the villagers to treat with the newcomers as members of their family. Next, he explained that Suzanne and her father emanated from a stock of charitable and dignified people eager to befriend them with a glimpse into their civilization. He ended by renewing a long-held belief that the visitors provided bold testimony that two distinct civilizations may live together peacefully.

Upon this final note the Bear Chief extended his arms overhead, eyes intent upon the heavens. The villagers, having surrounded Suzanne and her father, gave with uproarious cheers and foot-stomping, an outpouring which measurably increased. One by one, the Bear Chief, Colombe Blanche, Aboyant and the boys stepped forward to greet the new-arrivals. Each bowed from the waist and gave with a hearty handshake. In like manner villagers poured forth to extend greetings, yet, because of Suzanne's delicate condition, the Bear Chief called for an abbreviated session.

The first to partake of the foods and delicacies, Suzanne and her father thanked Raven and Little Bear who served each of them a heaping plate of venison mixed with berries, sweet potatoes, and stringed beans, a fond staple of the season, they boasted. A fruit compost followed, along with a thick, maple-flavored beverage: Colombe Blanche urged the boys to feed Suzanne, whereupon the entire village fell to partake of a noble repast.

By afternoon's end the banquet ended of its own accord. Rising from a post beside his guests, the Bear Chief summoned a young warrior. The young man kindled a fire brand from the grand hearth, and, coaxing the flame, he brought it to the Bear Chief. He passed it to James, speaking half in French and half in the native tongue:

"Come! Take this flame and light the hearth in your lodge. I will guide you."

*Cranebrook: a stream coursing through northwest Auburn, now largely covered and diverted

** The former Quill's Hill, now the site of housing tracts near Garrow Street Extension

Chapter Two

Intruders in Paradise
The Captain Introduced.
His Resourceful Assistant.
Terror in the Night.
Rescue & Recovery.

The British Expeditionary Forces of North America consisted of two integral units under a single field command, the captaincy. The first, a military arm, contained hardened soldiers chosen for their endurance in overcoming obstacles encountered for the most part in the vast, wooded heartland of colonial North America. Throughout the interior of the great and forested lands the soldiers built forts in which to house their numbers and to carry on trade with local aboriginal delegations. Radiating from each outpost came roads which the soldiers cut through the forest, in order to establish communications with others of their kind and to reconnoiter the native inhabitants. Garrisons of the day sat near a large body of water, or commanded the summit of a hill. The optimum fort occupied a hill overlooking a lake or river. The stark Fort Oswego and its lesser sister outposts shared these distinctions, so situated on a promontory about the mouth of Oswego Harbor, and the Forces resided there during the mid-1750s and 1760s.

The Forces' second unit consisted of an extensive surveying crew. Acting under the auspices of their commandant at Oswego, the crew ventured out in all four directions to open aboriginal lands for white settlement. Coincidental with the British siege of Montreal during the fall of 1760, white settlements proliferated along the frontier, spreading throughout the Lake Country and reaching far down into lands bordering the Susquehanna River and the homeland of the Delaware. On the continent British parliamentarians hoped to establish an English-speaking colony among these uncharted lands in the wake of the French retreat. Always at a loss for manpower, the last remaining French forces in the region departed, leaving strewn behind a scattering of poorly-equipped trading posts to conduct trade with a few loyal Iroquois. Soon, these remnants of French influence passed into history, except for one, largely unseen and unknown to itinerants.

Under the command of a Captain, the surveying crew, some several hundred strong and armed, traversed old French overland trade routes carved out long ago by the Iroquois and their French allies. Officially, the Captain sought to open up lands for settlement, often bordering native villages, while placating the inhabitants with plentiful gifts, mostly utilitarian, for easing the strain of daily living in village life. Irascible and insistent some of his crew claimed, the Captain nonetheless struck a chord of affection, however, grudging, within the hearts of many of his followers. Perhaps this allegiance traced back to his persistence and thoroughness in addressing seemingly impossible assignments, a challenge which he consistently solicited. His combative manner earned him a measure of loyalty from among men who otherwise resigned themselves to limitless common and repetitive tasks at their garrison. Thursday, September 7th, 1760 found the Captain camped about seven leagues to the southeast of the native village of Osco in high and rugged terrain in a locale considerably removed from the approved routes of travel. That afternoon, in a rare moment of leisure he departed from his chores, put his feet up and conversed with his aide, his voice hoarse and strained:

"Simmons! You pour a delightful pot of tea, Old Man. Good for what is ailin' ya, heh?"

"Aye, Cap'n. Never one to turn down a compliment. Hot enough to drown that pain in your gouty leg?"

"Fraid I am a goner in that department, Simmons," Captain Worthy returned, removing his extended leg from the top of a whiskey cask, a remedy he devised to relieve pain in the lower extremity and ankle.

"Such is the curse of the Good Life," he lamented. Seated, he rubbed the leg vigorously. He rose and sat intermittently, testing the painful limb against the hard earth. "Ah needs me rest, lad. We have an arduous venture awaiting us." He sipped at tea sparingly. Wincing, he appeared a man in grave thought, Simmons believed.

Although he traveled extensively with the Captain, Simmons understood him solely from a professional stance. He knew not of the man's guarded beliefs or plans, nor did the Captain offer to disclose them. What Simmons said next brought the Captain out of his sedan in a manner borne of alarm:

"By the way, Cap'n, I have a curious thought. We have ploughed through these forests well-nigh a fortnight. Where are be bound to, I dare ask?" He calmly stepped back to sip his tea, his eyes on his superior.

Gathering himself, the Captain looked straight ahead. Avoiding Simmons' glance, he replied as one delivering a speech: "Simmons. We are at once upon a major and dangerous mission. We are entrusted to persuade the inhabitants of these lands to join in allegiance with the Crown."

"Pardon my intrusion, Sir, but we seem to be moving in circles, keeping to the shadows."

The Captain pawed the earth with his uninjured limb. Spitting out his tea, he quipped angrily: "Simmons. These forests abound with opportunities in many forms. In our labors as surveyors we want to claim that which is good and avoid that which may bring us ruin. We want to apportion these lands among our friends and divest them from our enemies. It is a difficult process. May I advise you that there are evil sorts nearby who want nothing more than to chop off our heads and mount them on a stake." Wincing, his index finger crossed his throat. He resumed a seat on a pair of thick cushions.

"May I assume that we are stalking an enemy, Sir?" Simmons asked innocently, in anticipation of a more definitive explanation.

"We simply want to stay out of harm's way, Simmons," Worthy returned, anger subsiding. "Our goal is to learn the disposition of the Native. Is he friend or foe? This is a *new* task for us, but not beyond our means," he smiled, confident in his reply.

To Simmons the Captain's romp into the uncharted forest constituted an unprecedented departure from the Force's regular duties. In truth, neither he nor any of the crew knew their destination. Is the Captain simply lost and afraid to consult him? He must form his questions carefully, lest the Captain deny him further access to his thoughts. The Captain spoke again:

"We will talk more on this, but not today. We depart on the morrow early, before the sun rises. Tell the men to catch some rest. They are to retire early this evening if they are to be fresh and alert." He placed his leg upon a cask and fell to massaging his thigh. Before Simmons departed, he called to him in jest: "Simmons! Since I made you Cordon Bleu yesterday, what have you thrown together for this evening's dinner?"

Simmons dashed off the remains of a cup of tea and, hastening to a long banquet table, stripped away a protective mantle. Beneath lay a grand variety of delectable foods, the makings of a herculean feast, which he spent the better part of the day preparing. He took a moment to wax eloquently about his gastronomic creations. "The forest's treasures, Cap'n, prepared by your faithful servant and steadfast crew. Pleasing to the palate."

The Captain, sarcastic wit in full play, retorted, in spite of recurrent pain: "Oh, spare me the details, dear man, and tell me what you have brought."

Determined to deflect the Captain's sarcasm, Simmons continued: "I have assembled foods, which on the Continent, would attract members of royalty." He pointed to grouse, quail, pheasant, and turkey, all turned to a golden brown. Beside them sat trays of roasted boar and venison. In turn he unveiled servings of summer squash, corn on the stalk, stringed green beans, sweet potatoes, roasted nuts and roots, rhubarb and spinach. Moving along the table Simmons displayed bowls of berries and melons. "For beverages I have hot chocolate made from cocoa leaves, a brisk corn beer flavored with molasses, and, of course, hot tea." Stepping back, he admired his labors. "I may have forgotten something." He stroked his chin.

"No, no! Not at all, my good man. You are to be commended—praised for producing a feast fit for a king. The Crown will be forever in your debt. William Pitt will soundly laud your efforts, correct, Simmons?"

"I am not beyond accepting praises, Sir," Simmons replied, taking care to agree with his superior. He relinquished any further attempt to engage the Captain in conversation concerning the Force's destination.

The Captain patted his stomach affectionately. He tested the swollen ankle by taking a turn about the table. Wincing, he abandoned the effort by announcing retirement to his tent, but not before tossing out a wry bit of humor tinged with sarcasm: "I leave you now, Simmons. I only hope that your preparations make me forget the agony I face with every step I take. You are Cordon Bleu," he snapped. "You are expected to make small miracles. Carry on!" he bellowed.

* * *

Relieved by the Captain's departure, Simmons heaved himself into setting out dishware and eating utensils for the men soon to take their places at his table. He reminisced about the feasts he prepared back at Oswego, his home base. Each Saturday he prepared a sumptuous setting for all residents. Saturdays represented the end of the week's labors for the surveying crew and the men came to table famished and almost at the point of calling out for food and drink. He did not disappoint them. He relished the post of principal chef, a departure from the characteristic role of aide-de-camp. He occupied both posts simultaneously, adapting to their special requirements. His ability to learn quickly and to make the necessary adjustments in approach to them earned him praise from the men in general and from the prickly Captain in particular. He knew that because of his masterful capabilities he would be one of the last to incur the Captain's wrath on those days that his superior scolded and chastised everyone within sight. Overall, he believed the Captain callous, a man hardened in the face of life's pitfalls, one who never emerged from calamity a victor on his own terms. Nevertheless, he owed the Captain at least a small debt of gratitude for having named him to what turned out to be two rewarding posts: aide-de-camp and head chef.

He set about to review the food-preparations of the crew. He established strict standards of cleanliness and insisted that all associates observe them. On the trail cleanliness often meant the difference between living and dying a slow, agonizing death where contagions borne by flies in his opinion entered foods preparatory to serving them. To guard against such infestations he boiled all vegetables. He placed fruits in packed ice in an icehouse lined with sawdust. He seasoned and roasted all meats. He never mingled meat wastes with the meat itself and thoroughly washed the latter. He boiled all culinary utensils after they served their purpose in food preparation. That done, he looked forward to making pies, choosing fruits native to the region. These fruits he did not store, mixing them into his crusts moments after they came in from the fields. To the crew's delight he often cut designs into pie crusts, absurd miniature etchings of his associates, and occasionally of his superiors. His crew begged him to make a design of the Captain, and the result, a thin, stooped body supporting a pompous and inflated head, brought the Captain's wrath down upon the entire baking staff, himself excepted. He denied a part in the plot and the Captain's anger mounted and he made wild accusations, subsiding after Simmons offered him a sample of one of his famous cherry cobbler pies.

The inspection complete, he reverted to the role of aide-de-camp. Essentially he must allocate seating for the members of the entire surveying crew—about seven hundred strong. Earlier, at his direction, men toppled tall trees and with saws, nails, and hammers, converted them into tables, benches and chairs, items to accompany the men wherever they chose to travel in the woodlands. So many men must be fed that he divided the Force into packs or "shifts" and fitted them with time-constraints at table, a schedule to be strictly observed, so that all may dine in relative ease and comfort. He kept a map, a large parchment. It became a seating-arrangement. On it with charcoal stylus he drew four quadrants at two abreast. He assigned each pack to a quadrant, each of which loosely merged with its neighbor. He counted the number of men in each quadrant and prayed that the final tally came to seven hundred "seated souls," he liked to think. After some manipulations the grand tally stood firm and he breathed a sigh of relief.

His tally completed none too soon, he looked up to find the Captain emerging from his tent. The man's guttural rumblings preceded him, as though urging the men to take up places at the fully-stocked tables. The Captain paused to stand at the head of one of them. He gazed long and hard at the plethora of foods stretched before him. Thrusting both arms forth, the Captain seemed poised to lay claim to all of the succulent delights which met his eye. Securing solid footing, he winced and drew himself to full height and addressed the hungry multitude:

"Gentlemen, we meet this evening on the eve of a great and noble undertaking. Before dawn we will sally forth from this place into the interior, a region wrought with mystery and dangers. We will rely on our collective strength to carry the day. His Majesty has laid claim to this forest primeval and the treasures which it holds. He trusts that we are able and fit enough to secure this forest and its lands for the Crown. Of course there may be native denizens who know not of our coming and less of our purpose. His Majesty asks that we hold these lands in trust for the native, and, in so doing, to protect these lands and their residents from needless exploitation and most assuredly from confiscation and devastation by lesser men than we, those whose souls are infested with evil plots. In the process we hope to establish a colony here to care for our progeny and their offspring. The same gesture we extend to the native denizens. His Majesty asks only that we share the largesse of the Crown, which He impartially distributes, with all newcomers to these lands who swear to Him their allegiance. One day, God willing, a government of laws will take root here to treat with all equally, both white man and red.

"I am told that native-dwellers have guarded these lands for centuries. They have built an entire civilization around these lands supported by the grand elements of earth, water, wind, and fire. Some say they are the first settlers of human-kind to live here. On first glance they have done well, but alas, they are too few in number to reap the full bounty of these lands because of their sheer prodigiousness. We will, therefore, with His Majesty's sanction, assist the native-dwellers in the task of administering to the land, thereby developing the forest to its full point of fruition for the good of all. In conclusion, I need not stress the privilege which His Majesty has bestowed upon us as we go forth to labor in these lands for the good of our brethren, for ourselves and our posterity, and for the good of England." His voice increasing in volume, the Captain shouted the final words, tossing his tricorn high overhead, a tactic which brought the men to their feet in thunderous acclamation. They hooped cries of joy and stomped the earth with their heels, even beating the tables with coiled fists, the callous maneuver bringing glass and dinnerware to collide along the length of the massive oaken tables.

The Captain, reveling in the ardor which his speech engendered, thrust arms and shoulders skyward. Chanting praises of the homeland, he lowered his arms over the seated masses. He relished such assemblies, particularly this one to which he emphatically gave a stamp of approval. The men picked up the chant, and, forsaking dinner, joined in their leader's vociferous tribute. Sharply he ceased calling. He raised his arms and the multitude quieted, whereupon he threw back his head and growled in a deep bass:

"Let us eat and make merry!!"

Simmons distributed tallow candles at the tables, for he anticipated the dining to continue late into the evening. The men fell to devouring the food with abandon and periodically shouted cries of approval, washing the meal down with rounds of beer and whiskey, tankards which willing bearers poured for them. A "tally-ho!" shouted here, brought about a "go!" shouted there. No one, particularly those who preferred to dine in peace, escaped the boisterousness of the spectacle. In general the Captain tolerated such outbreaks, although he confided a disdain for them to Simmons, who shared the Captain's point of view. By late afternoon both men retired to tented quarters where they dined leisurely, viewing the gaiety from a distance.

The dining continued into the evening, the scene a portrait of frenzied enthusiasm. With succeeding courses the men broke into song. The emerging darkness brought about the telling of tales, ventures in which ordinary men accomplished extraordinary feats, the seeds from which legends are born. Progressively a coolness descended upon the revelers and the men lighted fires about which they gathered to spin tales. Some played at darts, ran short relays, even danced with fancied partners. All the while beer and whiskey flowed liberally throughout the camp and in the resultant darkness, the men relied upon the campfires and vivid imaginations to mark the surroundings. Some reported seeing grotesque figures leaping out of the camp fires, ebbing and flowing effortlessly among the shadows which the flames cast on all objects roundabout. Winged creatures, drawn by the flames, buzzed overhead frantically in search of mates. Others of their kind hunted for minuscule prey, snatching them out of mid-air. On the grounds four-footed animals hunting after food sought after each other. Essentially the men found themselves in an arena teeming with nocturnal life that made of the campfires beacons by which to pursue, capture, and consume food.

The men by all accounts stood inured to the frenetic movements being put into play around them. Occasionally they stirred when bodies in the night nearly collided under their noses, as with the winged creatures and the fireflies. Prominent wherever the brightness of the camp fires merged with the lengthening shadows of the forest, many of the creatures great and small developed uncanny and disproportionate shapes and sizes in the eyes of the naive observer who followed their random pathways through the ethereal and pervasive darkness. Some of the men reported that the stark contrast between the bright camp fires and the blackness of the night drove them into confusion whereby they lost the ability to mark exactly what passed before the eye. They told of lone, winged bodies in their field of vision simply melding together in a smear or blur, leaving one out of balance and shaking his head in confusion. It is a temporary condition, some men claimed, which leads one to reach erroneous, albeit exaggerated, decisions with relation to the height, weight, and size of a body, and its distance from one point to the next. Add to this sketch plentiful amounts of beer and whiskey, they claimed, and you have the makings of a fairytale, not unlike those which the men spun liberally that evening in the dark and thick forest.

* * *

Apart from the main gathering two men conversed. Wrapped in blankets in the cool evening, they huddled beside a camp fire. They tossed on logs, sending sparks adrift in the darkness and the flames crept higher and burned brighter. Not long before they arrived overland from deep within the colony of Pennsylvania, and, along with their comrades, made camp along the crest of a high ridge overlooking one of the many valleys midway into the colony of New York. During the journey they struck hard beside the Susquehanna River. One of the men remarked about the journey to a companion:

"Dobbs. I have a mind to buy a patch of land when my obligation expires." He poked the earth with a stake.

"You may choose between the rolling hills of Pennsylvania or the deep valleys of New York," his partner, replied. "In the end, Densmore, you will have fetched a valued piece of property." He drew a blanket nearer.

The man, Densmore, stared straight ahead, his eyes coming to rest on a region in mid-air where the bright flames of the camp fire dissolved into the palpable blackness of the forest canopy. Within this framework of intensely quiet and thick blackness, the eruption of any sound great or small became magnified in the hearts and minds of the observer so that the mere snapping of a twig fell upon the ears with the ferocity of an exploding cannon ball. Unable to confide in their senses, the two men sat in rigid disillusionment, gazing blindly into the black night. Burning twigs from the fires popped. Hot sparks danced wildly overhead. Flying bats screeched in full flight. Panthers screamed at each other over a fresh kill. This flood of spontaneity in an otherwise rapt stillness engendered within the men a state of urgency wrought with fear, for they possessed no means to curtail the wealth of sights and sounds which invaded that tiny zone of privacy which they set aside for themselves. Ironically, a part of their being did not care to see the nocturnal proceedings come to an end. Many comrades assigned macabre meanings to the goings-on, perhaps the best way to explain the unexplainable.

Densmore gave a sudden start. Recoiling in his blanket he exclaimed:" There is a woolly beast on your flank, Dobbs." He pointed nervously to his partner's left.

"Mind you, now. I see nothing but stars and fireflies. Have another swig of ale and let us spin our tales."

"There will be no more story-telling tonight. Up and off with ya," Densmore called, rising. Cautiously he retreated toward the main camp, calling over a shoulder: "The meat! Where did you hide the meat?"

"Hungry are ya?" Dobbs retorted. "It is here by my side." He held out a piece of venison, but Densmore running frantically, called over his shoulder: "Put your legs under you and fly like the wind!"

Momentarily Dobbs settled back to enjoy the warmth of the fire. A quick glance about him produced no signs of alarm and he attributed his partner's abrupt departure to the need to empty his bowel. Nevertheless, peering into the blackness, he remained alert for the slightest disturbance. Unpredictably, the blackness gained substance. A dark, round mass rolled toward him. It tread heavily, so disturbing the soft earth beneath him. It gave forth with gruff vocal sounds and a stale and rank odor preceded it. The leviathan now thrust itself upright, presumably standing erect. So close it stood to him that he caught glimpses of flashing teeth, flared nostrils and barbed claws protruding from its bulk and fear set in, for he realized at long last that he stood defenseless in the path of a bear—a hungry bear. The beast headed straight for him and Dobbs, his wits about him and still clutching his cherished piece of venison, flung it at the giant, dropping it expertly at the behemoth's feet. To his relief, the bear dropped down on all fours, swooped up the prize and, turning to the rear, rumbled off into the night.

Densmore, meanwhile, returned with a small band of men. He did not ask after Dobbs' welfare, but instead demanded to learn the route of escape which the creature pursued. Dobbs, vexed by his partner's callousness, refused to give details and assigned little importance to the entire incident. In vain he attempted to explain to Densmore's followers that the bear came only for food, and, having attained it, moved on. He understood at last that the men came to hunt the bear and to kill it. The smell of tobacco clung to their clothing and they reeked of beer and whiskey and yearned for excitement, even at this late hour of the evening. Finding Dobbs reluctant to support them, they pushed him aside and moved off into the blackness, torches in hand.

From a distance Dobbs followed the hunters. When he heard shouts thrown up around him, he knew that the men held the bear in their sights. He secured a hiding place and, peering out, witnessed what he feared most: The men stood circling the bear, taunting the creature, which, having no innate fear of human-kind, stood by aloof, bent upon consuming its catch. One of the men lunged forward, stabbing the beast with a bayonet. The bear forsook its meal and chased the man. Hooking him with mammoth claws, the beast tore into the man's leg, tearing it open. Roaring, it charged another man, whereupon several of the hunters discharged muskets into the animal, severely wounding it. The men pursued the bear. In retreat the bear absorbed volleys of gunfire and, before it fell dead, it turned to face a man giving chase at its flank. Seizing the man by the neck, the bear shook him so violently that the man's head tore away at the shoulders. The vanquished bear fell over the man's remains, leaving the hunters to separate the two prostrate figures.

The hunters dragged the beast back to camp, a short distance away. Someone cut off the bear's head while another skinned it, after which they hoisted the limbs atop a tall pole on the parade grounds of the camp. With the skin washed and dried, men took turns wearing it, taking tours on the grounds and jesting with each other. At length the men tossed the skin upon the flames. In turn the men roasted the carcass, ate part of it and discarded vast sections at random. Once again beer and whiskey flowed and the men, chiefly the hunters, broke into melodies, songs of old which extolled the feats of the mighty hunter who felled the proverbial savage beast.

Dobbs remained apart from the conviviality. He disdained the comportment of certain fellow-comrades, for to him the attack on the bear represented a strike against Nature and all of Her creatures of which human-kind formed a part. For some people the bear held human-like qualities, he knew: strength, power, grace, and endurance. An intelligent animal, the bear learned much in the same manner as human-kind: through trial and error. 'We are not that much different from one another,' he concluded. At that point Dobbs came to believe that the camp consisted of two distinct bodies: the one which enjoyed the wilderness and its creatures and the one which sought to subdue all that is wild and free.

He noted the lateness of the hour. His trail watch stroked the beginning of a new day. In the back of his mind he anticipated Nature's revenge upon the men who upset Her delicate balance. In the killing of the bear he believed that the hunters robbed the earth of the single great benefit which the bear conveys to the human species— curbing population growth in species whose high proliferation compromises Nature's ability to feed all creatures during lean periods. Nature will respond, he knew. He did not know when, or in what form, but he knew that the inevitable beckoned.

Growing sleepy, Dobbs recalled a story from youth which his father told him: 'His father's neighbor raised sheep-herding dogs. A farmer with whom he traded coveted one of the animals, the neighbor's favorite dog. One evening the farmer lured the dog with scraps of meat and spirited the animal away. The neighbor scoured the countryside with a party of supporters, but to no avail. On the second night the dog returned to its master, ruffled, but satisfactory. Stuffed beneath the dog's collar the neighbor caught sight of a bolt of bright, multi-colored cloth. Spots of blood clung to it and the neighbor determined that the dog fought valiantly to escape. What is more, the neighbor recognized the cloth, part of the sleeve of a shirt worn by a man whose home he frequented on many an occasion. With the dog in hand, the neighbor visited the farmer. He confronted him. The dog barked loudly in the farmer's presence who reluctantly admitted culpability, made all the more convincing when the dog pinned him against a tree. There the farmer remained until the neighbor called the dog away hours later.' This story ended with no loss of life, but deep within his bosom Dobbs sensed a constant, ominous feeling. It first began with the incident of the bear.

The forested plateau on which the Captain settled provided him with a temporary refuge. An island within the woodlands, it gave him sanctuary against ambush, while furnishing him the space he required for accommodating a large crew. He may come and go as the situation dictated and because of the seclusion of the camp, all subsequent maneuvers fell under his purview, subject to his stamp of approval. No one, he believed, knew that he occupied the crest of those deeply-forested highlands set between two finger-shaped lakes.

The Captain, however, knew not of the resourcefulness of the native inhabitants. From the moment he departed lower Pennsylvania, Delaware scouts marked his path northward. Along the way they gave their allies reason to understand that an intruder moved through the region. Thus, the Cayugas, who regarded the Delaware as members of an extended family, learned of the Captain's approach early-on. They passed knowledge to their neighbors, the Seneca. Meanwhile, the Onondaga, the Keepers of the Flame, and the Oneida, the People of the Standing Stone, learned that the Captain led a great number of soldiers through the heart of the Five Nations. Soon, all inhabitants north and west of the Susquehanna learned of the Captain's coming. The friendly French, snug in a trading post beside Lake Onondaga, learned of it also. At a hastily-held meeting at Onondaga, everyone, red and white, decided to watch and remain alert.

The Bear Chief, warrior-chief of the Cayugas, went one step further. He dispatched three scouts to reconnoiter the Captain's maneuvers. Known for bravery, the three men reached the camp during the height of the revelry and expertly concealed themselves within a stone's throw of the Captain himself. It is with great grief that they witnessed the slaughter and dismemberment of their clan brother, the bear. The bear, a living symbol of Nature's power and beauty, became a sacred talisman to the Cayugas, so much so that families named male sons after the bear and young men performed rituals of manhood in the bear's honor and glory. Now this heroic symbol lay shattered and torn and the scouts yearned to express pent-up grief without betraying their hiding place to these peaus blancs whose foul deed they came to hate. One of them, then two, then three, loosed arrows into the darkness and, after the missiles descended, the scouts uttered a death's howl and moved off to grieve before returning to their village.

Behind them they left a camp consumed by fright and consternation. All gaiety drained from the soldiers the moment that three of their number, felled by arrows, collapsed to the earth to breathe no more. Soldiers carrying torches convened near the fallen where they were able to do little but comfort them during the remaining moments of life. Simmons hastened to the scene and the Captain, hobbling, followed suit and as either man debated how to treat with the casualties, the majority of the men who stood aside grew restive. A howling suddenly broke free of the thick forest, too close for many. The men fell back in fear and agitation and a sizable body took flight. Forsaking firearms they ran headlong into the blackness, mindful of putting great distance between themselves and the awful scene behind them. Simmons attempted to forestall the exodus to no avail, and gaining momentum, the flight turned into an evacuation. Soon Simmons stood alone, calling orders that went unheeded. The Captain too vanished from view. Deserted, Simmons turned to the three casualties. He gave them water and cleansed their wounds, but despite his care, he found them since expired. He grieved their loss, yet he feared for the runaways, who, running in a mob, knew not the lay of the land nor the secrets which it held.

The crew initially ran in a collective body. Soon they broke into packs, blindly heeding instructions, in order to disillusion fancied assassins who pursued them. A few of the men carried firebrands, but, for the most part, the full moon furnished the sole beacon through the foreboding night. Firearms, clothing, and supplies lay back in camp, undisturbed. Someone found a shallow stream bed and, coming together again, the men secured solid footing along its sandstone bottom and surged recklessly ahead. No one took note of the distance covered, nor did anyone call for rear-guard action, or attempt to set up a defensive perimeter. United by fear, the men looked to the stream to lead them out of the forest. Several may have held other thoughts, but to voice them meant having to be left behind to face the unknown, and so, everyone ran together, a great amorphous mob fleeing from doom. Dobbs ran with the mob, not out of choice, for he held other thoughts. He ran because he feared the crew's wrath in case he decided to remain behind. Their taunting would remain with him for the remainder of his days in the Forces. Deep in thought, he allowed himself to drift toward the rear of the pack.

The stream broadened. At first shallow, it deepened and the men dodged rocks in their path, but maintained course. Gradually the stream flowed faster, yet no one posed concerns and the men picked up the pace accordingly. From up ahead rumbling sounds, however faint, drifted back among the ranks and one man remarked that the earth beneath his feet shook. The night became cooler and up ahead mist formed and rose high, closing in about the fleeing mass and the once barely audible sound became a thunderous roaring. Dobbs, aware of the pounding of his heart, no longer heard it beating fiercely in his chest for the roaring, constant and tumultuous, crashed against his ears, deafening him.

Up ahead the pack broke into three segments. Two segments ran to either side of the rushing stream and came to an abrupt halt, leaving the main body to plunge straight ahead. It is this body that seemed to disappear from view without so much as leaving a sound. Dobbs drew up short, but the men to his rear carried him along and within moments he drifted off and away, his legs no longer gripping the earth beneath him. For an instant, suspended in mid-air and bathed in cool vapors, he believed himself transported into a more peaceful world. In the next instant, his entire posterior from neck to haunches exploded in pain and he lost consciousness, neither seeing nor sensing anything more at all.

Far above him, on the brink of a precipice, crew members stood on either side of the stream, delving into the darkness below them. Separated from fallen comrades, the survivors registered grief in all of its forms. Some men cried openly. Others moaned. Some stared blankly into the blackness. Nevertheless, all grieved the loss of fellow crew members, those who fell over the precipice at the point where the vigorous stream precipitously dropped out of sight. The survivors counted themselves among those who made a split-second dash for the shoreline and now, on either bank of the river, they stared hopelessly down into the abysmal chasm which claimed so many lives. Now, beset with the pain of lives lost, coupled with the omnipresent fear of ambush, they stood mute as sheep about to be led to slaughter. By dawn they moved away from the precipice. Seeking shelter among the shadows and tall grasses, they waited until the dawn before sending someone off to summon Simmons.

* * *

With the break of dawn, Hastings, an eager and apt officer in the Forces, stepped forward to assume command. Tossing aside warnings of sudden attack, he volunteered to go for supplies back at camp and to enlist the aid of Simmons and the Captain. Meanwhile, he instructed one Goodrich to ascertain the losses suffered with the approach of morning. He gave everyone reason to understand that upon his return every able-bodied man would engage in the process of rescue and recovery. Taking one man with him, Hastings set out boldly, back-tracking the crew's original flight along the river bank.

The disaster at the river unknown to him, Simmons set about trying to impose a stamp of order upon the camp, itself a scene of chaos. After burying the three deceased, he moved to recover articles and furnishings which the men in flight cast aside with abandon. He sighed at the enormity of the disarray before him, all the while keeping an eye alert for the Captain. With the morning sun breaking through the forest, his thoughts ran to the men, none of whom returned from the previous evening. He longed to restore the camp before the men, any of them, made an appearance, and it is by keeping an eye to the single path leading from the camp that he noticed two figures striding smartly toward him.

Hastings, calm, in spite of having witnessed a tragedy, recited the events of the late evening. Simmons listened attentively, and, as his colleague spoke, began to assemble articles from the grounds to enlist in effecting a rescue— most certainly a recovery. Bringing forth three wagons, he loaded them with litters, gauze, antiseptic, splints, towels, drinking water, and a whole host of implements intended for probing the soil. Finally, he loaded portable chairs, the very chairs which earlier ringed the banquet tables, along with lengths of rope. Speaking rapidly, he explained:"We will give the survivors something to sit on while we haul them up from the depths below." Hastings and his companion managed a weak smile and the trio set off with their baggage. In addressing this urgent state of affairs, no one spoke of the Captain.

By mid-morning many of the survivors amassed at the precipice. Finding sure-footing, they glimpsed below the rim. Some recoiled in horror, but all knew that they must take bold steps to devise a plan to bring their comrades living and dead back to the heights. A grim scene of human suffering visited those who cast a glance over the precipice. Beginning halfway down the escarpment men lay in clusters, having come to rest upon boulders, rocks, branches, the outgrowth of bushes and saplings, and even upon each other. Not everyone perished, for observers on the heights noted movements among those who fell within the more resilient fauna. Then came the moaning, that cry of suffering which only those too injured to speak are able to utter. Further below, at the base of the ravine, many men lay immobile, but sporadically signs of life emerged, for men on the heights reported the movement of an arm here and a leg there— and always the continuous moaning.

Dobbs stirred. Knees and ankles bloodied and in pain, he nonetheless stole a glance about him. Beneath his posterior two comrades lay inert. Dead upon impact, he silently thanked them for having saved his life. A third man lay beside him, whom he recognized as Rice. Rice stirred and Dobbs called weakly to him, taking care to make light of the disaster with a bit of humor:

"A fine mess we have fallen into, Mr. Rice."

"In more ways than one, Mr. Dobbs."

From within a boot Dobbs extracted a trail knife. An uncommon knife, it more resembled a small sword. With difficulty he sat upright, although he feared his legs broken. Reaching about him he pulled and cut at a growth of vines protruding from the escarpment, explaining to Rice:

"I will fashion these vines into a rope. How are your arms?"

"My left is numb, but I am right-handed."

"Good. I will cut and weave them into a lariat. Try to stand and throw it upward where someone will take it and pull us up against the face of the cliff." He looked upward where the man Goodrich managed to find a foothold slightly below the face of the precipice. There Goodrich secured himself and urged the men above to throw a line to him so that he may anchor himself to a boulder capable of supporting his weight.

"Dobbs! Why not make a sling?" Rice called. "It is stronger than a lariat—something that you are able to straddle and two men above will pull on either end. Up, up, and away," he gestured.

Word of Rice's plan spread rapidly and within precious minutes surviving crew members on the heights chased after vines and branches. Many kept knives. Forming squads, they sought young, supple vines and branches to weave together to form ropes and slings. Goodrich, first to finish, anchored himself aloft before lowering himself over the precipice, coming to stand on a boulder to the side of the escarpment. Meanwhile, men labored, interweaving the strong, coarse strands of material. Intent upon the task at hand, no one reported that the once-coursing stream slowed to the strength of a trickle.

The man Goodrich received the first of several man-made ropes. Tossing an end down to Dobbs, he instructed him to fasten the rope about the waist. That accomplished, Goodrich proceeded to drag his comrade ever-so-slowly laterally across the mound of brambles upon which he lay. He estimated that Dobbs lay at a depth of twenty meters from the rim and some fifteen meters from his own position. In pulling Dobbs, Goodrich noticed the accumulation of large rocks to the side of the chasm, half-way down. To him they resembled a primitive staircase. With perseverance he may be able to pull Dobbs to one of the boulders after which the poor man may gradually ascend to the heights with the aid of a sling or additional rope. He shouted his thoughts to Dobbs who heartily endorsed them, but reported a great lack of strength in his legs. Goodrich lavished him with assurances and Dobbs, crawling over mounds of leaves and the bodies of fallen comrades, wrapped an arm around one of the boulders. Men on the heights cheered and someone dropped down beside Goodrich with a second rope. Together, the two men, heels digging into the soft earth, hoisted Dobbs toward the heights, where eager men lay flat on their bellies and, extending arms over the rim, hauled Dobbs steadily upward to rest upon the heights.

A general cheer erupted among the men on the heights and from below Rice demanded to be carried aloft on a sling, a true test of the device, he offered. In the growing light of the morning he reported seeing more men in need of rescue. They lay beside many who perished. Two men at the rim, holding either end of a tether line, tossed the saddle-like sling to him, leaving Rice to straddle it in the manner of a rider mounting a horse. Rice insisted that the men haul him straight upward against the escarpment, thereby bypassing Goodrich. The men thought little of his demand, but more of preserving his wishes and proceeded to haul him upward, and Rice soon became the second man rescued.

One by one men scaled down the staircase-like boulders, ropes in tow. Pressing to the chasm's floor, they probed for signs of life among the human remains. They exerted great care and dexterity picking among the mass of arms and legs heaped upon a soggy, brush-strewn terrain. It is the composition of the native soil at this point that may have spared the lives of many men, serving as a giant sponge that cushioned one's fall. Where bones collided with boulders however, only death followed, either quickly, or over the course of the late evening, but it came, nevertheless. In due course the rescuers hauled more men to the safety of the heights from the depths of the chasm, outfitting them on slings and calling ahead to their associates on the rim. Secure upon his boulder, Goodrich coordinated all aspects of the rescue. In so doing, he noticed that the supply of ropes and slings grew thin and he longed for the arrival of Hastings.

Suddenly, a resounding cheer resonated over the heights. His thoughts running to the arrival of Hastings, Goodrich, clutching the boulder, thrust his shoulders back sharply so that he may glance upward for signs of his colleague. He may have loosened a grip on the boulder, for his legs gave away in the soft earth and he plunged straight down on his posterior, successively bounding over several of the boulders which comprised the cascading staircase. He lay dormant on his back-side. Pain cut through his limbs so incisively that he found himself unable to call out. Weakly he lifted an arm. Exhausted, he lowered it with a grimace. The exuberance of the men at both extremes of the chasm told him that Hastings stood nearby and that, in their celebration, they neglected to tend to him. He fought to remain awake until the men returned to their senses, once again going about the process of rescue and recovery. Again, lying fully-extended on his back, he raised and dropped an arm. After what seemed an interminable period of lying in pain he heard concerted voices beside him. Hands reached out to him, probing him gently. He grimaced in pain, but did not resist efforts to transfer him to a waiting litter. At length he recognized the voices of Hastings and Simmons. He told himself: 'I will live' and lost consciousness.

At Hastings' command, all available men flocked to the wagons to gather the supplies sorely needed for the casualties. Soon the heights beside the stream lay consumed with life-saving devices. Hastings stepped lively to where wooden chairs lay in rows. He ordered ropes to be fastened to the chairs preparatory to lowering them to the bottom of the chasm. A squad formed. Men placed themselves shoulder-width apart, each holding a chair affixed to a rope. They wrapped additional ropes about their waists and other men stood behind them pulling the ropes taut in order to grant them a firm footing along the rim's smooth surfaces. At a given signal the men lowered the chairs the twenty meters to the bottom of the gorge into the waiting arms of associates. They in turn transferred the tethered chairs to the injured, delicately placing each casualty in a sitting position, then tugging on the rope in a gesture to haul away. The exercise repeated itself so successfully that the chair-lift soon became the chief means of effecting rescue. No incidents leading to injuries occurred in either preparations or transfer and at midday, by most accounts, the last survivor crested the rim, coming to rest on the heights.

Simmons addressed each survivor's injuries from the moment a wounded man reached the heights. He employed the entire arsenal of medical supplies with a coterie of appointed aides following closely behind him. He and the staff cleansed and set broken bones and treated, stitched, and bandaged lacerations. They applied splints to gross fractures and expeditiously removed limbs damaged beyond repair. The number of amputations remained low nonetheless, due, Hastings believed, to the receptive composition of the floor of the gorge where scores of men lay wounded and wailing in pain. It is the floor, he noted, unlike the gorge's rocky abutments, that consisted of decomposed grasses, limbs, and leaves and occasional shrubbery, all of which absorbed the full force of the men's weight upon landing. He praised the labors of Simmons and his aides during a respite, after which he called for the removal of the dead.

Laborers methodically arranged the dead in rows along the depths of the gorge and, tying them securely to a succession of chair-lifts, called for them to be hoisted straight upward along the face of the escarpment. In short order the heights above the precipice became a temporary resting place for scores of fallen soldiers. Hastings placed them in rows set opposite the stream from the wounded in a clearing bordered by saplings. He ordered the saplings cut down, covering the deceased with leaves and branches in order to ward off vermin and scavengers. He walked among the deceased looking for signs of the Captain. Finding nothing of interest, he conferred with Simmons, notably about the Captain's fate and the emerging matter of burying the dead.

"I have looked for the Captain to no avail, Simmons."

"In his crippled state I doubt that he has tarried far off."

"These men deserve a proper burial at Oswego, Simmons. Do we have sufficient transports?"

"Yes. We have transports. How many? I do not know. What do you propose?"

"I propose that we return to camp, bring the transports back here and search once more for the Captain."

"Hastings. In all of this we have not been attacked. What do you make of it?"

"That, my good man, is yet another mystery in the wealth of mysteries we encountered today."

* * *

A thunder clap and then the skies opened. In a midday cloudburst, sheets of rain mixed with hail stones pounded the earth, sending all able-bodied men running to find shelter. Simmons and Hastings covered the wounded with canvas tarpaulins, leaving a scarce few for the remaining crew-members. The once-diminutive stream regenerated itself. Gaining in size and strength, it began to course mightily over the precipice in a reprise of its ferocity. The waters lapped at the heels of the recumbent wounded, leaving laborers to carry them to higher stretches of the heights. Along the eastern bank of the stream where the deceased lay, the surging waters overflowed the bank, inundating neighboring lands. The soil grew saturated and began to break apart in sections along the gorge's rim. Clumps of earth slipped over the waterfall in turn. Rescuers, bent on aiding the wounded, literally turned a blind side to the deceased who lay exposed, awaiting transport. A soldier, otherwise occupied, cast a glance after them. He called out a warning to his mates:

"Look!! The cadavers are afloat."

Simmons and Hastings took heed immediately. Seizing grappling poles, they waded into the fierce waters from a position on the stream's left or western bank. Flanking the right bank and pressed against a protruding boulder, corpses, having slipped modest restraints, appeared poised to enter the swirling waters, perilously close to the gorge's rim*. The strong currents ripped at the men's extremities. A persistent undercurrent strived to draw them beneath the surface. The stream's sandy bottom began to pull away from them. They bent low in order to maintain a tenuous grip on the yielding, swirling bottom. Uppermost they knew that scarce precious moments remained between salvaging the dead and leaving them to hurtle over the waterfall. Tentatively the pair hooked into two cadavers. Steadfastly they pushed them back toward the tenuous bank, compressing them tightly against a boulder. Simmons held them in place while Hastings tore away heaps of mud from the bank. He pounded and kneaded the mud with bare hands, compacting it against the boulder where it grew in size and density. Soldiers on the bank tendered saplings to the two officers. In turn the two herded the remaining cadavers against the muddy bank, whereupon they pressed the saplings into service. In effect the officers built a corral out of the saplings. Thrusting one end of a sapling into the soft bank, they rammed the opposite end against the mud-encrusted boulder— giving the cadavers to nestle tightly within a cordoned-off corral. A burst of rescuers waded into the stream to lend support. Stumbling in the turgid waters, many came to within a meter of slipping into the gorge. Grappling hooks spared some of them. Increasingly the situation demanded that one make bold choices: saving oneself, saving a comrade, or saving the deceased. In the rush of events, the distinction between the three choices became blurred, then utterly indistinguishable, with the result that several rescuers poured over the waterfall into the murky crevasse. In response laborers constructed a sapling barrier. Launching the apparatus into the stream, they lashed it between two boulders forced into position, the better to forestall the loss of still more valued lives.

* * *

The rains ceased. The intimidating waters of the stream began to subside and the skies greeted all below with a burst of sunshine. Rescuers latched on to ropes and, bounding over the escarpment, repelled against its unyielding face while descending to the chasm's floor. There they reclaimed those who fell victim to recent calamities— the living and the cadavers in like measure. Ironically they went about the grim task with exuberance and in the course of inspecting the depths, they learned that not a single soul from among the late rescuers who plunged over the falls lived to tell about it.

Upon the heights a new danger took form. Animals emerged from the forest in the late afternoon to forage and to hunt. The largest of them, bears, required meat and they are not above consuming carrion, especially when it lies open and vulnerable. Smaller carnivores, crows and squirrels, readily take advantage of a ready-made feast. These creatures and more came forward after the abatement of the rains, while Hastings and his crew set about restoring the accommodations of the wounded who lay back among trees in a glen. A wolf howled and the crew glimpsed a bear making off with a cadaver, having broken through obstacles placed in its path. The thought of frightening the beast with firebrands gained little support. Given the dampness pervading the landscape, tinder, those shreds of wood essential to creating a flame, simply did not exist. The men's thoughts ran to their firearms, but these lay back at camp. In desperation a party of men circled the bear when it returned to snatch another meal. Shouting, they pelted the beast with stones. It dropped its meal and ran off.

Hastings declared the rescue and recovery at an end. He called a meeting whereupon he allocated wagons to accommodate the fifty-five deceased. Everyone moved to higher ground. Pitifully short of transports, Hastings ordered cadavers to be layered one on top of the other. The wounded occupied all remaining transports taken from camp where that ghastly horror struck. When the columns came together to begin the trek back to Oswego, he ordered a squad to find safe passage over the flat lands beyond the gorge. Upon the squad's return, the two-columned caravan departed the macabre scene with heavy hearts.

Granting the gorge a wide berth, the columns plunged into the forest. Laborers hacked through underbrush, cutting a path to the marshy lowlands. These in turn led into a wind-swept clearing of tall grasses. The men soon found the land able to bear the weight of the wagons without difficulty. They set about marking soft and low places—small bogs into which a wagon may slip. Occasionally that once-tumultuous stream came into view. No longer a tempest of fury, it flowed in the guise of a bland trickle, coursing languidly over the sodden terrain. The wagons too cut through the rudimentary path. Coming to rest on the grassy plain, they paused to await further instructions. Anticipating Hastings' approach, everyone swooned from the heat of the day. Flying insects in myriad swarms cascaded down upon the men, investing exposed flesh, sending them reeling over the plain, seeking cover. They placed sacks over their heads and stepped along tentatively at Hastings' urging. Apart from these misfortunes, the men found the beauty of the plain refreshing, where the vivid colors of the late summer merged with the softer tones of early autumn. They crossed the stream once again where it trickled through a low-lying recess. Harmlessly it flowed away, a thin, innocuous ribbon. The men caught glimpses of mounds of earth along the way: great hump-backed behemoths of mud, some with deep orifices, molded over generations by rushing waters and fierce winds.

The plain climbed into an undulating hill. The caravan negotiated its gentle slope without incident, coming to rest along a ridge running the length of the hill's summit. Here Hastings called a halt in order to develop with Simmons an alternate means for conveying the wounded. Principally, Hastings sought to alleviate the discomfort befalling those who rode in the incommodious, wood-planked wagons. Desperate, he cast about for suggestions, settling upon one Watkins who proposed the adoption of a method germane to the natives of the region.

"I have heard that the aborigines carry loads by means of a litter pulled by man or beast. They fasten two long boughs together at one end and tie them to the horse's harness. The boughs must trail along the earth on either flank of the animal. Skins are pulled across the boughs, making a framework of sorts. Drawn tight and lashed to the boughs, they support a heavy load. A man or stout woman may serve in place of the horse. I see that you have already felled many saplings. We have sufficient horses to complete the arrangement. I say that we do it."

"Splendid idea, Watkins. Let us see to it." The two men conferred, then rejoined the party. Hastings asked Watkins to divulge yet another thought.

"That I shall, Sir," he began. "The natives gather much more food than what they hunt. Much of it grows in the wild. Plentiful, it will sustain a village. Within a stone's throw there are many delights." He counted on his fingers: "There are mushrooms, roots, berries, apples, cherries, honeysuckle pears, sunflower seeds, and, of course, there is corn."

"Yes, Watkins. We must see to it immediately. Come with me. I will order a detail to build these litters of yours and one to search for edibles. We must hurry. Daylight is wasting." He ushered Watkins before him to the stream where he made a series of announcements, after which he appointed him in command of the project and went off to confer with Simmons. He found Simmons changing dressings:

"Any sightings of the Captain?"

Simmons, jaw set firmly, rose and approached his colleague: "Strange, but I accounted for every last soul but him. There are signs of him everywhere . . . clothing in his tent . . . his boot prints on the grounds . . . his tobacco spittle . . . even the knob of his cane in the earth. A prisoner, or a hungry bear's dinner, no less."

Hastings listened intently: "He is here. He is much too cunning to fall captive or be killed. He is in hiding. I believe him the victim of a seizure. He crawled off to recover in privacy before taking to the trail again."

"Simmons replied soberly, arm around his colleague's shoulder. "Let us send one more detail out to look, one more before we depart."

The pair walked among the wounded, pausing to give the men water from precious stores. They shifted them to different positions when they complained of soreness. They inspected wounds, daubing them with strong spirits and quinine. They beat back flies which began to gather on exposed flesh. To combat the congregation of flies and other air-borne insects, they ignited firebrands, then muffled the flames and fanned the plumes of smoke into the abundant soft vapors. Hot and intense labor, they drank liberally from water-flasks. Occasionally a man expired. Laborers carried him off to an open field to be wrapped for subsequent burial. Solemnly they loaded the deceased into wagons, one beside the other, then one stop the other. Once filled, the wagons assumed a position at the rear of the caravan bound for Oswego. Hastings vowed to inter the deceased at Fort Ontario: the garrison in which they originally quartered.

Watkins assembled one of his horse-lifts to demonstrate its usefulness. He laid two saplings down, a space between them. Crossing to one of the wagons, he returned with an armload of furs and skins. He crossed to the wagon again, carrying back an assortment of bows and arrows. He lashed two of the skins between the saplings, drawing them tight. With an aide holding the apparatus upright, he lay back on it to demonstrate its strength. Although delighted with Watkins' maneuvers, the men gave him to understand that the articles in the wagon posed a mystery to them—items new and foreign—for never in traversing the wilderness of late did they solicit or seek or openly procure native possessions.

Hastings inspected the lot. He concluded that the articles belonged to a private cache. He looked at Watkins, awaiting an explanation.

Watkins claimed innocence on the matter, having stumbled on the articles by accident. Men searched the wagon, finding pieces of the Captain's clothing. Hastings called a meeting: "These articles may belong to the Captain, but without his presence we shall have to postpone drawing hasty conclusions. May I remind you, however, to accept no gifts from the natives we happen to meet. Watkins. You may carry on."

Watkins drew a crew about him. He brandished a bow and arrow. "Gentlemen. We shall be hunting shortly to feed our hungry; however, we do not wish to excite the natives who live here. An arrow flies silently and is as deadly as a musket ball." He produced a series of baskets salvaged from the late evening's banquet. "We will fill these with the delicacies that the yonder fields and hillsides have reserved for us." His eyes sparkled and he appeared buoyed up by what the afternoon held in store for him. "Shall we be off, gentlemen?"

Eagerly the select crew followed him: Watkins promising to return early with palate-teasing delights. The remainder of the Forces harnessed the horse-drawn litters, loaded the wounded and brought the ensemble in line before the wagons of the deceased. A small party dropped back to dig fire pits and to bring out roasting spits.

With Hastings and Simmons in command, the caravan would make a final pass through the original camp grounds, a scarce two kilometers south, or downstream, in search of the Captain.

True to form, Watkins returned shortly, with baskets laden with fruits and tender morsels. Some of the men killed wild boars and turkeys on a romp through the hills and the thoughts of making the final feast a great one may have hastened the return to camp.

Dinner proved all too short in duration, but the succulence of the meats and additional treats made the effort worthwhile. Aides fed the wounded and no one went hungry. On Hastings' orders, the regulars buried the remains of their meal on completion and assumed a marching mode.

Watkins, a newly-arrived celebrity of sorts, rode slightly to the rear of Hastings and Simmons, who spoke softly with each other. Ostensibly they objected to burying the deceased at Fort Ontario, burned three years earlier by the French (1).An alerted Watkins listened, drawn by the two officer's secretiveness. He heard scant details:

"Yes. The Captain still lives," Hastings yielded. He always rises to the challenge of the unknown."

"He owes us an explanation, Hastings. His absence raises serious doubts and questions that reflect upon us."

The observant Watkins caught sight of a luxuriant hide, reminiscent of the articles in the private cache, protruding from beneath the pommel of Simmons' mount. Simmons and Hastings spoke guardedly, yet certain gestures indicated that the piece formed the basis of conversation. The pair took pains to put adequate distance between themselves and the sojourners, leaving Watkins begging to learn more. He remained intrigued, however, by the clandestine bent of the two officers. He assigned the event to memory: his repository for the oddities that took place on this day during this most uncanny and fatalistic journey into the wilderness.

*Carpenter's Falls: south of Skaneateles, NY and north of New Hope in the Bear Swamp National Forest

(1)Borneman, Walter R. (2006). The French & Indian War. Chapter 5: *"That I can Save England."* Harper/Collins

Publishers. 10 East 53rd St., New York. NY pgs:: 68-69

Chapter Three

Breaking New Ground
The Bear Chief Holds Council.
The Yorks Befriended.
Suzanne Forms A Friendship.
The Corn Festival Begins.

Led by the fleet Cerf Courant, the scouts of Osco ran ceaselessly through the night, their objective to find and report to the Bear Chief. Masters of the rigorous terrain, they made haste where novices may falter. In so doing, their tenacity and resolve, together with intermittent patches of moonlight, guided them along pathways of their own creation. Propelled by anger and a sense of disgust in witnessing the barbarism of the peaus blancs, the men ran in a single unit, joined by a common goal. They quickly closed the seven league gap between Osco and the scene of the slaughter of brother bear. Drawing up beside the great camp fire at Osco, Cerf Courant signaled his men to halt. Overhead the brilliant moon smiled favorably upon him. In spite of the tragedy of the late evening, he envisioned peaceful days for himself and all of the villagers.

Although early in the new day, bright coals still glowed in the great camp fire. He brushed his hand over the warm hearth stones. The many footprints in the soft soil told him that a meeting took place by the camp fire not long before. His senses told him that something of importance took place. He picked up his pace, crossing the grounds to the door of his leader's lodge where he called softly at the front portal. A sleepy Colombe Blanche greeted him and he deferred speaking with her, asking her to grant him an audience with her husband. She insisted upon speaking however, and her words startled him: "My husband has guests. He has given them a lodge and is now speaking with them. They are of the peaus blancs. Come! I will bring you."

Colombe Blanche led Cerf Courant to a lodge next to her own. Inside, seated beside a modest fire, her husband conversed with two guests: a white man and a young woman. The guests occupied two of Colombe Blanche's finest blankets, usually reserved for important occasions. The young woman spoke French, Cerf Courant observed, the language that the Bear Chief spoke when meeting with others of the white flesh. While his guests ate and drank, he gestured to Cerf Courant to join him by the fire. He introduced the man as James York and the young woman as Suzanne, his daughter. He allowed his faithful ally the opportunity to pronounce his guests' names, once, twice, thrice, until James York and Suzanne laughingly gave their approval. Cerf Courant gripped the hand which James York offered him. Smooth to the touch, it held a strength that rivaled his own and his initial hesitation subsided. Comfortable speaking in French, he gave his account of the tragedy to which he bore witness.

"Fearless One. Many peaus blancs visited our hunting grounds yesterday in the region of the Great Falls. Le Pecheur, myself, and another watched their movements long into the night. They feasted and played at games and made loud conversation until the moon reached its zenith. Then something terrible happened." He paused, his voice trembling, but he continued at the Bear Chief's urging:

"A brother bear wandered into their camp. He may have been drawn by their food. Certainly the gaiety attracted many creatures of the night. Men sighted the bear. I believe they are soldiers. They chased him and poked at him with sticks. The bear stood his ground against the men. This angered them and one of them stabbed him with a lance. The bear chased the man and killed him and killed another before other soldiers fired at him with their loud fire-sticks. Not content with leaving brother bear to die, these soldiers cut off his head and hide and put them on display and mocked his remains. I and the others grew sickened by the sight. We wanted to kill the soldiers, but they are too many. In our sorrow we aimed our bows high and fired our arrows in a great arc over their camp. We heard the screams of men in pain and we fled, coming to rest on your doorstep." He wiped his face free of tears and continued:

"Fearless One. We believe these soldiers to be partners of the Devil Spirit and we know not what to do. We ask for your wise counsel." He fell silent, awaiting a reply. All eyes turned to the Bear Chief.

He rose quietly. He stepped back to face those in attendance and, in an air of confidence, began in French: "Recently a series of events have taken place which are altogether new and different to the residents of Osco. We villagers have no historical means of treating with them to the extent that many of us are confused and fear-struck. Perhaps these events are tests of our strength and valor which our Creator has visited upon us. If this is true, then the coming of the soldiers and the slaughter of brother bear are the means by which our Creator has chosen to force us to grow and develop as a People. We all know that in coming together and forming strategies for treating with misfortune, we will turn out so much the stronger and continue to reap the benefits which our Creator has reserved for us. I believe that our concerns are great enough to merit the attention of the Clan Mothers. As you are well-aware, they are the governing body of our People. Their collective wisdom will guide us in approaching these new events ranging from the summer storm, the arrival of our welcomed guests, and the soldiers who lurk at our doorstep."

He pulled from his pocket a gold-encased round object suspended from a thin, golden chain. Upon consulting the surface of the object he exclaimed: "We will meet in one hour with the Clan Mothers in their lodge." Deftly he pocketed his shiny object and prepared to depart the meeting when Cerf Courant inquired about the piece. "Ah, mon ami. This is a gift from Henri Marchand. He calls it la montre à la chaîne— the watch on a chain. It divides our day into twenty four equal parts or hours. You have only to look at the needle to learn the hour of the day. I must go now." He gave la montre to Colombe Blanche who called Cerf Courant to her side. She guided him in counting the hours with her, holding out a corresponding finger as she spoke. She explained that the large needle gave the hour and the small needle gave segments or components of the hour. "It is now 10:20," she recited, demonstrating with her fingers. "It is much improved over our counting method. Perhaps Monsieur Marchand will give you la montre and we will talk more about it." Cerf Courant nodded and departed the lodge.

Colombe Blanche directed her attention to her husband's guests. "You have heard the name 'Henri Marchand.' He brings us gifts through the year. They are very useful in the managing of a household. Concerning la montre, all the principal leaders of Osco have them. You will meet him one day. He comes from a fortress in the land of the Onondagas, our kin to the east. He supplies our basic wants in exchange for some of the skins and furs our People have taken from the creatures of the forest. He is good man and has traded with us for many years. He has befriended the Onondagas when food grew scarce in the winter seasons. Many of them have taken residence in his fortress and remain in his employ through the seasons. He has given us to understand that he will protect our interests as long as we continue to protect his interests. I am not fully knowledgeable of all that he speaks, but I have confidence in his friendship and sincerity."

Soon a courier entered the lodge. He announced to Colombe Blanche that the hour of the council with the Clan Mothers drew near. She invited James and Suzanne to accompany her. They must adopt the role of observer, she said, for they are not members of the village and do not speak the language of the Five Nations. "You must think of the Clan Mothers as members of your own family," she spoke, noticing a degree of hesitancy on the part of Suzanne. She took the young woman by the hand and, smiling, escorted her and her father over the camp grounds to one of the largest lodges in the village.

Suzanne counted five women seated around a stone hearth in the center of the lodge. An ample fire spread its warmth throughout the entire structure. In contrast to the morning's coolness, she welcomed the soothing warmth of the fire. It sent little shivers through her limbs and the flesh on her arms rose up in minute bumps. The women sat stoically with legs crossed on thickly woven mats (2), their countenance fixed straight ahead. With eyes darting back and forth, they otherwise sat immobile before their guests. They wore tunics and leggings stitched with long, flowing streamers, each woman wearing a costume unique to her own design. The stunning yet subdued colors reminded Suzanne of the autumnal season fast approaching. She and her father sat opposite the women on mats. Colombe Blanche sat between them and invited her guests to partake of the beverage beside them. Suzanne sipped from her cup. She delighted in the sweet taste of the mixture. Curious about the beverage, she longed to inquire after it, but, in light of the implied solemnity of her new surroundings, she declined.

The Bear Chief entered the lodge. He wore a tunic and complementary leggings. A long row of stitches in either seam of his leggings accented his height which, Suzanne estimated, rivaled her father's. He expended a few moments extracting his montre and trail calendar. Replacing them within his uniform he announced his findings in French, a language which pleased Suzanne immensely: "C'est aujourd'hui vendredi, le 8 de Septembre: It est dix heures trente au matin."—Today is Friday, the eighth of September. It is 10:30 a.m. He sat beside Suzanne's father and without ceremony began to speak to the Clan Mothers:

"The summer storms have sent two strangers to our doorstep. I have met with them and found them to be friendly, for they returned the kindness extended to them after I and several others pulled them out of serious difficulties. In my mind they remain strangers no longer. On the other hand there exist those of the white flesh who present a much different image. These are soldiers who entered our hunting grounds unannounced, conducting themselves more like children than men. In their wild actions they attacked and slaughtered one brother bear, the symbol of our clan, not to partake of his flesh, but to desecrate him.

"Nature is both cruel and kind, we know. We know that following the havoc of the summer storms a new day full of promise shines bright and clear upon us and we go about our lives with a renewed sense of purpose. This is the fickle way of Nature. I ask: Is this the way of the peaus blancs? Are they as wavering and changing as Nature? Cruel one day and kind the next? We know that we are unable to change the vagaries of Nature. This we have learned to accept. Yet we ask how there may be within the community of the peaus blancs those who profess goodness and those who present evil. On this matter we are sorely confused."

One of the Clan Mothers spoke, the eldest of the entourage, Suzanne estimated. "Thank you for inviting our council, Bear Chief. You desire to learn the meaning of the messages which the peaus blancs have sent to you. Thus far these messages have confused you and, as a result, you know not how to treat with these newcomers. We of the Clan Mothers believe that the peaus blancs are of two distinct camps and have sent you two distinct messages. However, you must regard them as a product of Nature in the same manner that we are a product of Nature, and, as such, subject to all of Nature's rewards and shortcomings.

"Your two guests seated before you come in peace. They have come a great distance, one wrought with pain and hardship in order to seek your guidance. They seek the truth in a matter vital to them and they have learned the stories of your beneficence as they sought your place of residence. Therefore, in their period of need they desire your friendship and counsel in securing the truth. They trust in your ability to deliver the truth to them. In return they will repay you with kindness and become allied with you in all of your endeavors far into your life.

"These peaus blancs arrived without women or children. Therefore, they are not part of a family that looks after its own kind and comes to share the land and its wealth with all whom they meet. No. They have come with broad trappings, provisions to sustain them for long periods in the woodlands. They come in a great, consuming body, ready to convert the woodlands and all people in it to their own purposes. They remind us of an invading army of locusts. They carry booming sticks. Not necessarily evil, booming sticks are a threatening instrument when their owners force the innocent to obey commands unconditionally. In evil hands booming sticks are evil instruments.

"Of these peaus blancs we believe they are driven by their own greed. It will be difficult to communicate with them because they do not speak our language, nor do they stand still long enough to learn of our ways. At first glance they appear intractable. We believe that you must observe these men carefully. You must also shore up your defenses to secure your People's security. They speak words which are strange to us and pose the threat of danger. Keep the peaus blancs at a distance. Never let them escape your vision."

The Bear Chief stood before the Clan Mothers. He praised their knowledge and appreciation of his concerns regarding the new-arrivals in his land. He then asked the Clan Mothers to grant James and Suzanne York an audience, a motion unknown in his opinion throughout all of Iroquoia.

Suzanne stood before the Clan Mothers. Initially she paid tribute to the Bear Chief for having rescued her and her father and for having welcomed them into their home. She then found favor with the religious tone of her host's statements: "His is a religion founded on nature and nature stands for the renewal of life. Christianity holds the same view, that one's religion is a renewal of life. Our two views, although taking root in two different parts of the world, are surprisingly similar. I find this very interesting and believe that, by exchanging knowledge, we will come to form the beginnings of a strong friendship."

"Your thoughts are accepted and demonstrate a maturity beyond your tender years, Mademoiselle York. You have shared a part of your history with us, something that comes as a surprise to us," one of the Clan Mothers returned. "Before you resume your place, we would like you to agree to serve as interpreter in matters where French is spoken. This is a post that brings one into the confidence of those who make decisions affecting a great many people. You may begin immediately. Do we have your agreement?"

A nervous, yet honored Suzanne fought to maintain composure: "Yes, yes. Of course, Madame."

"Good. I believe that your father wishes to speak. You may usher him forward."

James York rose. Facing the Clan Mothers, he began slowly: "My daughter and I and the soldiers of the white flesh are called English in our homeland. We come from two islands on the far side of a great ocean, but that is the extent of what we have in common. Specifically, I am Irish and come from the smaller of the islands. For centuries my people and the English have fought hard battles. They are mostly over the governance of our land, but a religious difference has most recently served as a point of divisiveness between our two islands. For the most part the English have prevailed in battle because of their superior strength in numbers and weapons. Now the English have come to your country. They have overgrown their island. It is too small to feed and clothe them and they come here to take away that which they lack at home." He yielded to the Bear Chief.

"I have heard of this great ocean. Our brothers, the Mahican and Delaware to the east have encountered these English. They have told me that these English came ashore in a thick mass. They paddled great canoes equipped with giant wings that unfolded when they caught the vapors. Never before have my brothers seen such a sight. The English did not stop to speak with my brothers. They plunged into the forests to hunt and trap. They stole away with women and the young. They killed with their fire-sticks those who resisted. Worse, the English left behind dreaded maladies which mowed down our brothers, killing many more than the fire-sticks. To their last breath my brothers have vowed to fight these English. I ask: Do these English soldiers carry the same evil intentions? I call upon your guidance, Clan Mothers." He deferred to James York.

"I put great merit in the words of your leader. However, there is one more reason, I believe, for the English presence here in your country. They are at war with the French. Across the great ocean they also wage war against the French. They are trying to drive them from their colonies the world over and claim them for themselves. The English presence here is yet another example of their unlimited ambition to pursue the French. Do the French and English not rival each other for your trade?"

"Yes," a Clan Mother spoke. "They have also clashed at French forts along the St. Lawrence."

"Do not forget that the French burned Fort Ontario not long ago," another replied.

James York continued: "You may be placing yourself in a dangerous position between two stubborn rivals."

The eldest of the Clan Mothers (3) spoke: "We too have heard of this rivalry. We have been put upon by both rivals who, in their own way, wave gifts under our noses in an effort to earn our allegiance. We tolerate their persistence, but privately laugh at their stupidity in trying to destroy each other."

A heretofore silent Clan Mother asked to be heard: "It troubles me that these rivals rush to shed blood over the land which we of Osco and all the villages hold in stewardship for Nature. Although we act as Nature's surrogate, we are prohibited from altering Nature for our own self-seeking purposes. This includes the senseless killing of another. We are like children and Nature is our mother. Therefore, all of us, even the peaus blancs, are children of Nature. We are all subject to Her laws. They are binding and unbending, but they grant benefits to those who will follow them. I believe that you, Monsieur, desire to live within Nature's boundaries. In this manner you will be able to reap the benefits that Nature has in store for you. Therefore, we Clan Mothers, acting as Nature's representatives, may be able to help you resolve a burning question. I trust that you came here with such a question."

"Yes, Madame. I have a wife. Her name is Caroline and someone took her from me and Suzanne by force. It is possible that the thief lies amidst the English who have found their way into your country. I say this because not long before she vanished certain Englishmen of persuasion visited our holdings, offering to purchase them. We, of course, refused, whereupon a member of Caroline's family died a mysterious death and she herself vanished. In searching for her we chanced upon a friendly French garrison whose commandant is on friendly terms with the Bear Chief. Given the magnitude of the task in finding Caroline, he pointed out that the Bear Chief has key allies throughout this country, some of whom may possess knowledge relevant to Caroline's disappearance."

"Thank you, Monsieur York. Let me ask. You claim no relationship to these soldiers? You came here out of your own accord, not by subterfuge or evil design?"

"Yes, Madame."

"You say that the peaus blancs steal people from their *own* kind?"

The Bear Chief intervened on James' behalf: "It is possible that the English who stole away women and children from our Delaware allies also stole away with Madame York."

"The taking of another is not unique to the English," a Clan Mother spoke. "Our brothers, the Seneca, have long sought after and taken members of foreign nations."

Another Clan Mother spoke: "The Seneca take others in order to replenish their numbers, many of whom have fallen in wars, died of starvation, and fallen to contagions which the peaus blancs spread among them. That is not the same kind of *taking* of which Monsieur speaks."

"This is true, Madame", James spoke. "It is common among some men to sell captives into slavery for a great price. Those with laudable traits carry a great premium. At the very least they serve in the masters' households."

"That is an extensive practice among the peaus blancs," a Clan Mother said. "Unfortunately for the nations, the peaus blancs pursued the practice upon opening trade relations with us. Some nations, growing dependent upon them, have rendered their own people dishonor by adopting the practice unto themselves. Tell me. What qualities does your wife possess?"

"Caroline is a loving and caring mother. She has raised two intelligent children. Suzanne is testimony of her qualities. She is a first-rate cuisinière and homemaker who is equal to any man in the home or in the field. She is not afraid to speak her mind and others seek her counsel. I am a very fortunate man." He fought back tears.

The Clan Mothers held a brief conference, after which the eldest addressed James York: "Monsieur. We believe that these men will neither sell nor kill your wife. She will be held as a servant, we believe, to a man of high station. At bottom he will trade her away for someone or something of similar value, if, perhaps, she fails to meet his needs. Keep in mind that the greater her qualities, the more her master will cling to her. This may cause disagreements along the way, some with severe consequences.

"We believe that once you find your wife, you will find who has taken her. We further believe that you came here of your own accord, unattached to external or foreign ties. You know not of these English, nor do they know of you. Your sacrifice and pain in coming here proves that your burning question is genuine and sincere. You have earned our support and that of the Bear Chief. Confide in him and you will find the solution to your concerns. This council is ended. Go in peace."

* * *

The Bear Chief and Colombe Blanche escorted their guests from the lodge. With Suzanne interpreting, James asked the Bear Chief to intervene in his search for his wife. He paused to reflect. The little party came to a halt around him, awaiting his remarks. When he spoke, he indicated that finding Caroline York called for a collective effort of major players. He introduced the name of the tradesman, Henri Marchand, a valuable ally and a reliable friend. "Monsieur Marchand travels the Lake Country from top to bottom. He is among the first to learn of developments of great magnitude, after which he confides them to me. He is due to arrive during the Corn Festival, a good occasion to meet with him."

James detected a note of hesitancy in his host's demeanor. In light of his favorable audience with the Clan Mothers, he anticipated more enthusiastic support. While he entertained these thoughts, the Bear Chief asked a question which put James's reservations about his host to rest:

"There is no one among the English who are assisting you on the matter of your wife?"

"No. Not at all."

"The English know *not* of your plans to find your wife?"

"This is true. I labor alone and confide in those whom I deem trustworthy."

"I find it difficult to believe that no English will come to your aid."

"Suzanne and I find ourselves in a delicate position. If we approach the English to press for Caroline's return, one of three events will take place: They will arrange for Caroline's release upon receipt of a large ransom. They may disavow knowledge of her, or they may have Suzanne and myself jailed for making false claims. Such is the influence of the English high command in the Lake Country. A ransom I am unable to pay. Moreover, it is highly unlikely that a mere commoner, is able to obtain an audience with a member of the established command."

"You say that you are prevented from addressing others of your kind because they occupy the high ground?"

"Exactly. There are certain customs which keep us apart."

"And which make enemies of friends."

"Yes. You have it."

"Yours is a strange community, Monsieur York. I am not able to live in such a community. We have no such hard and fast divisions at Osco, or throughout the Confederacy. You have taught me something important."

Both men looked up to see Chien Aboyant running toward them. The little man stopped before the Bear Chief and, tugging on his sleeve, whispered a message in his native language. The Bear Chief, expressionless, nodded in understanding and approached James and Suzanne York: "Many English soldiers have died. They plunged over a waterfall not far from Osco. It is the Great Falls. Something frightened them. There are rumors that they feared an attack from hostile natives and fled for their lives."

Suzanne translated quickly from the French, then ran sobbing into her father's outstretched arms. "Father! If the soldiers attack the village the Bear Chief will never come to our aid. We will never find mother." She broke into tears, flinging herself upon James's chest.

Her father tried to console her: "Dear daughter. The Bear Chief believes that we have no ties with the soldiers. This is good for us, but lays bare our unfortunate set of circumstances. The worst that may happen is that we are forced to search for mother on our own. Think of it, Suzanne. Unknown to all, we are free to search to our heart's content, silently, drawing no attention. The thought remotely has merit, however grim." He drew her chin to his chest and patted her head and his soothing words calmed her.

The Bear Chief took note of the compassion between father and daughter. "We will follow the council of the Clan Mothers. We begin by building our defenses of the village. Aboyant! Follow these English and report to me their whereabouts." He turned to James York: "The English know not of our village. We are free to build our defenses without interruption. How do you see this matter, Monsieur York?"

"These English are impulsive. They tend to follow the commands of a single leader who is well-equipped for open-field warfare. He knows of no other ways to engage an enemy. Knowing this, we must fight them in ways new and different to them. Here. Let me show you about fortifications."

With the Bear Chief at his side, James bent over the earth with a sharpened stick. He etched a form of earthworks into the soft soil, speaking as he labored: "This is a *rampart*, a great mound of earth overlooking the palisades. From the summit one may rain arrows down upon an invader. Inside are channels where one may take shelter in the event of a siege. One of them attaches to a tunnel going underground leading to the rear gate of the village. From there the safety of the forest awaits."

"This is good counsel, Monsieur York. I will present the matter of your wife to Monsieur Marchand. By your hand I conclude that we have reached an agreement." He offered his hand to James York and the two men thus inaugurated the beginning of a friendship.

An elated James made an observation. "I have a likeness of Caroline. Let me send for my daughter." To his rear Suzanne heard him speaking and, taking her leave of Colombe Blanche, scurried off to her lodge. Returning shortly, she beamed radiantly, producing a small box clothed in velvet. Obligingly, she handed the box to her father. James approached the Cayuga chieftain and delicately removed the lid. "Go ahead. You may hold it."

Carefully the Bear Chief peered within the box. Inside a portrait framed in gold bore the likeness of a beautiful woman. Young when sitting for her portrait, the woman wore long blonde tresses gathered at the neck. With blue eyes, porcelain complexion, and prominent cheekbones, she appeared tall and self-assured. A faint smile crossed her lips and her glowing cheeks bore a hint of powder. The Bear Chief looked from the image to Suzanne and back again, making comparisons.

"Yes. She bears a strong resemblance to Suzanne," James spoke.

"Father. If Aboyant took the portrait with him he may be able to show it to others on his travels."

"Suzanne. The portrait has survived the summer storm. It must never leave your hands. After all, it is one of a kind, the last possession of our home, less the clothes on our backs."

"Please forgive me, father. Wait! Let me show it to Aboyant. Let me test his memory." She scampered off.

She returned shortly with the quixotic Aboyant. He held the box to his heart, then transferred it to his forehead, then back again to his heart. He spoke in French: "I will never forget such a beautiful face." Kissing the portrait, he returned it to Suzanne, smiled and bowed and went to stand beside the Bear Chief: "I have chosen my men, Fearless One. You will have me to go now?"

"Yes. Take provisions for five days and report to me your findings, however small. Agreed?" Aboyant bounded off. The Bear Chief asked to inspect the portrait once again. He traced his fingers around the oval-shaped gilded border. "I have seen this brilliance before," he confided to James. "I have two small stones which give off this brilliance. My wife believes they bring Bonne Chance to the holder."

"That is Good Luck, father."

"Yes. I am quite aware of that, dear daughter."

Suzanne addressed the Cayuga leader. "Mother sat for her portrait on her anniversaire"—birthday. She held out a thin golden chain attached to the frame. "The ensemble is called a *locket* and goes around the neck of the woman." She demonstrated.

The Bear Chief nodded with understanding. "We have such things here at Osco," he confided.

"Oh! A locket?," Suzanne exclaimed.

"Non! Pas du tout. Des anniversaires"—No! Not at all. Birthdays.

Suzanne broke out in laughter, followed by her father to a lesser degree. The Cayuga leader permitted a slight smile to cross his lips, unaware of the humor which he inadvertently manufactured.

James York regarded the locket. He spoke to his host: "Truly, many men covet this locket dearly."

"I understand. They are drawn by her beauty and stature."

"Thank you, but it is because of this." James's fingers traced over the gold-laced border of the piece. "Some men in my world are drawn to kill or steal for this amount of brilliance."

"The ways of your community are indeed new to us, Monsieur York. For us the brilliance holds no value beyond its beauty. We take delight in a thing of beauty and share it with our friends. We never think to covet it—to hide it from others of our community. A thing of beauty is to be enjoyed by all." He made sweeping gestures, pointing to the locket with one hand and to the clear, blue sky with the other.

"Let me tell you about the brilliant stones, Monsieur. My wife keeps them in her pocket. When she puts on a new costume she puts the stones into a pocket. She held them during the summer storm. She held them upon your rescue. She brought them to the council with the Clan Mothers. Something good took place at the end of these events. Your locket is for you what the stones are for her. As long as you hold it near you, nothing harmful will disturb you or your family."

'How eloquent,' Suzanne thought.

"Tell me," James asked. "What do you wish for with your stones?"

"I ask for good fortune to shine upon my hearth and home."

'Utterly brilliant,' Suzanne thought. 'He speaks pearls of wisdom which rival those of heads of state.'

"You have spoken the words that Suzanne and I wish for in our prayers," James returned.

The Bear Chief stepped back. A tugging at his clothing diverted him. He looked down to see the cherubic faces of his sons greeting him. He tousled their hair. They squealed in delight. He pummeled them playfully, then called them to attention and introduced them to his guests.

"The small one is Raven. He has eleven years. The taller one, Little Bear, has thirteen years. They are full of life and almost as difficult." Again the delicate smile crossed his lips.

"They are so beautiful, Monsieur," Suzanne remarked. The boys promptly scurried behind their father's back, their faces crimson.

"They approve of you, although you have more years," Colombe Blanche offered. "They are at an age when the world opens up for them. It is a wonderful place for them. Every day is a day of discovery and adventure. You remember those days, do you not, Mademoiselle?"

"Yes, and I miss them dearly." She thought a moment, then added: "Perhaps that is what I enjoy about my stay here . . . ummm, discovery and adventure."

"My sons have begun to study French," Colombe Blanche offered, coming to stand beside Suzanne.

"Soon they will be as proficient as their father", Suzanne returned, cheerfully.

"By the way, thank you for interpreting my husband's words for your father. You are very talented."

"French is one of my enjoyments. At home I have books in French . . . mostly on affairs of state."

"You will be famous one day," Colombe Blanche conceded.

"Oh no, Madame. At home it is the men who hold sway in affairs of state . . . supported of course by a strong woman. Here the Clan Mothers make policy. This is good, but my community is not ready for women . . . at least not at the present period in history."

"Indeed! That bit of knowledge astounds me. After all, the woman makes up one half of the household in your community as well as in mine. By this practice you are throwing away one half of your strength as a community."

"I agree, Madame, although I have not thought about it in exactly your terms."

"Our chief sachem says that it takes a calamity, such as a war, for changes to take place."

"At home we believe that through hard labor and sacrifice changes take place."

"We have not known this always to be the case, Mademoiselle."

"Nevertheless, Madame. I have the sense that we have known each other through the ages."

"I have the same sense." Colombe Blanche laughed, lightly. She gripped Suzanne's shoulder and they walked on, the boys scurrying along behind them.

* * *

"We have yet to take our guests on a tour of the village," Colombe Blanche called to her husband.

"I welcome the pleasure. The thought has not escaped me," the Bear Chief condescended.

"I am not the first to think of it?" she chided.

"Hardly. I sought only to await the proper moment."

"The day is not long enough, my husband," she called.

Turning to face his wife, the Bear Chief grasped her hand, and, pulling her to his side, set off in bold steps. Suzanne held fast to Colombe Blanche and all the members of the entourage picked up the pace appreciably, although not necessarily with great satisfaction.

The little party reached the main portals of the village. On either extreme of the entrance laborers broke out picks and shovels. "They are building two of your mounds here," the Cayuga chieftain explained: "They will also build one at the postern gate. They will carry mud from the river bank to make them firm. They will cut channels into a corridor beneath them." He walked the grounds gracefully, taking pride in his presentation.

"You see that our men and women labor together," Colombe Blanche pointed out to Suzanne. "The women fill the carts with mud and the men pull them. While the men build the mounds, the women bring the tools to the site and wash them clean when they are soiled."

"Where do your tools come from?" Suzanne asked.

"Henri Marchand brings them. He has a post to the east."

"What does he ask of you in return?"

"Friendship." She explained tartly:

"To join fast our friendship he brings us fire-sticks with ball and powder in exchange for some of our furs and skins. I bake bread in an oven which Monsieur Marchand presented me for my anniversaire."

"You have a trade relationship with Monsieur Marchand, it appears."

"Yes, Mademoiselle. He supplies us with our hard goods." She pointed to an iron kettle (4) beside the central camp fire. "We have an anvil for making spear tips of iron. He has also given us wooden bowls and plates and dining instruments. Every household has enough for a family of six. It is more than trade, I believe."

"His generosity is boundless."

"We exchange clothing with him. We supply him with deerskin leggings for the hard winters and he brings us long women's dresses of cotton. Indeed, Monsieur Marchand is generous. Some of our foods are not native to this region. Monsieur Marchand brings us potatoes and tomatoes from the gardens at his post. You must see it one day."

"Life is better for you with Monsieur Marchand at hand?"

"Yes. We have become dependent on him for many little pleasures of life. Of course we supply his needs as well. He once said that we are the eyes and ears of the Lake Country."

"You have a genuine interest in each other, Madame. Friendship."

"Yes. Friendship."

"What articles does Monsieur Marchand value of you the most?"

"Our furs and skins. He sends them half way across the world where they become luxurious garments for those who walk and ride streets paved with stone."

"Are there enough for you and the rest of the world together?"

"No. This is what concerns me. Through close relations with tradesmen, our native specimens have dwindled to the point of disappearing from our homeland. This makes me sad. Our men know it, but they have been bitten by the peaus blancs' bug of greed and rush to satisfy it. We will survive if we are able to maintain our distance from them. We must seek friendship with boundaries."

'Such an astute woman,' Suzanne thought.

"What do you hope for in your friendship with Monsieur Marchand?"

"Monsieur Marchand asks no more of us than we are willing to give. Moreover, ours is a small community and the bug of greed has not chosen to reside among us. We remain secure for the present."

"Are there not others who long for your trade?"

"Oh! The English. They have visited our neighbors to the east and west. They have plentiful goods, more than the French, but they do not offer friendship. Unfortunately, some members of the Confederacy have chosen to trade with them. They are, I believe, in grave danger. We believe that the English come to take away the lands of the People by means of clever devices. They are masters at deception and before one realizes, his lands are gone from him forever. Our Delaware brothers know full well of what I speak."

"You are very knowledgeable about present-day affairs. How do you remain abreast of events?"

"My knowledge stems from my husband, the Bear Chief. His father Moray, is the uncle of Tah:gah:jute, and brother of his father, Shikellimus. Tah:gah:jute became the famous orator of his People, the Gayogoho:no. Tah:gah:jute has traveled the countryside speaking out for his brothers, who strive to hold on to their precious lands. At this moment he is in the land of the Ohio near Fort Duquesne with our allies, the Delaware. They have been pushed further west and Tah:jah:jute is speaking with officers of the government to stake them a final claim, one which they may hold forever. This is so important to him that he has brought his family to the Ohio country."

"This is incredible, Madame. Please continue."

"Tah:gah:jute first saw the light of day here at Osco. At an early age his father took him on sojourns to most of the villages of the Confederacy. They met with the leaders of the day, both native and peaus blancs and put their trust in many of them. It is in the Delaware country that Shikellimus became friends with James Logan of the Penn family. Logan supported the Delaware land claims in his council chambers, so pleasing Shikellimus that he baptized his son with the Christian name of 'Logan.' Messieurs Penn and Logan have since passed away, leaving strained relations between the Delaware and the peaus blancs. All this has given rise to Tah:gah:jute's presence on the Ohio, for this is where a good portion of the Delaware have gone."

"The Delaware are in search of a homeland?"

"Yes. They have also grown tired of the promises which the Ohio leaders have made."

"This is most unfortunate. What are your thoughts on the matter?"

"Tah:gah:jute and others will try to talk in terms of peace. Failing that, there will be war." Colombe Blanche turned way her head with these words, wiping away tears. When she spoke again, her tone seemed uplifted:

"Do you intend to remain long among us?"

"As long as you will have me."

"Good. You may teach my sons French. You interpret very well and the Frenchman takes to the field too much. The boys need constant instruction if they are to learn the language."

"I am honored. I will begin tomorrow." Suzanne embraced her hostess about the shoulders.

"Tomorrow begins the Corn Festival. It runs for seven days. Custom dictates that we attend and participate."

"I understand. We have a later rendez-vous, Madame." Suzanne shook the hand of her hostess.

"Very good. Come. My husband calls for us to join him on his tour. We must give him our full attention, or he will shrink away and not speak to me for days."

"You seem very content here."

"Yes. I am. I hope that you stay long enough to enjoy this place as much as me." Again they hugged and waited for the Bear Chief to join them.

* * *

The Bear Chief ushered the small party to the great camp fire. There, women roasted ears of corn on iron grilles, donated no less by Monsieur Marchand. Nearby, other women pounded corn kernels into a meal and from there into flattened cakes which they in turn heated over the grilles. Once turned to a golden brown, the women piled them into bowls, covering them with maple syrup. Further along, women made corn soup. They supplemented the stock with stringed beans, mild and hot peppers, onions, and corn off the husk, stirring the components until well mixed and heated to suit the most discriminating of palates. Moving along to a fourth venue, the Bear Chief invited Suzanne to sip from the contents of a large urn standing within a woven basket. Suzanne raised the urn and, tossing back her head, drank from the long, narrow neck of the urn. Immediately she winced and her eyes watered, but she swallowed the potion, giving a guarded look over her shoulder to her host.

"Strong, but tasty. What is it?"

"Whiskey. Corn whiskey, Mademoiselle," her host replied, his countenance placid.

Beside her Aboyant rolled his eyes and turned down the corners of his mouth. "You will be sick tomorrow, Mademoiselle," he uttered cautiously.

"Not unless I become sick now," Suzanne returned, sardonically.

The little man dashed off, returning with a goblet of water.

"Thank you. So much better. I believe that I will live," she spoke, blushing.

"The Corn Festival begins with a procession. Then there are dances," Colombe Blanche offered.

"Do not forget the stories, mother," Little Bear interjected.

"Yes. There are stories. Very colorful stories," she laughed, tousling her son's hair.

The procession moved to one of several banquet tables. The Cayuga chieftain took delight in reciting the variety of entrées prepared for the villagers. Suzanne noted that they went from light to medium to heavy in composition. At Colombe Blanche's invitation, she chose a plate of sweet potatoes, roasted meat rolled between leaves of boiled cabbages, and corn cakes flavored with syrup. Her father, James, stacked roasted slices of meat topped with onions and green peppers between two thick pieces of bread. Behind him Aboyant selected a thick paste made of roasted squash mixed with nuts and berries. He spread the mixture between two slices of bread. The three shared a pumpkin pie for dessert.

"There is a story behind the choice of pumpkin at the Festival," Colombe Blanche spoke. At Suzanne's inquiry she explained: "The Pumpkin has always wanted the Festival to be dedicated to itself, but lost favor to an overpowering Corn, which is our traditional food. In its victory over Pumpkin as the People's choice, Corn set out displays at all the banquet tables, save one. This is reserved for Pumpkin in the form of desserts, for Corn believed that Pumpkin made pies the envy of all of the contenders for dessert at the banquet tables."

Suzanne nodded in appreciation of the tale, yet knew not whether to count it as genuine lore or Colombe Blanche's attempt at humor. She decided against pressing the matter, for she determined that the tale succeeded on both counts. Pleased with the tour, she grasped her hostess by the hand and they continued their review.

Colombe Blanche invited Suzanne to taste one of the many pies. "Of course you know that the village mothers make these. This one has grapes, berries currants, sweet potatoes, roasted meat, cinnamon and sugar. Do you have a name for it at home?"

Suzanne tasted the pie. "Back home this is called 'mince pie.'" She rubbed her stomach affectionately.

"We simply call it la tourte remarquable—the outstanding pie— and save it for special occasions. My husband, the War Chief, is the spokesman of the Corn Festival. He is the living symbol of the first War Chief of our people, Wenenhs. We are The People of the Swamp, the Gayogoho:no. He came from Goiogouen, a village overlooking Lake Gayogoho:no to the west of Lake Osco. The lake drains into a great swamp on its northern border. There our People first took root some four centuries ago. I was born in the village of Goiogouen (5), the principal village of our People. It sits on a hill and has many lodges which are warm in winter and cool in summer. Many visitors came to our village over the years. Of these, les Français are the most frequent. We began trade relations with them and adopted the ways of their religion, Catholicism, in order to demonstrate the sincerity of our friendship with them. Behind our hill lies a deep gully hemmed in by trees. A strong stream flows in the spring and the animals which we savor come out to feed and are never too far from the reaches of our keen hunters.

"My village grew in size and stepped over its bounds and one day our Clan Mothers decided that some of us must move off and build another village. I believe, however, we moved because the missionaries no longer came among us, something that made many of us sad. Only a child then, I remember walking to our new village on the shore of Lake Osco. We named our village Osco as well, for one of our number glimpsed the lake from a hill and marveled at its beauty and serenity. Come! I will show you our fields."

Colombe Blanche led Suzanne beyond the village to the north where there stretched row upon row of corn, squashes, melons, beans, and berries. "Some of these grew by the hand of Nature," her hostess replied. "Others grew with a helping hand and a strong back." Once returned to Osco, Colombe Blanche gathered her sons and everyone in the little party sought out the giant elm of Tree of Peace (6). Colombe Blanche explained that, according to legend, the five nations of the Confederacy formed a union long ago while seated under an elm. Known for its durability, the elm down through the ages reminded the People to seek strength through unity, the best stratagem for fighting external threats and adversities.

"The procession is about to begin," Colombe Blanche announced to her guests. The Invocation comes first."

The Bear Chief appeared. Standing before the Tree of Peace, he rose to his full height. A large gathering quickly formed in a semi-circle before the Tree with all eyes turned toward him, the War Chief. Ultimately, he raised his arms to the skies and all became quiet. Seated between Colombe Blanche and the boys, Suzanne watched with eagerness and when the Cayuga chieftain began the Invocation, she traced his every word with her lips.

"Hearken, that peace may continue unto future days!

Always listen to their words of the great Creator, for He has spoken.

United People, let not evil find lodging in your minds.

For the Great creator has spoken and the cause of Peace shall not become old.

The cause of Peace shall not die if you remember the Great Creator."(7)

His Invocation completed, the Bear Chief held out a string of black beads on an adorned belt. Touching each bead, he circulated the belt among the Elders of the village. One of the Elders stood and, coming forward adorned him with a headdress of deer antlers.

"Now you are Mentor of the People of the five nations," he spoke, reciting from ancient script.

Another Elder rose. From ancient script he spoke in praise of the Bear Chief. "You shall be proof against anger, offensive actions, and criticism and your heart shall be filled with peace and goodwill for the welfare of the People of the confederacy."

Now the villagers gathered into a tight circle and took up the chant of welcoming him as Mentor:

"You who walk among us do so with thoughts of goodness and dignity to provide for our welfare and secure our future against all hardships."(8)

The Bear Chief gave a short statement of recognition: "It gives me great satisfaction to merit your confidence. I will perform my duties to the fullest extent of my ability and serve as long as I hold your approval. Now let us enjoy this great Festival."

Dancers poured out into the clearing surrounding the Tree of Peace. Joining hands, they formed a continuous line and danced through the pathways of the village. Approaching the central camp fire, they split into two lines, danced around it and closed ranks again. The dancers, representing ears of corn, wore masks of bark and reeds. Stalks covered arms and legs. They danced in pairs, two abreast. They heaved from side to side. They jumped straight upright. They ran short bursts of speed. They turned, stopped and leaped into the air. Always moving, they represented the arrival of Corn, the King, Colombe Blanche reminded Suzanne. Other dancers, wearing pumpkin masks, tried to chase away the Corn dancers, but lacking sufficient numbers, gave in to them, yielding the field, according to ritual.

Soon the entire village rose to dance the Family Dance. Partners held each other at arm's length and made wide circles around the great camp fire. Suzanne danced with Little Bear and Raven simultaneously. Next to her Colombe Blanche danced with her husband. Occasionally he whispered into his wife's ear and Suzanne noticed her cheeks turning crimson more than once. Many of the dancers exchanged partners, but Colombe Blanche and her husband remained inseparable.

Dancing gave way to storytelling. A venerable hunter broke forth with: Why the Raccoon Wears a Mask. "A certain native kept a fastidious garden resplendent with many crops. A raccoon longed to steal the goods and one evening made good on his promise. The native vowed revenge. He covered his crops with mustard seed and when the raccoon returned to dine he became covered with it. It burned his eyes and muzzle, forcing him to cover his face with cool, black mud from the stream. At that point the Great Spirit visited the raccoon telling him that he would forever wear his black mask as punishment for stealing the native's goods."(9)

A second storyteller presented: The Mouse That Prevented a War. "Mice have always enjoyed the field crops which grew near villages, particularly the corn. One of the mice overheard the War Chiefs planning to make war on an enemy. They feared that the Chiefs faced defeat and with it the loss of their corn crop. The mice decided to destroy the War Chiefs' weapons. Waiting until dark, they chewed their way through the Chiefs' bows and arrows.

The next day the War Chiefs discovered their loss and the Great Spirit visited them. In great fear they aborted their mission, thus saving the corn supply for themselves, the mice and all the creatures of the forest" (10).

With each story play-actors performed sketches. Dressed in special garb they paused at intervals to absorb the many acclamations which the audience tossed their way.

The telling of stories ran late into the evening and the villagers went to sit by the great camp fire to take advantage of its warmth and glow. Among the audience sat dancers wearing grotesque masks depicting huge pumpkins and the heads of buffalo and wild stags. Some of them carried fire brands, and rising, they swayed from side to side, linking arms and moaning in an incessant low monotone. The shadows of the night grew deeper and the fire's flames leaped higher, all of which sent intermittent shivers along Suzanne's spine. Little Bear and Raven huddled close to her on woven mats which their mother brought for them. The dancers tossed treats among the crowd, especially for the benefit of the children in attendance. These consisted of berries and other fruits wrapped in little balls of corn meal. For the parents and elders of the village they tossed out sacks of popped corn.

The dancers grew bolder. Taking running jumps, many vaulted over the camp fire. Landing securely, they grabbed lances and launched them one by one into a ring anchored in the soft earth. In the center of the ring stood a large wooden carving of a stag's head. Colombe Blanche explained to Suzanne that the dancer who threw his lance closest to the stag won a rendez-vous with the maiden of his choice. "It is a way for unmarried men and women to meet each other," she said. "Nothing out of the ordinary takes place."

Two combatants came forward. One wore a pumpkin's mask and his opponent a corn mask. At a given signal, the rivals conducted a mock battle to the death. Brandishing knives and war hatchets, they hurled at each other, wildly shouting. Blades came ever closer to flesh, but, in the end, neither combatant suffered injury, nor lost a drop of blood, for they practiced their maneuvers long and hard during the summer season before putting them on display. Suzanne shivered again and Colombe Blanche explained the history of the event to her in traditional terms. The contest ended with Corn slaying Pumpkin and preserving for at least one more season the reign of Corn in the hearts and minds of the villagers.

And then the Festival ended, a further segment to come due later in the year, Colombe Blanche conceded, one of five principal festivals celebrated throughout the Confederacy during the lunar year. Suzanne departed the grounds with the boys at her side. Colombe Blanche and James York followed. Slowly the small party made its way back to the lodges. They walked quietly, tired from the long day of feasting and taking part in the Festival's robust activities, yet beset with fond memories. The coolness of the late evening made Suzanne sleepy. Beside her the tired boys struggled on wobbly legs. Looking about her, Suzanne noted the obvious fatigue inhabiting all members of the party, the indefatigable Aboyant no exception. Regretfully, a languid Suzanne bid her hostess a quiet good evening and headed off to her lodge to retire.

Restless and unable to fall asleep, Suzanne cast off her blankets and addressed her father: "I believe that we have much in common with these people of the forest." She sighed. "The dances. The feasts. The People's love of the land. Their love of life. It is beyond my fondest dreams. A fairytale come true. Am I really here?"

James York gave a summary of the villagers at Osco: "This festive season has brought out the several sides of these villagers, who, in spite of what comes to pass, will always be of strong spirit and united in purpose."

"I am amazed, father, by the legend of the Pumpkin and the Corn. We are not the only ones to adore our myths."

"Not at all, dear daughter. Myths have a way of drawing people together the world over. We are testimony to that." He yawned and rolled over in his blanket.

"Well done, father. I believe that I will go to sleep now."

"Suzanne! The locket. How did you happen by it?"

"A man gave it to me the day that mother disappeared."

"How do you mean?"

"A man approached me as I waited with the wagon for mother. He spoke briefly in words that made little sense, ending with: 'your mother is safe and well,' and departed."

"You thought nothing of it?"

"I knew not what to think. I found myself in fear and denial."

"But you did not tell me."

"You have enough worries without one more, father."

"I understand. Lord help us."

"Mother is in trouble. Is she not?"

"Yes."

"We must find her." Suzanne began to sob.

James sat up and looked about in the dimly-lit lodge. "I believe that we are no longer alone, Suzanne. I believe that we have landed in a good place." He leaned over his daughter's prostrate form. Their eyes met.

"I know. I know. I am better now. Father?"

"Yes."

"I planned to tell you . . . after a bit."

"I know, Suzanne. Get your rest now."

"Good night, father."

"Good night."

(2)Kimm, S.C. The Iroquois: *A History of the Six Nations of New York*, Press of Pierre W. Danforth, Chapter V: The Home, (1900) pgs: 25-26.

(3)Van Sickle-Wait, Mary & Heidt, Fr., William The Story of the Cayugas: 1609-1809, Book I__Iroquoia. Dewitt Historical Society of Tompkins County, Inc. Ithaca, NY (1966) pgs: 55-56.

(4)Williams, C.L. Topical Review of World History, Chapter *9:Exploration and Colonization*, Topical Review Book Co., 131 North St., Auburn, NY pgs:(1952) 89-90.

(5)Wikipedia, The Free Encyclopedia (2005): *Goiogouen*, The Wikimedia Foundation, pg: 1.

(6)Callison, James P. (1999) The Iroquois Constitution: *The Great Binding Law*, Tyhe University of Oklahoma Law Center, Norman, OK, pg 1.

(7)Callison,(1999) pg. 5.

(8)Callison, (1999) pg. 6.

(9)Cooper, Leo. *Seneca Indian Stories*, The Greenfield Review Press, Greenfield Center, NY (1995) pgs: 9-12.

(10)Cooper. (1995)pgs:21-25.

Chapter Four

Ominous Clouds Gather
The Captain Lives.
Seeds of Contention.
Three Biographies.
Adventures on the Trail.
The Runaway.

The Captain stirred. Captain James Worthy, acting commander of His Majesty's British Expeditionary Forces, Division of Surveying, destination, the Ontario frontier, stepped forth from his berth, a hollowed-out tree trunk in which he voluntarily sequestered himself for the better part of two days. He subsisted on grasses and roots, the very same materials which concealed him in this, his hideaway, carved out by a stroke of lightning on a day long lost to the ages. For water he passed his tongue over droplets of early morning dew which clung to these grasses and roots. He left his cocoon only to relieve himself, after which he reentered his berth and pressed weary limbs hard against the rough surface of the forbidding hollow, pulling the grasses and roots over him until he effectively blocked all hints of daylight from penetrating his refuge.

He longed to move his limbs freely, unencumbered by the confines of the worm-infested trunk, where insects ran at random: his body a bridge over which they crawled to distant parts of the enclosure. Pain ran along his spine. His joints stiffened: signs that his ravaged body sent him demanding that he seek prompt relief. With the heat of the new day pressing in around him, he breathed with difficulty and, foregoing caution, stepped out of the enclave in order to stretch his tired limbs and otherwise renew ties with a world which he so abjectly abandoned not long before. He headed for the tall grasses beyond the camp grounds, the gouty foot making the journey a belabored and painful ordeal.

He loathed yielding to the irrepressible demands that his organs systematically thrust upon him. He knew presently that he must seek an uncharted, remote site in which to cleanse himself bodily. The maneuver, ever-pressing, altogether inconsequential in its totality, consumed his total consciousness. It rose up, leaving him temporarily defenseless and open to sudden attack. It is with eyes and ears attuned to the slightest movement in his surroundings that he entered the tall grasses. He thought back on his good fortune during the confusion at camp. 'The gouty foot may have saved his life.' The persistent inconvenience of a permanent limp, so shaping his outward demeanor, compelled him to find a retreat nearby and quickly in which to relieve himself, a place hidden from wandering eyes where he may respond to bodily demands, after which he may return to the hollow trunk, his sanctuary.

Lowering himself amid the tall grasses, he found solace. Rising, he emerged. Exercising due caution, he stole back toward his retreat. Nearby, the grasses rustled and crunched under a heavy weight, a sign that he shared the woodlands with an intruder. He turned in the direction of the sound, hand fixed upon a pistol. Apprehension growing, it subsided when he recognized a familiar voice:

"Captain! It is **you!!** The Saints be praised!"

"Simmons, lad! At last we meet!"

The Captain smiled a toothy grin and accepted his aide's firm grip and responded with one of his own, taxing his waning strength to the limits.

"I see that you still have a powerful hand."

"The last of my attributes, I assure you, Simmons."

"Are you all right, Sir?" He brushed bits of bark and grasses from the Captain's backside.

"Nominal, Simmons, nominal. By the way, what happened to you, lad?"

"Our men ran headlong through the night." He paused to catch his breath. "Many of them fell over a water fall and perished." He looked away in sorrow.

"Ah! Those blasted wretches. They are the scourge of the earth."

"If you mean the invaders, Sir, frankly I did not see any invaders."

"You will not see them until they want to be seen."

"If you will allow me, Sir, I believe the whole affair a great misunderstanding."

"We will see about that, lad. Needless to say, I am furious. In the mass confusion of that evening, I set out in search of our men. After the dust settled I scoured the countryside on foot, a most arduous task for me." He gently rubbed his ankles. "You see. Our horses ran off with the men and I found myself stranded."

"You walked in the night, Sir?" Simmons asked, a note of incredulity in his voice.

"Yes. I thought it too dangerous to light a flare."

Simmons noticed a number of horses in the camp's stockade. He made a mental note of their presence.

"They came back in the early morning of their own accord," the Captain conceded, aware of his aide's alertness.

"How did you spend the night, Sir?"

"I set out over the camp grounds. I looked for traces of an enemy in camp. Alas. I found little, save these." He produced a handful of arrows with flint points. "That is all. Plagued by exhaustion, I curled up into my blanket and spent the night thinking of the Forces during happier days."

"It is good to have you back, Captain."

The remnants of Hastings' corps entered camp, a portrait in great disarray following the mass evacuation. He and several others surrounded the Captain, eager to inquire after his well-being.

"I much prefer to hear of your exploits, Hastings. Please carry on."

"Very well," Hastings returned. He recalled the bravery of Dobbs, the heroic acts of Goodrich and the ingenious organization of Simmons. The men shouted hurrahs with each name brought forth.

"I am not the hero of this occasion," Simmons called out, regarding Hastings.

At the sound of his name, the men reserved their loudest acclamation for Hastings. He, in turn, uttered a subdued "thank you" and retired into the background.

"I am proud of you, gentlemen, proud of you all," the Captain beamed. "Let us eat and drink before we take to the trail. Our mission awaits us. The best days of the Forces are close at hand. There is plenty of food and drink to go around. Simmons! You are still my aide. You have not forgotten how to set a table, have you?"

"Sir. In all sincerity, my men long to return to our base to care for their wounds and to bury their dead. The wounded need the care of a physician. Oswego has such a man. The men are weary. What is more, we need transports to carry everyone. Before we are able to move out, we will have to make a number of them."

"That is understandable, Simmons; however, do you think that if we beat a hasty retreat to Oswego we will arrive in one piece? I think not. Those savages will set upon us from every direction until we are reduced to dust. Do not forget. They know the land. We do not. We have only one choice, Simmons, and that is to crush them before they are able to muster their allies. I say that we root them out. Then we will be able to travel at leisure to Oswego."

The views of both men found support among the soldiers, who stood approximately evenly divided in their sentiments. The Captain, however, fought for his point of view. Unleashing a tirade, he appealed to the soldiers' sense of purpose:

"What are we doing here in this land if we are unwilling to defend it from heathen barbarians? Yes, we are tired. No one is more tired than I. Yet, we are soldiers. We are able to rise to the occasion when others among us have fallen by the wayside. It is we who are the ultimate saviors of human-kind and that alone makes us members of a very select and private assemblage. Think of it, men. We are the elite of this frontier. What a privilege it is to serve with the Forces." He strode briskly before the soldiers. Clenching his fists, he spoke at the top of his voice. To many of the men the Captain's aggressiveness and determination to succeed rekindled in them a spirit of enthusiasm which the tedious, overland journey up to that point all but extinguished. At first they stood in silence, digesting his words, before ultimately breaking out in rousing hurrahs. They spoke among themselves:

"Say, mate. The old man looks as though he will fight an entire army singlehanded."

"If he is ready for one so weary, his heart must be in the right place."

"I say that we join him. Give him his last hurrah!"

Hastings joined Simmons. The two men stood in disbelief over the Captain's insistence on routing out an invisible enemy.

Simmons pressed a point upon Hastings: "I retrieved the arrows from the men slain and they looked nothing like those which the Captain presented."

"Now that I think of it, Simmons, I find it difficult to believe that he conducted a search by night with only the moon to guide him."

"He lied to us. He never left the camp grounds. Keep this to ourselves."

"You have my word. He is bent on his mission, it appears."

"And he has the support of the men."

"Half of them. Listen. We have no grounds on which to depose him, but we may be able to extract a compromise from him." The two men conferred, after which they approached the Captain. He, in turn, called a general meeting and made an announcement:

"I must tell you that in my pursuit of the marauders I followed the tracks of two men. I briefly caught sight of their backs. They wore the garb of the Forces, most likely trophies of their kill. I fear that they stalked us in no uncertain terms. They are watching us this very moment. That is why I urge us to hunt them down." Minus his walking stick, he shuffled about, pausing to peer behind trees, a wild caste to his eyes, made all the more aghast from the disheveled appearance of his hair, streaked with tufts of grass and laden with shreds of bark from the tree trunk in which he, unknown to the men, spent the night. His words brought cheers from the multitude. Simmons and Hastings exchanged glances before the Captain spoke once again:

"Of course we shall return to Oswego. Never let it be inferred that I care not for my men. We will split our command. Listen closely. A well-armed party will escort the wounded and dead back to our base. They will go in transports. I have prepared conveyances for them now as I speak. Everyone in need of a conveyance will have one. The remainder of our forces will pursue the enemy. They will consist of two parts: cavalry and infantry. Our cavalry, will feature our marksmen. They will lead with rifles and bayonets. Behind them our infantry will consist of our foot soldiers. They will bring our cannon on transports, as well as our stores of lesser firearms and ammunition. We will enjoy a light repast before we begin our journey. That is all, gentlemen."

"Is this a war, Sir?" someone asked.

The Captain whirled in the direction of the speaker. He spoke not to one, but to all assembled: "In attacking our corps, these marauders have also attacked the Crown. In my opinion that is the worst form of insult to heap upon our sovereign and his secretary, Pitt. King George and Pitt alone have convinced the Parliament to send us here to tame these wild lands, thereby making them fit for settlement for our countrymen and all those who come in peace. I ask you. What is more noble a cause than that? We are the path-finders of the next generation who will lay down cities and towns and roads, linking them to the fine traditions that we ourselves have known in our native England." Speaking in a deep baritone, he paced to and fro, thrusting his arms forth to accent a point. Suddenly, his demeanor changed. His voice became meek and mild and he repeated the question put earlier:

"Is this a war, you ask?" he stated.

His eyes bore into the multitude. Small and piercing, they invaded one's very thoughts and more than one soldier looked away, seeking relief. Expanding his chest, the Captain spoke slowly, carefully enunciating: the teacher speaking to his students. "Let me answer that. It is more about a parent chastising an errant child. In this case the Crown is the parent and the natives are the children. Of course we act in place of the Crown. That makes us the parent. We shall praise our children when they are good and punish them when they err. Above all, we mean them no harm, for we love our children." His voice trailed off and he grinned broadly, saying: "We are justifiably going to dust off the little rumps of our errant children."

At first, laughter, then applause, intermixed with hurrahs, reverberated through the bestrewn camp site. The Captain bowed deeply before his audience and any bold effort to derail his momentum at this point stood doomed to failure with the Captain's acceptance of the men's generosity.

"He enjoys more than half support now, Hastings."

"This is true, Simmons. This is true."

* * *

Not everyone fell in line with the Captain. One man asked: "Do you foresee much opposition from the French in this land, Sir?"

"I believe that the aims of the French differ greatly from ours," the Captain shot back.

"They have established trade routes with the aborigines, Sir," another man stated, apprehensively.

"We do not care to usurp French trade routes," the Captain shouted.

"How do we avoid a confrontation with the French if we punish the aborigines, Sir?"

Incensed, the Captain whirled, turning on the man: "Let me remind you that it is **no**t the French who suffered dearly of late, assaulted in the sanctity of their camp."

Dobbs, recovering from light wounds, asked to speak: "Sir. In all truth we do not know that we suffered an ambush. Our chattels remain intact, save that which we ourselves destroyed during our flight."

The Captain approached Dobbs. Standing head to head with him, he spoke distinctly, a portrait of self-restraint.

"Perhaps, my good man, we shall wait to be ambushed before we act. That is what you are saying, is it not?" Weary and tired, the Captain's voice crackled as he spoke.

"Not exactly, Sir."

"My good man. I am in charge of some six hundred lives, less dead and wounded. I am not willing to pretend that an act of *no* consequence took place on this site. On the contrary, to do nothing is to give free rein to villains everywhere to ambush us whenever they have a need to spill blood. In a flash we will become the whipping boy for everyone who has an axe to grind." In anger he tossed his plumed tricorn high over his head. Retrieving it, he slammed it over his head, and turning to Dobbs, pointed at him menacingly:

"I do not believe that you would allow an aboriginal band of stone cutters to accost you. Let us do what our armies are trained to do." He asked Dobbs to recite the three steps of treating with an opponent.

"To reconnoiter, pursue, and subdue, Sir," Dobbs recited obediently.

"Exactly. I see that you know the duties of a soldier. Now let us practice them!!" He looked behind him to support from Hastings and Simmons. Meanwhile, the two conferred among themselves:

"If the Captain has erred in judgment, he does so on the side of caution," Hastings offered.

Simmons supported his colleague: "The Captain merely wants to take steps to make certain that we are not attacked unawares. We have lost far too many lives at this point." He spoke in a conciliatory voice and in general held a solid following within the ranks.

"I say that we enjoy the feast the Captain has promised us," a man called.

The multitude burst into laughter, the call having diminished the tenseness of the moment. The Captain pronounced the assembly dissolved and Simmons brought out the remainder of his stores. The men, eager to cast discord aside, reached greedily for the food, knowing it must last them until they reached Oswego.

Dobbs, somewhat embarrassed by his encounter with the Captain, dined with two of his colleagues. An observant man, Dobbs spoke freely, albeit guardedly:

"For a man in the Captain's compromised condition to travel the woodlands in the dead of night is a bit far-fetched for me, gentlemen."

"Dobbs is correct," Rice stated. "One's first concern is one's own security. Other matters come afterward."

The man Watkins spoke: "The Captain claims to have seen two red men. In the middle of the night I find that incredible." He stirred his tea. "What is more, no one, not one of us reported such a sighting out of the entire corps."

Rice and Samuels believed that anyone walking in the night required a torch to light the way. "The Captain claimed not to have carried a torch," Rice stressed.

Simmons happened upon the little party. He attempted to mitigate the men's fears and concerns, although privately he shared them strongly: He addressed the dissenters:

"I have traveled beside the Captain over many sorties. In my opinion he is a selfless warrior who puts the needs of the corps first in his thoughts and deeds. He tends to think little of himself in the face of danger. Perhaps this leaves the impression that he is careless or lax in his duty. In the Captain's defense I say that it is more convenient for the novice to assign blame than to bring forth practical alternatives. We do not enjoy the best of circumstances at the moment, nor have we chosen the Forces because we seek peer-approval. In truth, gentlemen, we have only ourselves to hold accountable, given our shortcomings. Let us band together and, from a position of strength, move on to accomplish our objectives. Thank you for hearing me." His demeanor calm and unruffled, Simmons turned smartly and departed the grounds. A round of applause followed him, the men, still dining, came to their feet.

Dobbs and several others held a private meeting. Dobbs offered the observation that the Captain deliberately absented himself from his command when most needed. Further, he seemed not to have a solid grasp of the captaincy, a position which demands strong leadership under stress. Dobbs acknowledged that more than once the Captain placed the lives of the men in grave peril, the most obvious that of the incident at the falls. It is the men themselves, he held, who made the important decisions of the command, not the Captain, who consistently paid little homage to the true heroes of the expedition.

Dobbs' party believed that Simmons and the Captain offered opposing approaches to treating with conflict: Where Simmons is able to put forth broad strategies to resolve conflict, the Captain relies on threats and innuendo to force adherence to his point of view.

"Is this an example of a difference in approaches to leadership or in the men themselves?" Watkins asked.

"Simmons has an expanded view of circumstances. The Captain is concerned with what lies immediately before him," Dobbs offered. "Perhaps this is why they have tolerated each other so long. The one picks up where the other leaves off."

"This is good, Dobbs. I have thought the same," Rice stated.

"They are two faces of the same coin. Although of different design, they complement each other to precision", the man Samuels added.

"Excellent, Samuels. My sentiments exactly," Rice congratulated his colleague.

"Either way will get us killed, mates," Watkins interjected.

Everyone laughed, leaving Hastings to put into perspective the function of the Forces in the Lake Country: "I reserve my final opinion of the Captain; however, he said something that made me proud to be a soldier: 'We are the Keepers of the Peace in this wilderness. Our labor is wrought with uncertainties and danger lurks at every turn in the road, yet we are willing to put our heads on the block.' This calls for a special person and, looking about me today, I see a mass of special people. We are one and all dedicated to our labors and willing to make sacrifices in order to achieve the greater good. Yes, men!! We are special. On this I agree with the Captain."

Hastings' followers voiced approval of his presentation and wanted to hear more of his delivery. He left them with an astute observation: "I am one to believe that out of tragedy comes eventual triumph: The losses that we suffered at the falls have taught us a valuable lesson. They have reminded us of our mortality, as well as the enormity of our task as Keepers of the Peace. Indeed! The falls has frightened us into accepting this new mantle. We are not quite at the level of comprehending the vastness of our obligations, but, as members of the Forces, we will apply ourselves fully until we have mastered the task."

He retired to the rear following a second round of acclamations, and, it is perhaps this series of speeches that swung the last of the Captain's challengers into line behind him.

Someone asked Hastings, the officer who conducted the rescue at the falls, for a concluding statement.

"Putting aside our thoughts of the Captain, we have come to grips with something of significance: It is we who are entrusted with the care and maintenance of this land. Our task is a privilege which our sovereign has bestowed upon us. He has recently gained confirmation as George III (11) and it is no accident that he expects to secure great accomplishments from us. Our sovereign speaks to us through the Captain and in light of this relationship, we are duty-bound to execute the sovereign's will." The men stood enthralled and begged for Hastings to continue.

"Very well, gentlemen. I say that we hold the future of this land in the palms of our hands, for, based on our participation, we may one day inherit this region. We will raise our flocks and children here. What we do now affects the destiny of our descendants. Let us hold our heads high and keep our muskets oiled. Your sovereign and the frontier, and, not in a small way, your Captain, depend on you. It is a matter of principle."

* * *

The men burst forth to shake Hastings' hand, heaping praises upon his eloquence. They cut short their meal. They voted by acclamation to abort the customary after-dinner rest and asked for permission to break camp immediately in preparation for the engagement yet to come. Simmons and Hastings beamed approval, and, attendant upon the exultation, the Captain emerged from his tent shouting 'hurrahs,' arms raised in a gesture of victory.

Upon this high note, Simmons directed the industrious Watkins to prepare to remove to Oswego, in light of the general lack of amenities on hand. Watkins chose an efficient crew. The men began by converting all possible forms of conveyances into transports: They stripped seats from wagons and lined the floor boards with straw and grasses. They placed splints, dressings, and blankets in each wagon. They fashioned table ware, knives and spoons into crude surgical instruments. They brought whiskey for antiseptic purposes and loaded quantities of Simmons's potato stew for meals. They fastened the now-renowned litters to cavalry horses, each litter capable of drawing one soldier. They brought along all remaining life-lines, ropes for securing the wounded to life-sustaining contrivances.

The eager Watkins introduced the possibility of sending an advance-delegation to Fort Oswego to advise the commandant of the Force's pending return. Simmons, his immediate superior, rejected the suggestion, citing the need to refrain from perilous undertakings when on the open trail.

With the number of improvised transports growing, the question arose of how best to dispose of the deceased. Up to that point the dead lay in shallow graves, following Simmons' orders. Watkins proposed exhuming the remains and transporting them to the base-camp, Oswego, where many of the fallen during their lifetime spent the majority of their careers. The two men spoke at length without reaching consensus, yielding to the Captain who happened upon the scene.

The Captain summarily dismissed Watkins and conferred with Simmons. Watkins, nevertheless, overheard the Captain's conversation and grew nauseous over his superior's remarks:

"Simmons! I do not condone the employing of scarce means, such as transports, to carry away our dearly departed. With or without an escort, the way is treacherous. We do not need to become open targets for the marauders. The spirits of these departed have passed on to a greater reward. Let us leave them where they lay."

Watkins doubled back on his tracks, coming face to face with the Captain: "In all due respect, Sir, I believe that our deceased deserve a final resting place at Oswego. It is their home-base."

The Captain stood stroking his fingers through patent leather gloves, carefully squeezing out the minute creases in them. He chose to avoid facing his antagonist and spoke as though from a prepared text:

"In light of our casualties, we need every suitable transport available. The road to Oswego is long and filled with many turns and perils. What is a man to do under such extreme circumstances?"

Watkins stood his ground: May you be more explicit, Sir?"

Turning to him, the Captain spoke in a condescending manner: "It is fairly simple, Watkins. We have a limited supply of transports. In truth we are hard pressed in all matter of supply and provisions. Yes. We need to find more of them and quickly, but we will never have enough, given the enormity of our losses. We are not prepared for contingencies, one of which may lie around the next bend in the road. Therefore, the deceased remain where they have fallen. I am not callous or indignant. I believe it rather touching to inter the deceased where they have fallen. It will forever be a hollowed place." He returned to rubbing his fingers.

With Simmons in attendance, Watkins addressed the Captain once again: "Sir! To bury the victims of the gorge here is to forever brand them culpable of a catastrophe not of their making. I believe that their memories need to be preserved at Oswego where they went about their duties as soldiers. It is Oswego where they lived and laughed together as members of a family in a home away from home."

"My dear Watkins. We must act with dispatch if we are to apprehend the murderers of our men. Now is not the occasion for whimpering sentimentalists. Look about you. The corps is ready to move out and we are having this little discussion. There is ample opportunity for it when we reach the comparative security of our base. At any moment we may be descended upon by wild aborigines. Any further delay may be disastrous. That is all!! Simmons! Come here I want to talk with you."

The Captain drew Simmons aside. The two men spoke passionately. Abruptly the Captain withdrew, leaving Simmons to approach Watkins. He smiled wistfully, putting him at ease.

"The Captain lauds your views in garnering transports. He places you in charge of securing more—making them, perhaps. He yields to your great concern for the men. That done, he has assigned Goodrich the task of removing the dead and wounded back to Oswego under escort. In turn he will pursue the marauders with the bulk of the Forces."

"We need more transports desperately. I will use my wits to find them," Watkins returned.

"Begin with the carts. There are sleds as well. Look for litters drawn by horse. You may have to fell and plane trees," Simmons replied.

"Yes Sir. There are wagons which may be outfitted for casualties. I will make a kind of ski also."

"See to it. We lack for daylight. Do the best with what you have."

"Yes Sir. So be it. You have no argument from me."

"By the way, you may take with you the medications you have put together. We move out in three hours."

"Thank you, Sir."

* * *

Sgt. William Watkins first saw the light of day in County Tipperary, Ireland in the year 1730, in the town of Tipperary. His father, a baker by trade, rose faithfully each morning at dawn to bake the breads and cakes which his mother sold out of their home, a spacious front porch converted into a store. Both husband and wife enjoyed their labors, a calling to which they devoted their attentiveness and abundant skills.

The eldest of five sons, young William assisted his parents in the bakery, applying exemplary care and knowledge to familiar labors gained under his parents' tutelage. He learned the administrative and sales components of the family bakery and took over completely when his father suddenly expired prematurely, some say from excessive labor.

At sixteen years William left formal education behind him, a decision he welcomed, but one which his mother scorned. Possessed of a vivid imagination, he devised a plan to appreciably increase the family's income. He would sell to the military, to the soldiers and sailors who frequented the bustling town of Tipperary along its wharves where it met with Galway Bay. He set up shop on Broad Street in the shadow of the Bay. In due course William established a loyal following of clientele and he enlisted the assistance of two of his brothers. The family knew steady prosperity for seven years, but at age twenty three his mother died of consumption. His two brothers drifted away from the firm and William found himself alone in the world. One day he promptly sold the bakery and the following morning, with a supply of currency, leaped aboard a merchantman bound for the New World.

He longed to inject greater meaning into his life and to fill the void which haunted him, stemming in part from the death of his parents. However, he also sought adventure and the freedom it provided to search for a career and it is the desire to break with his past that he accepted the post of Provisioner of Stores & Measures aboard the H.M.S SEAFARER on her maiden voyage to the Niagara frontier. The ship set sail on a sunny morning in the summer of 1759, bound for His Majesty's recently rebuilt fort of Oswego. He eagerly looked forward to beginning a new stage in his life in a career as a soldier in His Majesty's Expeditionary Forces.

The SEAFARER entered the upper St. Lawrence after three weeks at sea. Sailing over calm waters, the vessel began a long descent down the river, reaching Lake Ontario after six days. Fort Oswego lay one day away and the vessel pulled into the grand harbor below the fort by the following midday under a warm sun and clear skies, to some clearly a good omen. Sgt. Watkins reported directly to Lt. Horatio Simmons, Chief Provisioner and aide-de-camp to Captain James Worthy, chief surveyor of the British Expeditionary Forces on the Niagara frontier.

He found his immediate superior, Simmons, a pleasant associate, although a little aloof. Well-schooled in his craft, Simmons chose him to keep order among the garrison's stores. For Watkins, his charge consisted of making accurate accounts of all provisions and supplies and providing periodic reports to his superior. He labored directly with the Keeper of Stores, Henry Van Schaack, who also dealt in fur-trading with the local aborigines. The Keeper stocked a storage depot laden with furs and skins. When aborigines came to trade, Watkins accepted and inspected their wares, and handed out utensils and other items for their personal use, a function which called for periodic and timely replenishment of the items to be offered in trade. He always dealt fairly with the locals, giving them value-for-value and soon earned their respect, if not admiration. He remained in sole command of the Stores whenever Van Schaack conducted fur-trading missions in distant regions of the Great Lakes.

Where Simmons wore a dapper white linen uniform studded with brass buttons and a gleaming white shirt with starched collar, and patent leather boots, Watkins preferred attire befitting the trail: buckskin shirt and leggings gathered at the knee and high-buttoned boots. Aside from their dress, Watkins soon learned that he and Simmons shared a penchant for professionalism in their labors, an occupation which called upon one to have a vivid imagination and innovative curiosity. So it is that they devised a varied diet for some seven hundred soldiers and additional family members who sat at their tables three times a day.

Watkins also went about the grounds on maintenance and repair assignments. During his watch he mended chinks in the palisaded walls, leaks in rooftops, kept the grasses mowed and otherwise attended to a host of prosaic projects. What defined his uniqueness however, stems from his having developed ways to make life in a garrison more amenable. For one, he set aside space for a court on which the men may play Dock off the Rock, a game he introduced, similar to shuffleboard and played with mallets. He built an archery range in another space. On the parade grounds proper he assembled seating for out-of-doors gatherings, covering the sector with a canvas-like top to ward off rain and snow. In another corner of the grounds he built a heated bath house, warming it with a wood-burning stove. Simmons approved of his endeavors and asked Van Schaack to augment his monthly stipend a full ten percent, a request which the frugal Keeper reluctantly granted. Watkins infrequently caught a glimpse of the Captain on the grounds, but spoke to him sparingly, and then, only in passing. To Watkins life at Oswego presented him with opportunities to employ his special talents and he looked forward to each new day with enthusiasm.

—

Horatio Simmons, thirty five years of age in 1760, began life in London. Of English-Irish heritage, he attended Catholic grammar schools, where he enjoyed foreign languages, ancient and modern, to a great extent. His fondest memory of school days concerned his playing Caesar in the play, Caesar's Gaulic Wars, in which he recited all lines in Latin. In his science class he designed a scaled map written in Spanish of the oceanic route of the Armada in its ill-fated quest to conquer Great Britain. He excelled in mathematics and his map displayed the precise measurements of a competent surveyor.

Always eager to learn, he spent countless hours alone reading, so much so that his parents thought him awkward in community gatherings, yet young Simmons dispelled their concerns when he rallied young men and women to his side with stories he gleaned from his reading, principally stories of wars and battles. One of the tallest in grammar school, his high cheek bones and thin, pointed nose, gave off with an air of mastery to others and no one questioned the authenticity of his tales. At home he cultivated a garden where he grew unique fruits and vegetables throughout the year, enough to feed his immediate family and some kin.

People sought after him for his knowledge and skills and he welcomed their solicitations. He considered his abilities in organization and planning two of his major strengths, particularly when they led him to delving into the root of a matter. An only child, his parents held great visions for him.

His father, a banker, secured him a post in the loan department of his bank where the young Simmons met with clients from diverse backgrounds, almost all of them embarking on new adventures requiring the investment of capital. Some of his clients held a keen interest in the great continent across the ocean where a merchant may open shop in any one of the burgeoning new coastal cities. Their stories filled him with wonder and when his assigned holiday came to pass he set sail for the New World. He landed in Boston and hired out as a cartographer's assistant, an assignment in which he planned many of the streets of the little city which engineers would soon carve from surrounding forests and marshes. His family and employer parted with him amicably.

In his second year a malaria infestation devastated many laborers, killing several colleagues. In desperation he fled Boston, seeking similar labor in lands untouched by maladies. He recalled reading a billboard calling for yeomen to staff the newly-reconstituted fort at Ontario. It lay at the edge of a pristine forest and beside a broad harbor next to a small, but expanding settlement. He and a small party of acolytes boarded the only means of transportation, a coach, and headed west. Disembarking at Albany they collared a river schooner and followed the Mohawk River west to Oneida Lake. From there they cut overland to the northwest, living off scarce provisions and whatever the land provided. Impoverished and hungry, they passed through the nascent settlement aptly named Oswego and arrived at the garrison itself in September of 1758 at a period when the military command readily sought skilled hands to apprentice in many and varied capacities.

The young Simmons produced a letter of introduction which his father acquired from the Banking House of London, the parent institution of his father's bank. The letter itself carried a brief note, stamp, and signature of the Chief of Employment Liaison, a Jacob Isaacs, who praised the perseverance of both father and son and, before the day passed into history, young Simmons found himself in the employ of the British Expeditionary Forces, destination, Oswego, the Lake Country. That very evening he dashed off a missive to his father, telling him of his good fortune. He posted it the next morning on a ship headed east out of the St. Lawrence before he departed on his first assignment with a Captain Worthy. Over the following year he would accompany the Captain on many a journey into the interior and fulfill several obligations which the Captain preferred upon him.

The Captain, principal surveyor of the Expeditionary Forces, traveled the length and breadth of the Lake Country, mostly north and south of the regions bounded by a series of glacier-formed lakes which he liked to call the Five Fingers. During the British siege of Montreal, a swarm of colonists passed through the Lakes region in the heart of the Iroquois Confederacy. Coming from the east, many of them at the invitation of speculators sought to settle along the Lakes. Others came to join the forces of Gen. Wolfe, who subsequently took Montreal the following year. The British Crown, anticipating a British victory, opened lands for settlement(12) and the Captain, under orders from his commandant, surveyed the lands, dividing them into tracts, then lots, for family-dwelling. With little regard for the natives living near the Lakes, the Captain performed a series of studies consistent with surveying. He needed an assistant and the young and industrious Simmons measured up to expectations.

The new aide-de-camp regularly forwarded correspondence to the commandant, Lord Carleton, the last to inspect a message before it reached its destination. He often caught glaring errors in the text with respect to the Captain's assessment of his responsibilities. He found that the Captain heightened his own importance by diminishing the status of others around him. He also tended to embellish his accomplishments, however trite. He found the Captain manufacturing tales in which he emerged the hero after engaging the enemy in vigorous battle. He said nothing, reluctant to report such discrepancies, thus granting tacit approval to his superior's errant ways.

—

James Alfred Worthy came from Manchester, England, a coal-mining enclave set against the shadow of its giant neighbor, London. He began life in the year 1711 and took his middle name from his grandfather, Alfred, one of the managers of the Bristol Co., Ltd., a leading coal distributor. His mother, a nurse, once told him that she bore him during a fierce winter storm and that he would henceforth manifest traits of insatiability and irritability.

His father followed in the footsteps of his own father, Alfred, He labored long hours in the mines until respiratory failure forced him to retire prematurely. The burden of family support now swung to young James's mother whose modest income barely supplied the needs of James and his three brothers. Increasingly she looked to James Alford, her eldest, to bear some of the burdens of family support.

At age sixteen James formally entered the labor force, becoming the leading family breadwinner. He abandoned formal education so that he may be able to devote more hours to his labors on the docks of London. There he loaded and unloaded cargo and packaged freight for shipment the world over. His employer paid him promptly in hard currency each Friday, giving James the opportunity to visit the many shops and stores which lined the market district. He developed a sense of awe over the wealth and variety of goods entering from world markets and knew that one day he would visit these far-off places.

He equipped ships for at least six months before accepting an invitation to learn the cooper's trade. An apprentice's mate, he earned free room and board while he learned to construct barrels according to specifications. He learned to take measurements, operate a bellows, bend iron in a hearth and shape and treat oak and other hard woods to form into the desired product. His obligations bound him firmly to his labors and not until Fridays did he steal away homeward, laden with gifts of foods and household supplies for family members.

One day a barrel he produced inexplicably rolled from its berth. Gathering momentum, it struck young James on his ankle, knocking him to the floor and passing over his leg. He picked himself up quickly and, although he suffered no broken bones, he walked with an unsteady gait for the remainder of his life.

On paydays James gathered with colleagues at the paymaster's shed. There he listened with rapture to the mariners' tales of overseas adventures. The Americas drew his particular attention, a land where scantily-clad aborigines shared the forests with wild beasts: a place where both subsisted entirely from the land's bounty. The mariners' tales stirred within him a sense of burgeoning freedom of expression. He fancied the Americas the center of a new way of life, one in which, given his skills, he may accumulate status and wealth.

He devised a plan. Saving his wages, he allotted a portion to his mother for the care of the family. He brought a brother into the cooper's trade at home in order to sustain the family, after which he set sail to Boston where he sought to set up a cooper's shop in this larger and more lucrative venue. Now twenty years of age, he found a position with the Handy Co. of Boston. In three years the owner made him a junior partner in the firm and the name became Handy & Worthy, Ltd. Two years later James married and moved from the loft above his shop to a residential corner in Boston proper, a locale frequented by young and married sorts of advanced means. With the birth of a son, James asked for a well-deserved holiday in order to visit his aging parents.

Once at home he found his mother dying of consumption and his father gravely ill. Soon after, he received a report from Boston and learned that his employer suddenly passed away, leaving him without an income. Back in Boston he considered purchasing the firm, but lacked sufficient means. All along he heard of developing opportunities in the Americas for skilled artisans in forts along the frontier. With his wife's consent he enlisted with the British Expeditionary Forces in Boston, determined to make the life of a soldier his next and final career. On a cold and dreary autumn day he bundled his small family together and departed by coach for Fort Oswego on the shores of Lake Ontario, his credentials and portfolio among his most cherished possessions. En route he poured over surveyor's manuscripts, vowing to learn them thoroughly before interviewing with the fort's commandant. His coach dropped him in a clearing beside an inland lake*and the determined James walked the remaining twelve leagues to Fort Oswego without incident, his family intact. Upon his arrival he interviewed for and secured the position of chief surveyor for the Lake Country, a range covering most of the central and southeastern sections of the New York colony. The commandant placed him at the head of the fort's surveying unit, some five hundred men, and he struck out on his first assignment less than a day after having crossed the threshold of his new residence.

James found ready employment because a series of British victories against their French rivals systematically dispossessed the French of vast stretches of territory— lands which the Crown offered for sale and speculation. Eager to establish a colony, the Crown opened these lands for settlement, unmindful of native residents who held the land for centuries. Nevertheless, coincidental with James's arrival in 1759, the French had lost Fort Niagara, following an intense bombardment by Col. Massey of His Majesty's forces. The blow forced the French to yield port access to Lake Ontario, paving the way for British incursions into the interior of the continent (13).

Fort Frontenac, on the inlet of the St. Lawrence, fell to Gen. Bradstreet in 1760 (14). During the same period, British regulars began displacing the Delaware, or Lenni Lenape, occasional French allies, from their homelands, forcing them ever-westward. William Pitt, the new prime minister of Great Britain, decided to reconstruct the devastated Fort Ontario and other garrisons which the French burned in 1757, a move designed to inaugurate his vigorous policy of colonization of the interior of the New York colony. To winnow the mercurial Iroquois away from French influence, Pitt named Sir William Johnson secretary of internal affairs in North America to ply the Iroquois with gifts and promises of British support against traditional enemies.

All of these developments introduced a more visible British presence in the colony and British subjects as well as colonists from the eastern colonies rapidly moved to fill the void created upon the ouster of the French and Delaware. With offers of cheap land, free rein to form their own legislatures, and religious tolerance from the Crown, thousands of immigrants descended on the Lake Country in the years leading up to the conclusion of the so-called French and Indian War.

With the capitulation of Montreal in the fall of 1760, the British claim to North America stood complete and James's services grew even more in demand. With Oswego his base, he traveled widely charting new lands, and securing them with residual forces. His marriage suffered, however. Wed to a man who seldom crossed her threshold, both spouse and child returned to the Continent after a year on the frontier. James stood inflexible to her pleas to transfer, bringing the marriage in all practicality to an end. Still a lieutenant, he aspired to the captaincy, a rank imbued with greater rewards and privileges. In his travels he infrequently persuaded landowners, including a few Delaware, to part with their lands for a negotiated price. He especially sought rich farm lands near bodies of water deep enough to float shallow draft vessels. He received a monthly allowance and enjoyed complete freedom of movement and decision-making authority in choosing parcels of land. Frugal, he found ways to stretch his allowance. In so doing he lived off the land when practicable and relied on subservient natives for clothing and meals. He learned that by doling out blankets and mirrors and combs and the like, he gained access to the minds and hearts of many native peoples, if only temporarily.

Harboring no constraints to bind him to conformity, James put together a plan to supplement his allowance. On visiting a native village he boldly asked for a quantity of furs and skins. In return he gave out modest articles in exchange. At length he offered more articles for human flesh, namely children and young women. He found this task uncomplicated: He found that families who lost male leaders to war and disease readily offered him younger sons and daughters with the understanding that he feed and clothe them in their stead. In trading for the young people, he performed a vital service to the village, he determined: relieving the families of additional mouths to feed during the lean days of mid-winter. Ultimately the villagers benefitted, he concluded. He did also, for he passed the goods and young people off to traders on his route for a tidy sum. No one thought the lesser of it, for certain not the corps, the bulk of whom came from the streets and wharves of London and Dublin. The commandant knew nothing of his enterprise and the corps, gullible to a man, went along with his indulgences and flights of fancy for a few additional guineas in return.

James corresponded regularly with younger brother, Nathan, in Boston. Nathan's earnings as a cooper helped to sustain his elderly parents, both of whom suffered from illnesses well-advanced. In late September of 1760, both parents passed away. James, occupied on the trail, received word of their passing a solid week following funeral services. He regretted his absence, but attributed it to one of the unforeseen hazards of his occupation. He grieved privately once he returned to Oswego. Shortly thereafter he countered his sorrow with happiness for, in a brief ceremony, Lord Carleton awarded him a captaincy. With a simple handshake and words of praise, Lord Carleton handed James a new jacket emblazoned with the captain's stripes and a certificate framed in embroidered gold leaf. James hung the certificate in his bedroom. During those instances when he slept at the garrison, he glimpsed at it before pulling back his coverlet. It became his final memory before he drifted off to sleep.

* * *

Simmons glanced at his trail watch. "Four-on-the-clock," he muttered. A pocket calendar furnished him with the day and date: Friday, September 8th, 1760. He would later learn the historical significance of the date: the Fall of French Montreal to Lord Amherst. He crossed off the day with his stylus and returned the calendar to the deep pocket in his leggings. He longed to leave this cursed place of death and when the Captain called for officer's assembly he hurried to join Hastings on a green patch under a broad tree to await final orders.

"We are departing under the terms of our agreement, gentleman," the Captain spoke crisply. "Hastings. You will lead one of our two columns over the frontier. Goodrich has already departed with our dead and wounded. Watkins, the able man, put together a whole string of transports for them. Astounding!! Bring trusty firearms, all." He consulted map-charts, perusing them diligently, staring long and hard at the etchings of terrain.

"Simmons. We will skirt the scene of our disaster and follow the marshy ground northwest until it breaks into the low rolling hills beyond. From thence we will march straightaway and search for friendly villagers to aid us in our search for the marauders. Questions?"

"No, Sir," Simmons replied.

"Excellent. Give the word. Let us be off!"

The Captain himself rode in a sedan, a box-like rig equipped with pillows and blankets. Running the length of either side, two poles fastened to the under-carriage enabled bearers to lift the contrivance. Supporting the sedan on their shoulders, the bearers transported the Captain over land too challenging for him to negotiate without assistance. An overhead awning dropped down at will to ward off precipitation and the sun's rays.

Marching in two side-by-side columns, the men registered high spirits and broke out in song. Upon entering the marshy land, some of them made note of vapors rising lazily overhead. Thick, yet translucent, the vapors enveloped the column, whereby the soldiers' faces and exposed extremities gleamed with moisture. Some of the men volunteered tentative explanations for the phenomenon, but everyone adopted Watkins' conclusions:

"It is the heat of the marshy ground mixing with the coolness of the upper vapors. The two meet overhead and the result is water which is heavy and falls in droplets or a mist." He stated his case soberly.

"What makes the heat?" someone asked.

"Beneath us are grasses and leaves and branches in various stages of decay. These, along with strong rains, soak the ground under direct sunlight and heat builds up."

"That is like the peat bogs back home," a man with a pronounced Irish accent stated.

"Yes," Watkins returned, "but your peat bogs have lain undisturbed for centuries, building up layers so thick that the heat does not escape. They grow hard and resistant."

"So they have no mist, you say?"

"Yes, or that which blows in from the sea. If you study the land it will teach you things."

"I believe I learned something today," a man replied, laughing. "But, you know, the more I studied the Captain, the less I learned about his true age."

"Everyone within the little circle of onlookers laughed.

The marshy land emptied into a great rolling meadow. The columns closed ranks and, forming companies, the corpsmen tread steadfastly through the tall grasses which rose up to meet them. Occasionally they approached a clearing and the Captain, ever-alert for a human presence, ordered a search of the immediate region. In particular, one clearing confirmed his belief that a war party of aborigines made camp not long before. Upon inspecting the site, one of the corpsman bounded back to the columns to report to the Captain.

"I have found the earth blackened where they made a fire, Sir."

"Good! Take me there. How far?"

"Half a league, more or less."

"Good. I will take a horse. Simmons! Bring me my trusted steed," the Captain bellowed.

Reaching the site, the Captain dismounted and allowed the corpsman to guide him to a footfall of interest. Indeed he found a patch of blackened earth within a clearing strewn with scorched rocks. Grasses curled and frayed lay in disarray along the margin of the site.

Additional corpsmen assigned to the scene found no signs of human footprints or discarded utensils. Bewildered, the Captain and Simmons stood aside in contemplation of what lay before them.

Nearby a statuesque elm rose straight upward, so tall that it seemed to touch the sky, one man cried. His concern brought others running to glimpse at the tree and they came away with the belief that its height and breadth gave it a special ranking, a majestic tower set among a field of lesser structures in the forest.

"Simmons! Come here! Look at that tree!" an excited Captain called.

"It certainly is a wonder, Captain. I have never seen larger."

"Take a good look, Simmons. The trunk coming down. The trunk. What do you see?"

"It is open. Peeled back like the husk on an ear of corn."

"Good, Simmons. Anything more?"

"It is black, brown, almost burned in places, Sir."

"My thoughts exactly, Simmons. Tell me, Simmons. If you drew a straight line from that opening down to the earth, where would you end up?"

Simmons extended his arm upward at a 60 degree angle. Taking one step backward, he looked beneath him. "I am standing on the blackened earth, Sir."

"What do you make of it, lad?" The Captain raised his voice.

"My God. Lightning, Sir!! Lightning struck the tree."

"Exactly. It started up there and ended down here." He gestured as though giving directions.

"So much for your theory. Where does that leave us?"

The Captain quashed a direct response. "Our little respite is ended. Assemble the men. We move on."

* * *

Maintaining double columns, the men marched ahead. The terrain became exceedingly undulating, the landscape a series of hills and valleys at close intervals. Tall grasses sprouted from the floor of the valleys and where they grew thickest, water gathered and the immediate surroundings became marshy and muddy. Although they marched side-by-side, the rise and fall of the land intermittently engulfed a portion of the marching body while leaving a considerable flank exposed. Essentially, those at the head of a column rose to full view while those at the center rode in partial view, leaving the rear section in full descent. A situation ripe for ambush, the Captain remarked that the procession resembled a giant serpent, hard on his heels, rising and falling, twisting its way along a wavering course.

The Captain placed the cavalry unit in the forefront of the procession, followed by the foot soldiers, leaving the heavy cannon, bringing up the rear, replete with six eight pounders, capable of firing a screeching ball upwards of 500 meters. He transported the cannon in wagons, two per conveyance, equipped with their own stocks on sets of wheels. When needed, soldiers were disposed to remove the rear gangways of the wagons, pulling the pieces to the earth from whence they rolled them along to their destination, aided either by man or beast.

Simmons, the Captain's liaison and surrogate, cut a wide berth beside the procession and, from his vantage point, endeavored to keep the entire assemblage within the field of vision. Riding to and fro, he stood erect in the saddle, the better to peer between the hills and valleys of the irregular terrain. At one point he came to a halt and waited for the entire body to pass before him. To his dismay a cannon-outfitted wagon failed to come into view. Spurring his mount, Simmons galloped to the rear of the cavalcade. He fastened upon the deep valley coming up fast before him. Dropping down into it, he picked his way through boggy soil before gaining clearance to dash along its breadth. True to his fears, he glimpsed what he feared most: an overturned wagon lying on its side in a pool of mud invested with choking reeds and rushes. Upon closer scrutiny, two cannon lay toppled in the wagon and one of them pinned a corpsman so tightly that the soldier writhed in pain. Dismounting, Simmons confronted a circle of helpless corpsmen bearing down upon the victim.

"Break out the shovels! Hurry! This man is injured!"

From a saddlebag Simmons extracted a bundle wrapped in canvas. A drawstring on the bundle allowed him to unfurl the entire package over the soggy soil from which he carefully removed a handful of medical necessities.

Two corpsmen dug into the soil below the disabled soldier, gradually excavating a shallow trench roughly equal to his proportions. Heeding instructions, the man predictably rolled into the trench, conceivably relieving the discomfort to which the hard earth subjected him, whereupon Simmons issued another command:

"Bring me two horses and two stout ropes. Then follow me!" Striding briskly, Simmons secured one end of the rope to the saddle of a horse. Clutching the remainder of the rope, he wound several loops around the mid-section of the field piece. He secured another line to the exposed wagon wheel, its free end to yet another horse. At a given signal the horses strained in reverse, applying pressure systematically to both devices. When the wagon wheel met with the earth, a second soldier pushed against the imbedded cannon from the opposing side, lest it topple from the wagon. The maneuver set the cannon upright and men rushed in to fasten it to the wagon board. The remaining cannon, having broken its moorings, lay on the earth. Restoring it to the wagon posed a less arduous task.

Simmons inspected the man's limbs, searching for broken bones. He tore aside the man's legging where he caught sight of blood stains. "Ah! I found it. Hand me those supplies!"

He washed the man's wound with alcohol and cleansed it with spirits of iodine, the latter a syrupy, red liquid with a strong odor.

"This will burn," Simmons replied. "Do not mind. If it is still strong, it will burn." He applied a generous amount to the wound. The man turned his head and bit his lower lip.

"Those splints! Hand them to me"! Simmons called. "Bring me the gauze and swathing as well!"

While he set and wrapped the man's leg, Simmons called for a soldier to go to the lead wagon, his field hospital, and bring back a pair of crutches.

"Hop to it! I want him ready to walk by the time you return!"

At the head of the cavalcade the Captain waited patiently, fending off all inquiries to send assistance to his aide-de-camp with a standard response: "Simmons has not called for help; therefore, he has the situation under wraps."

Back at the site of the incident, Simmons ordered the two wayward cannon to be inspected. Next, he swept off the floor boards of the reclaimed wagon before meticulously arranging a quantity of dried grasses on them in the form of a rudimentary mattress. Buoyed up with crutches, the wounded man allowed a soldier to escort him to the wagon where two pair of strong arms lifted him on board.

"There you go, mate," Simmons called, jubilant. "You men! Haul those two pieces to the head-board and fasten them securely. Put a stock behind them to prevent bucking. Give our patient plenty of comfort." He barked a command and slowly the procession resumed the march.

To everyone's delight the rolling terrain gave way to a gently rising plain bordered by maple, ash, and oak trees. Watkins, riding in the vanguard of the assemblage, identified several species and entertained questions in general about the foliage. Ahead, a swarm of birds inhabited a grove of trees which stood beside a fast-flowing stream. The Captain called a halt and sent several men to get water and to investigate the trees, thereby stalling the campaign, an odd stroke for him, Watkins thought. When he looked again after the Captain, he found him conversing with Simmons. Some of the men, having rode ahead, returned swiftly to the Captain's side.

"They are apples trees, Sir and the water is fresh and cool."

"Outstanding! We will take a brief respite and indulge ourselves," the Captain replied in a pleasant manner.

Simmons appointed a small party to gather apples and water and the men dashed to the site, baskets and buckets in hand. They found themselves in competition with other creatures of the forest. In the rear of the apple grove, deer stood on hind legs to reach the fruit. Bees with yellow stripes cut frantic patterns overhead. Unruffled, the men pressed forward. They stopped short, however, when a piercing scream drove them backward. Two of the men crept forward. They happened upon a young cougar feasting on a fawn. The cat charged the men, goring one, leaving the other to run off in fright. The horses, inherently fearful, bolted and ran, taking all arms with them and leaving the remaining man stranded. The other ran ahead to alert the command and Simmons immediately dispatched marksmen to the scene. The cat however, seeing itself threatened on several fronts, struck off into the forest, leaving its meal behind and a badly-mauled soldier.

Once again Simmons came forward to rescue a soldier in need. He reported that the man's thick trail jacket may have prevented a more serious injury. He cleansed and wrapped a wound to the man's arm, after which the expedition prepared to move out. Warily, a detail procured a few apples and a little water, a far cry from the anticipated bounty that everyone craved.

* * *

The plain entered into a gradual descent and small trees dotted the landscape. Here and there the columns crested a knoll or plateau which allowed an unobstructed view of the countryside. At one point the Captain called a halt and bade Simmons and others in his vanguard to come join him. He stood upon a lofty prominence or ridge bestrewn with coarse grasses flanking what appeared to be a lake many meters below. Many gazed down longingly at the meandering blue ribbon. Gaining in breadth, it terminated gently across a lengthy expanse of broad, sandy beach (15). Northwest, beyond the beach, slender plumes of what appeared to be smoke wafted lazily skyward.

The Captain turned to Simmons, a thin smile crossing his lips. "There you have it, lad: the refuge of our marauders." He waited until the entire body approached the plateau before continuing:

"There is a village* down there. Look after that smoke rising. Soon we will pay the villagers a visit, on our terms, of course. Simmons! We will camp here until dusk after which you will convey our six pounders down the ridge and plant them on the beach opposite the village. I will approach the village with the cavalry. The infantry will descend the ridge and remain hidden in reserve to our rear."

The sweeping announcement gave the men pause. Some stood stoically. Others bristled. Simmons bade them to rest and eat a light meal of dried foods. The men fell to and conversed lightly. They spoke of the stark contrast between the detached and unassuming life on the trail and the challenge which lay before them, an undertaking demanding full commitment that came suddenly, forcing them to make serious choices. They broke off into small clusters and ate and gradually they moved apart and ate in silence.

Watkins spent the respite in deep thought. In tracing the developments of the past twenty four hours, he came to a sobering conclusion: He decided that the Captain intended to attack the village all along. He led the men on this foray, he believed, because the exercise fulfilled a personal ambition. Marauders notwithstanding, the Captain held designs for the village, for he went to great lengths over forbidding terrain to pursue a fancied pack of villains. What is more, he believed, 'the Captain stood willing to risk the lives of the men in order to pursue self-seated goals'. He may be incorrect in his assumptions, he thought; however, further events would either confirm or dash his suspicions. Not one to lie idle, a man who believed in creating his own destiny,

Watkins decided to press his concerns upon Simmons, perhaps on the Captain himself. His jaw set firmly, he found Simmons dining alone and asked for permission to join him. His inquiries placed the aide-de-camp on the defensive.

"Have we found our enemy at last, lieutenant?"

"I beg your pardon. How is that again?"

"We seem to be moving toward a confrontation of our own making."

"The Captain has good reason, I assure you."

"Is the price of losing even more men worth the cost, lieutenant?"

"The life of a soldier is wrought with ups and downs . . . not so different from the rest of human-kind."

"I, for one, prefer to have a choice in how I live or die, lieutenant."

"Are you in defiance of our mission, Watkins?"

"The *mission*? The men have long asked themselves the substance of this sortie. I question the capacity of an officer to plan my life for me down to the smallest morsel of my existence. How about you?"

"**Watkins!** You knew the travails of this occupation well in advance of joining."

"That is beside the point, lieutenant. You know deep down the folly of this engagement." With each remark he crept closer to Simmons, leaving him little space in which to dine.

"You are a talented craftsman, Watkins. You may want to confine your enthusiasm to what you do best."

"Very well. I quit the Forces. They have exceeded the scope of authority. I will return to Oswego on foot and demand an audience with Lord Carleton." His voice gained strength. He rose to depart.

"Hold on, there, lad. Let me have a word with you," an irritated Captain intervened.

"Too late, Sir. I am off."

"To defy your superior is a court-martial," the Captain called behind him.

"Then try me before the King's court at Albany," Watkins returned. He began to descend the steep hill.

"Not unless I shoot you first. Seize that man!" the Captain shouted.

The Captain pursued Watkins in halting steps. A mean feat for him, he knocked him to the ground and tried to pin him until assistance arrived. Watkins tossed and turned violently and effectively shook loose of the Captain's grip. Rising, he lunged feet first down the face of the ridge, at this point a steep declivity which favored a sure-footed woodsman in his youth. Dressed in trail moccasins, Watkins dug his toes into the hillside. Taking powerful strides, he surpassed the slower and gout-ridden Captain, who crawled back to the summit and mustered a small party of bewildered soldiers to pursue Watkins.

Watkins, taking advantage of a lead, enjoyed early success in the flight. Stepping sideways, he grasped at rocks and branches to aid him in descending the prominence. Ahead lay the lake itself. A tree-lined bank interspersed with bushes and hedge rows separated him from the water's edge. With the daylight growing short, shadows began to form amidst the greenery. Near the bottom or base of the hill he paused to take a deep breath and to sketch in his mind a route of retreat, and then he heard the shots. They came from behind him, high up on the ridge. One! Two! Three! His shoulder burned with pain and then went numb. Blood streamed along an arm and, stripping off his head scarf, he stanched the wound, then, keeping low, he made for the cover of the trees.

Among the trees lay leaves, great mounds of leaves. In layers, wet and dry, they lay undisturbed over the course of several autumns past. Beneath them the earth, soft and moistened by rainfall, crumbled under his footsteps. With a plan hastily formed, he deviated from precipitating straight downward and, cutting to the left, headed for a dense pocket of leaves and underbrush. With bared hands he dug frantically into the soft soil, carving out a shallow berth great enough to contain him. Taking a final glimpse of the surroundings, he marveled at the deep shadows which engulfed him and the leaves and shrubbery which shielded him and there, in a tomb-like refuge, despite the sharp pain in his shoulder, he lay back in repose, confident of waking up on the morrow.

Reaching the base of the hill, pursuers fought against the looming darkness and the Captain's entreaties. Searching through the grasses, they found no traces of their quarry. Moving ahead to the water's edge, they turned aside layers of leaves by hand and foot, their clothing and exposed limbs slashed by brambles. From atop the hill the Captain hurled curses and threats at them. They decided to end the search. Calling a short meeting they planned to fire their weapons and report to the Captain that Watkins died while refusing to surrender.

"He will ask for the body," one soldier offered.

"We will say that Watkins drowned in the lake while trying to escape."

"How do we place him in the lake?" another asked.

"See that boulder? We will have Watkins standing on it and firing at us. We returned fire and he toppled off into the lake. How say you?"

"It is worth a try. It is too dark to search without flares and flares bring out the curious."

"Exactly. Who wants to fire first?"

The plight of Watkins, his confrontation with the Captain, his pursuit, the entire drama which ensued on the trail, in effect, nothing escaped the watchful eyes of Chien Aboyant and a small party of scouts. Tracking the columns since they departed the devastated camp site near the falls, Aboyant prepared to search for the soldier who fled amongst the trees and bushes before Lake Osco. The scouts carried lances. They waited until the man's pursuers abandoned their search before silently creeping along the shoreline of the lake. Walking side by side, they began to painstakingly probe the undergrowth with the blunt end of the weapons. Before long a scout took a keen interest in a particular location. He crept forward. Tossing aside mounds of leaves, he motioned to his partners. Soon, the remainder of the delegation carefully withdrew the exhausted Watkins from beneath his shelter. Too tired to speak, Watkins dropped his head and lost consciousness.

"This man is wounded," a warrior spoke.

"I touched his chest. His heart still beats."

"This is good. We will take him to the village."

"He is a peau blanc. He may know the other peau blanc at the village."

"Then he may tell us why he has come here."

With great care the men strapped Watkins to the back of the sturdiest scout and made off silently.

Meanwhile, Watkins' pursuers mounted the hill. They encountered the Captain on the summit. With hands on hips and legs astride, his countenance stern and unforgiving, he challenged the men to deliver a favorable report without uttering a single word. Hard put to face the stern task-master directly, the soldiers masterfully manufactured an artifice, replete with their own accounts of heroism and sacrifice which culminated in their quarry's unmistakable demise. Content with having posted a victory over the hardened Captain, the men climaxed the hill, exuding success from every pore. Brushing past him, they bustled to return to the expedition. Coiling, then leaping forward, the Captain sprung at the men, hurling forth with the burning question they so painstakingly prepared for while below:

"Where is the body, gentlemen"? an exasperated Captain demanded.

"He slipped below the water after my ball struck him, Sir."

"We searched for his remains in the grassy-clogged waters to no avail," another soldier volunteered.

"Darkness halted all attempts to haul him up, Sir. With your permission we will try again on the morrow," a third soldier offered, petulantly.

"No, gentlemen. That is not necessary. That is all for today. It would take the entire command to find our man, judging from your account. Perhaps another day. We are hard-pressed to move smartly along. Who knows what tomorrow will bring?" His spirits dashed, the Captain retreated to his tent, grumbling incomprehensibly.

(11)Williams, C.L (1952), Chapter 19: *The British Empire*, pgs: 168-69

(12)Borneman, Walter R. Chapter 16: *Montreal to Michilimackinac*, (2006), pgs: 249-252.

*Lake Neatahwantah in Fulton, NY

(13)Borneman, Walter R. Chapter 13: *Battle for a Continent—Or Is It?* (2006) pgs: 194-200.

(14)Borneman, Walter R. Chapter 9: The Bateau Man (2006) pgs: 144-150

(15Merrill, Arch (1951): Slim Fingers Beckon, Chapter 3: *Owasco*, Heart of the Finger Lakes Publishing, Interlaken NY pgs: 22-24.

*Osco: The Cayuga village at the head of Owasco Lake in the vicinity of a current traffic circle.

CHAPTER FIVE

Flint & Steel
Sanctuary.
A Call to Arms.
The Battle for Osco.
Requiem for the Dead.

Unable to fall asleep, Suzanne stirred restlessly in her bedroll. The enormity of her life thus far consumed her. She considered herself exceptional in light of the developments she both witnessed and took part in shaping. At home her friends and acquaintances pursued exclusively in their dreams what she encountered on a daily basis. In a sense she too lived a dream. She dreamt of making fast friends of the Bear Chief and his family and all of the Gayogoho:no. She dreamt of learning their language and folkways. She dreamt in sharing parts of her early years with them. Most important, she dreamt of her hosts inviting her to partake of their way of life.

In her dreams she held the luxury of constructing events to her liking. Her dreams held pleasant memories and ended on an uplifting note. No one ever died or became gravely ill. Nevertheless, conflict arose in her dreams: the contest between fantasy and reality. She adored the former, a product of her own imagination, but she viewed the latter with skepticism, even fear, for she knew that reality is housed in a realm of uncertainties and unpredictable developments, some of which abound in danger, even death. Aware of this dichotomy, she turned ever-more restlessly in her bedroll, struggling to reconcile these two conflicting forces. Alas! She failed and her inner spirit released her from further torment. Eyes wide awake, she sat bolt-upright.

On this night, vivid images of her sojourn in a new and different land formed the nucleus of her reverie. Therefore, the Great Festival, her exchanges with Colombe Blanche, her antics with Raven and Little Bear, and more, held special meaning for her. She threw herself wholeheartedly into interacting with others, for she made a pact with herself to learn the elements of survival in this new domain. She committed herself to gain the utmost knowledge with regard to her surroundings for two reasons: She truly enjoyed the realm in which she found herself and she believed that her arrival coincided with the approach of great changes on the frontier. In short, she wanted to be a part of history-in-the-making, and, if possible, to leave her mark upon it.

She thought briefly of her mother, adrift on the frontier and stood lost without her, her mother whom she tried so much to emulate. For her own peace of mind, however, she needed to jump back completely into reality. Rising, she crossed over to the 'counting frame', the means by which the villagers marked the time of day. Colombe Blanche explained the process of counting to her before placing her in charge of keeping the time for the villagers. She proceeded to review in the silence of her lodge the workings of the device:

The counting frame consisted of a series of hollow, interconnected reeds coiled into a loose spiral and placed within a square-shaped box opened on the top. The time-keeper inserted beads into the coil at one end. By manipulating the frame, the time-keeper set the beads into motion of their own accord, the beads tracking through the reeds. Because of their varying sizes, it took a full twenty four hours, a full cycle of the moon, for the full complement of beads to complete the journey through the frame and emerge through a small hole where they dropped into a pottery jar. At any given moment one may discern the time of day by counting the number of beads having emerged and dividing that sum against the total number of beads. She decided to test the system and compare its accuracy to the time on the trail watch upon her wrist. She found four beads in the jar. Out of a total of twenty four beads she performed the division and came away with 1/6th of a day having passed. Multiplying by twenty four, she came away with four, or four o'clock on the hour. Yawning, she glanced at her watch.

It read 04:15. Already an additional bead began to emerge from the frame, about one-fourth of the required distance. "Satisfactory," she heard herself say, "but I prefer my watch overall."

Wide awake, with the light of the moon to guide her, she crossed to the open hearth. There she put an iron kettle on the fire. Her father lay fast asleep. She washed quickly with warm water before preparing breakfast for the both of them. She planned a hearty meal of hominy cakes, grouse hen's eggs, fried strips of boar meat, a hot tea, the taste of which posed a mystery to her, and chilled berries in a bowl. She must remember to thank the boys for having brought her the berries. She liked their enthusiasm, generosity and sense of thrift. Briefly, she stepped outside her lodge to admire the alignment of the stars. She stole away whenever possible to study their configurations. They brought to mind days of peace and serenity, ingredients of a perfect world: her world of choice.

A commotion near the great camp fire drew her attention. By the light of the moon she discerned a party of young men speaking rapidly and struggling with a heavy burden. One of the men broke free and rushed to her side. She recognized the dancing steps of Aboyant and raised her hand to greet her host's faithful ally. He spoke in French, the universal language of the Iroquois:

"Mademoiselle. We have found one of your own. He is wounded and needs care. He has much blood. Please tell your father."

'Breakfast must wait,' Suzanne told herself aloud. She aroused her father. Already awakened by the disturbance out-of-doors, James ran to join the young men. Upon glimpsing the wounded man, he directed the Aboyant crew to carry him into the lodge and to lie him down upon the straw mattress trimmed with 'down'. James inspected the poultice of moist leaves and mud which the warriors placed over the unfortunate man's shoulder. Weakly the man lifted his head and uttered:

"I have been shot."

"This is true, friend, but we will help you," James replied, soberly.

Eyes upon the man, James accepted a hot cloth which Suzanne pressed into his hand. Removing the poultice, he cleansed the periphery of the wound. The man registered no sign of pain, whereupon James looked up knowingly to his daughter. She brought forth James's trail knife and a bottle of one hundred proof rum. Passing them to her father, she restrained the man's arm, leaving James to administer to him.

"Take a deep breath and hold it, lad," James spoke.

Suzanne held a candle as her father poured the rum into the exposed wound. Grasping a knife, James probed into the loose flesh, turning the blade knife ever-slightly. With a surgeon's skill he located an obstruction lying against the man's shoulder bone. He lifted it with the knife until it surfaced. Dousing his fingers with rum, he pulled out a musket ball the size of a small walnut. The man winced, but did not cry out. Beads of sweat formed on his brow and Suzanne responded with a cloth dipped into the cold water of an urn.

James applied a fresh poultice of mud and grasses which Suzanne molded into a paste. He left a small opening for drainage of the wound, whereupon Suzanne inserted a hollow reed beneath the poultice and covered the wound with layers of swathing. Privately she gave thanks to the French tradesman for having brought medical supplies to the village. She brought water in a gourd to the man who took strong drafts through parched lips.

"Father. He must be starved. He needs a good cleaning," she warned.

"Stay with him. Keep him awake lest he fall asleep forever," James advised.

Suzanne put pillows beneath the man's head and shoulders. She returned to making breakfast, not for two, but for three. Soon she fed the man from wooden bowls and spoons while he lay dormant. Together with her father, Suzanne ate breakfast beside the man and maintained a vigil throughout the morning. A bit later the man signaled that he wished to speak to his hosts. Suzanne crept close, lending an ear.

Slowly the man related a harrowing brush with death to James and Suzanne. In the narrative the man warned of imminent dangers lying ahead for the native villagers and their confederates. He refrained from naming his assailants largely because of fatigue, yet he left James and Suzanne with the unmistakable impression that they must act quickly to avert disaster. Suzanne caught bits and pieces of the man's pleas:

"All of you will be killed. You must move away from here quickly. Leave everything. Run!" he murmured. He endeavored to rise in order to augment his remarks, but James restrained him judiciously. Father and daughter regarded each other soberly, eyes fixed upon each other. At that moment the Bear Chief entered the lodge and crossed to the man's bedside. Aboyant and the fleet runner, Cerf Courant, followed, giving Suzanne to understand that the visitors held particular concerns regarding the uninvited guest.

"My scouts have saved this man from death's door," the Bear Chief spoke in French. "He has endured much pain in order to come among us. I want to learn of his story from his lips."

Suzanne volunteered to convey the man's story in French for the benefit of the Bear Chief. The man began by giving the name of Watkins, an assistant surveyor for the King's forces in the Lake Country. He related that in fleeing from marauders, many colleagues fell to death over a great waterfall only hours ago. His superior officer, he continued, believed that local natives attacked him in a moment of weakness and that he sought revenge. He refrained, however, from injecting privately-held thoughts into the discourse.

"In his tormented mind my leader seeks to punish many for the errors of a few."

Listening intently, the Bear Chief spoke: "You ran away from your own human-kind because you know the difference between what is good and evil in this world. Those who refuse to acknowledge this difference are abhorrent to you and make you sick enough to run away from them. You believe in pitting good against evil. We, the People of Osco, have held this view since early in our history."

He then spoke at length about the incident in the camp of the peaus blancs: "My scouts witnessed the ravaging of our Brother Bear, a living symbol of our People. In expressing grief they acted out of sorrow, not malice. A lesser People may have sought immediate revenge. We intend the peaus blancs no harm; however, this unfortunate incident is bound to bring out the true character of the players, that is, the peaus blancs and us. Unfortunately, irreversible forces are already set in motion so that the ultimate contest between our two camps will be played not in the councils of reason, but on the battlefield."

With another reference to Watkins, the Bear Chief addressed the gathering: "This man has made a great sacrifice in coming to our village. His own human-kind knows not that he is present, so much so that his death at our hands will not give them cause for concern. However, for this man to return to his human-kind advances the prospect of his death at their hands, for he poses a threat to his leader. By his defiance this man has become a captive of his own truth and righteousness. Strangely, we the People, complete strangers to him, deem him worthy enough to live *because of* his truth and righteousness." Swiftly the Bear Chief raised both arms over the head of the prostrate Watkins: "Fear not! You are safe with us. We do not openly seek your friendship, but the presence of two of your kind strengthens your standing. You are therefore welcomed to reside at our village where you will be able to manifest the very qualities which you have so aptly demonstrated." His delivery completed, the Bear Chief touched Watkins lightly upon the forehead. Suzanne finished her translation and Watkins forced a smile to cross his lips, but the tears in his eyes bespoke his true feelings.

* * *

The Bear Chief turned to Aboyant, addressing him in the language of his People:

"So:was-Ho:nghweh! Desa:driheh!"—Dogman! Hurry!

"Go to the ramparts and tunnels and man them with archers," he ordered.

He called Cerf Courant: "Move the women and children by underground passage to the rear of the village."

Recalling Watkins' warning about a possible cannonade, he spoke to another aide: "Send warriors to the grasslands by the lake shore. Look for the great booming engines. Be prepared to silence them once I give the command."

Ever since James York advised him to build ramparts, the Bear Chief regarded him seriously. In earnest he concluded labor on the fortifications, an endeavor which diverted him from the traditional occupation of preparing for the Great Corn Festival. Because of his attentiveness, the mounds rose quickly, a tribute to the speed and dexterity of the laborers. He personally supervised the construction of the imposing works, employing a large crew to dig into the earth, gather it in heaps and clusters and shape it into resistant barricades. The labor delayed the beginning of the Festival, but the Clan Mothers accepted his explanation with reluctance, prompting the Bear Chief to comment further: "There must be four mounds, one for each corner of the village, and they must peak slightly above the palisades, enabling archers from the heights to train their bows on the enemy below. Over the seasons the mounds will present a firm resistance to all threats. Honed by the wind and the rain, they will harden. Air-borne seeds will land and sprout, preserving the shape of the mounds. Within the mounds corridors and storage spaces will provide several benefits: They will preserve foods and supplies, including weapons, shot and powder. They will provide additional living places. They will furnish a means of escape to the populace in event of an attack. The corridor running the length of each mound below ground will lead to the postern gate and the forest beyond." Observing the labor, the Bear Chief grew pleased with the efficiency of the crew, aided in no small part by the shovels and axes which his ally Henri Marchand extended to him in exchange for a cache of furs and pelts. A wise move, he thought.

An aide ran to him with an urgent report: "The peaus blancs draw near. They come along the valley floor and are approaching the grassy plain at the head of the lake. They have booming engines and have set them on a rise within striking distance of the village" Trembling with fear, the man spoke in fits and starts. The Bear Chief calmed the man by assigning him the task of conducting an evacuation of all the lodges. The mounds now opened to occupancy, women, children, and families equipped with modest provisions, departed for the underground chambers. Men and warriors, on the other hand, proceeded to staff the parapets or walkways atop the palisades. Each defender carried a supply of arrows and a bow, lances, a fire brand and a musket.

"What are you to do, Fearless One?" an aide apprehensively inquired of the Bear Chief.

"I go to meet with the peaus blancs on the grassy plain with some of my finest warriors. I will ask why they are dressed for war when I come in peace."

Word of the threat of a military invasion spread quickly through the village. Recovering from his wound, Watkins lay in bed in the York's lodge. He insisted upon keeping abreast of developments and peppered Suzanne with questions. She came to change the dressing and bandages twice that day and to serve him hot meals. Otherwise, she dashed off to the ramparts, toured the grounds of the village, and met with Colombe Blanche and the boys, all the better to learn the popular mood or tone among the villagers. During her tour she learned of the Bear Chief's order to remove to the underground chambers of the mounds. Cutting short her visitations, she hurried back to the lodge and Watkins. There she prepared provisions while he told of his desire to offer services to her and her father. In rapid fashion he recited accumulated skills in carpentry and engineering and of the need to seek vengeance against his accuser. She listened impatiently while scurrying from one room to the next. After what seemed an eternity, she appeared next to his bedside equipped with two crammed backpacks. Driven by a sense of urgency, she interrupted Watkins' discourse, speaking in a tremulous, yet insistent voice:

"These are for you. You are going underground."

"I must get dressed."

"I have aides to help you."

"You are not going?"

"Of course. A bit later." She left him in the hands of two assistants.

Suzanne entered the grounds where a great number of villagers made for the chambers. Watkins was swept past her, borne in a litter. Colombe Blanche and the boys called to Suzanne. She waved and nodded in agreement and watched as the crowds swept them along, then dashed swiftly up a stairway leading to the parapets. Standing on her toes, she peered over the palisades, her eyes embracing the grassy plain which struck off from the plateau before the village and ran unbroken to the beach head. Caught by surprise, she inhaled sharply and peered below.

Arrayed on the plateau, warriors formed a defensive line before the main gate. Two columns deep, they ran the entire length of the eastern portion of the village. Beyond, on the grassy plain, still a comfortable distance from the plateau, soldiers sat on horseback going through the motions of moving into formation. The flash of an occasional scarlet tunic gave her to assign a British origin to the mounted men. She looked to her left and spied a band of warriors hiding among the river's tall rushes. The warriors swung sharply into view, whereas the soldiers knew nothing of their presence. Looking about, Suzanne retrieved a pair of lenses tethered to the parapet. She looked over the heads of the soldiers and behind them. There, hard to the rear of their camp, the sinister muzzles of field pieces poked through a bed of thick rushes. Putting aside the lenses, she absorbed the entire landscape, knowing that from her vantage point she remained the sole witness to the drama about to play out on the grassy plain. For an instant, macabre images of sabers flashing and men falling entered her field of vision, threatening to linger. She shook her head in an effort to dislodge them and breathed a sigh of relief when she heard her father's voice.

"Suzanne! Come down from there! You are in danger!!"

She dashed down the stairway and into James's waiting arms. "How remiss of me, father."

He led her to the entrance of the underground passage where Colombe Blanche greeted her.

"Watch her for me," he called and hurried off.

Suzanne embraced her hostess, then begged to leave, claiming the need to retrieve an article from her lodge. Colombe Blanche reluctantly consented, but sent an aide to follow her. Suzanne, however, dashed off to the parapets once again before the aide appeared.

—

The Bear Chief and attendant warriors entered the grassy plain, shoulder to shoulder in two columns. Back-to-back, they steadfastly advanced upon the adversary. He and a few principals were mounted. En route he dispatched Aboyant to surreptitiously lead a small band through the tall grasses to lend support to the warriors hidden in the river's rushes. Beside him rode the fleet runner, Cerf Courant, second in command. Halting the columns, the Bear Chief chose Cerf Courant and a band of archers to walk with him to the enemy's lines. Save for the sound of gliding moccasins, silence reigned supreme on the plain. Soon he halted, having come to within fifty meters of his adversary. He called out in French, the universal language of the frontier:

"Vous d'un sentiment anglais, je voudrais de faire votre connaisance. Il y a beaucoup a discuter. Je vous envoie une flèche brillante. Tenez-la en haute et je saurrai que vous avez le vouloir de faire ma conaissance."

You of an English nature, I would like to meet with you. We have much to discuss. I will send you a flaming arrow. Hold it on high and I will know that you are willing to meet with me.

An archer released an arrow. A multitude of eyes guided it to earth where it burned brightly before languishing.

A runner retrieved it from the grassy plain, breathed new life into it, and, carrying it back among the Red Coats, waved it aloft. The maneuver precipitated the advance of a small party of Red Coats. Led by an officer dressed in white, the men, in full battle array, marched up to the Bear Chief and, forming a semi-circle, came to rest before him. With eyes upon the Cayuga sachem, the presumed leader rode forward. Halting, he briskly stripped off a pair of leather gloves, and, dismounting, stood at eye level with his counterpart, extending a hand. A thin smile crossed his lips. He spoke in French:

"Bonjour, Monsieur. I am Simmons of His Majesty's Expeditionary Forces. With your permission I would like to speak."

The Bear Chief nodded with aspect taciturn, and Simmons continued: "To my astonishment I find this land inhabited. It is very beautiful. You have a fine home here."

"To my People, taking the hand of a stranger signifies the exchange of friendship between them. Friendship creates a strong bond and may only be broken under extreme circumstances."

"You have my promise of friendship, Monsieur."

"This is good, yet deeds speak louder than words. You have come a great distance to meet with me for a reason very important to you. I grant you the opportunity to speak first."

The astuteness of the Bear Chief unnerved Simmons, forcing him to choose words carefully: "We of His Majesty's forces have come to visit this land, to enjoy for ourselves its grandeur. We intend you no cause for alarm."

"This is good to learn," the Bear Chief replied, aware of the man's tenseness.

"There is one manner of concern to me and my men. It appears that late last evening our camp fell victim to an ambush. Bowmen slew three or four of my men. The remainder panicked and fled headlong over the land. Many of them in the dead of night fell over a waterfall and perished. It is a terrible end to the lives of so many worthy soldiers."

The Bear Chief remained unruffled and stoic.

"We believe that the assailants have fled to this village. We want to make certain that they pay for their crimes in a manner agreeable to us both. We ask for justice." Simmons stepped back in anticipation of a response.

The Bear Chief spoke slowly and calmly: "It grieves me that you have suffered losses in this land, a place where beauty unfortunately walks side by side with death. You forget that you are strangers to the forest and are not skilled in its ways. By seeking our council from the beginning, you would not be lamenting your losses now. One must study the forest. In doing so, one strikes a balance with Nature and Nature shines brightly upon him."

"I assure you that we come in peace," Simmons responded contritely.

"Your appearances betray you, Monsieur, for you have come dressed for battle at the break of day."

"One must prepare for contingencies. Is this not true?"

"In my mind a greater question comes to light: By your presence you wish to hold my People hostage while you search for evildoers. I remind you that you are guests in this land and are duty-bound to yield to the conventions established by your host in deference to his long-held practices."

Simmons bristled. "We have come to take charge of the evildoers. Certainly your practices apply to evildoers."

"All peoples, Monsieur, maintain rigid practices in spite of threats from without. You lead us to believe that this land is in a state of war. I give you my reasons: First, you approach my village without sending an envoy. Second, you arrive with soldiers dressed for battle. Third, you attempt to conceal your booming engines. Most of all you assume the undeniable guilt of men in my village. There are no evildoers here. To speak the term aloud is to brand my followers with a false label: one of doing harm to innocent bystanders. In my mind's eye your personal losses followed accidental, unplanned maneuvers by unskilled yeomen. I look about me now and that is who I see. Your misfortune is a matter of innocence among strangers in a strange land."

Composing himself, Simmons asked a question: "How have we brought about our own misfortune, I ask?"

"You have tried to subvert Nature to your own ends. After all, you slew Brother Bear, a living symbol of Nature. In anger, Nature took revenge upon you. Now that Nature has exacted a penalty you must go your peaceful way. We have forgiven you, for we are Nature's creatures and ask that you live in accordance with Nature's plan."

"You are trapped, Monsieur, trapped by the very Nature which you serve."

"No, Monsieur. We are guests of Nature, You are as well, but choose not to recognize it. We have formed laws to help us follow Nature's way and have prospered. However, Nature is unforgiving to those to bend those laws."

"You are well-versed in your beliefs, Monsieur," Simmons returned. "On the other hand your beliefs do not reach out everywhere, for we do not live by your laws. Perhaps our ignorance of your laws has led to our misfortune, but it remains that my men have perished needlessly because of events set into play by men of evil intentions."

"Once again you try to condemn the People of Osco for the foolish acts of your soldiers. Nature treats with foolish men severely. Whereas I may forgive you, Nature does not. This is good, for, in the long run Nature brings order and balance to the world, a world which foolish men running wild are disposed to destroy. I have studied your laws. They are rooted in Nature under a Supreme Being. One of your laws holds that one must not kill another out of anger, or design, or for personal gain. Another of your laws forbids you from stealing the goods and wife of another. Your Supreme Being has passed these laws down to your people where your law-making bodies have accepted them. The both of us, Monsieur, respond to a higher power. You have yours and we have ours and the similarities are more numerous than the differences. That is all I have to say."

Simmons, taken aback by the wisdom of the man before him, made a final appeal: "Tell me. How do you treat with evildoers— those who commit foul deeds?"

"We banish them from the village, and in extreme cases, from the Confederacy."

Simmons looked his counterpart directly in the eye before replying: "We hang them."

"Yet another difference between us, Monsieur. By banishing we grant one the opportunity to mend his ways. Hanging, like death itself, is terminal, severing one from all ties with the living and eventual repatriation."

"Perhaps our differences are too great to remedy, Monsieur", Simmons returned, reaching for his gloves.

"The day is still young," the Bear Chief replied, free of sarcasm.

"I must speak with my immediate superior. If you will excuse me. Before I leave, how are you called?"

"I have several names, but as chief of my village I am called L'Oeurs Debout—The Standing Bear."

"Very regal. It fits you well. I wish you success." Eyes fixed upon the Bear Chief, Simmons mounted quickly. Smiling confidently, he gestured with his tricorn, then, spurring the mount, trotted to the rear of the command, entourage in pursuit, the main body having taken fixed positions on the plain.

Suzanne watched the entire meeting unfold before her eyes. Although not able to overhear the principals, her lenses enabled her to study their faces and gestures. She gave particular attention to details and when the tall man dressed in white retreated, she made note of his figure. Overall, his features and carriage compelled her to follow him with her lenses to the extent that she tarried on the parapets longer than intended. She put the lenses aside, consumed in her thoughts, then redirected them to the man in white. Back and forth she alternated until a small pang of fear crept into the pit of her stomach. It lay there, heavy, and her breathing came in starts. Ill at ease, she tethered the lenses and, fleeing the parapets, made for the companionship of Colombe Blanche and the boys.

* * *

Having sent the aide Simmons to speak with the leading figure of the village, the Captain reclined against a tree on the plain to the rear of the camp. Limbs aching, he possessed neither the stamina nor desire to bargain with the aborigines. Now that he glimpsed Simmons galloping toward him, he hoped that he reached success in putting together an acceptable agreement with the aborigine leader. Regardless of the aide's success, however, he irrefutably intended to attack. Painfully he pulled himself to his feet upon Simmons' approach.

"His name is L'Oeurs Debout—The Standing Bear. He says there are no marauders among the villagers, but he does not dismiss the possibility that our men died by accident."

"Arrows true to their mark are no accident," the Captain growled.

"Apparently the bear which we slaughtered is sacred to the natives. They or others nearby may have acted out of grief for their loss."

"We both have our losses to bear, evidently."

"He says that our lack of understanding for his customs brought about our tragedy at the falls, that no one in particular is at fault. A sad set of circumstances."

"Is that so? An unfortunate accident is it?" the Captain ranted, glowing red about the jowls.

"He does have a point, Sir."

"He will feel the point of my bayonet," the Captain rapidly drew a forefinger across his neck.

"He is a religious man. He says that our killing the bear is an affront to Nature."

"Oh, balderdash!! He simply does not want to come to terms with his crimes. There are no excuses for what he has condoned. My lenses have not lied to me. From where I sat, this savage has captivated you with his oratory."

"I must admit that he is most eloquent in speech. His followers must truly put their faith in him."

Shaking a finger menacingly, the Captain retorted: "He has them under his spell as he has with you."

"What do you propose, Captain?" Simmons asked, curtly, masking his annoyance.

"The commander who will not lead has an army that will not fight," the Captain stormed.

"Sir, in all due respect, I wish to relinquish my command of this expedition."

"It is true. You have been smitten. Go back to your pots and pans. This excitement has restored me. I will take over the reins." He gestured wildly. Bringing forth a cane, he stomped the ground, walking in circles. He called over his shoulder: "Before you go, have the men break out knapsacks. We will take a short repast and respite."

"Very well, Sir."

The soldiers reclined on the plain and ate a dried and cold meal of pork and beans. The Bear Chief, ever-wary withdrew his columns to the plateau before the village gate. Within the village, archers assumed positions on the ramparts. Meanwhile, from deep within the Captain's ranks, a horse cavalry moved forward, taking up a stance in neat rows behind the recumbent soldiers. At the Captain's call, a young adjutant, one Lennox, emerged from among the spirited steeds. Receiving a note from his superior, he read it aloud as instructed:

"Gentlemen. Assume your battle stations. Divide into four equal columns, two deep and two across. March upon the village. Commence firing at 50 meters. Columns will alternately fire, reload and fire, pouring a steady hail of shot at the enemy. Commence cannon firing once the columns reach 25 meters from the village. Upon entering the village, change to pistols and sabers. Take prisoners when possible, especially women and children. Look for valuable articles such as furs and pelts. You of the horse-cavalry are to remain in reserve until called when needed. Now, in His Majesty's name, let us march on to victory!!"

The Bear Chief attained the plain. Runners broke off from the main body. Streaking through tall grasses to the immediate north of the plain, they alerted Cerf Courant's warriors concealed within dense undergrowth. They in turn broke into two bands to correspond with the two-columned infantry on the march. On the plateau before the village, the elite guard remained in reserve, poised to strike upon command.

Cerf Courant waited until the infantry marched beyond him. The bemused regulars, keeping in tempo with fife and drum, paid no heed to peripheral maneuvers, their eyes fixed straight forward. To all intents and purposes, they viewed the runners as a body of discordant runaways taking flight. The astute Cerf Courant placed his brother, Fox Tail, in command of one of the two bands. Together, keeping low, they led the warriors slowly forward. Approaching the infantry from behind, the warriors set up a fierce howling, once the soldiers stood exposed. Dashing wildly, the warriors encircled the soldiers. Wielding war hatchets, they selected prime targets, leaped into the column to make a kill, then sped away to reform—a body in motion, always moving. Suddenly they yielded to archers among them who pelted the invaders with a hailstorm of arrows. Reformed again, the main body leveled broadsides at the confused infantry, which broke apart and set up a defensive perimeter. Fixing bayonets, the startled infantrymen huddled in compact squads from which they struck out with pistol and musket during those few moments that the warriors came into the line of fire. Having gained the upper hand early, a party of warriors fled to the rear of the enemy camp where they located the three booming engines. Stuffing the muzzles with stones and grasses, they set fire to the surrounding reeds and rushes before stealing back to rejoin the assault.

The infantry, although divided into segments, fought valiantly. The men in squads fired in measured sequences(rising to fire, then dropping down to reload while a second squad fired). A most predictable maneuver, the warriors waited until the soldiers reloaded before striking in full force. Making necessary adjustments, however, the infantrymen met the warriors' advances quid pro quo. A resurgence among the infantry brought the horse-cavalry into the battle, spurred on no less by the infantry's great display of resolve in the face of impending disaster.

These new developments did not elude the Bear Chief's watchful eye. Secure in a bunker beside the plateau, he summoned by means of Aboyant, the archers, who maintained vigil atop the protrusive ramparts to his rear. At a given signal, the archers released flights of arrows high above the plain. Descending, the deadly missiles fell true to the mark, dropping many a horse-soldier where he sat astride his mount. Horses fell also. Other horses threw off riders and ran wild over the plain. Struck by momentary success, the Bear Chief instructed the archers to release fire-arrows upon the plain. Sufficient numbers of the missiles occasioned blazes to spring up where they struck dried grasses, sending man and beast reeling beneath the pungent odor of billowing smoke intermingled with the repelling stench of burning flesh. Surviving cavalry vacated the plain in all haste, leaving dead and wounded where they lay.

The resourceful Lennox responded. He exhorted sufficient numbers of the exhausted cavalry to reenter the fight whereby they charged at the warriors who crept forward to reclaim the plain. The Bear Chief ordered the elite guard to mount and encircle what remained of the horse-cavalry and infantry—pressing them into a constricted circle. There ensued fierce fighting at close range with sword and bayonet pitted against war hatchet and war club. Clearly the field belonged to the most able of belligerents, a battle of attrition, remarkable in the form, not strategies employed: While warriors dodged and twisted with every turn, the soldiers stood in a tight circle, stationary, striking as a unit.

The fight raged on interminably. Ever-aware of early losses, the Bear Chief, adhering to counsel, decided to withdraw all forces before they may grow irretrievably high. 'Better to grant the besiegers a hollow victory than lose the precious core of the fighting force,' he reasoned. Overall, the soldiers presented a superior force in terms of numbers. More significantly, they held possession of the three sleeping giants, or booming engines, which may be resurrected, he feared. On the other hand, the Bear Chief believed that he held the advantage of subterfuge over the enemy, given his predilection to exercise stealth by harnessing the surroundings to desired ends. Unknown to advisors, he began to organize a plan of stealth in anticipation of a reversal on the plain. He acted none too soon.

Without warning the encircling warriors abandoned the fight. The maneuver allowed remaining cavalry and infantry to take repose. They did so without inducement, laying down arms to partake of a respite full on the plain. There they cleansed and wrapped wounds, gathered the dead and wounded, and nibbled at hardtack and biscuits. Meanwhile to the rear of their camp, teamsters, under the guidance of Lennox, revived the heretofore doomed cannon— affably named the Three Sisters. Cleaning muzzles and removing grasses from the pieces, the teamsters hitched them to three horse-drawn wagons and hauled them side by side onto the plain in full view of the retreating warriors. The maneuver incited the Bear Chief, for he assembled all forces before the palisades into two columns extending over the breadth of the plateau. A log bridge separated the plateau from the village. Beneath it flowed a robust stream, invariably an offshoot of the lake Osco. With removable planking, the bridge may be disassembled to discourage the entrance of itinerants into the village. Laborers set about to do so. In the village proper archers manned the imposing ramparts behind the palisades. They stood equipped with instruments capable of wreaking great havoc upon an invader.

Angered by what he termed an ostentatious display of cowardice on the part of the defenders, the Captain urged Lennox to bring the cannon into prominence. The three pieces lumbered forward, the teamsters calling out to each other the number of meters necessary to score a direct hit upon the village gates. Again, hidden from view, the Bear Chief watched the odd procession limp closer to the home he truly loved. Curiously, he withdrew the elite mounted guard and when a party of horse-cavalry dislodged a pocket of warriors from the rushes north of the plain, he made no attempt to counter-attack. Facing no discernible resistance, the three war machines secured a suitable position on the plain. Gunners, however, kept them at a comfortable distance from the warrior-invested plateau. An initial salvo shattered the venerable timbers of the portals, sending great shards of blackened and burning wood in all four directions of the compass. Oddly, no harm befell the defenders. To a man they stood outwardly unmoved by the explosions, suffering the acrid smoke and burnt powder to filter down upon them.

For Lennox the aerial assault provided him with the impetus he needed to rekindle the soldiers' spirits. Cheering heroically, the battered infantry and exhausted cavalry, ran headlong toward the village portals. The Bear Chief, through Aboyant, called upon the elite guard to meet them before the plateau. Spread across the canopy-like mound of the plateau, the elite guard fired into the swarming horde—two columns in full swing. Supporting them, archers on the ramparts above rained down a steady stream of arrows and musket balls.

Beset upon from multiple quarters, the besiegers withdrew, stumbling over their dead in retreat. Those soldiers who crossed the log bridge turned away to seek shelter along the far bank of the stream. There they dug burrows into which they may conceal themselves. They cowered in fright until a subsequent set of cannon bursts prompted the oldest and bravest of them to set out anew over the bridge. Braving endless rounds of shot and arrows, soldiers constructed rudimentary causeways over the stream in places where the waters trickled slowly. Plunging into the forest, they gathered small trees and saplings, which, together with boulders, made for a tentative walkway across the stream. The undertaking, in various stages of completion, men heaved themselves over these crude pilings. Gathering in a knot of heaving flesh, they pushed mightily across the plateau to the very gates of the village. Many fell precisely into a solid line of fire, yet they refused to abandon the fight— often stepping over fallen comrades in order to gain the plateau. To the defenders the raw determination of the besiegers far outstripped their superiority in numbers, or endless supply of powder and ball. The battle wore on, hotly contested. For the Bear Chief, his store of shot lay perilously low at the moment that the teamsters on the plain swung the largest of the three cannon into service. It sat perched on a knoll in tall grasses north of the plain, its deadly bore aimed at the village portals.

In desperation, an aide ran to the Bear Chief: "Fearless One! I have a warrior who will silence the booming engine with a simple command from your lips."

"He will need a horse. Does he have a horse?"

"He found a runaway standing by the rushes. Look! He is mounted and ready to ride."

Following the aide's extended arm, the Bear Chief spied a young horseman half-hidden behind tall pines near one corner of the palisades He carried a lance.

"He plans to ride out and kill the soldiers by the booming engine, Fearless One."

"He dies in vain. The soldiers are too strong for him."

At that point the Bear Chief unveiled a portion of a plan to launch a counter-strike, to be set into motion by Cerf Courant. He explained to a selected few that Cerf Courant was to slip onto the plain with a small party, kill the teamsters and guards and stuff the great behemoth so that it may cough no longer. He reasoned that the soldiers, preoccupied with storming the plateau, were hesitant to give chase—fearing at the least a ruse. While he spoke, the loyal Cerf Courant collected a party of young warriors and slipped into the tall grasses surrounding the great booming engine. Silently the young men issued forth— instruments of death in hand. Bounding from concealment, they methodically slit the throats of the teamsters who milled about the great beast in anticipation of orders. Not a sound escaped the dying men's lips. Treating with the great cannon, the warriors filled its bore with heavy rocks and packed it with wet grasses. Rolling the cannon balls into a shallow ditch, they filled it with earth before creeping away with a supply of weaponry and the mounts of the newly-deceased. Bending low in the tall grasses, they traveled east beyond the plain where the Osco ran fast and deep at the base of a muddy ravine. There they tethered the horses and divided the weaponry amongst themselves and settled down to await the arrival of the Bear Chief with the second part of his plan.

Meanwhile, fighting grew so intense on the plateau that no besiegers took possession of the great cannon. Within his command post the Cayuga War Chief executed another order: He placed the entire elite guard in the direct path of the storming soldiers— infantry and cavalry all. Following, he ordered a number of archers manning the ramparts to descend and lend support to the guard. Exhausted, the besiegers gave no ground. They may have perished to a man, save that they held ample supplies of powder and ball which they spewed forth unrelentingly. This factor alone kept the defenders at bay, forcing them to withdraw into the village itself. During the next precious moments the archers retreated under heavy fire, leaving the frenzied soldiers to storm the village proper. The Bear Chief viewed all with alarm. He began to fear for his family and fellow villagers. Angered, he lashed out to meet this most recent of challenges.

He summoned still more archers. Many of them, sharpshooters, they flung fire-arrows into bundles of straw placed about the village portals. Billows of dense smoke stung the eyes of the besiegers, filling their lungs with contaminants. A good number of them elected to retreat beyond the fractured gates in search of the fresh vapors abounding on the grassy plain. Many collided with incoming waves of soldiers on the ravaged log bridge. These two competing forces fell at loggerheads, stalling the siege, and creating an impasse which played into the hands of the defenders. In the next moment scores of archers emerged from every conceivable corner and crack of the ravaged palisades. They found excellent targets in the form of the confused soldiers and were able to forestall a full-scale rush upon the village proper. Joined by members of the elite guard, these defenders forced a full retreat and regained the plateau.

While the fighting raged above them, the villagers, with Suzanne, Watkins, and James, wound their way along the underground passageway. Forging ahead through the dim channel, everyone carried thoughts of reaching the postern gate—a secret to all but the villagers. Notably, each man, woman, and child carried basic articles of clothing and backpacks of food. Ascending a stairway to the gate, they made silently for the thick forest beyond where they took up shelter in earth-hewn bunkers on the far side of Eagle Mountain.

From the command post, the Bear Chief peered upon the scene of battle: Before him lay corpses festering under the warmth of the midday sun. The elite guard, although taking the fight to the marauders, fought under the strain of exhaustion with fewer numbers. Archers lay dead, young men who, in more salubrious days, he invited into his lodge to visit and to make light banter with his sons. Chilling signs of death and destruction took place most notably about the plateau, followed by a series of ghastly scenes at the ruptured bridge and stream. The village proper held fewer dead, but all vestiges of civilization had been irretrievably maligned or eradicated. He hung his head in mourning. Aboyant sent him word that all residents, including his family and honored guests, escaped to the security of the forest. Sorrowfully the little scout noted that a number of residents, children and young women, fell hostage to the soldiers.

The Bear Chief breathed a heavy sigh and bestowed upon Aboyant the sober task of calling a halt to the fight and to vacate the village fully. He believed that in so doing the weary soldiers would not pursue him, nor seek the villagers' means of escape. Slowly he unfolded the second part of a plan to confederates: Although many warriors accompanied the villagers to Eagle Mountain; others withdrew surreptitiously with Cerf Courant to the thicket-invested ravine above the Osco, There everyone awaited the Bear Chief's arrival with a plan of which they held sketchy knowledge. Already scouts reported that the soldiers, having won a Pyrrhic victory with the departure of their adversary, sat upon the earth to soothe fresh wounds and aching bodies. They cleansed and wrapped injuries and ate hardtack and biscuits. Indeed, the bales of smoking grasses drove many of them to camp farther along on the plain where the vapors ran cool and refreshing and it is there that they eagerly devoured dried rations and floated guttural epithets of no consequence. Presently, the man in white, accompanied by an older sort, approached survivors of the fatigued corps before the ravaged portals. The pair strolled about, pausing to make cursory inspections of the living, the dead, and the dying. The older man spoke:

"This place has a stillness, Simmons," he confessed, in a whisper.

"The dead do not speak, Captain," his junior officer returned.

"Alas, we have won the day, Simmons. Yet, looking about, I wonder what *precisely* we have won."

"That, Sir, remains the eternal question. For some, it is never answered." He glimpsed at the impassive countenance of his superior.

"Find Lennox for me. Bring him here," the Captain barked, his animosity sparked.

At the young adjutant's approach the Captain issued a series of commands: "Take a crew and go into the village. Look for articles of value. Furs and pelts do quite well. If there are young people, bring them along, women in particular. Yes! Women! Bring the women!! I understand that you uncovered a few villagers in a crumpled lodge. Yes! Bring them along."

The adjutant's jaw tightened. His mouth stood agape upon hearing the Captain's words. He looked about sheepishly, then back at the Captain, whose riveting gaze he met head-on.

"It is all right, son. The village is abandoned. Anything of value belongs in a more secure place."

"Understood, Captain," Lennox stammered. "I will see to it."

"Good. Take some of our transports and load them with your findings. By the way, the men's respite has expired. Tell them!"

"As you wish, Captain."

"And, Lennox. Torch the village. We do not want it to fall into evil hands, do we?"

"No. Of course not, Sir," Lennox stammered, at a loss for words. He hurried off to arouse the men from leisure and to prepare them for the impending task.

The Captain turned to Simmons who posed a poignant question: "What of the dead, Sir? What shall we do?"

"A recurrent theme of late, Simmons." He stroked his chin. "I say that we bury them here, here where they have fallen--- here where they gave their all." He looked about him. "Find me such a place where they will lie undisturbed."

"On this I wholeheartedly agree, Sir." Saluting, Simmons started off toward the village.

"Wait! Hold it, Simmons! We have not completed the matter at hand." He gazed upon the billowing dark clouds overhead. Striking out blindly with both arms, he called: "They are *here*. They are watching us. They are here. They are watching our every move— waiting to strike." He drove a fist into the palm of his hand. "We must find them and defeat them entirely!"

"Are we up to the task, Sir?"

"That goes without saying, lad. Go and tell Lennox to assemble a detachment of horse-cavalry here beside the stream. We depart immediately. We will squash all vestiges of resistance. You are in full compliance, are you not, Simmons?"

"Why, yes, Sir. Enough said, Sir." Dutifully Simmons turned on a heel and made for the village grounds.

* * *

Abandoning the command post, the Bear Chief absconded to the agreed-upon place of seclusion at the foot of the ravine overlooking the Osco River. Descending the steep slope, he met with Cerf Courant and the others whom he designated to carry out his novel plan. On the plateau before the ravaged village meanwhile, the two officers still conferred affably, unaware that he had made the transition.

Shallow at the point where the warriors flocked, the Osco lay at the base of a generous embankment, a robust declivity of hard, clay-like sand which rose steadily upward, spilling over onto the grassy plain. The expansive and barren shoulder provided in its descent a slippery surface which the most able of woodsmen broached with caution. There, hidden among forbidding underbrush, the Bear Chief's select band received instructions. Some reached the refuge with horses taken from battle. Others arrived on foot. All, however, came with weapons. Now everyone leaned forward in rapt attention.

Mounting the mud-mired embankment, the Bear Chief gazed west over the pathway carved out by so many of his ancestors. It led to Eagle Mountain,* that lone sentinel of strength and solidity—symbols of the Peoples' core traits. Studded here and there on both sides with trees and thick bushes, the pathway skirted the village proper and headed for the base of the mountain some 500 meters distant where it debouched. It housed shrubbery and dense bushes. Intermittently tall maples and oaks sent their limbs arching over it to the extent that sunlight rarely penetrated the fierce canopy during the bright, warm days of summer when the trees were in full foliage. Those who walked the pathway under those conditions spoke of the supreme beauty of Nature, but with words of trepidation, for the inherent eerie stillness set against a backdrop of deep shadows forced the timorous heart to beat faster. The perfect place to hide, the Bear Chief recalled from the days of his youth when he and his comrades trapped deer in the thickets ripe for the taking. Berries grew aplenty at the foot of the great mountain, so bountiful that he often ventured from Guiogouen to gather them. Of the embankment he knew since early days its capability of concealing large numbers of men. Along that precipitous slope he played at war games in his youth with Cerf Courant and Fox Tail and other virile young warriors.

The Bear Chief's faithful band awaited final instructions. Descending the declivity, he gathered everyone together: He placed Aboyant in charge of concealing half of the band among the trees and foliage midway along either flank of the pathway. He watched as warriors setting out on foot merged seamlessly with the surroundings. They occupied the second half of the pathway until its terminus at the mountain. There they met with the first of the villagers who staked out a section steeped in coppices. It is there that they listened to reports of the ravaging of Osco.

Emerging from the ravine, the mounted warriors, the second half of the band, set up a raucous whooping at a given signal. Led by Cerf Courant, they urged their mounts over the crest of the embankment, whereby they dashed along the pathway in full view of the soldiers encamped on the plain. According to plan, they slowed when approaching the section of heavily forested canopy. Their ceaseless clamor bestirred the soldiers who rose from taking leisure. The Captain ordered Lennox to lead a cavalry chase with sabers drawn.

The mounted warriors paused once they achieved the midpoint of the pathway. Behind them Lennox bore down heavily, prompting them to turn and fire. Fleeing, the warriors ran at a fixed pace, displaying no signs of fear, while keeping out of firing range. A determined Lennox called out to his men. All the while the warriors persisted in a dogged, measured flight. Imbedded along the pathway, where Aboyant's force lay concealed, scarcely a leaf turned in the soft vapors. Again the mounted warriors allowed the cavalry to shorten the distance between them. Ahead loomed the majestic mountain. The warriors' whoops and cries intermingled with the sobering clatter of sabers. Eager for battle, Lennox challenged his men. Reaching the base of the mountain, the fleeing warriors divided into two segments. Encircling the promontory, they rode to left and right, invading the thickets and forest fastness which rose up to consume them.

Bewildered, Lennox called for a halt, the better to study conditions before him. The men prepared for a respite. Some set aside weapons. Others strained in saddles. The bulk of the cavalry came together at the base of the mountain where they pondered how best to spend an indefinite period of enforced idleness. This brief interlude of quietude, however, rapidly dissipated when scores of screaming warriors tore into the cavalrymen's flank. Pouring out from behind trees and bushes, the warriors drove the cavalrymen into a tight body. Joined by Cerf Courant's mounted warriors, they let fly with lances and arrows at the hapless horse-soldiers before diving for cover. The cavalrymen attempted to select targets from among the elusive band. They fired into the swirling throng which split into segments and retreated upon the flash of gunpowder. Reassembling, the warriors attacked in waves, striking and retreating. Lennox ordered the men to fix bayonets, while others resorted to pistol and ball. Surrounded, the cavalry stood resolute to drive back the enemy.

Lennox ordered the men into squads. Those who applied thick arm bands succeeded in warding off the murderous blows of the war hatchet. In banding together, the horse-soldiers compelled the warriors to break apart into smaller packs—making of their thrusts less frequent and easier to absorb. Lennox stood poised to reduce the warriors into small cliques whereby he may advance upon them, press them together, and ultimately annihilate them with saber and bayonet. He failed, however, to reckon with the versatile ingenuity of the warrior. Armed simultaneously with a hatchet and a hunting knife, the warrior possessed two weapons for the lone bayonet or saber of the soldier. In the hands of an agile, young warrior who leaped and thrust from side to side, the hatchet and knife delivered crushing and deadly blows upon an unprepared adversary.

The fighting raged on hotly, each combatant master of his own unique brand of warfare. They may have struggled indefinitely until the Bear Chief sought to press for a successful conclusion of the fray. Striding to the apex of Eagle Mountain, he summoned a band of the mounted elite guard to join battle. The guard summarily surrounded the horse-soldiers, a maneuver replete with hoops and calls, that sent consternation flowing through the ranks. Amid the confusion, a few cavalrymen, followed by a general exodus, abandoned the fight and fled to the shelter of a neighboring cornfield. There they cast about digging trenches from which they fired at will. The Bear Chief halted any pursuit, lest the foe gain the upper hand. In passing, he explained to Aboyant that he cared not to accumulate great losses, nor trample the cornfields which his villagers held sacred.

The roar of musketry reached the ears of the Captain, who, inspecting the village ruins, supervised the selected looting of marketable commodities. In response, he dispatched a second column of cavalry over the canopied pathway. In the cornfield, meanwhile, the horse-soldiers' hot discharges set fire to rows of corn stalks lying parched under the late-summer sun. The horse-soldiers beat a conspicuous retreat, ranging blindly through the smoldering corn. In flight they happened upon other comrades advancing from the village. Disgorging accounts of the ambush, they gathered beside the newcomers, bound by the common tie of revenge. The Bear Chief, on the other hand, seized upon the opportunity to lead the warriors back among the trees and bushes of the pathway. There they waited impatiently, aware of the pervasively low cache of powder and ball in reserve. A cautionary Bear Chief limited each warrior to two volleys.

Lennox, the young adjutant, did not flee the cornfield. When the flames raged through the stalks, he carved out a wide berth in the earth with a bayonet and, covering himself with mosses and grasses, concealed himself from view and from certain death at capture. He watched with interest the warriors assuming positions among the trees and bushes. He strained to devise a means by which he may warn his comrades of a resurgence of hostilities. Above all, he feared that newly-arrived cavalrymen may unwittingly stumble into an ambush. He placed the lives of the command over that of his own, and when he discerned the familiar clatter of hooves upon the hard pan of the trail, he knew that he must act immediately.

Casting aside the trappings of his hiding place, Lennox rose to full height and strode out upon the pathway, exposed without adornment to his God and to the enemy. Emboldened and fearless, he awaited the approach of the complementary force. When first he sighted the column, he waved frantically, a signal that all was not well. He fell to stepping lively over the trail, calling the sound of a wolf in distress. Faces gradually came into view before him, and making recognition, he called out the name of the lead horseman who brusquely curtailed the detail's forward progress. Straining in the saddle, the leader called out to Lennox who broke into a sprint to intercept him. Running, Lennox called out the alarm to take cover and the lead rider galloped toward him in all haste. Lennox reached out to mount a steed which the leader held for him. It became the final act of his short life, for a flight of arrows pierced his innards and he slumped quietly to the earth.

Although unable to save himself, the ill-fated Lennox may have saved the lives of dozens of comrades. No sooner did his lifeless form strike the earth than the entire relief column of cavalry dismounted and, deserting the trail, secured cover along the far left shoulder of the pathway. Unwittingly, they disembarked opposite the Bear Chief's hiding place—the trees and bushes on the right shoulder. Soon, volleys tore over the pathway, many of them finding the mark.

The warriors' barrage failed to rout the horse-soldiers. They responded with brisk fire. Heated exchanges took place without leading to marked results. Presently a strange development occurred: The horse-cavalry heard no more from the warriors. They talked among themselves, and concluded that the warriors ran out of shot. To test the belief, some of the men constructed counterfeit soldiers out of corn stalks. Covering them with ill-fitting garb, they tied them to cross-beams and held them overhead while squatting in hiding. Within moments the mannequins bristled with arrows. Subsequently, the soldiers settled upon the flight-path of the arrows and, making hasty calculations, fired directly across the pathway into the trees from whence the missiles issued. They cheered when screams of agony poured forth from the forest and, gathering together, send a small band in pursuit of the enemy.

Pursuing an elusive target in close quarters proved a daunting task. The cavalry learned that advancing in squads within the dense forest provided the warriors with the opportunity to break into small packs, disperse, then come into formation behind them. Returning to more familiar practices, the cavalry regained the pathway, hoping to draw the warriors into the open road. Almost immediately they withered before a dense volley of musket fire. The warriors followed, brandishing war implements. Forsaking muskets, the soldiers drew pistols and sabers, formed a defensive line, and engaged in hand-to-hand combat. In the absence of Lennox, they found themselves unable to gauge the enemy's size and strength. They fought tentatively at best, and perhaps, naively, held a portion of their strength in reserve under cover. The warriors, on the other hand, provided no surcease to the weary soldiers, charging the defensive line in orchestrated waves. In desperation the corporal of the guard bid the sheltered reserve to enter the fray. They arrived none too soon and together both units drove the warriors back across the pathway and into the forest. With the passing of daylight, all forms of combat became more intermittent. By early evening the horse-soldiers realized that the enemy had taken flight once and for all.

Exhausted, yet relieved with the cessation of the fight, the men rose from shelter, however timorously. They poured over the pathway when one of them fastened upon a light team drawing along two of the wayward cannon. Close behind, a third cannon, the greatest of the three, plodded ponderously. The gunners in charge bent to the task of discharging a duty which by then remained no more than perfunctory: They stationed the three pieces beside each other, filling up the trail, and, at the corporal of the guard's suggestion, discharged them in the vicinity of the warriors' last known stand. Minutes became an hour and when no volleys or counter-attack evolved, the teamsters and attendant soldiers sat upon the hard pan, weapons tossed aside.

In the absence of a retaliatory strike, gunners stumbled over themselves with excitement, and began to prepare to deliver a fusillade. First, tamping the muzzles with powder, they followed with a shovel—full of grapeshot for each bore. Next, they adjusted the range of the cannon by elevating them on the rear apron of the crude wagons. There remained the sole chore of igniting the fuses, a task to which sprung two eager yeomen. At that moment a deep voice called out three sharp commands from deep within the forest, a piercing voice which produced spontaneous results, for any and all remaining warriors in hiding fled headlong in a body into the deep fastness, their footsteps pounding heavily over the carpeted forest floor.

"Gao:nodahse! "—You come over here!

"Desa: driheh! "—You hurry!

"Sanigohaeda:s:geh?"—Do you understand?

The Bear Chief having spoken, warriors retreated before the hot iron balls of shot which gave chase after them. Most ran successfully through the trees and underbrush and lived to see another day. Unknown to the soldiers, all surviving warriors amassed on the far side of the mountain where the Bear Chief met with them. In precious few moments he doled out praises to one and all, a gesture which drew the villagers around them with like praises. In due course the Bear Chief stood apart from the assembly. He climbed the mountain where he maintained a silent vigil. Taking neither food nor drink, he peered stoically through the trees for hours.

The soldiers refused to wait and watch. A number of them flocked to the gunners' side where they lavished them with praises. Others rejoiced over what they believed a divinely-inspired reprieve from certain death: They rolled on the hard pan. They kicked up their heels. They performed somersaults and hand-stands. In stark contrast to the gaiety of the moment, great carnage lay on all sides of the celebrants. A sobering realization, the wash of corpses, and one in particular, brought the mirthful conviviality to an aborted end: A celebrant discovered the body of the valiant Lennox. Bending low, he cradled the well-admired lieutenant in outstretched arms and, brushing through a maze of merry-makers, lay him at the feet of the gunners' mates.

"We need to go back to the village and bury him. The Captain approves, I am certain," the man stated simply.

"The Captain is choosing a place for all the deceased," another man offered.

"Who wants to go for transports?" another asked.

The men looked at each other. No one volunteered, perhaps out of fear of what may lie in wait in the great thick forest bearing down upon them. At last, one Owens chose a small escort, and, placing Lennox upon a horse-drawn litter, cut a melancholy path back to the scarred Osco. Meanwhile, the horse-soldiers began the grim task of gathering the dead and wounded from the rather far-flung battle grounds. After posting a light guard, they learned that the task at hand remained too great for them alone without aid from members of the principal command. Shortly thereafter the pathway hummed with transports— four-wheeled wagons with a great depth and high sides. By late afternoon all ten of the wagons stood filled with cadavers. A ponderous cargo by all accounts, each transport required four horses— two more than the usual team. Owens insisted upon the removal of all weapons from the battle sites. Understandably, muskets, pistols, sabers, knives, even belts and whips, all manner of weaponry, made way for the village along with the deceased on board the transports. Not surprisingly, the horse-soldiers returned with few mounts. Those found after the fight stood idle, rummaging. Many of the men simply became dispossessed of their mounts in the heat of battle, leaving them to amble disconsolately back to the village to grumble to comrades. Some of the more cantankerous among the cavalrymen attributed the patent loss of horses to the warriors' insatiable demand for meat— a delicacy on the palate for some, a means of transport for others.

"For sure they do not plan to eat them!" one horse-soldier complained.

"Perhaps," an astute Owens deduced. "They have food. They want them for the same reason that we want them."

"To ride?"

"To ride and to hunt," Owens continued, soberly.

"To say nothing of the beauty of the beasts," another added.

"I am sure that the aborigine's tastes rival our own. This is one reason why they are riding and we are walking, mate," Owens offered. "Buck up! We have been spared our miserable lives to fight another day."

* * *

From the heights of Eagle Mountain., The Bear Chief awaited the soldiers' departure. By early evening all warriors had gathered at the site—shaken but resolute. Discerning no cause for further precautionary measures, the Bear Chief gathered all residents about him. He designated the mountain and environs a camp in which to address the needs of the wounded. From that moment the women, traditionally-skilled in caring for others, set up field-stations, equipping them with poultices to apply to wounds. They also cleansed lacerated limbs, and stitched open wounds and affixed wooden splints to torn appendages. The severely wounded they tied firmly in litters stuffed with soft grasses. Hunters and gatherers went out in search of foods, for everyone must be fed during this most trying period. Until further notice, the mountain became the new home of the villagers. Few complained, owing to the unadorned beauty of the mountain and its surroundings.

On one occasion the Bear Chief led a party along the gentle slope to the mountain's summit. Essentially a hill, the prominence stood tall, overlooking a rolling plain of tall grasses, where multi-colored blooms tossed and turned in accord with the gentle vapors visiting the slope in summer. Shallow ridges cut across its girth, descending into clefts and dales holding pockets of dense brush. Sturdy oaks, maples, and ash trees, symbols of strength and longevity, dotted the surfaces.

Attaining the summit, the little party held an all-encompassing view of the countryside below, where streams and trails meandered off into oblivion, insignificant from this advanced height, and where one may stretch out a hand and touch the sky, —yea, touch the face of the Great Creator. Those who indeed reached out longed to gain a sense of power over all earthly challenges and they came down from the mountain exhilarated, speaking words of great wisdom to friends and relatives and before long the lethargic stamp of melancholy abandoned the camp. True to expectations, the villagers established residence among the clefts and valleys of the mountain which sheltered them against wind and rain and from predatory incursions. The cautious Bear Chief assigned a light guard to stand watch preparatory to retrieving the deceased from the fields of battle. He brought with him many of the horses, which fell into his hands during the fighting, for purposes of transport.

The horse-soldiers, on the other hand, deflated in body and spirit and visibly shaken from the loss of Lennox, returned to the ravaged Osco. Stripped bare of its attributes, the once-robust village lay smoldering in ruins from the torch. The foundation stones of the former great council fire remained the sole recognizable property extant. It is there that Owens found the Captain and the aide, Simmons in intense debate over a matter of great importance, although for different reasons: The grounds over which they quarreled consisted of a circular enclosure of calloused hard pan beat down by the heels of countless residents who saw fit to tend to the great council fire. Large stones set congruently to each other marked the enclosure's circumference, and, at a glance, the imposing configuration sat at the village's epicenter. A pit or basin in which items may be prepared for consumption, occupied the center of the enclosure. The pit too stood rimmed by stones, although of a lesser bulk and consistency. Owens walked across the enclosure, marking off 60 paces or 18+ meters. He brought his measurements to the Captain and Simmons, who debated the overall size and location of the enclosure. Yielding to expediency, both officers summoned a crew with picks and shovels to break ground, their ultimate decision resting upon the resistance of the earth. Gradually the forbidding earth broke apart with steadfast applications from a determined crew, leaving Owens to declare it the crude beginnings of a burial site.

While the crew labored, the Captain produced a leaf of paper from which he read the names of the fallen soldiers in the battle of Osco. Then, walking about the stones surrounding the pit, he recited the names again, inscribing an X on the earth before each stone. Proudly he noted that not one of the deceased did he omit from a place of final repose. Owens thought that he saw a tear flow down the craggy cheeks of the man he deemed a stern task-master. From that moment forward he augmented the manner in which he viewed the Captain.

The digging continued far into the afternoon. The Captain declared that Lennox be the first to be interred, following preparation for burial. He grew insistent that a brief ceremony be held for the adjutant so-enamored by his men. One of very few to be interred in a rudimentary coffin, Lennox lay facing the rising sun, hard by the largest of the stones fronting those guarding the basin. In lieu of a chaplain, the Captain himself led a memorial service of his own choosing. He wept noticeably during the delivery, eliciting similar responses from among the congregants. His delivery concluded, the Captain buckled at the knees and sought Simmons's arm in leading him away to his tented quarters. Soon, however, he composed himself, and returning to pressing matters at hand, directed that Owens and Simmons bring forward the remainder of the deceased. In all, sixty separate plots formed three concentric circles around the pit or basin, in effect an inner circle. The laborers tamped a mound of earth into place over each grave and fixed a row of stones running lengthwise over each mound to hold back hostile elements. The Captain sighed in satisfaction when learning that, according to his calculations, every last member of the deceased reposed in uniform in relative comfort. He stood quietly to the side observing procedures and when the end came, Owens observed him with head bowed and hands wiping tear-filled eyes.

Following burial rites, the Captain called for everyone to convene for a moment of solemnity. Simmons brought forth a book of prayer and several of the soldiers read eulogies taken from its text. Standing near the fallen Lennox, the Captain read from the book. He chose a passage that regaled the life of an enthusiastic and promising young man, cut short in battle. Finishing, he walked away slowly. The entire command then broke into two segments, and, convening on either side of a grave, faced each other, touching sabers overhead, while Simmons read a final passage over each fallen comrade. Thereafter the eulogy service ended and the men became free to grieve for a short period, preparatory to abandoning the ruins of the village. In the lengthening shadows of the late afternoon, members of the command scurried to and fro loading sacks of booty taken from various sources: foods from the underground caverns, furs and hides from cold storage bins, and dried logs and tinder for kindling fires. Before the arrival of early evening the command assembled on the plateau, the scene of unbridled conflict a short while ago. There they formed into a long column and, fording the moat, headed out to the northwest. An appreciable lack of horses hampered the command's progress. Yeomen soldiers performed at least one duty of the noble steeds: hauling numerous wounded over hilly terrain in hand-drawn wagons. No one complained, however. In departing, the command moved out in silence, each man struggling with his own thoughts of what took place that day.

The Bear Chief noted the passage of the soldiers from his refuge on the mountain. Once the besiegers disappeared over the horizon, he led the warriors upon the grounds of the once-proud village. There, struggling against the onset of darkness, he began to gather the deceased casualties of the battle. The purloined horses proved most useful. Laborers fashioned cradles from saplings and, lashing them to the animals' backs; they placed fallen comrades upon them in well-defined rows. Many warriors resorted to carrying the dead by hand. Binding them to their backs, they walked to the periphery of the former central camp fire where they lay them at the foot of the great stones which formed the outer boundaries of the enclosure. In all, some sixteen warriors came to rest along the fringe of the former community hearth. They lay in a great circle. Each one reclined before one of the great stones of the camp fire's exterior, each stone bearing the name of the deceased, etched into the smooth sandstone-like surfaces by a skilled artist and cutter.

Originally the Bear Chief intended to occupy places within the enclosure— approximating the central pit or basin, the communal core of Osco. Preempted thus by the besiegers, he conferred with Cerf Courant and other leaders, and all agreed to allow the interred soldiers to remain where they lay in an observance of respect, not necessarily for them, but for the rite of burial in general, one of many rites which the Cayuga held sacred. In the end the Bear Chief reasoned that the larger, more impregnable stones which gave rise to the outer wall formed a distinct barrier between essentially two different burial sites. By his account, the sixteen warriors enjoyed the posthumous benefit of luxuriating in a spacious bed of alluvial soil, a refuge set apart from all others, in particular, those who occupied the inner circle nearest the basin. Standing back, the Bear Chief observed the scene, the placid countenance breaking into a thin smile. He summoned the ancient Iroquois rites of burial (16):

Laborers placed the deceased in shallow furrows, not over four feet in depth. The warriors lay with arms folded across the chest, arrayed in full battle dress, accompanied by preferred weapons of choice. A personal memento followed them into the after-life. The women prepared the bodies for burial and all living members of the once-thriving village descended upon the site to witness the ceremony, over which he, the Bear Chief, the War Chief, prepared to preside. By agreement, the villagers elected to move on to new lodgings so that the Spirits of the Dead may be able to roam freely over the land that the deceased once knew in life.

Gradually, the circle of witnesses tightened around the burial site. Colombe Blanche and the boys came forward, along with James, Suzanne, and Watkins. Colombe Blanche related that the Lords of the Confederacy invested her husband under the Iroquois Constitution with the authority to conduct the burial ceremony to the exclusion of all others. In his address, the Bear Chief paid homage to all Iroquois warriors of late who fell in battle, paying the ultimate sacrifice under the most extraordinary of circumstances. Speaking from the outer ring of the former great hearth, in the shadow of the fallen Osco's defenders, he quoted from the ancient oral text of his ancestors:

"I, Hnyagwai:Hahsenowa:neh—The Bear Chief—speak for those unable to speak for themselves. Now we have become reconciled as you start away. You were once warriors of the Five Nations' Confederacy and the United people trusted you. Now we release you, for it is true that it is no longer possible for us to walk about together on the earth. Now, therefore, we lay you here. Here we lay you away. Now then we say to you: 'Persevere onward to the place where the Creator dwells in peace. Let not the things of the earth hinder you. Let nothing that transpired while yet you lived hinder you.

"In hunting you once took delight. In the game of Lacrosse you once took delight and in the feasts and pleasant occasions your mind was amused; but, now do not allow thoughts of these things to give you trouble. Let not your relatives hinder you and also let not your friends and associates trouble your mind. Regard none of these things.

"Now then, in turn, you here present who were related to these men and you who were their friends and associates, behold the path that is yours also! Soon we ourselves will be left in that place. For this reason hold yourselves in restraint as you go from place to place. In your actions and in your conversation do no idle thing. Speak not the idle talk, neither gossip. Be careful of this and speak not and do not give way to evil behavior. One year is the time that you must abstain from unseemly levity, but if you are not able to do this for ceremony, ten days is the time to regard these things for respect."(17a)

With head lowered, the Bear Chief reverently abandoned the hallowed site. Approaching the family members of each of the sixteen fallen warriors, he spoke to them a message of condolence "Please go to cheer your minds once again. Rekindle your hearth fires in peace. Put your house in order and once again be in brightness, for darkness has covered them. If you shall do this, the black clouds will roll away and the bright sky will become visible once more. Therefore, you will live in peace in the sunshine once again."(17b)

Women brought out stores of food. Adhering to tradition they built a fire and the villagers gathered around a small corner of the former central camp fire. There they ate a modest meal of roasted meats, nuts, berries and fruits. A period of mourning followed, greatly abbreviated in order to allow the villagers to accumulate belongings and depart the ruins quickly in advance of incidental invaders bent on retaliation. Some of the residents expressed concern about moving. Colombe Blanche quieted their fears by announcing her husband's imminent speech.

The moment of departure drew near. Suzanne appeared at Osco's shattered portals, her modest belongings wrapped in a box and tied to her back. She stood with Fawn, her new friend, the young woman who tirelessly cared for Watkins during his convalescence. Orphaned at an early age, Fawn was befriended and later adopted by Colombe Blanche when both lived at Goiogouen. The dear maiden set off waves of passion in Watkins and he seldom left her side at Osco. Suzanne hoped that Fawn may be able to draw significant details from Watkins relative to her mother's whereabouts. He appeared reluctant to communicate with her openly until that final afternoon in the village when Suzanne conceived of an inducement to arouse his curiosity in her mother.

Within a cache of meager belongings she found a portrait of her mother encased in a silver compact, tethered by a golden chain, a gift of her father on their wedding anniversary. Miraculously the locket survived the summer rains and numerous other calamities. Displaying it before Fawn, Suzanne asked her friend to take her to Watkins where he immediately seized upon it as a subject worth exploring, He began by drawing a close similarity between her and Caroline, whereupon Suzanne lamentably related the story of Caroline's abduction, so prompting her prolonged search. In a flurry, Suzanne disclosed her mother's appearance, attributes, and culinary skills, yet when she spoke her mother's name, Watkins' alertness heightened appreciably when he began speaking extemporaneously of a woman named Kerry.

"At Oswego there was a handsome woman who served the officers at mess. She sat with one exclusively, the Captain, and we yeomen believed her his servant or concubine, for he never let her out of his sight. We yeomen became enamored of her golden tresses, blue eyes, and stately figure, and when she served Irish stew on Saturdays we fought each other to find a place in line."

Suzanne beamed with delight. "Yes. That is mother. So, we may find her at Oswego?"

"No. To our dismay she up and vanished one day. Rumors have it that she refused the Captain's advances and he sold her into bondage, or worse."

"Tell me the worst."

"The Seneca may have her. They often adopt able mistresses into the Confederacy. They have need of replenishing losses from wars and maladies. The congenial ones they keep. The incorrigible ones they sell or kill. Aunt Kerry is a valuable asset to whomever takes possession of her. The Captain may have sold her at Kanandesaga, for having refused his advances. He tended to bring her along whenever he went on sorties."

"Trafficking in humans!! How disgusting!! Does the commandant know of this activity?"

"Lord Carleton has suspicions, but has been unable to secure reliable confidants from among the men."

"How sad!! Is trafficking accepted procedure on the frontier?"

"It is until a law is passed against it, and even at that, there are those who will defy it."

"I need someone to penetrate this wall of silence."

"Far be it from me. The Captain believes me dead. If he learns that I live, my life will not be worth a rotten hen's egg. The Chief—the Bear Chief! Learn with whom he trades, the French, I believe. Find the French tradesman and you will learn of your mother's fate."

"Provided I find her. How do I keep her safe? All of us?"

"The evildoers(s) must be brought to trial. If they are soldiers of the Crown, they will be jailed, dismissed from the corps, and forfeit all pensions and wages."

"It is an approach worth taking. I must find an ally." Gritting her teeth, Suzanne slapped her thigh.

"There you are." Colombe Blanche called softly to Suzanne. "Come. My husband is about to give his farewell address. You will learn of your new home now." She swept along everyone in her path: Suzanne, Fawn, Watkins, and the boys. They walked to the plateau, where villagers, hauling possessions, began to flock. The resonant voice of the Bear Chief greeted them. Looking up, Suzanne beheld a tall, regal figure before her:

"We move to the lands once frequented by the great orator of our People: Tah:gah:jute (18). He first ascended these Round Tops when a youth to find inspiration to guide him along the path of peace. He is now with the Delaware, speaking on their behalf before those who wear the powdered wigs. I have chosen these Round Tops for I wish to be able to make good choices for my People in the image of Tah:gah:jute. We are at war with invaders into our lands. It will continue until the invaders give up the fight, or are all killed. Join me in the Pledge of War in which we ask for strength and courage." (19). With bowed heads, the villagers recited the brief oration.

The end came solemnly. One by one the villagers touched the hearth stones of the valiant warriors who died in battle. They formed a long, gently-sweeping circle in keeping with the outer confines of the former communal hearth. Passing beneath the ravaged palisades of Osco, they walked slowly with heads bowed out of reverence for the deceased. Weaving to and fro, the procession headed due north over two ranges of rolling hills. Their new home lay immediately beyond: a series of spacious slopes capped by grass-covered, earthen mounds: the Round Tops.*

Colombe Blanche displayed the golden stones to Suzanne: "They will bring me good fortune, I trust."

Suzanne noted to her hostess: "This locket has brought me good fortune. It is more than a prayer."

*Eagle Mountain corresponds to the former Quill's Hill, now a residential tract in southwestern Auburn, NY

(16) Van Sickle-Wait, Mary & Heidt, Jr. William. The Story of The Cayugas: 1609-1809 (19660 pg: 55

(17a&17b) Callison, James P. The Iroquois Constitution: *Funeral Addresses* pg: 18

(18) Merrill, Arch. Slim Fingers Beckon. Chapter 3: *Owasco and Auburn: Lakes Country Metropolis*: Empire State Books, Interlaken, NY (1951) pg: 25

(19) Callison, James P. The Iroquois Constitution: *Rights and Powers of War*. pgs: 15-16

*Fort Hill Cemetery, Auburn, NY

Chapter Six

Signs of Unity.
Signs of Conflict.
The New-Arrivals.
Architects of the Round Tops.
The Summit.
The Case of Caroline York.

The morning found Watkins drawn up into a coil in a thick, woolen blanket. The coolness of the new day awakened him, in this, new residence at the Round Tops. He sat up. Bleary-eyed, he yawned and looked about him. Intuitively he pushed backward on his heels, retreating from his blanket. A giant shadow enveloped his sleeping space, giving him pause for concern. Sheepishly he glanced over his head and glimpsed a great hardwood climbing endlessly toward the pale-blue sky. Balking at his innocence, he slapped his thigh in anger. He rubbed his backside in an effort to relieve the stiffness from his limbs. He chastised himself for having slept in a fetal position with arms and legs tucked tightly to his chest.

His stomach growled, emitting pangs of hunger. His stomach always growled when breakfast drew near. Customarily he took his first meal of the day at about eight hours. He reached for his trail boots. They served him well over the years, dating back to his days at the bakery, when he assiduously rubbed them with oil to make them last a bit longer.

Reaching inside a boot, he pulled out a trail watch. The other boot held a trail calendar. He noted the time: 08:15am, his gnawing stomach a reliable prognosticator of the dinner hour. Retrieving the calendar from its protective sleeve, he circled the date with a bit of carbon: September 9th, 1760, a Saturday. Replacing the watch and calendar, he drew the boots on slowly. Stretching, he stood and performed a series of twists and bends in order to stir dormant muscles. Taking tentative steps, he peered upward through the trees and found that an azure sky replaced the pale-blue, assuring him of a warm and pleasant day.

Back home at this hour he baked the breads and little cakes for the many townspeople who frequented the family bakery. Scores of military folk visited his shop also. To prepare for such a surge, he rose at five hours most days of the week. Although fatiguing, the labors carried intrinsic rewards. He enjoyed the brisk activity and meeting clients' demands. Now fully awake, he realized that his new life on the frontier carried its own share of challenges. Here on the frontier he intended to be successful in meeting them, perhaps to the point of becoming a master of his surroundings.

Usually clean-shaven, his face sprouted a mass of stubble. He needed a shave and a bath. The bandaging needed to be changed, although the swelling in his shoulder subsided considerably and he retained full movement. For the moment these necessities must wait. The gentle vapors of the morning spurred the aroma of cooked meat toward him. His stomach growled. Hunger growing, he patted down rumpled hair, straightened his wrinkled buckskins and headed off to find the origin of those pleasant emissions which besieged his senses to no end. He soon met with success.

In a small clearing he found Fawn beside a camp fire. She turned what he presumed to be griddle cakes on her iron skillet— assuredly an object of trade. A pot boiled, emitting the unmistakable aroma of coffee. A second skillet held strips of bacon and eggs frying. Beside her lay a sumptuous bowl of berries. Looking up, Fawn greeted him with a few well-chosen words of English, an obvious tribute to Suzanne's teaching.

"Good morning. Sit down, please." She spread a strip of canvas on the hard earth.

"Eat!!" she commanded, bringing her hand to her mouth to demonstrate.

He began eagerly, sampling from the several bowls she placed before him. Stealing a glance at his hostess, he marveled at her beauty: the long, black hair, the deeply-set eyes, the supple yet strong body. 'All that a soldier needs. Good food and a good woman.'

"Good. Very good." He forced out the words to show his appreciation.

Fawn smiled politely. Touching a shoulder, she whispered: "I will clean you now." She scampered off to prepare a dressing. His eyes followed her. She disappeared beyond one of the great earthen mounds.

Suzanne paid him a visit. Perky and jovial, she, like Fawn, exuded comfort in her new home. He told her of Fawn's progress with English. She blushed scarlet and admitted to a burning desire to develop Fawn's facility with English, her newly-found tongue, in both reading and writing skills. She began to go into the details of her approach to teaching. She alluded that, through Fawn, she may be able to extend instruction to the villagers.

"I like the almost coffee," Watkins interjected, changing the theme of the conversation.

"Do not be alarmed, Monsieur. It is called chicory, a substance long known to the villagers. Do not ask me about its origins. I asked a villager and he took me to a tree and pulled off a piece of bark and put it in my hand."

"Bark? Tree bark?"

"Bark!" she laughed. "Tree bark!! Your friend returns. She may be able to help you with that," she replied, pointing to his beard with a hint of sarcasm.

"Now, Suzanne. A man's beard is his property. After all, you know I must remain anonymous."

"Anonymous, yes, but unrecognized, no. I am sure the mites of this place are very pleased that you have chosen to live among them. Let Fawn help you. Here she comes."

He decided against challenging Suzanne. Gulping the remainder of breakfast, he sat in silence as Fawn washed and dressed the wound with what appeared to be army-issued cloth. Finishing, she led him back to her camp fire where she helped him remove his boots. With a cloth she demonstrated how to wash using one hand. Next, with a bar of soap made of lye and ashes and other ingredients, Fawn made a rich lather. She applied it to the cloth and dipped the cloth into a pot of hot water. She handed Watkins the soapy cloth and vacated the premises as he stripped to wash his anatomy. She returned shortly with a change of under garments, a pair of men's hose, and a clean shirt. He dressed. She turned her back and rummaged through a leather bag. Turning back to him, she held forth a razor.

Following Fawn's instructions for shaving with one hand, Watkins soaped the stubbly beard. Fawn applied a whetstone to the razor and from her little bag took out a pocket mirror. She held the mirror before him while he scraped off the growth of beard. He winced when reaching those difficult corners of the mouth and under the nose and ears. She struggled to contain her laughter, enjoying his anguish. He stuck his tongue out at her in mock anger. In response she took away the hand mirror at the moment when he brought the razor across his chin. He yelped in pain and blood flowed freely from a small incision. Fawn acted quickly. She stanched the blood loss with a cloth dipped in warm water and instructed him to keep it in place on his chin. Scurrying off, she returned with a mud poultice which she applied to the wound. Watkins stood impassively, more embarrassed than injured.

"Now you have two wounds," she said in a light-hearted manner. "I must go to Suzanne. I will come back to you later," she called over her shoulder, skipping away.

She found her new friend on the grounds writing in a book which she termed her journal. She tried to make entries each day, she told a curious Fawn. "It may prove noteworthy one day," she confessed. Suzanne went on to ask for Fawn's approval in planning a breakfast for Colombe Blanche and the boys in order to show her appreciation to them for having aided her and her father. Fawn tried to dissuade Suzanne, citing Colombe Blanche's innate shyness, but Suzanne determined to press on. Her breakfast prepared, she called for Colombe Blanche only to learn of the absence of her hostess from the camp grounds. Reluctantly, she began to believe Fawn's message. Forming a plan, she dispatched Aboyant to find her, but he soon returned empty-handed. In desperation Suzanne set off with Fawn and Aboyant. Together they scoured the immediate vicinity and it is Aboyant who found Colombe Blanche seated in seclusion at the base of a hill and staring blindly into the distance. Her sons frolicked nearby. Aboyant spoke with Colombe Blanche before approaching Suzanne. He begged her to listen to him intently.

"She is disturbed that you prepared breakfast for her," he explained. "By custom the woman of the home prepares and serves the meal. By your actions you are depriving her of her duty."

"Oh, I am deeply sorry," Suzanne wailed. "Please tell her that in my land these things are done as a matter of course out of simple kindness."

Aboyant bounded off and returned a few minutes later. "She will come to breakfast provided you allow her to prepare breakfast for you one day." He grinned capriciously, then asked: "Do you have a birthday soon?"

"Why, yes. At the end of October."

Aboyant bounded off again, leaving Suzanne speechless.

Returning, the little man bowed deeply from the waist: "She will prepare a meal for your birthday. You need to tell me the day of your anniversaire—birthday. You must tell no one. If you agree, she will come to breakfast now."

"Yes, yes. I agree. The 14th of October." She repeated it in French. "Mais oui. Je suis d'accord. Le quatorze d'octobre".

Again Aboyant disappeared to deliver the message. He returned shortly, leading Colombe Blanche and the boys and the little party returned to the camp site. There they found a renewed Watkins bedecked in fresh apparel. He beckoned Suzanne's guests to partake of Fawn's breakfast, whereupon he sat down for another course to Fawn's delight. She beamed approvingly, her features radiant. Her manner gave Colombe Blanche to understand that Watkins meant something extraordinary to her and she subsequently hastened to join in breakfast. The boys sat beside their mother giggling and exchanging words known only to themselves.

Watkins inquired of James York, prompting Suzanne to outline with a sense of pride her father's undertakings.

"Father took breakfast early this morning. He went with the Bear Chief and Cerf Courant. They brought one of the field pieces from Osco and are placing it at what will become the entrance to the Round Tops. Father is making a carriage for it. He found a saw, hammer, and nails in the underground stores at Osco and packed them before we departed. A wise move, to say the least."

"Indeed, Mademoiselle. How did the tools come our way?"

"Father says they came by way of Lake Onondaga where a French tradesman keeps supplies for use among the natives. Usually he gives them in exchange for articles of trade."

"This Frenchman. He trades directly with the Bear Chief?"

"Yes. They are on the best of terms, I am told."

"There you have it, Mademoiselle. You must go to the Bear Chief and have him introduce you to the tradesman. If he is the wide traveler that you imply, he will know all the stories and myths coming along the frontier."

"He may know of mother?"

"Exactly."

"Before you arrived, the Bear Chief agreed to help father. We waited for the tradesman during the Corn Festival, but he did not appear, and nothing more came of it," She sighed, hanging her head.

"Fear not. You have taken the first steps and are to be commended. What brings you so far west?"

"There is a French outpost near Lake Onondaga. Father and I told the commandant about mother and he suggested that we come here to speak with the Bear Chief."

"Interesting. I did not know of such an outpost. Is this outpost also the retreat of the tradesman?"

"Understandably. I believe so."

"Find him! Speak with him! Travel with him if you must! He knows something. Little, perhaps, but something."

"Thank you, Monsieur. Colombe Blanche is expecting me. We will talk later."

—

She regarded Watkins as a new ally. With this in mind, she merrily joined Colombe Blanche to plant seeds, many of which her hostess salvaged from the battered Osco. They lay in urns on the grounds. She found Aboyant separating them into sacks, one for each species, prior to planting. Colombe Blanche began to label each sack with their contents. Suzanne asked to help and her hostess handed her a carbon stylus and leaf of paper. While Colombe Blanche identified the seeds, Suzanne labeled the slips of paper, inserting each one into the sack. She lost count of the number of sacks, but committed their contents to memory: corn, green beans, squash, pumpkins, onions, broccoli, sweet potatoes, berries, currants, and peaches. The boys came along. Holding clamshells, they explained that they planned to dig furrows for the seeds. Suzanne beamed satisfaction and the boys told her that they intended to visit the south slope of the

Round Tops which held rich, loamy soil. They begged their mother to take them on her tour. She reluctantly consented and, full of cheer, the boys volunteered to lead the party. They soon came across the Bear Chief and James York, finding them engaged in building a mount for the field piece. The Bear Chief directed the boys to a large crop of blackberries along the eastern slope, and the boys begged their mother to allot them two of her baskets for picking them. She scolded them mildly for abandoning the party, yet relented when they promised to fill baskets to the brim.

Suzanne took up the clamshells in the boys' stead and she and Colombe Blanche went about digging furrows and planting seeds. They kept the boys in plain view and agreed to summon them at midday for a lunch of wild berries. The women labored long and hard in the warm sun and at length Colombe Blanche insisted on resting. Her stomach turned upside down, she reported, and her eyes burned. She began to sneeze repeatedly and her eyes became swollen and red.

"Ah! You have the Summer Sickness," Suzanne announced, confident of the analysis. She picked a handful of yellow blooms on long, slender stems. "See! Goldenrods. They are all about. You must leave this place and wash with warm, soapy water. Then, you must drink a hot potion and cover your head with a hot towel. You will be better by tomorrow." She summoned the boys. They raced headlong to her side, their baskets overflowing, not knowing of their mother's plight. When Raven reached Colombe Blanche, Suzanne warned him not to touch her. In the same breath she reported that Colombe Blanche remained in no grave danger. The boys breathed a sigh of relief and Little Bear begged to tell a story of an excursion along the slopes in hopes of reviving his mother's spirits.

"I have a honeycomb," he rejoiced. "I played a trick on the bees. I held out some blackberries and while they ate them, I took their honey." Smiling, he luxuriated in his own cleverness.

"Why are you holding your arm? his brother Raven asked."

Little Bear paid him no heed and continued singing praises to himself.

Raven brushed alongside of his brother and pulled back his arm to reveal red welts the size of small raisins. "What are these?" he asked, suspiciously.

"The bees are smarter than I thought," Little Bear confessed in embarrassment.

* * *

Suzanne laughed and the aggrieved Colombe Blanche pushed forth a weak smile. The boys took light of the matter and the little party set a contented pace back to camp where the boys began to prepare the berries for dinner. Suzanne found Fawn and together they went in search of her father. They encountered him standing on the southern slope, trying to speak with the Bear Chief with the few native words he thus far assimilated. Suzanne translated her father's words into French for her host, the universal tongue of the frontier:

"I will build a large cabin with living quarters downstairs and sleeping quarters upstairs. It will have a pitched roof with bark shingles over slate. The kitchen will have a stone hearth running the length of one wall, complete with chimney. There will be chairs and tables for the living quarters and closets and bureaus for clothes and personal articles. A wooden stairway will connect both floors. There will also be a cellar for storing foods and dear possessions. It will be below the kitchen and connected by stairway." Deep in thought, James rubbed his chin.

"Windows! There must be windows, father!"

"Not to worry. I am told that the tradesman will bring windows."

"Then this man of mystery really exists?" Suzanne walked back and forth inspecting the new cannon mount.

"Within the week. It is always following the Corn Festival, I am told, dear daughter."

"Good. I see you have been studying. Tell me more about the cabin, father."

"There will be hardwood floors covering all of the rooms. The cellar will be hard pan. For the present one must go out-of-doors to a facility to attend to bodily functions. Indoors there will be a bathing room with tub and sink with water pumped from a well." He smiled luxuriously and continued:

"The bathing room will be next to the kitchen and its hearth. Water will be heated on the hearth and brought to the tub and poured in by the bucket." He gave a feigned demonstration.

"Excellent, father. Who will live in this house?"

"Our host and hostess will have the first dwelling. Others will shortly follow."

"You will do this alone?"

"No. Not at all. Watkins has volunteered. We will also train a number of the native men to wield a hammer."

"Absolutely amazing!!" She ran over and hugged James. "Where will you put the beast?" she asked, referring to the six-pounder.

"Directly at the southern gateway to the village. No cannon shot, of course—a monument, no less."

"A monument celebrating the victory of good over evil," Suzanne quoted, standing beside the cannon.

"There will be a palisade around the entire village," James continued." There is no need for parapets. The hills themselves make outstanding look-out points. Storage will be underground. A moat will run side-by-side with the palisade. A tunnel will lead the villagers away from danger in case of an attack." He scratched his head: "Have I forgotten something?"

Watkins overheard James and offered suggestions. "It is good to build cabins for all of the families as soon as possible. The winters are long in this land and the climate changes at the drop of a hat. Each cabin must be single-family in order to preserve family ties and intimacy, something that the long-house of old did not provide. On the other hand, unmarried males for example are probably better suited to live in communal homes, much like those of the long-house (20). Does this make any sense?"

"My sentiments, exactly, Watkins," James returned. "When do you want to get started?"

"You give the word." He bowed graciously before James.

"I am certain that our host will approve of the plan, Watkins. Let me speak with him," he called, walking away. Returning moments later, James's face blushed with excitement, something rare for him: "The Bear Chief asks for stables for the horses and one structure to house their provisions." He smiled, then continued: "He wants a structure large enough to hold all the tools and contrivances that he expects to acquire."

Watkins laughed softly, but confided to James that he and Suzanne must first cultivate the Bear Chief's friendship as a prelude to securing aid in finding James's wife. On that point both men agreed and shook hands.

—

Word of the men's proposals spread quickly through the rolling hills and from everywhere volunteers young and old came forward to offer services in building a village which fulfilled current expectations. The Bear Chief directed Aboyant and Cerf Courant to form teams in order to begin felling trees. He cautioned against removing the thick stands that bordered the periphery of the Round Tops, however. For the Bear Chief the trees held a sacred significance and also provided a circular line of defense around the entire camp. Calling the laborers together, he sent hunters out to bring back fowl and deer for a feast he planned to give before the commencement of the cutting. The darkening sky gave him to understand that the day grew late. Subsequently, he deferred the project until the following day. Meanwhile, he urged all laborers to set aside the necessary tools preparatory to an early start on the morrow. Privately he thanked his friend, the tradesman, for having donated the valued instruments.

Everyone feasted until late that first evening. Exercising caution, the villagers refrained from sparking camp fires. They built instead a central pit, lined with stones, to become the sole hearth of the camp. That first evening the Bear Chief posted a light guard atop the taller mounds. He himself sustained the watch and wherever he walked an air of enthusiasm permeated the camp. Presently Colombe Blanche came to stand beside her husband, her stomach pains having appreciably subsided:

"It is good that these newcomers have come among us, my husband."

"They are good. Bear in mind, however, that their needs are great."

"Tomorrow is the Sabbath. Remember that no labor takes place on the Sabbath."

"Thank you. Under the circumstances, I forgot. Very well. Spread the word." Beside him Watkins appeared dejected. "I trust that you understand," the Bear Chief addressed him in no uncertain terms.

At that point the Bear Chief chose to speak at length on the Sabbath and his faith, ostensibly for the benefit of Watkins. The usually soft-spoken, reticent speaker launched into the role vigorously:

"All of the villagers are Christian. Long ago, men of the Long Frock visited my ancestors at their principal villages near the lake to our west*. They brought us trade goods on which we have become dependent. They taught us the French language and asked for little in return. During their tenure they asked that we observe their religious practices together with our ancient ways and we found that the two go hand-in-hand. Along with the tools brought to us, our quality of life has improved. We came to trust in the brothers of the Long Frock, for they endured numerous hardships in order to be with us. They lived in poverty, ate little, demanded no tribute, and, to an extent, enjoyed the pain of suffering, an ordeal which our Seneca brothers frequently visited upon them. They asked only that we recognize their Saviour as our Saviour. We held no exceptions to their wishes and Nature treated us kindly, so we acceded to the Long Frocks' wishes.

"The Long Frocks set out schools in our villages in which they taught us their cherished beliefs. We have long honored these beliefs in our own ways, but we cared not to offend the Long Frocks. Their teachings reminded us of the inherent strength of our ancient ways and we became stronger thereby because the Long Frocks insisted that we actively practice religious observances. I recall their teachings: 'Do not murder another. Make your enemies into friends. Respect the wife and property of your neighbor. Do not steal the goods of another. Do not lust after the flesh of another. Give to those who have not.' These are all good beliefs and we try to follow them, although some brothers stray from the path. I, for one, see their goodness and have observed them among the members of my village. Long after the Long Frocks departed our lands, I continue to observe them (21).

"It has not always been the same with our brothers to the west and north. They frequently conducted purges in which they persecuted the men of the Long Frock. Perhaps they are not as patient and understanding as we. Our numbers have always been less numerous than theirs and we came to welcome newcomers into our villages, for we looked for ways to acquire new thoughts in order to enrich the quality of our lives. We also have fewer enemies than our other brothers. At some point the men of the Long Frock left us. They abandoned us to their teachings which we highly regarded and practice to this day."

The Bear Chief brought Colombe Blanche forward: "My wife has accepted the teachings of the Long Frocks, one of the first in her village. When still a young girl the Long Frocks came to her village and, bearing gifts, spoke with her father, a wise and honored chief. Her father allowed her to study with them until she understood their teachings. Her instruction culminated on a Sunday when one of the Long Frocks immersed her in the waters of our lake in a ceremony which everyone in the village attended. The ritual is called Baptism and she became the first in her family to be inducted into the church of the Long Frocks. In passing, the Lord of the Forest welcomed her also, giving her the wisdom to set a good example for her children and to approach life with a heart full of humility.

"She wears the Cross, a symbol of our new faith. The tradesman brought it to her and asked her to wear it around her neck to protect herself from illness. It helps to keep her pure in thoughts and speech. After we wed I became baptized. My sons followed and we all wear the Cross. It is of gold and brings us more in favor with les peaus blancs, for gold is a substance dear to them. A priest from the French fort arrives most Sundays to conduct the Mass. He stays in a home which Henri Marchand, the tradesman, built. Monsieur Marchand lives there during his trips along the frontier. We will visit him one day."

His speech ended, the Bear Chief announced his intentions for the disposal of the horses gained in battle. He called Aboyant, Cerf Courant, and Watkins. "Brothers. I award a horse to each of you. Remaining horses I give to my sub-chiefs, to my wife and to my sons. I have set aside a number of them for laboring in the fields. Also, I believe that they are good for carrying messages to our brothers. We must treat with them wisely." Turning to James York and Watkins, he asked: "Etse:geh:ogwatge:nihs:oh?"—Are you coming to our meeting?

Speaking to Suzanne in French, Colombe Blanche translated her husband's remarks. Suzanne in turn translated from the French into English. Colombe Blanche explained that on Sunday evenings the villagers commonly attend a vigil in which they ask the Lord for strength in meeting personal objectives and in combating adversaries. Usually the vigil takes place out-of-doors around the central camp fire, and indoors during the rains, she continued. James York and Watkins readily assented to attend, whereupon, they partook of the Bear Chief's sumptuous feast and spent the remainder of the day discussing the merits of their labors.

Sunday dawned: the York's first Sunday in the nascent village. After a light breakfast Watkins met with James York. He discussed a proposal to outfit a hearth in homes for all families of six members. He brought the proposal to the Bear Chief who favored it, concluding that a great stone pit* lay some two leagues north of the Round Tops in which lay great slabs of stone ripe for the taking. Given the recent species of labor-saving devices to fall into his hands, the Bear Chief expressed confidence in removing the stones without difficulty. and in bringing them back to camp in short order. On this day of reverence the Bear Chief spoke at length for the benefit of the guests:

"I chose this place because it lies in seclusion. It is Nature's conception of a fortress, securely guarded by hills. It lacks but one feature which at Osco flowed in abundance: water. There is a stream which flows from near Eagle Mountain. It comes this way, but splits into two branches**. One branch goes to the northwest. The other comes straight toward the Round Tops, ending in a bog beyond the southern entrance to the village. We need to deepen the bog and make a passageway for the water to flow into it and out of it. Then we will have fresh-flowing water to drink and to give to our horses.

"It is difficult to find the exact source of the stream, but knowing that Eagle Mountain is surrounded by mystery makes it easier to say that Nature herself created the stream from nothing at all. If we are able to harness the waters from Eagle Mountain and bring them to our village, then we will know that Nature approves of what we do. Remember that Eagle Mountain has helped us to hide from invaders. I believe that all events tied to Eagle Mountain will bode well for us. Therefore, I am convinced that Eagle Mountain is the earth-bound home of the Great Spirit. I have thought so since my youth.

"On the eve of passing into manhood, my father took me to Eagle Mountain in order that I may accomplish a feat. We camped for several days on a slope. Eating little and sleeping less, we braved the cold night vapors. All the while my father kept watch on the horizon. He kept an eye keen for the sight of an eagle returning to its nest. When an eagle finally appeared, my father sent me to pluck a feather from its wing while it sat on the nest. I baited the grounds around the nest with meat from a fresh kill and when the eagle came to eat them I threw a fishing net over it and reached inside and plucked one of its feathers. Then I cast off the net and walked swiftly down the hillside. The eagle did not follow me. It returned to its nest and watched me. My father met me at the foot of the hill. He told me that I passed my test into manhood for several reasons: I did not show fear. I chose a sound plan to defeat my opponent. I treated my opponent with respect. I carry the eagle's feather to this day. It is in a hidden place."

After conferring with the Bear Chief, James York announced a plan for diverting the stream at Eagle Mountain. He called for a series of declining terraces to lead the water to the bog before the village. He planned to build a dam there in order to convert the bog into a pool with both inlet and outlet— thereby creating a steady flow of fresh water. The depth of water in the pool depended on the volume of water coming down the terraces. In spring the waters all around tended to flow freely. The overflow would draw small animals and deer and water fowl to the pool where they may be hunted. He yielded to Watkins.

Watkins proposed lining the watercourse with strategically-placed rocks in order to prevent the erosion of the stream bed during the spring and summer rains. He also believed that underground sources of water lay abundant in the region— given the number of shallow streams coursing to the northwest. Therefore, he suggested digging for wells, a means to supply running water to the new homes under construction.

Cerf Courant expressed a need to establish a series of watching-posts along the margins of the new village. Accordingly, the guards must develop a system of alerts to danger which they change at intervals in order to confuse an enemy. He also suggested storing many diverse foods for consumption in lean periods, especially during droughts when the supply of wild animals dwindles below the level of subsistence.

Aboyant stepped forward to be heard. He carried one of the muskets retrieved from the field of battle. He called for all able-bodied men to become skilled in its use. He suggested scouring the battle sites for shot and additional weapons, claiming that he possessed a small arsenal of arms and shot which he accumulated during returns to the Osco battle site.

* * *

The Bear Chief vowed to weigh all proposals during the remainder of the day and to begin the arduous task of choosing among them before the seasonal warmth appreciably deteriorated. Above all, he assigned the construction of cabins his top priority, with all other matters decidedly essential, yet peripheral to his central objective. The camp remained in repose for most of the afternoon. When the hour of the Sunday vigil loomed near, everyone congregated to a lofty mound to hear the Bear Chief's opening remarks:

"Villagers! Look around you. We have guests among us from distant shores. They chose not to come here by their own hand, yet once they entered our domain they found peace and tranquility awaiting them. They have come to learn from us. We, in turn, will learn from them. In building a new village we all have learned to labor together for a common good, a goal which is blind to differences in race and stature. We are all equal before each other and before our Creator. This is how He looks upon us. May we have the strength and good sense to continue our labors in praise of Him." He dedicated the vigil to the newcomers in camp and asked the villagers to come forward to greet them. At this point, James and Watkins delivered written copies of all proposals and made short speeches of appreciation to their host, the Bear Chief, and hostess, Colombe Blanche. Shortly thereafter everyone broke into small parties to enjoy a feast prepared by the women of the village.

Suzanne chose the hiatus in ceremony to seek after the Bear Chief, whose friendship she longed to develop. She confided to him her fear that the man who attacked Osco was the same British officer who abducted her mother.

The Bear Chief listened intently and at once uttered the term: gaya:dahneh:skweh—kidnaped—under his breath. Suzanne, her aspirations elevated, continued: "I know that your friend, Marchand, trades with the Seneca and that they accept prisoners from near and far to replenish depleted numbers. They also sell prisoners. If my mother is among them, Monsieur Marchand will be able to buy her back for us."

The Bear Chief consoled the eager young woman: "I enjoy good intercourse with Marchand. We supply each other's needs; however, he is first a tradesman and will charge a handsome fee in searching for your mother. In a sense you will pay twice, for Monsieur Marchand must meet the Senecas' price, if indeed your mother is their prisoner. Do you have the means to pay?"

James York interceded: "Our means washed away with the summer storm. I propose to exchange my labor for Caroline's freedom. Suzanne will join me. Have we not proved of value since first we met?"

"You have been most admirable guests," the Bear Chief returned. "I will speak with Marchand and you will have all fees excused. Without speaking, the search will be difficult and dangerous. You may be killed, but ultimately that is the true cost you must be willing to bear to achieve success. Your boldness and daring have fortified you to make this perilous journey, but they alone will not guarantee you achievement. Do not fear!! I will recommend you to Marchand. A word of caution! Do not give your true names to strangers who come before you for they may fall upon evil ears. You will most assuredly pass through Kanandesaga, a Seneca town where everything, human and otherwise, is bought and sold or exchanged throughout the day without regard to ownership, past and present. Do you agree to all of this?"

"Yes," James replied.

"I agree," Suzanne followed.

"Good. Let us go to the Summit."

The Bear Chief led James and Suzanne York to the Summit, the tallest mound of the camp, a locale he set aside for special occasions. Unlike other prominent mounds, the Summit rose up conically from a broad-based hill, forming a plateau at its apex from which speakers may address an audience or upon which meetings may be held. Centrally-situated, the northern flank merged with the surrounding denseness, while the remaining three flanks resembled a leisurely-rolling plain descending unobstructed into the lower reaches of the camp. From the Summit one enjoyed a liberal view of the landscape. The little party sat upon woven mats and covered their extremities with woolen blankets to fend off the damp vapors which tended to accumulate there. The closely-knit circle in which they reposed instilled within Suzanne a sense of intimacy with her surroundings and of course with the Bear Chief whom she regarded in a new light. Her host spoke:

"I come here to seek the counsel of my uncle, Tah:gah:jute," the Bear Chief opened. "It is said that he visited the Summit (22) to call upon the Great Spirit to help him make wise decisions. Perhaps that is why he is widely known for his speaking and is sought after when major questions must be decided concerning the People's fate. He has not lived here for a while, but his memory burns deep in the hearts and minds of the villagers. This is a good day for story-telling. I have not heard your stories at any length since your arrival. I need to know more about you so that I will be able to help you in your quest." He looked directly into James York's eyes, prompting him to speak:

"Suzanne, her mother, Caroline and I, came to the Susquehanna region three years ago. We answered a call from Caroline's uncle, Charles. He ran a prosperous farm and knew through our letters of the failure of our first farm along the Chesapeake. He offered us lodgings and food in exchange for our labor. Charles greatly valued the addition of our three hands. Near Charles' holdings a British unit camped. They came to open new lands for white settlement. The local Delaware objected to the intrusion even when offered compensation and often disagreements erupted, but Charles quelled them by assuring the Delaware that the British meant no harm. For a certain period all remained quiet. Yet Charles learned that the British wanted his land also. He refused all compensation and united with the Delaware to block further British expansion. His neighbor, a Quaker, held influence in the provincial legislature and Charles once led a Delaware delegation to speak there. Following his appearance, the British made no further demands and all seemed in order for the moment."

The Bear Chief asked to speak. "The Delaware have treaty relations with my People. We are free to hunt and fish on their lands and we call each other brothers. We are the keepers of the north lands and the Delaware are keepers of the southeastern lands in a region going from Le Grand Lac Ontario to the upper Chesapeake. Their concern is our concern. Recently they are alarmed over the loss of ancestral lands. The peaus blancs ply them with gifts and currency and unfortunately some of my brothers have parted with these lands. Secretly, British soldiers have enlisted the aid of willing Iroquois to drive off the Delaware and take possession as a reward. This my brothers scoff at, for they know that the British have no intention of surrendering what they deem theirs to another party. With this in mind, I and the members of my village, believe that the attack upon Osco is one more example of the British desire to chase all of us away from our inherited lands." He yielded to James York.

"We are coming close to the connection between the British and the disappearance of my wife. Charles served with the colonial militia. After he retired from duty, he exercised a pension and bought the lands which became his farm. He raised fruits and vegetables in a year-round project requiring constant attention. To that extent he employed neighboring Delaware. He found them loyal and industrious and when drought or famine struck their villages, Charles welcomed them to reside with him indefinitely. They lived in cabins in his fields which they tended on a daily basis. A firm trust grew between Charles and the Delaware. He saw them both commonly linked by the land on which they resided— the land sought after by greedy agents. He believed that strength in numbers posed the best defense against a wrongful takeover, thereby lessening the tendency of the British to display a show of force. Nonetheless, the British came back on more than one occasion in small delegations to offer incentives to sell. Charles still refused and, when absent, Caroline spoke for him. One day a party of Delaware found Charles dead, washed along the shore of the Susquehanna which flowed nearby. Caroline and I made inquiries to government officials. They produced no results and officials deemed his death an accident. We knew that Charles did not know how to swim and we struck out on our own, making inquiries of the populace. Still we came away empty-handed, but in the eyes of some of the people I read the signs of fear. Out there someone knows, but is afraid to speak. Shortly after we exhausted our search, Caroline disappeared from market, usually a safe haven for her. In full daylight someone snatched her away. Out there someone knows something vital to my inquiries. I must find this witness, for Caroline's sake, for Charles' sake, and for my own peace of mind."

The Bear Chief spoke: "I now understand your reason for being here. We are, you and I, linked by common causes: You have frequented the land of our brothers and have labored with them side by side. You are aligned against the same enemy as we. You want to guard your lands against invasion. Most important, you search for justice for the ones whom you hold dear to you. Tell me. Do you have any private thoughts on this matter?"

"Suzanne and I have concluded that the leader of the Osco invasion is the *same* officer who ran off with Caroline. We offer in evidence the observation that his expedition is the only command to have reached out beyond Oswego and into the Susquehanna region. Watkins, your guest, has spoken to me of this command's travels. He dare not return to the command for fear of death. Therefore, I find great merit in his account."

The Bear Chief resumed: "You have demonstrated your goodness of heart to the People over and again, Monsieur York. I do not question your allegiance, or the burdens which you carry. When you go before Monsieur Marchand, I trust that you will conduct yourself in an exemplary manner. The labor of a trail-hand is difficult. You will see yourself performing the same tasks each day in an effort to stay alive. Your only redemption lies in the new challenges which each day brings you. What is most important, you will be able to keep your eyes and ears open for signs of Madame York. It is good of you to go, for you alone are in the best position to name Madame York. Tell me. Do you have a son?"

"Yes. I have a son. His name is Matthew. He serves with the British marines in Newfoundland. He does not know of his mother's plight, nor is he aware of where Suzanne and I are at present."

"You are in a most delicate position. At any moment your son may be called to defend any of the forts along the great waterways of the east and west. If you ally with Monsieur Marchand you become an enemy of the British and they will hunt for you. You may be held prisoner in a fort which your son frequents and he may be present at your hanging. British seamen master the great waterways. French soldiers hold inland forts. This makes for constant tension between them. It is strange that two great bodies fight over lands they do not own. It is the land and its riches that they desire and they are willing to crawl over our dead bodies to grab it for themselves, each in his own way. It is for this reason that I form no permanent alliances with either of these rivals. I try to buy satisfaction from both of them, knowing that sooner or later one of them will hold sway and come to me and my brothers to dictate terms of surrender. You will meet Marchand. He will smile and bring you cheer, but you must realize that he is a pawn in a much larger game. These rivals will try to convert you to their way of thinking. Remember, stripped to the bone, you must never surrender that which makes you whole: the love for yourself and those whom you hold dear. These no one may take from you and it grieves our rivals to know this. They sit up late at night gnashing their teeth in agony over failure to gain our full surrender. You and I, however, rise up with each new day, happy to be alive, for we enjoy life.

"We enjoy each other and we are full of hope that a bright tomorrow is on the horizon and in our own small way we labor to build such a place. For this reason I will intervene for you, for this place we inhabit is in a constant state of change and we, Nature's humble servants, need to bring about change for the better of all. This is my message for you today."

For a long moment James sat silent. Suzanne uttered not a word, but when James glanced at her, streams of tears poured down her cheeks. A light vapor moved in and the skies turned gray and the little party sat motionless, each aware of the other— each consumed with private thoughts. The Bear Chief spoke, the deep voice breaking the stillness on the mount:

"This man, Charles. I recall my Delaware brothers telling me of his skill in producing great yields. A generous man, Charles shared his knowledge with my brothers and they came to develop a liking for the land as a valued treasure. They raised an abundance of foods which held them through the hard winters when the creatures of the forest became scare. Indebted to Charles, no longer do my brothers rely on the four-footed animals to keep them from starvation. No longer do my brothers freeze in the cold winters when bear skins are unavailable. Charles secured blankets and boots for them, often from the very British who wanted to buy his lands. To clothe my brothers Charles often donated excess yields to the British garrison in exchange for clothing, although I doubt that the British stood aware of this development. I do believe, however, that they eventually learned of his beneficence and sought ways to quell his enthusiasm. Perhaps this is why he died. Charles owned many hectares and my brothers performed a multitude of services for him. Services that other land-owners paid for came without a price to Charles, for my brothers esteemed him greatly. Perhaps this is one more reason for someone to kill him. We shall perhaps never learn who killed Charles, but we must believe that it is someone who took exception to his good fortune."

"We are deeply indebted to you," Suzanne spoke between tears.

"You owe me nothing, Mademoiselle. Your call for assistance is but one more voice crying out in the wilderness. It is the voice of all native families who long to preserve cherished ways. Your call has charged me to exercise my duties of chief, one of which is to protect my People's inherited way of life. Therefore, it is good that you ask for my assistance. It is better to ask sooner than later."

"How will you proceed?" James asked.

"I will seek the counsel of neighboring chiefs and allies. I am familiar with many of them from my youth when my father took me with him on journeys to their villages. At an early age I traveled the length and width of the Iroquois domain beside my father. He sought to form strong alliances with his neighbors as a means to thwart an enemy. I did not know that he intended for me to one day follow in his footsteps. Looking back, I am happy that he brought me along."

"Will we meet with Monsieur Marchand soon?' Suzanne asked.

"Yes. Of course. Let me tell you my reason for going to him. Let us say that I find strong signs of a killer. Perhaps I will find the killer himself. In order to bring this killer forward, I will need the support of a well-esteemed peau blanc, for who other than a strong ally will believe the word of a chief whose name is not recognized in the councils of the white men?"

"If we find mother. If we find the killer, your name will be widely recognized," Suzanne replied.

"I may then have to flee for my life. Recognition brings out one's enemies."

"It also brings out one's true allies, those necessary to carry the day," James said.

Rising, the Bear Chief spoke: "This is a theme without end. We have done well here. The Summit forces those who choose to meet here to speak candidly and without deception. I have seen that happening today. The day is growing short, yet we have accomplished much. Let us prepare for tomorrow." That said, the Bear Chief drew a blanket over his shoulders and slowly descended the Summit. James and Suzanne followed. Neither spoke, each one remained consumed in thought.

* * *

Returned to camp, James and Suzanne encountered Watkins. The inquisitive look in his eye compelled James to attend to him despite the late hour. He stole a glance at his trail watch and calendar, committing the findings to memory: Monday, September 11th, 1760, and launched into discourse:

"Our host has agreed to help Suzanne and me search for her mother. He has one great concern, one that affects us all: There are no established laws on the frontier which reach out to strangers and new-arrivals. I have learned that, in the interest of profit-making, the British and French have suspended all semblances of judicial prudence in a push for riches. The Bear Chief gives the attack on Osco as an example of such preoccupation. In the case of my wife, Caroline, he concedes that witnesses must be chosen who will speak on her behalf."

"I understand your plight, James. I for one am prepared to stand up for you when the occasion presents itself. My testimony alone, however, will not lead to a conviction. For that you will need the testimony of others close to the body of conspirators who are willing to come forward. This is not the first case of abduction to cross the frontier, but if it succeeds, it will *truly* be the first. For myself I believe that there are *several* predators out there. They may not be aware of each other, but they labor in close proximity to each other. This is what I fear. The difficulty for us is that examples of wrongdoing on the frontier suffer from lack of exposure and a lack of prosecution in courts of law. You and I know there are no courts of law in existence to treat with them. There is something more: a widespread inertia among those in power to admit of misconduct and neglect within the military establishment. The Crown equates a move against the military to an assault upon its very own hierarchy. Unfortunately for us, the military is at odds with disobedient natives, yet it is these natives whom we must turn to for allies."

An angered Suzanne entered the discussion: "You are saying, Monsieur Watkins, that a few wrinkled old men in starched shirts are keeping my mother under wraps?"

"In a rather blunt way, yes, Mademoiselle."

"I see that my mother poses a strong threat to those in power, both here and abroad." She thought a moment before speaking again: "My mother is very persistent. She will pursue her quest for justice indefinitely."

"The proper forces must be marshaled, Suzanne," her father offered.

"Let me see, father. We have the Bear Chief, an esteemed tradesman who has yet to reveal himself, and a living witness in the person of Watkins." She counted her allies on her fingers, feigning an air of defiance.

"You will need a diversity of allies to press your case, Suzanne," Watkins offered.

"I have a thought. I believe that finding mother and her abductor will lead us to solve the larger matter."

"The larger matter?" Watkins asked.

"Yes. This talk about 'Justice' on the frontier. Father. I never thought about it before, but I believe that you and Watkins are correct. That is the larger matter. Justice, and plenty of it!!" She struck her thigh affirmatively.

"You are out to break the mold, Suzanne," Watkins submitted.

"I prefer 'iconoclast,'" she returned, head held high.

"A what?"

"Iconoclast. It means one who shatters accepted beliefs and practices."

"You will have your hands full. Tell me. How do you come by such a term?"

"I am a product of St. Mary's Academy for Girls. Member of the school newspaper staff. Wrote about human interest events." She jumped on the words, pushing them forward. Turning toward the right, her back arched and ramrod straight, she finished with a smart salute into the horizon.

"You turned eastward," a curious Watkins commented.

"Yes. Of course. The sun rises in the east. In its ascent, it gives birth to a new day filled with new challenges. Also, the promise of a better world looms omnipresent. It is school tradition."

"Such spirit. To whom does she owe it?" Watkins asked, perfunctorily.

"Whatever I am, I owe to my mother," Suzanne chirped.

"Suzanne too is persistent," James stated. "I have *two* of them to contend with," he laughed.

"Mother is very independent," Suzanne cut in, hoping to rescue her father from embarrassment. "I wager that at this moment she is conceiving of a plan for escape. In so doing she will have struck a chord for human justice. That is why we must find her." She pushed back tears.

His curiosity aroused, Watkins turned to James York: "Tell me more about Caroline."

"The disappearance of Caroline I consider a mystery. It has saddened me greatly. Caroline customarily took our produce to market on Fridays in the afternoon. She traveled with an escort, sometimes with Delaware, always with Suzanne. Caroline rode by wagon. Suzanne followed on horseback. The route led two and one half miles to the town. Beside her stand in the town of Bay's Berg, Caroline unwrapped her goods and counted her currency. Suzanne assisted. She often visited other merchants nearby.

"On the day in question, Caroline departed for town with Suzanne. Nothing seemed out of sorts. Many townspeople frequented the open-air stalls of the market district. It lay near a military post and His Majesty's soldiers made a practice of coming in to spend a portion of their stipend. With the townspeople and soldiers, the district resembled a stockade filled with livestock— all milling together in continuous motion. I myself stayed at home. Crowds do not please me. Caroline always reported to me the events of the day, however ordinary. Caroline put in a full day. Arriving at eight hours, she left at five to prepare dinner at home.

"According to Suzanne, Caroline disclosed to her that a man came to her stand to order purchases. They came to a handsome amount and he requested that Caroline deliver them to his bailiwick. She thought this strange, for he appeared capable of carrying them under his own strength. The man persisted, stating that he intended the purchases for comrades at the post, who, earlier that day, set out on field maneuvers. In truth a body of soldiers recently engaged themselves in clearing fields outside of town in order to make way for row houses for soldiers' families. The man appeared too insistent, however, and despite his reassurances, Caroline rejected his invitation. The man produced the credentials of a purchasing officer and wore a full military uniform. Caroline cited the need to remain close to her stand and the man initially dropped the matter. He came back later to suggest that she make a delivery upon closing her stand, and again Caroline refused, giving a need to return home. He departed with reluctance, yet gracefully.

"Caroline made note of the man's appearance and dress. She reported her observations to Suzanne for posterity: He stood of medium height and weight, hair black and flecked with gray. He gathered it in a bow behind the neck. Although in military attire, he wore the colors of no particular unit, nor did he wear the characteristic emblem associating him with a unit. He wore black, shining boots, well-polished, which came up to the knee and a set of spurs for goading a horse. For a man who claimed to have spent the day on horseback, he appeared all too clean and dressed in the manner of a land owner, natty and spruce, one who seldom approached a horse. He spoke in a scratchy voice, the result of excessive cigar-smoking no less, and leaned upon a gilded cane, an instrument which in no small way aided his gait and complimented his dress. The piercing blue eyes frightened Caroline and she sought every occasion to look away from him. Caroline believed him a man accustomed to commanding others and one who expected full compliance: characteristics not compatible with the likes of a purchasing officer, nor with her own standards for a spouse. Therefore, she held reservations about his genuineness and bid him a curt, yet polite refusal.

She maintained her station, witnesses agreed, until closing, when she closed her stand and awaited Suzanne's arrival.

"Suzanne came for her mother as planned. She found no trace of her whereabouts. Caroline's stand, however, stood full with all wares intact, a sign that Caroline left not of her own free will. Confused, Suzanne searched the immediate vicinity. She called upon neighboring vendors and spoke with habitual consumers. Bits and pieces of knowledge gushed forth, but nothing of lasting substance. At this point the town's constable came forward. He tried to fit together a portrait of the so-called suspect from a description that Suzanne rendered— taken solely from her mother's reflections. When Suzanne turned up the word 'military,' the constable withdrew services, stating that he, a civil servant, lacked the authority to make inquiries of the military— the dominant arm of defense in the community.

"Suzanne spent the major portion of the afternoon asking questions at random. Our dinner hour came and left, prompting me to go look for her. I found her with the constable pleading with him to break with tradition. Perhaps in deference to me, he promised to make local inquiries. The constable furnished us an escort home and offered to form a search party consisting of yeomen farmers who charged a modest fee."

The Bear Chief interrupted at this point: "You have been pursued by evil men who covet your possessions, Monsieur York. They know that you will search for your wife, and when you do, they will take possession of your lands. The abduction is one more example of the determination of these men to force you to quit the frontier. They are beset with greed. Among others of my kind this condition has played out through the ages. In succession the Algonquin, the Huron, the Erie and many more Peoples have coveted the same lands for themselves, pushing out their neighbors. Greed drove them to covet and greed brought down their civilizations at length. Sadly, they never learned from the errors of their own self-serving ways and are no more recognizable as nations. We, however, of the Gayogoho:no, never descended into these depths. We believe that this land is too large and stuffed with treasures to become the property of a single owner. We believe, therefore, in sharing the land with all who are prepared to care for it. If one cares for the land, the land will provide for him (23). Perhaps, this is why we the People still reside with homes and a civilization intact. We have always built strong foundations.

"Let me speak more about your wife: It strikes me strangely that Madame, whom you lead me to believe, is of sound mind and body, has chosen to remain with her abductor. Not once did I learn of her attempts to escape his grasp. Something has prevented her from exercising her will. The man holds a weight over her head. If it falls, someone very dear to you will be killed. In so doing, Madame York is willing to endure pain so that you and Mademoiselle Suzanne will be spared the brunt of it. In the long run, Madame will make use of her grit and guile to pull free of her abductor. I do not know when that day will come, but it will certainly come."

Turning to James York, the Bear Chief delivered a somber message: "You must think of the one who allowed this presence of evil to enter into your life. There is a certain someone, if you are fair to your senses."

"Suzanne. Help me with this," James pleaded.

"Father. There is no one," Suzanne insisted.

"Nothing out of the ordinary? Think!!"

Suzanne counted out her fingers her functions at market with relation to her mother: "Ride to market. Set up the stand. Bring Daisy* to the corral. Feed Daisy. Buy flowers for the mantel. Go window-shopping. Return for mother. No, father. There is nothing different."

"You spoke with no one, never?"

"No!! Wait! There is a man—a tall man dressed in a white uniform. He confronted me in front of the flower shop. He asked all sorts of questions about Daisy—so many that I wish the horse was able to speak. I told him of my urgent need to depart and it is Daisy who saved me. She knocked into the man as I adjusted her harness and he promptly stepped aside." She thought a moment. "He is rather young, fairly attractive, hair behind the neck, is clean-shaven. Ah!! He has a cockney accent, which tells me he hails from London. He may be of the military, but his uniform is that of a landed gentleman. I believe he tailored it personally for himself. He is well-groomed, without a beard, and is accustomed to riding, judging from his knee-length boots." She tussled her locks, prodding her memory.

Tears poured down her cheeks. "Father!! While I spoke with him, mother disappeared."

"It is an old ruse, Suzanne. He delayed you so that an accomplice may capture your mother."

"Father. I must confess. During the battle of Osco, I stole away to the parapets. I found a pair of lenses and trained them on the Bear Chief. He met with a distinguished-looking man. They spoke at will. Father! That man! His gait! His attire! Everything about him tells me he is the *same* man who confronted me with Daisy."

"That is astounding, Suzanne. By the way, your story has spared you a sound scolding."

"I recall the man of whom you speak," the Bear Chief offered. "By his manner he is an accomplished man. In speaking with him, he insisted on putting forth his own accomplishments. He turned deaf ears to my arguments. It is his own brashness that opened the battle. Monsieur York. Do not be fooled by strangers who hold themselves out as friends. The constable of whom you speak appeared almost out of nowhere. He offered you aid for a price. If you accepted the offer, your life may have been cut short. He has his own interests in mind, not yours. He is part of a greater plan to malign you— worse, silence you."

James continued: "The constable offered an escort to Philadelphia, where he claimed a garrison lay to grant greater assistance. He demanded that I start out immediately. I refused, for I thought he acted too hastily, when earlier he demurred. Suzanne and I waited until the following day before setting out alone. No one pursued us and we adopted the theme of two strays: an officer and his daughter, who lost their command in the wake of the Indian wars. Walking due north, we followed the Indian Trail (24). We made a practice of asking pedestrians about our two *lost* friends: an officer and his lady, also detached from their command. We gained results, all reports indicating that our party held a two-day lead over us hard by the trail bound for Oswego."

Watkins spoke: "I recall that the Captain made regular sallies into the Pennsylvania country. He kept hard by the Susquehanna. It provided cheap transportation for bateaux. He visited rising settlements to enlist crew-members for the BEF survey team. His maneuvers began in earnest with the British capture of Fort William Henry (25) last year and the reoccupation of Fort Oswego. The fall of Niagara two years ago and the storming of Montreal as we speak (26), have furnished him with an abundance of confidence that a sweep of French holdings is not far distant. Soon, droves of settlers will overrun this land and the French will see themselves running back to Canada. I, myself, do not care to see that day. One such sally took me to the gates of Osco, you will recall James. True to form, the Captain withheld vital details until they became self-evident. Casting off the Bear Chief's peaceful intentions, he opened battle.

"With regard to Madame York, I first laid eyes on her during the evening mess at Oswego. She served the officers at table, doting on the Captain's every whim. He never furnished an explanation for her presence, and we men fancied her his wife come to visit. On the other hand, the Captain never spoke of having a wife, leaving us to believe her a refugee abandoned on the trail whom he befriended, worse, a prostitute whom he employed for special services. She prepared excellent meals and we men always looked for her graceful demeanor to grace our humble settings. I remember her from a distance: Tall, blonde, easy on the eyes, she dressed exclusively in long skirts and sleeves, wearing a bonnet. She prepared the officers' meals. I remember some of the men saying that the Captain saved her from a band of marauding savages who wiped out her entire family. This may or may not have merit, but whatever the case, she clung to the Captain closer than a new pair of riding gloves. She and the Captain did not converse freely with each other. Of course he has always been one to sit and brood at length. Madame kept to her own quarters by all accounts and the two of them, to my knowledge, did not share the same bed. At first glance they seemed a couple united by necessity rather than by the heart. I may be remiss, but I do not believe so. One day, a particularly gray day, she appeared no more in the dining hall. Her absence set tongues a wagging and for every man who questioned her absence there sprouted a new explanation. Of course no one questioned the Captain himself. Men do not simply approach the Captain with questions. He is a man who prefers solitude."

"I understand, Watkins. Tell me. What accounts for Caroline's disappearance in your eyes?"

"James. I have asked myself that very question more than once. I never knew them to argue openly. You and I know that between two people there is more to the pudding than meets the eye. For myself I find it difficult to believe that she ran off unescorted. I *do* believe however that Madame and the Captain came to a stark disagreement. Their relationship, whatever its substance, died on the vine, never truly developing. They came to a fork in the road. Madame is extremely talented in the kitchen and will not have difficulty entering into a new bond of servitude."

"Servitude. How cruel!" Suzanne wailed.

"Unfortunately, Suzanne, this is the situation with your mother," Watkins returned, penitently. "Her cooking and domestic skills command a fancy price on the market, the black market, where goods are bought and sold at will. No fool the Captain, he has reaped a fine reward in furs, or pottery, or precious stones in turning her over. If I may play devil's advocate, he has earned much in excess of his yearly stipend. Where there is a demand, someone will fill it."

"This may not be her situation at all," James postured, hoping to allay Suzanne's fears.

"This is true, James. Let me continue further. Up to now we have assumed that the seller profits from a sale. In the case of Madame York, she also profits."

Suzanne gave Watkins her full attention. "Oh?"

"Wherever she finds herself Madame will be allowed to live comfortably, although not far from an overseer, for she has other outstanding qualities which reach beyond the household. Any scoundrel who walks her on his arm gains great status among peers. By now she has learned to employ her attractiveness to her benefit."

"I do not know whether to praise you or scorn you," James returned.

"This is the way of conditions on the frontier, James."

"Tell me. Provided that Caroline remains in servitude, do you envision her captor in truth selling her?"

"A soldier, James, spends many idle hours on the trail. He may accomplish great deeds, but many of his days smack of idleness and solitude. A soldier lives to serve, but he plays a waiting game. A sheer lack of service tempts him to lash out, searching his soul for ways to make life meaningful in surroundings strewn with all-too-common banalities. Moreover, the soldier often sees himself apart from the mainstream of life, the forgotten warrior, sent far afield to appease the whims of his government. In the soldier's mind other people decide his worth. He is but a tool in their pocket. The soldiers I have known have accepted their fate. Of course, there are others who wish to defy the vicissitudes of their lot—if only for a brief period. It is these men, perhaps the Captain, who wish to create their own destiny, at least shape it to meet their needs. Am I going too far, James?"

"No. Not at all. Therefore, in taking Caroline, the Captain hopes to covet for himself that degree of satisfaction which the staid, military way of life has denied him over the years."

"Yes, and in this special circumstance, to plunder that which belongs to another, James."

James nodded, then spoke: "For a man who has been pressed into a mold so to speak, abducting Caroline is one way of gaining retribution from the very demons which in his mind have made him less of a human."

"Very good, James. To lose Caroline he must admit defeat, and defeat is a condition unacceptable to even the lowest soldier in the hierarchy. Extraordinary circumstances may push him to part with Caroline, say his very life hanging in the balance. Given that extreme, he may trade her off for a handsome price. Failing that, he will keep her under wraps indefinitely, unless brought to account, whereupon he will sell her, reap the profits and move on, for in the end he must save himself. Hence the evilness of her captor."

Suzanne, on the point of tears, gasped and James took a step backward.

"Bear in mind James that we are simply allowing our thoughts to wander. Madame York may be living in the lap of luxury to our knowledge."

"Far from it, I wager. Tell me. What dangers lie within human servitude?"

"There are the constant dangers of transporting one's prized possession to a safe haven. I am told, for example, that there are a flotilla of pirates who cruise the St. Lawrence."

"What do you know about them?"

"Like our enterprising Captain, they engage in the slave-trade. Unlike him, they have trade routes expressly established to carry a great number of captives. They go by either land or water, although they prefer the latter."

"What are the advantages benefitting these pirates?"

"Pirates sail light and fast craft, capable of eluding bulky merchantmen. They hide in coves and inlets and sail at all hours of the day. Someone snatched at Montreal will find himself at Fort Detroit in a matter of hours."

"I am not able to conceive of Caroline being thrown to the pirates."

"Does she have a temper?"

"She states her case. She is of her own mind."

"I ask, because stubborn and demanding women make for poor objects of trade. They are among those given up."

"I assure you that Caroline is aware of her surroundings. Her knowledge is not confined to the kitchen."

"I believe you, James. That may prove to save her in the long run." Watkins paused to collect his breath, then continued: "In thinking back and listening to your accounts, James, I believe that Madame's captor took a fancy to her. Therefore, I believe that she is safe for the moment. More so, I believe that her captor will hold fast to her against all temptations to the contrary."

James clenched his teeth. "I want to believe you, Watkins."

Suzanne consoled her father. "Let us put our faith in Watkins' wisdom. I have learned much here today."

"What are you writing, Suzanne?" Watkins inquired.

"It is a journal. It keeps my mind occupied in periods of stress." She smiled, briefly. "At this rate I will be able to create a treatise—at least a chronology." She put down the quill. Tossing back her head, she picked up the threads of her father's story:

"Removed from the constable's watchful eye, Father and I took matters into our own hands. We visited the surveying camp which lay next to Charles Martin's holdings. Again we assumed the role of officer and daughter in search of the officer and his lady from whom we became sidetracked— a perfectly innocent foil. A certain lieutenant treated us to dinner, giving us to understand that our subjects departed not long before with a small party for his base, Fort Oswego. He offered to escort us, but we graciously declined, a move I believe he thought strange. Father gave assurances that we required no assistance, claiming that we held good relations with neighboring settlers. The post commander gave us two horses along with rations and early the following morning father and I resumed our search, confident of having fooled everyone of substance.

"We kept hard by the course of the Susquehanna, tracing footprints along the path bound for Oswego. Looking for distinctive foot prints, we found many attributed to soft-soled foot wear. Others we assigned to the military where the hard heel of a boot cut into the pliant earth. I looked for a telltale impression so traceable to mother: shoes with pointed toes pressing into the soft soil of the trail, feet spread fairly closely together. Once found, I looked for supporting evidence: bits of women's clothing, shoe strings, a button, and then I spied it: A *daisy*. Not any daisy. It is the kind of daisy that my little colt Daisy favors. Strange that it is lying in a field of clover—tossed no less by a passerby. Father and I searched the rushes. We found more daisies, not scattered, but placed by someone: someone who wanted to leave a trail. What is more, someone crumbled the leaves, but left the flowers whole. Father and I determined that this is the act of someone calling out for help: Mother. At home mother was wont to crumble the leaves of withered daisies. She alone raised these flowers in our garden. They came from Charles Martin's collection, and, to my knowledge, no other kept that kind of daisy. I brought a supply of them for Daisy to nibble on those days that mother and I went to market. They grew so well under mother's care that she did not protest when I snatched them up. One day a man, an artist, sketched Daisy eating her flowers. He gave the sketch to me. I have it back at our home." Suzanne shed tears briefly:

"Father and I came across a farm house. We called upon the owner, a Monsieur Evans, a member of the Society of Friends. I poured out my story to him and showed him the daisies. He immediately walked to the mantel over the fireplace. He came back with a small bouquet of daisies: identical specimens to those I held. In my excitement I believe that I dropped mine. Monsieur Evans took note of my anguish and told me how he happened to have them.

"Apparently a certain Lord and his Lady called upon Monsieur Evans not long before. The man spoke and the lady remained silent. The man announced that he and the lady lacked for food. A band of savages robbed him of his purse, their horses and food and blankets, the man stated, and he feared sleeping under the heavens once the sun set. He needed to reach Fort Oswego to report his losses to the commandant there. He said that he was a surveyor by trade, stationed at Oswego, but engaged on the lower Susquehanna. Monsieur Evans fed the pair, gave them blankets and a pack of provisions, and two mares from his stable. The man thanked him and left for the water closet. During his absence a strange happening took place. Madame, who earlier stood silently beside her mate, reached beneath her skirts and retrieved a cluster of daisies. She begged Monsieur Evans to accept them as a small token of her esteem for having come to her aid. She urged that he display them on the mantel strictly following her departure and when the Lord returned nothing more was spoken on the matter. Soon thereafter, the Lord and Lady bid farewell—she fully-reserved. Monsieur Evans, curious of the Lady's strange request, watched the pair's departure from a bay window, all the while assigning the incident of the flowers to memory.

"Monsieur pondered over the Lord's claim of having met with hostile natives. To his own knowledge the natives of the region held peaceful relations with the settlers, never quarreling with them. They and the Quakers of the countryside held out their hands in cordiality to all who crossed their threshold. The Lady, he recalled, chose not to speak in the Lord's presence, and, when at last she spoke, her voice betrayed a hint of distress, even fear. The Lady's hands trembled, giving Monsieur Evans to believe that she feared for her security. He attempted to delay his guests' departure in order to learn more about them. To this extent, he invited the Lord and his Lady to a church supper that evening. The Lady's eyes sparkled, but the Lord declined the invitation, citing the need to reach his destination with dispatch. According to Monsieur, they departed forthwith.

"Monsieur Evans offered father and me two Delaware to guide us through the Lake Country. He referred us to the French garrison beside the Lake Onondaga and to its commandant, Guillaume Le Rocher. Monsieur stated that the Iroquois of the Lake Country traded regularly at Fort Oswego and are currently at peace with the Delaware. In a kind gesture he asked the two guides to inquire of the Iroquois concerning mother. He outfitted them with gifts to trade for her release to the extent that she is in residence. Father and I took our leave. Monsieur's son, Justin, accompanied us to the French garrison where he presented the commandant with a letter of introduction from Monsieur Evans.

"During our journey to the garrison we rode ceaselessly, the Susquehanna our guide. Gradually the river shrunk to a trickle and our trail disappeared and we knew that we reached the land of the Iroquois. We entered a great valley, the Onondaga, and when we emerged, the soft, rolling hills erupted into a series of little hills or drumlins. We scaled the drumlins and kept to their top crest. Looking off to the west we spied a long and deep-blue lake* and when it came to an end we dropped down from the drumlins and came across a broad, dusty roadway. It ran east and west**and for a short distance shops and stores and homes sprung up along its shoulders. Etched with deep ruts, the pitiful road bustled with inhabitants in this little settlement* * * and no one paid us any heed. Our guides brought us to a natural spring where we drank from a well and filled our flasks. We lingered to catch our breath before tracking off to the northeast. We crested many more drumlins over five kilometers before they gave way to a broad plain. Near our journey's end our guides urged us to look ahead and from a distance we spied the outline of what the Onondagas call Lake Gannentaa.* * * * The garrison, our guides indicated, lay on a mount overlooking the lake and is reached from a stairway carved into the earth. Named Pointe Aux Bois, the garrison kept watch over the northern section of the Onondaga valley, the ancestral home of the Onondagas. Several Onondagas resided at the garrison permanently apart from their principal village to the south. They enjoyed good commerce with Monsieur Le Rocher whom they regarded as a friend.

"We stood on the far shore of the lake straining to catch a glimpse of the garrison. Even in the autumn season its palisades lay hidden behind stands of evergreens, a consideration its builders took into account. We saw nothing but the smooth, disk-like surface of the lake, butting against a sandy shore which trailed off to steep escarpments below the garrison. Our guides gave us to understand that the garrison stood on the site of a long-abandoned French fort. Le Rocher rebuilt the fort, intending it to serve as a center of trade with the local natives. Le Rocher installed a well-stocked trading post and staffed it with tradesmen fluent in the local tongue. Natives came to reside in the garrison during lean periods and moved their provincial village nearby. To all but the French and surrounding natives, the fort did not exist. It remained obscure, tucked away behind overbearing greenery, all very suitable to the French, Monsieur Le Rocher related, most congenially.

"Justin presented our letter of introduction. Upon reading it, Monsieur Le Rocher burned it, lest it fall into enemy hands. He set aside lodgings for father and me and dispatched two Onondagas to accompany our Delaware to Oswego. Father and I spent three restless nights awaiting their return. Once returned the scouts reported that indeed a woman of mother's features resided at Oswego periodically. They themselves did not catch a glimpse of her. They further reported witnessing a sale of sorts taking place deep in the forest by which several young people entered into servitude, the matter sealed with the exchange of currency and goods passing from hand to hand. Mother's likeness was not among those sold, the guides learned. No names were disclosed during the sale and so the guides came away empty, but when they approached the man who called himself 'Lord' and asked to purchase some of the young people taken, they met with stern opposition. The 'Lord' threatened the scouts with incarceration unless they depart the premises. He demanded to know from whence they came. At this point the scouts resolved to flee for fear of being forced to shed suspicions upon Le Rocher whose livelihood depended upon remaining anonymous. In the end the scouts lamented the loss of so many comrades— young men and women with whom they spent their youth. They brought these concerns to Le Rocher upon returning to Pointe Aux Bois.

"Le Rocher attempted to assuage our fears," Suzanne spoke. She quoted him: "It is good that you have chosen to take us into your trust over the English. There is a great difference between the French and the English: We would invite you to dinner and serve you food. The English would invite you and imprison you.

"Father and I conferred with Le Rocher about this principal difference. Father stated that the French came to the Americas in order to open trade with the native people. For France the Americas presented a vast repository of wealth in the form of fur-bearing animals: commodities to supply to an eager world market. Few in number, the French depended upon diplomacy to open and sustain relations with the indigenous inhabitants. It is the upper echelon of the French hierarchy which profited from gains made from sales— the serfs, or the majority of France's constituents, a stone's throw from abject poverty at all times, father told me, in speaking with Le Rocher.

"The English, father said, came to open colonies in the New World and flood them with English-speaking people who one day would pay taxes to the Crown, in part to pay for England's wars with France. Superior in numbers and weaponry, the English expected the native peoples to bow down before them. In the grand scheme of things the English conscripted native peoples to do their bidding. These natives labored in the fields and in the shops and in the mills. Fed poorly, they were paid poorly and many took ill and died. For those who learned a skilled craft it mattered little for they soon died from exhaustion or disease. Mother, he stated, is one more example of a helpless soul cast into bondage, for perhaps different reasons, but a servant nonetheless.

"Father and I continued speaking with the commandant, Le Rocher. He agreed with you, Watkins, that mother may be sold in the event that her captor no longer desired her services. He spoke of camps in which servants are readily sold. There are forts along the Great Lakes, for example. Then there is Kanandesaga, a Seneca town. It stands near the principal military road which cuts through the Lake Country, a road frequented by soldiers and traders alike regardless of their allegiance. All sorts of trading takes place at Kanandesaga, the commandant stated, and the resident chief, Cornplanter, offered little opposition, for the British bribed him with lavish gifts. They even built him houses of wood with pitched roofs and windows. The commandant's leading tradesman, Marchand, always placed Kanandesaga on his itinerary and it is he whom the chief, Cornplanter, favored over all others. The commandant gave us to understand that Marchand was preparing to make a sally into Seneca country very soon. He kept a house* near the village of Osco hard by the Genesee Road, a few rods north of the Bear Chief's village, the Round Tops. He urged father and me to visit Monsieur Marchand. He wrote a letter of introduction and we took our leave shortly thereafter.

"Our host, the commandant, proved a generous sort, Monsieur Watkins. He provided us with a canoe light enough to carry and ample dry rations and a map of our destination which his cartographer prepared for us. Father and I explained our penurious position and the commandant roared with laughter, for upon his arrival in the Lake Country he too held nary two farthings to rub together. He expected Monsieur Marchand to dip into his wealth of knowledge of the Lake Country and extract the means by which to secure mother's release. We parted on amicable terms and set out on foot, our canoe in tow. Walking due west, we traveled next to what our map termed the Seneca River**. Eventually, when our legs tired, we launched our canoe. I took the stern and father the bow and, despite the steady pull of the waters over my paddle, I enjoyed myself greatly. Oh, if mother only knew!

"Following our map, father and I paddled due west until we came to a portage. From there we carried our canoe along a straight and narrow path due south. A scattering of shops and dwellings rose up along the way* * * but for the most part we found ourselves removed from human-kind. We continued south and the land rose and fell for a good four kilometers. Soon we heard waters rushing over rock and

went off to our right through a grove of trees to have a closer look. We
spied a fresh stream running briskly*and decided to launch our canoe
in order to spare our weary bones. On our map a village took shape
further south where the stream flowed north from the outlet of a quiet
lake. Beside the stream, the commandant reminded us, lived the War
Chief, The Standing Bear, or Bear Chief, friend of Marchand and
one open to visitors, especially those in need or distress. We no sooner
launched our canoe when the skies turned gray and winds whipped up
around us. Waves formed in the stream and pushed us against rocks.
At one point I lost my paddle and father labored frantically to keep our
little craft afloat. When our canoe burst apart at the seams, father and
I found ourselves swept along with the current. The fierce waters threw
us boldly upon a bar, a lump of earth covered with stout, long grasses.
It is there that we clung until a stroke of good fortune came our way."
She glanced with admiration toward the Bear Chief.

"Now, Monsieur Watkins. I believe that you know the story of
our venture into the Lake Country." Eyes swollen with tears, Suzanne
poured out appreciation for the Bear Chief's intervention on her behalf.
He, himself, stood beside her, a model of stoicism.

"I wish to sing praises to the commandant, Monsieur Le Rocher,
for listening to my story—also for providing father and me with a map
and provisions on our journey. I also wish to thank Justin Evans for
leading us into secure hands. He is homeward bound, but knows that
he carries our good wishes with him. The labors of his father must not
go unheralded. Monsieur Evans gave us shelter and provided us with
worthy guides who led us straight to Monsieur Le Rocher. Truly, The
Society of Friends is alive and well. Now that we are with new friends I
wish to give praises to Colombe Blanche. She made my stay at Osco and
beyond one of great joy and personal satisfaction. I hope to meet with
Monsieur Marchand and from the stories I hear about him he is another
example of the goodness which this frontier has produced. Together, all
of us will unite to do what is right in order to bring mother back where
she belongs. Wherever she resides at present she would be proud to learn
that so many good people carry her image in their hearts and minds."
She then fell backward, exhausted from the lengthy speech.

The Bear Chief stepped forward. He renewed a pledge to intercede
on behalf of his guests. He praised Henri Marchand for cultivating
lasting friendships among his People with worthy peaus blancs. In a

similar vein he held out the willingness of the tradesman to aid in the search for Caroline York and to bring her captor(s) to justice. He ended by saying that Monsieur Marchand, in the tradition of the French missionaries, holds the People in high regard as well as all newcomers such as Monsieur and Mademoiselle York— all of whom he deemed new friends (27). He offered to loan warriors to search for Madame York, although he himself preferred to remain at the Round Tops. With everyone having been heard, the Bear Chief pronounced the meeting at an end and in an ample space before his cabin he built a fire. Colombe Blanche and the boys placed sweet meats upon it and Fawn brought out bowls of tender legumes. Everyone partook of the light meal, delighting in it and in the company of each other.

At one point Suzanne reached out to her host. Touching a sleeve, she uttered:

"Nya:weh:a:ohe!—Thank you for the light in the darkness!"

(20)Taylor, Colon F. & Sturtevant, William C. The Native Americans: *The Indigenous People of North America.*

Salamander Books, London. (200) pgs: 232-233

*The villages of Goiogouen, Tiohero, and Onnontare occupied heights above Cayuga Lake's eastern shore near Great Gully Brook in the Town of Springport

(21)Merrill, Chapter 4: Far Around Cayuga's Waters pgs: 60-61

*A quarry in the vicinity of York Street in Auburn, NY

**Numerous streams pass through southwestern Auburn, NY. Many have been covered or drained or diverted.

(22)Merrill, Arch. Chapter 2, pgs: 24-26

(23)Moses, W.J. Handbook of Fort Hill Cemetery. Publishers: The Fort Hill Association of Trustees, Auburn, NY (1853) pgs: 34-35

*Suzanne's yearling colt who had an affinity for flowers.

(24)Wait, Mary Van Sickle. *The Story of the Cayugas.* Chapter 8. Dewitt Historical Society of Tompkins County, Ithaca, NY (1967) Map: pg: 234.

(25)Tanner, Helen H. An. Atlas of Great Lakes Indian History: *Inter-Colonial Warfare.* University of Oklahoma Press, Norman, (1987) pg: 46

(26)Tanner (1987) pg: 47

*Skaneateles Lake

**Genesee Street in Skaneateles

* * *Precursor to Skaneateles

* * * *Onondaga Lake

*Marchand's home stood at the corner of Washington & W. Genesee Streets in Auburn, NY

**Early artery of navigation traversed by Iroquois and tradesmen

* * *Early Weedsport, NY, known as Brutus

*Owasco River

(27)Selkreg, John H: Landmarks of Tompkins County, New York, Chapter One, D. Mason & co., Publisher, Ithaca,

NY (1894) pg: 2.

Part Two

DESTINY'S CHILDREN

CHAPTER SEVEN

Forging Alliances
New Partnerships.
Maple Grove.
Henri Marchand.
On The Trail.

Morning. The 11th day of September in the year 1760. A calm and cool Monday morning. Watkins marked the day off on a trail calendar. He secreted it within his boot along with his watch-on-a-chain. Extracting the watch, the hands read 8 hours and 3 minutes. He yawned and turned in the bedroll. The thick native blankets in which he wound himself trapped the warmth of his body beneath him. He loathed to toss them aside and step out into the crisp, autumn day. He spied the sun breaking over the horizon and its position corresponded with his watch's reading. Satisfied, he returned the instrument to the boot.

Gripping the boots, he brushed away accumulations of the previous day. He turned them upside down. Tapping them on all sides, he looked for insects and other minute forms of life which seek out warm, dark places in which to hide from enemies and also to search for prey more minute than themselves. He paid especial attention to the predatory insects and snakes that lie in dark places poised to sink venom-charged fangs into unwitting subjects. His knowledge of life on the trail taught him that the majority of bites proved harmless to man, yet the occasional exception brought death within minutes to the unprepared woodsman. He inspected his boots thoroughly, making the process a part of a morning ritual.

He regarded the boots an extension of his lower limbs, and, unable to fathom life without them, he removed them once a day prior to retiring and before bathing, understandably. He polished them dexterously. He did not require a festive occasion to compel him to perform all the necessary functions to transform his English leathers into a handsome work of art. On the trail he labored more fastidiously to achieve the same effect. A man given to order and predictability, he polished the pair daily, rain or shine.

Fawn once remarked about the brightness of the boots. He mused that they served as a point of interest which initially drew them together. Fawn liked to prepare breakfast for the Bear Chief and the rest of her adopted family and she considered him a fitting guest. He would join her soon at the abbreviated camp site he constructed during his first day in his new home. He longed to commend her for her culinary skills and to converse with her on matters more substantive than the regal footgear. He buffed them until his image greeted him. That done, he sat back.

Today marked a day of construction. In an agreement reached with James and the Cayuga War Chief, he offered his services to the building of residential cabins for the new inhabitants of this, the Round Tops. He looked forward to James's companionship, a man with whom he shared a love of the out-of-doors. His daughter, Suzanne, although a lass of sixteen years, exhibited a great deal of maturity for one so young. She approached new challenges with the self-assurance ascribed to a family matriarch. Upon her mother's disappearance, Suzanne deftly stepped in to fill a lingering void. Both she and her father adapted quickly to the changes that the frontier thrust upon them. They seemed to gain enthusiasm with each new challenge with regard to converting unpleasant conditions to a distinct advantage. In sum, he believed that Suzanne and her father thoroughly enjoyed life in the woodlands, a place which afforded them the rare opportunity to learn the valuable lessons which they may put into practice for many years to come.

Back on the Continent any sort of structured collaboration between James and himself held precious little hopes of success. There, the deep rift between the two major churches in England set up traditional barricades over the years to keep him, a Protestant, and James, a Catholic, apart forever. Here in the Americas, on the other hand, survival of the species human-kind called for the development of strong, interdependent relationships which cut across all barriers, religious and otherwise— barriers that people threw up to keep foes at a distance. He drew the drawstrings tight. Next, he washed with water from an urn. The morning ritual complete, he set off to take breakfast— a meal which Fawn prepared each morning.

Two thoughts occupied him this fine morning: the coming construction and Fawn. With relation to the first thought, he must complete all principal construction before the onset of winter— perhaps two months away. Cabins for all residents must be built. Many of the amenities, such as running water, may have to wait until the following spring, but the basics must be installed from the present: solid floors, walls, and roofs, hearths and chimneys, room furnishings, and doors and windows. He and James planned to train a number of native men in the art of woodworking. He looked forward to the challenge. He wanted to begin the undertaking in earnest under James's supervision so that upon James's ultimate withdrawal he may have accumulated the skills necessary to lead the construction successfully on his own.

He considered Fawn. He wanted to cultivate her friendship. She remained at his side during two vulnerable points in his life: that of wounded soldier and that of refugee. At Suzanne's request she treated and wrapped his wound, yet her personal attentiveness helped him to forget the fear and isolation that haunts all runaways who seek refuge in foreign quarters. He looked forward to seeing her each day. Certainly her features drew him to her. With long raven tresses, large green eyes, a svelte figure and light, coppery complexion, Fawn possessed the external qualities of a rare beauty. She did not thrust her beauty upon him, but kept it in reserve, much in keeping with her demure, almost timid manner. During moments together she occupied herself fully with making him well— sparking within him dreams to last a lifetime.

The first of the guests to descend to breakfast, Watkins greeted his hostess, then promptly took up a place on the hard earth before she may return the greeting. He watched her carefully. On a skillet Fawn turned corn cakes, taking care to equally brown both sides. She brought him a cup of chicory before bounding to another skillet to turn a host of fried eggs. She mixed strips of ham taken from a boar hunt with the eggs. Bowls of berries lay nearby, plucked earlier by Raven and Little Bear. Crossing to a deep kettle, Fawn stirred the hot contents slowly. Smiling with satisfaction, she scooped out a ladle-full of the corn mash and poured it into a bowl into which she applied a generous portion of maple syrup. She beckoned him to begin eating. She watched him, as he probed with the one good arm, looking for a sign of approval of her cooking skills. He beamed broadly and scraped the bowl clean, motions that carried a universal meaning.

His hunger visible, Fawn hurriedly scooped up a ladle of fried eggs. In haste she brushed her fingertips over the hot ladle. She cried out in pain, borne of shock. The eggs flew awry. Desperately she licked her fingers. Watkins leaped to her side. Plunging her hand into an urn of cold water, he urged her to hold it in place. He dashed off to retrieve an urn of bear grease which he kept in storage. He wiped her hand dry and applied the viscous material liberally to her hand, covering it with a clean linen wrap. Tears flowed freely down her cheeks. He wiped them away delicately, holding her close to his chest for precious seconds. She offered no resistance. Choosing to lay her head upon his shoulder, she looked up at him. He gazed down at her, longingly.

Footsteps announced the arrival of other guests. Watkins allowed Fawn to withdraw from his bosom, whereby he opened a blanket for her to sit upon. In a role-reversal of sorts, Watkins assembled her breakfast and served her: he with one arm bandaged and she with her hand wrapped. It went awkwardly, their feeble attempts to feed themselves drew the attention of the guests, yet no further incidents took place. One by one guests came forward to assist them in obtaining additional helpings and gradually they ate their fill. Watkins, speaking for Fawn and himself, extended his thanks to everyone for interceding during this delicate moment and everyone settled back, ate, and made small conversation. They spoke of tasks to come, duties to be performed in assembling a village. Apparently no one witnessed the short, tender interlude of Watkins and Fawn—no one, save Suzanne. She voiced her concern to her father:

"Father. Watkins ate very sparingly of his plate."

"Perhaps he is not hungry, dear daughter," James returned.

"With Watkins such is never the case," she laughed.

"He did have his hands full for a while, Suzanne," James conceded.

"I believe you, father—but not in the way that you think," she smiled.

James cast his daughter a blank look.

"Not to mind. I will tell you one day."

The Bear Chief, his breakfast consumed, looked about and one by one the guests finished eating and prepared to meet the new day. Watkins, in spite of his injury, insisted on taking part in the construction and went off with James. The boys and their mother chose baskets to take on a hunt for berries and mushrooms. Suzanne remained behind to assist Fawn in preparing for the next meal of the day.

James introduced Watkins to the current project: repairing a broken wheel. Having survived the battle at Osco, the spokes of the wheel lay shattered in places. James wanted to instruct his young charge in restoring the wheel by making use of the excellent tools which Henri Marchand donated over the years. He selected lengths of wood which he sawed and planed. He drilled notches into the stock of the wheel and inserted the new spokes, securing them with nails which he drilled with a hand-held drill. For a finishing touch, James fitted a new iron casing or strip to the wheel's rim. He drilled holes intermittently, and, inserting iron nails, pounded them securely into place.

"Almost done, lad," James announced. "We have yet to soak our wheel in brine. Bring me that bucket of water."

"Brine, you say?" Watkins asked, pulling a large tub of salty water to the work site.

"Yes, Watkins." James placed the wheel in the solution and stood back to admire his labor. "You have to soak the wheel two or three days. The brine helps the spokes to expand, thereby fitting tight all around the rim."

"Ah! I understand. Spoken like a true son of the sea, James."

"On the contrary, Watkins. I have never been to sea—only something I read about back home—from Caroline's library of books. A vast collection." Wiping at his eyes, James turned his head away for a brief moment.

"I understand, James," Watkins replied, soberly.

The two men passed to another station where natives notched and planed logs. "These will soon be walls," James spoke, proudly. He led Watkins to a neighboring site strewn with mud. He handed him a large ladle and quipped: "We need to seal in the spaces though. I believe I have found an occupation for you, Watkins."

"You are very kind, James," Watkins cajoled. "It is good to know that one is thinking of me in my delicate condition." Together the two men looked at each other and laughed, rejoicing in the humor.

While James planed logs, Watkins stirred the contents of a giant mud cake with the one good arm. They conversed with each other, but not about the project:

"It is important to remain out of sight of strangers, lad, during my absence. You will have occasion to go beyond the village proper and you will meet with English-speaking men. Keep your contacts to a minimum and tell them nothing about the Round Tops."

"Way ahead of you on that score, James. I value my own hide dearly," he returned, pinching a wrist. "By the way, James, it concerns me how you will proceed against the Captain if indeed he is the true culprit."

"I will make inquiries over the countryside. This Monsieur Marchand of whom I hear much seems like a valuable tool in that regard." He stroked his chin. "Once the culprit is made known, I must set a trap for him and lure him into it." He set aside the planer. "Of course, a conviction depends on the abundance of evidence and the willingness of witnesses. So far I have you, lad."

"Let us not forget the testimony of Madame Caroline, James."

"We must find her first. When we do, what tribunal wants to admit the testimony of a woman—on the frontier, no less?"

"You will need strong evidence, James. I believe the term is 'incontrovertible.' It must come from within the culprit's circle of companions. Fat chance of that!! The military sticks together like molasses to fly paper."

"Think hard, Watkins. There must be a few seeds of discontent brewing within your old corps."

"Indeed there are, James. I must think on it long and hard. In the meanwhile let us pursue Madame Caroline's relationship with the Captain. Think, James. Why did he take her in the first place from your farm? To punish her for having refused to sell her land? That is what we *first* believed. This is not the full reason, however. James. In his own blighted way, the Captain *loves* her. He removed her from Oswego in order to punish her for rejecting offers of affection. He aims to break her resistance by taking her on the trail—giving her a glimpse of the hard life—to break her spirit to the point that she begs forgiveness. Yes! Yes! James. That is the manner of the Captain." Watkins pounded a fist into the mud pile and inadvertently smeared the pasty substance over his cheek.

"The thought has crossed my mind, Watkins, and you know the Captain much better than I. He alone stands to lose her attention more than any other man." James put aside the planer. "I agree with you. We are looking for a lone culprit—the Captain."

"All the more reason to take up a search at once. You need to spread the word along the frontier. Word travels fast—especially when accompanied by a generous bribe."

"That will never happen, Watkins. You forget that I am without means."

"That is why you must consult with the tradesman. I learned of his influence by listening to your stories. I did not know until now that his presence went a long way in keeping the peace between the native peoples and French partisans."

"I know that I have heard it said more than once, but how is the tradesman able to help me directly, Watkins?"

"Listen, James. The tradesman already is trusted among the Iroquois. Of late, however, the British have made inroads into his territories. Also, they are but days from sacking Montreal. He is looking for ways to endear the Iroquois to him and the French. What better way than to capture the British officer who steals women and burns native villages?"

"Hmmm . . . You are saying that . . . ."

"I am saying that the tradesman will enlist the help of the natives to capture the man who would burn their villages. According to our theory, he is the *same* man who has stolen Madame York. A victory for the tradesman solidifies his position with the Iroquois at a moment when the French need allies. It also brings Madame back to you. Think of it, James."

"I have not thought of it in those terms."

"What is more, James, you have an ally in the War Chief, the Bear Chief. He is the tradesman's friend and will come out in support of Madame York."

"How are you so certain?"

"He sees Madame through the eyes of her daughter, Suzanne. You see how well Suzanne moves among the residents? Do you remember that he thought the image on the locket to be of Suzanne?"

"Yes, yes. I remember. You have good vision, Watkins."

"I owe it to my years on the trail—looking out for my hide." He laughed a subdued laugh. "Bear in mind James that Monsieur Marchand is free to roam in places which are foreign to you. With his established reputation he may do for you free of charge that which is certain to cost any other man a king's ransom. I know that the commandant at Oswego considers Monsieur Marchand a strong rival for the trade of the Iroquois. He knows not where the tradesman resides, but the very name, Marchand, gives him cause for concern."

"And you, late of Oswego, know that all too well, Watkins."

"I consider myself on a new career, James . . . say . . . ambassador of human justice."

"A most noble undertaking."

"Let us say that I am trying to redirect the current state of affairs." He paused to allow the words to settle. "Simply, I oppose everything that Britain stands for in the colonies."

"It is good to have an ally."

They shook hands and took up the labor once again.

They labored in silence until Watkins drew up from a task. "There is something more, James. The Captain seems to have suffered a lack of judgment with the tragedy at the falls. For one, he divided his forces. He sent a number of the dead back to Oswego under a small escort. Essentially this move betrayed his position to an enemy. It left the men open to attack where they escorted in all sincerity a convoy of mere corpses. A waste of manpower if you ask me. Second, he raided the village with the remainder of his forces. In the process he lost a good deal of men on the field of battle, and let us not forget the skirmish with the cavalrymen. He escaped with plunder, I am told. It is his way of justifying an attack."

"Tell me, Watkins. How does the commandant at Oswego hold with unprovoked raids on local natives?"

"Lord Carleton applies British law with a thick brush. An officer convicted of inciting unrest among the populations is subject to dismissal from the service, a fine, and incarceration."

"How about dealing in human flesh?"

"The laws are less precise on that score, James. The indentured system is alive and well in the colonies. It is the colonies that breathed new life into the system, given the great amount of labor required to turn idle fields into producing bountiful yields. From a distance, it is not an evil system, for it has saved many a wretch from homelessness and starvation. Of course, the manner in which the system obtains laborers is another matter. Some indentured servants are either volunteers into the system or encouraged to join. Others, mostly from the native populations, are forced into servitude. They gradually move into the indentured system provided they are able to survive the demands and constraints which new owners place upon them. Therein lies the great flaw."

"The manner in which they are chosen?"

"Exactly. Many of the soldiers at Oswego are indentured. Agreeing to terms, they chose to enter His Majesty's service for a certain period after which they may withdraw and collect a pension for the remainder of their lives. I, for one, volunteered, but that is beside the point. There are also those at Oswego, who labor there intensely day after day. They have come from the native populations— a few from elsewhere. In general they serve at the whim of the post commander. More than likely they are the property of an owner or captor. He decides their fate and many do not see a second winter. These are the true slaves, James. They are paid in kind, not in wages, or not at all. The master has full reign over their very existence. The master encourages slaves to curry favor with him by telling him of any plots in the works to overthrow or kill him. He extends a small privilege to those who so come forth. Then, in the black of night he advances upon the evildoers, killing the plotters. I have seen this happen, James. More than once the Captain has been associated with these doings, although I have not witnessed it at first-hand."

"It strikes me odd that the Captain's maneuvers have eluded Lord Carleton."

"Lord Carleton is a preoccupied man, James. He came to the region to rebuild Fort Ontario which the French burned in 1757, I believe. He is also committed to opening new lands to white settlement. In the process he has built a town to the east of the fort. All of this consumes men and materiel, leaving scarce little for reconnaissance over errant ne'er-do-wells. He has heard rumors to be sure, but lacks the invasive methods by which he may launch an investigation. Without direct evidence, the commandant is left with rumors, nothing more, leaving the Captain, and others like him, at liberty to claim the defense of justifiable retaliation in a time of war."

"Of course, Watkins, I understand your point. In my opinion, however, in pursuing the Captain, the successful prosecutor will not attack the theory of self-defense." He paused to measure his words.

"Go ahead, James."

"In my opinion a successful prosecution must proceed along the lines of 'excessiveness' and 'exclusion'—that is to say, did the accused exercise excessive force to meet objectives when lesser force may have accomplished the same ends?—and, did the accused prevent more peaceful methods for settling a conflict from taking place?"

Watkins considered the terms carefully.

"Let me provide you with some illustrations."

"No. I understand, James. You have thought long and hard on this matter."

"In my search I will speak with those who met with our captor. I will write down what took place among them. The day and date are important. I will put together a journal of my travels and present it to the tribunal when called upon."

"For the prosecutor who interprets your journal there is instant fame, James. James!! We may be on the threshold of striking a blow for justice—human justice.'"

"I will settle for having Caroline back."

"Who will write for you, James?"

"Suzanne. She is an excellent scribe."

"So I have heard. So I have heard."

The two men shook hands and once again fell back to the project at hand.

* * *

In the early afternoon of that first day of labor, James and Watkins walked to yet another site. They descended the southern slope of the Round Tops to a low-lying stretch of land bounded by a marsh. Equipped with axes and shovels, they planned to remove patches of sod to apply to the wooden pitched roofs of the soon-to-be cabins. They found a party of villagers already engaged in sod removal. They labored under the watchful eye of the Bear Chief.

He, in turn, greeted James succinctly and handed him a leaf of parchment. It contained a list of particulars of supplies needed to address the task of construction. James discussed the request earlier that day with the Bear Chief and Suzanne committed the request to paper. To James's knowledge, Marchand would honor the request later that day.

Requested Supplies & Necessities

From The Stores at Pointe Aux Bois, Le General Guy Le Rocher, Commandant

12 September 1760, Ano Domini

For The Village: cast iron ploughs(2), anvils (2), hammers (10), chisels (6), muskets w/ ball & powder (20 pcs.), nails, (20) boxes of 40 ea., saddles, (2), harnesses (2), lariats (40, planers (6), saws (6), axes on handle (6), leather gloves (10 pr.)

For The Households: towels (washing & drying) 40pcs, hand soap (bar or cake) 60 pcs. Also: tallow, needles, thread, also: flour, sugar, salt in 40# drums. Also: flatware and cutlery for 20 families. Also: serving dishes, trays, cups & tankards. Also: talcum, clean linen wraps, quinine, rubbing alcohol, sodium salts & toothbrushes & hair combs and mirrors.

Respectfully

Bear Chief X_L'Oeurs Debout

The Bear Chief signed his universal name, The Standing Bear, next to his colloquial name, Bear Chief, making an X at Suzanne's guidance.

Aboyant, hard by the Bear Chief's heels, appeared on the scene. Doffing his hat, he beamed and bowed deeply from the waist. His maneuvers portrayed that he bore good tidings. With a wave of an arm he beckoned everyone to follow him. Effortlessly he bounded over the conical drumlins of the Round Tops. Pressing due north, he topped a final drumlin where he paused to allow the little party to overtake him. At once, Suzanne and her father found themselves on a broad, dusty road, a principal artery, and beyond it, an imposing mansion boldly faced them.

The home sat on the crown of an expansive hill. A lone yet prominent structure, the three-storied dwelling provided its inhabitants with a commanding view of the landscape and surrounding woodlands. Chimneys sprouted from the roof, one for each of the four fireplaces on the first floor. In the center of the flat, gabled roof sat an exterior observatory, a square-shaped cabin with windows and doors to which a small party may retreat to enjoy mutual companionship. To the immediate south lay the drumlins of the Round Tops. Beside the home to the west a broad path took shape.* It began where the dusty thoroughfare crossed in front of the home, the Genesee Trail, and ran north along the down slope of the hill where it butted against a fast-flowing stream: the Osco River. A thick grove of trees surrounded the home, at once furnishing shade to the occupants during hot summers and complementing the innate beauty of the iron work fencing and the solid-gray granite blocks of the residence. The luxuriant boughs veiled the home in perpetual tones of mauve and purple, softening the hard and austere lines of the granite façade. A pair of miniature, iron-clad lions, jaws agape, crouched at either foot of the stone stairway. They guarded the massive oaken door leading to the foyer of the home. Come the slightest of breezes and the delicate shade trees beside the lions cast dancing shadows over them in such a manner that they sprouted signs of life with eyes blinking and jaws straining. Especially on those gray days of autumn, the lions projected a most-sinister aspect to all newcomers approaching the mansion. A broad walkway of segmented slate ran between the foot of the entrance and the dusty thoroughfare known as The Genesee Trail.

Breaking from the party, Suzanne rushed ahead to pull down the wrought-iron clapper placed prominently over the oaken door. Her father's document in hand, she stood on tip-toes to tug mightily on the ponderous device. It flew from her grasp, soundly striking the metal plate beneath and sending a crisp, smacking report deep within the mansion with the ferocity of a rifle shot. Suzanne lurched backward, coincidental with the door's opening seemingly of its own volition.

A lank, spare man peered out at her through thick lenses. Hands on hips, he gave forth with an effete demeanor, emitting a barely-audible greeting in a voice which chirped arrhythmically, not unlike that of the timid canary:

"À votre service, Mademoiselle. Je m'appelle René. Welcome to Maple Grove. Monsieur Marchand awaits you within". He turned sharply, retreating along the long corridor connecting the inner rooms.

"Enchantée," Suzanne returned, eager to speak in French. Now that the main body joined her, Suzanne followed the servant, her gaze fixed upon the bold-striped wall coverings of the foyer. René led the party sharply left to a large room outfitted with divans, sofas, and chairs: to Suzanne, museum pieces all. A room of comfort, it featured Persian carpets spread over glistening hardwood flooring. In a far corner sat a harpsichord finished in rich cherry wood. In an opposite corner a globe of the world occupied a shell-like cradle which sat upon an engraved table, its surfaces highly polished.

"Welcome to le salon, mes amis," René squeaked. He escorted the party about the room.

"Here we have a spinet: forerunner to the harpsichord," René spoke affectionately. "Monsieur often plays for guests. He sings as well, but I prefer his playing," he chirped, wincing, pleased with himself.

The party approached an immense fireplace. It occupied most of the room's west wall. Suzanne stood before it in wonder, eyes racing back and forth over its appointments, keeping in step with René's discourse:

"The façade is white marble interspersed with black marble. The wings or buttresses extend into the room and may be folded back. The mantel is also marble: thick to support Monsieur's goblets and tankards coming up before you."

"The fireplace holds half a chord of wood, but Monsieur does not go to that extreme." Holding a chute, he explained: "Monsieur likes to come downstairs at night to fill the chute with pieces for the next day." René pointed to a large iron box: "Monsieur places the box in the fireplace filled with pieces. After they burn, he scoops out the ashes and buries them out-of-doors. Ashes have a way of rejuvenating the soil," he claims. "He so dislikes soot and ashes indoors," René whispered, flicking his fingers in an arc overhead.

—

Suzanne almost burst out laughing. Containing herself, she walked to the wall to take a closer glimpse of the portraiture. There, in a long row above the fire place, the portraits of several distinguished-looking patriarchs reigned, suspended in perpetuity. Dressed in their finest, they bore faint resemblances to each other and presumably sat for their portraits at approximately the same age in their lives, most likely not long before they expired. All of the figures appeared old, yet regal and statuesque, the full line of the Marchand family running back generations. Housing each figure, broad frames, trimmed in gold leaf, seemed to breathe life back into these ancient specimens. René offered a brief description:

"You see before you five generations of Marchand. Beginning with the grand patriarch, Alexandre, on the left, we end with Marcel on your extreme right. In the center you have, Adele, Monsieur's late wife. All of the men gained fame in wars in Europe and lived and died there. Only Monsieur came to live in America. He collected these portraits upon the dissolving of his predecessors' estates. They represent, in most cases, the final treasures remaining among his family's earthly possessions."

René walked beneath each portrait. "You see how they are dressed in civilian attire? They disdained wars, all wars, yet they served valiantly and rose to great heights. Monsieur clearly follows suit."

"A handsome lot they are," Suzanne heard herself say, unable to muster more eloquent terms.

"A skilled artist is able to fashion wonders," René returned, a thin smile upon his lips.

—

Suzanne walked beneath one of the four bay windows. Neck straining, she gazed directly upward. Each window descended from a point below the lofty ceiling to the wainscoting which stood about knee-high from the floor. She counted eighteen panes of glass secured within stout frames. The window casements protruded from the wall, allowing a great diffusion of light to flood the salon on those days when the sun burned bright in the sky. Giant tapestries clung to the windows, flowing and cascading downward like a waterfall flowing over a precipice. A rich crimson, they came to within a finger's width of brushing against the gleaming hardwoods. A hand-crank allowed one to open a row of panes along the bottom of each window, a function which Aboyant eagerly performed. Playfully he wrapped himself in a tapestry. Then, stepping out, he bowed low and mouthed "à votre service." René stepped in and pulled the tapestries back, securing them to the casement.

"There, there, my little friend. Now you have no fear of getting snared," he quipped. If vexed, he did not betray his emotions, and the little party moved on.

—

The guests now stood before the east wall of the salon, a section devoted almost entirely to bookcases stuffed with volumes. She measured off thirty paces with her feet between the first and last bookcase. All of a deep mahogany, they stood at shoulder-height. Glass doors permitted one a cursory inspection of the volumes without having to turn the gold-encrusted knob over the latch about halfway along each door. Heavy, thick volumes occupied the lower shelves and lighter-weight books the uppermost. Someone once told her that one may learn much about a man by knowing his literary tastes and Suzanne set about to test the assumption.

Bending low, several French classics caught her eye: Spirit of the Laws by Montesquieu; The Social Contract by Rousseau, works she heard of but never read. Above them she recognized The Prince by Machiavelli, Praise of Folly by Erasmus and Locke's Treatises on Government. The upper shelves held works bound in heavy paper, written by contemporary French, English and German authors. René gave her to understand that many of the books came as gifts to Monsieur from the authors themselves, authors with whom he commiserated while in Europe.

"Monsieur hopes to write his own book one day after he departs the frontier. A noble exercise—writing."

"Yes. Very much so. I agree, René."

—

Her father called her attention to the wainscoting in the salon. Back home James called it 'trim' and for a modest sum one may install a plain version of it. Here, however, beauty and artistry came together to render an elaborate portrait of the sea dashing upon the shore, where the waxing and waning of the frothy waves stood out in bold relief, capped in ivory by a master craftsman, etched with chisel and hammer into the sturdy oak panels, all polished to a high gloss. Above the knee-high wainscoting, colorful wall coverings rose up to the ceilings where they butted against plain-white panel borders. The coverings' design delighted Suzanne: a forest green background overlaid with thin, vertical strips of gold, blue, red, and orange.

"Monsieur believes the covering brings the forest into the home," René explained, touching the wall.

Suzanne nodded in agreement.

—

The room and furnishings captivated her and, stepping backward, she lost footing and plunged into a cavernous lounge chair. Its depth consumed her arms and legs and she fell back, helpless, knowing that she required the assistance of a comrade to pull her upright. Aboyant came to the rescue. She waved him off. Embarrassed, she sat back in the chair's luxurious leather folds and imbibed the salon's splendor. She took note that the abundance of sumptuous divans and ottomans provided the guest with an unobstructed view of the salon's appointments. Beside each stood a small table furnished with an oil lamp equipped for light dining and reading, exuding the trappings of comfort and leisure to be enjoyed by the many, not the few. In such surroundings guests invariably lingered longer than they intended. In a neighboring corner a stately grandfather clock pealed the hour. Suzanne turned to it. The height of a tall man, it contained small compartments along the façade, which, according to René housed a chess set and tea set. He showed her a sample of each, after which he extricated her from her snug berth.

—

With René's guidance, the guests passed to the rear of the salon. The Bear Chief paused at the foot of the grand staircase. Standing at the foot of the staunch balustrade, he glanced studiously along the stairs. His eyes followed the flow of the elegant, broad hardwood steps. His fingers traced the polished handrail. At first broad, then gradually diminishing in dimension, the steps rose steadily, finally disappearing around a turn leading to upper rooms. He remarked on their majesty, that, given their splendor, they reminded him of a gateway to a higher realm where celestial beings frolicked and that whoever ascended the steps passed from this world into the next.

Little shivers broke out along Suzanne's shoulders and spine upon hearing the Bear Chief's analogy. She dispelled it rapidly. Ahead, a new section of the mansion opened itself to scrutiny. René led the guests through an arched portal into the dining quarters. She lingered momentarily to absorb the intricate detail of the arch's embossed paneling. The paneling rose straight upward from the hardwoods, its surfaces embellished with miniature gargoyles in high relief. The gargoyles, Suzanne learned, represented Biblical figures. Where the paneling met at the arch's apex overhead, facsimiles of the Holy Father and Lucifer, the Christ and the anti-Christ respectively, hurled challenges at each other, their images carved in durable oak for the sake of posterity.

The dining quarters held several appointments in common with the salon, namely, wainscoting and wall coverings. On the other hand, the vast dining table marked the room's uniqueness. Its gleaming, rectangular surface reminded Suzanne of the ice rink she frequented back home: smooth and square and polished. The table comfortably seated eight guests on high-back chairs which rolled back and forth on tiny wheels. Amply cushioned, the chairs also came with arms carefully channeled in a kind of arm-rest to allow the guest a measure of comfort while leaning on the chair or pushing forward. A Persian carpet ran the length and breadth of the room, permitting a modest margin of the hardwoods to shine through. The carpet's deep blue heightened the aesthetic value of the walls papered in pastel blue. Against two neighboring walls china closets and serving stations took up residence. Above them, lining the walls, a raft of great oval-shaped mirrors trimmed in gold filament, and suspended from gold-plated chains, bore down upon the guests. A room devoted to candles, every admissible surface supported an exquisite exhibit of them. Suzanne learned that a French artisan designed the center piece of the dining room table, an oval-shaped silver platter adorned with stems and leaves through which rose up a bank of candles in bejeweled mounts. In the middle of the ceiling, a massive chandelier in the form of a wagon wheel thrust out candles from the tips of the numerous spokes. René proceeded to light some of them with a long straw dipped in wax. Each of the sideboards held displays of fruit in bowls, ready to be eaten, and next to each bowl a candle burned brightly.

* * *

Adhering to strict standards, René placed the guests according to their relevance. Therefore, Suzanne and her father sat on the right side of the table—a place of prominence— and the Bear Chief and Aboyant sat opposite them. Collectively they sat to the immediate left and right of the head of the table respectively, a place soon to be occupied by Henri Marchand. Dutifully René stepped briskly about, methodically pulling foods from the small compartments within the serving stations. For an opening dish or precursor, René served salads. He called them 'garden salads' and each one sat in a bowl of thick lettuce beneath articles taken from Monsieur's extensive gardens: radishes, cucumbers, slices of sweet onion, peas and carrots, miniature tomatoes. Fine strips of ham and cheese followed. René handed each guest a bottle of sauce mixed with wine vinegar to apply at leisure.

While the guests dined, René stood idly by, eyes trained upon every movement. Casually he consulted a time piece, after which he moved once again to the serving stations. Upon flinging open the doors, a waft of steaming vapors followed him into the room. Donning gloves, he lifted out a large tureen, and, cradling it, set it gently on a serving cart. With a ladle, he dipped the precise amount of a hot, thick fluid into the small cups placed beside each guest. His task completed, he resigned to a corner of the room and chirped meekly: "Hot oyster stew fresh from the Chesapeake."

In an effort to engage René, James remarked about a former liaison with the Chesapeake region and complimented René on the soup's consistency. His host, however, politely ignored him, and fell to the next task: filling the water glasses. Chores completed, he crossed to the far side of the room where he entered an alcove. Emerging seconds later, he announced: "Monsieur Marchand arrives." He motioned the guests to rise.

A robust man of medium height swept into the dining quarters. Despite a broad girth, he moved on nimble feet. Dressed in a gentleman's finest attire, the man sported a black outfit, complete with ruffled, white collar and shirt sleeves. He wore leggings gathered at the knee above white silk hose. He wore black patent leather shoes. The patriarch beamed a broad smile, and, bowing slightly, walked to the head of the table where he scooped up a generous portion of walnuts. Taking small bites, he glimpsed at the guests one by one, making certain that his smile remained with them. He proceeded to greet each guest with a firm handshake before taking a place at the head of the table. Once seated, he leaned forward and introduced himself in terms imbued with friendly authoritativeness:

"Good afternoon, my friends. I am Henri Marchand. I understand that you have a request to make." He looked from guest to guest, a cue for Suzanne to retrieve her father's document for supplies.

She passed the document to her father, who in turn passed it to Henri Marchand. The tradesman perused it lightly before handing it to René. "I believe that introductions are in order," he quipped, looking at Suzanne.

Suzanne spoke her name and that of her father, expecting to engage the tradesman in conversation, yet quite the unexpected occurred with the man's next remark: "Very well. Good! Let us eat!"

Roast turkey, the principal course, arrived and René filled the guests' plates with mashed potatoes, candied potatoes, squash, and green beans. Monsieur Marchand elected to bypass the salad and soup. He made straight for the principal course. Suzanne spent the next several minutes observing him, trying to gather words to describe him, a diversion in which she freely indulged since arriving in the Lake Country. To Suzanne, Marchand appeared to be a man of tenaciousness and resolve. The broad shoulders and stout neck supported ample and thick facial features. At a distance his head and hands seemed too large for his body, but these attributes served him well, she believed, for, given his larger-than-life aspect, one is compelled to devote to Marchand one's full attention when in his presence. He truly is the master of his castle, she believed.

At length Marchand lay aside his dining utensils. Suzanne sensed a willingness to speak and she perked up her ears and her interest grew accordingly.

"My dear friend, the Bear Chief has conveyed to me your story, mes amis. I am deeply moved. You have sacrificed your earthly comforts and personal fortune to strike out on a trail of danger and uncertainty. To go to these lengths out of love for another demonstrates strong commitment to family. In spite of this low point in your lives you have chosen to perform admirably while under the Bear Chief's supervision. For this he is very grateful. You have arrived in the Land of the Lakes at a moment when the two leading nations of the world are at war with each other for ownership of these lands. I am told that my adversary is about to subdue Montreal. It is the final stronghold of French influence in upper North America. In the absence of an effective counterstrike, the balance of power in these lands will swing to him. For we French on this side of the St. Lawrence, our days of unrestrained liberty may be coming to an end. Perhaps no amount of intervention on the part of the French will stem the natural flow of events—but it may delay them. I speak not of intervention in the traditional sense with flint and steel. I speak of something more incisive and enduring and elusive than a musket ball. I speak of restructuring the contemporary scene. Let me be more explicit:

"James and Suzanne York. You seek my aid in finding Madame York. Ordinarily I am reluctant to undertake such a venture. It speaks of putting a great deal of my men in harm's way, many of whom may pay the ultimate price for valor. On the surface I have nothing to gain and everything to lose. On the other hand, my friend the Bear Chief tells me that Madame's situation affords me a 'golden opportunity.' He has given me to understand that our adversary has usurped his authority with regard to the treatment of peace-loving people. In sum, for one who is a guest in these lands, he has seen fit to run off with his host's property and possessions and to put to the torch all that remains of which he is unable to absorb. Those properties and possessions which he steals he converts to his own benefit or offers for sale. His climb to power is at the expense of those unable to speak for themselves. These are not the ways of a mighty nation. Certainly they are not the ways of France in North America.

"I am not prepared to leave these lands in the hands of corrupt and unscrupulous men. I will challenge them by appealing to the popular will—on the field of battle if necessary— but more importantly in courts of law where the voice of the people may be heard without fear of recrimination . . . all of the people, for I intend to fight for all of the people of the Lake Country. If my efforts are successful, popular opinion will flow to my side, so strong that the claims of my adversary will fall by the wayside and *la fleur de lis* will live on in the hearts and minds of the people."

Eyes aglow with enthusiasm, Marchand struck the table frequently with his fist, a move that both accentuated his statements and brought René scurrying from the kitchen to his side. He found himself conveying the same message to his servant frequently: "That will be all, René. Thank you."

"We start out early on the morrow. There will be four of us, your friend, Aboyant included." Turning to the Bear Chief, he requested the services of his ally and swift runner, Cerf Courant. With a nod the Cayuga sachem acknowledged the tradesman's request.

"This is a challenging journey, Mademoiselle. You are welcomed to remain at Maple Grove."

"I choose to accompany my father. We console each other."

"Very well spoken, Mademoiselle. We begin our venture by seeking support from members of the Confederacy. We will bring a small party of warriors from the Round Tops and will have ample rations and firearms. I will introduce you as my niece and your father as my brother. You must not indulge strangers with stories of Madame York—particularly our allies. They may take a dim view of sending forth valiant warriors to save a woman. No disrespect intended."

"We understand," James answered, speaking for himself and Suzanne.

"Bon. You will find supplies waiting for you at the Round Tops—courtesy of Colombe Blanche and a helpful colleague of hers."

"That would be Fawn," Suzanne smiled.

"Ah, yes. Fawn. A most vivacious young woman." He coughed when pronouncing her name. "Before I forget, take this list and see that you bring all of the articles on it with you." He handed the list to James who read it aloud:

Provisions for Travel by Foot

1. *Changes of Clothing*: stockings, under garments, cotton or linen shirts (full sleeve), trousers (wool), a cap or broad-brimmed lid (to guard against exposure), back pack (secured by chest and shoulder straps), boots (long distance, shoes (short distance.

2. *Personal Properties*: soap(bar or cake), towels, leather gloves, flasks of water, matches, flints, dry swatches(for starting a fire), iodine(bottle), quinine, rubbing alcohol, bandages, linen

patches, wood splints, pocket knife, needle & thread, thread for dentifrice, pocket mirror, scissors, note papers, pens with ink supply. Also, the 'necessary papers.'

3. *Required*: Musket and shot and powder, also pistol with same, hunting knife, dried foods for back pack, fruits and green leafy vegetables, blankets for wearing and sleeping, portable canvas tent, trail map, trail watch and calendar, compass.

4. *Other*: horses (one per voyager) travois (two per party of four).

James folded the paper and placed it in his shirt pocket, whereas his host handed him yet another document. He stressed that it came from his superior, Gen. Le Rocher, a letter of introduction to the Seneca chieftain, Ga: yant: hawah: geh, the Cornplanter. Written in French, Suzanne begged her father to allow her to read it aloud. At first teasing her, James relented in the end and Suzanne read the document to the small congregation:

Le Billet A' L'Introduire
Destiné Pour Le Grand Cheftain
Ga:yant:hawah:gah

Mon chère compagnon: Ce billet se trouve destiné pour l'emploi de trois passants de bonne qualité. Pendant ce moment, ils font des voyages par La Terre des Lacs. Ensuite, faites-moi le plaisir de s'occuper de leur sauveté parcequ'ils sont engagés dans une oeuvre de grande signification, nommément la commerce à partir de nos deux nations renommées: la France et le Peuple des Iroquois, ceux qui se sont accordés de travailler ensemble pour toujours.

De cette maniere je mets entre vos mains les plus competentes, les suivants—Monsieur Henri Marchand, Agente de la Commerce, le Pays du Nord; M. Jacques Marchand, le frère et Mlle. Suzanne Marchand, la niece. Il y a aussi deux compagnons avec eux.

Je me pose comme ton compagnon eternel, Guillaume Le Rocher, Commandante de la garnison Pointe Aux Bois parmi les Onondagas de Gannentaa. Je sais bien que tu honneras ma requête au nom de notre amitié.

Guillaume Le Rocher Le 12 de Septiembre de1760

Au Nom de Notre Sauveur

Suzanne went on to translate the document, stating that General Le Rocher asked for safe passage of the Yorks and their escort on a mission of vital importance to the growth of good relations between France and the Iroquois in the Lake Country.

"Merci, Mademoiselle," a merry Henri Marchand returned. "You will be passing into the land of the Seneca and the domain of the Cornplanter. He is very much attuned to the comings and goings of travelers in his country. You must conduct yourselves as guests. Do not act too passionate, and, above all, do not endeavor to deceive him. He is my dear friend, but many Seneca have bitter memories of the French dating back to the last century.* Your letter will carry you through safe passage. Have no fear."

He rose and motioned to the guests. The little party repaired to yet another elaborate room, which the tradesman designated the 'drawing room'. There René served cake and strawberries and offered claret to the men of the party. For Suzanne he produced a glass of butter milk in lieu of the wine and to her delight she enjoyed it.

She set about inspecting the room's appointments while the men conversed. In a word the room reminded her of a museum—a storeroom of antiquities, replete with unique specimens befitting either the collector or connoisseur of art. She approached an immense roll-top desk. Aligned with small drawers, each drawer labeled alphabetically, she sat in the high-back chair which faced the desk. She sensed René's presence behind her.

"Each drawer holds a map corresponding to the letters that you see. Ah! Here is India." He opened the drawer and pulled out a map of linen on canvas, drawn tightly over a slim, wooden rod. With Suzanne's help, he unfolded the map and placed it on a nearby table. Stepping back, he smiled crisply.

"Monsieur has maps of all the major nations of the world. He has traveled to many of these places." Hands on hips, he rolled his eyes in envy.

"Suzanne almost burst out in laughter. "Simply amazing," she replied. "Oh! There is Calcutta."

She walked before the great fireplace. Framed in white marble and ebony, its polished surfaces glistened. Stooping beside it, she caught a glimpse of her face peering out at her. Behind her René gave her to understand that the precious stones came from the valley of the Nile during one of his master's voyages to Egypt. Busts cast in bronze occupied the entire length of the mantel. Inscriptions written on small cards beneath them identified each character. Suzanne read the cards and learned that all of the characters held high rankings in the military from England to Europe and Asia. Two massive world globes stood on either flank of the fireplace. She casually spun one of them in its cradle while crossing to the harpsichord.

A more contemporary instrument than the spinet, the harpsichord occupied the center of the room. It rested on two deep Persian carpets, each set in shades of blue, red, and amber. Sofas and chairs, and the customary oil lamps stood nearby in small clusters, all facing the instrument. Suzanne stood back to admire the room at a distance: blue painted walls descending into carved white wainscoting waist-high and white corniced molding merging with the ceiling. She found herself nodding approvingly once again. Turning, she faced René and the remainder of the guests.

"Come sit by the harpsichord. Monsieur may play for you in a bit." He wheeled along a cart of refreshments. In the next instant a vibrant Marchand pulled aside the bench of the harpsichord, and, brushing away imaginary particles of dust, deposited himself brusquely. Beaming broadly, he broke out in song, nimble fingers tickling the ivories with fervor, the voice a pleasant bass:

> I left my love in Mandalay
> T'was on a bright and sunny day.
> She almost won the best of me.
> But my true love is the rolling sea.

Concluding the piece, he laughed uproariously, jowls a rosy red. Everyone reciprocated, breaking out in laughter. Jumping up, Marchand approached the guests, smacking beefy hands together. Walking to and fro before captive listeners, he spoke, making ample gestures:

"Let me tell you how I happened to come to this land of lakes. I am one half of a partnership of two. My partner, the one with the fertile mind, is Richard Clement. Several years ago Richard opened a trading post above Lake Champlain. He asked me to join him. We came from Quebec province where the fur trade ran briskly. Iroquois and Hurons from the western Great Lakes flocked to our post with articles of superb quality. We sent them on their way up the St. Lawrence to mother France where they became headdresses and coats for the stylish denizens of Paris and beyond. We grew prosperous. I decided to venture further south. I made my move when French soldiers sacked Ontario. Richard remained behind. Initially I set up a post near Albany.

"All went well for a short while. However, British traders moved rapidly into the region. They traded exclusively with the resident Mohawks, supplying them with goods in exchange for their furs. The two formed a compact which in effect prohibited exchanges with others such as my Iroquois and Hurons. Slowly my lines of supply dried up and I found myself at a disadvantage. In a fit of anger I moved on a whim to Pointe Aux Bois. Truly a dilapidated post, I restored it, yet endeavored to keep its presence a secret to all but my closest circle of associates. I traded locally, confining my routes to the east and west along the Genesee Road corridor, and soon struck up a friendship with your host, the Bear Chief. In the meanwhile, the French soldiers vacated Ontario, leaving me 'high and dry.' They also surrendered Fort Frontenac and Niagara to the British. Not to run, however, I persisted in pursuit of my dream and here I stand before you today, the leader of a small, yet active post.

"In looking back on history, I believe that Richard and I filled a need in the lives of the natives. Once our French missionaries quit the heartland in the last century, the natives fell into disarray. For lack of a firm theological model, they began to quarrel among themselves. They fell to the despicable task of taking prisoners. They killed some of them and sold many others into slavery. Indeed, your adversary, James and Suzanne, is no stranger to the sale of human flesh. In our own way Richard and I changed this most barbaric and crude practice. At our posts we simply reintroduced a Christian ethos into daily life while furnishing natives with needed goods and services. Our posts always supported a chapel, the doors of which stood perpetually open. We welcomed all-comers into our posts and drew no lasting or harsh judgments against anyone. Perhaps these are the true reasons for our continuance to the present day. For certain it is not the French military that gave us stability. To speak of, there is **no** French military.

"Richard and I witnessed great changes coming over the natives following our treatment with them. In general, the natives have regained their communal functions: They adhere more strongly to family traditions. They think in national terms, not in pockets of isolation. They are conscious of how their actions affect others. In the achievement of these ambitions, new leaders have come to the fore: Cornplanter of the Seneca and the Bear Chief of the Cayugas strike a resonant chord. These men have the ability to draw large numbers to their side and, because of this development, I bring to them my allegiance."

He looked about him. The room fell silent. "Enough about me," he roared. "Let me hear from you. Mademoiselle! I understand that you are an accomplished songstress. René is passing out song sheets. Please lead us in a few bars. Page 3, no. 4, please. Ready?"

Too late to refuse, Suzanne joined the tradesman in song, who recited from memory. She elbowed her father, a move which ignited a chain reaction, for James, the Bear Chief and Aboyant loaned their support in chorus. They sang several pieces until René advised his master that everyone eat the strawberries and cream before they turned sour. The music and singing ended abruptly with the tradesman making an announcement:

"All of you may sleep here this evening after you gather your stores. We leave at 6 hours tomorrow." He escorted the guests through the foyer and out the great door which René held open for them. Suzanne scurried over the slate walkway. Crossing to the roadway, she turned and waved in appreciation, before rushing to gather her belongings and returning to the mansion.

* * *

A new day dawned. The ever-vigilant Watkins rose early at 5 hours, this Tuesday, September 12th. Although the building of the Round Tops proceeded on course, most residents still slept under the stars in bedrolls. Near him Fawn rose. She prepared a breakfast for Watkins and for the soon-to-be travelers who spent the evening at Maple Grove. The thought of sleeping in a bed of 'down' gave Watkins reason to stretch his limbs in an effort to remove some of the knots which accumulated overnight. That feat accomplished, he fell to the task of bringing forth the last of the necessities for his new friends. He read from a list which he marked off with a stylus. Fawn came to stand at his side. Together they pronounced the terms on the list. He congratulated her for her eagerness and spontaneity. Soon the travelers fell in around him. Amid handshakes and farewells, the Bear Chief made known the intention of staying behind in order to supervise the construction at the Round Tops. Watkins looked forward to laboring with him.

Colombe Blanche joined Suzanne. Pleasant and professing a broad smile, she requested that Suzanne open her palm. She dropped her 'stones' into the precocious girl's hand and made a gesture over her closed fist. She spoke softly: "May these brilliant stones bring you good fortune on your journey, dear one. May they aid you as they have aided me." She spoke in French and Suzanne cried tears of happiness and both women embraced each other, after which Suzanne returned the stones to her hostess.

Marchand appeared. He summoned the sojourners and, following a small repast, everyone trooped outside to the tradesman's barn. There, awaiting him stood eight members of the Bear Chief's home guard. The tradesman brought out horses. Presently Watkins arrived with the provisions and supplies and in very short order the little party abandoned the barn. They marched over the pathway leading to the front of the mansion where they paused at the end of the slate walkway. One step beyond, the Genesee Road, the gateway to all points west, rose up to meet them. René waved to the little party from the front steps and without any ceremony the sojourners departed Maple Grove and its fine tapestries and luxurious settings and set out to challenge the unknown.

In the role of tradesman Marchand traveled the Genesee Road incessantly. Once a narrow and crevassed pathway, the road gradually developed into a broad, straight-forward artery which passed through the heart of the Lake Country. It stretched between Albany to the east and the shore of Lake Erie to the west from whence travelers continued either through the Great Lakes system or over rough inland roads into the interior of North America. Initially a native trail interconnecting native villages, the road underwent a series of name-changes in its trek westward. Following white expansion into native lands, engineers, serving chiefly with the military, saw fit to plane and widen the road. They hacked down burdensome obstacles and drained nearby lowlands to discourage flooding of the road during the wet season and the icing of it in the winter. Neither native nor white lay claim to the road, for it held the distinction of being an asset to all— the one well-developed and continuous artery to the west. For Marchand the road enabled him to travel to distant reaches of the Confederacy where he plied his trade with villagers who depended upon him to sustain their way of life. In all likelihood he helped to develop that way of life, owing to the quality of goods he introduced. In exchange he received token valuables, furs and such, but more importantly, he received the friendship of the unpredictable and semi-bellicose Iroquois.

He owed recurring successes to the Genesee Road. He esteemed it so highly that he built Maple Grove next to it. He procured the stones for the mansion by following the Indian path outside of his door to the west. It ran north through swampy and hilly land beyond a great open pit lined with gray sandstone. The Bear Chief escorted him with a selection of volunteers after a particularly uplifting trading session at the Round Tops. There, in the bowels of the earth,* he extracted the building blocks for the home. The Bear Chief too took samples of the stones in order to build new structures with the faithful Watkins. For Marchand, the road proved a great benefit and he thought of it in glowing terms. Unfortunately, not everyone traveled the road with the best of intentions. He recalled the march of Count Frontenac, late, of the 17th century. In a bid to conquer the Mohawks and Onondagas, Frontenac pillaged the Dutch-held enclave of Schenectady in February of 1690. His warriors traveled by snowshoe over the snow-encrusted Genesee Road from due east. Sacking the compound known as the Stockade (28), they traveled on during a subsequent sally to destroy the central village of the Onondagas. Thus, in some quarters of the Confederacy, enmity still persisted against all things French.

He recalled how the Bear Chief sought to build a village beside the road because it afforded him free rein to travel to all points east and west throughout the Confederacy. For the Cayuga sachem the road served as a means of communication, transportation, and escape, the latter in the event of an unsustainable siege. One further advantage of the road lay in its strategic value, for he who controlled the road governed the movement of supplies and war engines fielded by an adversary. In sum, The Round Tops, largely unknown by those outside of the Bear Chief's circle of decision-makers, depended heavily upon the road for the security and well-being of its residents.

—

The sojourners traveled briskly. Marchand planned to visit Cayuga villages in order to make inquiries of Madame York and her supposed captor, the Captain. Following the sack of Osco, the Captain's whereabouts vanished from the customary reports that he received from scouts. This situation concerned him greatly. He knew nothing of the man, save a rumored perfidy, the thought of which gave rise to a decision to scour the western villages of the Confederacy.

For the first stop on the tour, Henri Marchand chose Chonodote. Situated at the foot of Lake Tiohero** on its eastern shore, Chonodote lay four and one half leagues straightaway west of Maple Grove. En route the road rose and fell over a series of drumlins. Gentle at first, they rose in pitch until the final drumlin, which plunged down sharply to the lake. The dwellings of the village occupied three tiers of earth, each one carved from the drumlin in well-manicured rows. They faced the lake and one ascended and descended from one level to the next by means of ladders set at intervals among the tiers. One entered the village either by canoe from the lake, or by dropping over the fast-cascading drumlin, the latter approach designed to discourage invaders. Beyond the village the land lay open and undulating and it is here that the villagers raised fruits and vegetables. The rains tended to create small pools of water where the terrain rose and fell and the villagers diverted the flows sufficiently to water the crops during warm springs and dry summers. An agrarian band, the villagers relied more on bountiful yields from the fields than hunting for meat. In late fall and winter they caught and ate fish from the lake. The villagers traditionally kept foods in storage and with the change in seasons they always ate well. No one starved.

The villagers took great pride in the fruit trees. They inhabited the spacious rolling plains and slopes above the lake where the spring rains provided abundant moisture for growth. The villagers stored the seeds of the fruit trees in underground urns deep in the soil, thus perpetuating the crop for generations to come. The trees yielded apples, cherries, and the favorite: peaches. In neighboring sections of the plains the villagers planted corn, squash, stringed beans, onions, melons, pumpkins, and mushrooms. Everywhere scores of berries hung from suspended arbors.

Marchand visited Chonodote four times a year— or once each season. He brought articles and utensils which the Cayugas put to daily use, which, according to reports received from the chieftain Stag Deer, greatly improved the villagers' way of life. In return Marchand accepted woven garments and moccasins and beaver and fox furs and deer robes and blankets. The villagers especially looked forward to receiving rifles and pistols with shot and powder, for they proved more reliable than the bow and arrow in felling large animals. A day of celebration prevailed during the tradesman's stay at this and other villages where goods and conversation flowed freely.

Word of his impending arrival usually preceded him and small children would lead him down the steep drumlin to the Stag Deer's quarters. On this day, however, despite the pleasant assurances emanating from the blue skies above, no one came to meet him. Marchand halted at the crest of the drumlin to listen. He heard nothing. All fell silent. A heavy knot rose at his throat. The mild vapors blowing in from the lake carried the faint scent of smoke. The knot descended to his stomach where it lingered. Breathing with difficulty, he ordered the sojourners to descend to the village with haste. A crowd gathered outside of the Stag Deer's lodge. Marchand brusquely opened a pathway, and there, in a dusty lane, he bent over a lifeless boy which the chieftain clutched to his chest. Their eyes met and the Stag Deer wept openly. He carefully passed the boy to another and rose:

"Look! They have killed him. My son. Look at my village. They have burned it!"

On all sides lodges lay smoldering— contents scattered. Children wept and crept close to their mothers. Men stood defiantly together. Some clutched spears and war hatchets.

"Deyojia:n:edo:t.—Stag Deer— Who did this?" the tradesman asked.

"Les Peaus Blancs. They have killed my son. I did not give them what they wanted and they killed him."

"How many are they?"

"Many. Yet they followed the commands of a few."

"What are you able to tell me now?"

"They came looking for furs and hides. They found them, but they are not enough so . . ."

"So they tied up our children and ran off with them," answered a woman nearby.

"Who are these men? I will find them."

"You are not enough. They have booming engines and long rifles."

The tradesman glanced at James before addressing the Stag Deer. "These are the same men who burned your sister village, Osco. They are trying to steal your goods and sell your children."

"What are we to do, my friend?" the Stag Deer grieved.

"We will join together and deliver to them a surprise attack so strong that it will crush them."

"I am so aggrieved that I will be of little value to you, my friend."

"Let me tell you that I came to you in search of these men. I heard rumors of their misdeeds. My friend James knows full well of their chicanery. He lost his wife to these men." He ushered James before the chieftain.

"Is this true?" the Stag Deer asked.

"Yes," a melancholy James replied. He held Suzanne's hand.

The tradesman brought Suzanne before the chieftain: "She is the daughter of this man and has lost her mother to these rogues. Suzanne?"

"We have come to help Henri Marchand find my mother. He is a good man. With your help he will seek vengeance for your loss." She produced the locket bearing her mother's portrait. The chief waved it off.

"Tell me what I must do, Monsieur Marchand."

"We must gather forces quickly and move against the interloper. We will join with my commandant who will lead his forces from Pointe Aux Bois."

"What is this Pointe Aux Bois, Monsieur?"

"It is my station here on the frontier. It is good that you know not of it, for my commandant and I prefer to keep its whereabouts unknown to evil eyes."

"I will go with you, but others must follow."

"Good. You must remain behind to grieve, but give me your warriors. Next I visit the Sandpiper at Tiohero."

"This is a good choice, Monsieur. Look! My warriors are thirsty for blood. They will follow you."

"May your son rest in peace forever. By his death may others know freedom."

"Yes, Monsieur. This is good. My son has not died in vain."

"Tell me. Is there one man who stood out above the rest?"

"Yes, my friend. An older man with a fierce countenance barked orders at his underlings. They jumped out of fear when he spoke."

"You are doing well, Deyogia:n:edo:t. Something more?"

"He carried a walking stick, for he walked with a limp."

The tradesman looked to James and Suzanne. They nodded in agreement.

"You must stay with us and celebrate this day of mourning, Monsieur" Stag Deer requested.

"That I am unable to do. My quarry gets further and further away by the moment."

"Take my warriors and bring me prisoners to appease my grief, Monsieur."

"That I will do. You have my word, Deyogia:n:edo:t."

—

The village of Tiohero (29) shared its name with the lake that it bordered. Situated some two leagues northwest of Chonodote, Tiohero* consisted of a cluster of lodges over flat yet marshy ground in the midst of a broad and unencumbered plain. Over the years the men of Tiohero built up the land. They carried in great quantities of earth, converting into a plateau that portion of the plain given over to their dwellings. Over the surrounding wetlands the villagers raised bountiful harvests. They enjoyed prodigious yields of fruits and vegetables and corn and peaches grew in abundance. Beyond the wetlands grassy marshes and bogs sprang up, giving rise to a natural network of defense against invasion. Mosquitoes and other pesky creatures swarmed continuously during the summer months and the villagers held them in great esteem, for not once during their occupancy of the plain did they suffer an attack from marauders. Migrating species of waterfowl nested permanently on the marshes and the villagers made their eggs a dietary staple. By summer's end the marshes dried out and the earth split into fissures and the birds flew south to winter quarters, but they always returned the following spring to hunt the tadpoles, grubs, and young frogs of the rebounding marshes.

The villagers called themselves the 'People' and they built lodges close together over their man-made plateau. During the spring rains men fortified the lodges with mud taken from the bogs and shored up any rifts in the broad, flat plateau. Under the summer's sun the lodges and plateau turned impenetrably hard, strong enough to hold back the fierce winds that whipped over the plain during fall and winter. A causeway built of stones over mud pilings ran out to the beach on the eastern shore of the lake and provided the most convenient means of access to the village. When lake levels rose after sustained rains, only the lowlands below the causeway flooded, thus keeping the principal artery high and dry, and, of course, the lodges perched on the plateau. All that the People required for daily subsistence stood in close proximity to the plain and its marshes and bogs. Large animals clung to the large forest to the west of the village and in winter the men paddled over the unfrozen lake to catch fish. The People enjoyed life in the Flats. The little island lay tucked into a corner of the wilderness and they named the region 'Les Plaines de Boue'—Mud Flats. When they dined in the evening the People rejoiced over the abundance which Nature provided them and the comparatively secure surroundings in which they found themselves.

No one kept watch over the outer reaches of the plateau that singular evening when the villagers gathered in their lodges for dinner. Everyone dined at approximately the same hour during the first indications of sundown. Families with children assembled around hearths in the sturdy lodges which locked out sounds from without. Presently, Oh:nehsi:yo, the venerated chieftain, rose to attend a favored dog. Tethered outside the lodge, the animal broke out in sharp howls and dashed inside to warn its owner of impending danger. Oh:nehsi:yo studied the landscape from his front doorway: the causeway, the beach, the lake front. At first all appeared calm, but the dog's incessant yelping gave him reason to heed the animal's cries.

Glancing toward the horizon, Oh:nehsi:yo glimpsed movement along the narrow beach head. A long column of figures marched over the beach and, breaching the causeway, headed directly toward the village. Blades of steel glistened under the setting sun and the crunch of heavy boots striking the hard earth drove him backward in recoil. He ran inside to gather the family. He sent the children to warn his neighbors and within precious moments villagers made a dash for the marshes and bogs and the forest. Warriors remained behind and it is they who suffered the first blows from the 'booming engines.' Soldiers followed and swiftly took up positions on the plateau. With rifles and bayonets, they went from lodge to lodge searching and looting. They made a pile of valued articles, mostly furs and hides, and pushed ahead to the lowlands. There they plucked small children from a mother's arms and shot at those who resisted them. A few final bursts of cannon fire wiped out many lodges and in short order the invaders withdrew, boisterous and bawdy, spoils in hand.

—

Marchand's band crept along the shoreline. Tiohero lay close at hand. Cerf Courant pointed out to the tradesman the profusion of human tracks in the soft earth. On the tradesman's suggestion, he followed them inland and over the causeway. Returning in a matter of moments, he reported his sightings:

"The village is in ruins. Everyone has run away or been killed."

Hoping to find signs of life, the tradesman barked out a command: "Search the marshes and woodlands! Bring me a live body!!" His ranks soon swelled with warriors. They spread over the plain and, returning, produced survivors of the ambush which leveled their village: Among them, Oh:nehsi:yo. He lamented:

"The rogues brought down our lodges with the 'booming engines.' We all dashed for the marshes and the leader of the pack, an older man, threatened to kill my warriors unless I led him to my cache of precious furs. I obeyed, ready to sacrifice my one life for the sake of many. I know now the folly of my act, for the older man intended to kill me outright. A younger man in his command persuaded him to spare me in case more treasures lay in hiding. I remember the older man's eyes— dripping red in the corners—dripping with red—the color of blood. I have never stood side by side with the Devil until that moment. His followers seemed in a hurry to move on and he released me, but not before carving my neck with a blade." He lifted shoulder-length hair to disclose an ugly red stain running the width of the neck above the shoulder.

The tradesman unpacked one of many medicinal bags and attended to his dear friend. Applying antiseptic to the wound, he wrapped it in linen cloth, while observing him for signs of exhaustion. You are most fortunate. The scoundrel did not care to kill you. He wanted to teach you a lesson . . . that he is able to conquer you at leisure." He spoke soberly and with conviction. "What are your losses?"

"A few died protecting children. We hid in the rushes. The soldiers did not follow. They sank in the mud. I lost my full complement of furs. *Your* furs. Do not hate me."

"On the contrary. What are a few skins to our friendship? When you come to Pointe Aux Bois, new supplies await you as always."

"Who are these warriors before me?"

"They are from Chonodote. They are going with me to Kanandesaga. I will seek the Cornplanter's help."

"He trades with the British. The men who attacked us spoke their language."

"Cornplanter *hates* the British. He coddles their favor, but tells me their secrets."

"I want to kill this brutish coward. Take me with you."

"Give me fifty of your best warriors. I will send for you soon." Marchand prepared to mount.

"You have it. When you call for me they will be ready."

"Thank you, my dear friend. I leave you now. We both have affairs to attend to."

The tradesman mounted his trusty steed. He directed a number of warriors to remain behind to assist Oh:nehsi:yo in rebuilding lodges. Turning to the remainder of the party, he shouted: "On to Kanandesaga!" Behind him a resilient Oh:nehsi:yo uplifted both arms in a gesture of victory.

The tradesman stepped up the pace. He wanted to reach Kanandesaga before nightfall. It lay less than twenty kilometers to the northwest of Tiohero on flat, expansive land. He kept to offshoots of the Genesee Trail before striking off into the high grasslands. He wanted to avoid early detection and the tall grasses and soft, rolling hills furnished excellent cover. He longed to see his ally, Ga:yant:hawah:geh, the wily and astute Seneca chieftain.

Kanandesaga,* the current capital village of the mighty Seneca, held a dubious reputation in the region. On the one hand, residents cultivated a great variety of crops over extensive stretches of irrigated lands. Planters and gatherers, the Senecas raised enough foods from the luxuriant soil to meet their own needs and also to furnish to other villages of the Confederacy. They raised crops largely unknown to others, in many cases original, and consistently produced a surplus which they stowed away for lean periods. They often exchanged surpluses for scarce items such as iron kettles, wool mittens, blankets, and, of course, rifles and powder. They traded early in their history with the French. Later, the

British stepped in and built log cabins for the Senecas in expectation of becoming exclusive agents-in-trade.

The Senecas, however, distrusted the British. Privately they viewed them as arrogant and abrasive toward the People and driven by a singular interest: the possession of native lands for white settlement. Although the Seneca preferred the quality of British goods over those of French, they lingered among the latter who lacked the military strength to subdue them—much less hand over the Lake Country to numerous settlers. The new chieftain, the Cornplanter, courted both camps: He accepted British goods and supplied the French commandant at Pointe Aux Bois with warriors to conduct reconnaissance and to supplement thin ranks. Neither camp knew the full extent of the Cornplanter's involvement with its rival, but suspicions ran rife throughout the region, The new chieftain, the Cornplanter, played both camps off against each other in excellent fashion.

Trafficking in 'human flesh' took place regularly at Kanandesaga. The Senecas looking to replace populations devastated by wars, death, and diseases, avidly sought to bring new life to the council fires. Usually the practice stayed within the native community, but occasionally unscrupulous white agents brought native captives and even homeless white children and women to villages in exchange for rich furs and hides and the rare gold nugget or coin. Largely young women and children, to the exclusion of adult males, the captives began a new existence as servants at Kanandesaga or at any of several native villages in the Lake Country or beyond. Surplus or non-amenable captives went to distant forts, most of which rimmed the Great Lakes. The fort at Oswego fell into that classification, and, indeed, Lord Carleton dipped into that ready pool of conscripts with eagerness on a regular basis. The thought of free labor served his vain, self-serving interests. He justified the practice of conscription as an act of saving poor, homeless wretches from a life of unending servitude at the hands of ruthless agents. Some of the native conscripts eventually gained liberty, but most remained bound to masters. Many died on the very spot where they served from diseases generated by encroaching white populations. A few lived to learn valuable trades.

A practical man, the Cornplanter took advantage of a poor situation. He readily accepted conscripts in trade from the agents who lined the trading arena of Kanandesaga, for they brought him much-needed goods. Nevertheless, he refused to sell a conscript for profit or gain. On the contrary, he released most to villages and other locales for which they expressed a desire, or merely returned them to their own homes in secrecy. Again, residual conscripts went to forts as objects in trade, there to live according to their wits and any good fortune which befell them. He confined no one indefinitely. Under his purview, everyone learned of his or her fate in due course and most departed Kanandesaga in better shape than when they arrived.

Fully-aware of Kanandesaga's dual reputation, the tradesman entered the village with the expectation of renewing old alliances with the Cornplanter. Apart from other villages, Kanandesaga lay open to scrutiny. Residents threw up no barricades to exclude foreigners. Neat cabins with pitched rooftops sat in rows facing each other on lanes carved into the soft soil. The village boasted a blacksmith shop, storage barns, granaries, foundry, trading post, a trading concourse, a crude barracks, a dog-racing track, general store, and two churches, all established by those seeking to curry favor with the unpredictable Senecas. Beyond the village proper the residents tilled fertile fields in which delectable crops became the envy of the entire Lakes region—transforming Kanandesaga, despite its shortcomings, into a prominent, regional trade center.

The tradesman found the Cornplanter (30) out-of-doors preparing a meal at a hearth beside his lodge. Dispensing with an entourage, he approached him alone. They spoke in French:

"It has been a long while, Ga:yant:hawah:geh." He extended a hand.

"Too long; however, I see that you arrived in time for dinner." They shook hands.

"Unfortunately, I did not come to dine with you."

"Yes. I know. You are too stern of countenance today. Something is troubling you."

"I do not want to lay my troubles on your doorstep."

"You have done so in the past and everything turned out for the better. Remember, Monsieur?"

"Yes. Of course. I have a letter for you." He handed him the Le Rocher letter of introduction.

The Cornplanter perused the letter before asking the obvious question: "How am I a part of your plans?"

"Chonodote and Tiohero have been ravaged by marauders. I believe that it is a maverick British party eager to disrupt the lines of the fur trade which I established in the Lake Country."

"I have not heard of this. It must have taken place very recently."

"Yesterday and today to my knowledge. I fear it is part of a greater scheme to drive Onontio from the Lake Country."

"This is serious, Monsieur Marchand. Now I understand Monsieur Le Rocher's concern."

"Earlier the same rogues sacked Osco, I believe."

"What will you have me to do?"

"I am putting together a plan to intercept these low-bellies before they grow too strong and confident. Of course I need your warriors in support. The warriors you see here are from Chonodote. Those of Tiohero are due to arrive by arrangement. Together, our combined force will join with soldiers from my sanctuary, Pointe Aux Bois, in a surprise-attack that will crush them in a single coup."

"Where do these low-bellies reside?"

"Sources tell me that they rendezvous at the base-camp, Oswego. I tend to believe them for they have superior weapons and a sizable column: signs that they are bound for a provisioned garrison."

"Fort Oswego!! I did not know that the British Crown approves of sorties upon simple villages."

"Councilors of the Crown do not as a matter of course. By the same token they push away all related public inquiries, Ga:yant:hawah:geh. There is something more: These low-bellies have seen fit to kidnap young children and women: *native* children and *native* women."

The Cornplanter stood silent, his features unchanging, and Marchand pressed on:

"Have you seen new faces traversing the grounds in recent days?"

"It pains me for you to put that question, Monsieur. I am sure it is a part of your duty. No! Not since our last bleak harvest did I accept new conscripts. Look at my home. It is most modest by your standards. I do not grow rich from accepting assignments of human flesh—for certain, not those of my own breed."

"This is all well and good, mon ami. Let me ask you this: I seek a white woman, tall and blonde, who may have come to your village."

"Why do you ask?" The chieftain met Marchand's gaze directly.

"Her husband and daughter have come with me. Le Rocher, my commandant, has written a letter of support for them. I have it with me. They are his guests, for they have no place to call home. Therefore, they are my guests, Sources tell me that soldiers have taken the white woman by force."

"A woman of such features is easily remembered, my good tradesman, although she may have escaped my inspection. If that is the case, she has entered in disguise for reasons known only to her."

"I am told that she appeared during the presence of a British officer. He walked with a limp and may have been her escort."

"I recall such a man. He came with a small band of soldiers; however, a woman did not come with him unless . . ."

"Yes . . ."

"Unless the woman came in disguise to deceive men otherwise moved by passion to desire her."

"Ga:yant:hawah:gah. I am told that a man came here with a woman. Perhaps she is not the one I seek—but a woman nonetheless." He produced Suzanne's locket, revealing the comely portrait.

"Monsieur. You make life difficult for me. I enjoy great commerce with your Le Rocher. The man of whom you speak came here with a troupe of followers. In my study of them I noticed one among them who may have been a woman, for she walked in the way of all women. She clung close to the man and spoke little. The man, your officer, was cruel and harsh toward the helpless wanderer. I paid him with an inferior supply of furs. He did not know the difference. Word of the sacking of the villages preceded him and I did not want to incur his wrath, nor place the lives of my warriors in danger. He departed almost as soon as he arrived— satisfied with the paltry allotment. The blonde newcomer, whom I deemed a woman, I placed with the Jemison (31) woman. Forgive me that I was not forthcoming, but I did not want to see additional castigation fall upon her. Mary Jemison has lived here a great while(32). The two became friends and prepared meals in the commissary. The blonde woman loved the children and began to teach them the English tongue. I took her to be one of high station and allowed her to bed in her own cabin. I kept her apart from the roving eyes of the soldiers who come here, but one day the man of whom you speak returned to claim her. She did not betray our secret and went off with him quietly. She left me a message to deliver. I put it in a special place. I found her charming and did not place her in the corral where new refugees go, despite the crude man's instructions. Excuse me." The Cornplanter entered his lodge and soon returned with a slip of paper containing a message scrawled in ink. Written in English, the tradesman read it aloud for the benefit of his host:

Dear Beloved Husband

I am enjoying my holiday in the lake country to no end. Already I have visited several native ruins: Chonodote, Tiohero, Osco. I plan to return to my home base with my escort party before setting out on new adventures. My consort watches over me. Do not worry. Watch over our daughter and son and I will engage you again at my first opportunity. Your loving wife, Carrie

The message in hand, the tradesman dashed to James York's side. He read it and summoned Suzanne.

"Father! It is mother. She has left us a cryptic letter. All along she has traveled with the marauders. Look! She will be in touch again, I believe."

"Yes, Suzanne. She also is en route to Oswego, if I am correct. We must go to her."

Together, Suzanne and her father accompanied Marchand to the Cornplanter's cabin whereupon the tradesman calmly prevailed upon his estranged friend to loan him the support of warriors. The sage chieftain looked into Suzanne's eyes, bright with anticipation. She stood straight and ram-rod stiff and effected a welcoming smile, a tall slim and handsome young woman who bore a strong physical resemblance to the woman in the locket.

The Cornplanter approached father and daughter. He stood silently beside them as they spoke fervently of the woman with the blonde tresses. At times the girl wept. Her father consoled her. Both fled to the tradesman to seek reassurances. At length the chieftain, taking full cognizance of the proceedings, turned to Marchand and made a statement most bland and casual:

"Monsieur Marchand. I believe that I am able to honor your request. How many warriors do you want?"

*The beginning of current Washington Street in Auburn, NY, at that point an Indian trail.

*Here he referenced the attack of the Marquis de Denonville upon the Seneca village Gannagaro in July, 1687 in Genesee County near present-day Victor, NY

*The former quarry in the northern section of Auburn, NY

**Cayuga Lake

(28)Taft, Grace (1913) pg: 3

*Commonly named 'Cayuga'

(29)Merrill (1951) Slim Fingers Beckon pg: 65

*Destroyed by Sullivan-Clinton campaign in 1779. Now part of Geneva, NY.

(30) Abler, Thomas S. Cornplanter: Chief Warrior of the Allegheny Senecas. Chapter 2: *Before The American Revolution.* (2007) Syracuse University Press, pgs: 13-32

(31)Abler (2007) pg: 7

(32) Merrill, Land of the Senecas. American Book-Stratford Press. New York, NY (1949) pgs: 122-124

Chapter Eight

---◆•◆•◆---

The Road to Ontario
The Campaign Begins.
The Bear Chief's Address.
Complications.
The Boatmen.
Neatahwantah.

Upon departing Kanandesaga, Henri Marchand presided over a considerable band of devotees. In addition to his escort, he gained forty warriors from Stag Deer and sixty five from the Cornplanter. Moreover, the Cornplanter intended to release about twenty five conscripts as soon as they received clothing and rations. The Sandpiper promised to send him thirty warriors, a figure they agreed upon before he departed from the ruins of Tiohero. He marched briskly and about four leagues east of Kanandesaga he ordered everyone to rest and wait for the arrival of the combined forces. He estimated that with the addition of the Bear Chief's volunteers from the Round Tops and Le Rocher soldiers from Pointe Aux Bois, he stood to gain close to four hundred fighting men. He selected a deep gully rimmed with trees and brushy growth in which to spend the evening and, with the approach of dusk, everyone set about eating cold rations.

Suzanne, reserved and quiet of late, approached the tradesman. She voiced her apprehensions over her mother's fate. "I know he is your friend, but do you believe that the Cornplanter told us the truth?"

"I believe that he desired to preserve our friendship in this uncertain period. Yes. I believe him."

"I am amazed that mother found the pluck to write that message."

"She is indeed a brave woman from what you have told me. Remember that the Cornplanter chose to show us the message. That tells me that he is in league with us. At this moment he is outfitting conscripts. By tomorrow morning they will be with us. Do not forget that, by fighting with us, the conscripts avoid spending miserable lives in the bowels of a roach-infested fort. The Cornplanter is one of our best allies. I must tell you that he is no stranger to the whites. He himself is half-white by birth. Still a young man, he took a white woman for a wife. Unfortunately, she died in childbirth. Perhaps you did not notice, but he speaks the English tongue well. He is always looking for ways to advance the lot of his People. Although the western Seneca have favored the British on more than one occasion, he leans toward the side of the French— not to forget his earlier defense of Fort Niagara. He committed warriors in a valiant, yet unsuccessful effort to save the fortress. For the present we French are friends and the British are enemies and I intend to preserve that arrangement."

"I am honored to serve with you, Monsieur," an enthusiastic Suzanne stated.

"Do not become too self-assured, Mademoiselle. We have a steep road ahead of us. First, we must topple our quarry from his home-base on the Ontario frontier. This comprises freeing prisoners at the forts stationed there. Then we must free our quarry's traveling captives. Third, we must make certain that our conscripts do not run away or defect to the other side. Forth, we must strive to keep our losses low, or else our whole movement will dissolve. Nothing to it! Heh?" He laughed, teasing Suzanne.

She returned the laughter, then: "It strikes me odd that we march with native conscripts to help set free native captives. By implication the two seem opposed to each other."

"I am pleased that you introduced that thought, Mademoiselle. You are an astute lass. Let me tell you that the success of our campaign depends heavily upon volunteers: conscripts and captives. Among the captive natives, or prisoners, there is an abundant collection of young men who are eager to join us in battle. They fight for two major reasons: First of all, they want to defend their homeland and the native way of life and we French have elected to support these efforts. Secondly, fighting presents them with an opportunity to reclaim their place among peers. These men have all suffered deep setbacks, losses which diminished their standing in the eyes of their comrades. By volunteering for service, they hope to perform brave deeds in battle and redeem themselves, so to speak. Does any of this make sense, Mademoiselle?"

"Why, yes, Monsieur. I have not thought of it in such profound terms."

"That is understandable. You are young. You are still learning the ways of the frontier."

"I must ask, Monsieur, why people of such opposite backgrounds see fit to brave eternal hardships and conflicts in order to come together."

"By this you mean . . . ?"

" . . . The whites and the native populations."

"In a word, it is *trading*. It is through trade that different peoples come to communicate with each other. Communication builds a knowledge of others, which, in turn brings about a toleration for those of a different stripe. Trade creates an interdependence between two opposing camps, so to speak. Trade breaks down barriers between peoples. For the moment at least they are all equal. One may not exist for very long without the other's support. This is not altogether good or bad. It is something like the marriage of a man and a woman. It is a relationship founded upon supply and demand, which, in the end makes both camps so much the stronger."

"You make a fine instructor, Monsieur. This is indeed my lesson in philosophy for the day," Suzanne quipped.

"It is more than philosophy. Someday someone will put together a new term for it; however, one thing is certain: We are making history as sure as we are standing here."

Suzanne took a step backward. She thought for a moment. "Yes. You are correct, Monsieur. I am so honored to have been chosen for this historical moment." She reached for her journal and made an entry.

"Speaking of history, Suzanne, down through the ages great moments in history owed their success to earlier, smaller events."

She put aside the stylus, eyes upon the tradesman.

"The Spanish captured Montezuma to be sure. Was it for the gold he owned? In the short run, yes. They ultimately wanted to establish an empire and this they accomplished in the long run."

Suzanne nodded in understanding.

"John Smith wed Pocahontas. This we know. Was it out of love? Was it to keep the peace with the Powhatans? Perhaps; however, in the long run his soldiers gained dominance over her father's lands, which led to the collapse of that kingdom and the rise of the English. There are many more examples, Suzanne. Some of them are chronicled in my books. Why am I leading this campaign? Perhaps I enjoy living the part of a student of history."

"A noble venture, Monsieur. Now I know that my mother is part of a greater experiment." Head held high, she breathed deeply. She turned to her father.

James patted his daughter's head. "Your mother is caught up in a plot more complicated than the two of us have the ability to solve. We are with friends, however. They will see us through. One day the three of us will sit back before a warm fire and think of this day of how far we have come."

"I suggest that we try to get some rest, mes amis. We have a full day tomorrow," the tradesman replied.

James addressed the tradesman: "What do we know of our adversary at this point?"

"I have two scouts in the field. They have reported our quarry heading toward Lake Ontario. Their base is no doubt the Fort Oswego. We will follow and wait for him to camp. It is better to intercept him before he reaches the shelter of his garrison. At that point we will be at full complement. I suggest that you retire for the evening."

"Thank you, Monsieur."

"Monsieur York?"

"Yes."

"Spread the word. No one is to light a fire, much less a match in the darkness."

"Yes, Monsieur."

"Monsieur York?"

"Yes."

"We will find Madame York."

"I know, Monsieur. I know. Good night."

"She is but two hours ahead of us."

"Thank you, Monsieur. Good night."

Unable to sleep, Suzanne rummaged through her back pack. She sought out the foodstuffs which Colombe Blanche prepared for her. She settled upon the sausage-filled biscuits and corn cakes. Her meeting with the tradesman delighted her. Through him she learned increasingly more about the woodlands in which she found herself. She moved on to sample a rolled cylinder of dough filled with venison and packed with berries. Thirsty, she drank water from a flask in her pack. Still restless, she longed for companionship. She summoned Aboyant, the self-appointed night watch-guard to come dine with her. True to form, the little man danced to her side. His capricious grin struck a note of frivolity in her and she decided to tease him in a playful manner.

"My dear Aboyant: The more I adore your name, the more I find it a bit cumbersome—not for you, but for others to pronounce. Truly you are not the Barking Dog that your name says you are."

A solemn-faced Aboyant spoke in English: "Madame Colombe Blanche gave me my name a long while ago. It has always sat well with me. It is like an old friend. I have not thought of changing it."

"You care not to offend her?"

"Perhaps. But everyone knows me by Aboyant, although it is far from my birth-name."

"Oh?"

"My true name is Great Bear," he returned, proudly.

"Hmmm. 'Le Grand Ours.' Do you find it attractive?"

"Yes. But some say it is too similar to the name of the War Chief."

"I understand. Colombe Blanche's husband. Hmmm. Go ahead! Pronounce your name."

Aboyant pursed his lips and slowly squeezed the French name out into the open.

"Very pleasing to the ear. I will call you 'Grand Ours' from now on."

"If it pleases you, Mademoiselle. Now I have two names: one for every day and one for special occasions." He went through a series of pulling and stretching movements, contortions of the arms and legs, made all the more difficult, for he sat on a blanket beside Suzanne, spine ram-rod straight. He laughed lightly, pumping his arms and legs. The moonlight illuminated his antics.

Suzanne started to break out in laughter, but in the next instant her father appeared beside her, his finger to his lips, gesturing to her to remain quiet. Abruptly she waved off the little man who returned to his camp vigil. She longed to learn more about the tradesman's purpose on the frontier. Quietly, she addressed her father:

"Father. Do you believe that the tradesman's success bears heavily on the fortunes of his king?"

"A most observant question, Suzanne. In my opinion, King Louis is plagued by war debts. On the Continent he has launched invasions upon European kingdoms to which he has committed thousands of soldiers and millions in pounds. On the surface he is doing this in order to establish French colonies dependent on French trade. Deep down though he hopes to thwart a strong British presence in those regions which have come to threaten many of France's possessions in the far corners of the world. At the same time Louis finds himself besieged by his administrators in the Americas to pump more men and materiel into a sustained colonial effort. Again, more debts. On the field of battle the once vast French military has succumbed to British military reprisals, a lack of munitions and supplies, and shortages in food and clothing. Aside from these harsh truths, Louis is trying to build up his navy to rival that of England. Thus far he has known disappointment, for he is unable to challenge England on the high seas and his treasury is in sore need of replenishment— given his presence on two continents. In a desperate move to curtail expenses, Louis has suggested, upon his minister's advice, the abandonment of funding colonial growth, at least in North America."

"That explains, father, why there are so few French posts in the Lake Country."

"There are bound to be even fewer, Suzanne," a sober James York replied.

"The tradesman is left to his own devices on that score, father."

"It appears that every man must shift for himself, Suzanne."

"Is there any salvation, father?"

"The tradesman hoped to develop the native fur trade to the point of bolstering Louis's treasury. And then there are the natural deposits."

"Natural deposits?"

"Beneath the surface of the land in Pennsylvania are deposits of coal. Coal may be diverted to homes for heating in winter, for cooking at the hearth and for converting iron into everyday articles such as rims for wheels, cooking utensils, heavy arms: cannon and howitzers."

"Rifles?"

"Yes. Rifles. Of course."

"A land worth fighting for, father?"

"I believe that our host will deliver a good fight: however, he has scant support from across the waters. There is, meanwhile, a new threat on the scene."

"Oh?"

"William Pitt, the new Prime Minister. He has begun a vigorous policy of colonization whereby he plans to divest France of all New World territories within two years. Louis is so concerned that he is tempted to relinquish all territories below the St. Lawrence in order to save Canada (33). It is rumored that Montreal and Quebec are so weak that they will fall as easily as snapping a twig with one's fingers. Montreal may fall at any moment. There is all the talk about it on the frontier."

Suzanne gripped her father's shoulder: "We are moved to find mother quickly."

"Yes. Regardless of the outcome, we have the best people on our side. Do you receive that impression?"

"I do. What more have you learned, father?"

"I have heard that Louis believes the natives to be an arrogant and warlike lot and that, following a major setback, he is prepared to cede the Lake Country to the victor." (34).

Suzanne gasped. "What will become of the Bear Chief and the tradesman?"

"They will be exiled from the territories. Worse. They will be taken prisoner. I also do not rule out their sudden demise at the hands of madmen. Perhaps William Pitt will make use of their resourcefulness and grant them a reprieve. That is a remote possibility, however."

"To swear allegiance to the Crown?"

"Yes, in exchange for their lives."

"Life is cruel, father."

"It is not always the good who triumph, Suzanne."

"Let me understand you, father. Given Louis's poor leadership, the tradesman is left to his own devices and everything that takes place from here onward reflects on him. Correct?"

"Well put."

"Well now. Let us give the tradesman our undying support. Let us make this campaign a success. Let us find this abductor of women and children and spit him back into the hind quarters of the British cur which gave him birth." On her feet and pacing to and fro, Suzanne struck a fist into her open palm repeatedly and struggled to keep her voice low. Her limbs burned with fervor. She breathed deeply. Aboyant noticed the profound change in her and interrupted the vigil to stare at her. James York took a half-step backward, but otherwise offered no comment. Out of the darkness the tradesman emerged.

He produced a folded sheet of linen paper. Opening it, he spread it over a blanket, and, by the light of a golden moon, invited James and other principals to gather around him.

"It is a map of our campaign route," he announced with pride. "You see how we move along the Seneca River from west to east. We pick up the Bear Chief's warriors here where the Northern Trail ends, then move on to the Onondaga-Oswego crossing where Le Rocher joins us. Everyone pushes due north on the Oswego River, the last leg of our campaign." Wearing a broad smile, he studied the faces of his audience.

"When does the Sandpiper join us?" James York asked.

"He is en route by war canoe over the Seneca River. I expect that by daybreak we will see him."

"How do you know all of this?" a curious Suzanne asked.

"I have been generous with my scouts and they have been generous with me," the tradesman quipped.

"Are there any pitfalls along the way, Monsieur?" the usually taciturn Cerf Courant inquired in French.

"Ah. So good of you to ask. I almost forgot. There are two cataracts on the Oswego River below our objective. We will need to go around those obstacles by land, unless we cross the river directly. We may have to scuttle all boats." He anticipated James's next question: "Le General Le Rocher is coming by bateau from Lake Onondaga. There is a fording place where the Seneca River meets the lake. It is of small consequence, but the bateaux are bulky and heavy. After he makes his crossing, he will push north on the river to the cataracts. We, of course, will bring up our canoes. At that point we must make an important decision. Do not ask me of it now," he demurred, fingers tracing over the map.

"Do we know where the enemy is at this point?" Suzanne asked.

"He is following the south bank of the Seneca. He needs to make a crossing and I expect him to take advantage of a low stretch in the river: a sandbar, perhaps, and make a crossing. Otherwise he must travel as far as the Onondaga /Seneca crossing—a longer, more tedious route."

"What do you make of him as we speak, Monsieur?" James asked.

"He is eager to return to his home-base. He will travel by the shortest route. He may stop for a respite, for the men are on foot and his horses need food and water. He has been afield continuously without seeing to immediate needs. He is tired, yet cautious. He does not know that we are in pursuit."

"How do you know that?" Suzanne popped up.

"He has posted no rear guard, Mademoiselle. It is not a case of neglect. He simply believes that he is moving too fast to be overtaken."

"And is too strong to be defeated," Cerf Courant added.

"Yes, mon ami. This too is true. Aaah!! Let me tell you that the four principals, namely Stag Deer, the Sandpiper and the rest all have copies of this map. If you look closely in the margins, it tells you where the principals are expected to be located at a particular interval. You see that the Sandpiper is due to pass the point on which we stand between 2 and 3 hours tomorrow morning." He stepped back, smiling with satisfaction.

"You are indeed the artisan, Monsieur," James York conceded.

"I am unable to take full praise for this opus. It comes from the fertile mind of Guy Le Rocher."

"But how do the principals know when to start out?" a puzzled Suzanne inquired.

"Excellent question, Mademoiselle." He withdrew a trail watch from his pocket. "All of my principals have these," he smiled. "I have two remaining." He tossed a watch to James York and Suzanne.

Before James and Suzanne may register appreciation, the tradesman again reached into a pocket. He withdrew two small booklets bound in leather and fitted with a stylus. Tossing them to them, he asked them to inspect them carefully.

"How delightful!" Suzanne squealed. "Calendars." She busily flipped through the blank pages. "Now Watkins has nothing new up on me," she giggled.

"They will prove useful in your travels, Mademoiselle," Marchand spoke, paternally. "Now. Let me see. What have I forgotten? Oh!!

Incidentally I have asked Cerf Courant to be the point man of our expedition. His firm friend, the Bear Chief, has given me to believe in his qualities of leadership. I for one have noticed the strict calmness under stress and keen knowledge of the countryside. If no one takes exception, I nominate Cerf Courant for point-guard." He applauded facetiously and the Yorks and Aboyant reciprocated.

"I still insist that we get some rest," the tradesman reiterated. "Today has become tomorrow. The Sandpiper will be with us soon." He paced back and forth.

"That is why you are still awake, Monsieur. You are worried about the Sandpiper," Suzanne returned.

"Worried? No! Concerned? Yes! Let me see. Our new point-guard must be properly equipped. Come here, Monsieur Cerf Courant." He summarily outfitted him with a back pack of foodstuffs, a rifle, pistol, trail knife, a box of phosphorous flare sticks, compass, a tin of ashes to darken the flesh beneath the eyes, a bar of tallow, which, when mixed with water, made a paste to ward off insect bites, a trail watch which he found by accident, and, finally, a bird-calling device which resembled a wild turkey's chirping. He took a few moments to establish a warning code with Cerf Courant regarding the device— the details of which became their sole property. Soon thereafter, Cerf Courant, bristling with new possessions, walked off into the pitch-black night to begin a vigil.

"For where is he bound? "a curious Suzanne inquired.

"The first assignment. He is to watch for the Sandpiper's arrival and call to us the moment he sees him." The tradesman sought approval. In the next instant Suzanne observed him talking over a shoulder, whereupon, two dark forms came dimly into view behind him. Barely discernible in the darkness, they came to a stop in front of her, two tall warriors emerging from the darkness, speaking not a word. Her heart skipped a beat and she stood poised to cry out in fear as the tradesman casually approached the men, extending a hand.

"Bienvenu, mes amis. Qu'est-ce qu il y a?"—Welcome, my friends. "How goes it?"

He made no reference to Suzanne's plight, introducing the men to her with the usual grand gestures:

"This is Dark Moon and his comrade, Two Bears, two of my scouts, compliments of Ga:yant:hawah:geh." He conferred with the men before breaking off to speak with James York.

"They tell me that the Sandpiper is on his way. They will stand guard here while we try to get some rest." With that he retired to a bed roll, all the while indicating to Suzanne and her father to do the same.

—

Still restless, Suzanne lay awake in a bed roll studying the stars. Alone with her thoughts, she enjoyed the tranquility of the night and longed for the night to continue indefinitely. She lost count of the hour until she heard a faint rustling beside her. A voice called to her softly: "Awake. Awake. We must be on our way."

She bolted upright. "What is the hour, father?"

"A little past two in the morning. The Sandpiper has arrived. It is a new day." He promptly marked the date on a trail calendar: Wednesday, the 13th of September. "We are departing soon."

She found the tradesman sampling a leg of turkey while avidly addressing the Sandpiper. She ate dried grains from her back pack and approached the two men, the better to hear Henri Marchand's delivery. He grinned broadly, a familiar posture when delivering a speech.

"Ga:yant:hawah:geh has been good to me. Personally I believe that it is the 'white' side of him that convinced him to join me (35). I am fighting in good company. I am fighting to uphold the legacy of de Champlin, my boyhood hero, who brought this vast land within the grasp of *La Fleur de Lis* (36). I am fighting for Montcalm, the savior of Montreal and architect of Ticonderoga. I am fighting to honor the missionaries de Menard and Le Moyne, who brought Christianity to this land. I fight to uphold Le Rocher's place in the Lake Country: Le Rocher, the one and constant friend to the native populations. I also fight for the day that this land will have its own form of government, one in which men and women of many origins will call each other by their first name and live side by side as neighbors and friends." He bowed deeply before the small audience gathered before him. Cerf Courant and the Sandpiper came alongside and together the three campaigners fell to studying trail maps. Presently the tradesman broke away to address the campaigners in full:

"We depart shortly. I urge everyone to take a light breakfast. The sausage rolls are excellent. I took the pains to place tender fruits into these tins. Believe me. I know." He held up a small, cylindrical tin complete with a lid. "Your fruits and vegetables will remain fresh inside. They are ready for the long haul. Do not forget to bury the remains of your meal. Keep the tins, however," he laughed.

Events moved quickly. The guides, Dark Moon and Two Bears, filled a wagon with provisions, hitching it to a stout horse. Everyone broke camp together, operating in near-silence. A column formed. Cerf Courant took a place at the head. Behind him rode the tradesman, followed in turn by James and Suzanne York. Aboyant and the two guides, and the Stag Deer's warriors followed, leaving Cornplanter's conscripts to bring up the rear. Suzanne looked about her, but failed to locate the Sandpiper.

"How soon you forget, dear daughter," James York reminded her. "They have taken to the river. We are going to accompany him on land."

"How confusing," a tired Suzanne in need of sleep, mumbled. She dropped her head low in the saddle. Her mount chose its own path.

The column left the security of the gully to skirt south over brushy lowlands. With the dawn a number of hours distant, the tradesman depended on the guides to lead him through the darkness to the shore of the Seneca River. The party plodded along tentatively, ever-wary of dangers, yet, in due course, the river came into view, its glimmering surfaces illuminated by a full moon. Cerf Courant ran ahead. Returning, to the fold, he confirmed the Sandpiper's location, thus dispelling all fears of the chieftain's whereabouts.

The tradesman warned the campaigners of sunken holes beside the riverbank, holes deep enough to hobble a horse or break a wagon's rim. He brought out another concern: "This is the season of the mosquito. Coupled with black flies, they carry infestations which will kill the innocent sojourner. There is not a profound remedy to my knowledge. I have found that they come out when the sun reaches its zenith at midday. Therefore, we will want to have completed our trek along the river by then. Questions?"

No one stirred and the pace continued. "Oh!! Before I forget," he mused. "Snakes are attracted by the heat of the day and tend to rest on the river bank. They like warm places and are not opposed to residing in a traveler's boot. Thrashing about in the water arouses them. They become angry and bite. It is not you campaigners that I fear for. It is your horses. An unwarranted disturbance will set them to bucking, bringing the rider to capitulate into the river. Well, then. You know the end of this little tale."

Suzanne looked beneath her mount and breathed a sigh of relief. Others of her party followed suit. Soon the tradesman called a halt, and, facing the swollen ranks, spoke slowly and distinctly: "Please do not consume food along the way. All of our food comes with wrappings. One tends to discard the wrapping. It attracts curious creatures of the forest. In turn, wandering eyes may spy the wrapping and conclude that a passing unit camped here. Our unit!!" Smiling coquettishly, he whimpered in the manner of a chastised child at the hands of a scolding mother.

All along the river walk clouds of early-morning mist rose above the surface of the water. Soft vapors pushed the mist landward where it billowed and thickened and curled around trees, obscuring the campaigners' vision, making travel difficult. For a short period the loss of visibility ground the expedition to a halt. A commotion behind her drew Suzanne's attention. Aboyant left her side in a rush to investigate. Others in the party joined him. She heard splashing and shouts of anger and, then, nothing. Soon, Aboyant returned to the column. She leaned far astride in the saddle, the better to see him. He blurted out a report:

"Horses fell into the river. One man has drowned."

"What are we to do?" Suzanne asked, alarmed.

"We are taking the victim with us, Mademoiselle." He noted her concern." If we bury him here, animals—worse yet—the enemy may find him and track us."

Suzanne nodded in understanding. Men placed the body in a wagon and the tradesman signaled the column to advance. Under Cerf Courant's guidance the column pressed doggedly eastward along the misty pathway.

* * *

Early that morning the Round Tops lay saturated with a thick cloud of mist. Plumes of heavy moisture hung suspended in mid-air, flowing between the conical hills, descending to envelop the grounds on which the residents slept. Early-risers found themselves bathed in beads of water which lingered upon their blankets and all exposed extremities with equanimity. Everyone longed for the sun to burn away the obfuscating mist while they dug deeper into their bedding.

The Bear Chief, an early-riser, paid little heed to the mist. Drawing a blanket tightly about the shoulders, he donned the emblematic bonnet of a chieftain and made for the center-most mound of the nascent village. Here, at the mound of Tah:gah:jute, he paused before climbing the short, well-worn path to the summit. His sons prepared to scamper after him before Colombe Blanche restrained them. At the summit the Bear Chief bowed his head in contemplation. He looked below the base of the mound where the logs of a new home lay stacked in neat rows preparatory to assembly. He looked to the north where the gabled roof of Maple Grove poked through the thick cloudy cover. He looked to the south entrance of the village where that one lone remnant of the Battle of Osco, a six-pounder, stood vigil. Tall and straight and stern of countenance, the Bear Chief turned to face the collection of residents who gathered on the plain below him. He discerned Watkins among the throng, surrounded by a party of warriors. The address that he planned to give centered upon these very warriors, men whose spirits he hoped to kindle prior to their taking the field to join Henri Marchand. Fawn stood beside Watkins, his steady companion of late. In the background Colombe Blanche tended to culinary pursuits— the boys clinging to her. Her kettles held foods for warriors in anticipation of the imminent campaign.

Rising to full height, the Bear Chief held his arms aloft. Everyone fell silent. Colombe Blanche ushered the boys to the mound to hear their father speak. He spoke in French, although he greeted the bystanders in the native tongue: "Sge:no! Gao:dehswe!"—Hello! Come over here all of you!

"Today you embark on a historic journey. Never before have you been called upon to go forth from your village to defy a predator. Yes, there is a predator along the frontier who is determined to drive us away from our cherished lands. He also is determined to drive away any and all of our allies. It is not only we of the Nations Iroquois, but our staunch friend and ally, Guy Le Rocher and the undaunted Henri Marchand, who are in danger of becoming dispossessed. We have already witnessed a sample of this predator's self-serving ways with the sacking of our dear Osco. This predator is omnivorous. I do not believe that he has passed from the scene. At this moment he covets the treasures of other villages in the Confederacy. These are mere trifles to him, for his unquenchable thirst for riches compels him to rape the countryside. He searches in a quest that will never end, for his lust holds no bounds. In draining our life-blood, he hopes to dissolve us as a People. I say to you that no man has the authority to do this. The Creator put us here. The Creator is greater than any man, white or brown, and all must defer to the Creator's will, for, to contradict the Creator is to deny His existence and authority. What is more, in his stead the Creator has named us, the Haudenosaunee, to care for His domain here on earth and I intend to carry forth the Creator's intent to its fullest extent. This is in keeping with the legend of our Hiawatha. He received orders from the Creator those many years ago on the shores of Lake Onondaga when he sat with the Keepers of the Flame, our brothers and sisters, the Onondagas. We must unite to castigate this interloper who poses in the uniform of our sometimes trading-partner, the English. We will restore our People's dignity once again and drive the interloper from our lands and waters and forests.

"Already our brothers from the western villages march to join us. According to my sources, they suffered grave losses at the hands of this interloper. Our friend, Le General, Guy Le Rocher, also joins us at the fording place of Lake Onondaga. With our combined strength we will drive the invader back to his place of origin beside the great lake, Ontario. From there he will sail away on a 'sailing bird' and harm us no longer. His grip on us will be loosened once and for all and our brothers at Chonodote, Tiohero, and Kanandesaga and all points of the Confederacy will be avenged. Let us march on to victory." Arms overhead, he waved them in a sign of victory to the accompaniment of a rousing acclamation from the spirited assembly.

At the Bear Chief's invitation, warriors and residents partook of the foods which Colombe Blanche and Fawn prepared. In that predawn setting, surrounded by low-lying clouds of mist, the villagers assumed a festive spirit and a general atmosphere of conviviality permeated the camp. Warriors gathered weapons and in twos and threes returned to the mound to receive marching orders. The Bear Chief did not disappoint them:

"Follow the Northern Trail* out of the village. You will meet with the Seneca River. Wait on its banks. You will join forces with our brothers and follow the command of Henri Marchand. I myself am remaining behind to supervise the completion of our homes and village before the winter sets in." At that point the Bear Chief descended the mound and joined his wife and sons at breakfast. Everyone dined in leisure, but several of the warriors called for the supreme leader to join them on the trail.

"Eh:kne:geh?"—'Are you coming with me?' one man asked in disbelief.

The Bear Chief reiterated his reason for declining: "I must stay to do the building."

"Sanigohaeda:s:geh?"—Do you understand? he asked the man.

"Nyah:weh, hnyagwai:Hahsenowa:neh. Oneh:ni:egade:di."—Thank you, Bear Chief. I will now be on my way.

The Bear Chief neglected to give the true reason for declining. During an earlier meeting with the tradesman he agreed to remain apart from the active campaign in an effort to preserve the anonymity of the Round Tops, and, more significantly, the guests: Watkins and James and Suzanne York. He believed that the success of the campaign depended on the utmost secrecy of the Round Top's location and the security of key witnesses. For the present the Bear Chief's patented response silenced further inquiry.

In terms of weapons, a respectable number of warriors chose the musket with powder and ball, gifts of the tradesman for the most part. However, traditional weapons predominated: bow and arrow and lance. The overwhelmingly favorite weapon proved to be the war club. Light in weight, it may be wielded by hand in the manner of a hammer, or launched at an adversary with a swift arm-thrust. One may also parry with it in close quarters, making short, knife-life bursts. Similar in handling to a slashing saber, it may be brought down heavily upon the exposed flesh of an enemy. The warrior took great pains in assembling a war club: tapering the shaft, choosing a suitable stone or piece of iron, wrapping the finished product in water-resistant sinew. In the end he painted it or added strips of hide or otherwise embellished it with signs of his own identity. Either simple or elaborate, the war club drew praises among the warriors for its versatility, durability, and balance.

Weapons and foodstuffs chosen, the warriors reconvened at the mound to choose an interim leader of their party. Eventually the man called Fox Tail came forward. Bronzed and tall, a brother of Cerf Courant, he carried the Bear Chief's recommendation. Hair braided, he smiled the kind of smile a fox sported after making a kill. Fox Tail assembled the warriors in a column of fifty earnest young men. Turning on a heel, he headed due north, out of the village's immediate environs. A few rods later and the party crossed the dusty Genesee Road and headed down the narrow native trail which flanked Maple Grove. In silence they descended a hillside which disappeared at its base into marshy ground. Turning east, the party skirted wetlands and followed a vibrant stream, named Osco, several rods. Turning north, they crossed the stream at the fording place**. Fox Tail called a halt to tell the warriors that the Northern Trail began beneath their feet and ran straight ahead over hills and lowlands to the Seneca River where a hamlet of hunters and lumbermen lived. The Marchand map gave the location as Weed's Basin. Despite a sudden downpour, the column moved out briskly. The rains pushed aside the thick, low-lying clouds of mist and soon bright blue skies heralded the beginning of a comfortable autumn day.

* * *

Marching under clear skies, Fox Tail's warriors reached the Seneca River at its junction with the Northern Trail in a scant one half hour. The Sandpiper's warriors awaited him, canoes drawn close to the river bank. To the east the sun began to rise, poking tender rays of light over the horizon. The two forces paused to await Marchand's arrival from the west. Upon arriving, the tradesman fell to perusing a raft of maps, the preponderance of which sent a bevy of confusion through the ranks. An annoyed Marchand summoned James York to lend him support in reading them:

"James. What do we know of the enemy?"

"He travels with many prisoners. His soldiers are battle-tested; therefore, he is confident of his ability to offset an attack. He is not in a great hurry to reach home and he is looking for the makings of a camp in which to rest his soldiers."

"Yes. Good, James. Come look at this map." He directed James's attention to a section which he circled with a finger. "Do you see a place to set up camp with suitable surroundings?"

The tradesman made a cursory inspection of a map. "What is this, James? A swamp? A lake?" His finger outlined a substantial body of water situated about six leagues south of the Ontario-Oswego complex of forts.

"That, mon ami, is Lake Neatahwantah* an inland lake— a relic of the ice age. I am pleased that you chose it. I thought along the same lines, Monsieur. It is my theory that our adversary is going there to rest before he makes a final burst for his base." He inspected the map further.

"Look, James! There are deep woodlands on three sides, filled with prey, no less. This open space is beach. Sandy or clay, it offers a flat, well-drained surface on which to pitch tents. To the north are grassy fields—the better to take refuge— even make part of an escape route. I think we have it, James," he exclaimed, folding the document.

"Are we able to surprise him in such a location?"

"Of course that remains to be seen; however, there are several advantages for us: For one, he knows not of our existence or presence. Two, we have a mobile strike-force which is able to strike and flee quickly. Third, the woodlands and grassy plain make excellent staging grounds from which to launch an assault." He looked up approvingly at the taller man, a gleam in his eye.

"What do you think, James?" the tradesman asked, in a demeanor begging for a response.

"The novelty of it. The boldness: moving quickly and striking from several points."

"Ah, James. Good! I believe you have struck the proper chord: Striking from several points *at the same moment* will carry the field for us."

"I fear for Caroline. Her exact whereabouts are unknown. She may be with our adversary."

"She may be with his *captives*, James. If this is true, she will be under guard: usually to the rear of the main body. We must separate the captives from the soldiers."

"Easier said than done, heh, Henri?"

"Not necessarily. If they camp, the captives will be cordoned off in seclusion. When we strike, one arm of our forces will free the captives."

"And if they do not camp, Monsieur?"

"Then we lay siege to their main base—after we seal off any routes of escape."

The tradesman sought to encourage James. "Let us hope that he camps for our sake. A victory for us will bind the warriors to our cause indefinitely and help us to set the terms for a suitable peace."

James listened attentively. "Do we take prisoners once we are successful?"

"A good question." Stroking his chin, the tradesman elaborated on the matter: "With prisoners we may negotiate for peace on our terms. Prisoners present a 'bargaining chip' which we must exploit to our advantage, given that we are in the minority before British military might. Prisoners stand to become a tool to make us look strong at the expense of our opponent. Believe me, James. Now is the moment to appear strong. The whole world is watching. This may very well be Onontio's last opportunity to preserve his standing in the Americas." He paced back and forth, wringing his hands.

"What is your greatest fear, Monsieur?" James asked soberly.

"My greatest fear? I have several. For one we rely on an army of volunteers—volunteers against seasoned soldiers. That leads to missed opportunities—failing to recognize opportunities as they arise and taking the required steps to subdue the enemy." He stopped pacing to glance along the Northern Trail for signs of the Bear Chief's band.

"If I may offer advice, Monsieur, your *native* forces are seasoned fighters. They are driven by a passion to avenge losses. In my view, you have made good choices."

"Look, James!! Bless my weary heart!!" Hat in hand, the tradesman ran down the Trail as quickly as his broad girth permitted him. Other principals joined him and, soon, emerging into the sunlight of a new day, strode Fox Tail with the Bear Chief's unit. He grinned broadly and sought out his brother, Cerf Courant, and the two men firmly embraced each other. Their joy spread among the campaigners.

"Everyone take a short respite," the tradesman spoke loudly, in order to make himself heard above the confusion which the coming together of so many bands generated. He retired to speak with the Sandpiper.

"Oh:nehsi:yo. How are the conscripts? Are they trustworthy?"

"They are good, Monsieur Marchand. Look for yourself. Do you see any of them running away?" He laughed and patted the tradesman on the shoulder.

"Did you feed them before you left Kanandesaga?" the tradesman asked, still worried.

"Yes! Wild bear meat. Raw!!" He laughed loudly, making light of the tradesman's nervousness. "I rode the waters of the Seneca during the darkness to meet you. I rode without stopping and my hands are numb, but I made it in the presence of great camaraderie." Nodding, Oh:nehsi:yo acknowledged the oarsmen.

Glowing with confidence with the choice of warriors, he pressed on:

"The conscripts are worthy young men. They rowed me here. Granting my warriors a favor, they relieved them of the burden. Without the conscripts to row, we may all be walking." He spoke with conviction.

Seeking to preserve friendly ties, the tradesman bowed low and spoke: "That is why I asked Ga:yant:hawah:geh to send his conscripts. I knew of their loyalty," he returned, embracing the chieftain.

Disturbed over what he deemed the tradesman's lack of sensitivity regarding the conscripts, Oh:nehsi:yo nevertheless accepted Marchand's embrace. He whispered into the tradesman's ear: "I have brought you forty able warriors and forty able conscripts. I see no difference between them. Thanks to Ga:yant:hawah:geh, they go together very well."

The tradesman remarked in all humility: "It is good to have friends like you. Now let us move on to victory."

"I will accept nothing less, Monsieur Marchand," Oh:nehsi:yo returned. Brisk for his years, the slightly-stooped chieftain, sun-beaten form weathered and furrowed, moved off. Returning shortly, he held a long bow aloft, presenting it to the tradesman.

"I have many of these aboard—gifts from Ga:yant:hawah:geh. The arrow carries a great distance farther with this." He clenched his fist. "Of course I too have the musket." He smiled to an aide brandishing a long rifle.

"My canoes are extraordinary, Monsieur. They are what the English call 'warships.'" He laughed sardonically and the two men shook hands, whereupon Oh:nehsi:yo directed the warriors manning canoes to prepare to depart.

The march resumed. Fox Tail's men fell in behind the Stag Deer's warriors. Briefly, the two bands spent precious moments to renew old acquaintances, climaxing the rendez-vous with hoops and shouts, much to the tradesman's dismay. Not one to arouse the tradesman's acerbity, Fox Tail joined Cerf Courant and both brothers passed to the head of the column. By arrangement, Marchand boarded the lead canoe. He brought James and Suzanne aboard. Aboyant, never far from Suzanne's side, begged to go along. The last to come into line, the conscripts and warriors from Kanandesaga, brought up the rear of the column. Marchand reminded everyone on land to look for signs of the enemy's crossing of the Seneca. Thereupon, the march resumed once again.

By late morning Cerf Courant reported sighting the conflux of many tracks on the muddy bank. They ran in profusion before mysteriously disappearing. He sent Fox Tail ahead to retrace them while the column plodded on. Gradually a pattern emerged whereas the tracks appeared, only to disappear. Fox Tail offered a resolution:

"He is looking for a fording place. He wants to cross to the north bank. So far the river is too high. The many horses tell me that he looks with great care."

"The best fording place is where Lake Gannentaa* meets with the Oswego River," Cerf Courant offered.

Fox Tail remained adamant: "No! No! That is not where he will cross. On a clear day the sentries of Pointe Aux Bois will pick you off. He will make a crossing well in advance of the fording place. Look for sandbars in the river or other high points."

The column and canoes set the same beat in order to keep abreast of each other. Marchand and Oh:nehsi:yo kept a vigilant eye on the trees and greenery lining the north shore of the river. Overhead the sky stretched forth in an endless blanket of deep blue and with visibility thus enhanced, little if anything escaped the watch of the observant principals. Presently they pointed boldly skyward —maneuvers that alerted everyone. Suzanne and her father observed a thick circle of birds on the wing. Periodically, birds broke from the circle to spiral downward. Oh:nehsi:yo called a halt to operations and an eager Aboyant begged to go ashore to reconnoiter. He returned shortly, breathing heavily:

"It is the remains of a hunting party. They took a number of deer, built a camp fire and ate their fill, and carried off the remainder."

"But he has not crossed over yet, has he?" the tradesman asked.

"No. He has not. His tracks are many on the south shore," Fox Tail answered.

"I understand. He has gone hunting for meat, no less. This is true?" the tradesman asked.

"Yes. He has entered the river at this point." Fox Tail traced a line in the muddy bank.

"Hmmm. He has boats at his disposal," the tradesman deduced.

"It is *not* a boat," Cerf Courant interjected. He made a series of hand gestures before drawing an object in the mud. The principals gathered around him.

"Oh!! A pontoon!" Suzanne exclaimed. "He entered by pontoons." She jumped up and down in excitement.

"Yes. That must be it," the tradesman conceded. "He came well-prepared and tried to throw us off in the process. We are learning more about him with each turn. This is a foe well-equipped to live on the frontier." He slapped a thigh: "Now we know of his little secret." He laughed lightly.

The expedition continued on course, the campaigners on land and water keeping apprised of each other's presence. Privately, Marchand reviewed the conscripts' performance thus far: 'They required no supervision and consisted of young native males, untested in battle, new to the immediate countryside. A willingness to abandon the confines of Kanandesaga, coupled with strong exuberance, made of them worthy members of the campaign and worthy of his trust'.

Cries rang out. Instinctively Cerf Courant and Fox Tail called a halt and the marchers grudgingly ceased operations. The brothers raced to the rear of the column. There they found three young men, writhing in pain on the muddy bank, Marchers gathered around them, powerless to assist them. The scene failed to dismay the two seasoned scouts. Sternly they barked out commands:

"Gado:goht! Gatge:se: Gatgahtoh!, Fox Tail called."—Let me pass through! Let me look at it!"

The onlookers lingered without backing away.

"Sago:ne:k!"—Move yourself away, a grim-faced Cerf Courant threatened.

He poured through the pack of bystanders, some moaning, some docile. Before him lay the three young men, ankles securely snared by iron traps—traps planted to pin down large animals such as bear and moose. Blood issued from where the teeth of the traps creased the flesh of the young men.

"Ta:desagye! Ahgwih:hehsye!"—You keep still! Do not touch it! Cerf Courant ordered the stricken youth.

Marchand and Oh:nehsi:yo hastened ashore. Fox Tail conferred with the two principals and in a matter of moments returned to the side of the stricken youth, an iron bar in hand. He handed it to Cerf

Courant. Kneeling beside the first young man, Fox Tail pulled mightily on the two inter-locking strips of the trap, the pair of serrated, iron teeth tugging at the victim's flesh. The teeth parted only slightly, yet, with great resolve, Cerf Courant jammed the iron bar between them, creating a gap along the course of the strips. Together, both scouts forced the strips wider apart through a combination of pulling upward on the iron bar and forcing the strips apart by hand. All the while a concerned Marchand held the trap firmly to the earth. The young man screamed, yet obeyed Cerf Courant unfalteringly.

"You pull foot out now," he called.

Wearily the young man obliged. Someone offered him a cloth and he wiped away excessive blood. Marchand called for a bag of medical supplies which Cerf Courant pressed into his outstretched hand.

"Sanohgwadrae:geh?"—Do you have medicine?

The tradesman brought out a bottle of bromine. He wiped the wound at the ankle with the brown, antiseptic compound. He applied a coating of iodine, a bitter, reddish-brown compound, a known healing agent. Taking a clean linen cloth, he wrapped the young man's ankle, binding the cloth with a length of deer hide drawn to the fineness of a string.

"Voilà! C'est très bon!"—There! That is very good," he spoke, stepping back and wiping his brow.

Fox Tail spoke to the youth: "Dehsda!"—Stand up!

Slowly the youth complied, whereupon Cerf Courant intervened:

"Esane:yo! Ahgwih:hehsye! Sanigohaeda:s:geh?"—It will heal! Do not touch it! Do you understand?

Cerf Courant expressed gratefulness to the tradesman, who called for a litter for the young man. The fate of the two remaining youth loomed imminent. Applying time-honored skills, the two scouts extricated the victims by mid-morning without serious repercussions. The Sandpiper believed that going by canoe afforded the young men greater comfort. He chose three warriors in the canoes to replace the wounded youth on land, after which he placed all three victims in canoes, their extremities wrapped in gauze. During the transition, Marchand and Cerf Courant stood aside to reflect on the turn of events:

"It is unexpected to find bear traps in these parts of the Lake Country," the tradesman began.

The pensive Cerf Courant spoke: "They are not bear traps. They are for the beaver—and for *you*."

Fox Tail studied the position of the sun: "He has gained the advantage of putting a great distance between us."

"He knows of our presence, perhaps," the tradesman asked.

"No! He lacks scouts to tell him of an enemy in the wings, In lieu of a rear guard, he has placed out traps to ward off an enemy," Fox Tail offered. "He may have stolen the traps from peaus blancs settlements. They have traps to hunt the beaver. The beaver is highly desired by the peaus blancs throughout distant lands."

"Exactly. Yes. That is the origin of the traps. They have been set to snare the first wretches who set foot on them," the tradesman reasoned. He looked about him. The principals appeared restless to move ahead.

"So be it. Let us go about our affair," he uttered, in a mixture of relief and resignation.

Marchand dispatched Dark Moon and Two Bears to reconnoiter the enemy. Aboyant, too restless to remain dormant indefinitely, sought permission to search along the shoreline for signs of a crossover. Marchand consented and the little man set out to scour the riverbank. He kept close to the reeds and rushes which grew in abundance in an unbroken line beside the marchers' muddy trail. From her canoe Suzanne caught glimpses of her little friend bobbing up and down like a bird looking for worms. She laughed to herself, but understood the significance of the task. She brought out her journal.

The marching column advanced in silence. On the river the oarsmen pulled in a steady beat, keeping abreast of the long defile. The morning became afternoon and the remainder of the day appeared destined to descend into monotony when Aboyant dashed headlong down the trail, having abandoned the dogged searching. He summoned the leaders to call a halt. Fox Tail yielded to Aboyant's demand and once again the expedition rested prematurely, both segments coming to meet along the riverbank— a communal buzz spreading through the ranks.

Aboyant brought Fox Tail and Cerf Courant with him as he ran back to a selected place by the riverbank. He scurried to the waterline, pushing back reeds and rushes. He pointed ahead to mid-stream where the river bottom rose up to form a substantial island running north and south from shore to shore. He stomped down upon the bank, making bold impressions in the soft soil. He gestured toward the island. The brothers came up quickly.

"Look! Look! They go through here!" He ventured out into the river.

The brothers watched. Others came to observe the source of the little man's excitement.

Entering the river, Aboyant clambered onto the sandy spit of land.* "Look! Look!"

The tradesman joined the brothers. Training a pair of lenses on the place, he nodded, handing the apparatus to Cerf Courant, who in turn accepted the tradesman's conclusion:

"Horses. Many horses pass through here," he spoke. He motioned for Aboyant to come ashore.

"The river is low here," Aboyant gushed forth. "The marks in the earth are deep. Many men riding many horses. There are two sets of prints beside each other. They rode two abreast and broke through on the opposite bank through the rushes."

"They rode due north—north to Oswego," the tradesman declared. He searched haphazardly through pockets for a map. Failing to secure it, he called upon James York who produced a copy of the valued parchment. In all haste the tradesman unfolded it over the dried grasses of the trail. The two men fell upon it—scouring it.

"He is heading straight for the lake, James. He either has a map or knows the region well. He will camp there. Do you see this marsh, James? It falls back from the lake to approximately where we stand. He will skirt the marsh and come up beside the grasslands to the right leading to the beach. He has a broad lead over us. Nevertheless, that gives him less of a reason to suspect us. Good!" Jumping up, the tradesman threw back his shoulders. Fingers snapping, he called for all to hear: "We have them within our grasp!"

Several campaigners registered impatience. Cerf Courant spoke for them:

"Gyahde:dih! Desa:dri:heh!"—Let us get going! You hurry!

The Stag Deer stole a glance at the map and hastened to speak with Marchand: "It is in all certainty Neatahwantah. The Bear Chief and I know it from our youth. Our families camped there to hunt and fish. Every summer the Bear Chief's father took us there on the way to Oneida Castle. A sandy beach borders the eastern shore."

Beside himself with joy, the tradesman carefully folded James's map, begging him to conceal it from view. He called a short conference of the principals, asking each man for private thoughts on confronting an adversary.

Oh:nehsi:yo spoke: "We must attack through the forest. His booming engines are not able to knock down trees."

The Stag Deer proposed sealing off all avenues of escape and driving the enemy into the lake to drown.

"I believe that our smaller force is more mobile than his—able to strike quickly and withdraw." James conceded.

Cerf Courant approved of enticing the enemy to pursue them and leading him into a trap.

The tradesman reflected before speaking: "We will move on to rendezvous with Le Rocher as planned. We too will skirt the marshy grounds. We will approach the lake in a roundabout fashion—through the forest on the east side of the lake by way of the Oswego River. Everyone will walk into the forest and take assigned positions. Ah! Before I forget. We need to tell the General that we are drawing near our rendezvous." He wrote a hasty message on a leaf of paper and handed it to the tracker, Dark Moon. Secreting the message, the trusted scout set forth along the river walk at a brisk pace, leaving everyone to return to formation. The column and canoes picked up the cadence once again and the campaign recommenced in full swing.

* * *

Guillaume Le Rocher, Le General, stood in the center of the Commons at Pointe Aux Bois. There, at 11 hours in the forenoon, he awaited the arrival of the courier from the west, the runner bringing him word of Marchand. He welcomed the sunlight and clear skies as harbingers of good things to come. He paced to and fro, nervousness mounting, the way it always did whenever he undertook labors of major significance. Attuned to the slightest movement on the grounds, he turned swiftly at the sound of a faint rustling to the rear. Smiling, he extended a hand to the tall, spare man who slipped in beside him, the same man who bore him numerous messages over these past several weeks. He accepted the tracker's message, then waved him off to the commissary to enjoy a hearty breakfast. He glanced at the message and heard himself say: "Good! All is well."

He walked swiftly across the Commons to the bell-tower. Stepping inside the housing of the structure, he chose to ring the bell by hand instead of ascending the serpentine stairway leading to the carillons suspended far overhead. The tallest structure at Pointe Aux Bois, the bell-tower allowed one to observe the full length and width of Lake Onondaga, and, on exceptionally clear days, to see the Oswego River where it met with the lake at the fording place. He tugged on the thick rope twice and the bell sent out a bold and brassy resonance signaling the call to assembly. He initiated this function daily, but today held special meaning for him.

In twos and threes the men poured out of the barracks. Outfitted in the dress of an explorer, they wore the customary blouse, jacket and knee-length boots of the woodsman. Largely muted in tone, their attire featured seasonal colors: browns and greens and russet. One hundred and thirty men, a combination of yearling soldier and woodsman, took to the Commons, weapons and packs in hand. They formed into neat rows of ten across and at least twelve men deep. Assuming a parade-rest, the General came to stand before them.

At 46 years of age, the General marked the 10th year as commandant of Pointe Aux Bois. In the summer of 1750, he assumed the administration of an abandoned and dilapidated 'pile of scraps,' to quote himself and others. To his knowledge, no one, since the days of Frontenac, Governor-General of New France in North America, presided over the garrison (37) long enough to bring it within the spectrum of successful French trading posts. Local Onondagas occupied the site occasionally. Sir William Johnson, the British Secretary of Colonial Affairs deferred making the site the center of a growing English-speaking colony after the discovery of salt around the shores of the lake. Land agents tried to sell parcels of land to the highest bidders, but colonists of the period possessed little in currency, and such early attempts at colonization failed. Thereafter, the garrison and environs passed into obscurity until one Henri Marchand teamed with Guy Le Rocher. Together they revived a small part of the once-flourishing French fur trade by securing trading privileges with the local Onondagas. How long this experiment may endure remained unknown, but the General, standing before the corps on that bright and sunny day, remained vowed to fight for all things French.

A survivor of King Louis' foreign engagements, the General sought a safer, more profitable venue, one in which he may supplement his dwindling fortune. He expended much of the family wealth on leading a field command in Europe. He jumped at the prospect of immigrating to North America to participate in Louis' policy of cultivating the favor of the native inhabitants, whom Louis regarded as crucial in perpetuating France's toehold on Canada and the lands south of the St. Lawrence. Louis created agencies, bodies through which he may bring the *savage* native into the French fold. The agencies, three in number: governmental, religious, and entrepreneurial, required administrators to move among the native populations. The colonial governor headed the governmental agency. Priests and missionaries composed the religious arm, and artisans, craftsmen, and tradesmen constituted the entrepreneurial branch. Louis chose the General to administer to the needs of the tradesmen in the old French garrison on the heights beside Lake Onondaga. The General named it Pointe Aux Bois, for the structure occupied a 'point in the woods.'

Acting on behalf of the colonial governor, the General made all staffing appointments at Pointe Aux Bois. These included a head of stores and provisions, an adjutant of arms, a warehouse supervisor, a horticulturist, a culinary specialist, and a tradesman, among others. He named Henri Marchand, a newly-arrived merchant, to the post of tradesman and in due course learned that the man possessed a number of leadership qualities which at once embraced a number of outstanding positions. In concert with Marchand, the General opened the garrison's doors to the native. He willingly accepted gifts of furs and pelts and doled out ample quantities of goods in return. He held so-called trading days in which the Commons displayed a wealth of goods essential to the native's well-being. On a typical day he dispensed with iron pots and skillets, wool blankets, mittens, scarves, stockings, leather belts, tooth brushes, tooth picks, and combs, mirrors, soap, candles, dishes and serving trays, eating utensils, bowls, mugs and glasses. A cache of rifles and pistols along with shot and powder stood nearby for the avid hunter and each article for disposal carried a premium, usually a sum on an affixed label designating the number of furs and pelts required for the article's purchase. Trading grew brisk among the natives and word of Marchand's magnanimity spread rapidly throughout the Confederacy, in such a manner that inhabitants from the far reaches of the Lake Country came regularly to the tradesman's stores.

The General set standards of conduct for all who entered Pointe Aux Bois. He rewarded consistent good conduct by granting the privileges of access to his ample stores. A gregarious administrator, the General supplied the basic needs of the indigenous populations. This often meant opening the doors in the dead of winter to natives who otherwise went without food, clothing, and shelter. Throughout the seasons, scores of natives elected to reside permanently within the garrison. With the Onondagas the General went a further step in providing schooling in reading and writing in the English language. He also encouraged them to adopt the tenets of Catholicism and retained a handful of missionaries to give instruction in Catholic dogma.

—

The General stood before the corps. Lean and lithe, his attire that of a man dedicated to extolling the life of a professional soldier. He wore long hair about the neck, gathering it in a thick ribbon. He customarily donned a linen waist jacket with deep breast pockets, a pair of forest-green trousers, wide-brimmed leather hat, and black, leather boots climbing high on the calf. The long-sleeved shirt, white and starched with broad collar, ruffled slightly in the vapors which tugged playfully at the thick, flowing bandanna streaming from his neck. A strong leather belt gripped his middle. He pulled softly on a pair of black kid gloves and, standing at parade-rest, commanded the assembly to stand at attention and cease all chatter.

He called for one hundred volunteers to man a small fleet of bateaux. The flat-bottomed and ponderous wooden vessels lay sheltered on the beach below the garrison. His intentions announced, he waited a long moment for the words to take root. Earlier that morning, so many men volunteered for the expedition that he established a lottery under which men may become randomly selected. He settled upon one hundred and twenty five yeomen and silenced further requests by quickly departing the Commons. He led the brash and ripe youth to the gateway which opened upon the beach far below. Exhorting them down the steep stairway, he lined them along the beach in a solid, unbroken column and proceeded to deliver instructions in loading and navigating the bulky craft. Eager to learn, the recruits pressed forward, whereupon he brought out a vessel for the occasion:

"Always balance your load equally. Wrap perishables in oiled cloth. Pole in shallow water. Use oars in deeper water. Travel with a boatswain. Stay shy of submerged rocks and boulders." He looked about, expecting a raft of lamentations, but none came forth.

The General regarded the novices intently. "Excellent, men. Load your craft and take a short tour of the lake. I have marked off a course for you. You will notice that I have placed at least one native in each bateau. The native is an able boatman. You are to follow his lead and recommendations without question. Clear? Good! Have at it, men!! Come back in one piece." He effected a broad grin and withdrew to observe the unfolding of events.

The men, having loaded the bateaux, set out into shallow waters over a prescribed course. They poled and rowed and shifted their loads to accommodate the conditions of the lake. They turned at strategically-placed markers. Seated ashore with seasoned Onondagas, the General made note of the men's progress: One bateau listed dangerously, spilling cargo. Another became affixed to boulders below the surface. A third boat missed a marker and spun out into the lake adrift. The General wrote down these indiscretions and upon the men's return, he sent them out again with revised instructions. The Onondagas on shore laughed among themselves. Their levity served to encourage the men and on the second attempt they made a complete circuit without incident, returning to receive the cheers of buoyant comrades.

"Good. I am hungry. Let us all go for breakfast," the General called. The neonate boatmen scrambled up the heights of the bluff to dine in the mess hall, not knowing that the most difficult test awaited them. The Onondagas followed at leisure for they knew what lay in store for the yeomen.

Following breakfast, the General led the neonates to the water's edge once again. He loaded a bateau and, bringing a boatswain, rowed the craft into deep water. The yeomen watched from shore as he put the craft through a series of precision-like maneuvers. He executed combinations of racing, banking, turning, and sudden-stopping. At first glance the men learned of his expectations and vowed to emulate him. When called, they bounded to the bateaux with a vengeance. Sweeping out into the lake, they performed maneuvers briskly and adroitly with minimal assistance from the Onondaga guides. The General marveled at the sight before his eyes, yet withheld lavish praises upon the men's return, for he knew of the dangers germane to inland waterways which often dashed the hopes of many an aspiring, young boatman.

"You are now the leading boatmen of Pointe Aux Bois. Well done," he told them. He shook the hand of each man, roundly congratulating him.

The Onondagas gathered nearby to discuss the Le Rocher method of instruction. They believed that he set an attainable objective for the new crewmen. He taught by example, i.e., giving demonstrations. He invited participation and encouraged the men to openly evaluate their performance critically. Under the given conditions, the Onondagas believed the General a fit task-master bent on bolstering the men's self-esteem. They marveled at how closely his methods of teaching approximated their own. They surmised that in youth he crossed paths with at least one or several of their number. They took delight in knowing the man— the man who reminded them so much of themselves.

The General studied the horizon, an act he performed with regularity. Glancing toward the fording place, a scant half league to the north, he reached for a looking glass. He bore down on a mass of human flesh gathered at the narrow crossing point and spilling over into the shallows. He regarded the hour on his trail watch. It corresponded with the planned arrival of the allies. Confident that they did indeed arrive, he called out to the yearling boatmen: "They are here! Man your boats. Our moment has come!!"

Twelve boats, each bearing ten boatmen, disembarked. Pressing the craft into a column, the boatmen poled, then rowed out to deeper water where they headed directly toward the little isthmus separating Lake Onondaga from the Oswego River. The stronger, more adroit boatmen, buoyed up by the able Onondagas, led the way in the first four bateaux. The General kept to the last vessel in the column from whence he may direct commands to the body as a whole. The isthmus crept closer and the figures beside it grew larger and the sign he looked for came into view: By prearrangement, a warrior on shore kindled a firebrand and waved it in the direction of the convoy. Le Rocher exhorted the boatmen. They rowed faster. Beaching the bateaux, the boatmen scrambled ashore to mingle with the western allies. The last to step ashore, the General met with Marchand who announced that the total strike force stood at over four hundred souls. He passed among other principals, calling out praises at random, then settled down to establishing the order of departure.

"Our canoes will take the lead, followed by the bateaux. The regulars will keep in step along the shoreline. Oh:nehsi:yo and Henri Marchand will take charge of the canoes. The Stag Deer has the regulars. Cerf Courant and Fox Tail will scout for them. I will assume command over the bateaux. Since this venture is a product of Henri Marchand and myself, we are in essence the leaders of the campaign. Its success or failure falls back upon us. I thank you for your attentiveness." He immediately consulted with the tradesman, both men pouring over maps. Presently, Marchand summoned the principals together:

"There are two cataracts which fill a gorge crossing the Oswego River. The greater and more perilous of the two lies directly across our path. Our water craft need to enter the river when the gorge is filled in order to gain the other side and Neatahwantah. That accomplished, we will conceal our vessels and trek through the forest to our objective. My trusty scouts tell me that the enemy is comfortably encamped." He looked at the two scouts with approval.

"Entering the river at the cataracts presents the most direct passage for us. To cross elsewhere puts us short of our mark. I know that hazards abound, but we are worthy of the task, given our resolve to succeed. Some of you may want to linger. That is understandable, yet the campaign weighs heavily upon crossing the river."

"Monsieur Marchand. I have trained my boatman to navigate under ordinary conditions. Fording under these extremes presents a forbidding challenge," the General retorted, "in no uncertain terms."

Deyojia:n:edo:t, the Stag Deer, looked at the map, then conferred with the tradesman: "I know this place. There are two waterfalls with a chasm between them. Water from the river fills the chasm, then mysteriously drains out. While the chasm is filled, canoes may travel at will on the river. In my youth I have done so, shooting over the waters and daring the river to claim me. Look at me now. I am alive and well." Striking his chest, he went to confer with Oh:nehsi:yo. Returning shortly, he met with the tradesman and the General:

"My friend Oh:nehsi:yo is not opposed to fording the river at this point."

"Your canoes are much faster than my bulky boats," the General lamented.

"Your men are still untried, are they not, Guillaume?" the tradesman asked his colleague.

"What do the men say about it?" an anxious Le Rocher demanded.

"It surprises me, Guillaume, but the men are eager to cross the river."

The tradesman wiped his brow and turned to look upon the bateaux men. Gathered about Onondaga crossing, they talked enthusiastically and exchanged shouts of encouragement. "You taught them well, Guillaume," the tradesman replied.

"I taught them to prepare to die, Henri," the General returned. He went to stand with the men who gave him a rousing cheer and begged to go forth with the crossing. The tradesman looked about him as though weighing a great decision. Suzanne and her father —all the principals kept him in their sights. In short order he spun around and addressed the General and the Stag Deer:

"Are you averse to reconnoitering any hazards ahead which we may face?"

"No. Not at all, Henri," the General returned. He launched a bateau. Boarding with the chieftain, he set forth into the river to make an observation.

—

The Oswego set a straight course due north, posing no foreseeable hazards. Within a few rods, however, the sound of rushing waters gave the two principals to understand that the cataracts lay ahead. The General beached the craft and, together with the Stag Deer, set out along the shore to glimpse first hand one of Nature's masterpieces. They mounted a grassy knoll and peered into a chasm, a deep trench which churning waters sliced into the bed-rock over succeeding generations. It ran the width of the river, east and west, a vast cavity of solid, black rock. Empty at this juncture, a cavernous void descending endlessly into the earth, soon to become replenished by a resurgence of waters cascading into it from the northern rim. The two men watched and waited. The waters began to rise. Flowing faster, the waters crashed into the chasm's walls, sending foam and spume on high, drenching and blinding them.

The waters roared loud and piercing, deafening the two leaders. They looked away momentarily, and when they looked back the chasm began a steady ascent, filling the void. Overflowing the rim, the waters fled to low-lying plains, so sustaining small marshes which in turn supported a number of species of plant and animal life. The General studiously marked the filling of the trench on his trail watch. Again they watched and waited. Almost imperceptibly the waters began to recede. Flowing faster, they fled down the chasm's sleek surfaces, sending aloft spray and foam in a great plume overhead. The two principals bid a silent tribute to the spectacle before regaining the bateau and rowing back to the command.

"Who will be the first to cross?" the General challenged the men. "You have precious few moments to cross the river before it claims you." He found himself shouting in competition with the raging waters. Behind him the chasm filled once again. Plumes of water-laden mist exploded straight upward, once the rising waters climaxed the rim. Stiff vapors floated the mist over the boatmen gathered before him. He glimpsed the men: Hardy, eager countenances stared back at him. Men spattered with foam gleamed at him.

A boatman stepped out of the crowd. Carrying an oar, he motioned others to follow him. Lean men, cheeks and eyes blackened to ward off the sun's stinging rays, moved to within an arm's length of their leader. Soberly, in measured words, the man spoke:

"We are ready to hurdle the river, Monsieur."

The General regarded the man intently. "Do you want to go with the bateaux or follow in canoes?"

"The bateaux, Monsieur? The warriors believe that the bateaux are more secure for us yeomen. The hour has come for us to prove our mettle."

"Good! Wait for the chasm to fill. You have about two minutes to cross. Do you have a trail watch?" Not waiting for a response, Le General slipped a watch over the young man's wrist. "Now, go!!"

The boatmen set six vessels abreast of each other, facing the opposing bank of the river. They paddled strongly, taking shallow bites with their oars in order to maintain formation. Once the waters climaxed the chasm's rim, they dug deeply to gain speed. Misty spray rose to meet them, obscuring vision, and little eddies nipped at the bows, tugging the vessels to right and left. A few boats collided. Others wavered and fell out of formation. The two boats on either extreme of the column drifted recklessly. In a heroic turn, the yearling crew of the compromised bateaux fastened grappling hooks to neighboring craft in order to right their course. Two bateaux perilously hiked upward, sending cargo packs to the rear. Desperate, the yeoman-crew fought to maintain course before lashing the packs to the crafts' midline. With everyone accounted for, the vessels forged ahead. In the face of the roaring waters, the boatmen called instructions to each other, the substance of which embraced the shifting of one's weight over the midline of challenged vessels. On and off, men scurried fore and aft. In well-orchestrated form, the yeomen transformed themselves into living counterweights to the pulling and tugging of the unforgiving waters of the swollen river. Apart from the incessant heaving of the turgid waters, the bateaux men maintained a steady course with the application of these life-saving measures. Three of the six bateaux hurtled forward. Completing the crossing, they sought the shallows and awaited their comrades.

The crew of the remaining three bateaux back-paddled to maintain equilibrium—employing this stratagem in order to forego colliding with each other during a final dash to the shallows. Despite the threat which the receding waters introduced, the men in the laggard vessels never displayed signs of distress. Indeed, they heeded the shouts of the boatswains, and, pulling mightily on their oars, executed precision-like strokes with precious few moments to spare. All the while on all sides the waters began to descend. Steadily the waters receded to the point of giving rise to a gap between the water line and the uppermost rim of the chasm. The men fully realized that they must in all haste hurdle the bateaux over the rim or perish. They lunged at their oars. The craft ploughed forward toward the hard rock. With the hulls at the point of smashing into the rim, the men shifted their weight toward the rear of the vessels. The hulls lifted and the vessels subsequently skimmed over the hard rock, cresting the rim, after which the men poled swiftly to the shallows. Their comrades, having already reached the shallows under less trying circumstances, cheered them. These newly-arrived boatmen participated in no merry-making. Instead they shouted encouragement to the boatmen yet to follow them.

Having studied the trials of their comrades, all remaining boatmen took to the bateaux with zest and bravado. They awaited the General's call. The commandant studied the ebb and flow of the waters and, when the basin filled, he gave off a resounding shout and the bateaux men cast off together, a column of six abreast, all of a single purpose. They cut a straight path over the turgid waters, refusing to repeat the errors of their predecessors. In so doing they avoided the pitfalls of their comrades and arrived en masse downstream to commiserate with them. All eyes immediately fell upon the Onondagas, who steadfastly declined to ford the river by canoe—citing inherent dangers. The growing reluctance spread to Oh:nehs:yo's command. The boatmen who rested in the shallows expected the General to pass judgment. The commandant paced nervously and consulting his trail watch, conferred with Oh:nehsi:yo, commander of the native canoes. Bearing a pronounced frown, the bronzed and venerable chieftain walked among the canoe-warriors. His eyes met each man with a baleful stare. He spoke not a word and before he reached the last warrior, the lot of them dispersed, each man securing a canoe.

* * *

The warriors crossed without incident. Joining the boatmen, they congratulated them and any latent hostility died instantly. Meanwhile, the marching column boarded rafts fashioned from buoyant saplings. They brought precious little cargo. With broad-faced oars, they struck out over the water-filled chasm. They moved from east to west, a decided advantage, for no cross-current impeded them. They arrived on the western shore to join the bateaux men. Conscripts floated cargo by raft and concealed all vessels taking part in the crossing, leaving the campaigners as a whole to reform. Fox Tail discovered the narrow trail which penetrated the forest due west. Consulting yet another map, Marchand dispatched the two loyal trackers to reconnoiter the unsuspecting foe. Following at a comfortable distance, the long, seemingly-endless column stepped into the forest, where on all sides stillness prevailed and the trees grew thick and mighty, casting a giant shadow over all beneath. By all accounts the trail led straightaway to Lake Neatahwantah where, the principals believed, the British reposed in a state of unpreparedness.

The General demanded strict silence, a gargantuan request to ask of a body of strangers thrown together on short notice into non-traditional maneuvers. The marchers tested themselves: Competing with gentle vapors passing through the tree tops, they made not a discernible sound and moved in the manner of plodding antelope drawn to a water hole. Silence reigned supreme, broken when the leather-bound feet of the two trackers raced along the hard pan in search of Marchand. They came upon the willing ears of the General, Cerf Courant, Fox Tail, and finally the tradesman to whom they poured forth their findings, each man taking a turn at reciting a discovery:

"Many soldiers camp at the northern fringe of the lake in tents."

"They occupy themselves with preparing roasted meat on spits."

"Beyond the tents stands a circle of booming engines and a cluster of wagons."

"At the southern tip of the lake stands a stockade hastily-built where prisoners reside."

Dark Moon came to prevail over his companion: "A sentinel stands watch over the booming engines. Another stands beside the stockade and a third keeps watch on the trail where it comes to an end."

Asserting himself, Two Bears continued the discovery: "There are two men, likely officers, who stand apart from the others. One is older. The elder man does most of the talking. The younger man is his eager student."

The trackers begged Marchand to slip behind the two men who stood locked in conversation, for the pair spoke in terms unfamiliar to them over matters which may carry valuable knowledge. The tradesman sought and obtained the General's approval, and, selecting Dark Moon, broke from the trail. They stole into the deep fastness of the forest to the very environs of the enemy camp where they came to rest behind a thicket mere paces from the two engrossed officers. Standing motionless, the tradesman prepared himself to remain unnoticed: He contracted his spine into a rigid column. He reduced his rate of breathing. He touched nary a leaf nor twig. These and other measures, which he dutifully hammered into the yeoman soldiers at Pointe Aux Bois, he skillfully executed. Without further thought, he bent an ear toward the engaged officers, straining to come away with important pieces of knowledge. While Dark Moon kept vigil, the tradesman stood immobile: a model of self-discipline, his ear sharply trained ahead.

—

"How do we explain them?" the younger man asked the older partner, gesturing toward the stockade.

"We saved them, you will recall, from incessant fires in their village," the elder replied, bent over a cane.

"I understand, Sir, but a whole series of conflagrations in succession?" queried the younger, dressed in white.

The older officer spat into the sand: "You must bear in mind that renegade aborigines attacked us without warning, and in the subsequent mêlée, put their villages to the torch to drive us off."

"I understand, Sir. That leaves the question of the wagons with their chattels and stores of valuables."

"We have merely assisted the aborigines in securing their belongings against the fires raging about them. We are, you know, keeping them until the day that the aborigines recover sufficiently to reclaim them."

"Understood. That brings us to the matter of the white woman."

"A woman of her stature has loved-ones in search of her. She fears for their security and will do anything to guarantee it, lest they too fall captives. To that extent she poses no burden to us." He coughed, then faced the younger man: "Please do nothing to demonstrate to her that we know not the whereabouts of her family. She must continue to believe that we hold them hostage."

"Her daughter, the precocious one, has seen me full in the face," the younger man returned.

"You worry too much, my dear man. She is too terrified to ever rise against us. After all, she knows *not* for certain her mother's whereabouts. Do not forget!! Witnesses have incredibly poor memories. The woman is our ticket to freedom, as long as her whereabouts are unknown to her family."

"When are the rangers due?"

"Within the hour. They will take the wagon with the dark canvas and leave a payment under the seat of the wagon with the white canvas. Send them on their way quickly. Do not allow them to drop behind and drink. If our men ask you questions, say that I sent you to guard the wagons. That is all." The two men parted company, the elder man leaning generously on a walking stick.

—

Ears ringing with knowledge, the tradesman stole back to the waiting column where he sought after the General. The campaigners lingered on the trail, growing weary of delay. In the interest of pressing the assault, the tradesman deferred elaborating upon his discovery— save that great chicanery lay in the making. The General demanded nothing more, his intentions set upon advancing immediately. According to plan, segments of the column dropped away to take positions in the forest: Cerf Courant led a party south to a concealed position behind the stockade at lake's end. Fox Tail hid among the trees behind the cannon and wagons north of the lake. The major portion of the command congregated on the trail where it debouched. It comprised Oh:nehsi:yo's and the Stag Deer's warriors and the boatmen under the General's command. With battle stations drawn, the tradesman and the General withdrew to a tree stump in the forest. Securing a toehold, they gained a reliable perspective of the fighting units strategically situated to strike at a moment's notice— a simultaneous assault designed to stun and rout the enemy. They almost succeeded completely. The assault began the moment that Marchand tossed a rock-laden bandanna overhead. It bounced amid fragile tree tops, landing noisily in a pile of dried leaves.

Fox Tail's band rushed screaming from the forest, hatchets in hand. Bearing down upon the feeble guard, the warriors dispensed with them at will before turning to the soldiers gathered at the northern beach. Alerted, the soldiers cut a hasty path to secure rifles staked out in pyramid-fashion. Preparing the weapons, the soldiers clashed with the first wave of warriors that descended upon them. While some fired, many more fixed bayonets and went head-to-head with the hatchet-wielding warriors. The fighting grew intense and the carnage mounted. A clever young officer ordered a retreat to the lake shore where he reformed the men into a phalanx. There they assumed the traditional European form of defense: Leveling a series of broadsides, the soldiers repelled the warriors successfully until the point where they came to reload. An ensuing warrior barrage and headlong rush collapsed the phalanx, sending soldiers running toward the south beach or back among the cannon and wagons in the grove to the north.

Cerf Courant, meanwhile, stormed the stockade. He dispensed with the lone sentry, leaving his band to challenge the unyielding gates. Made of thick oak, the stubborn portals repulsed the repeated blows of the war hatchet. In turn, the slick timbers of the enclosure afforded the warriors no opportunity to scale the walls. Cerf Courant pondered the thought of firing the gates, but feared for the lives of the captives within. Soon a second concern arose. The soldiers who escaped Fox Tail's band scurried away from the beach and made directly for the stockade. Seeking shelter, they began to heave into the backs of Cerf Courant's band who surrounded the structure. Dropping down upon the sands before the beach, the soldiers formed a skirmish line and opened a withering volley, forcing Cerf Courant to quit the stockade-offensive.

At this point the Stag Deer departed the trail with his band in order to relieve the stockade. The surge of maddened soldiers displeased him, driving him in hot pursuit. He ordered warriors to fall upon the earth at the first sighting of the 'flash in the pan,' —the moment that flint met powder, releasing the deadly iron shot. To a man the warriors heeded the fearless Stag Deer. Everyone dived to earth, the screaming shot flew harmlessly overhead, whereupon in an unbroken wave the warriors plunged ahead, pinning the foe against the beach. The Stag Deer led the charge directly into the enemy's midst where he counted several coups. Unfortunately a musket ball split his ribs, bringing him down. He never ceased exhorting the warriors— not until he drew a final breath.

Meanwhile, those soldiers who survived the disaster of the aborted-phalanx made for the comparative safety of the grove— a cluster of trees and bushes sheltering the cannon and wagons. It is here that skirmishing broke out. Soldiers retreated to it, determined to make a bold stand. Firing from behind trees and boulders, the soldiers warded off successive waves of attack, a maneuver which tipped the tide of battle in their favor. In observing the turn of events, The General and Marchand decided to make a massive effort to bring the fighting to an abrupt demise. Turning to the conscripts among them, the two leaders decided to launch their collective talents. Eager to enter the fray, these untested innocents emerged in two units. The first came up tightly behind the foe. The second arm drew into formation along the beach in plain view, cutting off retreat to the south. Both bands fired in succession, driving the soldiers to the earth. They did not run, however. Reassembling, they returned fire, and taking advantage of the brief bewilderment which they engendered among the innocents, ran headlong down the beach to join those comrades battling the Stag Deer. The yeomen/conscripts pursued them. Shortly a great mixture of heaving bodies gave at each other from behind hastily thrown up barriers and shallow pits etched into the sandy beach. The General hesitated to throw into the mixture a gang of bateaux men, for fear of complicating the confusion.

An impasse in the making, no signs of a clear victory emerged for either campaigners or foe. Save for an unforeseen event, the fighting may have raged on indefinitely. Disturbingly, plumes of thick smoke rose from deep within the stockade. Fighting ceased. The combatants paused to gaze at the awesome spectacle. Rising from the midst of the smoke, a voice boomed loud and defiant. Turning heads, the voice commanded attention:

"I demand safe passage, or I will set ablaze the entire stockade!!"

The tradesman and the General ran to the scene, taking refuge behind a sand dune. Presently the doors of the stockade opened and a man, rather sooty and gaunt, ambled forward. Leaning on a walking stick, he stopped a few steps from the threshold. Beside him he held a young boy fast about the neck.

"I demand safe passage for my men and captives within, or I will fire the stockade."

The two principals, Marchand and General Le Rocher, conferred briefly while the man, whose appearance fitted that of the elder officer, hurled invectives over the beach awash with combatants in various stages of composure. Understandably, the two principals beseeched him to surrender in order to receive good terms.

"What? Surrender? You seem to forget that you are not the clear victor here. At any moment my men may turn on you. I have only to give the word and today will become the final day of your miserable lives." He glared at his men strung out along the beach in odd assortments. Some wiped at wounds. Some moaned in pain, while others rubbed the stains of battle from soiled tunics. All, however, wore the look of exhaustion mixed with dread.

"Look about you," the General spoke. "Do these men care to fight further? I think not. Better to stop now and live to fight another day than cast your fate to the wind."

"Surrender? Never!!" The elder spat into the sand. Casually he slit the throat of the boy in his grasp, letting him fall where he may. "Now do I have your attention, gentlemen?" Behind him the smoke in the stockade grew thick and pungent.

"Withdraw your forces! This is my final offer!" the man shouted. Brandishing a fire brand, he pivoted smartly and marched back within the flaming enclosure.

All fighting having ceased, the General called the bateaux men to the beach. There, before the stockade, they surrounded the foe, who in turn lay down arms in anticipation of receiving new orders from whomever came forth to issue them. Presently the elder reappeared before the stockade. He barked out a command. The heavy portals opened slowly to release a small yet prim body of soldiers. Carrying small arms, they formed a column on either side of the portals. Scores of forlorn women and children, young and old, issued forth to take positions between the columns. Advancing, demeanor one of contempt, the elder stood at the head of the motley troupe. He addressed Marchand and the General not by name, but as the leaders of those who chose to rise against him:

"If you believe that I trust your intentions, you are mistaken, gentlemen. That is why I am reluctant to turn my back to you. I will take these miserable wretches with me. They go to a better life. They are, after all, my assurance of arriving with my head still seated on my shoulders. Yes, you do want them. There is something more that you want, I am told. Something you have come this way to pluck from my grasp. That will have to wait for another day, I fear—if at all."

He stepped back among the captives. Returning, he held a woman by the wrist. Tall and blonde and statuesque, the woman exuded fair and handsome qualities, despite the abject circumstances in which she found herself. Unkempt, her long, blonde hair covered her face and she strived without success to push it under her collar. She seemed at one point to blurt out, only to subdue herself and stand meekly at the elder's side. Watching the pair a shoulder's width apart, one may conclude that they formed at the most a tentative alliance built on the distrust of one for the other. The elderly man pushed the woman forward— a cue for her to take center stage. Breathing deeply, she stood erect and addressed the entire gathering, friend and foe, who pressed forward to catch a glimpse of her:

"I am Kerry. The man beside me is my guardian. I have accompanied him on many sallies along the frontier. Although I belong to another, he is not willing to part with me. Believe me when I say that he will kill me and the others unless he is granted safe passage. I long to return to my true family. However, to ensure that no harm comes to him and these fine people, I ask freely that you grant him and all prisoners safe passage without reprisals. I know that you will honor my request or suffer these fine people to be consumed by the torch."

The woman's name struck a chord with Marchand. "She is indeed the wife of our James York, Guillaume." Putting aside a musket, he approached the man.

"This is a valiant woman who has suffered much pain and agony. Do you deny her a moment's peace before she leaves these parts?"

"Not at all, my good man. What do you have in mind?"

"I have her true guardian among my forces. Her daughter resides with me also. Do me the honor of allowing her to see them. The visit will please her soul and fill her with pleasant memories to accompany her on her journey and life's travails will be less harsh on her."

"As you wish. Keep in mind however, my promise to the lot of you. You must return her or suffer the consequences of your folly." He called the woman Kerry to stand beside him.

The General plucked James and Suzanne from seclusion in the forest. Suzanne recoiled at seeing a wash of corpses littering the path she chose along the beach. She forced herself to look straight forward. James walked along placidly, but knew that something of importance lay at hand. The General ushered James and Suzanne into full view of the captives. The elderly man barked a command. The captives opened a pathway and the woman named Kerry stepped out to confront the assemblage.

Sobbing, Suzanne ran to the woman and fell at her feet. Rising, she daubed her tear-streaked eyes and those of the woman as well. Kerry held Suzanne tightly. Suzanne brushed aside Kerry's golden ringlets and boldly faced her.

"It has been so long. Father and I believed you . . ."

"Dead? No, my child. Tested, but not vanquished." Caroline stepped back; "How have your captors treated you? You look well."

"Captors? No, mother. These are my friends." She gestured toward the tradesman and the General.

"Oh? I did not know." Caroline cast half a glance at the elderly man who stood smirking behind her. Turning back, she came face to face with James.

"My husband. My dear husband. I have missed you," she murmured, as though measuring her words.

James wiped tears from Caroline's eyes. His own eyes welled up. Tears streamed down his cheeks. He fought for words. "We will be together soon, my fair wife."

"If only in spirit, I cherished our days together." She sobbed lightly and, with arms wrapped about each other, James. Suzanne, and Caroline embraced.

The elder man stepped in between them. "We must postpone our family reunion until another day, my friends. Come, Kerry. We must be off." He sneered at James, who restrained himself. The scene crackled with intensity.

"Please allow me to gather my dead and wounded," the man demanded, addressing the tradesman.

There ensued a general cleaning of the grounds. A delegation from either camp set about selecting burial sites. The elder man assumed the lead, for he grew eager to depart. The General remained in the background with his force tending to wounds. He ordered fallen soldiers to be buried in a resplendent glen beside the lake. He placed the grave of the Stag Deer apart from the others. Beside it he placed the remains of the campaigner who perished in the Seneca River. Each man received his own plot. The tradesman ordered cairns of stone placed over each grave and in the end conducted a requiem Mass at the site in which the fallen were cited for bravery.

The elder officer buried his dead along the southern beach. The wounded he loaded on wagons, crowding them together, for he carried many casualties. He gave no parting eulogy, nor did he cite any of the deceased for bravery on the field of battle. His weary soldiers led the captives from the battle grounds, bound together in a continuous queue. In passing the stockade, the elder set fire to the rugged oaken portals before turning for the forest trail. No one from the Le Rocher command protested the maneuver and while he himself conducted the requiem, the elder pulled away, leaving a smoldering stockade to the care of another.

In the peaceful grove turned cemetery, Suzanne turned to steal a glance over her shoulder. She looked for her mother in the long line of departing captives. She waved at what she thought to be a pale woman with blonde tresses, but the marchers flocking together obscured her view. She choked back tears and then she spied a curious sight: A man, young and tall, wearing white, approached the elder officer. Handing him a plump envelope, he buffeted him about the shoulders. Accepting the envelope, the elder concealed it in his tunic, smiled, and shook the younger man's hand, whereupon the two sauntered to the head of the column, conversing lightly. Slowly the forest consumed the column and when Suzanne stole a second glance, the trail stood empty. She saw no one at all.

(33)Williams, C.L (1952), Chapter 6: *Early France*, pgs: 69-73

(34)Tebbell, John (1948) ed. The Battle for North America: From the Works of Francis Parkman, Chapter 8: *The Battle With The Onondagas*, Doubleday & Company, Garden city, NY. pgs: 382-383.

(35)Merrill (1949) Land of the Senecas, pgs: 112-114.

(36)Tebbell, ed.(1948 Chapter 3: *Champlin at Quebec*, pgs: 43-56.

*North Street, Auburn, NY

**State Street in Auburn, NY where it crosses the Owasco River adjacent to Auburn Correctional Facility

*Lake Neatahwantah lies on the outskirts of Fulton, NY and is entirely natural in origin

*Lake Onondaga

*A section of the Seneca River due east of Baldwinsville, NY in the Town of Clay. Shallow and narrow for much of the year, it is close to the Great Northern Mall shopping complex

(37)Tebbell. The Battle for North America: Part Four Count Frontenac (1948) pgs: 374-383

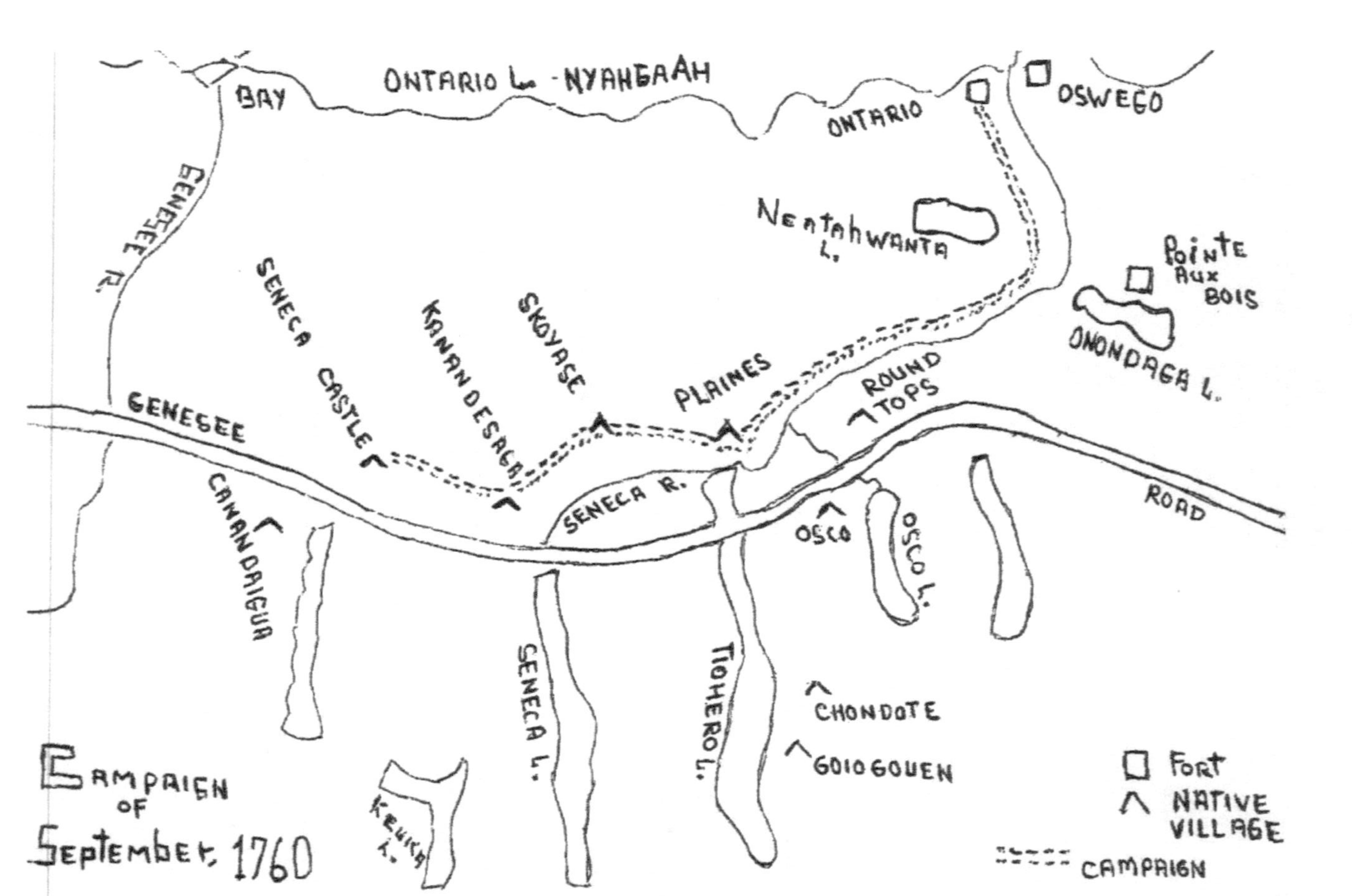

ONTARIO L. - NYAHGAAH
BAY
ONTARIO
OSWEGO
Nentahwanta L.
Pointe Aux Bois
ONONDAGA L.
GENESEE R.
SENECA CASTLE
KANANDESAGA
SKOYASE
PLAINES
ROUND TOPS
GENESEE
CANANDAIGUA
SENECA R.
OSCO
OSCO L.
ROAD
SENECA L.
TIOHERO L.
CHONDOTE
GOIOGOUEN
KEUKA L.
Campaign of September, 1760
Fort
NATIVE VILLAGE
CAMPAIGN

CHAPTER NINE

The Contenders
Principal Concerns.
Reverie.
Prelude to Battle.
Siege by Night.
The Aftermath of Battle.

Following his adversary's departure, Marchand reviewed the decision he made regarding the enemy's ordnance. Essentially he allowed him to vacate the battlegrounds with field pieces intact. Aside from taking possession of two lesser cannon, the tradesman sent him off under free rein with the bulk of his properties. He interred a number of enemy dead, left behind preemptively. He expected to hear protests on these accounts, not from his men, but from Le Rocher, co-commandant. He early formed the basis of treating with the Le Rocher inquiries, and, upon his colleague's approach, he delivered a cogent statement which left his friend satisfied without placing a strain upon their relationship.

"The field pieces are too ponderous for us to carry, Guillaume. From here outward the land is wet and marshy."

"We do not require another impediment in our path. We need to move swiftly."

"Granted, Henri. As for their deceased, I am comforted that you restricted them to a site apart from our own casualties. The ridge makes a suitable resting place." He nodded approvingly.

"That it does, Guillaume. Not too close to our men, yet in an acceptable location—despite the circumstances."

"There still resides a gnawing piece of uncertainty in my mind. Do you have an alternate explanation?"

"Yes. Yes. Of course. Out of respect for the dead, I stand against leaving corpses of any stripe to stiffen under the warm sun. Concerning his chattels, they are merely utensils common to any commander who fields an army. It serves us little to run off with them, Guillaume."

"I accept your explanation, Henri. Is there another motive to your decision?"

"Perhaps my benevolence will tell others that we French are a charitable people."

"One who cites examples of his benevolence is quoting from a self-serving text, Henri."

The tradesman grew out-of-sorts: "All right, Guillaume. I have done so in order to cast us in a favorable light among those who may seek to disparage the inherent goodness of the French command in the Americas." Pouting, he wrung his hands.

"Ahh!! Now I understand, Henri. Very well done," Le Rocher returned, laughing under his sleeve.

—

Suzanne sought after the tradesman, eager to explore an issue which ignited her enthusiasm. She began by recalling to him her mother's efforts to leave traces of her presence along the trail of abduction.

"Yes, Mademoiselle. I remember fully," the tradesman nodded.

"I believe furthermore that mother has searched for us in her own way for as long as father and I have searched for her." Alert. She held her head high, steeped in thought.

"Interesting. Please continue."

"We know that her captor made regular sallies to native villages to the west." She rubbed her chin. "She may have passed through each of the villages that our villain attacked—along with Osco." On that note Suzanne lowered her head to conceal her sorrow. She sighed: "So near, yet so far."

"In my opinion she has never been more than a day ahead of us," the tradesman concluded. "I believe that she has been so close at hand that we failed to recognize her. What does that tell you?"

"She traveled in disguise?"

"Exactly, Suzanne!"

"I remember Watkins telling me that mother's captor took her to Kanandesaga—presumably. She resided there for a lengthy stay at one point. Cornplanter is sure of it." Suzanne paced nervously. "My question is: Why did the brute take mother along on these rampaging missions?"

"It is my thought that he wanted to tether your mother on a short leash. He is enamored of her, I strongly believe. He feared losing her to a younger swain."

"Mother is not easily forced into compliance. She may have very possibly kept *him* on a tether."

"Oh?"

"Why, yes. She may have allowed him to come close before astutely pushing him away—enough to whet his appetite. A 'cat and mouse' act. It is what has kept her alive. This I believe she has done over and over with impunity. She has kept him in her sights as readily as he kept her within his sights. You do understand, do you not, Monsieur?"

"That is very believable, Suzanne; yet what do you say as to her incarceration?"

"He became angered over mother's constant rejections and struck back short of killing her."

"Ah, yes. That supports my original theory. There is one question, however, which concerns me."

"Yes?"

"Madame continued to play a game of 'touch and go' indefinitely when she may have . . ."

"Run away?" Suzanne interjected. "I thought of that and believe that she feared perpetual enslavement or worse: Death, if caught. She believed herself more secure in taunting the beast until father found her."

—

During the calm following the skirmish at Neatahwantah, the Sandpiper visited the principals. Drawing a blanket over his shoulders, he made a short speech, intending to soothe them:

"War brings out the true measure of the man. You, my friends, have conducted yourselves with bravery and valor. You will live to reap the fruits of your labors, for the Lord of the Forest approves of your deeds. War compels different peoples to come together to face a common foe. In war one's strengths come to the surface and all differences are cast aside. Those who do not follow such a path in war become consumed by it and flounder and perish." He stepped aside to admit James York:

"Let us burn the stockade fully," James called. "I, for one, refuse to lay my eyes upon a structure which pays tribute to evil in its several forms. I speak here of slavery, incarceration, abuse, humiliation, and the subjugation of a species." Angered, he lashed his arms out, reciting in order these several species of evil visited upon his wife. Suzanne stepped back, struck by his outburst. James hugged her and approached the tradesman, who, sensing James's sincerity, called out:

"Ah! So be it! Cerf Courant! Please do James the good turn of firing the stockade down to the last spar upon our departure." In the next breath he availed the campaigners of an assortment of foodstuffs laid out on blankets in the shadow of the graves. He injected a bit of sarcastic humor into his discourse:

"These gifts are from our adversary. He obligingly left them for us once I sent him off on his merry way."

"Once a tradesman, always a tradesman," the General bemused, buffeting his comrade about the shoulders.

The two principals dined beside each other, whereupon the General took the liberty to address a matter important to him:

"Henri. How do you propose to overtake a superior force with your lessor one?"

Perplexed by what he deemed an audacious claim and moot question, the tradesman nonetheless replied calmly: "By stealth, Guillaume."

"Henri. Be reasonable. Your bows and arrows against his muskets and cannon?"

"We bested him most recently, you will recall. We shall do so again."

"He will be ready for you."

"I have more than one trick up my sleeve, Guillaume." He reached for a biscuit.

The General put aside a dish. "Listen to me, Henri. Unless you dispatch him with one decisive blow, he will have your head swinging from a yard post. What has Neatahwantah proved?"

"It proved my theory: We are in extraordinary circumstances his equal."

The General grimaced: "Those, however, are few and far between."

The tradesman grew defensive: "We are new to battle. We performed admirably for commanders new to putting natives at death's door."

"We had losses you will notice."

"Small measure when compared to *his*, Guillaume. We are ready to start afresh. He, on the other hand, must snake off to lick his wounds."

"I grant you that one, Henri. However, this battle proved that we are unable to dispose of the enemy in a single blow. I hardly support your desire to pursue him."

"Guillaume. The enemy believes that he fought a band of wild savages, accompanied by a scattering of far-flung Canadians. He knows not of our French reserves at Pointe Aux Bois. It is not necessary that he know until . . ."

"We strike again?"

"Precisely. Thank you, Guillaume for your indulgence," Marchand smiled, impishly.

"Henri! We must protect our allies. To do that we must dip into our reserves. If we lose our allies, we lose the frontier."

"Continue." Marchand pulled on a turkey leg.

"Our native allies carried the day for us, but they also exposed themselves to the extreme. If our adversary retaliates, he will go after them."

"What do you imply?"

"We must commit our *own* men to a greater extent in order to maintain our allies' loyalty."

"Very true. For all of your concerns I suggest that you sit back and watch the second stage of my campaign."

"Oswego, no less."

"No! Ontario. We go after Ontario. Oswego is incidental. It is too strong. Am I understood?"

"Henri. Montreal is now under siege. If it falls, what becomes of our efforts? Nothing will prevent the Red Coats from descending upon us. Pointe Aux Bois will be exposed and destroyed!"

"That is why we must have a victory at Ontario. A victory will set him on his heels and give us the space to plan our next move, Guillaume."

"A 'touch and go' affair, I fear."

"Yes, Guillaume. Begin to entertain a strategy that has no rigid bounds."

"May I offer a critique?"

"Is this something new for you, vieux chapeau?" He laughed at the attempt at sarcasm and sighed: "I am going to hear you with or without giving my consent."

"Henri. First of all, you allowed the enemy to dictate the course of the battle."

Marchand, eating from a dish of berries, nodded, and cast a wan smile.

"Second, you based victory on a chain of events to take place. In effect they did *not* take place. The plan was too complex for your bands of natives to execute."

Marchand put down the dish: "My dear Guillaume. Although our forces possess superior skills unto themselves, they have never fought together in a concerted battle until this very day. You and I commanded a naive yet determined body of scrappers—red and white—pressing forward to overcome stout resistance. Yes, we abandoned the cannon, but it does not serve our purposes to acquire excess baggage. An army must travel light and prepared and that we are."

"You have my apologies."

"I submit that my enthusiasm outweighed my military prowess. Looking back, we came unprepared for contingencies. By comparison, the enemy anticipated our maneuvers before we put them into play. The fusillade that we sent over their heads comes to mind. For the most part I have faith in our forces. We will not repeat the same mistakes again." Fists clenched, he raised his voice.

"This is good, Henri. By the way, I will be sharing operations with you. We need to keep losses low—particularly among our allies. We lack the luxury of sustaining the fight without them."

"Thank you for the lesson in Colonial Relations, Guillaume," Marchand returned, sarcastically.

The General overlooked the remark. "Thank you for securing some of the wagons, Henri. They hold precious articles fit for trade. Because of your intercession, we are able to return these articles and remain worthy of our allies' trust." He gripped his comrade's shoulder firmly, drawing a comment from his steady ally:

"Fear not. All is not lost. Let us set our sights on freeing the captives, Guillaume." Marchand began to walk away. "It is good that we did not storm the stockade. There would be more cadavers to bury in that case. Our day in the sun is fast-disappearing, Guillaume. We must make a move now, or forever hold our peace."

"By all means, Henri. I am sending our dead and wounded back to Pointe Aux Bois by bateaux. There are fewer than twenty. I feared more." He buried all eating utensils in the sand. Other campaigners followed. Soon the column reformed. The boatmen and natives joined ranks and the column swelled in size, buttressed by three field pieces and three wagons of pelts and furs. The General consulted his trail watch.

Two hours elapsed since his adversary vacated the battle grounds— "enough for him to dispel all thoughts of our following him in hot pursuit."

Mounting, the General called over a shoulder: "He is well dug in by now, Henri."

"But not for long, Guillaume," his comrade returned, in a mood decidedly jovial.

The column closed ranks. All sub-sections fell into line. The Cornplanter conscripts brought up the rear, a position which delighted them, for no one came to stand guard over them. Steadfastly the campaigners retraced the path through the battle grounds. Behind them, the ruins of the stockade went up in smoke. Approaching the Oswego River, the column turned north to travel along its bank. Men dropped off infrequently to conceal canoes and bateaux in the tall grasses.

* * *

Captives in hand, the Captain and aide-de-camp led the shattered command toward Oswego-Ontario, their home base. The dead and wounded compelled him to travel much slower than anticipated, but he respected his men's wishes to bury most of the deceased at the principal garrison, Oswego. He feared no counter-attack, believing that parting remarks to the attackers sufficed to hold them at bay. Nonetheless, he posted a rear guard.

He reminisced over the battle at Neatahwantah, awarding himself accolades for astuteness. In effect he told himself that he 'survived ambush by virtue of wit and guile—turning the tactics employed by the marauding savages upon themselves. His chief ploy, crawling amid the limbs of fallen fighters, allowed him and his aide to seek shelter within the stockade, aided no less by a confederate. Once inside, he struck intimidation into the very souls of the populace, threatening them to the threshold of death's door. The attackers, accepting his threats at face-value, those savages and rag-tag Canadians, withdrew without calling his bluff. Craftiness won him back his properties and most of his weapons. Granted, he relinquished purloined furs and skins, but his aide received payment earlier for a delivery he made under the very noses of the enemy in broad daylight. And the prisoners? They did not revolt. They trusted in his ability to guarantee their well-being—these sons and daughters of chieftains whom he held in the hollow of his hand.

'That left the *woman*. During the fight she exhibited rare valor, ultimately keeping him from capture. Although she openly shamed him in speaking aloud, she must suffer no chastisement and remain a prized commodity: a *de facto* negotiator. The woman's family will keep at a distance from him for fear of his delivering on his original threat, and he will be able to breathe more easily. With the captives and the woman subservient to him, he will be able to travel the region at will preparing more lands for settlement. Of course he must capture the marauders, punishing them severely. For the present he must strengthen ties with Lord Carleton. He looked forward to good food and drink at the garrison.'

His reverie passed to Lord Carleton: 'The commandant generally accepted his accounts of events on the frontier without question. Lord Carleton preferred tending to the garrison's internal affairs, leaving him to tend to external matters. In spite of recent losses, he expected to receive Lord Carleton's full endorsement—amounting to granting him another season as Chief Surveyor. Already his tireless dedication to detail received notice beyond the Lake Country—finding credibility at the court of William Pitt himself. Praises received from abroad placed him in good standing with Lord Carleton, whose tenure at the garrison depended upon the ability to transform the surrounding forest into the center of an English-speaking colony. For both Lord Carleton and himself, the longevity of their careers owed itself to the successful interpretation of the sovereign's expectations.

'He recalled his labors relative to the frontier: The uncertainty of life, the inherent dangers, the brevity of small victories, the agony of disappointments—all these and more— sent mixed messages coursing through him, pulling his mind-set fiercely in either direction. He sought a release, a departure from these unrelenting, pent-up thoughts which drove him between bouts of tranquility and hostility. Perhaps that is why he indulged himself in clandestine operations so distinct from official duties. Rife within the military, pockets of corruption proliferated. Men of all stations supplemented modest incomes by secretly pilfering, buying, and selling select, often forbidden commodities—inclusive of human flesh—for a profit. Some accumulated wealth wherever it may be found before the travails of frontier life subjected them to sickness, poor health, enemy torture, a score of maladies, premature disabilities, even death. Forsaking caution, these men raced to enjoy life's simple pleasures while they held the ability to do so. At first he held himself above the contest, but, rising in command, he listened more frequently to others. He allowed them to pull him deeper and deeper into a way of life with saccharine-like qualities which promised great rewards for little investment. Embracing it wholeheartedly, he knew no escape and ran with it. No longer his *own* man, he became *their* man, a soldier among soldiers, struggling to survive in unforgiving surroundings.

'He prepared himself for an audience with Lord Carleton: the commandant sure to demand an accounting of operations this past fortnight: his presence in the native village, his rout at the hands of incensed warriors. He and Simmons would offer the explanation of self-defense against packs of marauding savages who attacked his camp. Lord Carleton knew not of the *woman,* one of the spoils of battle, whom he took along on sallies. He, Simmons, and a few others guarded this secret from the outwardly-pristine, stain-free commandant, a man who revered the uniform of the Forces and all of its trappings and privileges over the more mundane duties of the administrator. Deceiving Lord Carleton stood akin to scoring a victory on the battle field. For him deceit proved an effective tool in surviving life's pitfalls and shortcomings— so common to the military scene. He gloried in the new-found power and comfort which flowed through his limbs whenever he plucked this particular device from his bag of tricks.

'In his own mind he befriended the native. He did not steal him away to a life of uncompromising servitude. On the contrary, natives took delight in laboring at the garrison: They shored up the fort's defenses. They built and repaired walls and ramparts. They hunted for meat in the woodlands for the residents. In return, he fed and clothed and lodged them. He housed others of their kind during periods of famine and drought, sheltering them from frontier enemies. He asked little from them—a sampling of furs and skins from their vast stores along the inland lakes. Better that he take charge of them than the Dutch or French. Yes, he held prisoners—casualties of war to be released with the cessation of hostilities. Of that number he sold only the implacable, volatile ones to pirates and adventurers who plied the Great Lakes. He found it necessary to do so in order to sustain the fragile peace between the Forces and the savages, to bind tractable natives closer to the Crown, and to stem threats of native uprisings upon the base-camp.

'Lord Carleton gave tacit approval to the reassignment of garrison native laborers who refused to perform expected services effectively, but he knew not that he, James Worthy, secretly sold them into bondage. By his own design, everyone profited from the sales, receiving an income-distribution. Everyone from the factors to lowly garrison soldier received a reward, which in turn bought their silence and loyalty. Even the miserable wretches themselves benefitted, for they came to live another day in a new locale, often under improved conditions.

'Concerning Lord Carleton, he viewed him from a distance, never at ease when in his presence. He considered him pretentious and self-seeking. Born into wealth, Lord Carleton sought ways to augment his holdings. He openly expressed hatred of slave-trading, but knew he stood powerless to curb the surreptitious transactions springing up almost at will. He made a feeble attempt to collect revenues generated from suspected sales—the more to hold in evidence against the evil-doers. Despite circulating spies within the ranks, no one came forward to report upon a fellow soldier. Lord Carleton spent at least half of most days trying to collect evidence of trafficking. He spent the remainder luxuriating in the role of post-commandant which included procuring lavish trappings for his rooms, and making extended hunting forays into the woodlands. These two developments in particular accounted for his disdain of the commandant and with each clandestine sale a wave of satisfaction bathed him in a well of warmth, a glow permeating his entire being. The men supported him, those non-privileged, low-born yeomen of inferior rank to whom he doled out residual gifts. He recognized their sacrifices in ways that the commandant never approached, rewarding them thus and they thanked him by giving him unbounded fidelity.

'He thought of the rangers, those hardy woodsmen of English stock who provisioned the garrison with produce and meats. Among the first settlers in the region, the rangers knew the land and its inhabitants. He counted on them to bring him reconnaissance reports of native populations. Their efforts he rewarded with periodic outlays of skins and furs, which they sold in leading ports of North America. At Neatahwantah he set aside a wagon load of furs for them. They came for it, and in the thick of battle no one noticed their comings and goings. In short, all those within his employ benefitted from his broad embrace.' His reverie complete, he spurred the column into a brisk trot. Home lay a short distance away.

* * *

The General anticipated reaching Ontario/Oswego by dusk. There in the twilight he intended to deploy his forces along the periphery of the parade grounds—hidden behind the barriers which the forest provided. At a respite point he distributed forest-green tunics to the warriors comprising the front ranks. When marching resumed, everyone remained silent, leaving an uncomfortable eeriness to pervade the ranks.

Suzanne, growing restless, searched for the opportunity to break the unending silence. Spying Aboyant, she bounced to his side:

"Am I the only gay soul left on earth, my good friend?" she chirped.

Not awaiting a response, she pressed on: "My dear Grand Ours. Today is your fortunate day. I have a new name for you."

Aboyant, in spite of Suzanne's enthusiasm, registered no response. Finally he mustered a weak reply: "As you wish, Mademoiselle."

Casting aside disappointment, Suzanne gushed forth: "You are now Hnyagwail-lo:nhgweh—Bear Man. How do you say?"

Aboyant turned to address her: "I am honored to own one more name, Mademoiselle. By that stroke I now rival the Bear Chief himself. It is good to walk in the company of the mighty and esteemed." He said nothing more and took up a position in the column, leaving a confused Suzanne behind him.

—

Fort Oswego occupied a high, craggy bluff overlooking Lake Ontario. The fortress stood out prominently on the Henri Marchand map. It straddled a hard-scrabble, rocky plateau which descended sharply along sandy slopes to the beach head, some one hundred feet below. Built over a harbor formed from receding glaciers, the fortress stood watch over it as well as over the deep-keeled British merchantmen that cast anchors into the soft harbor bottom. Bounded by thick forests, the garrison, a symmetrical stone rectangle, rose up ominously from the plateau, at the northern-most terminus of the land of the Cayugas. It was there that the Cayugas, People of the Swamp, came to catch the large fish unique to the lake, having spawned in the St. Lawrence and traversed to the lake and harbor to mate and give birth.

The Cayugas speared the harbor's fish from canoes deployed in waves, forcing them together. During low tide, natives drove the fish toward shore, clubbing them with war hatchets. The fish, feeding on smaller specimens in the harbor, grew to great lengths. Strong and dominant, the fish repelled all newcomers, but proved vulnerable to the natives' schemes to lure them. The People returned to the harbor successively to reap the bountiful harvest. They set up camps, remaining until they took their fill. What they did not consume the People stored underground in urns and baskets lined with salt. The harvests took place two to three times a year with everyone from distant parts of the Confederacy regaling the great catches with colorful festivities. The fort, however, had not become a reality at that point.

Once constructed, the People moved further inland from beneath the fort's shadow. They frequented the smaller, glacier-carved lakes. They all but forgot the fort, yet from a distance they studied the men who came and went from it. They watched the men extract sand from the harbor bottom and beach head. Carrying the sand in baskets, the men mixed it with small pebbles in water, applying it to the fort's walls. For the People the fort assumed grandiose proportions and they shrank from it, warning family members that inherent evil resided within the walls poised to spring out upon them. With succeeding seasons the men thickened the walls to the length of a man's body, leaving the natives to conclude that no known force stood powerful enough to compromise them. They learned the name of the fort: Oswego. Perched imperiously on an imposing bluff, it cast a giant shadow over the harbor on sunny days and sent moon beams by night cascading to earth in bent, fragmented segments.

The British completed Fort Oswego prior to the outbreak of King George's War (1740-1748), as the Crown grew determined to protect its North American possessions from French inroads. It played an insignificant role in that conflict and not until the French & Indian War (1754-1763) did its name reappear on the lips of strategists and map makers. The British refurbished the fort prior to the outbreak of hostilities, erecting a second structure of lessor stature: Fort Ontario. It sat to the immediate west across the harbor, tucked away amid the folds of an undulating plain. Ontario absorbed Oswego's overflow of men and materiel, including a jail of sorts for captives and prisoners awaiting judgment. Small by the standards of the day, Ontario appeared remote and diminutive in comparison to Oswego.

Following the renaissance of the Fort Oswego complex, the French under General Montcalm swooped down upon it in August, 1756 at the beginning of the oncoming war. He attacked both Fort Ontario and Fort Oswego with a collection of native allies and Canadian militiamen, coming by canoe over Lake Ontario. So swiftly came the attack that the resident commandant abandoned both garrisons, surrendering unconditionally. Montcalm's force set about sacking the remaining stores and warehouses. His native allies insisted upon burning all combustible structures. Reluctantly the General agreed, drawing the line, however, at the butchering of residents and survivors of the attack. With both garrisons ravaged and scarred, Montcalm abandoned the region. He departed for Montreal via the St. Lawrence with 1700 prisoners and booty salvaged from the sinking of harbor merchantmen. En route he allowed some captives to escape in order to spare his men the expense of guarding them. He arrived at Montreal bearing ample spoils of war which he distributed throughout shops in the city. Remaining prisoners he sent into indenture or forced labor details.

Overall, the French victory at Ontario-Oswego bode well for them. The Iroquois swung allegiance to the French, giving rise to a vigorous trade which spread to many Great Lakes outposts. Pointe Aux Bois came into being, opening a trading post to local natives and sending tradesmen to all points far and wide. If the French are to be criticized, it is that Montcalm abandoned Ontario-Oswego prematurely. Within two years, however, the winds of war changed, allowing the British to rebuild the two garrisons as well as Fort Ticonderoga to the east. During the same period the Iroquois Confederacy solidified trade relations with the French.

For the moment the British suffered a strategic defeat. The Ontario-Oswego complex lay at the crossroads of trade routes accessible by land and water, many of which reached deeply into North America. On the surface the loss at Ontario-Oswego denied the British access to the interior by means of the Lake Country. Meanwhile, the natives in general demanded that the French take the lead in protecting them against age-old enemies and providing them with goods and foodstuffs during lean harvests. Eagerly the French acquiesced, filling the void created by the retreating British, leading to the balance of power in the Lake Country swinging to *la fleur de lis*.

French missionaries invested the Lake Country in the 17th century. One hundred years later, men such as Henri Marchand and Guillaume Le Rocher arrived to foster trade relations with native populations. Perennially deficient in numbers, the French extended the branch of friendship, which, when coupled with ample quantities of goods and materiel, drew the Iroquois to them. A reciprocal relationship took place whereby each camp supplied the needs of the other. For their part the French furnished a steady stream of supplies, in exchange for the Iroquois' setting up of a buffer zone between their hosts the French, and the rivaled British. The arrangement may have continued indefinitely, for the Iroquois viewed the French as a non-threatening species of human-kind. Where the French lived side-by-side with the Iroquois, the British established pervasive English-speaking settlements. Where the French respected the status-quo, the British created opportunities to persuade the natives to do their bidding.

It is this resurgence of a British presence that the General marched to intercept. He settled upon the rebuilt Fort Ontario, the lessor of the two garrisons. He hoped to sack it quickly with minimal loss of life. In his mind's eye, he longed to complete that which Montcalm failed to do. Beyond that, he hoped to draw British attention away from Montreal currently under siege, forcing them to redirect operations solely around Ontario-Oswego, where he may keep them under surveillance. Pursuing the aberrant British abductor of Caroline York provided him the pretext needed to meet this objective. For the present all allies stood fast beside him. They championed his cause and he would allow them to aggressively carry the fight while his finite forces remained in the background—unless of course matters changed dramatically.

—

These thoughts in mind, the General led the column forward. Presently he called a halt. Upon conferring with a scout, he addressed the gathering:

"We are but a mile from our adversary. He is camped on the Commons before Ontario. A number of prisoners are penned nearby. You all know your assignments. Let us move out quickly and quietly."

A guide reported: "I have killed one of their scouts. Before he died, he confessed to searching after us."

Marchand approached the General: "With a dead scout, our foe knows that all does not go well."

"All the more reason to move out immediately, Henri," the General retorted. Turning on his heel, he came face-to-face with Suzanne. Pale and weary, despite the sun's warmth, something troubled her, and he knew she stood at the cusp of disclosing her concern to him.

"Ma chère amie. We meet again," he spoke, softly.

A tear in her eye, Suzanne spoke plaintively: "Monsieur. When you send off the men, keep an eye open for mother." Tears welled, and she fought in vain to drive them away.

"Bien entendu, ma chère amie. I will search for her. I know how much she means to you." He hugged her about the shoulders. "Let me tell you a little secret."

Suzanne looked up appreciatively: "My father does not send me. I come of my own free will."

"Yes. I know, dear one. Madame means very much to me as well." He smiled: "Your desire is great. You show pluck. That alone is worth your mother's freedom. Tell me. How many years have you?"

"I have sixteen years, but I believe that I lived most of them in this place."

"I must confess, Mademoiselle, that in all my years of service I have never met a young woman of your tenaciousness." He clenched a fist to accent his point. Bending, he cupped Suzanne's chin in the palm of his hand:

"I will find her, chérie. If you must cry, let your tears be tears of joy. Tell me. What do you have in mind once all of this passes?"

"I enjoy the Bear Chief and his family. I want to take mother and father and live with them."

"Ah, yes. He is a good man. We will find your mother and your wishes will come true. That is my promise to you. Agreed? Remember. Out of sad days come good days. We do not know when that will take place. It is one of life's mysteries, but you are young enough to see better days. For certain this is true, by my word."

A meek Suzanne smiled approvingly. Le Rocher led her by the hand back to the column. Placing her astride a noble steed, he instructed Aboyant to guide her, making certain that she remained surrounded by her father and other nurturing principals.

* * *

With the approach of dusk, the Le Rocher column reached the periphery of the woodlands which ringed Fort Ontario. The Commons, an expansive parade grounds, spread out fan-shaped from the fort's main portals, where it butted up against dense stands of maples, oaks, elms, and box elders. Within this excellent form of cover, the column deployed into several segments: To the left on the western flank of the Commons, stood the Sandpiper's bowmen. Directly opposite on the eastern flank crouched the General and the riflemen, a force composed of the French recruits and bateaux men, and the Sandpiper warriors, Fox Tail among them. Marchand occupied the forest directly south of the main portals, together with the Bear Chief's volunteers: additional French regulars, and the Kanandesaga native conscripts— formerly prisoners, now warriors at least in name. Within this latter mixture James, Suzanne, Aboyant, and Cerf Courant resided.

Row upon row of tents occupied the Commons, temporary lodgings for the BEF, which, despite losses recently incurred, numbered over five hundred men—too many to inhabit the garrison proper. Huddled along the fringe of the eastern Commons, a stand of palisades formed a crude yet effective holding pen. Within, in various forms of repose and dress, lay the prisoners of Neatahwantah and residual captives. Before the main portals near the midpoint of the Commons, stood a rectangular, wooden platform. Logs laid on end lent support from beneath. A hand railing circumscribed the structure. A short flight of stairs mounted the platform, ascribing to the scene a stage-like setting.

The advancing darkness brought soldiers to commune on the Commons where they mingled with returning comrades. Filling every space available, they inhabited corridors among the tents. They strolled at random over the grounds. Over food and drink they enjoyed each other's company. Bursts of laughter punctuated the quietude of the cool, crisp evening. The rampant gaiety belied any resemblance to the horrors of battle which beleaguered the BEF most recently: Musicians emerged and the assembly sang songs to the tune of violins, trumpets, flutes, and fifes. Men danced with each other, giving rise among the Le Rocher party that the spectacle owed itself to the generous amounts of whiskey flowing freely. The gaiety showed no signs of diminishing and with the encroaching darkness the revelers lighted fires before the tents made from tightly-wrapped faggots of sticks. In rapid succession the bundles burst into flame, casting a deep red glow over the camp grounds.

A fierce, red ball rose overhead where the voluminous flames converged. It shone so brightly that it outlined in bold symmetry all semblances of human-kind ruminating within the canvas-covered tents. In silent protest, Suzanne and others of her party turned their heads away from the brilliant luminescence. Shielding bare extremities, she and others backed away from the intense heat. The revelers, reduced to a dancing frenzy, cavorted and turned wildly, unmindful of the flames. Frenetically they waved arms and dashed over the grounds, caught up in the passions which the flames kindled within them. All appointments on the grounds stood drenched in white light, save for the pen on the periphery housing the captives. Built in the shadow of tall fir trees, the pen became devoured by shadows with the lengthening of the evening. In similar manner, the awning covering the façade of the garrison's main portals blocked out all light below. Men passing in and out of the structure appeared to come from nowhere and disappear into nothingness.

Marchand and the General captured the merrymaking and spectacle of light through field lenses. They spoke not a word to confederates, invoking a code of silence throughout the ranks. As precipitously as it began, the dancing ceased: the revelers coming together about the platform. With bosoms heaving, the revelers chanted, swaying in a great circle about the platform—more suitably a stage. The climbing flames grew all the more intense, bearing down upon the revelers in a manner that stamped them with intimidating, blood-red features. From her sanctuary among the trees, Suzanne stared hard at one of the revelers. The young man danced in an ever-widening arc, coming within a half meter of her. Poised to flee, Suzanne kept her balance. From within her dark retreat she stared into the man's eyes. Frightened, she gave a start, seeing flames in the man's eyes—flames dancing and cavorting in competition with those that rose up around him. Dazed, she toppled backward, slumping into the arms of her constant companion, Aboyant.

Marchand's lenses searched the grounds. He detected movement within the prisoners' corral. The chanting in full swing, he spied a column of lowly sorts walking in lock-step toward the stage. Young native men, thin and disheveled, they walked with heads lowered and arms behind their back. A guard led them. Another guard brought up the rear. At a signal the young men paused before the stage, then in single file, each one mounted the steps, coming to rest in a line toward the midpoint. There, guards secured their ankles with chains to the floor boards. Rising, the guards scurried from the stage to the main portals where they disappeared within the garrison.

Three men issued from the portals. They strolled leisurely side by side. Approaching the stage, they halted. In turn, Marchand passed the lenses to others. All gaiety ceased as though by prearrangement. The revelers moved closer to the stage. Surging together, they formed a mass of flesh straining to catch a glimpse of the poor unfortunates. Pressing together, they fought for position with eyes and ears attuned to the miserable souls arrayed above them. Marchand studied the three men. The tallest of the three wore a suit of white. Mounting the stage, he bowed to the throng below which acknowledged him with renewed shouting. The man appeared young and physically in good measure. A sash about the waist held a gilt-handled sword, for all purposes ceremonial. Turning, the man held a hand out to a second man. His companion mounted the steps slowly. A cane in hand, he leaned on it severely while crossing the stage. Perhaps twice the age of the younger man in white, he wore the forest green trappings of the ranger. Tilting a tricorn, he nodded to his companion, yet spoke not a word. He stood of medium height and appeared fit with the exception of a slight paunch about the middle. He joined hands with the younger man in white, the pair standing at parade-rest.

A third man mounted the stage. The largest of the three, he sported an expansive girth. Broad, drooping mustaches imparted to his countenance a sinister aspect. The arms hung long and thick, trailing off to bulbous-like hands which opened and closed like the jaws of a gaping ocean clam. The large, square head, the features coarsely chiseled, suggested that the hand of the Creator carved him from a slab of granite. The protruding jaw completed the terminus of that slice of rock, which, running straight down from the forehand, allowed for a nose to issue forth. Long and aquiline, the nose, akin to an invasive tool, drove outward before terminating over the lip. A thick mane of black hair trailed from beneath a stocking cap drawn firmly over the head. He wore a full-sleeved linen shirt and thick leather trousers supported by suspenders. Rocking from side to side, the man grinned through tobacco-stained teeth. Marchand passed the lenses to Suzanne.

She bore in on the three figures. She stood on a boulder in order to gain greater advantage. Suddenly she gave a start, and losing her balance, slumped to the soft earth. Rising of her own volition, she breathed in short gasps and sought out Marchand. Motioning for paper and stylus, she eagerly inscribed a message for him. Marchand devoured the contents before bringing it before James York. Other principals followed. All gathered around James as he read:

"The man in white is the one who approached me at market the day mother vanished. I also saw him at Osco from the ramparts before the attack began."

The General's lenses perused the three figures. Coming to rest upon one of them, he whispered into Marchand's ear: "The large man is the sea pirate: **Black Jack Mc Knight**."

The General tendered the lenses to Marchand: "There is our man, the crusty one in the middle."

"Yes, Guillaume. The same one from Neatahwantah, unless I have missed the mark."

"He is the one seeking the favors of Madame York, Henri."

"With that said, she must be nearby, Guillaume."

"Stolen away in the garrison? The pen, no less! She is here. I know it," Marchand returned.

The two principals conferred with James York, after which the General disclosed a compelling opinion: "The three of them together tells me that they are united in a nefarious scheme to deceive and defraud. We are, gentlemen, about to witness that scheme first-hand." He gestured toward the stage: "I give you, gentlemen a *slave sale*."

James York took the lenses. "It is too dark to see within the pen," he lamented.

Marchand drew close to him. "In my view all three men have formed a plan to make a small fortune at the expense of these unfortunates. Each one has his own role. I suspect the dandy is the decoy. He prospects for suitable candidates, given that his superior, the crusty one, is lame. The crusty one is the leader of the three. The ugly one swoops up the captives and sails off with them. I suspect that any currency passes through Old Crusty first-off and hence down the line."

"I venture that Old Crusty's superior, Lord Carleton, knows not of the scheme, Henri," the General brought forth, adhering to a private thought.

"This is distinctly possible, Guillaume. However, it is unlikely for the soldiers *not* to know."

"They are sworn to silence, mon ami."

"Better. They have been paid off with favors or currency, Guillaume. After all, Lord Carleton has not been able to dislodge the evil which we witness."

"Henri. You know much of the ways of the charlatan."

"I have crossed paths with many diverse genres over the years, mon ami."

"Your knowledge may be of great service to our campaign, Henri."

"I have heard of such men in my travels. Now I stand before three of them."

"Let us keep them in our sights, Henri."

—

At that moment an unbridled commotion issued from the Commons. The General and other principals leaned forward. The revelers, soldiers all, surged to the platform, surrounding it. A guard hauled a young native forward, whereas the crusty man stepped behind him. He called out a price. Beside him the sea pirate called out a second price. The man in white beckoned the audience. Speaking of the youth and vigor of the subject, he asked for a vote.

By acclamation the rabid onlookers settled upon the initial offering, leaving the burly man to pay the crusty one a sum of currency. The bizarre exchanges progressed far into the evening—the revelers infrequently called upon as final arbiters in the exchanges between the older man and his burly counterpart. With few exceptions, the sea pirate met the crusty man's price—choosing the strongest and tallest of the captives. In the end, the crusty man counted his earnings and the two men shook hands ceremoniously.

Native warriors witnessed the sale. Registering distaste for the blatant acts, they retreated to the rear, covering their mouths for fear of crying out aloud. Others stood poised to fire muskets in protest, yet yielded to Cerf Courant's and Fox Tail's admonitions. Midnight brought about the sale's end. Newly-purchased youth plodded off to the garrison, firmly shackled. Those not purchased returned under guard to the confines of the holding pen. Slowly the great doors of the garrison closed after the young captives. Everyone watching in the forest knew that a significant event had taken place—one unique to the Lake Country. Warriors wept openly and all gathered to discuss the development. Fearing detection, the Sandpiper persuaded the warriors to confine all open grieving to deep within the forest, lest their plaints arouse suspicion.

Marchand stole to the General's side: "Guillaume. Let us slip the bonds of the prisoners."

"They are held in chains, Henri, and we do not have the key," he lamented.

"Guillaume. Cerf Courant believes that the chains are hammered into soft earth at the end of each row. One has only to pull them free, Guillaume. The guard stands in the shadows. It is good for us. Cerf Courant carries a sharp blade. He will end the guard's miserable life quickly."

"And what of the prisoners within the garrison?"

"Guillaume! Do you naively believe that they are cozily housed, fed, and furnished with luxuries?"

The General stood mute, his countenance a mask of confusion.

"Guillaume, my fine friend. Already the **Black Jack** has departed the garrison with his two allies. He has spirited away his prizes on a waiting ship, observing all the elements of alacrity and dexterity."

"And where is this ship, Henri?" a doubting Le Rocher asked.

"A cruiser in the harbor below, no less. Hidden at best. We must act now or all is lost. The garrison is not bolstered against a bold attack. It is ripe for the plucking. Think of it, Guillaume. We may be able to sack the garrison, rescue the captives and capture the villains in a single coup."

The General held a short conference. "Oh:nehsi:yo and Cerf Courant are for it. Henri. I too am with you."

"Good! Now let us be off and running!"

* * *

The General and others observed that the revelers returned to the tents and camp fires where they pursued each other's company. The tall flames permeated the darkness, richly illuminating the Commons. Musicians broke out in catchy refrains. Soldiers sat together to tell tales. Food and drink flowed liberally. To the General, no guards roamed the periphery of the grounds. The campaigners, however, watching from seclusion, shivered in the damp forest without the benefit of a warm fire. Huddled in the darkness, they sampled cold meats and hard biscuits, washed down with water from deerskin bags. Everyone waited for the tedium of the enforced vigil to pass. They longed for the excitement which an attack engendered. During the evening the campaigners awaited a signal to open an assault—each unit prepared for a unique role. The fighting soon began, not according to plan, but by means of an isolated incident which forced the General to respond prematurely.

Muted footfalls moved through the darkness. Sounds of bodies colliding and struggling fell upon the campaigners' ears. The sounds grew louder, erupting into barking, followed by a loud thrashing against the earth. The Sandpiper recognized the sounds and stole to the General's side:

"There are wolves among us, Monsieur," he whispered.

"It is the meat. I ordered all wastes to be buried," the General fumed.

"It may be the soldiers themselves," the Sandpiper conceded.

"For our sake I pray you are correct."

Cerf Courant joined the two men, arms dripping with scraps of meat. In disgust he tossed them down and stood idly taciturn.

"I do not want to learn from whence they came," the General sighed.

—

The disturbances alerted garrison sentries. Accordingly, a number of soldiers departed the works to invest the surrounding forest. Watching them, Cerf Courant hatched a plan: Crawling to the garrison, he held the meat scraps in hand. Secreting them beneath the shadows of the main portals, he crept back to seclusion. The baleful barking returned. Shots rang out from the garrison. Sharp cries pierced the darkness—then, nothing. Shortly, waves of laughter broke out among the tenting soldiers. Regaling each other, three of them laid claim to a pair of bloodied carcasses—wolves to be sure. They dragged them into the fort and sporadic celebrations continued into the night.

The General inspected his forces. A certain tenseness pervaded the camp. He scratched notes on a leaf of paper, summoning the principals. He instructed the Sandpiper to occupy the forest on the western Commons behind the soldiers' tents with seventy warriors. He directed Cerf Courant to bring fifty warriors, invade the pen on the eastern Commons and slip the prisoners' bonds, leading them to safety. He himself prepared to spread the regulars, bateaux men, and additional warriors to the south, placing them under Marchand until called upon.

About half past the midnight hour, the main portals opened, releasing a detail of laborers bound for the wooden stage. Before the garrison a second detail aligned the three great cannon into position, muzzles trained due south. Le Rocher followed astutely with field lenses. The stage disassembled, the laborers carried the cumbersome planks to within a few paces of the prisoners' corral. There, they stacked them into a great pyramid. Secreted within the enclosure, Cerf Courant and companions broke the captives' bonds while observing strict silence and cunning. Their charges paid them full attention and the entire operation proceeded unnoticed from without. Meanwhile, the laborers set fire to the pieces, after which they beat a leisurely retreat back to the Commons. Behind them the flames rose mightily, aided no less by gentle evening vapors. In quick succession the flames leaped to the pen. Cerf Courant urged his charges to quit the burning structure one after the other without arousing suspicions. He held great persuasion over them, for the charred walls withstood the flames until the last of the captives escaped before collapsing. A heretofore melancholy General Le Rocher beamed with pride when Cerf Courant and Fox Tail entered camp at the head of a long line of captives—browned but not burned.

A number of them produced knives and small arms, proving that they intended to fight fiercely against their captors once cornered.

"Fire at the stockade!!" a sentry screamed. The portals swung open to discharge a gang of water-bearing soldiers. They charged over the Commons. They doused the smoking embers— drowning all vestiges of the conflagration. Then began the process of looking for human remains. The fire-fighters found none. Calling upon comrades, a full detail began a modified search within minutes of notification, leaving soldiers to stumble about in confusion, anger, and bewilderment. Soon the call went out of prisoners missing. Away in the forest the captives settled among the campaigners. Plumes of smoke followed them. Many burst out coughing, giving echoes to resound through the forest and the principals to shudder with fear. Soldiers, aware that they no longer occupied the Commons alone, came together in a circle. Plunging into the forest, they affixed bayonets.

They surrounded a band of captives who became separated from Cerf Courant. Aware of the penalties for escape and capture, the General immediately surrounded the foe with his regulars, bateaux men, and the Oh:nehsi:yo warriors. Those captives with weapons pleaded to face the enemy, giving the General cause to enlist them. The soldiers, hardy and spoiling for a fight, held their ground, but fought poorly. Many perished from a lack of discipline. The warriors pressed forward in anticipation of scalping the dead and dying and cleaving the skulls of the wounded. The General called for them to desist, leaving the enemy to lick his wounds and drag off his dead. The battle may have ended there, but a sizeable pack of survivors ran straight into a squad of garrison soldiers bent on rescuing them. This heretofore beaten body of soldiers joined with their rescuers to continue the fight.

A short distance hence, south of the Commons, Marchand studied the budding predicament. He released several units: the Bear Chief's volunteers, all able-bodied former prisoners, and the Kanandesaga conscripts in a single body. Skirting the Commons proper, he brought them into position behind the soldiers. The strategy caught the foe unawares and with the General steadfastly advancing, the soldiers adopted a survival-mode of defense: Flanked on two fronts, they spun off into small units. Falling prone upon the earth, they selected targets at will. It is then that the Kanandesaga conscripts threw caution to the winds and made a bold strike in order to post an early victory.

Brandishing hatchets and knives, they dashed headlong into the fray. Dodging and weaving, they cut into the soldiers' line, killing many while suffering minor losses. In the face of such zeal, the soldiers, at the point of absorbing many casualties, fled back to the fort, some of them shielding themselves with warriors seized in battle. The General and Marchand halted pursuit for fear of striking them.

Many of those fleeing to the fort set up a defensive perimeter before the main portals running the width of the works. A brazen few tied captured warriors to the cannon, making of them human shields. They then released a fierce musket barrage into the forest at the unseen enemy. Soon gunners emerged to load the cannon. In response, the General and Marchand prepared to launch an aerial attack upon the fort with arrows from the point where the Sandpiper stood in concealment. The noble chieftain commanded a troupe of longbow marksmen. With the moonlight to guide him, the Sandpiper launched waves of the deadly missiles upon the gunners. Most died instantly, only to be replaced. Bolstered by their comrades' resilience, soldiers within the works rained shot into the trees at an enemy still unseen and unknown. Neither the General nor Marchand ordered a charge of the works in the interest of preventing the senseless slaughter of allies. Far into the early dawn the two sides continued to lunge at each other from concerted points across the great Commons.

A stalemate in the making, the General grew impatient. Calling the leaders together, he unveiled a bold plan: He proposed fitting the Sandpiper's arrows with tiny sacks of gunpowder capable of exploding on impact. The soldiers' bonfires still burned brightly, he noted. He proposed to spark them with the fire-arrows, spreading an impenetrable blanket of flames over the Commons, forcing the garrison to give up the fight and settle for terms. No one posed objections, whereby the General gave the order to commence firing. The Sandpiper chose the finest marksmen, sending them off to retrieve the necessary implements. Returning, the marksmen awaited only the Sandpiper's command to fire. He gave it with a wave of the hand, leaving them to step out of the forest. Missiles, guided by moonlight, flew silently. Striking on mark, they gave the gun powder to explode, sending shards of burning embers pell-mell. Arrows striking the façade of the works exploded, tearing the wooden palisades to shreds. On the Commons sparks ignited the canvas tenting and shrieking men ran for cover. Chaos among the soldiers mounted. A raft of arrows struck the guard-sentry house atop the works. Fitted with the tiny sacks, they wiped out the structure, sending hot embers streaming within the fort. When struck, the bonfires produced a heightened glow before exploding altogether, casting the Commons in a bright, white light. Attendant gunners and soldiers perished outright. Survivors fled into the fort to join comrades seeking refuge. In turn only a single unit of soldiers remained on the grounds. Forming a modest skirmish line, they fired wildly, but posed little threat to the campaigners.

Still the garrison refused to concede defeat. Abandoning the grounds, the single unit gained the fort's ramparts, there to fire down upon approaching reserves. Marchand responded with the longbow warriors who, coming out of concealment, rushed the works. To his dismay a resurgent band of soldiers departed the fort. Advancing to the cannon without, they righted them and began to load them with shot and flaming branches. Once released over the Commons, the branches exploded, lighting up the dark night and exposing the besiegers under a canopy of bright light. Furnished with illumination, soldiers streamed upon the Commons. Throwing up rude trenches, they began to hammer away at the incoming campaigners.

The General valued his men and allies too highly to lose them in a battle of no particular merit. He summoned an abandonment of the assault, withdrawing all combatants beyond the range of the enemy's cannon. Contemplating the next move, he met with Marchand:

"Their cannon are too strong for us, Henri. We will wait until the morning before storming them again."

"The situation will be much the same, with one exception: They may gain reinforcements."

"I expect their reserves, however impaired, to descend on us before first light."

"They have but few fit fighting men to challenge us, Guillaume. All able-bodied British are away with Lord Amherst who is sacking Montreal as we speak. I have detailed Cerf Courant and Fox Tail to block the path to Fort Oswego where there lies a skeleton force. Small wonder that we have not met with resistance from them. We may still carry out a humble victory. I say that we forge ahead. Tell me. Do the soldiers still hold native captives?"

The General stole a glance with his lenses: "I see them chained to the cannon behind the gunners."

"Good! Let us wait until the soldiers have cleaned the grounds of rubble and have retired to the works. They need to tend to the dead and wounded. They may post a light guard, for they believe we are frightened off. Nevertheless, during the night, but before the morning, we must spike the cannon and open a bombardment with our small pieces. We must also send flares over the walls."

"It is a simple yet untried plan, Henri."

"You are not convinced, I fear. Listen, Guillaume. Where do we stand now? Loggerheads? Unacceptable! We came to win and win we must!"

"What man will volunteer for such a mission?"

"Man? Men! I give you men, Guillaume! Any number of our campaigners will step forward. There is *one* unit above all which will jump to the occasion once asked."

"The prisoners of Neatahwantah?"

"The very souls, mon ami. They are ripe for vengeance. How better to cast off the shackles of their oppressors?"

"What is their condition? They look ragged and weary—hardly fit for a challenge."

"I have passed out rations. Before long I will ask for volunteers. Henri. Send the Sandpiper to me".

Guided by moonlight, the Sandpiper threaded a path through the darkness. En route, he stumbled upon an immovable object. It rose up to grab his ankle where it bore into the soft flesh. He chose not to pull it for he knew its identity from the first—an animal trap. Blindly he cast about, fastening upon a fallen branch. Wincing, he stripped it bare. Grasping it, he tossed it to where it came to rest beside the silhouette of a campaigner in the Le Rocher camp. The man turned to him. The Sandpiper called out his own name, whereupon the man and the General himself crept swiftly to his side where they set him free, soothing the ankle with antiseptic. The General appropriated the moment to speak of his latest plan:

"Your marksmen have served well. I need of them one more service. I need to fire the garrison's structures in the way of the hunter who smokes out a hive of bees from a barn. How say you?"

"I look forward to one more encounter with the devil," the chieftain replied, soberly.

"My thoughts exactly. When I give the word, send fire arrows over the main portal. My small field pieces will give you cover."

"But the booming engines, Monsieur."

"They will be silenced according to plan."

"I am always prepared for one more adventure, Monsieur."

"Bon, mon vieux ami."

"What of the captives chained in full view?"

"They too are a part of my plan. You will see."

"I will be watching."

—

The temporary cessation of hostilities produced the desired effect. Remaining enemy ground units retreated within the fortress. Soon the familiar sight of chimney smoke gave the campaigners to understand that the enemy had settled in for the evening. Marchand glimpsed a light guard on the ramparts. Another light guard braved the darkness, coming to rest before the main portals. They fed scraps to native male prisoners seized from the former pen, and the fierce skirmish on the Commons. The last of the bonfires died. The scorched façade of the works bore witness to the scars of intense heat. Although abandoned, the soldiers' tents stood maligned, yet intact. A light rain fell. It changed to hail with pellets bouncing from the hard pan. The General consulted with Marchand:

"These are most favorable conditions for my plan, Henri. Look!! I have back packs filled with stones. The volunteers are waiting in the wings. Let us not disappoint them."

"Agreed, Guillaume. It is too late to turn back." He laughed lightly: "After all, you need at least one friend to support your madness."

The General summoned Cerf Courant. The trusted scout ambled noiselessly to his side. In one hand he held a pair of boars on a leash. His brother, Fox Tail, held a young male boar. The men greased the animals. Cerf Courant released the beasts in the direction of the soldiers' tents, to which he secretly affixed scraps of meat. The two swine tore through the tenting in search of a tasty meal. Perhaps the redundant hailstones or the agitated soldiers spooked the animals, for they ran wildly, becoming entangled in support lines. Ripping at the canvas, they toppled tents which fell full upon them, trapping them in folds of material. The shrieking boars brought a drove of soldiers out upon the grounds. At least three of them stripped away the torn canvas whereby the beasts charged them before making a break for freedom. More soldiers arrived and the boars gored them. They strived to surround the beasts, driving at them from all sides. Ultimately the soldiers herded the two wayward boars into a corral. Butchering them on the spot, they fell to quarreling over the spoils. At that moment Fox Tail released the lone male boar. The ponderous beast tore over the Commons. Barreling into two soldiers, it gored them severely. Soldiers arrived to chase it, setting up another haphazard pursuit. Precious minutes flew away. The boar proved an elusive target. Finally, a single shot to the head brought the rampage to a sudden end. To an observant Le Rocher the entire episode consumed a lengthy interval, fitting precisely into his plans.

The incident of the boars brought many soldiers to the center of the Commons where, in the dead of night, they stumbled with great difficulty to apprehend three errant beasts. While the tumult flowed, six captives, newly-freed from the ravaged corral, stole silently to the garrison's façade. They came to rest beneath the giant shadow cast by the portal-canopy. Each young man carried a leather bag laden with small stones and thick grasses. They brought tamping poles. Their belts held war hatchets and pistols. Deftly the men fitted the stones and grasses within the muzzles of each cannon. They rammed them securely against the breech with the tamping poles. Laboring beneath the great dark shadow, the men prepared to depart as stealthily as they arrived. In a final act of defiance, they severed the bonds binding their comrades to the cannon and the entire troupe stole away together into the night. Returning to the General in the forest, these bold and brave campaigners graciously absorbed the praises which the entire body afforded them. The General dutifully recorded the day and date: Thursday, September 14th. He expected dawn to arrive at five hours and forty five minutes—coinciding with the next part of his plan.

Le Rocher, now General, turned to the principals. He instructed them to launch a decisive thrust upon the works. All parties agreed, prompting the General to tour the encampment with his firm ally, Marchand. Approaching the newly-freed captives they made note of their condition. In passing, the General found that one of them stood apart from the rest in both form and demeanor, preferring to remain in solitude. The two principals studied the remote figure from a distance. They confided to each other that the subject possessed features unique to a person of interest: The golden ringlets protruding from a black watch cap gave the two the impetus to approach and address the subject. The General led the way in greeting. Receiving no response, he plucked away the cap to reveal a woman in a man's clothing. He addressed her in French. The woman replied haltingly, whereupon he ushered her squarely before Suzanne. Leaving the two together, he proceeded on tour. Soon, Aboyant rushed to his side with the message that Suzanne lay prostrate at the feet of the mysterious woman. He and Marchand bounded to the scene where they aroused the stricken Suzanne. She awoke, and, speaking incoherently, pointed to the woman. Aboyant, meanwhile, summoned James York, who came upon a crying and tear-stained Suzanne. James crossed to the woman who sat nearby, hands covering her face. Touching her gently, James spoke reassuringly, all the while lowering her hands to her bosom. James spoke certain words to the woman—words known only to a husband and wife. Stirring, the woman looked up. Stepping back, James studied her countenance. Kneeling before the forlorn figure, he announced:

"Good God, Caroline!! It is you!"

General Le Rocher summoned Suzanne. James led his daughter and long-lost wife to the rear of the lines. There, the three consoled each other. Huddled together beneath the boughs of a great maple, the three sought shelter from a sudden downpour, gaining a reprieve from a battle-scarred landscape of chaos and evil.

—

Back on point, General Le Rocher peered through the trees. A misty rain descended—filling low spots with pools of water. Despite the rain, a light guard paced before the portals of the works. Aboyant came to confer with him. Much to the General's dismay, the quixotic little man emerged from the forest. He brandished a long sapling topped with a white handkerchief. His advance did not escape the alert guards and they allowed Aboyant to approach them. Under cover, the Sandpiper and Cerf Courant stood at the ready to the west and east of the Commons, respectively. Presently a figure issued from the works. A swarthy, clean-shaven hulk, the man carried a cutlass sheathed about the waist. His great bulk compelled him to stride stiffly in the manner of a stalking bull. He snorted frequently and wiped at his chin, drawing to mind a strong relationship with the buffalo— that great beast of the plains. The texture of his leather trousers and knee-high boots resembled the tough hide of the buffalo. With a square torso set over tapering legs, he projected a surly scowl that betrayed tobacco-stained teeth. Grumbling, he ambled over the Commons, a small body of followers at his heels. Halting, he folded massive arms over an expansive chest and leered down at the little man who stood a half meter beneath the protruding jaw. Withholding a name, the giant offered not a greeting, unless spitting on the earth before Aboyant's feet constituted his version of a salutation.

Aboyant stood firm. Reserving comment on the man's appearance, he peered upward at him, staff in hand. Stepping forward, he kicked loose the soil at his feet, jamming the instrument into the hard pan, eyes locked upon his bellicose host. Aboyant folded his arms over his chest in a self-satisfied manner. He doffed his characteristic and peculiar lid slowly. Bowing low, he emitted a sugary smile. Rising, he deftly extracted a sheaf of paper from his tunic. Opening it tenderly, he held it out to the leering giant. Grudgingly the man snatched the paper. Snarling, he handed it to one of his party, eyes riveted upon the little intruder. Hidden from view, the campaigners stood waiting with hearts pounding.

The big man's comrade read the message silently. Finishing, he broke into sustained laughter, sharing its contents with members of his party. Upon the big man's insistence, he read it aloud, still laughing:

"You are hereby instructed to abandon this garrison immediately upon pain of certain death. You are permitted to take all belongings

After laying down your arms. You may go in peace, provided you offer no resistance to the forces who surround you."

The big man shuffled toward Aboyant. Calling the little man closer, he stepped swiftly to the side in a single step, wrenching the sword from its sheath in blazing speed. Reaching overhead, he brought it straight down over Aboyant, intent upon cleaving the little man's skull. The wary Aboyant, a master of self-discipline, skirted to one side. Bending low at the waist, he allowed the blade to pass over him. Bolting upright, he pulled a blade from his trousers. He plunged it into the giant's chest as the blade of the sword completed its deadly arc. Gasping, the behemoth uttered not a word. He stood stiff-legged. His features became horror-stricken: The tongue gushed blood, darting between the teeth. The eyes turned red, bulging in blood-stained sockets. Aboyant dashed between the flailing arms. He extracted the blade with a vengeance. Kicking the giant's lower leg, he brought him to topple to the earth. The giant's comrades stood aghast, but otherwise did not pursue the little man. Aboyant turned his back to the ruffians. Wiping the blade against the fallen hulk's trousers, he sauntered from the scene without so much as casting a glance over a shoulder. At the point where Aboyant reentered the forest, the big man's comrades drew pistols. Indecision won over them, however, leaving them to gather over the still form, this giant of a man-beast silent forever. Confused, they broke for the works where they milled about in consternation.

In view of the events, the Marchand detachment revealed itself along the eastern Commons. He opened a fierce barrage of musket fire upon defenders amassed before the works. Unexpectedly they charged toward him. Gunners prepared to fire the great cannon. Discovering the pieces' shortcomings, they flew their hands up in anger, shouting profanities to the four winds. In response, Marchand seized the moment, sending forth the forces of Le Rocher, the Sandpiper, and Cerf Courant. A two-tiered column enveloped the entire eastern Commons, compelling the soldiers to drop to one knee before the works where they fired frenetically. The fight ran hot and bloody before the General executed a scheme: He bid the teamsters to roll the three light-weight pieces into position—two of them survivors of Neatahwantah. Primed and loaded, the pieces gave with a broadside along the face of the fortress, spewing clusters of grapeshot. Those who did not perish at first blow, heaved themselves into the charred fortress, there to seek shelter and burrow into concealment. A good number fled beyond the works, over the northern slope and perilously close to the harbor. There they hid in dense thickets, while others sought passage to Fort Oswego to the east. Tasting victory, the General trained the little guns on the works itself. He hammered it at short range. Scarred timbers crumbled. The main portals collapsed to reveal a blackened interior, leaving frightened soldiers to throw up their hands. The General, every bit directing the assault, halted further bombardment.

Those surviving soldiers eluding the assault fled below the ravaged garrison where they reached a series of stark conclusions: They realized the spiked cannon opened a turning point in the besiegers' favor. They knew that they sorely lacked for gunpowder and shot. They were unable to secure reinforcements from Fort Oswego across the harbor because of a besieger-blockade. Awaiting dawn's first light of the following day, they viewed themselves akin to a pack of refugees. Desperate, they named one of their number to open a route to Fort Oswego— one final burst to secure aid. The selected soldier crept out along the steep escarpment of the northern slope below the works' grim remains. Shifting among boulders and brambles, the duty-bound soldier sought the path of least resistance eastward—that opening which skirted the barricade of rocks and logs thrown up by the campaigners. At length he found such a passage way—a narrow trail cut by deer most likely during the rutting season. Keeping to the shadows, the soldier stirred not a single leaf, coming to within meters of Fort Oswego's outer limits. There, he halted in mid-stride. Looking for a company of His Majesty's forces in fighting form, he spied instead a collection of scruffy, unkempt campaigners, exercising maneuvers, their ranks streaming north to south in an unbroken line. Though lean, these campaigners appeared prepared to fight and it is this sighting which he mournfully brought back to his comrades in hiding.

The lot of them spent long moments reviewing the astuteness of the campaigners in achieving victory, however tenuous. They recalled the campaigners' clever employment of fire-arrows and small caliber weapons. They recalled how their own bonfires served as beacons to draw the enemy's fire—providing him with a useful tool in battle. Most disheartening, they recalled how fighting without a supreme commander left them at a loss to coordinate the fight— one to make necessary adjustments of men and materiel along the way.

During the murky pre-dawn a cadre of survivors appeared at the works' smoldering parapets. There they hoisted white flags of surrender. Elsewhere, commands in isolated pockets of the Commons threw down arms to sit on the hard pan, awaiting orders. The General himself appeared before the vanquished. He sent the Sandpiper's forces forward to receive prisoners. The soldiers offered no resistance. Walking willingly to the periphery of the Commons, they allowed themselves to be searched and taken into custody. Marchand and others counted one hundred and ninety five of His Majesty's soldiers thus detained. The residual force at Fort Oswego never proved a contending factor in the fight and the principals granted them asylum so that they may tell their story to Lord Carleton. At least one hundred and fifty of His Majesty's soldiers perished in the fight. Many ran off, according to Marchand. Le Rocher decided to take all prisoners to Pointe Aux Bois, there to set up conditions for negotiating a just peace between the belligerents. Meeting with the campaigners, Marchand praised them for carrying the day by means of conducting a wise interpretation of unconventional warfare, of executing guile effectively, and by exhibiting unbridled enthusiasm.

* * *

Le Rocher and Marchand repaired to the remains of Fort Ontario. In viewing the parched structures, the principals ordered destroyed all evil-posing trappings of the works. To that extent the Sandpiper's warriors set fire to the captain's quarters, the quartermaster's cabin, the soldiers' dormitories, the powder magazine, dining hall, the target range, the forge, and the officers' dormitory. Selected structures remained untouched. In deference to authority, the token force at Oswego proper invited the two commanders to a modest repast. Accepting in all sincerity, Le Rocher and Marchand strode leisurely over the main yard, making a cursory inspection of spared structures. These latter comprised the sutler's store, the chapel, the commandant's residence, horses' livery stables, granary, the storage depot, tailor's shop, one-room school house and elaborate flower gardens near the postern gate. The General spoke to Marchand:

"I am conserving certain vestiges of the works, for I want our adversary to know that even in battle I am a benign soul who observes the articles of war."

"Are you not granting our adversary unusual indulgences?"

"On the contrary. We have our enemy where we want him. I will present Lord Carleton with an ultimatum. Either he negotiates with us, or we will notify his superiors of his failure to secure the works—indeed, his failure to make necessary preparations for an assault. We have at our disposal the bulk of his soldiers—those who through poor leadership fell into a trap. Our trap. Moreover, those whom I have set free know upon whom to thrust fingers of guilt and idle tongues speak volumes, you well know. Therefore, Henri we are rest-assured that the commandant will treat with us on our terms—and soon."

"What of the precious skins and hides stored roundabouts, Guillaume?"

"They are the property of our allies who fought so bravely beside us. I propose that we restore them, Henri. We must look after our allies, not betray them, mon ami."

"My sentiments exactly, Guillaume."

The General prowled about the grounds of the ravaged works. Head bowed, he became the object of curiosity. Aware of the many eyes following him, he made an announcement: "I am looking for signs of the evil triumvirate: the crusty codger, the pirate, and the dandy, to be precise. You all are invited to join me. Where are they? One does not simply vanish from the face of the earth!"

James York approached. Having spent several hours in consoling Caroline, he learned of the General's interest in pursuing her abductor. He volunteered to search the grounds with a small detail.

"Excellent, James. Take Cerf Courant and Fox Tail with you," an ebullient Le Rocher interceded. "We are most likely looking for a concealed means of escape—something that by its very simplicity defies the senses."

Turning to Marchand, the General, in buoyant spirits, made known an observation: "I long expected to find these works sparsely defended, Henri. You recall hat General Amherst swooped into Oswego to recruit a force for his Montreal campaign. He took with him renegade Iroquois, New England militia, and British regulars (38). Montreal has poor defenses—an island without walls, ramparts, or gun batteries. She is doomed. We, on the other hand, are unable to retain the holdings that we possess indefinitely. France has too few soldiers at arms in the Americas. The majority are fighting in Europe, of all places. Let us hope to find the evil that lurked within these battered walls before we are unable to do so." He inspected the grounds, joined by two prisoners from the devastated Ontario, who volunteered to accompany him.

The pair, a Mr. Rice and a Mr. Dobbs, provided a historical commentary of Fort Oswego's extensive gardens. Le Rocher and Marchand learned that the gardens originally belonged to one Major Duncan (39) a sub-commander at the fort. Consisting of flowering blooms and vegetables, the gardens occupied the entirety of the rear grounds—approximately one half of the work's total land mass. Proceeding on tour, the two principals noted the tidy rows of pathways traversing the gardens where the specimens received tender care at the hands of the Major and a select crew of laborers. They never lacked for water and nourishment, according to Mr. Rice and Mr. Dobbs. Major Duncan planted an assortment of flowering trees in the gardens, namely lilacs, dogwood, and rose bushes. Many of the seeds and actual specimens he imported from the Continent. The Major also cultivated local yields which he gathered over the course of many sojourns into the Lake Country. His diligent labors received much praise from the body of residents living nearby the works. Over the years the Major furnished the burgeoning settlement of Oswego with choice vegetables, gradually extending his gardens into the growing community itself. Early settlers owed their well-being to the foresight of Major Duncan, who saw them through periods of drought and harsh winters. To many, Major Duncan was a preeminent early contributor to the growth of what became a thriving community. He formed a friendship with Lord Carleton while in residency, the pair going on hunting forays.

The two principals visited the storage depot, domain of one Henry Van Schaack (40), Superintendent of Stores. Mr. Dobbs and Mr. Rice eagerly gave a vivid account of Van Schaack, whose exploits in the fur trade were legendary among denizens of the garrison. More than any other man, Van Schaack developed the growth of the fur trade in the Lake Country. Traveling to Fort Niagara, Detroit and forts of the Great Lakes, he accepted the natives' peltry which came in from neighboring villages. At first he brought specimens to Schenectady before opening a route to Albany by bateaux plying the numerous inland waterways. Enlarging his sphere of influence, he displayed his wares to entrepreneurs in Quebec and New York City. From the latter locale his specimens found their way to London where he established trade agreements with houses of commerce. Van Schaack became London's chief consultant in trade relations among the natives with whom he trafficked. From modest beginnings, Van Schaack rose to a position of importance among the captains of the mercantile trade on both sides of the Atlantic. He cultivated a friendship with Sir William Johnson, Superintendent of Northern Indian Affairs and fought in the French and Indian War, helping to engineer a French defeat in a minor, yet critical battle. Both maneuvers put him on solid footing with

British military authorities in North America. His appointment to Fort Oswego represented the formal recognition of his labors to bring native fur trading within the Crown's purview. During the sacking of Fort Ontario, Van Schaack, according to Mr. Dobbs and Mr. Rice, was en route to Michilimackinac on yet another fur trading venture. He would revel in the sparing of his coveted fur-storage depot, the two concluded.

Proving a free-flowing font of knowledge thus far, the General thrust an image of Old Crusty upon the verbose pair from the recesses of his mind. To his delight Mr. Dobbs and Mr. Rice burst forth with a wealth of discoveries—observations long held under wraps and shared only between themselves. Tracing Old Crusty's known movements, they ran back to his preemptive strike against the village Osco, after which they studied him from a distance. Le Rocher learned that Old Crusty, Captain James Worthy, led two distinct lives. Officially he surveyed lands for white settlement. On the other hand he played the rogue interloper: demanding tribute from natives in the form of furs, skins, and the human species. He sold all for a profit and woe to the man who cast him in a poor light.

Mr. Dobbs disclosed that Van Schaack commonly reported shortages in specimens in the storage depot during the Captain's tenure. Suspecting theft, he confronted the Captain, which led to violent outbursts between the two of them. "To be sure, he never caught Old Crusty in the act, yet Old Crusty held keys to all principal buildings."

"Van Schaack became suspicious," Mr. Rice offered. "The Captain is in charge of the grounds, but offers no knowledge of what may have taken place. Their meetings often centered about the one making charges and the other denying all. More than once they almost came to exchanging blows."

A perplexed Le Rocher asked: "To where has this villain Old Crusty absconded?"

"I presume that he departed to attend to what he termed important affairs," Mr. Dobbs offered.

"In the midst of a siege? That is the extent of your knowledge, good man?"

"The Captain is a master of mystery with a talent to completely absent himself from others," Mr. Rice stated.

"What of the dandy? The man in white?"

"Simmons. He too seems to have vanished unawares. He is not among the dead," Mr. Rice continued.

"Very bizarre. Tell me. Why do you confide in me, gentlemen?"

"I speak for those whom the Captain has slighted. Many soldiers fell to their death because of his stubbornness."

"He attacked a native village and many more died. He is inept and crazed, I fear," Mr. Dobbs returned.

"He is not to be found when tragedy strikes. He has blackened the eye of the BEF," Mr. Rice contributed.

"At Ontario he played the role of a coward, my friend," Mr. Rice concluded.

"Yes. There you have it. In my sorrow I almost forgot. His indiscretions are many and tragic."

—

The Rocher party returned to walking the grounds of the scarred shell of the works. Occasionally they kicked up remnants of battle: arrow shafts, musket balls, and sundry objects. At one point the General struck an impediment that refused to yield of its own volition. On inspection, a knob or protuberance of sorts broke the surface of the hard pan. Bending, he dusted it with gloved hands. An iron handle came into being. Tugging it, he made several aborted attempts to dislodge it. One last violent tug and the hard pan split apart to reveal a rounded-iron cover, an integral part, attached to the knob. With assistance, the General turned the cover aside, discovering a black void which descended into the earth. He called for a torch, and lowering it into the darkness, found that the opening led into a pit or vault carved underground. The makings of wooden staves supporting the vault came into view. Fastening a rope to the torch, he lowered it along the cylindrical shaft or opening. Deeper it descended, his hands feeding the rope ever-carefully. When at its limit, the torch touched bottom, flickered, and died out. He retrieved the rope. Placing the line before him, he measured the distance traversed. Elated to no end, he made an announcement. "Gentlemen. I have found where Old Crusty went." Marchand joined him. "Who will be the first to enter?" he asked, patting a prominent stomach.

The General settled upon Fox Tail. Tall and lean, Cerf Courant's brother came forth, shovel in hand. Men scooped away clumps of earth. Fox Tail secured a rope around his waist and allowed himself to be lowered down the foreboding shaft. Marchand passed him a lighted torch and everyone gathered around the opening with interest. Striking bottom, Fox Tail announced that indeed he found himself in a cavern, the likes of which spread extensively. On the surface a crew widened the opening to admit several more men. They descended into a cavern and came to stand together at full height in initial wonderment. Capacious, the cavern stood equipped with a wooden ceiling buoyed up with stout timbers. Walls, smooth and planed, stood off to the sides of the gloomy, damp enclosure. Searching along the walls, the crew looked for an opening or exit leading to the exterior. In the dimness the men groped the walls, inspecting irregular surfaces for signs of a door or portal. Relying highly on the sense of touch, the men searched diligently, unmindful of the pent-up heat which their combined mass released into the confined space. One of them announced the makings of a door knob pressed hard against a wall. It turned to the touch. Earth fell away, pouring over the cavern's floor. A creaking or scraping sound ensued, guiding the man further. By touch alone, the man dislodged a door set upon ancient hinges. It opened at a second attempt to admit a breathtaking panorama of the great harbor, some two hundred feet below.

Beside himself with delight, the General descended to the cavern floor where he regaled the new findings. Overcome by the sheer weight of the discovery, he slumped to the makeshift floor where he covered his head in his hands. Renewed by the fresh vapors entering from the harbor, crew members gathered around him with torches burning brightly. Bit by bit, the men made a series of poignant discoveries: They found spent shackles, restraining ropes, remains of a fireplace, a stack of wood, a small cache of food stores, uniforms folded in an armoire, two small beds, and attendant sundries. A heavy, pungent odor emerged, making breathing difficult. Leaving the curious below, the General regained the surface where he sought after Mr. Dobbs and Mr. Rice for whom he held questions:

"Gentlemen. This is clearly the scoundrels' route of escape. You attest that it is unknown to you?"

Dobbs and Rice looked at each other. Rice spoke: "In all of my days in residence I knew not of this hidden place, nor have my comrades spoken to me of it," the man returned soberly, eyes upon Le Rocher.

"Strange that it may seem, but I believe you," the General confessed, stroking his chin. "Let me say that, judging from the circumstances leading to this point, the rascals reserved the place for escape when other means failed."

"With the exception of a slave sale or two, Guillaume," Marchand quipped.

"Yes, Henri. How thick are the three of them? Our villains?" he asked, looking from Dobbs to Rice.

"Simmons. He sticks to Old Crusty tighter than glue," Dobbs spoke.

"And the pirate?"

"Not too familiar with him. He comes and goes at leisure, but Simmons and Old Crusty are inseparable."

"There! You have it," the General shouted. "Old Gouty, the pirate and the dandy formed a conspiracy, most likely departing by separate conveyances: the pirate to a ship, the others by means unknown." He called down to the crew below: "Do you see evidence of tracks? Prints leading to the exterior?"

Struggling against the inherent darkness and recumbent congestion at their feet, the crew inadvertently stumbled upon a gruesome discovery: Thus, Fox Tail called to the surface. He reported the finding of cadavers stacked against a wall covered with loose earth. Presently he brought forth an inert form, a wizened and lank soul sorely maligned. The man lay covered in dust and soot, and wore the remnants of a red tunic and blue leggings. Fox Tail cleared passages along the man's eyes, ears, and mouth and prevailed on him to speak. Mr. Dobbs revived the man with smelling salts, claiming him a stranger. In short order the man sat upright. He begged for food and asylum. He gave his name willingly and claimed to have been left for dead. Le Rocher gave him nourishment in exchange for an account of his condition. He and others stood aghast by the tale of horror which the man spewed forth:

"The crusty Captain plucked me and some mates from a harbor merchantman," the man, John Stout, stated, wincing in pain. "He offered to reward me for lending him a hand in loading cargo aboard a vessel weighing at anchor. I and my mates heaved to. We packed and dropped bales of furs down the cliff to the harbor and loaded the vessel. Then we all met in the cave awaiting payment. There the Captain met us before a warm fire, looking every bit the gentleman. We expected dinner and wages. He shot the lot of us. A friend helped. I slumped between two of my mates. I played dead. I allowed them to carry me to a pile of my mates where they threw me down and covered me with earth and rubble. I believed myself more dead than alive until you came to find me."

"You remained in the cavern, wounded yet alive?" the General asked, recovering his senses.

"Sure as I am speakin' with ya.'"

"His friends. Who were they?"

"A pirate and a trim dude in light uniform."

"Were names exchanged?"

"Not a one, mate."

"Again. Why were you not killed?"

"They fell on me. My men. I played dead and held my breath. They covered us with sod and dashed outside. In a hurry they were."

The General pointed to Mr. Dobbs and Mr. Rice: "Do you know these men?"

"Strangers to me, mate." John Stout coughed generously.

Le Rocher made note of the man's clothing: "What rank are you?"

"Rank, you ask?" John Stout scoffed." I am a mere boatswain's mate. I lifted these clothes from a dead soldier. Mine were bloodied —dripping with body parts and the like."

Upon further inquiry the General learned that the Captain conscripted Stout and others from a merchantman, promising a handsome reward to transport what he, Stout, deemed to be native youth and precious furs, to a standing harbor vessel. Though not forced to comply, he, Stout, looked to earn just compensation and persuaded his mates to accept the Captain's offer. Stout's men urged him to accept, whereupon he complied with the Captain's request. Once finished, everyone came together in the cavern where the Captain drew pistols and fired, cutting the crew down, with the aide of the prim man, dressed in white. In their haste, Stout suffered minor wounds and vowed to live to tell his story. The two tore off immediately after committing the deed, Stout concluded.

Stout accepted a cup of water. Imbibing deeply, he continued: "I hope I have been of service to you, gentlemen." Leaning back, he closed his eyes in repose.

"You have been of immense value," the General spoke. He ordered Stout removed to Oswego proper, there to receive medical treatment, a bath, clothing, and a hearty meal. Turning to Dobbs and Rice, the General asked boldly:

"Are you willing to offer evidence against the Captain?"

"In exchange for my liberty? Yes," Dobbs returned.

"Guard your tongue, Chris. Your life will not be worth a rusty nail once word of your story reaches the Captain."

"Andrew!! I am not about to spend my remaining years in a dark cell."

"His tentacles reach far and wide, Chris. They will grab you and squeeze out your life's blood. Take Watkins."

"Yes. Watkins. He tried to forewarn those aborigines. Shot and banished. Gone. Gone forever."

"We do not know that for certain, Chris. His body was never found."

"I believe that he is still out there, Andrew—waiting for the moment to show himself."

"I hate to differ with you, but I think not."

—

A courier from Fort Oswego arrived. He asked the General to spare his garrison from native reprisals. Le Rocher gave with reassurances. In a gesture of friendship, he sent a detail to clear remaining obstacles from the obstructed pathway leading to the fortress. Task completed, the residents of the fort poured out to greet him, circulating among his men. The women and children of Oswego held a reception for the campaigners. Everyone associated with the occupational force sat down to a noble repast.

Among the first to attend the reception, the York family dined with the wife of Oswego's sub-commandant before accepting a guided tour of the campus. Unlike the battered Ontario, Oswego emerged unscathed from the fighting, and presented a number of stylish buildings set in the era of King George II. Suzanne and her mother took particular interest in a lone wooden cabin on wheels situated in a corner of the main campus. James turned to Dobbs and Rice and the two men unfolded the story of the quaint little structure.

The cabin, they began, served the needs of Major Duncan, assistant garrison commandant. He is attributed with having established the first frontier schoolhouse, to their knowledge. Portable, the cabin rested on logs, in turn fastened to wheels, enabling it to be rolled at will over the grounds. The Major believed in a well-educated body of soldiers and arranged for them to take lessons in conjunction with official duties (41). According to the two witnesses, following morning drills, the soldiers broke off into small squads to study inside Major Duncan's cabin. Assisted by traveling teachers, the Major introduced his charges to the full gamut of pedagogical lore—otherwise given in more formal settings. The two men took delight in reciting the litany of subjects studied within the little school: reading, ciphering, calligraphy, geography, Latin, Greek, comparative government, world religions, Iroquois dialects, homemaking, surveying, and Aristotle geometry. To better serve his charges, the Major hauled the school over the campus by means of a team of draft horses. He set up a time-table of classes so that over a week everyone received one full unit of instruction. He gave daily paper and pencil tests, a major exam or review to follow at month's end. He also reserved periods of instruction for the children and young adults of the garrison.

The Major divided the school into two sections: the first served as his bedroom; the second served as a library and dining room. The library stood stocked with books and anthologies donated by officers' wives and from the Major's private collections. Itinerant teachers often donated books and ships docking in the harbor brought materials from abroad. The Major furnished the walls and floors of the school with animal skins, providing blankets for his charges on cold and forbidding winter days. There, during the endless winters so germane to the Lake Country, in the absence of communications with the external world, human intercourse flourished. Soldiers and young residents clamored to avail themselves of the Major's offerings in this warm and bucolic cabin. Committed to the elimination of illiteracy among the soldiery, Major Duncan conducted classes throughout the year, making every effort to create conditions conducive to learning. For example, he allowed soldiers to borrow books on request for personal enrichment, setting up agreeable terms with them.

A youngster by the name of Annie Mc Vicar passed the summer and fall of 1760 at Fort Oswego (42). Among other venues, she frequented the Major's school, where, according to her father, Duncan Mc Vicar, an officer stationed at the fort, she took her first classes in reading and writing. Dobbs and Rice remembered her as an endearing and inquisitive little girl who possessed a great appetite for knowledge. Suzanne and her mother soon met Annie Mc Vicar. She delighted them with her innate intelligence, and patiently awaited her father's return after fleeing following the siege of Fort Ontario. Generally, Annie clung close to Major Duncan, and with her mother's permission, accompanied him on walks beyond the garrison's walls. The young girl greatly admired the out-of-doors, especially the varieties of waterfowl that visited the marsh lands. One afternoon Annie took Suzanne and Caroline York on a tour of the school. She shared her enthusiasm for learning with her two guests. The General remained for three days at Oswego, allowing Suzanne to teach a few classes.

"The little girl Annie brings out my nurturing qualities, Suzanne," Caroline spoke, arms encircling her daughter. "To think that one day not long ago I brought you along the path of erudition."

"Have I strayed so far from the tree, mother?" Suzanne chided.

"Not at all. You are an excellent student and teacher. Your lingering at the schoolhouse confirmed my belief."

"I am in need of an assistant, mother. Do you consent to join my classroom?" Suzanne asked in jest.

"By all means. Together we will take civilization to a new level. Good students often make good teachers, you know." She smiled to herself while looking out upon the horizon.

Suzanne meditated, then spoke: "I want to teach the young natives the way I taught Raven and Little Bear."

"That is entirely possible once we return to the Round Tops, dear daughter."

"What if the Round Tops no longer exists? What shall we do?"

"That reminds me, Suzanne. I want to do something for the native peoples—for women as well. Neither they nor we are recognized for the special qualities that we possess."

"The spirit of the pioneer has caught you, I see."

"It has caught you too, Suzanne. Yet you are not aware of it."

"We live in a man's world, mother. They make all the laws and rules."

"We are also surrounded by strong men. Strong men will listen. With their support we will make our ambitions known." She held Suzanne at arm's length, looking into her eyes.

"What do you propose, mother?"

"After the fighting dies down, I plan to go to Albany to speak on behalf of those unable to speak for themselves."

—

A great din erupted from among the residents on Oswego's main concourse. Aboyant ran to Suzanne's side and in a jumble of words announced the fall of Montreal to Lord Amherst. Annie Mc Vicar joined him.

"Will father be coming back soon?" Annie called.

"Yes, child," Suzanne returned softly, refraining from disclosing her father's true fate.

At week's end the hour of departure arrived. The campaigners bid fair adieux to their Oswego hosts. Reluctantly they began a tedious trek to Pointe Aux Bois. They kept to a circuitous route in order to confound enemy scouts. The prisoners won in battle, the principals placed under the watch of the Kanandesaga conscripts, whose prowess in battle gained them the recognition they so sorely desired.

Le General thought ahead: Once at Pointe Aux Bois, he would set about drafting the terms of Lord Carleton's capitulation.

(33)Williams, C.L (1952), Chapter 6: *Early France*, pgs: 69-73

(34)Tebbell, John (1948) ed. The Battle for North America: From the Works of Francis Parkman, Chapter 8: *The Battle With The Onondagas*, Doubleday & Company, Garden city, NY. pgs: 382-383.

(35)Merrill (1949) Land of the Senecas, pgs: 112-114.

(36)Tebbell, ed.(1948 Chapter 3: *Champlin at Quebec*, pgs: 43-56.

*North Street, Auburn, NY

**State Street in Auburn, NY where it crosses the Owasco River adjacent to Auburn Correctional Facility

*Lake Neatahwantah lies on the outskirts of Fulton, NY and is entirely natural in origin

*Lake Onondaga

*A section of the Seneca River due east of Baldwinsville, NY in the Town of Clay. Shallow and narrow for much of the year, it is close to the Great Northern Mall shopping complex

(37)Tebbell. The Battle for North America: Part Four Count Frontenac (1948) pgs: 374-383

(38)Anderson, Fred. Crucible of War, Chapter 40: *War in Full Career*, Vintage Books, NY (2000) pgs: 387-390

(39) Clark, Joshua. Onondaga, Or Reminiscences of Earlier and Later Times. Stoddard & Babcock, Syracuse, NY. (1849) pg: 374

(40) Van Schaack, Henry. Memoirs if the Life of Henry Van Schaack. Chapter 1. Mc Clurg & Co. Chicago (1892)

(41) Grant, Mc Vicar Annie. Memoirs of an American Lady. Chapter IX: *Continuation of the Journey*—Arrival at Oswego. D. Appleton & Co New York (1808) pgs: 65-68

(42) Grant, Mc Vicar Ann (1846) pgs: 59-64

CHAPTER TEN

Crossroads

Le General Meets Skenando.
Pointe Aux Bois Welcomes The Yorks.
The Captain Reemerges.
A Welcomed Visitor.
Matthew York.

The campaigners headed due east. They followed the northern shore of Oneida Lake and where the lake ended they turned directly to the southwest in the direction of Pointe Aux Bois. No one protested the roundabout tour, for everyone knew that they must protect the anonymity of their lone French post, or suffer the consequences of premature discovery. In light of recent British incursions into the Lake Country, their numbers held too few to offer sustained resistance to a siege by a superior force, and everyone therefore adhered to the guidelines of the two leading principals: Le General Rocher and Henri Marchand.

The General preferred highly wooded regions invested with low valleys with ample foliage. He marched the force of French and natives in two columns at close intervals so that each segment may keep watch over the other. The prisoners walked between the columns, secured by arm shackles and stout bonds, where the former ran in short supply. Fox Tail and Cerf Courant led the procession, followed in turn by the principals, the archers, the riflemen, and hatchet-wielding warriors. At the General's insistence, Marchand put Dobbs and Rice in the vanguard of the procession with instructions to lend an eye and ear to the surroundings. The three little cannon brought up the rear, along with two wagons laden with furs, pelts, shot, and gunpowder bound for Iroquoia. The campaigners maintained tight formation in order to reduce exposure to predatory elements. They kept up a steady gait and allowed no unnecessary discourse to pass through the ranks.

In his haste to return to home-base, the General neglected to collect his bateaux which he beached along the banks of the Oswego River. French explorers long ago adopted the bateaux from the onset of their quest of the Continent. The broad-beamed, flat-bottomed craft served French traders well so that anyone who spied a bateau on an inland waterway knew that the French lay hidden in the shallows. Again, to deflect attention away from Pointe Aux Bois, the General dispatched fifty men overland to secure the boats, his only claim to a marine force, and float them back to the base.

The campaigners followed a well-known Oneida trail, one that led them to within a short distance of the Oneida capital, Oneida Castle. Marchand urged the General to visit the village so that he may renew relations with his old friend, Skenando. He traded with Skenando extensively and the wise and venerated chieftain trusted him as a true friend. In the past Skenando provided him with useful knowledge concerning British military maneuvers. The chieftain possessed a remarkable talent for predicting the outcome of events long before they came to pass and after lauding Skenando's attributes before the General, the commander yielded to the tradesman's request. Consulting maps, he ordered a modest change in direction and the procession took a turn toward Oneida Castle. Although getting along in years, Skenando rushed out of his cabin to greet his old friend. He brought with him his wife and other members of his extended family. He embraced the tradesman firmly and gave him to understand that he held an urgent message for him:

"The white agent William Johnson has visited me, my friend."

"Yes. I have heard of him. He seems to follow in my footsteps of late."

"You may want to keep him within your sights, for he is an ambitious man."

"Tell me about him, old friend."

"He wants me to form ties with his British traders."

"What are your thoughts on the matter?"

"If I agree, he will flood me with expensive presents." He paused, then, "He will also bring in many more homesteaders than my People are able to tolerate."

"Our bonds must remain strong, for we are both under siege."

"From the same source," Skenando added.

"Yes. This is true, old friend."

"I understand that you stormed Ontario."

"Word of my exploits travels quickly."

"He will rebuild, you know. He will rebuild and come after you."

"I may ask you to support me, Skenando."

"I will if I am still in a position to do so."

"It will be a true test of our friendship."

"One that I am able to meet, my friend. Tell me. Do you have any of the Cayugas with you?"

"Yes. I have a band which the Bear Chief granted me."

"Ah, yes. The Bear Chief. He is cousin to Tah-gah-jute. On that aspect alone he is a fine man. Tah-gah-jute is half Oneida, you know. His father, Shikellamy, is Oneida. During his youth father and son visited me regularly. Later on the Bear Chief and his father came. Over two generations we spoke of severing the Covenant Chain* which my predecessors formed with the British. William Johnson became worried. He wants to keep us faithful to the Chain. He wants to buy our loyalty with lavish gifts. This means he wants to lock you French out of our lives."

"I enjoy our friendship, old friend."

"I do as well. Tell me. Have you ever met Tah-gah-jute?"

"No, but I know that he used to live near the site of the Bear Chief's new village."

"I did not know that the Bear Chief moved to a new village."

"He found it necessary to protect his flock from enemy raids."

"Ah!! More blood wars?"

"Not at all. British soldiers raided and looted his village by the lake."

"This is so unlike William Johnson to punish an ally."

"I thought them renegades. I pursued them to Ontario where I assailed their fort."

"Ah!! Now I understand. Do they know you? They will seek you out."

"They believe I am Canadian. You must keep my secret, old friend."

"Of that you may rest assured. I must tell you that, before he left for the Ohio country, Tah-gah-jute paid me one final visit. He went to seek peace for the Delaware, his cousins along the Susquehanna. The whites there pushed them back into Ohio and they are very angry."

"But does not the Pennsylvania legislature assure the Delawares of their native lands?"

"Face-to-face, yes, but behind their backs, no. You see, William Penn, their friend, has died, and many men, his sons included, have come to buy the land, even force out the Delaware. Already there has been bloodshed on both sides. The British have all but given ownership to the western Senecas."

"This is horrible, Skenando."

"Yes. They are trying to turn brother against brother—and I believe they are winning."

"This Johnson is a man of two faces, Skenando. He is not to be trusted. We must drive them out."

"We are too small and you are too few, but I am pleased that you fought them at Ontario."

"Thank you, old friend. Let us speak of more pleasant things."

The chieftain led forth several young children. In succession they shook the tradesman's hand, cherubic faces beaming up at him, coal-black eyes all the glow. They introduced themselves by name, greeting the tradesman in the English tongue.

"A young missionary **has visited us. This summer he taught the children to speak the English tongue. He plans to come back one day with more missionaries and teachers."

The tradesman ushered forth Suzanne and her mother. "I have two women with me. They adore children." He winked approvingly and Suzanne and Caroline allowed the children to surround them and touch their garments.

"They flock to you, mother," Suzanne squealed in delight.

"They have never seen blonde tresses before, Suzanne. Do you see how they speak in English?"

"It is simply amazing. We must thank the man responsible. Where is he?"

"Mr. Kirkland is making a missionary tour," the tradesman spoke. He looked from Suzanne to Caroline. "Look! The children think that you two are their new teachers."

Both women laughed. "Here is the opening you have been looking for, Suzanne," Caroline reminded her.

"It is very tempting to stay here, mother; however, I am unable to leave you alone."

"I still have father. You do remember your father, do you not?"

At the sound of his name James York entered into the dialogue: "I believe it a noble task for someone to reach out to another civilization with the hope of spreading faith and understanding. I am honored that not one, but *two* members of my family have chosen to enter into such a calling. You have my unrelenting support, ladies." He bowed from the waist and smiled impishly, but Suzanne knew that her father held the greatest respect for her views on administering to the natives, stemming no less from her charitable Catholic upbringing.

Skenando clapped his hands together and from an undisclosed source bearers came forward laden with an assortment of objects—all pleasing to the eye. He reached for the two long-rifles and extending his arms, the bearer lay them before him.

"Monsieur Henri Marchand," Skenando called, voice wavering. "I have for you two examples of my appreciation of our friendship. Please accept these rifles." He smiled and held them before the tradesman for inspection.

"Mon Dieu!! Magnifique! The wood is splendid. The steel of the finest. Heavy. I accept in all humility. I will not ask you from whence they came."

"It is good that you do not, vieux chapeau," the chieftain laughed lightly. "I am not finished." He summoned another bearer who brought forth a pair of pistols on a fluffy pillow.

"I wish to bestow these pistols to your worthy comrade, Monsieur Le Rocher. I have heard much of him, but until now he stood unknown to me."

The General stepped forward, and, bowing deeply from the waist, accepted the pistols from the bearer. Turning to Skenando, he embraced him about the shoulders and shook his hand firmly.

"The mark of a decisive man," he heard the chieftain state.

A small party of onlookers drew around Skenando. Bearers brought out pillows on which lay articles for women to wear: wrist bracelets and head bands. Not of any tawdry design, the articles festooned with bits of amethyst, garnet, and diamonds, glowed on close inspection. Made of strips of deer hide, the articles came embroidered along the border with colorful stitching. Skenando called upon Suzanne and her mother to accept them as a token of friendship. In all deference the ladies came forward to honor his request. The small gathering lingered for the final presentation. Skenando distributed trail knives to each of the male principals. One by one the General, the tradesman, James York, and Fox Tail and Cerf Courant, and Aboyant accepted the chieftain's gifts in all humility. With the day growing short, Skenando invited the guests to remain with him at least until the morn. Speaking for the campaigners, the General agreed and set about selecting a site in which to house the prisoners, after which everyone sat down to enjoy a modest, yet well-prepared dinner.

Before dining the General sought a conversation with Caroline York. "Madame York. The manner in which you reply to my questions will have a strong influence over the conduct of this campaign. May we proceed?" He gave no indication of the substance of the inquiries, and Caroline acquiesced without reservation:

"Very well, Monsieur. I am open to your questions. The campaign is dear to me."

"Bon, Madame. Please. During your abduction, did you on occasion share your bed with your abductor?"

Caroline blushed scarlet, a sharp contrast to her ivory complexion. Lowering her eyes, she looked away momentarily before coming face-to-face with the General. Suzanne sighed in dismay. James rushed to the General's side, seeking an apology, whereas the General adjusted the inquiry:

"Did your abductor ever force you to commit acts against your will?"

Smiling slightly, Caroline searched for humor in the inquiry: "If you mean in preparing his favorite dishes night after night, then indeed, he forced me. The penalty for refusing? Going to bed without supper. Let me assure you, Monsieur, that, under those circumstances, I did not refuse to serve him."

To the astonishment of James and Suzanne, Caroline responded wholeheartedly: "Did I share my bed with him? The answer is 'No.'" Watching Caroline's every word, James and Suzanne sighed in relief.

"Do you believe that your abductor acted on impulse or was wont to deliberate in his conduct toward you?"

"Oh! In capturing me? An excellent question. One I have asked myself over and over." Taking a deep breath and tossing back her head, Caroline placed her hands over her hips in contemplation. She spoke with conviction, a twinkle in her eye: "I believe that my abductor is a lonely man. He lacks the care of a good woman. On the other hand, he is intensely driven by his own demons. One such is a lust for power, something that he has acquired a thirst for. His lust drives him to make choices for his benefit alone. In the end he is never able to become friends with anyone—much less a woman."

"I assume that your days became very troubled, Madame. You have my sympathies." Thus far Caroline's disclosures confirmed the General's suspicions.

"I knew that I needed to survive. I wanted to join my family. The longer I remained alive, the sooner they would find me." She looked affectionately toward James and Suzanne. They joined hands with her and Caroline found new resolve with which to continue her story:

"Of course he more than once wanted to sleep with me. I found myself recalling to him the happiness I enjoyed with my family. On those occasions I stood at a terrible loss without you, James and Suzanne, at my side. He often repeated that I would never see the two of you again. I must *grow* to love him, he told me. You, James and Suzanne, are gone forever and there is no one out there to love me, save him. He took me on forays to break my spirit. He recalled to me the hardships of life on the trail and said that a life of wandering awaited me if I continued to resist him. No other man would want me, he said, for he made it known that I belonged to him and him alone.

"I found great satisfaction on the trail with the native children. I taught them reading and ciphering. The People came to ask for me when my captor appeared in their villages, and I no longer saw myself alone and unloved. This angered him immensely and he confined me in the prisoners' block at Kanandesaga (43). My jailor, the Cornplanter, witnessed my labors with the children and set aside private quarters for me to live and teach in. My captor did not know of this and the

Cornplanter always warned me of his whereabouts. Yet, one day he came for me. He pulled me back upon the trail with him. He forced me to carry the valuables that he stole from the People. Where others rode horses and wagons, I did not merit that luxury. It is only when confined to the prisoners' block along the way that I enjoyed a respite from endless walking." Stooping, she rubbed her ankles.

"He is a jealous man above all, Madame," a curious Le Rocher concluded.

"He fears losing me, not for his own sake as with an affair of the heart, but for the loss of power that goes with it. It is frightening to consider the lengths he will go to in order to bring me back to him."

"Thank you, Madame. If you will excuse me for a moment." The General took leave and met with Marchand, after which he returned to Caroline with an announcement: "Henri and I believe that you are in grave danger. Your abductor may do nothing, but that is unlikely. We believe that he will search for you. He knows not of Pointe Aux Bois, nor, for that matter, the new village in the hills. Henri and I are pleased to escort you to either retreat. Meanwhile, all locations in which you have resided need to prepare defenses." He looked knowingly at the Sandpiper and quipped:

"To capture a fox, do not chase him. Build a baited trap and let him fall into it. Madame York, out of no disrespect, you are the 'trap' of which I speak. Suddenly you are famous." Doffing his tricorn the General smiled and laughed lightly, a feeble attempt to lessen the pent-up tensions which noticeably transferred to James and Suzanne. Suzanne acknowledged the effort with a wry smile, sufficient incentive for him to persevere:

"Bon! Let us avail ourselves of our host's generosity and remain here until the morrow. For now let us enjoy his food and drink, for I know that we are hungry." For himself, the General chose to eat lightly and converse with Skenando.

"It is a custom to smoke the calumet of friendship with a new friend," Skenando spoke softly.

"I am deeply honored," the General replied, drawing a blanket tightly around the shoulders.

"We grow our tobacco here where we have abundant rainfall. The earth favors the tobacco plant."

"That is something I did not know. You do not get it from the Carolinas apparently."

"Not long ago it came from the Cherokee Nation. They are now conducting wars with neighboring bands who, out of jealousy, have destroyed much of the harvest."

"What do you do in the event of a poor crop?"

"That has yet to happen, but my friend, the tradesman has offered to step in."

"How much do you depend on good harvests in general?"

"A great deal. Although the forests are filled with animals, we prefer to cultivate the land. Our fields are large and everyone from small child to warrior takes a turn in them."

"This also is something new for me. You do not avoid meat entirely, however."

"We hunt to stock up for the lean parts of the year and of course for special occasions such as weddings, births, and funerals—of which there are several through the year." He passed the calumet to the General.

"It has a sweet, mild flavor. I expected otherwise."

"Yes. I have heard of the harsh British tobaccos. They are starved for sunlight because the British want to move them to market too quickly. That is not the case here."

"I am deeply struck by your candor."

"You are a genuine man. I am able to be candid with such a man. You must stay for a few days. Stay and watch our young men play their games and make fools of themselves."

The General laughed lightly." That is a luxury I am not able to pursue at this point, my friend. I must secure my prisoners at my garrison."

"When you go I will keep watch for your enemies and send you word of their approach." He drew on his calumet.

The General followed suit and the two men shook hands. Drawing the blanket tighter, Skenando took leave, but not before securing a promise from the General to stay the evening.

* * *

Friday, September, 15th. At dawn's first light the General rose. He consulted his trail calendar, circling the date. He roused the principals from warm cabins. He dined sparingly and while they dressed and consumed a small breakfast, he took leave of his gracious host.

"You shall not get rid of me so quickly," Skenando spoke. "I am providing you with an escort through the forests to your home."

"A most kind gesture, my friend," the General replied, eager to depart, yet reluctant to leave his new ally.

"We shall meet again. I see the look in your eye," Skenando returned. "Do not forget that we are alike, the two of us. Do you have all of your gifts?"

"Most assuredly."

"Then a part of me goes with you. Adieu. Till we meet again."

—

Under escort the victorious campaigners entered Pointe Aux Bois to the sight and sounds of games in progress. The General ushered the York family, Marchand, and Aboyant, to one of several banquet tables replete with food and beverages. There, they took part in a sumptuous repast, which seemed to flow interminably, while watching games of sport— common forms of sport during this season of the corn harvesting.

The Ball Game occupied an extensive portion of the grounds and took precedence over other activities. The General explained the Game to his guests: "In two teams of six to eight players, contestants seek to propel a small ball made of deer skin through their opponent's gate at the end of a small field by means of a stick. The Ball Game tests one's alacrity and patience and calls for manual dexterity and mobility. Although not limited by constraints of time, the Game often lasts for hours, or until contestants drop away, owing to fatigue. One earns a 'point' for driving his ball through the gate, and the team earning an accumulated majority of 'points' wins the game."(44) Allies of the contestants avidly voiced their support with shouts and whoops, to the extent that everyone on the grounds participated in the Game in one form or other.

In one corner of the grounds, players engaged in the popular Javelin Game. To an excited Suzanne, the General explained the mechanics of the contest: "One team rolls a wooden ring in front of its opponents, who, throwing javelins at it, hope to pierce the circle, thus starting the game at that particular point on the field. Members of either team, supplied with several javelins, take turns throwing them into the circle, from a regulated distance, with the intention of striking an opponent's javelin. A javelin struck is a javelin captured and the team accumulating the most wins the game."(45) Suzanne begged her father for permission to play. A reluctant James agreed and the spirited young woman dashed off to join with a team. She burst with glee on every occasion that her javelin found its mark within the circle. One strike spurred another and Suzanne went ahead to accumulate so many javelins that her opponents deemed her victorious. James took delight with his daughter's persistence and accuracy, yet the General recalled the ring having been stationed uncommonly close to her. He kept his observations to himself, however.

Cerf Courant and the Sandpiper arrived with their forces. Following a brief turn at the banquet tables, the men joined the games. Overwhelmingly, they chose competitions in archery, their marksmanship in the exercises replicating their recent prowess on the field of battle. Now, however, they took part in merely mock battles, these longbow men firing at both stationary and moving targets, albeit made of straw-men fitted with cloth.

From ancient days it became customary among the People to close the Festival of the Corn Harvest with the Peach Stone Game. The General invited the York family to watch one of the games already in progress. To begin, players of two opposing teams took turns rolling peach pits over a blanket. Painted black on one side and ochre-yellow on the other, contestants flung out their pits, looking for the blackened surfaces to appear, 'tokens', symbolic of prizes. Prizes ranged from a basket of corn to a pair of snowshoes. The former prize required a roll of eight black pits, and the latter, a roll of twenty-four. One lost a turn by rolling only one or two pits and one possessed a maximum limit of eight turns or rolls in which to claim his prize. One lost by exhausting his/her allotted turns. Popular among the People and their guests, the Game often lasted more than a day, with contestants sacrificing food and rest in pursuit of hoped-for rewards.

The York family spent the remainder of the day at the games and when nightfall approached, the General ushered them to a secluded sector of the garrison where a solid row of small, yet comfortable-looking houses stood. He stopped beside the first one— tree-lined with a front lawn: "This one is for you," he spoke softly. "Notice the chimney," he laughed. "I know that Madame is quite the mistress of the kitchen. It is yours whenever you choose to visit Pointe Aux Bois." He proceeded to lead the guests on a tour of the structure, pointing out its amenities:

"It has wood-burning stoves in all four corners. It is built for a family of four with a master bedroom and bedrooms for two others. There is a water-closet and bathing tub made of iron. Water comes from a well which is pumped by hand into the kitchen sink. For bathing and washing dishes you pump water into a bucket, carry it to the oven to heat it, then pour it where it does the most good." He brought out a wooden bucket, replete with handle and put on a demonstration. Then, later: "Let me see. There is a parlor, a dining room, a reading room, and, of course, here is the kitchen with cupboards and pantry." Lifting a door in the thick earthen floor, he peered down into a profound underground cavern. "This is your cellar, or, if you will, your dungeon, mes amis," he smiled. "Serves either purpose". To Suzanne he whispered: "Do not worry for the sake of Aboyant. He will be next door to you in the home which Monsieur Marchand occupies. I take leave of you now to allow you the remainder of the day to yourselves." Smiling, he doffed his tricorn and backed out of the house, pulling the heavy oaken door behind him.

* * *

James brought wife and daughter to his breast, hugging them firmly. "It has been so long without you, my dear wife." He stooped to embrace Caroline. She bent backward from the waist, looking into his eyes. "I will be in my room if you have need of me," Suzanne spoke softly, drifting away wistfully.

"My husband. I need you now, but we must talk," Caroline returned, wiping tears from her cheeks. She walked toward the master bed. Sitting, she tested the mattress, beckoning James to join her. "James, my husband, I am so frightened that he will come back and pull us apart. Do you believe that the General still intends to capture him?"

"Yes," James sighed, "but the General wants the rogue to search for you and fall into a trap."

"He is out there, James, this very moment searching for me—for us." She shivered.

"For the moment we are safe, my dear Caroline. He has yet to return to Ontario and face an angry Lord Carleton." He patted her hair and placed a blanket around her shoulders.

Caroline stood up abruptly: "Suzanne knows the man in white, James. That is why she became troubled at Ontario. Let me ask her something." Moving away from James, she summoned her daughter into the room.

A sleepy Suzanne joined her parents. Her mother's question revived her quickly.

"Suzanne. The man in white at Ontario. Where have you seen him before? Think deeply!"

Slowly Suzanne pushed out the words, thoughts she kept to herself for so long. "He led the soldiers who attacked the village at Osco. Seeing him at Ontario is like a bad dream. I wanted to make certain, but I know now that he is the man who spoke to me at market." She fought to hold back tears.

James jumped up "The old trick! He created a diversion while his Captain stole off with you, Caroline." He struck his head, with open palm, in amazement. "Now, I understand. The two of them planned everything from the beginning. There is much more to this than we know, Caroline." He came face-to-face with his wife. Pacing the floor, he asked her boldly: "Caroline. You have never met with the Captain at market or elsewhere?"

"No, James! What are you thinking?" she asked in alarm.

"Charles Martin! Did he ever speak to you of this man, the Captain?" he asked emphatically.

"He told me that one, perhaps two soldiers tried to persuade him to sell his holdings, not once, but on several occasions. He seemed concerned, but not in fear of his life. I did not press him for more details."

"Of course not. Unfortunately, we know the results of his refusal." James paced the room with firm strides.

"Yes, my husband. Someone murdered him. I am not able to accept any other explanation. Soon, thereafter, the Captain ran off with me. I have trouble believing that I live while poor Charles died." She daubed at her eyes.

"You are perhaps a trophy of his success, my dear wife. You are of no value to him dead. Alive, you make him a fine maid-servant and companion, someone who gained for him the respect he never earned outright."

"James. I never thought of it in such a way. Believe me. I thought of myself enslaved, not a companion."

"Given what we have seen, he is a man who needs to exert dominance, Caroline. I believe that this same rogue murdered Charles." He held his wife tightly about the shoulders, for she suddenly grew weak.

"Oh, James! How are we to learn the truth?"

James spoke rapidly. "We used to live in Delaware country, Caroline. We hired the Delaware to labor in our fields. They became our friends. Caroline! Remember that the Bear Chief is an ally of the Delaware? Not long ago he offered to help us learn the truth about Charles' death."

"Yes. I remember. It makes me weep that you went to such lengths to find me. The Bear Chief believes in you, James. We must go to him and ask him to honor his offer."

"Yes. Tomorrow Cerf Courant returns to the Round Tops. I trust him to carry our message to the Bear Chief. It is better that we remain here until we learn of the Bear Chief's decision." He gripped Caroline's hand.

"But, will he come, father?" Suzanne exclaimed.

"I believe so, Suzanne, or he will send a representative. This is yet another test of our friendship."

A worried Caroline wrung her hands. "And the Sandpiper, James. He must go to Kanandesaga to warn the Cornplanter of the rogue's presence on the frontier. I believe that the rogue will press the Cornplanter for his knowledge of who it is that attacked him."

"I think that we are without worry, Caroline. Above all, the Cornplanter sees himself as partner-in-trade to Henri Marchand. He does not care to dissolve that association. He hates the English. He released the rogue's captured natives to fight with us, you may recall."

"Very good, my husband. I see that my confinement has kept me unaware of developments, but I am learning quickly." She strode to her husband's side, taking his hand in hers.

"It is a matter of remaining in the shadows while we seek allies to fight the beast," Suzanne interjected. "Seems simple to me," she chuckled, stretching and yawning, overcome by her several days on the trail.

"Yes, exactly, dear daughter", James replied, enthusiastically. "Tomorrow morning before you rise, Cerf Courant and the Sandpiper will be well on their way with important messages. Thank you, Suzanne."

He patted her head. Pleased with Suzanne's incisiveness, James sensed the ending of the session.

"May I go back to sleep now, father?" Suzanne queried.

"Yes! Yes! By all means. Your mother and I are exhausted. You must be equally exhausted." He patted her once again and Suzanne departed the room, a mischievous smile on her lips and a twinkle in her eye.

—

The campaigners slept soundly that evening. The warriors found ample warmth and shelter in the stables and the night passed peacefully. A little past dawn of the new day Suzanne awoke to the pleasant aroma of smoked sausages coming from her cabin's kitchen. She found her mother over a hearth preparing breakfast. Caroline set a table with poached eggs, sausages, hot cakes and syrup, bran cereal, tomato juice and hot tea with cinnamon. "All home food, grown nearby— except the tea," Caroline quipped, merrily. A knock on the door brought her to step lively to open it, admitting principal guests.

Taking assigned places, the guests filled the small kitchen. Conversation turned on the campaigners' victory at Ontario with the General and Marchand handing out praises generously. On the parade grounds, the warriors enjoyed prepared breakfasts. A pleasant ambiance descended upon the garrison. Eager to depart, Cerf Courant and the Sandpiper announced their leave-taking with deep regret. The two allies pocketed hand-written messages to the Bear Chief and the Cornplanter in leather pouches, after which they loaded two wagons with furs and pelts bound for the People. Leading their respective columns, the two woodsmen departed Pointe Aux Bois at about nine hours that morning of Saturday, September 16th, according to the General, who dutifully observed the transition.

The York family, meanwhile, availed themselves of their co-hosts' congeniality. The General and Marchand took a special interest in acquainting their guests with the pace of daily life at the garrison in the form of a tour.

The tradesman insisted on visiting the shops. The shops, he explained, each in its own way, functioned to serve corresponding needs of the residents. The small entourage first visited a *cooper's* shop. There the craftsman went about his labors with enthusiasm. He walked to a tub of hot water from which he extracted equal lengths of trimmed wood, called staves. Placing the supple pieces between the jaws of a wooden press, the craftsman slowly applied pressure to either end of the staves, causing them to bow outward in an elliptical pattern. Summarily he locked the press with pegs, explaining that the hot water softened the wood, thus allowing the press to bend each stave into the desired form. The staves required a full day to assume their new shape, he stated, whereupon he and an assistant gathered up a handful from the previous day. With hammer and nails they drove the staves into an elliptically-cut base, after which they forced the entire ensemble into an upright position, wrapping the staves tightly with a length of rope. Together the men rolled the cumbersome apparatus to the *farrier*, who stood by ready to wrap iron bands laterally around the circumference of the apparatus: top, middle, and bottom. Already red-hot to the texture of molten iron, the bands melded into each other, once the *farrier* gripped them with heavy tongs. His assistant doused the melded pieces with cold water, bonding them, whereupon the *farrier* rolled the completed barrel back to the cooper for the final step in the process: the fitting of the wooden cover.

The *chandler's* shop stood next to the farrier's. The tradesman called it by its French name: le chandelier. Here the York family watched a craftsman making candles, which eventually would be installed throughout the garrison. With the candle an indispensable ally in the dark of winter, the tradesman kept the chandelier fully-employed and well-compensated. The craftsman explained that he poured heated fats from swine and fowl into molds to make the candles. A hollow tube running the length of the mold, held the wick or lighting element of the candle, the man stated. "I prefer the hair of the horse, which, when tightly braided, forms a strong bond against the fats. Above all, the horse does not mind a bit," He laughed. "I take it from the tail. There is enough left to shoo away flies." He laughed again. An ecstatic Suzanne made notes in her journal.

The York family continued the tour with a visit to the *butner*. His shop, a rather simple layout, stood awash in buckets of peach pits. The jovial young man invited James to observe him closely. Holding a pit in one hand, he ground it straight across with a sandy stone. Next, with a hand-held drill he formed two small holes in opposite ends of the pit. Grasping a leather strop, he ground and polished the pit until it became smooth to the touch and rounded in the form of an oval. Holding the finished product before James, the *butner* exclaimed:" Here you have the perfect button." He dropped it into one of several buckets at his feet. Smiling, he remarked: "It is the little things that keep this garrison in good order. We may survive without our firearms, but one is not able to brave a cold winter without buttons to hold up thick, heavy pants."

Suzanne took delight with the *crocker*. His craft, she noted, combined physical dexterity with artistry. The craftsman presented a lump of clay to her for inspection. Depositing it upon a potter's table, the man sprinkled the amorphous mass with water. Seated before the table, he caused it to revolve by manipulating wooden gears beneath his feet. While he pulled and twisted the clay in the manner of a baker kneading dough, the *crocker* stroked and caressed the grayish lump. Slowly it yielded to his ministrations. At once a neck formed and the base of the object grew stout and thick and when the neck resembled that of a goose, the man deftly thrust his fingers into it, forcing them straight through to the base where he spread them out while vigorously pumping on a pair of gears. The table purred like a well-stroked kitten. Shortly, the *crocker* extracted his arm in a swift movement, and to Suzanne's astonishment, not a trace of clay adhered to him. The *crocker* brought the spinning table to an abrupt halt. Throwing up his arms, he signaled the end of the task. He placed the finished product before Suzanne, an elegant water urn, three feet in height, with long neck and broad, round base, capable of holding twelve gallons. "It goes to the *farrier* shop to get fired," the *crocker* stated cheerfully. So saying, he lifted the heavy urn, walking it the few short steps to his friend, the smithy.

The tradesman ushered the York family to additional venues and, much to their satisfaction, they met with a host of skilled craftsmen in successive order. The resident-*cobbler* demonstrated the art of cutting and stitching leather for the making of boots. Next to him an *arkwright* put the finishing touches on a small chest for the storage of personal sundries. A *soaper* rewarded Caroline with a bar of soap which, he claimed removed the most stubborn of stains. Nearby the tradesman paused before a straw-model of a man. It stood upon a pedestal trailing bits of cloth affixed by slender wooden pins. To a perplexed James, the tradesman explained: "This is my new suit of clothes. You see how closely it compliments what I am wearing today? My friend, the *sartor* will tailor it to my proportions. Then I will have two fine suits.

Correct, Luis?" He patted the bespectacled man with needle and thread gratuitously on the shoulder and the tour continued.

The General joined the tour. He escorted the family to some favorite venues. At the *boulangerie* he explained the function of each of the principal craftsmen who turned out breads, biscuits, and cakes for the garrison. In turn the Yorks learned that the *meunier* selected from among various grades of flour that grade or consistency of flour that most suitably lent itself to production on a large scale. The *boulangers*, they learned, performed the actual labor, taking instructions from the *meunier*. A hierarchy of sorts existed among the *boulangers*, making use of the division of labor so that everyone exchanged roles in production.

"Everyone sooner or later performs in all of the divisions of the bakery," the meunier stated, "an arrangement reached through popular consensus. I must say that the *boulangerie* is loved by all at Pointe Aux Bois and I have no trouble persuading people to labor here."

The confectionery or *confiserie* comprised a smaller portion of the *boulangerie*. A craftsman aptly named Monsieur le Doux introduced his guests to an assortment of flasks. He tugged on a cork stopper of the flask labeled *ginembre*, and beckoned Suzanne forward.

"Ah! Ginger," she exclaimed.

"Oui, Mademoiselle. That is one of the many delights which I put into our cakes. There is also *la cannelle*-cinnamon—and *le citron*-lemon. Voici!" He gave Suzanne and her mother each a cake called *du pain d' épices,* which both women heartily consumed and identified as gingerbread. "We grow some of our *épices-spices*-on the grounds, but others come from France. There is a garden beyond this building. You must ask Monsieur Le General to take you there." He smiled and bowed and returned to his mixing table where he prepared more of his *pain d' épices.*

"Monsieur le Doux acted too soon," the General lamented. "He has already told you of our gardens. I will show you, nonetheless. Follow me," he laughed in good humor. "Our gardens may not be as extensive as those of Ontario, but they suffice."

The gardens lay across a rear stretch of the garrison. A campus unto itself, the gardens consisted of fruits and vegetables grown on either side of a broad aisle. Along this pathway and those lateral to it, attendants wound their way with buckets of water. Others carried shears to prune the vast collection. Still others raked away dried leaves and chased off pesky flies bent on imbibing tender shoots. "We raise foods from the New World and the Old World alike," the General noted to the guests. Next, the little party visited rows of tall corn, ripe for the taking, interspersed with squashes, melons, sweet potatoes, stringed beans and grapes on the vine. "Our resident natives tend to these crops. They have houses bordering the gardens where they remain the whole year. Some have even raised entire families here. Our grapes: *les raisins*, are from France, along with our *pommes de terre:* potatoes. We are trying to introduce them to the native populations."

Turning to Caroline, the General spoke in somber tones: "You are welcomed to stay here at Pointe Aux Bois indefinitely. It has all of the comforts of home—so to speak. For you, *la cuisinière,* there is *la cuisine, la boulangerie, and les jardins.* It is your second home, Madame, and, perhaps will become your favorite."

"I thank you for the attention you have paid the three of us since our arrival," Caroline replied appreciatively. "There is much goodness here at Pointe Aux Bois. I must, however, follow my husband. He plans to return to the Round Tops to honor his pledge to help the Bear Chief build a new village." She shook hands with the General in acknowledgment of the offer.

"It is not wise to depart these grounds with that evildoer on the prowl," the General warned Caroline.

"Yes. I am well aware, Monsieur. Last evening, my husband and I spoke at length about how to treat with him. James believes that he in truth murdered my uncle, Charles. I am certain that you want the rogue for reasons of your own—reasons which launched your strikes against him."

"It is a delicate situation, Madame. If I am to capture the villain for certain crimes, I run the risk of bringing the British army to my doorstep. My position here at Pointe Aux Bois will be exposed. Indeed, Pointe Aux Bois itself will lie exposed. On the other hand, to do nothing gives the rogue free rein to pursue nefarious deeds. To that extent we French will lose everything gained along the frontier and the aborigines will fall to the whims of a cruel master. I am ill-prepared to live to see the dawn of that day."

"I understand, Monsieur. We are all bound up into an all-consuming web. Free one limb and another is entangled."

"I must tell you that James is contemplating how best to bring about the rogue's capture. He is about to ask the Cayuga sachem to call upon friends: the Delaware. It is in their lands that the murder took place. They live near our original holdings. We lived with them in peace. It is James's hope that one of them carries knowledge of the murder and will come forward with a discovery."

"This is very good, Madame. It is good that you have confided in me. If your suspicions hold true and the villain is indeed a murderer, there remains the agony of bringing him before the bar of justice."

Caroline asked for an explanation and the General continued: "Your abduction, although real and painful for you, is no more than a myth in the eyes of the jurist. I say this, Madame, because of the indistinct qualities of the offense itself. Simply, abduction conveys different impressions to different people. What is abduction for you is a mere dalliance with a stranger to another. There is the question of consent on the part of the victim."

"You are saying, Monsieur, that abduction is one's word against another? Do I have it?"

"Yes. Standing alone without benefit of strong witnesses, this is true. This is your condition at present. However, if you are able to combine abduction with a more serious offense, say murder, and lay them at the feet of this villain, then you will begin to earn the support of those who will one day sit in judgment." He spoke slowly, measuring his words, looking away from Caroline.

"I understand, Monsieur," she spoke softly. "I need witnesses who will speak for me, you say?"

"Exactly. It is as simple as that and as difficult as that," the General returned, facing her.

"You once spoke of drawing him into a trap." She regarded him, wistfully.

"Your story of the crusty dog, your captor, tells me much about him. He is a man driven by his own ambitions, and one who may subsequently be deceived by manipulation. His own self-absorption will bring about his collapse, aided no less by my interventions. In the battle of Ontario I employed one such artifice: For example, because of a lack of a visible French force, he has come to believe that a band of aborigines and Canadians attacked him. In that vein he believes the attackers to be disorganized, for they carried out no executions and merely scorched the fortress, taking little in the way of spoils. In pondering why marauders may have spared the lives of the innocent at Ontario, he has concluded that they in essence feared his wrath and retaliation. I, however, by demanding that our besiegers carry out no mass murders of the innocent, gave him the false impression that his forces remained invincible in the region. His vainglory has thus surfaced, giving him to believe that the besiegers literally feared him so strongly that they spared many lives after the battle. He sees them as weak and therefore reluctant to oppose him. Meanwhile, our villain will continue to scour the countryside, searching out the native and stealing from him. His pursuit of the native thus elevates his own quest for power. In this manner he builds up an elevated view of himself. He does not know, however, that he has played into my hands."

"He believes himself supreme, you say?"

"Yes! Exactly, Madame."

"He knows not that he has been deceived?" Suzanne added.

"Splendide!! Mademoiselle!"

Caroline breathed deeply. "You are very wise. Tell me. Are you beyond his suspicions at this point?"

"Yes. He knows not of me. I am therefore able to move forward without trepidation."

Caroline gasped: "I understand. You planned the battle to give him a false sense of security."

"In a matter of speaking, Madame. In my own limited way I will help you Madame. Come!" He guided her by the hand through the garden pathways. "The dinner hour approaches. Where is Monsieur York? Where is Suzanne? Please forgive me. I talk too much and ignore my guests."

The General called for Suzanne and, at the sound of running footsteps, he turned to find her balancing water bucket and shovel in one hand against a pot of berries in the other. Reaching him, she exclaimed, in mock defiance: "Someone must tend to the gardens while you two are wasting the afternoon."

—

The York family spent this, the first of several days at Pointe Aux Bois in anticipation of the arrival of the Bear Chief. Caroline labored in her kitchen, preparing, among other delights, her favorite turkey pot pies. James circulated among the shops, where he learned valued skills at the hands of the craftsmen. Suzanne preferred the gardens, where, on warm, autumn afternoons, she mingled with the native residents as they cultivated seasonal vegetables and fruits and blossoms. During respites she walked from the gardens to the edge of the sheer cliff near the main gate of the garrison. There she scanned the horizon for signs of the Bear Chief. She marked each vigil on her calendar and reported disappointment to her parents with each passing day. Inwardly she began to pine for the Bear Chief and the way of life she spent with Colombe Blanche and the boys.

A new day dawned. Suzanne awoke early. She noted the date: Sunday, September 24th, a day of rest, according to her religious beliefs, to be spent in part by attending Mass. She helped her mother prepare breakfast over the hearth and when James joined them at table, Suzanne asked that they dedicate this Sunday Mass to the Bear Chief. She would pray that the Bear Chief accept her father's offer to intercede among the Delaware. His arrival would acknowledge acceptance of her father's plan, and, to a greater extent, acceptance of her and her parents into his extended family.

The York family set out to Mass at nine hours. En route to the small chapel, Marchand and Aboyant joined them. Suzanne enjoyed the singing which took place at Mass. The chorus consisted of the sons and daughters of the garrison's inhabitants, who joined with the children of resident natives. For Suzanne, the coming together of the two races represented a harmony which their combined voices brought forth in song. A missionary conducted the Mass. Addressing the congregation in French, the missionary spoke of invoking one's faith when meeting the challenges which the frontier visited upon the settlers— especially young children. He called for the formation of strong bonds among family members and Suzanne believed for a moment that the missionary fashioned the message for her alone.

The Mass concluded, the family accepted a Marchand invitation and walked with him to a venue dedicated to maple syrup. The tradesman held a cup below a spigot fastened to one of several maple trees. Stirring the viscous mass, he sipped from a cup and invited Suzanne to try a sample. She squealed with delight:

"How sweet it is! Mother! Father! Come and try!"

"Life is sweet," James replied. "Our reward for the travails we have survived."

Suzanne offered a cup to her mother. Behind Caroline, Aboyant held a cup, his lips trembling.

"These maple trees date back to my arrival at Pointe Aux Bois," Marchand exclaimed, proudly. He gazed at them affectionately. "Of course, the syrup is no secret. The natives have tapped into maple trees for generations. They donated the young plants to me and now you have the finished product." He bowed low, smiling broadly.

* * *

Approximately thirty-three kilometers to the northwest of Pointe Aux Bois, another scene took shape. There, upon the charred grounds of the former Fort Ontario, a solitary figure, bent over a walking stick, rummaged among the soot-choked remains of his once proud domain. Periodically he paused to relieve a persistent pain in the ankle, a pain which traversed the entire spinal column, terminating at the base of the neck. It brought about a certain rigidity which prevented him the full motion of the head and shoulders. Bent to the task at hand, he paid little heed to his infirmities while attempting to reconstruct the series of events which brought about the dismemberment of the Ontario garrison. He thought to himself:

'During my absence night raiders destroyed Ontario. They knew full-well that neither I nor Lord Carleton remained in residence. They must have tracked me. After freeing my hostages, they selectively torched the buildings. Strange that the storage depot and school still stand. They are taunting me. They made captives of the soldiers rather than kill them. Most likely they are savages following instructions from white men. They are Canadians who fought with the French— members of a raiding party who happened along in the dead of night while the soldiers slept. Yet. Why that night? Why Fort Ontario? They followed me. From where? Neatahwantah? Highly unlikely. I fought that rag-tag outfit to a draw and departed on my own terms. The frontier is unsafe. There are raiders out there. They waited until most of the men left for Montreal. Then they struck. Simmons is missing. So is the white woman.

'I left my post. Rue the day. Granted, I concluded a sale to **Black Jack**— earning a tidy sum. That is my own affair apart from my professional life. Lord Carleton knows none of it, but now I must answer to him. He too is not without blame. Did he not leave the post as well? Unlike him, I did something of merit. Is it not I who sailed to Niagara in order to requisition the transfer of sailors to Ontario to shore up the garrison's weak defenses? Did I not negotiate with Niagara's commandant Briggs for the transfer? Did not Briggs send a brigantine the length of the St. Lawrence to the Newfoundland territories? Yes! Briggs believes my account of the state of the frontier— that both Niagara and Ontario require an influx of men to fend off threats from marauding natives and their French sponsors. Never mind that I chose to leave Ontario on the brink of an ambush. The greater good is that I accomplished a major maneuver. I erred in judgment. In war this is common. I erred on the side of righteousness. I will beg Lord Carleton's forgiveness. He will not reprimand me too harshly, for he too is not without blame. Whatever the outcome, no one is able to claim that I am not a professional soldier.'

His reverie ended, he continued searching amid the rubble of the charred grounds. He cast aside burnt shards and embers, trying to draw a vision of their former state. His labors carried him the length and breadth of the grounds, head and shoulders bent low, pain coursing through his spine. When, at last he stooped to retrieve an object, he smiled inwardly with satisfaction, for he implicitly knew that he held an item applicable to vindication. With this evidence in hand, he summarily stopped searching further. The recurrent pain hastened the decision to do so. Before departing the grounds, he gave an audience to one of the few remaining residents of Fort Oswego who drew up beside him:

"Yes, my good man. How good of you to join me. I hold this spent shot along with arrowheads with shaft partially burned. I found them scattered hither and yon." He held a handful of the little iron balls in one hand and arrowheads in the other. "Look closely. Tell me what you see."

"The shot is fairly large for this region, Sir. The arrowheads look to have similar shafts of the same model."

"Exactly. Your eyesight has not failed you. Perhaps your memory of the battle is also sharp."

At the Captain's urging, the soldier forced himself to summon the events of that fateful evening, now several days past, events so rapid, so unforeseen, so overwhelming, that he stood unprepared to introduce them in other than the most fleeting of terms. He gave a sketchy account of the besiegers:

"Some of the men wore blackened faces. They may have been white, but no one spoke. For their costumes, they wore tunics and leggings of forest green, not unlike the French-Canadians. Clearly, natives carried the assault. They spoke but little. A leader did not emerge to my knowledge." He paused, searching his memory.

"Thank you, my good man. Lord Carleton has returned and we will present him with our accounts. I intend to propose a plan to squash these attacks and restore a semblance of order once again to the frontier. Of course, I require Lord Carleton's approval, but given the urgency of the matter, I expect to receive it in all haste. You are my witness."

"I am honored, Sir, to assist in restoring the army's prestige. My name is Caldwell."

"Very good, Caldwell. I salute you. Assemble a small task force and be ready to move out when I call for you. That is all for now."

Caldwell returned to his rooms at Fort Oswego. He set about preparing a roster of men to place on a task force, no sooner completing it when he received word that an impatient Lord Carleton awaited him and the Captain. Presently the two men entered the commandant's sterile, yet commodious parlor side by side. Saluting smartly, they awaited Lord Carleton's opening remarks:

"Gentlemen, gentlemen. I find it perilous to leave my garrison in the hands of those entrusted to care for it. What have you to say?" Striding firmly behind a voluminous desk, Lord Carleton appeared vexed and unnerved to the two subordinates. Initially he refrained from making direct eye contact.

Caldwell deferred to the Captain, who conducted a sobering litany— one of helpless soldiers prevailed upon by heartless marauders. He attempted to paint himself and his aide as victims who acted heroically with no thought to their own security. The enemy, the Captain reported, took advantage of the garrison's deficiencies in manpower, robbing and looting at will. (He chose to omit that a force one fourth the size of his own committed the deed.) The Captain explained that by previous arrangement he presented himself to the commandant of Fort Niagara in order to secure reinforcements. To his misfortune, he related, hostilities erupted at Ontario during his meeting with the post's commander. He succeeded in securing the aid of a warship of sailors from the Newfoundland territories, due to arrive soon, to replenish manpower among the northern garrisons of the frontier. Caldwell, he lied, bargained with the enemy and succeeded in having the gardens and other appointments spared from the torch.

Lord Carleton paced. Finally he elected to face his subjects. "I laud your efforts, Captain, during this trying period in our history. You certainly acted with valor, a point which you did not hesitate to impress upon me. It is only because of your interpretation of your duties that you stand before me now. You, Captain, in my absence, are in charge of the garrison. Unless, of course, a surrogate is appointed in your stead, you are charged to physically remain in residence in the garrison. There are no exceptions to this, you well know. You have served His Majesty long enough to know the simple truths and this is one of them." Lord Carleton measured each word, so that the scribe never missed a single stroke of the pen.

"I designated Simmons, Sir, to see to affairs in my absence," a contrite Captain returned.

In full possession of his demeanor Lord Carleton replied: "That may be true, Captain, but an appointment must go through the customary channels. What is more, I know not of your arrangement with Niagara. At the very least your conduct is suspicious. Nevertheless, the garrison may have been lost with or without your presence. We will never know, will we?" He turned to glare at the Captain. "The point remains, Captain, there has occurred a breach in leadership, a lapse in judgment, resulting in our loss and another's gain." He looked alternately at both men, allowing the words to take root.

"Sir. No one in my command knew of the forthcoming assault. The marauders caught us unawares. They exercised clever plans one after the other." Head low, he frowned in defeat. A gloom settled about him.

"All the more reason to maintain your post, Captain," Lord Carleton returned, raising his voice. Slapping palms together, he opened and closed his fists, a man on the threshold of rendering a decision: "I have the choice, Captain, of placing you under arrest, or to demand that you remedy the situation. With either turn, your career lies in the balance. I advise you to take steps to make amends immediately. To do that, you need to find these marauders of whom you speak in order to avoid incarceration."

Betraying no emotion, the Captain spoke: "Sir. I believe that I know the enemy. I have found traces of him on the grounds. Caldwell!"

Caldwell produced musket balls and arrow shafts, his hands trembling. Snapping them up, the Captain placed them on Lord Carleton's sumptuous, mahogany desk for inspection. For the commandant's benefit, the Captain reiterated the conclusions which he reached earlier on the grounds:

"You see, Sir, how this ball is larger in diameter than those in common use on the frontier? We believe it to have been made by a smithy, the same smithy who shoes horses— someone who inhabits a town or fort. I found many such examples, which leads me to believe that someone planned the attack."

Choosing the arrow shafts, the Captain continued: "Here you see the scaling of the arrowhead on the etched shaft itself. I found several of these—each one a copy of its predecessor. The same craftsman made these missiles at a single location. It is not by happenstance that this took place. The ball comes from the white man. The arrow is from the red man. The two came together to sack Ontario—two forces with a singular purpose in mind—an undertaking well-planned. I defer to you, Sir."

"It appears that you are determined to redeem yourself, Captain. You have some believable theories. You wish to put them to the test, but I stand between you and the path to success."

The Captain overlooked Lord Carleton's effrontery and pressed forward: "Sir. In an attempt to rescue my career, I offer to track these scoundrels. I will take no respite until I drag them before you. I ask only your indulgence to lead a task force into the interior, where, under the sign of peace, I will search for answers. To begin, I recommend Kanandesaga." He crisply saluted Lord Carleton.

"For any other soldier this request is an exercise in futility. You, however, know the woodlands well, Captain. You have bode well with the aborigines in the past— so you tell me. This sort of venture will prove a good test of your leadership, Captain, and may ultimately determine your fate. At any rate, it is the material from which colonels are made. Captain! I give you your task force, but I demand results. So be it! Go to it! This session has ended. Good day!" He saluted his subordinates, their signal to depart.

The Captain ushered Caldwell into the courtyard, where the aide drew a deep breath of fresh air. Turning to him the Captain chirped in a light-hearted manner: "So, Caldwell. Go ready the men. I told you of our leader's implicit faith in me. All is well." He laughed insidiously while Caldwell cast about uneasily, mopping his brow.

* * *

With the conclusion of the Mass, Suzanne and her parents became the guests of the General at his house for yet another breakfast. Suzanne invited Aboyant. Together, everyone set out to enjoy a morning of comfort and relaxation. A pathway led them hard by the front gate of the garrison, and Suzanne once again begged for permission to resume a vigil. James York secured from her a promise to abbreviate her visit, and a contented Suzanne consented before scampering away. Greeting the gate-keeper, she borrowed field lenses and tugged mightily on the latch of the palisaded door, standing on the tips of her toes to accomplish the feat. Stepping gingerly over the threshold, she found her footing on the top step of a stairway which descended sharply to the beach front. Winds whipping across Lake Onondaga rushed up the stairway to tug at her clothing, but she paid no notice to this persistent annoyance. Poised on the lofty perch, she scrupulously examined the lake shore.

She found good reason to linger longer upon this watch. Hard by the northern beach-head, two figures walked along the shore line. Too distant to discern with the lenses, she waited in expectation, her heart in her throat. At length, the figures crept closer, and, approaching the stairway, where it coincided with the beach, stopped to gaze upward. Grasping the lenses firmly, Suzanne bore down upon the figures. She paused momentarily before emitting a shriek of joy so strident that gulls squatting on the palisades took to flight. With arms aflutter, she beckoned the travelers to join her forthwith and only a last-second's decision borne of caution prevented her from dashing down the precipitous decline to greet them. Slowly the two travelers mounted the stairway, the fifty-three steps which Suzanne committed to memory. They spoke not a word, and Suzanne, in a fleeting moment, feared having acted presumptuously. Shortly, one of the pair addressed her by calling her name and Suzanne's fears dissolved in the wind, for the deep, resonant voice belonged to no other than the Bear Chief.

"Sge:no, Mademoiselle. Dajihah:dwadawihshe."—Hello, Miss. Let us rest a little while.

"Bien entendu, Monsieur. Suivez-moi."–Very well, Sir. Follow me— Suzanne smiled approvingly. Locking arms with the Bear Chief and Cerf Courant, she led the men back through the portals to Le Rocher's house where she hoped to find her parents engaged with him. The rare opportunity to bring all of the principals in her life together under one roof delighted her. She tingled with excitement.

Caroline caught sight of Suzanne through the front window of the house. Calling James, she rushed out-of-doors to greet her daughter and guests. Once indoors, Caroline deferred to her husband who made introductions, leaving her free to bedeck the dinner table with her favorite chinaware. Marchand entered and it is in this manner that the three architects of the Ontario campaign: The General, Marchand, and the Bear Chief, came together under one roof for the first time. Suzanne beamed a broad smile and her thoughts ran to what she planned for her journal that evening. The General prevailed upon his guests to sit, drink, and dine and everyone, with the exception of Caroline, who prepared appetizers, came to the table. Suzanne, looking about her, jumped from her chair. Taking her mother's place in the kitchen, she urged Caroline to join the others in her stead. Caroline quietly stole next to her husband, who hardly noticed her presence, for all eyes dwelt upon the Bear Chief.

The Bear Chief explained that Little Bear took ill over the past week, compelling him to remain with him through the day. "Because of Watkins, Little Bear is out of danger. Watkins wrapped the boy's chilled body in blankets warmed with heated stones and fed him generous portions of corn soup which Fawn prepared for the boy."

Turning to the reason behind his visit, the Bear Chief related that he intended to travel to the Delaware country by following the ancient hunting path along the Susquehanna. The residents there knew his People well, going back centuries, he continued. He looked forward to tending to James York's request and to rekindling old relationships. He preferred to travel by horseback, but arrived ill-equipped, he lamented. The General interceded, offering two hearty steeds from his livery. James presented the Cayuga sachem with a map of the farm—holdings he left behind in the hands of the Quakers. Sketching it rapidly, but accurately in pencil, he placed it in a cachet to keep it in good form.

Taking up a pen, James wrote a short letter of introduction on behalf of the Bear Chief to the Quaker family tending his farm. This too he placed in the cachet. Marchand presented the Bear Chief with a trail calendar instructing him in its use. He also prepared a back pack for each man, complete with dried foods, matches, kindling wood, flint, bandages and antiseptic alcohol. Caroline insisted that the visitors take along two of her turkey pot pies. She beckoned Suzanne to wrap them tightly in cheese cloth.

The Bear Chief acknowledged the General's solicitude, and turned to relating developments at the Round Tops. Watkins consumed a great deal of his attention: "The tireless craftsman continues to build cabins for the residents. There are kitchens with hearth and flue, parlors with fireplace and chimney, a dining room, separate bedrooms for family members, wooden floors, and below-ground storage pit. Chairs and tables and cupboards and walk-in closets, grace all homes, which comfortably house up to six occupants. One-floor exclusively, a few homes contain a second floor for larger families."

He envisioned no shortage of timber with which to build the medium-sized, yet comfortable homes. To ensure the propagation of the forest, he urged the cultivation of new trees and already, during the first season of the Round Tops, laborers began to place certain seeds into cultures for future generations to enjoy. Colombe Blanche, played a major role in the conservation of seeds. She kept seeds in urns in underground storage, namely peach and squash, and set aside a portion of the Round Tops for new tree growth and transplantation. "She recently devoted the western slope to the planting of corn and many other delights, reserving the eastern slope for berries. She has the lumps—bee stings— on her arms to prove it," he concluded.

James York asked the Bear Chief to describe the Round Tops to date. Taking a deep breath, the Cayuga sachem smiled briefly, giving the little party to learn that he was about to approach a favorite subject:

"An inner circle of palisades shields what I prefer to name the Interior Village. They completely enclose the dwellings within. There is a walkway circling the top of the palisades from which guards are able to keep watch over the village in general. An Exterior Village is planned. Consisting of homes, storage barns, and quarters for animals, it too will have a surrounding palisades. The cannon that we retrieved from Osco will sit before the village gates. The villagers enjoy drawing water from the stream which Messieurs York and Watkins take from the hill near old Osco. It still flows to the lagoon mere footsteps from the portals of the Round Tops. Fish and small four-footed creatures abound there, some of which we hunt. Small children continue to play in the glen near the lagoon by day. I hope to complete all major building before the snow falls."

Holding up a finger, the Bear Chief indicated that he wanted to make a final disclosure. Looking directly at Suzanne he spoke slowly: "Raven and Little Bear await your return, Mademoiselle. They have no one with whom to share adventure stories."

The General brought out a long calumet. Deftly he stuffed it with tobacco and kindled it over his open fire place. Offering it to Marchand, he asked him to make a wish or dedication, passing it in turn to the men of the circle. The tradesman took a shallow draft and spoke, asking for sustained good relations with all the native people of the region. He passed the pipe to Aboyant. The little man took a long draft on the stem. Coughing and sputtering, he uttered in French:

"Je souhaite à nous convoyageurs Bonne Chance"—I wish Good Fortune for our fellow travelers.

Cerf Courant took the pipe. He wished that the voyagers have the strength to repel all evil men sent to defeat them. The Bear Chief, next to take the pipe, thanked the Creator for seeing his son through the fever and for surrounding him with genuinely good people. Le Rocher, the last to take the pipe, wished for continued good harvests in the vegetable gardens.

Suzanne and her mother watched the proceedings from a distance. Suzanne believed that the men's offerings, each one unique, told quite a bit about each man himself. She shared her thoughts with her mother. Privately she made her own wish. She asked that justice be served her mother for the anguish she endured. She confided her wish to her mother who whispered to her that she made identically the same wish.

The calumet passed to James York. Holding it tentatively, he took a shallow draft and stated that he reserved the opportunity to speak about his son, Matthew York. He wished him well in his labors with the marines, but confessed that he longed to see him at his side once again. He began to launch into a lengthy discourse, covering his son's labors, for the benefit of his companions, interrupting himself when the Bear Chief and Cerf Courant announced their imminent departure.

At that point everyone accompanied the two men to the stables where they took up packs of provisions and found horses saddled and waiting. One by one everyone bid the men a successful journey, marked by firm handshakes and hugs of affection. Soon, back in the General's comfortable house, they convened before the fire place and James York broke into discourse:

* * *

"Matthew is my eldest. He exceeds his sister, Suzanne, by four and one half years. Let me see. That puts him at age twenty-two. He has been with the British Royal Navy since age eighteen. They prefer the term 'marines' and Matthew has sailed with them extensively almost from the moment he jumped on board the fleet at the Port of London. He always longed for adventure, willing to travel great lengths to find it and of late has seen his hands full of it. Together with his mates he maintains the fishing station at Newfoundland, along the Grand Banks near the town of St. John's." Pausing, he looked toward the General and Marchand. "With no disrespect toward you, gentlemen, the marines acquired most of the island after France conceded defeat of the fortress, Louisbourg in the late war (46).

"Matthew harvests cod from the ocean. He cleans 'em, packs 'em, making 'em ready for market. Not content with a single task, he has elected to occupy himself with other assignments: removing dangerous boulders from the river–St. Lawrence–and mapping new fishing grounds on the inner banks. Through thick and thin he is ready to sail to the interior to answer His Majesty's call to duty. Each day is unlike its predecessor, much to Matthew's liking. In his letters he told me that he will return home one day soon, but each letter carries a different post mark from different ports. I have not heard from him since I began searching for his mother. I look for the means to tell him that she and I and his sister are alive and well and in good hands. His letters are held by the family watching my home. He knows not of his mother's affair, nor of our whereabouts.

"At age eighteen Matthew rejected attending university, to the dismay of his mother and myself. He preferred to labor with his heart and hands, mark my words, while young, and with his head when old, he told me. I first introduced him rather indirectly to the sea. At home I raised great quantities of vegetables which I took to market in London.

They made their way around the world, feeding soldiers and sailors in the far reaches of the British Empire. Matthew often came with me. Down to the ships by the docks I took young Matthew. To me the place reeked of stale odors, along with dirty old men and vagabonds stealing everything not nailed down. More than once our hearty dog Fetch left his mark upon the backside of a transgressor. Matthew liked the little shops scattered along the docks, barely more than tents strewn haphazardly: hiding places for the money-snatchers who stole from the unwary.

"Matthew first toiled in a bakery near our home. He bought many necessities to grace our humble hearth. He held a fond interest for clothing and weapons. They came from far-off places, something to parade before his schoolmates. His dress is that of the woodsman, the tracker, the ranger— all men of hearty stock and bearing. A veritable arsenal filled our rooms, in the main, hunting rifles and pistols and every sort of knife. He developed a talent with all of his arms. He built showcases for them, setting them throughout our home at all points of the compass. They made a fetching sight and he dusted them religiously at his mother's insistence.

"Matthew loves animals. He brought home stray dogs and kittens when returning from school. He kept them in kennels, feeding them biscuits from the bakery in which he toiled. He sold some of the animals to shelters which trained them to guide the blind. He always liked to breach new frontiers, leaving the surroundings in better condition than when found. He kept Fetch to watch over baby Suzanne on those days when I went to market while his mother performed chores at home.

"During his youth he took the side of the oppressed. Among the young there is always one clod, larger and stronger than the rest of the lot who is aching to show his might. He usually strikes from behind, catching his victim unawares. Such a clod lived in the neighborhood and played cricket in the summer with many other boys from the neighborhood. He played goaler, where he occupied a space before the net. One afternoon, Randy found it satisfying to trip up Matthew's teammate, Lewis, a leading player. Lewis injured his leg in the process and left the game, putting his mates at a disadvantage. With cricket there is no replacement of players and his mates believed the game lost. Matthew decided to level the playing field. He and a mate double-teamed Randy, leaving another mate free to make the winning goal.

Other players followed Matthew's example and before the season ended, Randy refused to take the field whenever Matthew appeared. The coach finally dismissed him altogether and Lewis returned to play during the championships where he helped to bring his team victory. Matthew and Lewis became fast friends. They frolicked together and Matthew taught Lewis to shoot and fight with his fists. The two youths formed a firm bond, staying together, joined by common adventures, until Lewis moved away slightly before Matthew threw in with the marines. Both believed that their parting represented only a temporary separation.

"The wonders of frozen and barren Newfoundland opened themselves to Matthew. He forged a trusting relationship with the aborigines of the island. Knowing that they strived against great odds in a forbidding land, Matthew never forgot their humility. Their generosity and friendly ways appealed to him. They shared their food with Matthew, took him on hunting sallies and taught him how to prepare cod for the table. When days grew gray and cold and food became scarce for them, Matthew brought the natives to the stockade of St. John's where he set food aside for them. He gave them warm blankets and articles entirely new to them. At St. John's the natives sported mittens, laced boots, woolen under-clothing and pocket combs and brushes for combing hair and cleaning teeth. The natives esteemed his efforts and put him in their trust, all a part of His Majesty's plan, of course; nevertheless, the maneuver tapped into Matthew's own sense of propriety. Matthew learned bits and pieces of their language and hosted their La Crosse games on a frozen field near the stockade.

"My son enjoyed preserving the wild. I learned this through his letters. He labored to bring about an understanding of man for all things wild. On one such occasion Matthew hunted for walrus with native friends. They made a kill, but before they claimed the beast, a polar bear pounced on it. A companion shouted at the bear and the bear chased him in pursuit, hot on his heels. Matthew stepped in. He pelted the bear with cod and the giant forgot Matthew's friend in favor of an easier meal. While the bear ate the cod, Matthew and his friend hauled the walrus away. Later, Matthew told companions that he found the bear too impressive to be killed.

"Matthew's letter about the wolf pups left me breathless. He found two of them huddled together in a frozen hollow. No members of the wolf pack came to claim them and leaving them alone meant certain death. Matthew brought them to his rooms at the stockade where he raised them on goat's milk. The she-goat allowed the pups to live with her in a warm loft which Matthew built. The pups survived and became the love of the camp. They live there still and are unwilling to return to the wild. Matthew hitched them to a sled when he went into the interior. He considers them members of his family. A native friend, an artist, made two drawings of the pups in ink and Matthew kept one in his rooms and presented the other to the commandant. I have learned all of this from his letters, each one more engaging than the last. I believe that he has an interest in a young woman, but I have not received word from him since leaving home. I fear that he awaits word of my condition, but I have not the means to tell him of recent developments about the state of his family."

* * *

At St. John's Matthew returned to the stockade from a seal hunt on the ice to find a visiting ship nestled in the harbor. It bore the name Courageous and boasted the cannon of a man-of-war beneath a mast of British colors. He watched men unloading her. Presently a mate called to him to pack his bags and prepare to set sail. Filled with melancholy, Matthew grasped that this day marked the last of his days at St. John's for quite a while. He kissed his young woman friend goodbye. He packed a bag and, locking his rooms, brought the pups to the commandant for safe-keeping. He resolved to treat with the matter of the unanswered letters to his father another day. Leaping aboard the mighty cutter, he learned of his destination: Fort Oswego in the Americas by way of the St. Lawrence. At the ship's railing he hurled goodbyes to his lady-friend as the craft entered the river's mouth, sailing southwest into the interior of the continent. Catching the wind, the Courageous plowed along swiftly in an ice-free river, wider now because of his diligent efforts in clearing away boulders from the shoreline. Local natives lined the shore, shouting salutations. Pressing together in a solid mass, they stood close to the water's edge in order to glimpse the sleek, elegant craft slipping past them. Torn momentarily between two worlds—the familiar and the unknown—Matthew caught himself lapsing once again into melancholy. A sharp summons from below-decks redirected him and he dashed down the stairway poised to accept new duties.

Matthew learned from the ship's scuttlebutt that unfriendly natives rallied to burn and sack the garrison at Ontario. Allegedly someone in high station sent for the marines to defend the region while the commandant rebuilt the fortress. For himself, Matthew held a few beliefs about the aborigines, thoughts that he kept to himself: He believed them a hardy folk who endured much privation in order to provide for loved ones. In so doing they became dependent on white tradesmen for a large portion of their sustenance and livelihood. Where whites and natives clash, Matthew believed, came down to a disagreement over the distribution of available supplies. In rebelling he reasoned that the natives registered justifiable anger over aggressive predations upon native soil. He planned to restore the peace between the two camps by building Oswego into a central depot of supply to peace-loving and receptive natives. Of the war in the Americas, Matthew believed the native an unfortunate casualty between two contending arch-enemies on the world stage: France and England. In their own way, both contenders tempted the native with either grand offerings or a withdrawal of supply, alternating between the two— often in subtle ways. Either way, the strategy served to pull the confused native into accepting the terms of either the French or the British on most of the burning affairs of the day, in effect redefining the native's way of life. Increasingly, the native saw himself held hostage in his own land where control of supply slowly passed out of his hands and into the hands of a foreigner. When the natives attacked, Matthew believed, they brought with them these thoughts, the effect of which drove them to strike in anger.

In his Newfoundland whites and aborigines lived in peace, but native friends told him more than once that much racial discord resided in the Americas. He often discussed this matter with his lady-friend, Dewai. She had only eighteen years, but her living in a cold and barren land seasoned her beyond her years. For the women of her village the elders set the standards: She needed to be strong, yet resilient, and aggressive, not daring, in her bid to attain a modicum of comfort in a world where vital, life-sustaining resources are often scarce. The land not alone her antagonist, she resisted the advances of young men who longed to lie with her in buffalo robes in a warm cabin by the fireside. A comforting thought, yes, but too predictable an existence for her. She set her expectations beyond the accepted village standards where the obdurate leadership insisted that young females fulfill Nature's plan by succumbing unconditionally to primordial instincts. Most assuredly she wanted to enter motherhood one day, but along a course of her *own* choosing, a step beyond that of doing her so-called duty.

She longed to stand out from the crowd, not to defy her peers, but to celebrate her uniqueness, to extol the gifts which the Great Spirit gave to her and only to her in a special way. She excelled in athleticism since childhood, able to hold her own with any male of the village. She learned a second language, French, spoken by the tradesmen who frequented her village. She learned to write the language, keeping journals of the letters of the alphabet, each page holding numerous expressions before breaking off into sentences. She set about committing her native language to the journals, sounding each word in accordance with the alphabet, until she built complete sentences. When the Englishmen came to her village she spoke with them in their language, finding that the French and English languages employed the same alphabet, and, in many cases, the same or similar words. After diligent study, she learned to speak, read, and write in three tongues: French, English and her own native Cree.

She continued the study of French and English, developing fluency in the conversational mode, having the ability to converse freely with the merchants and strangers she met at market in St. John's. She moved ahead to the addition and subtraction of ciphers. This skill proved invaluable to her when selling her fine woven baskets and embroidered tunics for men and women. She learned to make such articles by watching her mother and grandmother by the fireside— often working far into the night to complete a piece. She went to market every second week of the month and found her wares in great demand for which she earned ample compensation. In turn she exchanged her earnings for hard goods brought by French and English merchantmen from across the great sea. She refused, however, to part with the occasional lustrous and brilliant pieces which the merchants called gold. These she saved in one of her woven baskets, the lid of which she lashed tightly into place.

It is at market that she first laid eyes upon him, the tall, well-built English young man with a shock of red hair and steel blue eyes which competed with a maze of freckles about the nose. The young man moved quickly among the displays of goods, searching for that one elusive article. He set a crisp pace, his outfit cleaned and pressed, clearly a man of substance. A smile on his lips, he spoke briefly with all the vendors, asking incisive questions. He knew about hard goods, she determined, and his wit and humor left a good impression among all with whom he commiserated. She learned his name upon inquiry and at home she consulted the alphabetic journals until she found "Matthew" at the top of the page under 'M.' She pronounced it over and over, even making it the theme of a light verse which she recited to herself and only to herself.

Matthew circled her booth once, twice, before stopping. He pointed to the tunic inlaid with porcupine quills along the sleeve, her favorite. Gesturing, he indicated to her that he wanted to hold it against his chest. She honored the request, and, handing him the garment, spoke in precise English: "This tunic will serve you well." Matthew took half a step backward, temporarily forgetting the tunic, whereupon his hostess proceeded to describe the garment in greater detail. Matthew, visibly affected by her command of English, stood enthralled with this bright native girl. Her complexion, a light golden brown, she smiled when speaking to reveal strong teeth of a pearly-white ivory. When she spoke raven hair flowed thick over her shoulders, and she looked upward at the tall youth through eyes the shade of the deep blue ocean. He looked momentarily at her fingers for a ring, a sign that she shared her life with another. Seeing none, he breathed a sigh of relief, blushing slightly when he discovered that she followed his every movement. They both laughed at once. He grew more at ease and she initiated their first dialogue:

"No. I am not married. Are you?" she asked casually.

He found himself blushing, partly due to her direct approach: Shuffling, he replied: "Hardly. I am a mere soldier by day and a cod-handler at night, ma petite. I have a stall here."

"Oh! You speak French! That is a most colorful language," she returned, a demure smile on her lips.

"You have witnessed the extent of my knowledge, I fear," he spoke, apologetically.

"No need to worry. I will teach you during your idle moments."

He posed a mild objection, regretting it as soon as the words escaped his throat: "My idle moments come too rarely. My sister, though, is the French scholar of the family. She taught herself, I believe," he smiled innocently.

They exchanged names. She pronounced 'Matthew' correctly, dragging the 'ew' through to the end. He stumbled over her name, calling her 'Dew:ee,' whereupon she readily pronounced it for him: 'Dew:ay'. They laughed once again over their mutual discoveries and set out walking the length of the stalls, row upon row of booths heaped with goods. Piled high, they all but choked off the constricted passage way, that narrow corridor interconnecting all the stalls. On more than one occasion Matthew collided with the delightful young woman in futile efforts to traverse the tight passage. Intuitively he drew her closely to him from about the waist and they crept along tentatively. She offered no objection, nor stepped apart from him when they reached the end of the corridor and looked out upon an open, grassy field.

"Moi foi! Your tunic! We left it behind," she exclaimed, grasping his hand.

"Not to worry," Matthew returned, her hand warm to the touch. "I must return to my stall. I left it vacant. You may make the tunic the subject of my next visit. I will trade you cod for it. How many cod is it worth?" he laughed.

"Enough to feed my village," she retorted, laughing.

They stood facing each other, laughing, he, holding both of her hands and looking down upon her, a full head beneath him, knowing they must part company, each one to return to previous obligations. He gazed at her intently, looking for one final moment into her azure eyes, beacons which aroused his passion and commanded his undivided attention. Reluctantly pulling away from her, he made an announcement: "Please be my guest at the garrison a week from Saturday. There will be a festival with games and food. Bring the tunic with you." He gripped her hand firmly for one brief moment before starting off toward his station. After several steps he looked back over his shoulder for her. Unfortunately for him, she already departed, leaving him with only her memory. Disgusted with himself, he kicked the ground, stirring up dust clusters, and strode head down back to his stall.

He spent a miserable following day, Friday, preoccupied with the thought of her coming to the garrison. He labored the entire day at the fishery giving out orders to the crew a little too aggressively, washing the same specimens of cod over and over, leaving the door to the ice house open, and forgetting to wash some of the larger kettles and skillets in the kitchen. Comrades noticed the change in demeanor and stood clear of him, reluctant to challenge him, for he outranked most of them. Everyone relished the close of the day's affairs and returned somberly to their homes, eager to put the day's maladjustments behind them. For himself, Matthew tossed and turned in bed, waiting for sleep to arrive, afraid to learn what the morrow held in store for him.

Saturday dawned. He rose with the first light of day, exhausted from lack of sleep. He rushed through his toilette and dressed. He gulped a few hard biscuits between drafts of hot cocoa, then, rushing to his desk, he set about planning the activities for the coming festival. Charged with the garrison's events, he established them around a theme: Daily Life in an English Garrison. He intended to throw open the portals to all residents and to his allies, the Cree and Micmacs. First off, for the benefit of guests, he opened the grounds to display the men and women of the garrison in their daily settings: at labor, leisure, and play. At a glance one came face-to-face with the blacksmith and his anvil, a mother baking bread at her hearth, youth playing cricket— among other examples.

He organized games for young and mature alike, games for all-comers to participate in. Among these stood: tug of war, stick-ball, darts, lawn tennis, quoits, lawn shuffleboard, pole climbing, pig-roping, rooster-chasing, turkey-calling, axe-throwing, archery, and many more . . . all planned simultaneously throughout the day. All along the route trays of freshly cooked foods and light treats awaited the discriminating palate.

Matthew brought music into the festivities. He employed residents to perform continually through the daylight hours and far into the evening. He chose instruments which in his opinion loaned a carefree atmosphere to the proceedings. By next week he hoped to have assembled musicians on violin, flute, piccolo, drums, and trumpet. Finally, Matthew planned the Grand Cotillion, a casual dance, more of a parade of participants. With the Cotillion men and women formed two opposing lines face-to-face separated by a generous space. When the music began the two lines walked slowly toward each other. Choosing partners, they paired off, man to woman, and danced a waltz. At length the dancers formed a great circle, man to woman, and strolled the perimeter of the space to the cheers of friends and supporters. The Cotillion lasted about an hour and marked the conclusion of the day's festivities.

The components of his plans assembled, Matthew submitted them for approval to the garrison's commandant. He received prompt authorization, after which he chose a staff from among the residents to assist him. During most of the week Matthew and his colleagues prepared the campus of the garrison to house a great influx of guests and itinerant travelers. Thoughts of Dewai still resided with him. They grew stronger as the days of the week progressed and when he returned to the stall in the market, he found his powers of concentration lacking. More than once he charged a pedestrian more than the stated price for cod. Some grew angry with him. Older pedestrians laughed and recalled to him the aberrant days of their own youth.

Saturday, September 23rd arrived. The festivities opened early as planned. Matthew made the rounds of the venues. Guests came from all over the immediate region: farm-families with children, soldiers from the garrison, St. John's residents, and of course Micmacs and Crees. On the basis of attendance Matthew believed the festival a success. He stood nearby sampling the opinion of the attendees. He liked what he heard. Occasionally he glanced hard at the guests, in search of a special face. The day wore on and he performed a vigil— stopping infrequently to dine and idly chat, an eye forever wary for his new-found friend. He visited most of the stalls with exhibits of rich native clothing and household utensils. Young native women displayed wares, but none of them reminded him of Dewai. A fellow marine challenged him to play at the field games, but he begged off, preferring to be alone in thought. The day wore on and afternoon became evening. Already the musicians began to assemble in the bandstand for the Cotillion. He caught himself nervously mouthing the tune to one of the waltzes— a staple of the festival.

The guests entered the parade field. Soon the music pulled them together in twos and the grand waltz lay moments away. From a distance he inspected each couple that strode past him. Several of his comrades chose partners and broke for the bandstand. They beckoned him to join them, but he waved them on ahead, content with observing the continuous flow of young men and women striding arm in arm over the grounds. He rehearsed how he would react should his friend appear with an escort other than himself. At first his temples rattled. Anger built up, but he knew that he exercised no claims upon her. This thought alone served to dispel the anger and subdue his passions and he set about gently toe-tapping the hard earth at his feet. Tiring of that he asked one of the servant girls for a waltz and to his surprise she accepted. He stumbled often and she called instructions to him. He obeyed, replying with curt "thank you's": the extent of his discourse with her. When the music ended she dashed off to her station without acknowledging him. Alone again, he watched children rushing to the banquet tables to snatch pits and pieces of food. A sense of abandonment crept into his consciousness. In the back of his mind he saw himself standing alone in a field, ripe with freshly-mowed grasses. The wind whipped up and the sweet fragrance of the grasses overwhelmed him. At peace, he stood motionless, hoping to invest himself with the reassuring fragrance forever. He stared straight ahead, imbibing the fragrance. He knew it from before. *She* wore that fragrance—his friend, Dewai. He turned about briskly, eyes wide-open.

"Is it too late to go dancing?" A soft voice called to him. She held the tunic. Apparently he did not see it. Breathless, he reached for her. He encircled her waist and bound her tightly to his chest. Her raven hair glowed in the ensuing darkness and the familiar fragrance of her flowed upward coursing through his clothing, impressing upon him her ambiance, her uniqueness. He searched for words with which to greet her. He settled upon something banal and trite.

"Ah! My special friend. I believed you lost to a pack of hungry wolves."

She laughed lightly. "Wolves there are, but not of the four-legged kind. Not to worry. I chased them off. I told them my escort awaits me with a waltz." She bowed low before Matthew.

"And a waltz it shall be." Clasping her about the waist, he led her before the bandstand.

"But the music has stopped," she protested.

Matthew signaled to the director of the ensemble. The young man smiled and struck up the musicians.

"Last call for Monsieur York," he grinned.

"How thoughtful," she demurred. "I brought along my brother. He fought off the hungry wolves."

She introduced her brother who gave his name in French and shook Matthew's hand in greeting. While the lad joined the festivities, she allowed Matthew to encircle her waist and lead her to the center of the parade grounds. "You will have to teach me. I do not know these steps," she smiled.

"With great pleasure, Mademoiselle." His eyes never left hers. They stood together, gazing at each other, the almost-perfect oval of her face catching the few remaining rays of the setting sun. The musicians settled in and played the Lovers' Waltz. Matthew recognized the title, but did not reveal it to Dewai. Instead he guided her through the turns without speaking a word. He held her close. Young women swooned at the sidelines, and reluctantly he held her at arm's length. Warm to the touch, her pleasant aroma invaded his senses, challenging his ability to make precise turns. Stooping, he pressed a cheek upon hers. He remembered her telling him that men and women of her Cree (47) village who promised themselves to each other sealed the agreement by touching cheeks. She pulled away, gazing up at him.

The waltz ended. They cut a path to the far reaches of the campus. He led her to a large shady maple. There they came to rest against its ample boughs, shielded from scrutiny. He kissed her cheek. Nibbling at her ears, he took delight in watching her shrink away, laughing in glee. An arm about her shoulders, they turned to watch the setting sun, now a golden orb sneaking below the horizon. When an evening downpour drenched the grounds, they huddled beneath the maple's sumptuous limbs, drawing closer to each other, sharing each other's warmth. It is here that they exchanged loyalties, he speaking the handful of Cree words which Dewai rehearsed with him. Twice they performed the exercise: in English and in Cree. She promised to write the short declaration for him on parchment so that he may hang it on a frame in his rooms. She promised to complete it on the morrow and carry it to him personally.

It is with great sorrow that he gave her to understand that on the next day he must depart for the Americas— there to serve his king, to do his duty. She spurned the term 'duty' since childhood, she told him, and made her objections clearly known to him. To her, 'duty' required human sacrifice with no assurances of rewards for having pledged one's faith and loyalty. It is a universal blight, she explained, placing the same insidious demands on all peoples everywhere. She feared losing him to 'duty' before their own exchanged loyalties gained meaning. She feared losing him to war, to sickness, and to a whole host of ugly calamities.

She demanded to retain a bit of him with her--something--someone to remind her always of him—her own way of rising up against and defeating the scourge of that 'duty', the thought of which brought her so much anguish. With a bit of him she would emerge triumphant over duty, for she wanted no other man and by their pledges they themselves wanted only each other. By her plan they would unite to produce, raise and care for a unique and special child, a testimony to her uniqueness, her ultimate victory over 'duty'.

They spoke at length, there beneath the broad maple in the autumnal downpour, bound closely together. It is then that Matthew prepared to give her a part of himself that would live into the next generation, far beyond either of them, that son or daughter conceived out of love—not duty.

*An agreement formed in the late 17th century which conferred the delivery of exclusive trading privileges regarding the native Peoples in North America to trade representatives of the British Crown.

**Samuel Kirkland, Presbyterian minister who visited and subsequently lived among the Oneidas, investing them with adaptations of western standards of living. Founder of Hamilton College in Clinton, NY.

(43) Parker, Arthur C. An Analytical History of the Seneca Indians. Chapter 14: *Kanandesaga or Old Castle*. The New York State Archeological Association (1926) pgs: 116-117

(44)Kimm, S.C.(1900). Chapter VIII, Games, pg: 38.

(45)Kimm, S.C., pg: 39.

(46)Parkman, Francis (Tebbell, J.ed,). The Battle for North America, Part Six: *Montcalm and Wolfe* (1948)

Chp.11. pgs: 615-626

(47)Taylor & Sturtevant (2002) pg: 197.

Chapter Eleven

The Searchers
Test of the Courageous.
The Captain Distressed.
Oh:nehsi:yo At Pointe Aux Bois.
Teedyuscung.
Watkins Makes A Choice.

The Courageous plied the waters of the St. Lawrence with ease, aided in no small part by the spirited zephyrs which gave the vessel a succession of gentle pushes. Light in weight for a man-of-war, the Courageous more closely resembled a corsair, that swift fighter with a raft of awesome cannon, port and starboard, able to cut tight, precision-like patterns with ease. For a smaller craft, the Courageous sported the rigging of superior ships: A jib and flying jib flowed generously from the bow's main mast, extending well beyond the bow itself. A broad main sail streamed back from a second main mast, somewhat taller than its predecessor, eclipsing the stern beneath it. The sails, made of strong, light-weight canvas, consumed oncoming vapors. Once caught within the billowing expansiveness, the zephyrs knocked about colliding with each other to lend a mighty thrust to the ship, giving it to plunge fearlessly through deep waters.

The vessel bore double rudders, affixed fore and aft to the bottom of the hull. They operated independently, and when set at right angles, served to brake the ship. A shallow keel midway between the rudders enabled the Courageous to draw into beaches at low tide, to turn sharply, and to displace water minimally, thus improving her stability. Her builders made her out of strips of red mahogany. Craftsmen all, they molded and shaved the strips, fastened them together with wooden pegs, covering the super-structure with water-repelling resin. The resin hardened with rock-hard consistency as the vessel sat exposed to direct sunlight while in dry dock. A double hull added an additional layer of protection against head-on collisions. Ninety feet in length by the English measure, the Courageous held billets for eighty sailors, each of whom shared a small cell with a roommate, complete with a bunk bed, top and bottom, wash stand, two folding chairs, a wall mirror, an antiseptic kit, a footlocker for rations, and a chamber pot. A small galley of sorts took shape amidships where a cook prepared a hot dinner once a day at 0:1800h. She departed St. John's with sixty marines, early that Sunday, September 24th, capable of holding twenty more men with relative ease.

In his bunk below decks Matthew finished a letter to his father. Folding it, he sealed the edges with hot wax, laying it aside. Concerning Dewai, he carefully omitted intimate segments of his life with her, discussing her in context with his comings and goings at St. John's. Customarily, a full month transpired before he received a reply from his father, a standard procedure running back to his arrival in Newfoundland some two years ago. His trail calendar gave him to understand that a reply stood past due. Any one or more reasons accounted for the delay in correspondence. Most obvious, the itinerant schooner to which he entrusted his letters may have met with foul weather. More than likely, the schooner lay idle in port waiting to capture a strong gust of wind sufficient to propel her past the treacherous Atlantic coastline. Of course, during this autumnal season, the Chesapeake Bay and incidental lands along the lower Susquehanna grew infamous for giving birth to violent wind storms. Waves leaping between land and sea flared up instantaneously to devour all vessels unfortunate enough to attempt the rolling waves. Even the deep-keeled schooner is not safe from danger, he noted. Schooners notoriously became stranded on the series of sandbars which straddled the inlets and coves of the Chesapeake Bay. There they lingered until dashed apart from high seas during the familiar hurricane season.

He decided to post the letter at Fort Oswego. There a courier would carry it by horseback along the Susquehanna to his father's home, hence sparing him the delays associated with delivery by sea. On his map the land route from Oswego to the Delaware country proved a great deal shorter than a sea route from St. John's south along the unpredictable Atlantic coastline. Without further thought, he resolved that, upon reaching his destination, his first task of the day consisted of posting the letter. He picked up his quill once again to draft a message to Dewai.

The Courageous kept to the shallows of the broad St. Lawrence, frequenting the myriad coves and fishing banks which constituted major portions of the irregular shoreline. At intervals the vessel weighed anchor while the crew took turns bathing in the refreshing waters. The stopovers provided the men with the opportunity to fish for all manner of edible specimens: tuna, shad, whitefish, shake, cod, and halibut, an endless outpouring of ocean-dwelling fish which migrated annually to the innumerable crannies close by the shallow banks in order to spawn.

On this occasion the Courageous pulled into a long, narrow lagoon. It held no marks of distinction, save that it opened into another somewhat smaller lagoon within. A narrow spit of land attempted to connect the two lagoons from north to south, but because of the rolling waters, never grew beyond a modest sandbar. Luxuriant white sands, the texture of fine sugar, covered the lagoons' beaches. They drifted to the water's edge where gentle waves pushing against the sands, carved them into minute hills and rivulets along the shoreline. On that afternoon the waters, deep and clear, reflected the brilliant azure of the autumn sky. The crewmen flocked to the ship's railing to partake of the breathtaking beauty of the sand and water in juxtaposition. In short order they plunged into the waters to bath and frolic. Others sat on the shore and cast for fish. A small detachment went ashore to look for vestiges of life. In the main the men discovered ancient fossils and burrowing crabs which they put into sacks. A few of the men reported seeing footprints and charred embers further inland. They declared them of recent origin. Aboard the ship one of the fishermen inadvertently snagged the line of an immovable object below the waterline. Diving below, his mates retrieved a sizeable anchor. It bore the legend of a privateer. One of the men brought up a cutlass, the favored instrument of pirates and soon the shoreline hummed with talk of a land infested with brigands. Driven by curiosity and a sense of adventure, a second detachment headed inland. Hacking away vegetation, the men plodded along furtively, eyes and ears tuned to a fine point. Soon they approached a forbidding sand dune. Silently a few of them ascended the structure. Rather than boldly crest it, the men peeped over the dune's summit. What they saw taking place below reviled them. Sickened to the core, the men crept back down and reported to their mates:

Apparently several surly-looking men, dressed in knee-leggings, short tunics with sashes girding the waist, stockings running to above the knee and black leather boots, occupied themselves with a small, defenseless band of young male natives. The lot of them carried cutlasses and wore long, flowing hair tied behind the neck. To a man they bore sinewy mustaches and stumbled about as though under the influence of the 'spirits.' Herded into a circle, their captives cowered in fear, fearing the worst. One of the villains produced a whip, and, to the delight of his companions, applied it liberally to the back of the tallest native. The youth's moans brought his allies to his side in a futile effort to shield him, whereas other villains laid into them in like manner, subjecting all to an interminable round of lashings. In the near distance a large, beefy man with ample mustaches stood over a hot fire. Laughing raucously, he urged his comrades to strike with impunity, all the while stirring coals with a cutlass. Piercing one of the coals, he pulled it from the fire, and, casually approaching the terrified young men, tossed the burning chip indiscriminately into their circle. Stepping back, he reviewed his handiwork. He laughed lasciviously when a young man, shrieking in pain, collapsed to the earth.

Greatly disturbed, the men of the Courageous repelled from the sandy dune. Bent upon rescuing the beleaguered youth, they gathered around Matthew York who met them at the foot of the slope. They determined the ruffians to be pirates and their victims, young natives plucked from villages to be sold into slavery (48). Two wooden pens at the scene gave Matthew to understand that the captives spent most of the day confined without the comforts of food and water. The marines concluded that the youth stood destined for a life of servitude in one of the many fortresses dotting the Great Lakes, perhaps worse, a fate akin to death, given the lashes the poor youth absorbed.

Matthew summoned his Captain forward, one Smythe. A young man, full of exuberance and charity toward others, he accepted Matthew's commentary with a look of horror. He detested the random flogging of children. What is more, he hated pirates and all they represented. Together the two men mounted the dune, whereupon Matthew spied a young girl whose willow-like stature and bearing made her in his opinion an item of interest to her captors. Terrified, the young girl sought refuge among taller males. A brigand pulled her from amid the assemblage and proceeded to lash her. Recoiling, she let out screams of pain, and, running barefoot, struck a course for freedom along the sandy beach. Her pursuer dropped back to prime a pistol before pointing the firearm squarely at her back. Dashing headlong, she dispelled all warnings to halt. Unknown to her, she headed directly toward the dune where Matthew and Smythe lay hidden.

The two young marines exchanged glances wrought with urgency. A human life lay in the balance and they alone retained the ability to preserve it. For an instant, images of the girl lying inert and bloodied on a wind-swept beach burrowed into their collective consciousness, boring deep within, lodging firmly in their mind's eye. Creeping pangs of guilt rose in the pit of their stomachs. Growing nauseous, they deduced that they must act in order to save her, if that meant restoring a sense of balance to the insane scene set before them. Without further delay, they tugged on their pistols, firing two volleys at once.

Two deadly missiles struck the villain. The center of the forehead and the pit of the stomach absorbed both shots, spewing forth the man's life blood generously before he slumped to the earth. The reports rang with such clarity across the sands that the man's comrades suspended all activities and ran to where he lay. Shouting profanities, they glimpsed the profiles of Matthew and his Captain, and, judging themselves in the majority, charged the dune, with pistols and rapiers in hand. Matthew and Smythe crept low behind the dune. They reloaded and prepared to deliver a broadside when a party of marines from the Courageous joined them at the most opportune of moments. Eager to aid their two comrades, the marines fired point-blank into the faces of the charging pirates. A great many fell away at once. Filled with enthusiasm, Smythe exhorted the men, who, in a body, rushed down the face of the dune with pistols blazing. Summarily they dispatched most of the villains and pursued those still alive into the forest. Smythe, fearing for his comrades' safety, called them back, but not before they killed several more, leaving the remainder to their own devices. Smythe conducted a count of the dead. To his surprise one pirate survived the ambush.

He begged for his life. Smythe ran to him, and, pulling the man to his feet, shouted:

"I need to learn of your leader. Who is in charge of this lot?"

The man hesitated. Smythe leveled a rapier before the man's throat. Still no response. He drew the sword into striking position at the man's ear. The brigand blurted forth a curt warning:

"He is **Black Jack**. He will find you." The man collapsed at Smythe's feet. Smythe, in turn, drew back to slay him. Matthew held back his comrades's arm. He advised him to interrogate the villain for important knowledge in exchange for granting him his life. Matthew won the argument and crew members dragged the wretch off to the hold of the Courageous. The native youth, having gained their freedom, flocked to the side of two, young marines. The young girl also came along, and after inspecting her for wounds, Smythe assigned her and other young females to a set of cabins on board the Courageous. Turning to the dead pirates, Smythe reluctantly decided to bury them on the field where they fell in combat. Matthew, in whom he often confided, believed Smythe's parting gesture noteworthy of a Christian, and gave approval. Ultimately he joined the burial detail. Methodically a party of marines set about the grim task of burial with the understanding to dig deep and quickly, their sole reprieve from the foul stench of the decomposing corpses which lay awash in blood and covered with flies and sprouting sand worms. The ritual completed, the burial squad raced to the nearest lagoon where everyone plunged into the refreshing waters in order to cast off the odors of death and gunpowder which clung tenaciously to the flesh and clothing.

Renewed, the crew trotted off to the Courageous, content to leave behind the land of death and depravity. A band of natives in tow, the men cheered when the Courageous came into view through the light mist rolling over the inlet. She bobbed gently in the lagoon with sails at half-mast. The sentry on board waved from his lofty perch on the main mast to signal that all was well. The crew trotted gaily along in cadence, yet in the next instant the sentry let cry a warning at the top of his lungs: "Ahoy!! Pirate ship at my back! Man your stations!!"

A well-disciplined crew, the marines boarded the Courageous and set out for their respective stations. Behind the vessel and blocking her route of escape, a corsair carrying five guns lay in waiting. Smythe shouted to the steersmen, who ably turned the double rudders at right angles, bringing into full view the ship's port side along with its entire battery of twenty pounders. Gunners and mates assumed positions. Meanwhile, a gangplank extending to the beach brought aboard the last of the young natives. Below decks marines scurried for weapons and shields. The foreign craft, somewhat smaller than the Courageous, flew no colors, but to the marines its origin was undeniable. A single-tiered ship, the corsair's main deck sat below the guns of the three-tiered Courageous, leaving the marines powerless to open a broadside at close range. Moreover, the guns of the Courageous did not pivot. Strictly stationary, they were designed for longer-range maneuvers—by all accounts, the length of a ship's distance away. Defiantly the corsair pulled in beside the Courageous at port side. A mere step, the length of a man's boot, separated the two vessels. Matthew counted one, two, three, five small cannon.

On the main deck of the Courageous Matthew and Smythe joined members of the deck crew at the railing. They looked downward into a maze of sinister faces, villains all, unshaven and unkempt, gaunt from lack of nourishment. A riotous crew, they railed invectives at the marines, their tattered clothing blowing in the wind, bodies festooned with scars and ill-attempts at self-immolation. To a man the throng cursed the marines liberally in terms which assailed the crew of the Courageous in general and the seaworthiness of the Courageous in particular. Their speech and saucy oaths confirmed the marines' belief that these brigands stood a breed apart from the rest of humanity.

A particularly despicable-looking character issued forth from the lot. He cast aside those of the crew who stood in his path and ambled with authority to the vessel's railing. Taller and larger than any of his confederates, the man incorporated the sum of their nefarious characteristics. He leered at the Courageous. Casting an eye at her crew, he fastened upon Matthew and Smythe across the way. Falling short of introducing himself, the villain snorted while pointing out the young natives on deck to his mates. He spoke in a deep baritone, well aware that his voice brought about undue distraction to the marines as it bounced back and forth between the two vessels. He taunted the marines with ingratiating speech, nonetheless making his intentions known:

"I see that you have kept my charges unharmed until my return." Sneering, he flashed a crocodile smile, his hands secured to a pair of pistols at his belt. Pulling on his long mustaches, he expanded his chest and blew forcefully through his nose, spitting its contents over the deck.

A disturbed Smythe gripped the railing of the forecastle. Faced with addressing this scourge of the sea, he momentarily suspended all pending concerns, and spoke firmly: "Your charges have met with misfortune at the hands of your mates. Fortunately for them, I arrived before they became lashed to a pulp."

"There are a few rogues among my crew, but I will weed them out and spare you the trouble of hanging them. I will also take those aborigines off of your hands." the large man returned, pleased with his response.

"It is no trouble to look after the aborigines," Smythe returned, a model of refined comportment. "By the way, I have cleared up the matter of the rogues. They will never molest anyone again. You will find their remains buried in the sand near the dunes."

"I congratulate you for helping me purge these waterways of riffraff. I will return your favor by taking the aborigines off your hands at no cost to you," he repeated, bowing and smiling lavishly.

"You are much too kind. However, I must tell you that I have plenty of provisions set aside and my great vessel is more than prepared to ensure their security." Smythe gestured approvingly toward the Courageous.

The big man grew more insistent. He spoke rapidly. "To wit. Your dear aborigines are on a level with street urchins. They have stolen from my food stores, attacked my crew with knives, and tried to seize my ship. They need to suffer the consequences of these misdeeds." He spat over the railing.

Smythe called out: "My dear man. Once the natives learned of their fate in your hands, they fought madly for freedom. Nothing less, nothing more. However, looking upon them now in their present wretched state, I find it difficult to accept your thoughts about their aggressiveness. Now, if you will allow me to pass."

The big man grew restless. "I do not intend to delay your departure, however, neither you nor I are going anywhere. You see, my ship is stranded with the keel lodged against the sandy bottom. I must wait until the waters rise with the tides before I attempt to wrench her free."

"That is strange, my dear man, for we share the same waters. My keel is free and I have the larger ship. Truly, the master of one's vessel knows its limits in unknown waters. Clearly you have failed to take precautions beforehand." Smythe stepped backward, exchanging glances with Matthew.

The big man drew back in anger. "First, you question my sincerity. Now, you question my captaincy. I hereby demand that you return my aborigines. Let us make it a contest. If you are able to sail by me before I dislodge my keel I will grant you custody of the aborigines down to the last wretched pup. If you do *not* succeed you will hand them over and I will take charge of them once I am free. Am I understood?" Without waiting for a response, the big man barked out orders to the crew milling noisily about the main deck. Meanwhile, Smythe met with crewmen to discuss the matter. A great many marines surrounded him along the port side, lending support. Unknown to them, sailors from the pirate ship began boarding the Courageous from the moment of the big man's engaging exchange with Smythe. Methodically they dropped into the lagoon from their craft's stern, a maneuver executed while the marines congregated on the main deck. Deftly the pirates swam to the abandoned starboard side of the Courageous, there to mount her at the water line. With her flank thus exposed to encroachment, the pirates sought toeholds in gunwales and port-hole openings, effectively pulling themselves upward hand-over-hand with the utmost of skill and dexterity. Moving with catlike tread, the villains padded along in moccasins. Attaining the top-most railing of the three-tiered Courageous, they dropped down to the top deck where they joined into tight packs to invest the ship's interior. Within moments they reached the rear of the main deck where they hid amid the rigging, casks, and hogsheads, there to await the opportunity to attack.

'From the outset, he, **Black Jack Mc Knight**, intended to board the Courageous in order to plunder her. It is no accident that he offered to parley with the young officer, who initially failed to recognize his intentions. That the young officer chose to discuss his offer gave him to understand that he may be easily drawn off guard long enough for him to precipitate an ambush. In their brief exchange he concluded that the young officer represented that new diplomatic breed of marine who preferred to talk himself out of a fight rather than soil his white kid gloves. So far he turned the young officer's glibness to his own advantage. Meanwhile, he saw something more as he bore in on the vessel: the gun-ports. From the moment his adversary swung to port side, he noticed the stationary mounts of his cannon. Not a single gun swung on a pivot. Therefore, the fight, if begun, must of necessity be fought hand-to-hand, with cutlass and pistol and no one equaled his men in hand-to-hand combat in all of the northeastern waterways. Soon this brash young officer would come begging at his heel for him to spare his command the misery of walking the plank and he would laugh in the whelp's face as he pierced his innards with a cutlass.' He smiled to himself a broad smile and laughed mightily— the signal for his sailors to advance.

Armed generously with instruments of death, the pirates emerged from concealment. They padded noiselessly to where the pool of marines stood about mid-ships on the port side. Their advance, however, coincided with the reentry of a squad of marines returning from below decks with weapons. Making straight for their comrades, the marines inadvertently stumbled upon the path of the pirates. Both sides reacted instinctively. While the marines fell to their pistols, the pirates drew cutlasses. Drawing first blood, several marines standing together, fired into the swarm of brigands, who, throwing caution to the winds, charged head-on with swords raised. They fell like matchsticks, but not before lashing out with incisive thrusts, bringing the marines to fall back and call for help. Their comrades gathered at the port side railing suddenly came to life and flocked to intercept the villains, effectively surrounding them and cutting off all avenues of escape. The fight may have ended there; however, scores of pirates invaded the deck from seemingly nowhere and a general mêlée erupted. From a distance the scene resembled a series of small contests all taking place at once with no one side emerging the victor. The full body of marines entered the fight, leaving no reserves. For the pirates, such proved not the case.

Bold and proud on the deck of his vessel, **Black Jack** maintained a constant vigil. Shortly he moved to take charge of the fighting. Bellowing out an order, he put into effect a second plan. With planks and ladders at the ready, his sailors boarded the Courageous at her port side. Her entire length overrun with raging madmen, the marines found themselves hard pressed to repel the invaders without abandoning the fight on deck. Aware of exposing themselves to a rear attack, a squad of marines broke away to beat back the boarding party. Desirous of driving his prey within a constricting web, **Black Jack** held fast to the Courageous with grappling hooks. When pulled taut, the sharp barbs dug into the wooden gunwales, becoming firmly affixed. Try as they may, Smythe's crewmen were unable to disengage them. Some died in the attempt— victims of a knife or ball in the back.

Matthew and Smythe fought side by side. The two marines rolled with the flow of the fight, but neither man counted a victory close at hand. Smythe challenged Matthew to devise a plan by which the marines may turn the tide of battle. Matthew looked about. Behind him stood the tool house, a stout shed holding instruments employed in navigation. Matthew crept to the tool house. Stealing within, he discovered bales of netting and a row of pikes, among other devices. He slipped back to Smythe, telling him of the find. His worthy commander released three marines to accompany him and Matthew retreated once again to the shed. Meanwhile, on deck the hand-to-hand fighting raged on unabated. No one noticed the small band of men exiting the shed, stooped over as though carrying a great burden. At Matthew's signal several marines broke off the fight. They moved back to assist him and his comrades who struggled to unfurl the netting. In the next moment the men gathered the netting and, raising it aloft, tossed it over the shoulders of the confused brigands, trapping them within. Pulling the netting taut from below, the marines stepped back. Retrieving the pikes, a number of them thrust the deadly spears into the netting where they effectively lanced the pirates like so many fish in a barrel, killing many outright. Seizing the moment, Matthew and his party carried more netting and pikes to their comrades who, in short order, netted and speared many more of the ruffians. From his station **Black Jack*** bellowed a command and the raiders fell back to gather the dead and wounded. Overwhelmed for the moment, they awaited their leader's instructions. For once the big man stood mute, jaw agape.

Matthew, on the other hand, hurriedly unfolded a plan before Smythe. "We need to put distance between the two vessels. Here is what we shall do: We need to hoist full sail, cut the grappling hooks and fire our cannon on the port side." Smythe barked out orders. In response, deck hands leaned on the winches. The main mast stirred, then rose steadily upward. On deck marines pushed past the vanquished pirates and snapped the lines holding the grappling hooks. Tossing them overboard, they assumed defensive positions before their stunned adversaries. Below decks gunners packed each cannon with a ball, then wadding, followed by gunpowder. At a signal from the lead gunner, the mates ignited the pieces— all twenty of them in a single stroke. The Courageous lurched violently to starboard. Those on deck not braced firmly to meet the explosion hurled violently forward. Men struck mastheads, barrels, each other. Most of them, pirates, lay silent and broken. The marines, aware of the plan, counted no casualties and during the second set of explosions, clung to each other fiercely. With the third volley the Courageous began to pull away from the pirate vessel. The main mast, fully engaged, billowed, having caught a favorable series of zephyrs coming in from the St. Lawrence. An alert boatswain spun her rudders to the 10 o'clock position, opening a noticeable gulf between the two craft. A broadside shredded the remaining mooring lines and boarding ladders, sending them overboard. Allegedly free from encumbrances, the Courageous drifted deeper and deeper into the lagoon, bringing her big guns in line with the mast of the marauding vessel. The zephyrs gained in strength and all of her sails filled, rising and falling over the rolling waters of the lagoon.

Black Jack stood immobile across the way. A score of pirates, sensing imminent defeat, jumped from the Courageous, leaving the dead and wounded to fall unattended. Some of them made toward shore, while others swam to the pirate ship where rope ladders carried them aloft. Suspending his vigil, **Black Jack** hauled in anchor, and, taking advantage of the gusty zephyrs, gave orders to abandon the lagoon. With survivors scrambling on board, he pulled the vessel swiftly to port, and, tacking sharply to the left, headed across the channel toward the open river, his stern flying in the face of the astute Smythe and valiant Matthew York.

The ease with which the pirates' cruiser departed the lagoon convinced the two young marines of **Black Jack's** crafty inclination to deceive. Before their eyes the cruiser started out smartly under her own power—the tale of a keel mired in mud a convenient invention designed to draw the Courageous into a fight. Smythe, eager to punish the wily pirate, ordered gunners to fire upon the cruiser before she made good an escape. He leveled the big guns at the cruiser's stern, confident that a few well-placed salvos would render her useless. Loading half of the cannon with grapeshot, the gunners cut down the cruiser's sails in a single volley. Other big guns responded with twenty pound shot which struck the cruiser about the stern— the force of the cannonade shredding her backside and opening rifts in her planking. **Black Jack's** visible weapons, five small swivel cannon, barked loudly, but harmlessly. With his vessel listing precariously, **Black Jack** gave orders to abandon ship. Beating a hasty retreat, many of the villains lowered dinghies. Others, to avoid delay, dived headlong into the waters. **Black Jack** commandeered a dinghy, and, launching it, fought back attempts to share it with others. A final cannonade set the pirate vessel helplessly adrift, crumpled for the most part, bobbing in the waters. On the Courageous the boatswain righted the vessel's rudders and the mighty craft, her sails billowing, caught the brisk vapors coming in from the St. Lawrence. She ploughed boldly out into the channel, her thick hull ramming the doomed wreck, sending it below the surface in bits and pieces.

Smythe lowered boats and marines set about plucking many of the fleeing villains from the lagoon. Most willingly surrendered and asked for asylum. Among the last to surrender, **Black Jack** snarled and sneered, yet otherwise allowed himself to be hauled on board without resistance. Smythe ordered the pirates bound to stanchions on deck, there to remain until the Courageous docked at Oswego. With regard to the unfortunate natives, however, he brought them aboard and housed them in cabins furnished with a bed and other comforts. He declined to search for the villains who absconded along the shore, choosing to leave them to their own devices. All exploits completed, the marines broke out bottles of spirits to toast victory, heaping praises upon Captain Smythe and his assistant, Matthew York. Meanwhile, the Courageous entered a channel en route to the St. Lawrence. She paused at the terminus in anticipation of a strong southwester. Instead, a brisk gale shot through her sails and the mighty vessel regained the St. Lawrence with a burst of speed, her crew bristling about the decks in fits of celebration.

* * *

Having convinced Lord Carleton of the worthiness of his proposals, the Captain departed Fort Oswego with a small band of explorers bound for the interior. Five men in all, the well-armed party carried ample food and supplies to last for three weeks. Each man navigated his own canoe, that sturdy and reliable craft capable of holding great quantities and moving with the utmost of ease over all manner of waterways. Following the Oswego River south, they turned west where it met with the Seneca at its junction with Lake Onondaga. The Captain occupied the lead canoe from whence he set a brisk pace. The hand-chosen crew, heeding an appeal for expediency, dug deeply with their oars. Taking no respite along the route, the men agreed to forego food and drink. Unaware of their destination, the men nonetheless threw their full trust behind the Captain, who rowed silently, determined to reach his objective before dusk, that Sunday, the 8th of October. Completing the three hour romp over the gentle waters, the Captain called a halt. Going ashore, everyone concealed his craft in the bulrushes and settled down to a brief repast in a glen near the shoreline. Once on the move, the little party headed due south over open and hilly terrain. They knew the land well, these explorers, having visited native villages along the way during the Captain's tenure as principal surveyor of the North Country.

A brisk walk of some twelve leagues brought the little party to a great meadow, devoted mainly to the cultivation of orchards of fruits and gardens of vegetables. At the northern extreme, the pitched roofs of framed houses and other dwellings stood out prominently against the deep blue sky of the late afternoon. Conversation among the men erupted, for many of them visited this region in an earlier period when they constructed these very dwellings for the Senecas in this village called Kanandesaga (49). It is here that they now returned, and the men, recalling vivid memories from gay days at the inn and the gaming tables and the trading stalls, laughed heartily. Slowly the conversation turned to tales of ribald accounts with willing women and it is here that the Captain aborted further talk altogether.

He led the explorers along pathways lined with two-storied houses, all of which championed windows of glass panes, chimneys leading to interior hearths, ample lawns and generous out-buildings. Children hard at play scurried to and fro' and young mothers tended to babies in cradles and hammocks, watched from a distance by village elders— the adult males having departed for the hunt. Looking to the left, then right, he chose a narrow pathway leading to the doorstep of a large house, perhaps the largest in the village. Stopping before it, he turned to the men, a smile on his lips, then called out: "John! John O'Bail!"*

A tall, elegantly-coiffed gentleman crossed the threshold of the house. Bronzed from the sun's rays of many summers, the man stood wrapped in a beaded robe, vermillion in color. Beneath, he wore a woolen red shirt and tanned deerskin leggings embroidered with shells and porcupine quills. Statuesque, he descended the porch steps, fixing his gaze steadily upon his caller, leaving the impression that he dressed himself for the express purpose of addressing visitors. He bowed slightly from the waist and the delegation, fixed upon his presence, patiently awaited his opening remarks:

"To my friends I am Ga:yant:hawah:geh. To all others I am John O'Bail."

Regarding the Captain, he asked: "How are you called?"

The Captain, seeking to establish amicable relations, spoke slowly and distinctly: "Ah, yes. I am called James Worthy. I come from Fort Oswego on behalf on my commandant, Lord Carleton. He requests your assistance in a pressing matter of great importance."

Already given to understand by the Sandpiper of the imminent arrival of the English, John O'Bail played the role of the naive observer and issued an innocuous response, nonetheless tinged with sarcasm. "I am not aware that I, a simple man of the forest, am able to come to the aid of such an omnipresent figure as your commandant."

The Captain wasted no words. "Thank you for hearing me. Lord Carleton desires to protect the frontier of Oswego, the gateway to your lands, from inroads by dangerous parties. Recently these parties have burned to the ground his fortress, Ontario, in an effort to open the whole countryside to a hostile takeover. You have known the commandant from days gone by. He has always looked after you. Not long ago his architects showed you how to construct homes to keep back the excesses of winter. He has given you weapons for hunting and utensils in exchange for your fine furs. Lord Carleton asks little from you. Your friendship suffices. He has known you to be honest in your treatment with him and the most knowledgeable among the residents of the forest. In the end he needs to apprehend these evildoers so that peace forever reigns between our two People. This is why he asks for your help."

John O'Bail betrayed no emotions during the Captain's delivery and James Worthy continued: "Allow me to introduce one of my explorers. Caldwell! Bring your articles, please." Caldwell came forward with arrow shafts and a cluster of iron shot, whereupon the Captain surrendered them to his host for inspection. John O'Bail dwelt upon the findings for a considerable period, turning them, tossing and catching them. At length he spoke with the aid of an interpreter:

"The points themselves are nothing special. They tell me nothing. The shafts are made of reeds. They come from the shores of the Great Lakes where rushes grow wild. The Huron and Erie live there—old enemies of the Seneca. Most likely they came from the region between Lake Ontario and Lake Erie where there is plenty of tall grass." He passed to the samples of iron shot.

"These are of an older origin. They are not the property of my hunters—nay, anyone residing in the Lake Country. "The owner of this shot fired an older weapon—a long, heavy rifle—the kind that Hurons may have offered in trade. The Hurons have always traded heavily up and down the range of forts bordering the Great Lakes—French outposts. They made other native populations angry with them, for they always came away with the most firearms and the best clothing, while flooding the trading posts with cheap goods. That is one reason that the Seneca went to war against the Hurons. In truth, the Hurons are our enemies. Our animosity goes back many generations (50). They are not welcomed to trade here at Kanandesaga. Whoever acquired the rifles for this shot came from beyond the Lake Country."

"Thank you" a somber Captain returned. "If you will excuse me for a moment." The Captain dropped back to confer with Caldwell and the others. Disappointed, he conceded that the chief did not tell him anything that he did not already know. In general the explorers believed that the chief knew more than he chose to reveal. Moreover, for the explorers, the chief dwelt too heavily on the Hurons, a nation that no longer counted among the leading traders of the day, in as much as the Seneca conquered them generations ago. Most French forts along the Great Lakes disappeared with the decline of the Hurons, the explorers noted. The possibility that one still existed stood remote, they conceded.

The Captain decided against pressing the chief further for greater details in Kanandesaga, his home-base, where he lived surrounded by partisans. He settled for gaining additional knowledge, conceivably to piece it together to form a series of links eventually leading to a prime suspect. He resumed his non-confrontational stance:

"You still trade with the French, do you not?" he asked politely.

"We at Kanandesaga open our doors to all who come in peace. There are the occasional tradesmen. They are known to come from Canada on their way to Acadie," (51) John O'Bail returned, his slow yet steady speech commanding the full attention of his audience.

The Captain offered an observation: "By your account, it is the Hurons who attacked Ontario, yet the question remains how they may have escaped the wary eyes of the Seneca warriors along the way, unless, of course, they arrived escorted by another party who shielded them and are strong enough to support their mission."

"To my knowledge, Captain, there is no party giving aid to the Hurons. Their day has come and gone and it is of no benefit to another party to rekindle the long-lost campfires of their nation at the expense of losing precious lives in the process." John O'Bail appeared unmoved by the Captain's inquiry.

No sooner did John O'Bail emit his words than the Captain drew a tentative conclusion: "It appears then that a small renegade body, perhaps Huron, struck Ontario with the intent to burn it down and rout its defenders. Does that interpretation agree with your understanding of the matter?"

"It is not by accident that arrows and shot found their way to Ontario. The question to answer is who among the denizens of the forest hated you British enough to attack you under a detailed and secretive plan. I support your thoughts of a renegade party. On the other hand, all of your major enemies are gone with the exception of a single unknown enemy small enough to escape detection. Herein lies your answer."

The Captain reflected a moment, then responded: "Going back in history, it is the Hurons and French who formed alliances in order to take over favorable trade routes. They attacked everyone in their path, in large measure the western Iroquois and their British allies. Is it possible for that condition to exist to this day?"

"A small force striking with cunning is, in my mind, more deadly than a larger force striking en masse. Such an event, when successful, tends to repeat itself. You are considering a major campaign for personal reasons and must ask yourself what you intend to accomplish in the end, and mostly, is it worth the effort and sacrifice? This is all that I know. I hope I have helped you."

In parting, John O'Bail offered the Captain and his entourage hot tea in crockery mugs. Slowly he backed away from them. claiming that he owed a friend on the grounds a visit. The explorers opened a path for him and the renowned leader walked stoically between the men, his manner casual, yet determined. In drinking the tea, one of the explorers found it too hot. He jumped back in pain, whereupon John O'Beal reserved for himself the final words of the session.

"Snigoha:k! Ahgwih:esa:seht!! Gado:goht!"—Beware! Do not drop it! Let me pass! He passed away slowly, leaving the interpreter to translate his final words.

The explorers exchanged empty glances. They expressed disappointment that the rendezvous with the Seneca chieftain produced not a scintilla of knowledge pointing to a suspect. To a man the explorers believed that John O'Bail kept many details in reserve, much more than he disclosed. A vexed Captain called upon the men to deliberate John O'Bail's words— those kernels of half-truths which their host lay at the explorers' feet. For himself the Captain struggled to form a hypothesis, a point of departure along which he may steer a steady course. He brooded. Suddenly he jumped to his feet:

"I propose, gentlemen, that, despite the results of the late war, it is the French who are our persistent enemy. They supplied the Hurons, or their surrogates, not only with weapons, but with the target itself— Ontario. It is the French who set the natives into motion, bidding them to conduct their bloody task in their stead. And so many are killed. So be it! There are multitudes waiting to sacrifice themselves— so dependent on the French has the native become of late. Think on it, gentlemen! The French have the most to gain, and also the most to lose. The poor native meanwhile is a tool, and a disposable tool at that, one willing to lay down his life for a few meager spoils of battle. Yes. I see it now, men. Come with me!!"

Confused, the Captain's adherents wearily followed him to the smithy's shop. There the Captain sought out and engaged the resident farrier— Caldwell hard on his heels. A dimly lit enclosure: wooden walls tarnished with soot, earthen floor baked a dull red under the heat of iron forgings, the shop to the newcomer resembled a burned out shell, maintained nevertheless to attract the curious visitor. From a distance a grayish pall hung over the shop, shrouding everything beneath it within a diaphanous veil. The emaciated and stooped farrier stepped forward. Soot-covered, he extended a grimy hand, his colors blending expertly with those of the atelier, looking every bit as ancient as his surroundings. Strewn about on shelves, walls, and tables lay artifacts, objects inherently germane to a smithy's shop, either abandoned by owners, or taken in trade for labor performed over justifiably lengthy periods. Holding himself out to be a collector of antiquities, the Captain produced the arrow shafts and shot, addressing the farrier in a casual, non-threatening manner:

"I have here four pieces of lead shot. I am looking for the rifle to which they belong," he smiled.

"Ah! Let me see, mate." Turning the pieces, the farrier remarked: "Old ones, they are. Large bore. Made special for the owner. A rifle past its prime." Stroking his chin, the farrier turned and walked to the far wall where, with difficulty, he pulled down a long rifle from a shelf. A weighty instrument, he held it firmly with both hands, placing it on a low table before his guest.

"Let me see that shot," he said, lips smacking. Deftly the farrier fitted one of the samples of shot to the muzzle of the rifle. Choosing a tamping rod, he pushed the shot deep within the barrel where it came to rest beside the breech. Smiling, he smacked his lips in approval:

"A perfect fit mate. This is you brand. Very few made. Any remaining on the frontier are strictly collectors' items, or have aged beyond repair. It is yours for a modest price, but I am known to accept objects in trade." He laughed, looking for approval from his guest.

"The rifle! Where is it made?" the Captain asked, turning a deaf ear to the farrier's speech.

"French-speaking Canada, mate. Look! Name is on the stock. A mite dusty, but a fine piece overall."

"Caldwell! My purse! Pay the man!" the Captain bellowed.

"In that case it comes to four guineas, or four pounds regular, if you do not have the gold, mate."

"Think nothing of it, my good man. Caldwell! Give our friend four guineas. Get some powder for 'er, besides." Exultant, the Captain pumped his host's arm. He praised the farrier for maintaining an interest in antiquities and for helping him to complete his collection of firearms. To Caldwell he turned:

"Now I may say that I am having a good day." Promptly he addressed the farrier once again: "Does your memory serve you well enough to declare by what manner you acquired this *magnificent* specimen?"

"But of course," the farrier recited, counting the coins. "A man came in with a broken spoke for a wagon. He left to make calls on the grounds. He returned in salubrious spirits and surrendered the rifle in payment. I dare say that I came out ahead on that affair. He spoke

English and French, he did. His French is better. A likable gentleman. A year ago, I believe. Maybe more. To my knowledge a man widely-traveled." Stroking his chin, the farrier laughed and continued: "You know. You always remember something about a stranger. When he laughed, his belly moved up and down. Certainly stole the moment. I think of him and his belly when I need to laugh."

The Captain nodded with understanding. "This man. Do you know his point of origin?"

"Oh, mate. These are difficult questions. From the east he came, I believe. I do not recall the name. He is a tradesman of sorts, I gather. He spoke easily with everyone here—the way of all tradesmen," the farrier stated, lips smacking:

"Are you staying for a while?" Without waiting for a response the farrier exclaimed: "My forge is hot enough to turn out forty pellets in a half hour. Worth the wait. Those pellets are hard to come by. Done?"

"No, no! My men are restless to return to the trail. Rest assured that I will care well for this piece," the Captain returned, stroking the barrel of the rifle. "You have been most generous, my good man. Gentlemen. Let us depart."

Behind him a bewildered farrier scratched his head. Mumbling to himself, he resumed a labor in progress.

The Captain made one final inquiry in the village. Passing to the trading tables, he cast about in search of a French-speaking bourse. He spoke with several tradesmen. He learned that there lay the possibility of a French trading post to the east of Kanandesaga, within a day's march. Known to but a few tradesmen, the post lay outside of the generally-traversed trading lanes. According to rumor, it opened but seasonally. Otherwise it served as a storage depot. No one in particular claimed it, and it fell into disrepair. Natives lived there periodically, according to local legend (52). By all accounts the trading post stood on a high bluff overlooking Lake Onondaga. The Captain surrendered a few more prized guineas while pausing to measure his successes that afternoon. A recurrent thought haunted him: 'With such a profusion of myths surrounding the post, it undeniably warranted investigation'. He promptly paid respects to the money-changers and, gathering his comrades, made haste in departing the village. Repairing to the canoes, the men pulled deeply on the oars, the better to reach Fort Oswego before nightfall. The Captain concealed the rifle in oilskin, placing it on the bottom of the canoe in which he rode, under a watchful eye.

—

Setting a rapid pace the explorers returned to home-base ahead of expectations. The Captain, laden with fresh discoveries, sought an immediate audience with Lord Carleton. In his mind's eye he envisioned the vile charge of abandonment of duty being wiped away with full status restored. Crossing the parade grounds in bold strides, he prepared to sing forth his accomplishments, in the end securing a command equipped to deliver him to the threshold of his adversary's sanctuary. He found, however, the usually quiescent parade grounds bustling with movement, a strange development in light of the advanced hour of the day. Remotely he feared that someone external to his entourage had come forward to announce discoveries, thereby robbing him of the opportunity to prevail upon Lord Carleton. Up ahead, a crowd of celebrants occupied the parade grounds between the commandant's offices and the blockhouse or lock-up. There a solid throng, a veritable human corridor gathered, having come together from all points of the garrison, a mass of bodies shouting and cheering and colliding.

Drawn by curiosity, the Captain pushed through the milling throng. Struggling, he wanted to see for himself what sort of attraction drew the crowd's attention so intensely. Before him a young woman swooned and collapsed. Stepping over her inert form, he found himself with an unobstructed view of what lay ahead: A parade of men, some twenty and more, secured by chains and irons, cut a path down the middle of the human corridor. Bedraggled and barefoot, they constituted a troupe of walking wounded, each man in his own way stumbling along, dragging a limb here, a foot there. Sorely unkempt, each man sprouted a month's growth of beard. Wearing tunics irreparably soiled and pierced with holes, the men moaned and grimaced in pain and discomfort. They cast their eyes downward in a futile attempt to preserve a modicum of anonymity in this most public of settings. Nevertheless, in passing through the human gauntlet, the lowly creatures fell prey to a litany of sarcastic barbs and chants which an aroused multitude hurled at them, a body feeding off of its own frenzy, scaling new heights of passion. Each man, a pitiful portrait of physical deterioration, projected a pallor of abject despair. Indistinguishable all, the Captain summarily dismissed them. Leaving them to their fate, he pushed past the heaving spectators and made straight for the commandant's quarters on the far side of the grounds. Behind him the din of the wild populace climbed steadily. He quickened his strides.

A loud roar halted him in mid-stride. He turned to find the throng lunging forward en masse, drawn toward a new development on the grounds. The incessant droning coursed in waves along the human corridor. He found himself hastening back to the crowd into which he once again immersed himself. At once the plodding wretches emerged before him. He saw nothing new here. Beyond, however, the multitude pressed hard on the flank of yet another wretch. This man, whom he viewed in earnest, exhibited features setting him apart from the other unfortunates. A large, beefy man with huge hands trailing mustaches from the chin, the shackled captive plodded along, grinning menacingly through clenched teeth. Defying the onlookers, the man spat liberally into the crowd, while shouting profanities at will. With bare chest expanded and shaggy head swaying, the man pulled indiscriminately against the restraints. Inured to the pain, his sheer bulk and ferocious aspect struck fear into the onlookers, who, acting in concert, shrank back from his approach and sought comfort among each other. The Captain stood firm, leaving the captive to pull up beside him face-to-face. The big man glared at him. Grinning sarcastically, he grumbled in a voice intended only for him to hear:

"Yes. It is I, your ol' friend, **Black Jack**. Remember me?"

The Captain hedged backward.

The once-vaunted pirate addressed him: "Now that we are neighbors, I came to collect my debts. I will begin by gaining my freedom first." Guards pulled him away. He offered no resistance.

Without a word the Captain turned and retreated through the crowd. A lump rose in his throat. A great weight settled upon his stomach. He beat a hasty path to Lord Carleton's quarters. An aide ushered him directly to the commandant's suite where he found Lord Carleton observing the events on the grounds through a grand parlor window. He waited long moments to be recognized, when, at length the commandant spoke:

"Welcome my dear Captain. You return so soon. Come see the spectacle on the grounds. We are about to have some uninvited guests reside with us for a while," Lord Carleton quipped, facetiously. "With this amount of excitement I almost forgot about you and your mission," he smiled. Drawing himself together, Lord Carleton continued:

"Something major has happened in your absence. A certain Captain Smythe and his marines captured a whole host of pirates on the St. Lawrence. Caught them in the act, he did, snatching up young natives to sell into bondage. How crass!! What do you make of it, Captain? Do you believe such boldness? Where there is a guinea to be made you will find a pirate." He pounded one fist against the other. Not awaiting a response, he proceeded:

"Captain, now that you are here, you will take bountiful comfort in what I am about to say. Smythe, fresh from Newfoundland, is charged with rebuilding Ontario, a move which you initiated in your own way, you will recall. Indeed, you merit praise, albeit delayed." Stepping forward, Lord Carleton vigorously pumped the Captain's arm: "There is a commendation in this for you, Captain". Studying the Captain closely, Lord Carleton asked again: "What brings you back so soon? You must tell me about your mission into the interior. Hmmm. Judging from the looks of you, all did not bode well. Tell me. Am I being presumptuous?"

"My apologies, Sir. I have a bit of turbulence in my stomach."

"Here. Have a sniff of brandy. Buck up, lad! Tell me your story. You will be in better spirits after you expound on your exploits." His arm over the Captain's shoulders, he walked him about the room.

The Captain asked for permission to sit, whereupon he slowly disclosed his discoveries in a bland, almost disinterested manner, his voice lacking its usual strength and sincerity. Finishing, he leaned backward on the Chesterfield, breathing deeply. Bending low to catch every word, Lord Carleton suddenly darted upright, elated.

"By your account you have performed admirably well, Captain. I always knew you to be the true woodsman. When last we met, you asked me for a command. You shall have it!! First off, I want you to meet young Smythe and a very courageous lad who labored incessantly at his side. Come with me."

Lord Carleton escorted a visibly shaken Captain into the main parlors where two young seamen sat engaged in conversation. They rose together at the commandant's approach, their uniforms blemished, yet whole. A beaming Lord Carleton began introductions: "Captain, I present to you Captain Smythe of His Majesty's cutter, the Courageous." The young officer stepped forward. Gripping the Captain's hand firmly he bowed, reciting the standard salutation. Retracing his steps, he ushered Matthew York forward, announcing him with a few well-chosen words:

"With quick and incisive thinking Matthew York truly saved the Courageous. The ultimate capture of the villains owes itself to his alertness. Clearly the Courageous is aptly named after him. Captain!! I present to you the marine who made it possible for me to be here today. I give you Matthew York, hero of the Courageous."

A blushing Matthew, unaccustomed to lavish praise, tendered a hand. The Captain took the marine's hand whereupon his stance faltered. Staggering, he buckled at the knees, with the result that the proffered hand turned into a helping hand as Matthew York installed the Captain upon a comfortable divan. Once seated he lay back, breathing heavily out of apparent exhaustion. Lord Carleton attempted to explain the Captain's condition to the guests:

"The Captain has come through a demanding journey in performing a significant operation for me. Reconnaissance, no less. A field in which he has few peers. He requires rest. Let us go below, gentlemen where I will be able to tell you of the Captain's recent adventures. Follow me, please," he smiled confidently.

Lord Carleton escorted Captain Smythe and Matthew York to the grounds proper, the site of the pirates' public humiliation. Now cast into the garrison's brig, the villains posed no immediate threat and the pregnant mob began to dissipate rather quickly. Coming to rest beside the lock-up, the commandant praised the Captain's labors in the interior for his guests' benefit. He created an engaging account of the man's exploits: First, he introduced the Captain's findings of the enemy's presence in the ruins of Fort Ontario. Next came the Captain's interviews with the Cornplanter at Kanandesaga. Third, he described the finding of a rifle, the likeness of which accepted spent shot found at the ruined Fort Ontario. Fourth, came the Captain's learning of the possible location of the enemy's sanctuary. So colorfully did Lord Carleton paint the Captain's labors that Matthew at once volunteered for an assignment under him. With permission from Smythe, Matthew temporarily resigned his duties at Oswego and ordered new clothing in preparation for a new role on the frontier. Darkness fell and after a brief supper the two seamen repaired to Lord Carleton's library to assist him in assembling a roster of soldiers to place under Worthy's new command. The Captain himself, meanwhile, purportedly disengaged from all that occurred around him, lay in full repose, a scarce ten footsteps distant.

"I am eager to tell the Captain that I am the *first* volunteer," Matthew York offered.

"You are the first after his aide, Caldwell, lad," Lord Carleton replied, shuffling papers.

"It is improper to wake him then, is it not?" Matthew asked.

"It will wait until the morrow. James Worthy has endured the limit of his surprises today," Lord Carlton smiled.

* * *

Ga:yant: hawah:geh, or the Cornplanter, knew well of the Captain's intentions during their meeting. Subsequently, he offered him precious little new knowledge in a gesture designed to delay the Captain's advance upon his friends at Pointe Aux Bois. Now he must make another turn: He must send an envoy to Pointe Aux Bois to advise Le Rocher to prepare for an attack. To convey the message, he chose a staunch ally, Oh:nehsi:yo—the Sandpiper. In order to deflect suspicion among British Loyalists along the way, the Sandpiper clothed himself and a companion in the trappings of a neutral hunting party. In addition, he waited a full day before departing: long enough for scouts to report to him signs of danger. Only then did he strike a course at dawn over the Genesee Trail to the east, beginning at Plaines de Boue, that section of the Trail less frequented by travelers than the more popular Seneca River to the immediate north. He expected to reach his destination before the sun fully rose. Bearing close to the early morning shadows, Oh:nehsi:yo moved at a quick pace, assured of passing along unnoticed. He skirted the northern fringe of the Round Tops, the first significant settlement beyond Plaines de Boue. It lay in darkness, its location known only to a few of his confederates.

Bearing due east, he encountered rolling drumlins, each prominence progressively more challenging. Descending the greatest and last of these, Oh:nehsi:yo plunged down the grass-lined face to find himself within visual distance of Lake Gannentaa. A short sprint around the head of the lake brought the party upon the sandy beach of the eastern shore. From that point he tracked north along the beach. Stepping lively, he looked for the familiar wooden stairway which ascended the sandy heights to the portals of the obscure French trading post. Above him on the sandy bluff, the crude yet welcoming post lay expertly hidden behind tall evergreens. Profuse trees and foliage occluded the entrance-way, effectively impeding inspection of the post from without. The tallest of the evergreens shielded the post's palisades from scrutiny. To all but a few of the closest allies, the structure existed not at all, or merely in the minds of students of history. Oh:nehsi:yo let out a cry, directing his companion to follow. He bounded vigorously up the stairway. Pushing aside copious boughs, he came to a standstill before the stern oak doors. Unexpectedly the doors swung open and a buoyant and bubbly gentleman emerged to greet him, hand extended. Oh:nehsi:yo eagerly took Marchand's hand, and pushed inside the enclave, his companion hard at his heels.

Declining food and drink, Oh:nehsi:yo insisted on meeting with Guillaume Le Rocher immediately. Marchand wasted no words and obligingly brought his guest before the post commander who greeted him warmly despite the urgency of the occasion. In a flurry the chieftain delivered the Ga:yant:hawah:geh warning of an impending attack. The General allowed him to finish before stepping back to compose a suitable reply:

"At last my presence has been disclosed. I applaud my adversary for having made my presence known to himself. Rest assured that I have taken steps to treat with him severely. Let me begin by stating that my adversary believes this place little more than a trading post and refuge for the poor, a tawdry and neglected camp bereft of soldiers and fortifications. From this moment, gentlemen, Pointe Aux Bois will defy my adversary's expectations to no end. To begin, I am assigning my regulars to the wooded thicket on the heights to our back. There they will remain fully-armed in trenches until called upon. Here on the grounds proper I leave soldiers in the guise of settlers and homemakers. In the many row houses you see before you are ample cellars carved out of the hard earth. Within, armed regulars will take up temporary residence, ready to spring forth at a moment's notice. Women and children will take shelter in the cellars. On the whole, I request the residents and natives alike to conduct themselves in the manner of daily living when on the grounds. They will be armed, however. I charge that our adversary will come to us in the guise of a traveler—perhaps someone who has lost his way. He will feign stumbling upon the works by chance, but we know this not to be the case. In any event we will take him on a turn of the grounds, for we are above all, gracious hosts." He laughed, pleased with his sense of humor.

"Please note this: Remember that he is a man of stealth and opportunity. These are his strengths and he will look for occasions to implement them. I will ask that he come in peace and to demonstrate sincerity by laying aside weapons. He will follow my suggestion, for he will see that we too are noticeably unarmed. The bulk of his forces, however, will be actively searching for a point of entrance."

"Does he not have the great booming engines, Monsieur?" Oh:nehsi:yo asked.

"Yes! He has the booming engines, but mark my words. They will sink into our sandy beach. He will find that he must fire them from bateaux; however, they are too heavy for bateaux. A single discharge will send the bateaux to the bottom of Lake Gannentaa. At any rate, I doubt that he brings bateaux. What is more, to fire at us from the heights is unlikely, given the sheer thickness of the undergrowth. Of course, our men in trenches there will gladly entertain our adversary with weapons common to the native. Combat will be hand-to-hand. We excel in it. We will have it no other way. We will beat our adversary at his own game, a game in which the chicken wins against the fox."

"What of our adversary when captured?" Marchand asked.

"A most suitable question, Henri. There are a variety of responses, but I believe that we must keep him hostage pending further British sallies bent on destroying us."

"That is a tall order. They may relinquish him to our care indefinitely."

"That is why we must capture his forces and hold them as well, Henri."

"We lack the capacity, Guillaume, and the endurance to withstand a siege."

"I have thought of that, Henri. In that event, with his men locked in our cellars, we will simply threaten to disclose Lord Carleton's shortcomings to the English-speaking world at the court of King George. Albany is but a courier's ride to the east."

"I see that as a remote possibility—if our principal captive still lives."

"I will see to that. We **all** will see to it. We hold all the high cards, Henri. Let us play them wisely."

Oh:nehsi:yo spoke: "Our enemy has stolen our women and children. He has robbed us of our furs by which we gain valued utensils and clothing. He has set fire to my village. He must pay dearly for his crimes. We of the People dispose of such villains quickly. You of the peaus blancs are afraid to make a decision unless it carries a benefit for you."

The General spoke: "I confess there are differences between our two camps, my good friend. Ultimately, gentlemen, the Captain must be exposed to his own people for the predator that he has become. You and I know that down through the ages people everywhere have made adjustments for the occasional thief. On the other hand they come to rail against the villain who extracts a great deal of pleasure from the misery he visits upon others. I say that we try him before the bar of justice of France. His sentence: banishment into exile."

Pessimistic, the tradesman Marchand spoke: "It is first necessary to capture him, Guillaume. He is bound to arrive well-reinforced and we know not the devices he plans to launch against us. Our plan appears well-devised, but we have only amateurs against seasoned soldiers." He sat back in dismay.

"I believe you, Henri; however, no one is without fault or flaw. On the other hand, I believe that his greed, fed by curiosity, will drive him into our waiting arms. Remember, gentlemen! We have already defeated our adversary on two occasions in which our wits and guile won the day. Success breeds success. Of course he knows not that men from Pointe Aux Bois labored to defeat him." The General raised his arm in a sign of victory.

Oh:nehsi:yo asked to speak: "All inroads against the enemy have been carried out in large part by the People. The enemy believes that it is the People who attacked him and he is likely to punish the People unless defeated. Your plan, Monsieur, must succeed for the sake of my People's posterity. All along you French have remained in the background espousing a strategy formed to draw suspicion away from yourselves and Pointe Aux Bois. This allows you the liberty to prepare a strong defense. Let us hope that you have followed a wise course. The fate of my People and of yours lies in your hands, Monsieur." In deep thought he bowed his head.

"You have discussed your views with Ga:yant:hawah:geh?," the General asked.

"Yes. He wants you to move under your own strength. He believes that your enemy will seek revenge against the People if they are seen fighting with you and you fail in your attempt to defend yourself."

"This is understandable, Oh:nehsi:yo. You have been a loyal campaigner. I shall miss your spirit and your longbow men." The General managed a thin smile and grasped his friend's hand in a demonstration of friendship.

"I have not abandoned you entirely, Monsieur. I have arranged for several select longbow men to join you. They arrive tomorrow," Oh:nehsi:yo returned, expressionless, his eyes meeting those of the General.

"You are indeed a true friend," Le Rocher beamed. "Come dine with us before you return home. I have some old acquaintances of yours to meet." Jumping to his feet, he announced the end of the meeting. He inquired into the whereabouts of the York family and, after expressing gratitude to his guests for attending, he set about locating them in turn. He came first upon James York, engaged in fortifying palisades with mud and clay.

"James. Oh:nehsi:yo has come to visit us. We dine soon. You must wash the day's toil from your hands," he chided.

James offered a hand caked with mud. Thinking quickly, however, he withdrew it and quipped: "A fine meal to end a day of hard labor. One of life's small pleasures. Of course I will dine with you."

James led Marchand and company to the kitchen where he found Caroline bent over a large and steaming tureen. She acknowledged everyone with a smile and curt bow before launching into a vivid description of the evening's fare:

"This, gentlemen is chowder. What you see is grown here in the gardens. Of course the shoreline of Lake Onondaga made a large contribution." She stirred the contents of her tureen with a wooden ladle.

"I have chosen potatoes, clams, turtle meat, red pimiento and greens. I mix them with milk and butter, a little flour, stirring gently. Then, I heat everything on my oven. When hot, I pour the contents into the tureen and stir until it thickens. Serve warm to hot," she smiled, hands on hips, her long white apron spotless. I hope you all are hungry.

I have enough soup for an army," she laughed, returning to her labors. "Suzanne is in the school. She will be pleased to see Oh:nehsi:yo," she called over her shoulder to the party. "Let us be off!"

Once at school, a room set apart from the church, the party found Suzanne conducting a lesson in front of a class of native children. Suspending her lesson, she ran forward to embrace the visitors, after which she invited them to review the fruits of her labors. At Suzanne's request, one of the students rose and read from a sampler, reciting one of the numerous tales taken from English lore. It espoused a moralistic lesson in the guise of a poem. The young man received a hearty round of applause, prompting another student to demonstrate skills in writing English in script. On the small chalk board behind him the student wrote a brief message of welcome to the party, beginning with: "To my teacher's guests."

One by one the students came forward to read examples of newly-acquired skills in writing cursive English. Paragraphs all and written extemporaneously, the passages reflected studious accomplishments. Oh:nehsi:yo, and all present, applauded each contributor. On a cue from Suzanne, the children rose. Tablets in hand, they read together from a prepared text, inserting the name of the Cayuga chieftain in English:

"Welcome to our school, Monsieur Sandpiper. We hope that you enjoy your visit. We are learning many new and wonderful lessons here. They will help us to better understand the world in which we live."

To Suzanne's surprise her students supplemented the presentation with an appendix: "Our teacher, Mademoiselle York is wonderful. We hope that she is our teacher for many years. She is our friend forever."

They sat down chanting Suzanne's name. Again the applause, followed by a blushing Suzanne bowing in all humility. Resuming composure, she turned to face her students, peering at them through tear-filled eyes.

"We have one more function, students, for our guests. Who knows of it?" she asked, daubing at her eyes.

A lone girl stood. She led the class in a verse. Beginning with the second line, her classmates joined in:

"Reading teaches us about others, people from near and afar. It brings everyone together to share knowledge and understanding. It makes us stronger and wiser in order to make the world a better place for all."

The guests filled the room with applause. Thanking her students, Suzanne dismissed them and convened with the guests, accepting praises with more self-assurance. Then, off to the dining commons everyone passed in order to partake of Caroline York's special foods from her own private stock of recipes. James York recited a brief prayer and the dining began in earnest. A chair beside Suzanne remained unoccupied. The General offered that Suzanne's friend, Aboyant, departed earlier in the day to gather berries. It is at that precise moment that Aboyant appeared, Suzanne reporting his entrance with a shout. She playfully badgered him for tardiness, while committing his catch to a large bowl which she placed in the center of the table. "Dessert has arrived," she jested, glancing at the ripe berries.

During the dinner the General asked the guests for a critique of his plan of defense. James York offered that the plan's success depended on the readiness of the garrison's soldiers. He concluded that fighting on one's own grounds offered an early advantage over a superior striking force.

Marchand spoke: "In capturing our primary antagonist, we must bring him to trial before his confederates rise up to free him. This calls for amassing evidence against him from among his own colleagues—a difficult task, in my estimation."

Caroline York asked to speak. The General granted her permission, given her untitled position of hostess of the dinner. "The greater issue here is the protection of those unable to defend themselves when attacked and molested by a stronger body. You all know of my abduction, but now I am told that women and young children from among the native-dwellers are mere prey and chattels to the great and powerful interests in contention for this land surrounding us. I am afraid that with the fall of Pointe Aux Bois, any hope for women and children will pass by the wayside."

Suzanne raised her hand and the General acknowledged her: "My mother is concerned with the creation of a new hierarchy which is driven by understanding, not fear. She believes that the English want to rape the land and all that goes with it. With this scheme, a privileged few will be able to dictate to the many. She hopes that, under a new order, the common folk will rise to the heights now enjoyed only by the privileged. To my mother I say, Amen. To that new day I say, Amen. To our friends among the People of the Lakes I say, Amen". She looked about the table. The principals sat with heads bowed. Now, beginning with the General, everyone uttered "Amen."

* * *

Traveling by day and night, the Bear Chief and Cerf Courant covered ground quickly. Now two days out of Pointe Aux Bois, they crossed into Pennsylvania territory. The land rose in height steadily, forming the foothills of the Appalachian chain. Avoiding the valley below them, they maintained the high ground. Shifting from ridge to ridge, the two woodsmen enjoyed the luxury of a breathtaking vista which the heights afforded them. In the valley the Susquehanna came into view periodically: at this point a thin stream, far removed from its rendezvous with the Chesapeake Bay many leagues to the south. They chose to lead their horses over the challenging terrain: rock-strewn hills, well-forested and denuded of vegetation, lest the animals grow fatigued and perish along the way.*

The Bear Chief sought an old hunting trail, one of several which his People followed into the Delaware country. He remembered his father and his cousin, Tah:gah:jute, taking him to the lush hunting lands of the Wyoming Valley during his youth. Both men once lived among the Delaware and their neighbors, the Friends. During his youth his cousin received the name of one of the Friends in baptism, the late province secretary, James Logan. As an adult many men called his cousin "Chief Logan". Often Logan and his father joined their brothers, the Delaware, or Tsa:ganha, in hunting parties in the autumn of the year, taking enough meat to last them through the harsh and cold winters germane to the Lake Country when snows and strong winds blew relentlessly across Lake Ontario from lower Canada.

After much searching, the Cayuga sachem found a suitable trail-passage. It lay near the settlement of Tioga. Overcome by intrusive undergrowth, the trail nevertheless proved navigable and he and his companion struck out upon it in bold strides, heavy muskets lashed to their shoulders, senses ever-alert. Before the day drew to a close, the little party anticipated reaching the village of the Bear Chief's ancestral ally, Delaware chieftain, Teedyuscung. Stopping briefly, he consulted his trail watch. It read 10:15h. Satisfied, he withdrew the trail calendar from his cachet pouch and circled the date with the bit of graphite which the General gave him: Saturday, October 28th, 1760. Next, he withdrew the letter of introduction which the General penned for him at his departure. Reviewing the terms, he took pleasure in this bit of respect which the French commandant extended to him. Beside Cerf Courant, the Bear Chief read the message aloud:

Par moyens de ce communiqué-ci je présente mon ami et allier, Le Chef a L'oeurs—Hnyagwai-Hahsenowa:neh du royaume Iroquois.

Veuillez de lui laisser passer par votre territoire sans travaux.

Il a besoin de trouver la vérité à une affaire mysterieuse.

À tel point, peut-être est-il possible de lui tendre la main.

Guillaume Le Rocher, General de L'Expédition Française à L'Amérique du Nord**

Teedyuscung lived near Shamokin in a village in the shadow of the British Fort Augusta in Pennsylvania, one of several strongholds established by his nominal British ally to forestall French advances westward into the Ohio country. Teedyuscung came into the public consciousness in his efforts to force a wedge between the Five Nations of the Iroquois, and their principal benefactor, the British representative of the Crown, James Logan: a Quaker. Overall, the Delaware felt threatened by the western Iroquois in particular, who laid claim to most of Pennsylvania, and who, sanctioned by the British, took steps to drive the Delaware from their ancestral lands. Logan, a British ally, tacitly sanctioned the Iroquois presence in Pennsylvania, given their ability to preserve their own neutrality in the midst of the competing French and British interests there. During the French and Indian War the Iroquois avoided permanent alliances with either great power while garnering favors and amenities from both. The Iroquois also provided what amounted to a colonial militia, keeping the peace among errant Delaware segments, making it unnecessary for the province to put together an official militia. Logan did not want to alienate either the Iroquois or British whom he believed the true power wielders of the region. He also felt indebted to Teedyuscung. In the end Logan deferred to the Iroquois' demands to keep Pennsylvania a protectorate of the Five Nations. This stance eventually brought him at odds with the chieftain who by now found himself betrayed by those whom he once counted as allies. He began to eye the French whom he originally abandoned (53).

By degrees the Iroquois slowly dispossessed the Delaware, becoming rich landowners. They regularly sold their shares to Philadelphia merchants, who, in turn opened up the lands to white settlement.

The Iroquois persuaded some of the Delaware to follow suit and, like the Iroquois, these natives prospered financially. White settlement became so rapid however, that the remaining Delaware sought aid in repossessing their lands, at least to cut short the massive migrations. The French, always seeking ways to counter British inroads into what they considered their exclusive trading territory, approached Teedyuscung and the Delaware. They offered them food, following a particularly poor harvest season, and arms, in exchange for their promise to conduct raids upon English-speaking white settlements. This, Teedyuscung agreed to do. Following General Braddock's defeat at the hands of a combined French and Indian force at Fort Duquesne, the Chief, acting out of expediency, aligned his followers with the French cause. At the same time, Pennsylvania's British-leaning legislators refused to supply him with arms and trade goods, all the more inciting his followers to make war.

Consisting largely of pacifist Quakers, the Pennyslvania legislature refused to vote for a measure of installing a militia and furnishing the Delaware with muskets and shot. However, pockets of anti-pacifist legislators caused such a stir in the assembly that it dissolved, choosing new leaders who, in effect, elected to help Teedyuscung, provided that he cease his raids and sue for peace. The Chief went a step further and solicited the new governor, Denny, for just compensation in lands lost. Governor Denny, meanwhile, privately entertained no thoughts of rewarding the Delaware, but, with the approval of the Quakers, openly presented the Chief with gifts and promised him a slice of the Wyoming Valley for a homeland. Teedyuscung promptly concluded a peace agreement and offered to turn a deaf ear to further entreaties from the French. He also insisted that the governor recognize him as the sole spokesman for his People, not the Onondaga Council of the Five Nations. (54)

Bent on preserving their autonomy, many Delaware moved west to Ohio, a region largely devoid of the aggressive Iroquois and white settlements. Back in the Wyoming valley, meanwhile, their brothers settled close to the Susquehanna, where they shared the land with whites, even embracing Christianity. The French arrived on the scene again, seeking trading privileges in Ohio, in what they termed a region worthy of development. They solicited the Iroquois to help bolster their meager military forces and to launch raids across the frontier upon encroaching British traders and accompanying military columns. Many Delaware, newly-removed to the west, joined them. Above all, the French feared a saturation of the Ohio country with cheap and plentiful British goods, a development assured of driving the native populations away from French forts strewn along the upper Great Lakes. History proved that where the goods went, the native populations followed, and with them the manpower the French sorely needed. Already, British traders followed the Delaware into Ohio. The Iroquois followed them also, but for the purpose of subordinating the Delawares' newly-acquired taste for independence. Initially the Iroquois sought to placate the Delaware by sending a Seneca representative among them with a variety of British trade goods (55).

The British hoped to stake a claim to the Ohio territory by building a string of forts to rival Fort Duquesne, all the way from mid-Pennsylvania. One man in particular, General Forbes, took charge of cutting a road through the dense forest. While construction began in earnest, General Forbes sought the approval of other decision-makers so that his labor may progress unimpeded. He soon heard from Pisquetomen, chief of the western Delaware, Governor Denny of Pennsylvania, and Pemberton, spokesman of the Quakers in the legislature. He lacked only Teedyuscung's participation. He contacted the Quaker agent, Frederick Post, who called a conference to be held at Easton in the land of the Chief's domain. Teedyuscung came to the conference, holding out hope of regaining lands lost to exploitation. He also wanted a reservation in perpetuity set aside for his Delaware. The Five Nations came in order to reassert control over him and to renew claims to the Ohio valley. Pemberton wanted to guarantee the Teedyuscung claims. Governor Denny came to preserve the lands and interests of the patriarchal Penn family: finally to conclude a peace agreement with the Delaware.

During much deliberation, Governor Denny secured the peace he wanted in four days at the conference after making extensive concessions: (He sanctioned the Delaware to seek negotiations with him directly, not through the Iroquois. White settlers may not cross the Alleghenies to open new lands. Pennsylvania or British traders may open a trading post for the benefit of the Delaware and other natives in the vicinity of Fort Duquesne). In exchange Denny received a host of British captives held from previous raids and skirmishes. Teedyuscung, however, received *no* lands, either former holdings or a reservation, nor did Pemberton, Post or other conference officials intercede on his behalf. Instead, officials referred the Teedyuscung claims to Sir William Johnson, the Crown representative of the five nations Iroquois, Johnson, long an advocate for the Iroquois, turned sovereignty of the Ohio region over to their governing council and Teedyuscung returned home deeply saddened. For the time being, however, the Delaware received a promise of political autonomy, along with supplies of trade goods and an assurance that they may live free of white encroachment.

For the French this so-called Easton conference signaled a death knell. Drawn by a cheap supply of British goods, the Delaware and other natives dissociated themselves from the French, who, now beset with a loss of manpower, recognized their own vulnerability. Retreating behind the walls of Fort Duquesne, they formed a desperate plan, and on one cool November day, set fire to the fortress and stomped off in advance of a strong British column (56).

Into this political morass stepped the Bear Chief, and firm ally, Cerf Courant. Both men knew nothing of the Teedyuscung ordeal until he recited his story to them from his own lips. In light of Teedyuscung's political misfortunes, the Bear Chief grew reluctant to solicit his aid. The Chief greeted him warmly however, after which the Bear Chief told him the story of Caroline York's abduction and the murder of her uncle, Charles Martin. Teedyuscung listened attentively, prompting the Bear Chief to go a step further: He then described Caroline York's physical appearance in detail, attempting to form a lasting impression. He paused when Teedyuscung signaled to speak:

"All along the Wyoming valley the British have established settlements. They have purchased lands from the Delaware and anyone who refuses to treat with them becomes their enemy. Concerning the York family, I have heard a story: They gained their lands following the death of Charles Martin. They shared them with the Delaware in the same manner that Charles Martin shared them. The British soldiers raided the frontier on several occasions, forcing the Delaware to move west with great droves of my People. Monsieur Martin stood his ground. Later, when Monsieur Martin refused offers of sale from the British, they killed him. They ran off with Madame York to frighten Monsieur York away from the lands that he so dearly cherished. In my view, Monsieur York made a clever move. He left the lands with Quaker neighbors in order to be able to look for his wife. The Delaware farm them. The Quakers still hold the land, but the British are reluctant to kill these peace-loving men and women. Instead, they have allowed the Quakers to grow their harvests unmolested, provided they distribute any surpluses in trade among the white settlers. To avoid bloodshed, this the Quakers have agreed to do. This is the situation at the moment I am told."

Teedyuscung maintained that he knew not who delivered the blow which killed Charles Martin. He held out hope that someone among the resident Friends or Quakers and remaining Delaware may be able to answer that question. He admitted that he often traded with members of the Friends' Society who lived in the vicinity of the York holdings. On every occasion they treated him in a friendly manner. With the Bear Chief's approval, he offered to make inquiry among the Friends, whom he described as being on good terms with their Supreme Being, a Being who stood firmly against murder and who mandated that they, the Friends, strive to bring those guilty of a heinous crime to a reckoning before the community. Teedyuscung believed that the friendship which the Friends demonstrated to him extended equally to all of his allies. This finding ultimately succeeded in convincing the Cayuga sachem of the Quakers' candor and sincerity.

The Bear Chief praised the York family before his host: James's labors in building a new village at the Round Tops, Suzanne's interest in teaching native youth, and Caroline's vow to expose not only her abductor, but all those who sought to imprison native youth in a yoke of slavery. He spoke of his cousin, Tah:gah:jute, who recently moved to the Ohio frontier to help keep the peace between new settlers and a large band of Delaware. He ended the speech by soliciting the Chief's assistance in ridding the frontier of those who would steal its youth and sell them into bondage. He read from the General's official notice to demonstrate his support among the French.

Teedyuscung listened attentively before speaking: "Making war on the whites did not bring me back my land. When I trusted their leaders, they betrayed me. I have since abandoned the warpath and now enjoy a moment of peace. Perhaps in honoring your request I will know greater peace forever. I understand that you have a number of supporters on your side. Perhaps they will remember me and my efforts to secure friendly relations with the whites. I am growing older with each day and

I seek peace before I pass altogether from this land. Peace is something that I may leave to my grandchildren with my passing. We may never find your murderer, but in honor of your cousin Tah:gah:jute, I will search with you so that you and your friends may know peace. We leave tomorrow."

—

The three men departed by canoe at dawn of the following day. The Susquehanna, now broad and fast-flowing, cut a determined path through virgin woodlands, interspersed with open, cultivated fields. The fields belonged to Quaker settlers, the Bear Chief learned, distinguishable by a single manor house and barn set at the rear of each parcel of land, hemmed in by knee-high stone fencing. Pitched roofs allowed rain and snow to dissipate with ease and operable wooden shutters encased thick glass windows, providing an additional layer of protection against the winter's cold and the autumn's strong winds. Scenes of order and cleanliness among the Quaker homes pervaded the senses as the swift canoe sped south along the river. Seated in the bow, Teedyuscung waved to sightseers along the river bank, men and women whom he recognized in this land of the Friends. Setting a fast pace, the little party kept doggedly to the task at hand. Fighting back fatigue, the Bear Chief and Cerf Courant looked to their host to deliver a sign of putting ashore. Finally it came and both men eagerly beached their craft and fell in step behind Teedyuscung.

Following a short burst over textured fields, Teedyuscung led the little party to the door of one John Rhoades, a Quaker. He introduced the Bear Chief as the cousin of Tah:gah:jute, or Logan, named for the Friend, James Logan. In presenting his credential from the General, the Bear Chief explained his relationship to the York family, including the abduction of Caroline York and the untimely death of her uncle, Charles Martin. He made it known that an evildoer lurked in the shadows, stalking at will, looting and smuggling for self-absorbed gain, a man in the service of His Majesty who betrayed his trust and built a career upon deceit and intimidation. John Rhoades summoned his entire family into the grand parlor. When he spoke, everyone pressed forward and the room grew tense with anticipation:

"The British tell me that they plan to trade with the Friends. They say that they will give us protection from roving bands of native warriors in exchange for our goods. I find something in error with that message. For one, we have nothing to fear from the Delaware and Shawnee who live beside us. It is they who help us to farm these lands. We have helped them survive through lean periods and it is they who have protected us against the Iroquois. Second, those Delaware who have not fled west still remain among us, for we have welcomed them with open arms. They are the original inhabitants of these lands and know best how to care for them. In our commerce with them we have loaned the Delaware the horse and the plow and invited them to farm our fields. They go about their labors happily. Charles Martin knew this when he entrusted us with his home and fields. Third, the British say that the French are unworthy stewards of these lands and must be driven off. Your document from the General, Le Rocher tells me that the French are our allies. We Friends do not trust the British. We consent to help you in our own small way." Jonathan Rhoades, eldest son of John Rhoades, prevailed upon his father to tell a strange, yet true story. "Oh, yes. Thank you my son," the elder replied, drawing on a corncob pipe. He breathed deeply, then began:

"I labored with Charles Martin in these fields. One day he told me that two British officers came to warn him of attacks along the frontier. They wanted him to move away to ensure his safety and offered him a sum which he refused. He described the men to me and before we went our separate ways, he asked that I ascend to his holdings in the event of his death or disappearance. I signed an agreement giving me ownership under those circumstances and no sooner registered the document with the clerk of deeds in Lancaster than I learned of his death. Early this year two officers came to me with a purchase-offer. They claimed that I lacked the strength to repel invaders. I told them that I feared no one, for I am a member of the Society of Friends. They went away without another word. Mysteriously, thereafter, brush fires started up at random throughout my properties. I grew sick all over. We have no local militia here, you know." He took a long drag on the pipe, and, trembling, concluded: "I must tell you that the two men who visited Charles and myself are cut from the same bolt of cloth. You must find them to solve the matter of Charles' death."

******

Construction of dwellings at the Round Tops accelerated. Watkins supervised much of the labor, sharing his knowledge with a hand-picked team of native men. To that extent all homes boasted pitched roofs, cellars fortified with stone-cut walls, and rooms to accommodate a family of six inhabitants. He equipped each kitchen with a spacious hearth for food preparation. Fireplaces adorned the parlor and dining room. In bedrooms small iron stoves burned hard wooden pellets, which emitted a sustained, deep-red glow. Artesian wells, activated by hand pumping, supplied water for washing utensils in the kitchen sink and also for washing oneself in the bathroom.

To bathe, one essentially took a shower by means of a wooden bucket perforated on the bottom. Suspended over one's head and attached to the bathroom wall, the bucket percolated water upon the bather below who initially filled it with water heated downstairs in a teapot at the hearth. Carrying the pot upstairs, the bather stepped into the wooden tub, stood very erect and loaded the bucket top side, then slid back a panel covering the bottom in order to release the water. One soaped oneself and rinsed at the same time, taking care to complete the task before the bucket drained. Agility and athleticism thus became determining factors in performing the ritual of bathing with the bather(s) devising variations on a theme.

The dwellings tended to cluster about the base of the many mounds from which the Round Tops drew its name. In the pattern of a concentric circle, the mounds provided additional protection to the inhabitants, shielding them from exposure to the high winds which frequented the region during summer and early fall. A wooden palisade elliptical in shape surrounded the dwellings. Along its rim a plank walkway, capable of supporting many vigilant warriors, imparted stability to the structure. Beyond the palisade laborers dug a moat the width of a horse-drawn carriage, lining its banks with smooth sandstone. Rainwater filled it to a three-foot depth.

The gentle western and southern slopes loaned themselves to the cultivation of staples: corn, stringed beans, sweet potatoes and gourds such as pumpkins. Colombe Blanche originated the project and now expanded it. The eastern slope, already a labyrinth of berry bushes, grapevines and fruit trees, continued to produce abundant yields, due in no small measure to Colombe Blanche's attentiveness. The northern slope, precipitous, a maze of tightly-knit coppices intermingled with lofty oaks and maples, stood pristine: a buffer against strong northern wind-whipped snows. With Fawn and the boys at her side, Colombe Blanche gardened, weeded, pruned, and released new seeds into the soil from her caches hidden underground in baskets, even within the mounds themselves. Watkins joined her at intervals and they discussed their respective occupations. He frolicked with the boys, who welcomed him as a surrogate, but she assumed all along that his true purpose lay in keeping close to Fawn.

Watkins met with Fawn between three and four days a week for an hour. He began to teach her conversational English, his native tongue, in response to her inquiries. Leaning upon his every word and intonation, she became an able student and before long Watkins discovered that her accrued passion for the language transferred unequivocally to him. She sent him subtle signs of tenderness: complimenting his handwriting, grasping his shoulder while he composed sentences for her with paper and stylus, meeting his eyes with her own for sustained periods. She dwelt upon his lips, teeth, gestures—the properties associated with effective speech. Her persistence made him uncomfortable, torn between conducting the day's lesson and returning his student's ardent gaze. A warmth kindled within him. His cheeks burned red and he feared that now she knew of his desire for her. He tried to deny emerging impulses. Drawing apart from her, he instructed her to read from the prepared text on the table before her. This measure served its purpose of diverting her attention from him, allowing him precious moments in which to compose himself, temporarily attenuating the message of deep sensuality which her eyes transmitted to him.

The lessons took them to the outer reaches of the village. They walked along the slopes: he pointing out objects and she naming them. He taught her to speak in short descriptive sentences. His tools: patience and praise. She responded well to his method of teaching by example. Follow-up lessons required her to recall the terms and phrases from earlier in the week. He asked her to keep a journal of the lessons after which he tested her over consecutively longer periods for memory and accuracy. Meanwhile, their walks continued. One such excursion took them to the abandoned grounds of her Osco, the village, by the lake of the same name. Briefly they toured the site where so many men fell during the siege of Osco and she placed a freshly-picked bouquet of honeysuckles in a woven basket and laid them in the center of the former great hearth. Bowing deeply, she crossed herself in the manner of all Christians and looked toward the heavens before rejoining her companion for a walk along the beach. Thoroughly pleased with her comportment, he stood taken aback by her sincerity; however, he refrained from complimenting her openly.

Along the water's edge wild flowers sprouted in many shapes and forms. She picked a large bundle, telling him that she intended them for Colombe Blanche. He winced, feigning disappointment, and, laughing, she threaded the stem of one of them through the loop of his collar. In tandem they scoured the beach looking for mussels. He looked behind him to find her tracing his footprints through the soft sand. Their movements, however subdued, startled a pair of wood grouse which took flight with their approach. He announced regret at not having a firearm with which to bring them down. She, on the other hand, rejoiced in the birds' escape, confiding to him that the grouse traveled in pairs— that they mated for life, and that with their death a nest of hatchlings died with them for want of parental care. She reminded him that for his lack of a weapon a small and vulnerable family gained another day on earth, a day to be together to tend to familial demands.

"We are not much different from the wild creatures," she stated, looking at him innocently. He hung his head, upset with his obliqueness in understanding a matter dear to her. Dictating the mood of the moment, she vaulted a fresh brooklet, beckoning him to follow. He slipped, stumbling in the soft sand and she reached out to him, offering her hand, pulling him to her side. She dropped her wild flowers in the confusion. He retrieved them, blowing away particles of sand. Bowing from the waist, he presented them to her for inspection. Laughing, she gathered them in her arms. He laughed, drawn by her spontaneity, and, taking her hand, guided her along the shoreline. They walked in silence, heads bent, tracing their tracks in the sand. After a few moments she halted and turned to him, her head coming to rest on his chest beneath his chin. His heart pounded and she made mention of it, placing her hand delicately over it, looking up into his eyes to exclaim:

"You are staying at the Round Tops, are you not?"

He chose a neutral stance, hoping to draw out her intentions:

"My labors are not yet complete. There remains much to be done," he stated soberly.

"This is good. I do not want you to leave."

He squeezed her hand and she continued: "If you stay, I will keep your house for you—the house that you made. Is that all right, Monsieur?" She took care to pronounce each word distinctly.

He watched her full lips rise and fall: "Before I met you I planned to go through life alone. Now I am ready to change my mind." He squeezed her gently about the waist.

She struggled to interpret the nuances of his speech, eventually emitting tears of joy, and, reaching up, she nibbled at his ear, setting into motion an unbridled sequence of events in which their pent-up passions, long quiescent, emerged triumphant. He kissed her and she returned his affection. He touched her and she reciprocated. They exchanged oaths of loyalty and fidelity, words which he helped her to form, after which, hand in hand, they began the trek home.

On reaching the village they spoke nothing of their tryst to anyone. They walked to where Little Bear and Raven occupied themselves with wild turkeys: listening to the boys' tale of having secured the birds. Originally the boys found two turkey chicks on the southern slope, and, fearing for their well-being, took them back to the village proper. There they placed them in a pen with seeds to eat, yet the forlorn chicks ate only sparingly. Raven suggested searching for the chicks' parents and they returned to the slope where they observed a hen and a cock frantically beating about the underbrush. The boys trapped the adults in cages of their own design, luring them with seeds. They let out peals of joy when the baby chicks stole beneath the adults' feathers to nestle. The boys tethered the adults to stakes within the pen and provided food and water regularly, vowing never to slaughter them.

When Fawn and Watkins found them, the boys decided to demonstrate how well the chicks and adults obeyed them. Taking turns, Raven and Little Bear called the two adults in succession with a unique call for each. Rewarding them with bits of corn, the boys turned their attention to the two chicks. They too responded to calls quite unlike those of their parents—in all, four distinct sounds. Fawn and Watkins marveled at the birds' intelligence, each bird answering to the unique call which the boys took great pains to develop.

"We shall never dine on these birds," Raven vowed.

"Let us ask mother to let us keep them indoors," Little Bear offered.

"They belong out-of-doors, children," Fawn warned.

"Then I shall sleep out-of-doors too," Raven insisted, stamping his foot and drawing laughter from the guests.

The encounter ended when Colombe Blanche summoned Fawn to the kitchen. She in turn grasped Watkins' hand.

"Come! Your services are needed inside," she ordered, in a jesting manner. Once in the kitchen, Fawn dispatched Watkins to slicing venison strips for dinner, leaving him with a fleeting kiss on the cheek. "When you finish, be sure to stir the corn soup on the hearth with the wooden ladle. Slowly!! It must not lump at the bottom of the pot. Slowly. Remember?" She disappeared to join Colombe Blanche in embroidering an afghan.

"Yes, Sir," Watkins protested, looking out of the corner of his eye. Dutifully he assumed the chores. In this brief period alone, he reflected upon this new station in life: 'Overall, his labors drew him into a tight circle of men and women who cared for him. He permitted himself to harken back to the early years at home: There, by virtue of his parents' devotion, he developed a sense of caring for others beyond caring for himself. Older than his siblings, he accepted tasks and chores designed to assist his parents in their rearing. To his parents he presented a third set of arms and legs to attend to his siblings' needs at home while they remained in a state of dependency. His brothers and sisters he treated with equanimity and they viewed him as a benevolent dictator: kind, but a dictator, nonetheless. Assisting his father in the bakery, he applied the same set of skills to administering over staff and laborers to the extent that the community at large grew to admire him and mothers yearned for the day that he may set up a household with one of their daughters. Here, in these spare moments at the village, he silently thanked his parents for caring for him, for instilling within him the seeds of leadership which he applied when his father prematurely died, leaving the bakery and his brothers and sisters without a firm course of direction. He not only took over the bakery, but became steadfast surrogate to his siblings. The family survived, and, at intervals, prospered. He questioned the decision to leave home on more than one occasion, but recalled that later, when the opportunity to advance his own agenda presented itself, he leaped at the possibility.

'Although dissimilar markedly from the living arrangement in Tipperary, he approved thus far of his lot at the Round Tops. He sensed the development of a strong bond between this new extended family and himself, especially with the advent of Fawn. All around him flowed strong signs of family-like intercourse: an unbroken chain of loyalty to maternal virtues, a dedication to duty on a community plane, a spirit of volunteering, the sharing of resources, and a deep sense of religiosity. For him Fawn embodied these virtues. She rekindled the virtues he learned at home, combining them with those he adopted here in this new home. She watched him grow with eagerness. His constant companion, she was in her own way every bit the teacher that he became when he gave her instruction.'

At one point that afternoon Watkins remarked about the great quantities of food which Colombe Blanche insisted on preparing. Fawn winked at Colombe Blanche. She in turn suspended her chores and sat Watkins down before her, whereupon she delivered an eloquent harangue in French to him, Fawn having given her to understand that Watkins understood the language sufficiently.

"Once a year we celebrate the Great Festival of Ripe Corn (57). We began at Osco as you may recall, and although forced to move, we conclude it here. By custom the festival is held in a long house. Of course we have no long house, but we have made adjustments. The corn we have here comes from last year's harvest, hidden from the pillagers of Osco. Beyond you see our *new* long house. It is a tent set on a sturdy platform and supported by strong beams. By tradition the long house belongs to me, for I am the wife of the Bear Chief or Standing Bear, War Chief of the People of the Swamp at the Round Tops. After preparing our foods in our homes we will consume them in the long house together during the entire festival. My husband usually presides over the festival. Now that he is away, we have no strong male leader from our village. I have settled that matter, however. Oh:nehsi:yo is coming from Pointe Aux Bois to take charge. You have met him, Monsieur Watkins, I believe. There are no games or feats of daring at this stage of the festival. We will listen to speeches in praise of certain entities: the next harvest, our new home, our health, and our continued happiness. All are invited to give speeches. Even women and children may take part. Of course everyone is invited to dine without restriction. At sunset the festival ends with a speech by Oh:nehsi:yo, then everyone retires to rest after so much eating and drinking." Smiling, she returned to her labors.

Joining Fawn and the boys, Watkins stocked the long banquet table in the rudimentary long house with dishes of rich offerings. He arranged them in a hierarchical manner: meats forming a centerpiece, surrounded by vegetables and fruits, everything in a great circle flowing outward from the table's center. Fawn came to stand beside him. Speaking softly, she locked her fingers within his and leaned comfortably on his shoulder. Nearby the boys strained their ears in the hope of catching some of her endearing terms. A stern look from Watkins, however, dashed their hopes, sending them back to their mother's cabin. Now alone, Watkins and Fawn walked the length of the table admiring the selections, as well as his handiwork. Feigning hunger, Watkins patted his stomach.

Well aware of his cajolery, Fawn intervened: "You must wait for the ceremony to begin, 'mon amour.'"

"How cruel. And which of these delights have you prepared, Little One?"

"Why, the corn soup. You stirred it. Remember?" she laughed gaily.

"Born to serve, dearest," he teased. "Hopefully we will avoid a downpour," he added, eyes upon the horizon.

"Have you brought your bedroll?" she inquired. "We may have to stay here through the night."

"Caught with all this food? Now that is a misfortune I am able to tolerate to no end."

They laughed leisurely, when suddenly she chose a more serious note. Clutching his hand, she recited: "I remember when you built the ramparts. You dug the pond for our water. You built the cabins of the village and the canal going around it. There is very little that you did not do. You did all of this because you want to help others more than you want to help yourself. It is very good that you came to visit us. We shall remember you forever. When we grow old we will remember you and before we die we will pass your memory on to the next gen–er–ation."

He aided her with the final word of her speech.

He watched her full lips as they formed the syllables. She tried again and met with success, after which she looked up at him imploringly, her head on his chest.

Gripping her hand, he kissed her long and hard on the mouth. She gasped, but otherwise stood still, savoring the moment. He released her. Their eyes met. Tears ran down her cheek. He brushed them aside.

"You have done so much for us and ask for nothing in return," she spoke, through tear-filled eyes.

Gripping her ever-firmer about the waist, he pushed out the words long concealed within his breast: "I ask only for you. Is that asking for too much? I want you with me. Together we will accomplish great things," he whispered.

He ceased speaking, for suddenly the heavens opened, releasing torrents of water over the camp grounds. Small hailstones pelted the tin roof of the long house, drowning out his words, yet by then, reading his lips, she had devoured them and pressed herself against him in acquiescence. Reaching behind her neck she released the colorful ribbon binding up her hair. The shimmering, ebony tresses cascaded to her shoulders, retaining her classic oval features in a framework of picturesque loveliness. Wistfully she tossed her head from side to side, her eyes never leaving his.

"It is cold and I have no blanket," she complained softly.

"Allow me, Mademoiselle," he intervened, wrapping his arms about her waist.

"I am better now," she returned, after a long moment. "Look!! We are the only ones out here!!"

"I think it has something to do with the rain," he jested, retaining a sense of humor.

"I am ready to move into your cabin now," she murmured. Her back to him, she enfolded her waist with his arms.

Gently he squeezed her: "Let us be on our way." Releasing her from his grasp, he kissed her quickly, then pulling off his tunic, he forced it over her shoulders, pulling it into place. Arm in arm they abandoned the damp confines of the long house. Skirting small pools of water, they made straight for Colombe Blanche's cabin, their steps quickening beneath the pouring rain. Stepping lively, they laughed over feeble attempts to remain upright on the slippery hard pan. Crossing the threshold of the cabin, they stood soaked, yet relieved to have escaped the full force of the deluge. Lingering momentarily, their minds raced to compose what they believed an important message to deliver to their hostess.

(48)Kent, Timothy J. Rendezvous at the Straits, *Slavery During The Fur Trade Years*, Chapter 16:Part VI, Silver Fox Enterprises, Wayne State University, Detroit, MI.,(2004) pgs: 592-607.

*Matthew and Smythe determined **Black Jack** a Metis: of French Canadian and North American native stock

(49)Parker, Arthur C.) An Analytical History of the Seneca Indians: *Kanadesaga or Old Castle*, The Time Presses, Canandaigua, New York, (1926) pgs: 116-117

*The Cornplanter

(50)Mohawk, John. War against the Seneca: *The French Expedition of 1687*. Publication of the Ganondagan State Historical Site, courtesy of NYS Parks Departmentt (2001) pgs: 1-16.

(51)Brasseau, Carl A. The Founding of New Acadia: *The Beginnings of Acadian Life in Louisiana, 1765-1803*. Louisiana State University Press:Baton Rouge, (1987) pgs: 72-75

(52)Parkman, Francis. Count Frontenac and New France under Louis XIV: Chapter XIX: *Frontenac Attacks The Onondagas* Little, Brown & Co., Boston, New York, (1880) pgs: 410-415

*They followed what is now Interstate 81 South out of Syracuse, NY.

**Simply, The message asked for safe passage for an important mission holding extensive ramifications

(53)Anderson, Fred The War That Made America. Chapter 1: *A Delicate Balance*, Viking Penguin Group, 375 Hudson St., New York, NY (2005) pgs: 6-16.

(54)Anderson, Fred Chapter 14: *Makers of War. Makers of Peace.*, (2005) pgs: 152-162.

(55)Anderson, Fred Chapter 2: *The Half King's Dilemma*, (2005) pgs: 18-24.

(56)Anderson, Fred Chapter 16: *General Forbes's Last Campaign*, (2005) pgs: 163-172.

(57)The Iroquois Constitution: *Religious Ceremonies Protected*, pg: 18.

PART THREE

THE CHANGING SCENE

Chapter Twelve

**Games of Chance
Black Jack Escapes.
The Captain's New Adventure.
A Plot Foiled.
Probing a Mystery.
Watkins and Fawn Forever.**

The cell or chamber in which **Black Jack McKnight** found himself effectively served to curb his bellicose displays of anger. The cemented walls of small, interlocking stones, together with a hardscrabble earthen floor, confined his sudden outbursts within the defined limits of this box-like rectangle. Given the thick and impenetrable walls, many forms of human intrusiveness, such as noises from without, never reached the ears of the sole occupant, so solid were the three-foot thick granite slabs. In an uppermost corner of the structure, a lone, tiny window fitted with bars admitted at the most dim rays of sunlight on those days when the sun burned bright. Through the window twice daily a jailer lowered a tray of food in a wicker basket on a rope secured to a hawser. A chamber pot occupied one corner of the cell, it too lowered and raised by the rope at day's end. An impregnable door of crude timber encrusted with ivy separated him from freedom. The cell measured 13' feet in height. Its base measured 16' in either direction, if one were to mark off the steps by foot.

Without an audience to witness his remonstrations, **Black Jack** settled down to living in a realm of silence. Save for infrequent bouts of rambling soliloquies, he spent this period of confinement in detached repose, seated on the hardscrabble floor, changing position largely to haul in daily meals and to exercise bodily functions. He walked somewhat to relieve aching muscles. He performed pushups: hauling himself up and down by the arms while prone over the floor, his chin always touching the hardscrabble. He lost count after one hundred or so repetitions. The great arms and chest grew larger and stronger. He took delight in the quietude, for it gave him occasion to think and to plan and he often drifted off to sleep, well-sated with self-made theories, a twisted smile upon his lips.

The keepers allowed him to eat with a full complement of utensils. They required that he return them on a serving tray— after which they received an inspection. Although living in a vacuum, the adaptable **Black Jack** remained nonetheless ever-active. With a knife he probed the irregular walls of the cell and picked away at the hardscrabble deck beneath his feet. Before long small fissures grew wider and deeper. He confined maneuvers to one lone corner where walls and floor converged. Digging steadily, he anticipated breaking off a sizable chunk of material within days, great enough to admit an entire upper body. A spoon enabled him to dig furrows between the small stones of the hardscrabble floor. Pulling away earth and creating a small crater, he delighted in his success and toiled so much the harder, always careful not to remove more than what he was able to replace quickly. He kept a log of his labors with a fork, etching a scar into the flooring with the passage of each day. His captors provided him with no lighting and may never learn of his handiwork unless they brought their own oil lamps inside to search. He doubted that highly, for he knew they feared him, feared that he may take their lamps away from them, douse them with the oil, set them ablaze, and escape. From a modest allotment of tobacco, he took care to cleanse all utensils before returning them: cleansing them with a mixture of saliva and tobacco juices, the acid-like strength of the combination cleaning and honing the surfaces that he tarnished during his labors. The dim light streaking through the window shone strongest in early afternoon and it is then that he became most productive.

Sitting back against the dank wall of the cell, he debated the proper course to follow in effecting an escape. A single choice occupied his thoughts and he alternately bandied about its merits and disadvantages. Simply, he fathomed tunneling out of the cell, a process well under way. The thought of escaping under his own devices appealed to him. Such a maneuver would allow him to scoff at his captors from a safe distance, taking delight in knowing of their discomfiture for having been played the fool. Most important, escape provided him with the opportunity to treat with his confederate, the man known as the Captain. The Captain owed him money for shipping his aborigines to far off places. However, having met him face-to-face on the grounds, the Captain knew innately that he intended to collect a debt long-due. The Captain also knew that no garrison has been built to restrain him indefinitely. Therefore, in his mind's eye, **Black Jack** summarized his account of the Captain:' Either the Captain will repay him once he escapes, or the Captain will take steps to kill him, either approach well within that shrewd devil's capabilities.

'Although confined to a cell, he saw himself in charge of the Captain's fate. He knew first-hand of the Captain's passion for human flesh, that endless reserve which earned him a wealth of guineas. Now that his own role in the slave trade suffered a temporary displacement, the Captain would be hard pressed to find another partner of his equal. He may attempt to go it alone, but that is unlikely since the Captain needed an accomplice to draw attention away from his more official duties. The Captain may rescind the whole affair, but that too he saw as unlikely, given the Captain's unrestrained greed. One thing lay certain: The Captain knows that he, **Black Jack**, presents a strong witness against him in a court of law. The Captain's exposure meant eternal banishment from his native England, at the very least. For himself, conviction meant death by hanging, after having been beaten and strangled. He feared no banishment, for he never held allegiance to any nation or monarch. He feared neither confinement nor the lash. He feared neither the gallows nor a pistol shot to the temple, for he planned to be long-gone before his absence became noticed. He, the skipper of an ancient Great Lakes skiff, which occasionally ran questionable cargo to inland forts, hardly fitted the contemporary description of an habitual criminal. He always traveled at will, suffering the four winds to pull him where they may.'

Lying back, he reduced this new relationship with the Captain to a single term: *threat*. He threatened the Captain because *he* knew enough concerning his exploits to see him convicted of trafficking in humans for profit—a high crime in certain halls of justice. He alone stood defiant before the Captain. Divulging the Captain's secret to the proper authorities translated into a conviction for him, unless the Captain agreed to come to terms with him along a pre-determined course. He lay back comfortably, but not too comfortably, for he never knew the range of thoughts crossing the Captain's mind.

A dinner tray descended, consistent with the arrival of dusk, precisely when the sunlight retreated once and for all through the small window. He expected the same fare: chipped beef over noodles with gravy, or a variation thereof, two slices of bread, hot coffee in a mug and a cup of water to drink. Hungry, he bit into the bread eagerly, the slices one atop the other. Immediately he struck a foreign body. Cursing, he spat out the bread, then fell to searching through the remains, retrieving a leaf of paper, crumpled, yet whole. Gingerly he unfolded the paper, eyes straining to discern the contents of a message written in script with the fine point of a quill pen: *"Tonight. The door to your salvation stands unlocked."*

Jaw agape, he stared at the message for a long moment. He dwelt not so much on the contents, but on the one who sent it to him. Slowly he settled on the Captain, the confederate with whom he joined to amass a small fortune in schemes, scourged by some, disavowed by others. It is the Captain, he thought, 'who, having gained knowledge of his confinement, chose to set him free, sparing him endless days in this stinking box. How thoughtful of the Captain. I have only to walk through the door to my freedom.' He placed the message on the serving tray. Before long a nagging thought gripped him, present from the moment he interpreted the message: 'How charitable for the Captain, or his designate, to take such a keen interest in his well-being.' He scratched his jaw. He thought about the frequency with which the Captain exercised charity to others during the course of their association. Not a single example came to mind. His stomach churned with the first pangs of fear. Bolting upright, the thought struck him that he is worth more to the Captain *dead* than alive. 'Beyond that door death awaits me,' he grumbled. He propped himself against a wall of the chamber, eyes wide-open, glaring into the opaqueness of the dismal, sweat-lined cell.

He thought on. 'He saw himself as a man of the moment. He liked to tell associates that he obeyed intestinal urges, those primordial drives which carried him through numerous adverse encounters, many of them death-defying.' The situation in which he now found himself satisfied all the requirements of extreme danger, barking on the threshold of death itself. Again he found himself compelled to choose between two poor alternatives: move along with the digging, or seek the path contained within the cryptic message. Neither choice furnished a guarantee of success. What is more, either choice severely tested the rational man's ability to choose between two relative unknowns. 'At his present rate of digging, he may not be free for an entire week, provided he had not been dragged off and hanged, or worse, starved to death. The message offered a quick and ready solution to his predicament' and, taking a glimpse about the sparse accommodations, he reverted to acting on impulse— thus succumbing to basic instincts.

He picked up the serving tray. Turning it over back and forth he estimated its weight and balance. Manipulating the oval-shaped, and sturdy silver specimen, he found it durable to the touch. He approved of the tray's tempered edges, tapering to a sharp trim along the perimeter. With thick handles on either elongated side, the tray may be pressed into a defensive capacity, shielding the face and vital organs against blows and punctures from without. On the other hand, the tray also assumed the status of an offensive weapon, an extension of the arm, particularly when swung forcefully in an arc, or launched in the manner of a discus. Overall, the tray's versatility appealed to him. Grasping it firmly, he cast a farewell glance in the direction of the accumulated diggings. Crossing to the door of the chamber, he turned the knob ever-cautiously. Predictably the door opened. Stepping out into the night, he held the tray flat against his chest, in the left hand— the left arm, the strongest— his throwing arm.

For a few precious moments he stood motionless sniffing the evening vapors, keen eyes searching the shadows for signs of movement. An ally, a brilliant harvest moon, cast down glowing beams. They fastened upon the tray, that silver and lustrous disk, which, in turn caught the moonlight and transformed it into spikes of white light, sending them scattering: so radiant that they illuminated a portion of the prison wall to his rear and a circumscribed space on the hard pan about his feet, temporarily blinding him. In deference to the intense luminosity he looked away sharply. And then he saw it:

A silent, silver-like streak sped toward him, aglow in stark contrast to the darkness, a slender, pointed projectile bound straight for his mid-section. Aided by the available light, he determined the missile to be a knife or lance. Too late to assume a defensive mode, he struck out with the tray. Swinging it in a great arc, he brought it down against the missile, intercepting its path, cutting it down, where it fell harmlessly at his feet. Immediately on a pathway he heard footfalls retreating into the night. Straining against the waning moonlight, he spied a form running from him, briefly glimpsing the lower legs of a man in full flight. Impulsively he planted his feet firmly, and with a side-arm delivery flung the tray full thrust across the mid-section to the horizontal, the sleek, oval disk tracking a fierce, scythe-like course. Ahead, a man crying out in a shriek of pain, collapsed to the earth. He ran to the side of the assassin, who sat rubbing a leg. Retrieving the tray, he glanced into the grimacing face of a man in acute pain, yet coherent, who signaled for mercy with one free hand. Angered, he denied himself intercourse with the man, nor did he attempt to interrogate him or demand an identity, lest the assassin make good an escape. He found himself entirely alone with the villain, anger mounting. Raising the tray overhead in the manner of an executioner, he brought it down repeatedly over the assassin's head and face, pummeling him senseless. The man fell back, inert. He searched the man's pockets, coming away with a large key on a chain. With anger vented, he tossed the tray away and spat on the ground beside the inert antagonist before dragging him off into a thicket of tall grasses.

He breathed a sigh of relief. Fleeting thoughts of confronting the Captain came to mind: 'After all, the Captain owed him for past deliveries: obligations for which he received no payment to date. Now he found himself in a position to demand payment, and with the aid of a select band he intended to collect on that obligation. To that end one final piece of handicraft remained:' He walked swiftly to the jail house next to his box-like chamber, a rambling, one-floor structure. He promptly inserted the assassin's key into the locking mechanism of the front door, the single-most door of the windowless jail, formerly an ice house, he recalled. The key turned in the door and all the cells in like manner. No one intercepted him. 'How strange,' but he did not tarry to seek an answer. In a matter of moments he led his bedraggled comrades off into the night, having secured their pledge to remain silent in transit. One comrade found two carts in a corner of the grounds, and, putting one atop the other, **Black Jack** and company noiselessly rolled the apparatus to a far corner near the abutments. Leaping aboard, they heartily vaulted over the garrison's topside. Dense ground cover cushioned them, and, uttering not a word amongst themselves, they scampered off into the black night.

* * *

A new day dawned. With the first rays of daylight Lord Carleton awoke to the sound of a loud rapping at the door to his quarters. Sleepy-eyed, he admitted the sentry of the guard for the northern sector of the garrison. Dressing hurriedly, he intercepted sporadic segments of the guard's speech, so rapidly did the guard discharge his words. Pulling on boots, Lord Carleton deduced that a man lay dead near the prisoners' block, that a jailer lay dead, and that all prisoners escaped unscathed. Bounding over the grounds, he shouted: "Bring the Captain to me!" Moments later he bent low over the lifeless form of a man covered with blood about the head and face. Looking up, he found the Captain at his side. Rising slowly, hands on hips, he appeared both aggrieved and angry. He turned the head of the deceased toward the Captain for inspection. He spoke loud and clear, the voice tremulous:

"Who is he? Do you know this man?" he fired.

In a disinterested manner the Captain replied: "The man, in spite of his wounds, smacks of one Lampley. A blockhouse guard. A new-hire, if I am correct." He approached the deceased man, nodding in the negative. After regarding him briefly, the Captain turned his back on the ghastly scene, returning to the commandant's side.

"You will notice, Captain, that someone dragged him here," Lord Carleton pointed to the matted-down grasses prevalent at the scene. "What do you make of the situation?" he asked, eyes red with anger.

"The jailer, Knowles, is missing, Sir."

The corporal of the guard approached Lord Carleton. Trembling, he made an announcement:

"The jailer, Sir. It is Knowles, the blockhouse guard. Most trustworthy lad, He is dead by the prisoners' quarters, Sir."

Lord Carleton whirled to face the Captain, voice rising: "Thus far we have two casualties and one accounted for. Captain! What guests have we admitted of late?" The audacity! The boldness of it! Murdered under our very noses." He shrunk back in despair.

"Our guests are the marines from the Courageous, Sir," the Captain intoned politely.

"I want the guest list with their names. Do you have it?" The commandant demanded.

"My man Caldwell has the list, Sir." The Captain called his name, not aware that Caldwell stood beside him.

"Yes, Sir. I have it. I will conduct a roll-call," Caldwell replied, retreating toward the guest quarters.

"See that you make haste, Caldwell," the Captain, at last aroused, called after the aide. "Unfortunate about Simmons, is it not? I miss him," the Captain spoke most mildly, changing the subject.

"You miss his meals, Sir, as well do I."

"The finest Cordon Bleu to grace a galley, Caldwell. Gone. Simply gone," the Captain returned, apologetically.

"He is alive and well. He is a survivor, Captain," Caldwell replied meekly, looking to continue.

"You are waiting to speak, Caldwell?" the Captain bellowed.

"Simmons is one of the few of us who is worth more alive to an enemy than he is dead."

"You have a point, Caldwell. In the coming days we will negotiate for him," his counter-part simmered.

Departing briefly, Caldwell returned with Captain Smythe and Matthew York. Smythe produced a guest list of marines, reading from it aloud. Matthew York accounted for the whereabouts of those cited, placing a mark beside each name. A tension-filled stillness pervaded the grounds, weighing noticeably upon Lord Carleton, who paced nervously, heeding every call. He ceased pacing when Matthew accounted for the last of the guests:

"Well done, gentlemen. Thank you. I see nothing disconcerting in the roll-call. Corporal! Remove this corpse. Captain! Meet me in my quarters at noon." Turning on his heel, Lord Carleton abandoned the grounds. Marching stiffly, he wore the look of a man in consternation.

—

Away on the beaches, far below the garrison, **Black Jack** led the band of fugitives through the early dawn. He searched and found a skiff, unguarded and loosely tethered, yet fit for employment. Before casting off the moorings, he asked for a head-count. One by one the men announced themselves, leaving **Black Jack** to echo their names. All appeared well until he sounded out the name of one Lampley.

"Lampley. Where is Lampley, mates?" The men looked about in bewilderment.

"I saw him with us in the jail," a man answered.

"No! Lampley never sat with us," another interjected. "Remember? He transferred sick to the hospital."

Opinions divided almost equally. **Black Jack** moved apart from the pack. He found a boulder to sit on where he thought long and hard about the incidents following the escape: 'The assassin dressed in a woodsman's mottled garb, the face dirty and swathed in a shaggy beard. The boots of a buccaneer fitted with spangles—*Lampley's* boots. Lampley: the least loyal member of the party' He jumped to his feet.

"My God! I killed Lampley!!"

At midday a concerned Lord Carleton faced a detached, yet attentive Captain in his quarters: "Captain. Permit me to review my findings with you. Your man Caldwell took a tally of the prisoners. There are ten, I believe, exclusive of the brute, **Black Jack**. They refused to give their names, at least true names, but in examining them, Caldwell wrote down distinguishing features of each man— a scar here, a broken tooth there, combined with the usual measures of height and weight. He built a portrait of sorts. Following, the prisoners went directly to the block house and Caldwell left a report in my rooms, the very rooms in which you reclined indefinitely, recovering from tedium." The Captain stood unresponsive and the harangue continued:

"Caldwell has completed an examination of the corpse. The man's height and weight conform to our man, Lampley. How do I know this? Caldwell discovered the man's name etched into his garments—his undergarments, to be precise. Caldwell also found gold guineas tucked away in a pouch beneath his belt. It appears that we have hired this Lampley in all-haste. He turns out for the worse. A soldier for hire. Caldwell, I give you, has recovered a bloody shirt from the cistern near where Lampley lay dead. It is standard issue. The ultimate assassin planted it there for convenient discovery. He is the one that we want," he shouted. "For sure, robbery is not the motive. What, then? Killed for sport by his own crew? I think not! Listen closely, Captain. After I left you exhausted in my quarters, I returned shortly to find you absent."

"I merely awoke and returned to my own rooms, Sir."

"Do you have a witness to that effect?"

"There is my native servant. Unfortunately, he speaks no English, Sir."

"That may be, but, in your capacity, you have the keys to all the units of the garrison. The jailer, Knowles, held *his* key to the blockhouse and he is dead and his key is missing. Known for honesty, the jailer did not loan his key to a crew of pirates. Captain. Have you your key with you—the key to the block house? It has a distinct marking."

"I do, Sir." He produced it for the commandant.

"Hmmm. Nothing out of sorts here. Captain, I have a theory: Our assassin murdered Knowles. That leaves Black Jack disposing of Lampley. In disguise as the jailer, that one-and-the-same-someone entered the blockhouse and bribing Lampley, filled him with the false hope that he may gain eternal fame by murdering **Black Jack**. Lampley, inane fool that he proved to be, in turn unlocked **Black Jack's** cell and attempted to murder him, but met with his own end, overcome by our scruffy resident-pirate and never getting to spend those guineas. How does that strike you?"

"I am aghast, Sir, that someone has gone to great extremes in an effort to sully your good name. If I may, Sir, how do you come to believe that this Lampley attempted to kill **Black Jack**?"

"The corporal of the guard discovered a bloodied serving tray resting near the crime scene. This means that the jailer, Knowles, was killed in advance of Lampley's encounter with **Black Jack**, for it is the jailer who regularly lowers the serving tray into the small window twice each day. This, I vow, shows that someone wanted to make certain of the jailer's death well in advance of the pirate's abandonment of his cell. This same lowly sort orchestrated the entire grisly affair from beginning to end. Lampley must die in his estimation to remove all foreseeable witnesses."

"What is the meaning of all this, Sir?"

"I have two questions which I plan to resolve, Captain. First, the true assassin has a connection with **Black Jack.** For whatever reason he tried to silence him, but failed, in my opinion. He is not a contented assassin at this point. Two. Not a *single* guard along the northern wall knew of the chicanery taking place. What is more, not a *single* guard patrolled the grounds during the entire escapade. How does that strike you, Captain?"

"Very strange, Sir. Conceivably there lies an agent among the guard?"

"I have thought of that, Captain, but I believe the answer is less complex than that. Do not fear. Our assassin's days are numbered." He strolled self-assured to a massive desk. Slipping into an arm chair he shifted some papers before addressing the Captain:

"You are about to depart on a new venture, are you not? The one that we discussed?" Without awaiting a response he continued: "Gather your men and make good on your journey. I expect a favorable report on your return. Rest assured that I am looking into this matter in your absence."

The Captain took leave, saluting crisply: "So be it, Sir." Crossing to the open door, he departed, closing it softly. Immediately Lord Carleton retrieved a slip of paper from a drawer reading: *"Tonight the door to your salvation stands unlocked."* Studying it briefly, he folded the note, placing it in a breast pocket. He sent for the corporal of the guard: "Smith. Bring me samples of the Captain's handwriting. Caldwell's also. Simmons as well. By the way, as soon as the Captain departs the premises, bring his native servant in to me. That is all. Thank you."

—

At the head of a column some two hundred strong, the Captain rode side by side with the new aide, Caldwell, a man devoted to performing at the same high level as his predecessor. Matthew York, who earlier appealed to Lord Carleton to join the contingent, rode behind with the regulars. Smythe remained at the garrison to assist the commandant in investigating the mysterious deaths of the jailer and Lampley. Caldwell directed a passing reference to the commandant:

"Lord Carleton appears driven to solving these murders."

"He is more driven to assigning blame. Have you noticed how closely he watched me? I am barely recovered from his baleful vigilance. Strange that he sanctioned my campaign in such a dismissive fashion. I am pleased, however."

"The lack of witnesses astounds me," Caldwell offered. "I regret having been preoccupied in the commandant's quarters all evening. Otherwise I may have seen something of importance."

"Do not fret, lad. It was necessary that I send you to acquaint yourself with all of Simmons' duties at the garrison as soon as possible. Neither you nor I were able to predict this tragedy. I must tell you that I have heard *rumors* of a plot to capture Lord Carleton. That is why I sent you and the guard to stake out the commandant's residence. We must protect our superiors. Correct, lad?"

"Yes, of course. Unfortunately the whole matter is a haunting ordeal."

"Caldwell. If anyone asks you, tell the truth of your whereabouts. You simply performed your duty to the best of your ability under extremely trying circumstances. You are not to blame." He smiled confidently.

"And you, Sir. Where were you during the tragedy?"

"While you attended to affairs within the mansion, I searched the residential grounds with a hand-picked crew."

"Looking for assassins, Sir?" Slowly, he realized the innocence of the question.

"Looking for anyone out-of-place who did not belong there, lad."

"Good, Sir. I deduced as much. We have nothing to fear, do we?"

"Nothing. Nothing at all, lad". He reigned in momentarily, yawned and, reaching for his trail calendar, circled the day and date of the year: Wednesday, November 1st, 1760.

"It is a new day and month, Caldwell, and new adventures are reaching out to us. Let us be ready for them and greet them passionately. Onward!!"

"Right beside you, Sir." Caldwell spurred his mount and out of the corner of an eye noticed Matthew York drawing the regulars into a tight column close behind. The Captain too noticed Matthew's advance and vowed to establish a certain distance between himself and this young, vibrant marine.

* * *

Departing Fort Oswego, the Captain followed the Oswego River by land to the southeast. Approaching the fording place with Lake Onondaga, he crossed without incident and struck out along the eastern shore of the lake, due south along the sandy shore. His eyes trained upon the hilly terrain above the lake, he looked for signs of a little-known post rumored to house inhabitants unfriendly to the Crown (58). In the back of his mind the thought of a career hanging in the balance drove him to find a link between that remote garrison and the destruction of Fort Ontario.

He carried four ten-pound howitzers, cannon suited for conducting a siege. He chose the cavalry to the exclusion of the infantry, owing to the preponderance of expert horsemen in residence at Oswego. Once he located the obscure outpost, he intended to drop in on the administrators to gain an understanding of the way of life there. He anticipated a cordial reception, confident in his own force's ability to put down a sudden uprising. Moving along the shore, he halted to split the column into two components, essentially placing the outpost and its environs between two bifurcated arms of the cavalry. The first arm was to follow the shoreline or low road below the post. The second, under an adjutant, was to take to the wooded heights or high road above the post, essentially not a road at all, but a maze of coppices, thickly-invested with brambles and tangle-weed. Between the two columns the post lay, if it at all existed. He himself went with the low road, along with two of the howitzers.

He brought with him a small number of native scouts, many of them having been snatched from the grip of **Black Jack**. 'Better my gain and his loss,' he thought. 'After all, **Black Jack** must not be seen traveling with young natives by day, especially those destined for sale.' He kept the scouts with him to look for a point of departure from the shore to the heights above where rumor told him the post lay under cover. Soon, some of the natives reported having spied a string of palisades running back from the peak of a high bluff. Hidden from observers a week earlier under dense cover in the final stages of summer, proud maples, elms, and oaks, having shed their leaves, allowed a portion of the towering palisades to stand exposed. Citing what they thought to be the semblance of a structure, the scouts searched for a route of passage along the shore leading upward along the steep, hilly escarpment. Howling with joy, they told of discovering a stairwell, replete with telltale footprints leading from the beach proper.

"We have visitors, Guillaume," Marchand spoke softly, peering through field glasses.

"By all means, Henri. The fox is in the hen house," the General replied, a mischievous gleam in his eye.

"Pass the word down the line, Henri. We are about to entertain a most welcomed diversion."

From the parapets the General spied a scene unfolding before him of many men milling together on the beach below. He watched the elder leader and retinue mounting the staircase. He admitted how wizened and spare the elder man appeared. The General raised an arm and the gatekeeper cranked open the great, oaken door, its weight bearing down heavily on hinges in need of lubrication. It opened hesitantly. The General smiled with satisfaction for having effectively denied the visitors an opportunity to catch him unawares. A slight snub, one may aver, but, upon opening the door under his own volition, the General in effect set the tone over the course of the proceedings to follow. He gave his title as 'Major' and introduced Marchand as the post's 'tradesman.' He invited the gaunt officer and vigorous aide to join him in conference in the rustic library of the post.

"Good day, Monsieur," the elder visitor intoned upon entering the post. "I am Captain James Worthy of His Majesty's Expeditionary Forces in North America. This is my trusted aide, Caldwell," he gestured. He waited for his hosts to respond, but the General merely nodded soberly, leaving the Captain to open dialogue:

"You have a tidy outpost here on first appearances, Major, tucked away in these hills. One would be hard-pressed to find you on command without the benefit of a map. Incidentally, in consulting my maps I found no trace of you. Have you been here for very long?" The Captain leaned back in a comfortable chair, eyes leveled upon the General.

"In terms of occupation, no, Captain. The post itself harkens back to the days of Count Frontenac. You may say that I am keeping it in memoriam. I want to assure you that he held a map of the region." Hands folded before him, the General invited conversation, looking every bit the military historian in a crisp uniform.

"Ah, the Count! He planted the seeds of a colony in the North Country, but failed to live long enough to see it through," the Captain hinted sarcastically. "With his death the fortunes of New France deteriorated, as I recall."

"A fortress bearing his name lived long after him, a trader's paradise," the General replied with confidence, reminding the visitor of Fort Frontenac at the gateway to the St. Lawrence (59).

"Understandably, Monsieur, but the structure's poor defenses made it easy pickings for adventurers."

The General pouted in disdain: "Adventurers you say? I say that it fell to the greedy opportunists and representatives of the Crown who destroyed it when its residents resisted a hostile takeover." He bore in on the Captain.

"There are always those prepared to take advantage of a calamity, Monsieur; however, you must take note that here in the wilderness it is the strong and defiant who survive intact. That leads me to my question, Major: You must rue the number of new settlements hereabouts. Enough to bear a grudge? Enough to swear an oath of vengeance?" The Captain leaned forward in the chair, shifting his weight, eager to press the discussion.

The General responded calmly, but with conviction: "Captain. We are so thoroughly occupied honoring requests of the aborigines and residents alike that we pay little heed to external matters. We are small, yet we harbor a strong belief that everyone everywhere is able to live together in peace. We are not alone in our belief."

"True. The Friends also subscribe to your belief. They live throughout the Lake Country and prefer the Word to the Sword. This is good, but by the same token, you obviously have no knowledge of the travails I have suffered."

The General leaned forward, eager for the visitor to introduce the thrust of his argument: "Captain?"

"My men and I have suffered great setbacks since first we set foot in this region. In surveying new lands for settlement we have been attacked by aborigines bent on exterminating us. Our parent headquarters at Ontario has been reduced to ashes, the smoke carrying for miles in every direction. Anyone who glanced at the skies during that horrible afternoon knows that I speak the truth about Ontario."

The General equivocated:" I have little knowledge of that event, but I ask: In all certainty are you able to point a finger at the aborigines?"

"I reclaimed arrow fragments from the ashes at Ontario. I also found musket shot, large shot—pieces common to an ancient weapon. Major. Do you make your own shot on the premises?"

The General launched into a brisk dialogue: "That we do. It is more practical than relying on outside sources. I am certain that you are familiar with that situation. Like many of our mainstays, we acquire our weapons through trade. Our tradesman Monsieur Marchand, travels to great lengths in search of goods and staples and, yes, muskets and pistols. They are one more example of the essentials needed for living successfully in the region. Of course we seek reliable specimens at a reasonable price. With regard to bows and arrows, we have found that they are in great decline among everyone in the region—instruments of the past."

"That is a fine specimen, Major. May I have a closer look?" The Captain pointed to the long-barreled musket suspended over the fireplace. Its glint and luster caught his eye.

"Yes. Of course. Henri! Bring your rifle over to the Captain, please."

Grasping the instrument by the barrel, the Captain stood it boldly upright. From a pocket he withdrew a musket ball. Dropping it into the barrel, he tamped it with a rod clear through to the breech. With a narrower rod, he pushed the ball into position beside the firing pin— leaving the unmistakable ring of metal-striking-metal to ring true.

"This rifle, Monsieur Marchand. Is it an object of trade?"

"Not at all, Captain. It is a gift from a dear friend." The Captain looked up, expecting an explanation and the tradesman continued: "A Delaware chieftain presented it to me for saving his village from starvation. The Major and I placed our post at his disposal after enjoying a bountiful harvest for the season." He smiled modestly. Fluffing the pillows about a high-back, he reclined comfortably.

"Very comforting, gentlemen. Let me recall to you that, beyond their required duties, my men have the additional obligation of serving the wretched savage, who is hard-pressed to care for himself. We praise him when he is good; we chastise him when he is evil. You have seen him from his good side. Without fail, we have seen him at his worst. Perhaps you have a special method of treating with him that you will share with us at another session." Not pausing to await a response, the Captain rushed forth with his agenda:

"Caldwell! Bring out the rifle I purchased."

Caldwell departed the room briefly. Returning, he carried a blue-emblazoned rifle, surrendering it to the Captain without a word.

Striving to prove a point, the Captain continued, extending the rifle:

"This too is a gift, gentlemen—a gift I purchased for myself. It bears a striking resemblance to your rifle, Major. I acquired it on the frontier, not too distant from this place." He studied the faces around him. The General and Marchand sat impassively.

"This rifle takes the same ball as yours, Monsieur Marchand." He dropped the shot effortlessly down the barrel, where it came to rest beside the firing pin. "Believe me! How remote is that possibility? How interesting I find this! Tell me, Monsieur. Have you ever been to Kanandesaga?" He studied the tradesman's posture.

Marchand rose and spoke: "Yes. I have been. Any trader worth his weight ventures to Kanandesaga. There, I have earned the loyalty of a strong and proud nation of Seneca. What are to me mere handfuls of common goods are bountiful windfalls to the lowly native suffering from pitiful harvests. How better to build the peace along an explosive frontier?" The tradesman resumed his place, pleased with his response.

The Captain persisted: "Do you find it rare that your rifle and mine share the same bore?"

"Not at all, Captain. These arms and many more have been bought and sold in numerous venues throughout the region, for the most part in exchange for goods and services. This is not a novel practice, you will recall. Allow me to take you on a tour of our post." He rose quickly, and the Captain, his argument attenuated, followed the tradesman. The General rose to escort Caldwell and everyone passed out-of-doors.

Once on the concourse of the post the Captain and Caldwell fell in step behind their co-hosts. The Captain's retinue joined them, a small party of eight, and everyone proceeded to the shops, housed in the large, wooden pavilion or industrial complex. The General brought his guests before the ordnance department where craftsmen stood actively engaged. Some constructed rifles from salvaged parts, or repaired them. Others poured lead for forming into shot. Still others cleaned and oiled barrels, breeches, and stocks. At the end of the line of production a number of finished pieces stood assembled with surfaces shining and stocks richly polished. The Captain made a keen survey of all operations, nodding approval, and the little party moved on.

In the courtyard proper the delegation passed among residents preoccupied with fortifying homes in preparation for the vagaries of the imminent winter season: They caulked windows. They filled structural gaps in exterior walls and planking. They cleaned chimneys from rooftops. They fitted shutters to window frames. Few paid little heed to the General and the visitors. From the community well natives drew water. Other natives passed in and out of the school house, a simple structure attached to the chapel. The trading post drew a number of loungers to the broad veranda, where comfortable benches and chairs enticed the itinerant to spend idle moments. Save for the gatekeeper and the guards standing watch in towers, no men of military stature frequented the concourse, an observation which the Captain quietly passed to Caldwell. At the tradesman's insistence, the Captain briefly visited the well-tended fruit and vegetable gardens, where native caretakers bid them to observe first-hand the results of intensive labors. Later, the Captain declined an invitation to dinner, claiming that pressing matters permitted him few indulgences. Beside the massive oaken door he took leave of his hosts with humility. His departure set into motion a heated and vicious chain of events:

The General and Marchand escorted the visitors to the gatekeeper's station, there to await the palpably slow opening of the ponderous door. Once ajar, the Captain's retinue commandeered the exit by knocking the gatekeeper senseless. Forming a phalanx, they barred further their hosts' ability to retrieve the stricken man. Unimpeded, the Captain forced open the main portals and summoned soldiers who stood in waiting on the staircase. In short order a swarm of them streamed along the perimeter of the concourse, bayonets fixed.

Matthew York, in command of a squad, but under no orders, allowed himself to be drawn along by the multitude, taking a position on the grounds. Other soldiers menaced the residents, herding them together into a tight circle. At this juncture the brazen maneuvers compelled Matthew to reassess his view of the Captain. Where earlier he described the Captain in terms of bravery and courage, he now ascribed to him the designations of tyrant and bully, far from the attributes of a stellar officer. At once he wanted to desert the Captain's command, but he fully feared becoming captured and jailed. Furthermore, although a guest of the commandant, Lord Carleton, he held pitifully little stature at Oswego, a condition that the omnivorous Captain Worthy was bound to exploit. In deference to taking flight, Matthew vowed to stand with Worthy's command until a more advantageous opportunity to voice opposition came to pass.

Initially flung aside, the General and Marchand sought a place of refuge. They found it in the guard-tower. Clambering up the stairway, the two principals rang the alarm, a large iron bell pivoting on a yoke which sent out a thunderous roar echoing throughout the works. The soldiers holding the gate dissolved, joining comrades on the concourse. Nevertheless, two of their number lingered behind to mount the steps of the guard-tower, swords in hand. The General beat them back, kicking at the heads and shoulders of the intruders from the moment they breeched the overhead opening leading to the palisades' upper walkway. Marchand appeared, plunging a deadly dirk into the first of several intruders. Soon the stairwell stood awash with crippled bodies. On the grounds invaders ignited firebrands and waited impatiently for the Captain's order to fire the buildings. The order never arrived. In an ironic turn the invaders found themselves fighting for their lives at the hands of the heretofore docile and disinterested residents: These placid folk, having tossed aside civilian trappings and suspending all chores, summarily produced firearms, secreted no more than an arm's length from their stations. Similarly, native residents, having gathered at the school in small clusters, broke out weapons. Both factions pursued the soldiers— in effect surrounding them. Meanwhile, women and children residents disappeared from the grounds as though by pre-arrangement.

The men of the post opened a coordinated attack, firing with muskets and pistols from all conceivable quarters. The suddenness of the maneuver repelled the invaders, yet they refused to bolt and run, for the Captain rushed in reinforcements through the open portal. In response the post's defenders brought into play a tactic which turned out to gain them an unprecedented advantage: Traveling in units, small pockets of menfolk alternately fired, ran to a new location, stopped, fired again, and dashed off to a new location— thus repeating the cycle. Their fluid transitions confused the invaders, who, for themselves, seldom moved beyond stationary heel-and-toe posturing.

The Captain ordered a third wave of soldiers upon the concourse. Matthew York led them. Unlike his predecessors, Matthew's squad isolated the traveling units and held them at bay with bayonets while awaiting orders. Falling back, the traveling units invested homes and buildings, all of which fronted broad and commodious windows. Once inside, they threw open the shutters. Ramming the barrels of six and eight pounders through the apertures, they discharged the pieces full into the faces of the onrushing soldiers. Loaded with grapeshot, the cannon coughed mightily, spewing forth minuscule, deadly missiles. Many soldiers fell, mortally wounded. Matthew's men pursued the defenders, but did not fire upon them. Fearing for the lives of his men, Matthew ordered them to cease fire and seek shelter on the hard earth. He set an example: With head and shoulders lowered, he approached the corpse of a fallen comrade in a section heavily congested with the dead— drawing it over his prostrate form. Many comrades replicated the maneuver, suffering random shot to spare them. Sensing defeat, the Captain sent up a flare with a starter's pistol, its sequined crystals descending from on high to sprinkle down over the heights above the post. Thereabouts, stolen away amid trees and undergrowth, the second arm of the Captain's forces lay in wait, nestled amid two eight pounders. They knew not, however, that they shared the heights with an equally-aggressive ancillary body of the General's rangers.

Emerging from concealment, the Captain's second arm descended to points above the palisades. They proceeded to loop the palisades with ropes, the better to lower howitzers to the concourse below. It is here that the rangers entered the fray. They preferred the hatchet and war-club, where the incongruous terrain rose up unpredictably, making the pistol and long rifle troublesome to manipulate. Their ranks swelled by native warriors, the rangers incited hand-to-hand combat, a technique in which they excelled. The Captain's soldiers, their cannon and firearms unable to counter obstacles thrown up by the forest, found themselves at a distinct disadvantage. Rangers severed the lines suspending the howitzers, sending them cascading to the concourse and away from the fight. With losses mounting, the soldiers broke and ran headlong, precipitating the rout which spread to their comrades below (60).

The Captain fled to the heights of a guard tower. There he hoisted a crude white flag of surrender, throwing up hands in submission. His men on the grounds, now fully surrounded, surrendered en masse, but Caldwell, the aide, eluded capture along with a small following. He escaped over the original path which he hacked out of the wilderness on the heights and began a circuitous route back to Oswego. On the concourse the General's units broke into squads in order to begin the process of receiving the enemy's capitulation. They blocked all conceivable exits with stands of timber. They searched the grounds for the dead and wounded. They stripped the soldiers of arms, confining the captives to barns and warehouses. Residents poured forth to volunteer services.

For that soldier who concealed himself among the dead in order to avoid capture, there existed the possibility of both defying death and living to tell about it. Another theme thus emerged: escaping under cover of darkness to alert one's comrades, then effectively leading them in an attack of retaliation. The General, well-aware of such clandestine measures, instructed everyone in his charge to search diligently to look for *stowaways* among the corpses. James York joined the searchers. Aboyant accompanied him, fetching souvenirs of battle, principally headgear, to complement a burgeoning collection. Many bodies lay in clusters, where grapeshot cut through their ranks, severing limbs—cutting short the lives of so many fearless men. To the novices among the searchers, the thought of separating masses of mangled arms and legs, presented an unbearable challenge. Many of them drew away, overwhelmed by the grisly life forms lying broken and disintegrating in the heat of the day.

Coming together, salvagers set about implementing a plan of disposing of the victims of battle. Laboriously they separated the dead from the near-dead, placing them in rows upon the concourse. Considering the wounded, the salvagers directed the post's medical officer to see to their needs. The remainder, principally *stowaways*, they ushered to the prisoners' quarters. In general, everyone, *stowaways* included, received medical attention in proportion to the extent of injury incurred, provided such injury remained within the realm of treatment, given the means at hand. Those severely injured faced the grim prospect of expiring prematurely. For that soldier who lay close to death, the women of the post took pains to make his remaining hours bearable, outfitting him with suitable comforts of home: blankets, warm clothing, a bath, good food, and engaging conversation. All the while the search for soldiers-in-hiding continued.

"I have something here," one of the General's soldiers called. The young man touched the flesh of a presumed corpse lying among a heap of the dead.

"Look! He is warm to the touch."

Others came forward to find a youth lying amid a pile of rigid corpses. James York stood among the observers. The youth, bloodied about the head and hands, lay face down, arms bent at right angles at the elbow. James felt for a pulse. Finding one, he turned the youth over on his back, revealing a face bathed in blood and eyes tightly closed. James called in vain to him. He sat him upright, resting his shoulders against the wheel of a field ambulance. He shook him gently about the shoulders. Reaching into his jacket, James retrieved a vial of paprika and black pepper salts. Shaking the mixture, James applied a bit of it to either nostril. He sat back to await results.

The young man acted reflexively to the strong mixture: His legs pulsated. He coughed. He sneezed. Opening his eyes, he shrank back from the sunlight. He rubbed his eyes vigorously. With the sound of voices, he opened his eyes again, straining to fix upon the flow of events about him. A hand touched his shoulder. He traced it to its source, his vision dimmed, yet unimpaired. He spoke: "Father. Is that you?"

James York fell to his knees before his son. Speechless, he stroked Matthew's face, caked in dried blood. "Water! Bring me water!" he called. Aboyant sprung up to steal a leather water bag from a passerby. Together, he and James scrubbed Matthew's face, James shredding his own shirt sleeves and sharing them with Aboyant.

"We have much to talk about," James conveyed to the prostrate form before him. We must go to my cabin. You are in danger here."

Two men suspended Matthew between them, leading him from the field. In her cabin Suzanne glimpsed the little entourage through a bay window. Upon glimpsing her brother she let out a tremendous howl, causing Caroline to drop and smash the pewter cup which held her late-afternoon tea. James entered the cabin solemnly. He sat the exhausted Matthew upon a divan. Caroline covered her son with a blanket, and everyone, including the peripatetic Aboyant, breathed a collective sigh of relief, sat back, and entertained thoughts about treating with the languid young man who sat before them.

Later that day Matthew stirred. Rambling incoherently, he insisted on telling his tale, although no one pressed him. Caroline set a bowl of her renowned stew before him and urged him to eat, but he talked on and on without respite. About him all eyes and ears hung on every word. Finally Matthew finished babbling. Nibbling a bit of food, he allowed Caroline to lead him to bed. He fell asleep immediately and the York family gathered around the fireplace to talk among themselves. Soon, the General called at the cabin. James York admitted him, only to find the commandant at the head of an armed guard. The General insisted upon speaking with him, stating that he wanted to provide the York family, who took shelter from the general mêlée, with details of the turn of events.

James invited the General to sit at table, but, when the commandant insisted on standing, James feared for the worst. Caroline and Suzanne joined him, whereby James beckoned the General to commence speaking. The commandant opened slowly and soberly: "Let me begin, my friends. It will please you that I have captured the nefarious Captain, the sole object of our interest these many months. From what I am able to piece together, the Captain visited our post after acting on rumors and hearsay gathered along his path of inquiry. These tales seem to equate Monsieur Marchand and myself with those who have advanced against him. Of course Henri and I admitted to nothing and in the course of our discussion the Captain, much in need of a victory, decided to storm the works. Our units proved too much for him and the fight ended shortly after it began. We suffered few losses, yet took on many prisoners of battle, the Captain among them." The General coughed lightly and looked directly at James York.

"We retrieved a prisoner of interest, however." He approached James and settled before him in a chair.

"In my tour of the concourse I believe that I witnessed you giving solace to one of the enemy, James. Some of your men brought him directly here to your cabin. This prisoner must be someone special to you." His words contained a hint of sarcasm, bringing Caroline to her feet:

"He is our *son*. He is *not* your enemy. It is not what it seems," she returned, emphatically.

"It rarely is, my friends," the General replied, apologetically. "You do know that he *is* a prisoner captured in battle and subject to the penalties withstanding."

James rose in defense of his son: "Matthew fought out of a sense of duty. He knows nothing of the Captain. Before meeting the Captain, Matthew spent idle moments aboard a ship writing me letters—letters I never answered, for I abandoned my holdings to search for his mother, you will recall. In the interim Matthew answered the call to defend the Oswego frontier. That is all. You have my permission to grill him." He started for the bedroom.

"That may not be necessary." The General looked to Suzanne. "And what do you make of this, Mademoiselle?"

"Matthew is brave and charitable. He left home to join the British navy so that my father may have only to feed three mouths instead of four—all at a period when our cupboards stood bare. I am honored to have him as a brother. He thinks of others more than he thinks of himself. He captured **Black Jack** and saved the aborigine children from a fate worse than death." Her voice grew in intensity. Tears flowed freely.

James York interceded for Suzanne: "Monsieur Le General. He is the same **Black Jack** we witnessed joining hands with the Captain on the eve of the slave sale. Matthew knew nothing of that arrangement. He came upon the pirate by happenstance. My son related to me his travails before your arrival. He has a witness—his ship's captain."

"I tend to agree with you, knowing your integrity, James. On the surface it appears that we have stumbled upon a way to rid the land of this Captain once and for all and the evil he has brought with him. Of course, if your son offers testimony against the Captain, he will gain an eventual pardon."

Caroline rose quickly: "Matthew brought the pirate before the commandant at Oswego who confined him. I trust that he remains there." Smoothing her skirt, she continued: "Matthew performed a most selfless act of rescuing a party of native youth from a life of bound servitude. He is to be commended." She sat down, ruffled, but confident of her delivery.

Steeped in thought, the General addressed the family: "Matthew is a true witness to the Captain's schemes. For that matter we are *all* witnesses stemming back to the night of the slave sale."

An enthused Caroline rose again: "Early in my captivity I witnessed the Captain's pillaging of native villages. He stole many of the precious furs destined for market—for trade with *you*, Monsieur."

James supported Caroline's testimony: "This tyrant has singlehandedly upset the balance of trade throughout the region. Here we have a well-paid surveyor who seeks to supplement his wages by engaging in black deeds. Caroline and I are not alone in our knowledge of his exploits. I have lived with one of his soldiers, a runaway, you may say, who risked life and limb to warn friendly natives of the Captain's presence in the Lake Country. Now that the rogue is captured, this runaway will provide you with a superior account of his days in service to the blackguard."

The General contemplated all testimony: "Now that we have triumphed over the Captain we have essentially triumphed over his commandant by the same stroke. Those who have escaped capture will report to him, but the commandant will not retaliate in my opinion, knowing that we hold many prisoners. I propose that we approach the commandant with what we know concerning the Captain. I venture that the 'dear man' knows nothing of his chief officer's chicanery."

"You have a plan in mind, I trust?" James offered.

"Yes. I will go to Lord Carleton. I will demand that he desist from opening settlements in the vicinity of Pointe Aux Bois. I will insist that he leave the garrison to rise or fall of its own will and that Henri be free to conduct trade with the surrounding natives. After all, the commandant's soldiers remain in our custody."

Caroline asked to speak, her eyes burning brightly: "You have no assurances that Lord Carleton will honor your request. You must pressure him further. You must demand that he try the villain in a tribunal as a *condition* of your releasing his soldiers. There is also the matter of our knowledge of his failure to secure Ontario from attack and his subsequent failure to subdue Pointe Aux Bois, both examples in which he allowed the incompetent Captain to have free rein. If Lord Carleton agrees to a trial we will keep these blunders a secret from the rest of the English-speaking world and sing praises of him to the court of St. James for having stomped out the seeds of evil within the British army. I say that this is a very tempting offer for him, gentlemen."

With all eyes upon her, Caroline pressed on: "Matthew has enjoyed a salient relationship with Lord Carleton. I propose that he approach him with our plan. James and I will accompany him, of course, Monsieur." (Caroline hoped that Matthew's audience with the commandant may cause the General to drop any charges he held against Matthew. At this point Matthew knew not of the Captain's abduction of his mother. Caroline deferred telling Matthew so that a subsequent meeting with Lord Carleton may proceed free of distractions). James reiterated the praises that Lord Carleton heaped upon Matthew during the **Black Jack** affair, together with Matthew's benevolent treatment of the native captives wrested from the pirate.

The General nodded in appreciation of Caroline's views. "Excellent, mes amis. I believe that we have a strong proposal. The Fates are with us. This is a rare opportunity to lash out against slave-trading. Lord Carleton, consumed by vanity and pride that he is, will want to be in the vanguard of celebrity."

"In order to secure his place in history, Monsieur."

"Exactly, Madame York."

"What of our prized possession?" Caroline asked, facetiously.

The General shook his head: "Our prized possession refuses to speak. He stands mute staring at the wall of a stable. Tell me, James.

How has your son related to the Captain during the period they have spent together?"

"At first he thought the Captain a fearless campaigner. He tried to become better acquainted with him, but learned that the Captain ordinarily stands aloof of the men. Today's battle introduced Matthew to the man's treacherous side. You must remember that Matthew knows not of the Captain's abduction of his mother. We have yet to tell him. In due course, Matthew will make a more-than-willing witness, potent enough to convince the commandant that he made a poor judgment in elevating this rogue to a post of seniority. In Matthew's own words the commandant looks upon Matthew as a leader of men. He assigned him to the Captain's force with a small command. In the battle of Pointe Aux Bois, Matthew exercised caution in directing a squad against the defenders. To my knowledge the squad produced no casualties among his men or the population."

"All of this counts in his favor, James. I have heard enough. In my mind Matthew is an invaluable tool in opening peace negotiations. This is a rare opportunity to bring all hostilities to an end and to deliver to the Captain his just desserts. We now have leverage to exert. I am confident that the commandant will welcome our terms now that we have half of his men in storage." Grinning broadly, the General pumped James's hand.

Caroline sighed in relief. Jumping up, she exclaimed: "I propose that we *all* visit with the commandant." Her declaration incited a lengthy pause. They broke into laughter when Suzanne entered the debate: "Now, mother. There you go stealing my good ideas again." She began counting on her fingers.

"What are you doing, dear daughter?," James asked. "Counting the scoundrels we have routed. One is for the aide, Caldwell. Two is for the Captain." She wavered a third and fourth finger. "The third is for **Black Jack**. The fourth is for the Man in White."

✳ ✳ ✳

At home John Rhoades held council with visitors: Teedyuscung, the Bear Chief, and Cerf Courant. The crux of the discourse revolved around Charles Martin. Ultimately John Rhoades confided that Charles Martin kept meticulous documentation with regard to his holdings. Although mostly in the form of accounting journals, he also kept a diary which he methodically nourished by means of daily supplements. A bachelor, Charles Martin wanted to leave a legacy of his comings and goings, particularly in the event of untimely death, given the pressures exerted upon him of late. He named John Rhoades caretaker of his estate before the Yorks' arrival. John Rhoades escorted the visitors to Martin's home, an estate largely vacant, yet regularly maintained. Separated by two gentle hills, the two homes sat in the basin of a fertile valley. With a front door key John Rhoades entered the Martin home. He proceeded directly to the library which stood beyond the parlor and dining rooms. Bidding his guests to sit patiently, he removed a large painting from the wall behind Charles Martin's roll-top desk. With yet another key he opened a wall safe and extracted a small wooden chest. Placing the chest atop the desk he opened it with a third key, withdrawing a thick, leather-bound volume. He summoned the visitors to his side.

"Following Mr. Martin's demise, I found some entries which may have a direct bearing on your inquiries, gentlemen." Adjusting his spectacles, he looked at Teedyuscung and declared: "They are in English." Teedyuscung, competent in English, nodded approval, leaving John Rhoades to open the volume, whereby he began to read selected pages marked with strands of colored string:

16 Apr 1759: Rec'd delegation led by Gov, Denny. Members incl., James Worthy, BEF, Horatio Simmons, BEF. Offer made to sell all properties to BEF for 2000lbs. Ster. Offer refused with vow to meet later.

21 Apr 1759: Wrote to James and Caroline York to come and assume operation of holdings and management of land.

19 May 1759: Frederick Post, Quaker agent for Delaware, raised, in presence of Worthy & Simmons, initial offer to 3000 lbs. Ster. Offer refused based on inadequate compensation for harvested produce and lack of suitable provision made for resident Delaware. Vow to meet later.

23 May 1759: James and Caroline York and daughter arrive to assume new duties.

12 Jul 1759: James Worthy, leading a small delegation, offered to purchase all lands and holdings for 4000 lbs. Ster. Final offer. Stipulated that John Rhoades disengage himself from association with resident Delaware and remove to Quaker territory in SW Pennsylvania. Offer refused and complaint entered at BEF military post.

With the fifth entry, Teedyuscung registered displeasure, fearing the conveyance of all properties to rival, chief Pisquetomen. He believed that Charles Martin held a similar view, a stand that eventually proved fatal to him. The Bear Chief called John Rhoades aside, after which he, John Rhoades, began a dialogue in review of Charles Martin's final hours. He spoke slowly and distinctly:

"Charles and I labored in the fields along with the Delaware. On that day it rained off and on and we found ourselves sitting in Charles' barn waiting for the rain to quit. Not one to sit idle, Charles jumped up and announced the intention of having a plow-handle repaired. He went off to the British compound, plow in hand, with a few Delaware, bound for a smithy— the only smithy within several miles. He met the Captain on the trail and dismissed the escort, asking the Delaware to return later that day. That is the last anyone saw of him alive. That afternoon the Delaware returned for him. Failing to locate him, they shouted and quarreled among themselves, so much so that a number of men left their farms to search for him."

"Who are these Delaware?" Teedyuscung asked.

"Members of a select crew. Charles held certain natives dear to him. Most departed for Shamokin after the tragedy." John Rhoades spoke hesitantly, a hint of sadness apparent.

"I will find them. Are there other men knowledgeable of the tragedy?" Teedyuscung asked.

"They are yeomen farmers. Friends, if you will."

The Bear Chief suggested that they separate and begin a search: Teedyuscung to go to Shamokin, and he and Cerf Courant to visit the Friends. With everyone agreed, the conference ended and the men took stocks of provisions in preparation for the journey. They agreed to meet again at John Rhoades' home to review the findings.

———

Teedyuscung traveled swiftly to Shamokin where he always enjoyed the friendship of fellow Delaware. He expected to make bold discoveries after holding a series of inquiries. He readily located Charles Martin's select crew. Everyone lamented over the gentleman's fate, yet no one volunteered to come forward. Teedyuscung demanded to learn why there prevailed such a reluctance to become engaged:

"We follow King George, nowadays," a man replied. "He has promised us new lands and plenty of gifts."

"King George is in his homeland beyond the Great Lake. He does not speak for you," the chieftain countered.

"This is true, however, his servant, the Captain, walks among us," another man declared.

Without citing the journals of John Rhoades, Teedyuscung replied: "At this very moment your friend the Captain meets with Governor Denny and Monsieur Post to remove all Delaware from ancestral lands. He has lulled you to sleep with whiskey and cheap trinkets and you are like soft clay between the fingers."

"How is that possible when Sir William is building a fort for us?"(61)

"Where is this fort?"

"Ontario. Sir William is rebuilding it after the Iroquois burned it."

"A mere trading post where you will be encouraged to exchange your valuable furs for more cheap trinkets. These are the very measures that Charles Martin fought against. Is he to have died in vain?"

One of the crew members yearned to speak: "The Captain met us on the road. He offered to escort M. Martin to the smithy in the event of a disturbance and we believed him. M. Martin dismissed us and we went home."

His candor brought another man to speak: "The Captain reported M. Martin's death to us the following day after making the rounds. He said that M. Martin drowned by accident. He said that he found him by the water. We brought M. Martin's body to the Friends for burial. We found a plow handle lightly buried in the mud next to the body."

Another man came forward with a vivid account: "The Friends said that M. Martin suffered a blow to the head, a blow delivered by a heavy tool. They examined the body before burial. M. Martin suffered great injuries."

"Such as injuries from a plow handle?" Teedyuscung asked.

The two natives sighed: "That is a question we ask ourselves over and over," one of them replied.

"The plow handle. Where is it now?"

"We left it with the Captain who vowed to present it to Gov. Denny and open an investigation. The Captain also told us that he found M.

Martin's horse near the body. He raised the possibility that his horse threw him and that M. Martin struck his head and drowned in the shallow waters of the river."

"What has become of the investigation?"

"Nothing that we know. The Captain and the governor have been drawn away from it by land matters."

"Where are they now?"

"The governor has gone to Philadelphia to speak with the two sons of William Pitt. The Captain? He has vanished."

"What are your thoughts on this entire matter?" Teedyuscung asked in earnest.

"We do not know what to think."

"We find it difficult trusting any of the soldiers."

"We are so afraid," another native offered.

Teedyuscung attempted to mollify the men's fears: "That is why I have come. I am looking for M. Martin's killer. I remember him as our friend. With his death we have not only lost a friend but our voice among the whites in their assembly. I need your support in arriving at the truth. Are you with me?"

"Yes! Let us do this," a man called. "Our hearts will beat with happiness when that day arrives."

"So be it, my brothers. I leave you now, but I will return one day."

———

John Rhoades led the Bear Chief and Cerf Courant to the homestead of Glenn Joseph, a Friend. There, in the library cheerfully illuminated by a brilliant hearth, he introduced the Cayuga sachem to a small party of Friends as the first cousin of Chief Logan, the famed Cayuga orator and namesake of James Logan. A vivid discussion then began. Glenn Joseph spoke first:

"At Charles' insistence I and a small body escorted him to the British military post. The soldiers in residence occupied themselves by scouting new lands for settlement. Charles occasionally visited the post to reinforce his customary refusal to sell, despite receiving sugar-coated offers. He also visited the smithy often."

"The surveyors at the post record new deeds and otherwise help new-arrivals adjust to their surroundings. They perform worthwhile services in general, I believe," another man contributed, in terms favorable to the British post.

"Monsieur Martin maintained good relations with those at the post, you say?" the Bear Chief asked.

"Yes. By all means, He did not fear going to the post. Despite the refusal to sell, the soldiers extended him goodwill, reluctantly at first, but genuine nonetheless," another man offered.

"They called him a stubborn Old Codger," a man said, chafing with latent distaste for the term. "Land sales have taken place so quickly that Charles' stubbornness became akin to food for conversation."

"It is with good humor that the soldiers entertained thoughts of Charles, you say?" the Bear Chief interjected.

"For the most part, bearing in mind that the humor they dispensed took its origins from Charles' sincere refusals."

Glenn Joseph rose: "Under peaceful conditions we surrendered Charles to the soldiers. Let me be more precise."

"Three men took charge of Charles Martin. The Captain, the ever-present aide, Simmons, and a spirited officer, Hastings." Glenn Joseph recalled the Captain's concern in providing an escort, citing unstable frontier conditions. Ironically, however, Glenn Joseph never recalled an eruption of hostilities between native Delaware and British soldiers. He attributed the relative peace between the two camps to the ability of Teedyuscung to bring feuding parties to the conference table. For him, the Captain's insistence of an inherent evil presence on the frontier seemed exaggerated— even out of place.

The Bear Chief pointed to several mysteries in accounts given thus far: Allegedly Charles Martin rode with the soldiers to the post yet, on his return he apparently set off *alone*, according to reports which Glenn Joseph gathered. Furthermore, no one at the post came forth with details of Charles Martin's demise, according to Glenn Joseph. Moreover, no one, save the Captain, announced Charles Martin's death, Glenn Joseph recalled.

"Did Charles Martin in truth reach the post?" the Bear Chief asked through the interpreter.

His inquiry caused heads to turn among those gathered, not the least of whom was Glenn Joseph.

"I assume that he did. We all assumed that he reached the post."

"You made inquiry among the soldiers?"

"Yes. We spoke with the Captain of the Guard."

"How about this Hastings and Simmons?"

"They went about their field duties on the trail, I am told."

"It is all very convenient when there is a murder afoot."

"We have posed the same question to ourselves. At this point I may say that the investigation still continues."

The Bear Chief summarized his thoughts for the Friends: "I say that a soldier, one or more, killed Charles Martin. I say that he looks like any other man and that you have borne witness to him on several occasions without knowing of the evil that lurked within him. You may also know the man, but are afraid to name him."

Glenn Joseph flushed scarlet red around the jowls. Several other attendees shuffled nervously in their chairs.

"You say that he set off from the post alone?" the Bear Chief asked, returning to a previous point.

"Yes. Apparently the smithy mended his plow quickly and Charles wanted to trust his own judgment by leaving lone. This we learned upon inquiry."

"Did the injury to Charles Martin compare with a blow to the head or a fall from a horse?"

The question opened new considerations for Glenn Joseph. He paused a long moment, then answered: "The men preparing his body found considerable swelling about the lips, cheek, and eyes. This conflicted with the blow to the head when deciding what ultimately brought about Charles' death." He paused again, then: "If you ask me, someone beat poor Charles to death." He choked back tears.

* * *

Standing beside her kitchen window, Colombe Blanche prayed for the rains to cease. The arrival severely hindered the culmination of the Corn Festival. In the absence of the Bear Chief she assumed the administration of the ancient incantations of her village. She recited a passage adapted from the oral language:

"Hiawatha. You who have brought us a bountiful harvest, despite adversities along the way, we honor you. The very rains which you sent us to grow our great yields have provided us with a surplus. We ask that you direct your goodness and generosity to our brothers, the Delaware. They have known lean harvests since the arrival of les Peaus-Blancs. They need

something to rejoice about and your rains will prove a welcomed benefit to them." She crossed herself in the Christian tradition. Taking up a vigil at the rain-streaked window, she gazed silently into the gray, stark skies looming menacingly.

Raven and Little Bear stood at their mother's side. Outside the cabin the rains beat fiercely against the windows, streaking them. Curious youth with boundless energy, the boys grew restive. They longed to be out-of-doors calling challenges to each other from the tantalizing heights of the Round Tops. On bright and sunny days the boys devoted a great part of their waking hours to adventure: They explored the lands adjacent to the village, a region invested with numerous points of interest: Eagerly they chased rabbits scrambling to reach the safety of their warrens. They pursued foxes up to the mouth of their dens. They flushed pheasants out of thickets. While meandering they ranged north of the village where the hills gave way to marshy flat lands and shallow bogs, home to colorful waterfowl and to one long and angular bird with sticks for legs and a long, narrow beak. When it flew its giant wings cast a shadow over everything below and it soared effortlessly and leisurely. The boys marveled at its flight. Cheerfully they reported many adventures to their mother while she waited patiently for the skies to clear. Amid gales of self-generated laughter the boys reiterated their discoveries to each other with an eye to their mother who maintained a stoic vigil and spoke not a word to them. They challenged each other to divert her attention. Raven made the initial attempt:

"The man Watkins has a lady-friend," he giggled.

"Yes, I know, child," Colombe Blanche whispered, eyes fixed upon her window. "Fawn and Watkins make a dear pair, yes?" she asked rhetorically.

"They hold their heads together. They stand in the rain holding hands. How silly!" Little Bear claimed.

"Not silly to them, children. They are in a state of union. It is what brought your father and me together. Union has a way of rising above common concerns of self. With union, two act as one. You will learn that one day." She turned to face the boys and asked: "What have you two been doing this afternoon?"

The impish grin on the boys' faces gave her to take a closer look at her two young sons: "Oh! Your leggings. The mud. Where have you been? Wait! Do not tell me! The Swamps!"*

"We only stayed for a short while," Raven confessed.

"You boys know that the Swamps are too far from the village. The land is soft. It will swallow you and we will never see you again. You must learn to follow your senses, not your desires," she scolded, facing them.

"We tried to be careful, mother," Little Bear whined, hoping to regain his mother's favor. Penitently the boys hid their faces in her skirts, hugging her, all the while poking at each other playfully.

Undeterred by the boys' antics, Colombe Blanche called attention to their leggings: "What would Mademoiselle Suzanne say about your muddy leggings?"

"She would be beside us step-for-step," Raven submitted.

"She would also teach you to care for your clothing."

"When is she coming back?" Raven asked.

"When it is safe for her to travel, my son."

"I am not afraid. I will go for her," Little Bear returned, defiantly

"Who will escort you?"

"Watkins will go. He is brave and strong."

"He is very much occupied, child." Colombe Blanche sought to end this round of pestering. She made the boys an offer: "You may venture to the Swamps with Suzanne upon her return. She will guide you and watch over you and you will be safe."

"Then you will not be angry with us any longer?" Little Bear asked.

"No. I will not be angry with you any longer," Colombe Blanche returned in mock-jest. Laughing softly, she tousled Little Bear's hair, then beckoned to the boys quietly, yet firmly:

"Now go change your muddy leggings!"

She glanced out of her window: "Look! The rains have stopped. The Festival is spared!"

The boys squealed in delight. Whispering, they agreed that, indeed, their mother persuaded ancient deities to chase away the rains. Caught up in this new discovery, they scampered off to do her bidding.

—

Watkins escorted Fawn to his home. Built in the manner of all of the new homes of the Round Tops, it presented appointments altogether fascinating and mysterious to her. He led Fawn on a tour, demonstrating their usefulness. She discovered his rocker. Sitting in it, she allowed

Watkins to instruct her in guiding the apparatus with the bowed runners. She came close to pitching herself out of the chair until she reasserted her self-confidence following a few well-chosen words from her host. Moving to the wash-tub and wash-board, Watkins demonstrated the method of washing clothes. Choosing a pair of socks, he transferred them expertly between both pieces of apparatus, alternately dunking and scrubbing them. Fawn watched, enthralled. With a pair of bellows Watkins breathed new life into the simmering logs in the fireplace. Under a steady hand, the flames leaped upward, comfortably enveloping the room with heat. Bringing Fawn to the library, Watkins ignited an oil lamp perched on a reading table. A small wheel at the base of the lamp allowed him to turn up the wick. A bright glow filled the lampshade, sending slim tendrils of light radiating along the walls of the room.

Fawn stood in awe of the devices. Momentarily speechless, she spewed forth with 'oohs and aahs', much to the delight of Watkins. She marveled at the mirror suspended over the sink in the bathroom and giggled hilariously when introduced to the water-closet in the corner. At length she and Watkins returned to the kitchen where he opened the door to a wooden ice-box. It stood the height of the average man. On the bottom lay chunks of ice submerged in a bed of sawdust. Two shelves above held fruits and vegetables from the autumn harvest. Cool to the touch, Fawn registered approval of the ice-box with suitably placed fits of elation.

Fawn stood fast at Watkins' side, catching his every word and gesture. Her zeal excited Watkins. He ushered before her more and more appointments and devices and waxed prodigiously about them. She acknowledged his commitment to detail with each presentation, touching him about the waist and shoulders, smiling radiantly in approval of the furnishings. At a certain point she passed her arm across his shoulders behind his neck, her soft fingers coming to rest at his ear. She slowly traced a pattern over the ear, repeating the movement, ultimately bringing his disclosures to an end. He ceased speaking and, turning to her, embraced her fully on the mouth, a sustained, warm expression of subdued passion. Neither spoke. He embraced her neck and cheek and her forehead, and seeing her eyes closed, he kissed them as well. His arms snug around her waist, she arched back to savor the moment and he pressed forward, his lips caressing her covered breasts.

She exhaled sharply, then giggling, she pulled away from him, her head half-turned back toward him, a smile on her lips.

He moved beside her and whispered into her ear: "I have not showed you everything."

Guiding her hand, he led her to the bedroom. His feet on the floor, he sat upright at the side of the bed, pulling her into position beside him. Her fingers probed the mattress, feeling the thickness of it. Again, something new to her, she sat, then rose and sat over and again until he restrained her, holding her arms by her side. She dropped back on the mattress, arms outstretched, absorbing the comforts of this new attraction. Reaching beneath her extremities, he pulled her legs from the floor, tumbling her slender form upon the bed, then, turning her lengthwise, took up a position next to her. For a long moment they lay face upward, sharing a common pillow rich in goose feathers. She probed it steadily, striving to push more of the softness beneath her shoulders, smiling when he relinquished it to her and lay beside her, watching her. She broke the silence between them:

"I like your house. I will stay here now."

His hands moved over her, feeling her warmth. She allowed him to tarry before gently pushing his hands away.

Inadvertently she disturbed the core of his passion, which, although concealed within leggings, transmitted a poignant message. She withdrew her hand, and, leaning over him, gazed longingly into his eyes:

"My People believe that when a man lies with a woman, she becomes his wife. Am I your wife?"

Reaching up, he kissed her on the mouth. "What does that tell you?"

"I must know!" she insisted, pummeling his chest in a gentle staccato.

He restrained her, then commenced to chant: "Yes. You are my wife, now and forever."

She pouted: "You took so long in making me your wife. I took you for my husband from the beginning."

He stared at her quizzically, prompting her to elaborate: "During your sickness I lay with you night after night. No one knew that I lay with you. To be discovered is to be exiled from the village. Then no man would want me for a wife. You did not know, for you spent most of your day sleeping," she explained, displaying a hint of anger.

"You fed me? You bathed me?" he sat up, stroking her hair.

"Yes! Everything. You hold no secrets from me," she confessed, her hand moving to his thigh.

Curious, he sat up: "You did not wake me? How did I eat?"

"You always woke long enough to eat my hot soup. It saved your life," she conceded, her hand at his chest.

"No. *You* saved my life." Reaching out, he pulled her to him, locking her in a fervent embrace. For a long moment they sat holding each other. Eventually he declared: "You never speak of your family. Do you have a family?"

Pushing him away from her, she daubed at her eyes, brushing away tears: "My parents. They are dead."

He turned away in dismay, but she pulled his chin toward her, insisting that he listen to her story. Their eyes met—his, opened-wide, hers, misty with tears. She began:

"Les peaus blancs killed them. They came in the early evening before the sun set completely. Their leader called for a council of the villagers. My father gathered everyone before the council fire in the center of my village—men, women, and children. Their leader separated the young from the old and demanded our furs, the price to pay for ensuring the peace, he said. The villagers came unarmed and my father carried his calumet, the pipe of peace. Their leader made a brief speech which no one understood and began loading our furs into a wagon. Into another wagon he forced many of our children. My father offered him the calumet, but he scoffed at it. My father asked him how the taking of children ensured the peace and the leader came to where my brother and I stood.

"Take the furs, but leave me my children," my father shouted, the last words I ever heard him say. The man struck my father with a sword and killed him and when my mother threw herself over my father's body he struck and killed her too. My brother and I wept over our parents and the man mounted a horse and swept up my brother and myself and rode off— the two of us screaming. We rode into the early evening, drawn over the man's saddle. He found delight in striking our backside. At last I broke free and jumped from the mount. I ran to a thicket, but my brother did not escape. The man carried him off and I have not seen my brother again. I pray that he is well. I pray that the thief is found and suffers."

Watkins patted her head and held her close: "I am so sorry. I did not know. No one aided you in your village?"

"The soldiers destroyed my village. They killed those who did not flee. My father, a brave and proud man, stood up to these rabble. For him his family and village came above thoughts of property. He surrendered his life so that many villagers may flee with their lives." She touched Watkins' shoulder: "Tell me that he will not be forgotten. Tell me that his Spirit lives on through the two of us." Sitting upright, she rested her head upon his chest.

Her testimony so moving, Watkins struggled to find words in reply. In drawing her ever-closer to him, his eyes welled up and his throat grew dry, then reluctantly the words flowed in a torrent, pressed together, barely audible "This man. Do you remember him? His appearance. Are you able to know him on sight?"

"I see two visions at night before I fall asleep. The first is that of my father. He smiles to me from his new home above. Below him is *that* man, smiling a surly smile, speaking in a whining voice. The two visions fight with each other, moving back and forth and around and around in my head, yet my father always wins the contest and keeps his higher position while *that* man grins and whines below him. There are nights when I do not sleep, when their battles are very long and I lay in the darkness waiting for my father to chase him away, but he is wounded and unable to complete the challenge and *that* man comes back to molest me while my father tends to his wounds. I am able to fall asleep only after my father strikes him down. Then his vision chases the evil man's vision away—but that is not for very long. One good thing survives out of this. I always see my father's face when I awake in the morning. He still smiles and speaks tender words to me, words from my childhood, and they provide me with the strength to go out and face my day. So it has been every night for five years and more."

Watkins dried his eyes. He cleared his throat. He repeated the question: "Do you know this man?" After a few moments she replied: "I know him by sight—by his voice. I will know him if I see him again. I pray that I live long enough to find him, for I will kill him and in so doing my father will be set free—free to roam the heavens with his fallen brothers—free to release his Spirit to guide me and protect me here on earth."

Deeply moved, Watkins asked the somewhat banal, yet essential question: "How is it that you came to live with the Bear Chief?" She anticipated the question and recited for him lines well-rehearsed in his native tongue:

"I come from Gayagaanha (62) near the crossroads of many trails through the land of the Gayogoho:no. It is close by Goiogonen, the first home of Colombe Blanche and the Bear Chief. The soldiers ravaged large parts of Gayagaanha. They took away our youth and our valuables and the Bear Chief moved everyone to Osco, a new home which he built for the People. It lay on a secluded plateau at the edge of the forest overlooking the shore of a beautiful lake. The Bear Chief believed the site large enough to give rise to a growing population. Tucked away into the side of the plateau, the location stood sheltered by the towering firs and pines. The village that sprouted up remained safe from wandering eyes until the soldiers discovered it and attacked with a vengeance. That is when we first crossed paths, you will remember. The Bear Chief fought them off and many soldiers went to be with their creator and no more did we suffer attacks. The Bear Chief may have rebuilt Osco, but he chose instead to go to the Round Tops. This is when you entered into an alliance with him and the white family and began to build a new village with strong defenses. It pleased me that a peau blanc chose to occupy himself side-by-side with the People."

"And it pleased me that you would bring a *stranger* back to health."

"You and I are *strangers* in our own way, but when we are together we are strangers no longer."

He marveled at the wisdom of her words, telling her so: "Fawn. I must tell you that I believe in your words, but something more has brought us together—our disdain for the same scoundrel. You see, I believe your parents' murderer and the man who marked me for death are one-in-the-same man. He will be captured one day, I assure you and we will no longer have to live in fear for our lives. We will know happiness and be free to live and love the remainder of our days on earth." He clenched her hands in his. Pressing them firmly together, his eyes met hers.

"I will know no true happiness until I learn of my brother's fate," she whispered.

"We need to capture the beast. Believe me, there are forces in play this very moment. That is why the Bear Chief left for the Delaware country. He believes the rogue to be tied to the disappearance of the white woman."

"I knew something unusual to be afoot. The Bear Chief does not willingly abandon the Festival. He took with him his ally, Cerf Courant. He left so suddenly that no one told me of his departure, not even you, Monsieur Watkins."

"There are so many questions to be answered: questions I do not have answers for at this point. I knew not where to begin. Please forgive my *gaucherie.* No offense intended."

"And no offense is taken. I believe you". She asked to speak partly in French, a tongue which she taught Watkins of late. He nodded in assent:

"You are not like other peaus blancs, although you come from the same roots. In your joining forces with the Bear Chief, you have been able to do your greatest good: helping others among the People. In taking your power from him, you follow a great leader who leads by example. He is the most recent in a long line of chieftains who so reached out to help his People. Like him, they brought the Gayogoho:no from the edge of obscurity to the prosperity that they enjoy today. Our early leaders, such as Orehaoue, partnered with the French to bring valuable tools of trade to every home in our villages. Shikillimy (63) guarded the People's southern border along the Susquehanna, opening a friendly alliance with the Delaware and keeping intruders at bay. One of his sons, Tah:gah:jute, so mastered the white tongue, that he became an orator speaking in public councils to heal the wounds between the People and the peaus blancs. A close cousin, the Bear Chief/Standing Bear, followed Tah:gah:jute's life closely. He endured sarcasm from the People for befriending white settlers who moved into his lands. You have lived and labored with him. You know that he bears hatred against no one. Like the chieftains before him, the Bear Chief believes in truth and justice. He labors to achieve it for everyone. If you say that he is seeking after an enemy, he is evermore seeking after truth and justice and you are—we all are in good hands."

Her incisive mind left an impression upon him. He saw her in a new light. No longer the compliant and conciliatory maiden, traits which first drew him to her, she became for him a keen observer of her surroundings, one who took pride in having been born in a most transitional period in her People's history and one who longed to make her own mark upon that period. To that end she possessed a penchant for helping others, learned at the knee of the one who rescued her, the master of Osco and the Round Tops, his mentor no less, Standing Bear: the Bear Chief.

Brushing his cheek with her lips, Fawn scrambled from the bed. Reaching behind her neck, she untied a thin, strap of leather. She reached beneath her shirt. Bringing out a light-weight frame fastened to the strap, about the size of a small portrait, she called him to approach. Gently she placed the object of interest, her Sampler, a strip of hide drawn tightly between the margins of the frame, in his hands. The makings of a passage sewn into the hide in multi-colored threads came into view. The message, definitely in French, challenged his modest command of the language. She stated that the passage expressed her People's understanding of Nature. Additional threads adorned the borders of the frame, bringing the inscription into prominence. He made a brief inspection of the passage, silently searching his repertoire of French words and phrases. She stood before him silently, gazing into his eyes, a smile on her lips. After a long moment he read the passage aloud in French, then, pausing, he rendered an interpretation:

"The People have known bleak days from the past. Now their days are munificent, reflecting that history takes place in cycles, from good to bad and back again, from highs to lows and back, all in keeping with the force of the circle of which the universe is made. Within this arrangement we are permitted limited freedom of movement and decision-making, yet we are by design prohibited from altering the overall sequence of historical events, for they are under the dominance of the circle, also known by many as a Higher Power." Watkins caught himself wiping away tears from the corners of his eyes.

"You must place it on your wall," she declared, elated. Now that we are united, my possessions I share with you. Here. I will do it. She crossed briskly to the room housing his modest library. There, above a stuffed armchair, she hung her Sampler, suspending it from an iron nail which she hammered into a stud-post.

"Now you have something of me to remember. Pray that you will always keep it."

"I shall always," he whispered with a kiss to her cheek.

"Good! Now let us go to the Festival" She reached for his hand. "You will want to hear Oh:nehsi:yo speak."

(58)Chase, Franklin H. Chronological Index of Onondaga History in the Documentary History of the State of New York. *Syracuse Journal*, March 2, 1903

(59)Parkman, Francis Count Frontenac and New France under Louis XIV, Chapter 3, (1880) pg: 27.

(60)Lamb, Martha J. The Magazine of American History. Kessinger Publishing Company, (2007) pgs: 524-525

(61)Borneman. Book Two: Mr. Pitt's Global War. Chapter 12 *Falling Dominoes* (2006) pgs: 193-194.

*Aptly named the Swamps, the region which came to encompass Water, Dill, Garden, and lower North Streets in Auburn, NY, remained periodically submerged in water until drained by white settlers in the early 1800's

(62)Taft, Grace E. Cayuga Notes. Chapter I. Antiquarian Publishing Do., Benton Harbor, MI. (1913) pg: 5

63)Taft (1913) pg. 6.

CHAPTER THIRTEEN

Turning Point
A Plan of Action.
Lord Carleton's Uninvited Guests.
A Grim Discovery.
Watkins Is Honored & Wed.
A Man Betrayed.

Matthew spent nearly two days convalescing at Pointe Aux Bois. He emerged from bed chambers in his parents' cabin to take nourishment and to attend to bodily functions, but otherwise remained apart from intercourse with family members. James and Caroline observed his daily coming and going with interest and concern. On the third day of self-induced confinement he displayed a bit of enthusiasm when he asked his mother for a bowl of her esteemed oatmeal topped with maple syrup, a breakfast favorite since infancy. His return to the family circle provided James and Caroline with an opportunity to open a dialogue with him. James sat opposite Matthew. Calm, James allowed him the luxury of savoring the meal before beginning soberly:

"Welcome back to the land of the living, son. Did you rest well?"

Stretching, Matthew scratched his head: "Forgive me for acting so far-removed. I am trying to recover my bearings." Again a scratch and then: "Whatever happened out there, father?" Barely audible, Matthew appeared tired and distraught. Dark circles hung beneath his eyes.

"I found you lying on the cold, hard earth, half-frozen and shaking with fright. Do you remember it?"

Matthew put aside a spoon. He threw back his head. Covering his ears with his hands he proceeded to repeat in a heightened voice: "The men! Did they make it? Are they all right?"

Suzanne came to sit beside him. She stroked his arm, but James still held the floor:

"Some of them made it, son. Others died. You are fortunate."

Matthew displayed no signs of hearing James. "I led quite the fight! Did I not? Tell me I fought well," he exclaimed. He rapped the table before him, sending the silverware to scatter wildly.

Caroline approached Matthew. Sitting beside him, she forced herself to smile: "Matthew. You are at Pointe Aux Bois. Your father and Suzanne and I live here in this French post. We have lived here for most of the past year due to trying circumstances. Life has been difficult, but we have survived in part because we are surrounded by strong friends. You, however, tried to capture the post at the head of a squad of his Majesty's soldiers at the insistence of their leader." She spoke almost in a whisper, struggling to remain dispassionate. Her delivery completed, Caroline sat back regarding her son.

Matthew stared straight ahead, countenance expressionless. Suddenly he reached out, striking his forehead with a fist: "Capture the garrison? Kill my family? No!! He looked directly at Caroline: "Mother. Is that you? How is it that I am here?" He spoke rapidly, his words melding together.

Caroline looked to James for guidance, whereupon he reiterated in abbreviated form the Le Rocher account of the short yet intense battle at Pointe Aux Bois. He looked for signs of remembrance in Matthew's eyes.

Matthew sighed, then blurted: "Am I a *prisoner*, father? Are we all *prisoners*? Where is the Captain? He will set matters straight." He looked about the room. Lowering his head to his chest, he breathed deeply, showing signs of distress wrought with confusion.

James replied calmly: "The Captain is a prisoner. **We** are not prisoners, son. **We** are among friends here."

"Father. The letters I sent you. Did you receive my final letter? No! Of course not. By then you left the farm on your search and you came here." Matthew rubbed his head vigorously: "I did not expect to find you here. I have never heard of this place. Do you believe me?" he asked plaintively, speaking rapidly, words in a flurry.

"Yes, son. I believe you," James replied calmly. He patted Matthew's head. "Let me tell you my story—at least a part of it. Are you ready?"

"Yes. Yes." Matthew panted. "Oh, I am so confused." He held his head in his hands. "Oh! I have such a tremendous headache. Please tell me what is happening—someone." He stared wide-eyed ahead, sitting on his hands, tipping at the edge of the chair. To begin James told him of the Captain's effort to seize the post.

Matthew sat calmly, expressionless, betraying neither thoughts nor emotions. James touched upon the battle in segments, for he did not care to burden Matthew with details at this tender point in recovery. He allowed Matthew to absorb the few sketches that he handed out to him, waiting for him to enter the dialogue once memory served him better. At length Matthew asked the question which James and Caroline loathed to hear, for it compelled them to respond in ways which may bring him undue stress. Looking from James to Caroline and back again, Matthew asked:

"Are you saying that the Captain is at the root of *your* troubles?"

"Yes, Matthew," James replied, soberly, gripping his son's arm.

"That is a great load to place on one's doorstep," Matthew returned, shrinking back.

"Your mother and I are prime witnesses to the deceit and madness, son. I know you placed faith in him, but . . ."

"He told me that I was out to defend the Expeditionary Forces from attacks by heathens and foul French," Matthew interrupted, looking away momentarily. When again he faced James and Caroline he did so through watery eyes— red and bloodshot. He wiped away copious tears, but to no avail. Sighing, he hung his head low. Sobbing freely, his chest rose and fell. "He deceived me too, you say?"

Seated beside her brother, Suzanne spoke reassuringly to him: "You did not know any of our travails, Matthew. Do not despair. Mother and father are about to visit with the commandant at Oswego. Do you want to accompany them? I believe that the meeting will do you a good turn."

Matthew sighed: "Here I sit, a prisoner of the French and soon to be banished by the marines. The marines! I gave them my whole life." He wiped tear-filled eyes. "I am in Nowhere Land. I belong to no one—a living corpse abandoned in the wilderness." He threw up his hands in abject surrender.

"You belong to us—your family. We will never abandon you, Matthew," Suzanne returned.

When Matthew spoke, he slurred the words: "If I may speak with the Captain."

"He will speak with no one, Matthew. Mother and father will tell their story to the commandant. He will compel the Captain to speak, unless, of course the commandant condones the Captain's exploits."

"No, no. Nothing of the sort. The two of them are distinct opposites. Each man has his own view of the frontier. Like myself, Lord Carleton stands quite unprepared for what you have to say." He looked about him, as though wrestling with a great burden. "You say the Captain is a prisoner. Will there be a trial?"

James sensed Matthew's return to a state of harmony. He decided to relate the rationale for seeking an audience with Lord Carleton: "Matthew. General Le Rocher believes that **you** will be able to offer testimony against James Worthy, for you have served with him first hand. By your own deeds, Lord Carleton holds you in high esteem. Your testimony will go a long way in establishing credibility as a witness if they carry the support of one such chief officer." He laughed lightly. "You may emerge from all of this a hero. If there is sufficient criminal evidence gathered, there will be a trial. It will be inevitable."

"Are there other witnesses, father?"

"Yes. Some of them are known to you. Your mother, Suzanne, and I of course are willing to serve. Others are scattered about the territory. They are being sought even as we speak. Some are reluctant undoubtedly and must be persuaded. It is a matter of seeking the truth—something that we your family stand for and hold dear."

"It appears that the Captain has left an impression upon many throughout the land. I will want to meet with these witnesses. Perhaps we will learn who the Captain really is after all. Yes. I will meet with the commandant."

James smiled. "Good, son. We *are* a family again. Come into the parlor. I want you to meet someone."

A beaming General pumped Matthew's hand, urging him to strike a trail immediately. He led Matthew to the parlor window where he pointed out a mounted escort in the waiting.

"I hope they have not come for me," Matthew remarked in jest. Everyone laughed, whereupon Caroline served Matthew a light meal. Rising at the end, he embraced his mother and donned a favored trail hat, a broad-brimmed, leather piece fitted with a pheasant's feather. "This always brought me good fortune," he spoke with assurance.

On the concourse the General handed Matthew the reins to a fast trotter. Choosing mounts, the family swung into position behind him, leaving Matthew and the General to lead the procession out of the post. Aboyant remained behind with Marchand, much to Suzanne's dismay. The little party descended a steep bluff directly north of Pointe Aux Bois, gradually curling down to the beach front and the low road. A short distance away lay the crossing point from Lake Onondaga to the Oswego River. Their objective, Fort Oswego, lay to the northwest at the river's end.

The General brought an escort of rangers. About twenty strong, each ranger carried stores and supplies to sustain him for fourteen days. Each one carried a pouch of dry rations in a saddle bag on horseback. A staunch girdle about the waist provided accommodations for a shot-bag filled with lead pellets, a powder horn filled with black powder, a pistol with holster, knife with scabbard, a hide or sack filled with drinking water, another hide of medicinal compounds, a pouch of tobacco, and a small carton of matches and chips of flint. Across the shoulders each man suspended a bedroll. Habitually the bedroll held items of toilette, rolled into a compact cylinder: one or two changes of undergarments and stockings, a woolen shirt, laces for trail boots, and writing and eating utensils. Slung over an available shoulder each man carried a musket, long and heavy, but effective at intermediate ranges. Each man also carried trail watches and calendars, gifts from the General. Marking on a calendar, he asked the men to do the same. He called out the readings: "Sunday, November 5th, 1760."

A number of rangers believed that the General brought too few men along on what they determined to be a hazardous journey. They feared reprisals from armed bands and voiced concerns to him when barely beyond the palisades of Pointe Aux Bois. In the interest of preserving the mission, the General called a meeting at the Onondaga crossing, gateway to the Oswego River:

"This much I know with certainty from my reconnaissance. Lord Carleton is unable to spare additional men to pursue me. Pointe Aux

Bois is secure at this point. Do not forget. We are holding over one hundred and fifty of his men there. It is unlikely that he will request men from Canada where His Majesty's soldiers have expended a great deal of men in taking Montreal and Quebec To do so opens him to sharp criticism and censure. I dare say that this disturbance in the Lake Country merits the attention of the Crown to any great extent. Nay! The Crown knows nothing of it, and will not as long as the commandant remains open to our terms. Also, gentlemen, I believe that in moving forward, a small force casts us in the light of negotiators as opposed to warriors. Questions?"

A ranger called: "We have no further questions. C'mon men. Let us move out. Daylight is a wasting!"

Before embarking anew, the General proposed building a strong case against the Captain by engaging Lord Carleton's full support in bringing him before the bar of justice. To that extent he announced the intention of conducting a Gentleman's Agreement with the commandant, in anticipation of reaching favorable peace terms before word of Lord Carleton's defeat reached King George's chambers and the irrepressible William Pitt— a man well-known for vindictiveness. A student of history, the General noted to the men that, following the death of the benevolent William Penn, the frontier became a region hotly-contested by British land agents and corrupt governmental officials who exercised unscrupulous measures in separating the natives from their lands. They fought hard to take that which was not by decree theirs. Here the General clearly alluded to the Captain without calling him by name. In closing, he gave the impression that Lord Carleton was more tractable and posed less of a threat to French and colonial interests than did the Captain. He neglected to discuss the circumstances leading to Penn's fall from grace: having become embroiled in political turmoil at home, spending less and less time in Pennsylvania, relinquishing influence over Pennsylvania's affairs, and falling victim to scandal at home (64). Nevertheless, with Penn's death, George III ascended the throne and the religious and political freedoms which Penn inaugurated in the Americas stood to pass from the scene as the new monarch prepared to establish tight reins over colonial possessions. This last included inexorably the Iroquois.

The General, ever the student of history, having recognized the transfer of power in the monarchy, looked for one brief moment during the period of the interregnum when he would be able to proceed with his own designs on his own terms in treating with what he termed the British Problem in the Lake Country. For him that moment arrived with the death of George II prior to the ascension of George III. Therefore, he saw nothing amiss in drafting terms of peace for Lord Carleton at a moment when the commandant, his command awash in slave-trafficking, stood too weak and embarrassed to oppose him. In sum he believed Lord Carleton amenable to terms, in as much as he intended to present them in a more generous and conciliatory package than any which Parliament would prefer upon him. Where he viewed Lord Carleton more of a victim at the hands of a treacherous colleague, Parliament, he knew, would see him as an administrative failure and castigate him harshly.

It is this logic that the General disclosed to the little party in council. Again he asked for commentary and Caroline York insisted that the terms call for (1) the relinquishing of the soldiers taken at Pointe Aux Bois in exchange for the court-martial of James Worthy on British soil and (2) the termination of slave-trafficking at Oswego and like British-held garrisons. At that point the General advised James that he brought him along to lend support to Caroline's demands. He advised Matthew that he brought him along to open a dialogue with Lord Carleton, for he knew that the commandant regarded Matthew highly. He then read from a list of intentions: "I propose trying one James Worthy in the presence of Lord Carleton for crimes against human-kind, including, but not limited to theft, abduction, physical abuse, slave-trafficking, and murder for the purpose of personal gain or profit." The principals applauded heartily, whereupon, without further delay, the campaigners struck out once again on the trail in a state of lightheartedness.

* * *

Under clear skies the campaigners followed the least deviating of pathways. Upon passing the treacherous falls near Neatahwantah, they reached the outskirts of the stony works at Oswego in only three hours by the General's watch. Matthew called out to the guard's tower, gaining immediate entrance for himself and principal others. He made small banter with the guards before passing to the commandant's residence, fending off all manner of glances from curious bystanders. In transit no one demanded that the party present credentials, due in part to his celebrity. On the contrary, men offered to accompany Matthew to the commandant's parlors. Bringing up the rear, the General took delight in observing the degree of deference paid to Matthew. Greetings flowed freely to the young marine, intermixed no less with nuances of doubt and consternation from among some of the more inveterate skeptics.

With gait restrained and posture ram-rod straight, Matthew mounted the flight of stairs of the commandant's spacious porch. Aspect sober, his general appearance reflected the solemnity of the occasion. Behind him the escort of twenty rangers split equally into two columns of ten at the foot of the stairs. Coming to parade rest, the men faced each other from opposite sides of the walkway, eyes locked in concert across the way, rifles with bayonets attached astride the right foot. Once Matthew mounted the stairs, the men gave a salutary click of the heel in unison. They stood tall in stiff waistcoats, polished boots, and trail breeches, full and gathered at the knee. Having gained the porch, Matthew extended a hand to a familiar figure, coupled with an approving nod and a smile of acknowledgment.

"We meet again, Mr. Smythe. We have been apart far too long."

"Come indoors, Matthew. Your host, Lord Carleton awaits you."

He entered a cavernous set of rooms, the walls of which rose to a towering height, enclosed beneath a dome-shaped ceiling. He fondly recalled the previous visit with Dana Smythe and Lord Carleton not long before. He crossed to a comfortable divan where he seated himself.

"The commandant, Lord Carleton!!" boomed a voice, heard, but not seen.

Matthew jumped to his feet. Doffing the trail hat, he bowed lightly.

"That will not be necessary. Remain seated, Matthew," a spirited Lord Carleton replied, briskly crossing the oak-empaneled flooring, heels clacking beneath him. He extended a hand, whereupon Matthew took the opportunity to introduce members of the primary party.

"Pleased to meet with you, Mi'lord. Allow me to present my father, James York. Beside him is my mother, Caroline, followed by my sister, Suzanne. Last of all there is my dear friend, the General Guillaume Le Rocher."

"Come and sit, gentlemen and ladies, one and all," Lord Carleton returned cheerfully. Gripping Matthew's hand he guided him to an expansive table, a highly-polished, rectangular work of art finished in mahogany. It stood in the center of the spacious room, its sculptured legs tapering into lion's paws. Upon seating himself, Matthew glowed with pleasant surprise when his image bounced upwards to greet him from deep within the table's veneered surfaces. Lord Carleton's manservant placed Dana Smythe to Matthew's right. To his left he placed the General, followed by James, Caroline, and Suzanne York. Seated alone across from the visitors, Lord Carleton called for iced-tea and crumpets to be served.

"I find it exceedingly difficult to conduct affairs on a dry palate," he intoned, the baritone voice filling the great hall. Sipping tea, he continued: "Although you arrive unannounced, let it be said that I conduct my public affairs in the tradition of the gentleman." He smiled and a degree of expectancy enveloped the room, although the visitors appeared well at ease. He whispered instructions to a servant and the man strode briskly through a portal. "I await the breaded pudding topped with vanilla and raisins. One must not conduct affairs on an empty stomach," he recited, eyes gauging the guests.

Suzanne made no secret of her hunger. Once dessert arrived, she ravished it while the elders dined leisurely. Finishing, she shifted about, casting half-glances at Lord Carleton, eager for the council to begin. A state of readiness mounting, she knew that her reservations spread to others of the party. After what seemed an endless delay, Lord Carleton dismissed the servant and called for the meeting to begin. In a most casual manner he addressed the General:

"This meeting lacks for one principal guest."

"Ah, yes, Sir. I have him safely stowed within my garrison," the General returned, facetiously.

"His aide. Do you have him as well? Simmons is the name."

"If you mean a certain officer in white garb. No. I have him not."

"You have a great deal of my men, according to my new aide, Caldwell."

"They are in my charge and well cared for."

Lord Carleton threw back his hands: "Caldwell has returned, so much the worse for wear. I ask: How am I to operate this garrison without my regulars, much less repair Ontario?" He wiped imaginary contaminants from his starched tunic and pushed aside dishware.

"You have to adopt new strategies for fighting on the frontier. Caldwell is yours, by the way. I do not want him," the General quipped. While his words hung over the cavernous hall, he began anew: "Sir. In all due respect, I do *not* want your regulars, nor my *principal guest*, for that matter. I have barely enough stores in reserve for my own residents to see them through the coming winter. You are invited to reclaim your regulars." The General allowed the words to linger.

"And what do you ask of me in return, Monsieur!" Lord Carleton asked demurely.

"You and I shall establish an exchange. A trade, if you will, Mi'lord."

"Allow me to make a conjecture, Monsieur. You propose that I grant you the prerogative of confining my chief surveyor in exchange for releasing my own men to my custody." He smiled tartly, fingers tapping the table.

"You are partially correct. I propose to return your soldiers on condition that you place my *guest* on trial, cease all movements against my post, and clean your ranks of slave-traders."

Lord Carleton said nothing for a long moment. When he spoke he feigned a light protest:

"A trial? For whatever reason, my good man?"

The General turned to the York family: "I give you *four* reasons, Lord Carleton: Meet James, Caroline, Suzanne, and Matthew York." He alluded to the principals with a grand sweep of the arm.

Instinctively Lord Carleton challenged them to offer testimony worthy of acceptance in a court of law:

"By all means, let them speak, Monsieur. Let us begin with James. James York, you say? Very well. Speak! James York."

James took the floor unabashedly: "Thank you, Mi'lord. I have longed for this audience for an eternity. My wife's abduction at the hands of James Worthy brought me to the Lake Country in search of her. My daughter Suzanne and I followed bits of evidence and rumor over many dangerous paths. Eventually all roads pointed to the Captain and once I discovered my wife, she chose him as the true culprit who spirited her away from home. Along the way I enlisted the aid of General Le Rocher and a host of friendly aborigines. In the process of finding Caroline, I learned that I stepped into a situation far more complicated than the abduction of a woman."

"Continue James, if you will." Lord Carleton leaned forward with interest, fist tucked under his jaw, eyes locked upon James's every word.

"My knowledge of the Captain goes back to my residency at Osco. He stormed Osco, a village of the Cayugas. He pillaged it. He burned it. He rode off with furs and native youth. Suzanne and I lived in the village at the request of the good-hearted chieftain who saved us from a raging storm. We witnessed the Captain's madness first-hand. Unknown to him, Suzanne and I followed him while he continued in the same vein to pillage native villages over the countryside. I did not know initially that he forced my wife to ride with him. She, nothing short of a prisoner against her will, he planned to keep as a consort and servant. Native youth, I learned, he sold into slavery with the assistance of confederates. My companions and I tracked the Captain here to Oswego, where, in the dead of night, we witnessed a most bizarre spectacle taking place: the sale of young natives. He is indeed an evil man. I defer to my dear wife, Caroline."

Lord Carleton took additional tea, gulped it down, and, calling the aide, whispered quickly into his ear. The man scurried away through a portal. "Please continue, Madame York."

Caroline, exercising due restraint, spoke:" My abduction coincides with my first meeting of the Captain. Every Friday I ventured into town to sell my produce. James and I kept a farm on the Susquehanna in Delaware country. My daughter usually came with me. We resolved to stay within calling distance of each other. On a particular Friday, which I shall always remember, we became separated and the man fitting the Captain's description lingered at my booth long after other people moved on. He asked me about some goods and when I turned to fetch them, he scooped me into his arms. He stuffed a cloth into my mouth and put a blindfold over my eyes and rode off with me to a remote location. I remember hearing many different voices around me—much laughing—the sounds of men coming and going. Under threats of injury to me and my family, he forced me to travel with him in exercises against the peaceful natives. He once jailed me in the corral of a Seneca town for refusing to bend to his wishes. He henceforth brought me to Ontario on a forced march, confining me in a pen on the grounds of the garrison. It is the attack of my husband's companions which set me free.

"On the eve of my rescue the Captain and an ugly, burly, scowl-faced man held a sale before the gates of Ontario. Beneath the full moon and blazing camp fires the Captain turned over a generous number of young natives to that man. The spectacle galled Monsieur Le General and the native warriors who came with James in search of me. They witnessed the entire transfer of these defenseless humans into slavery. The Captain and the ugly man and one other, a dapper sort, disappeared into the bowels of the fort, following the sale. Incensed, the natives laid siege to Ontario, subduing it. They did not torch it, however. The fall of the garrison led to my freedom. Other native captives of the Captain found freedom with me. The warriors sought after the three evil men without success. James later found an underground cavern beneath the ravaged grounds. In a far corner a doorway opened to the steep bluffs leading to Lake Ontario. However strange, James found the remains of human habitation in that cavern equipped to support a family of five or six for a fortnight."

Lord Carleton sat speechless. He took a few notes. "Your story is fascinating, Madame. My chief surveyor's nocturnal maneuvers come as a surprise. The cave poses even more of a mystery." Sipping tea, Lord Carleton spoke with conviction: "I believe your story has merit. The cave explains the rapid disappearance of the accused. Upon my inquiry, I recall the Captain telling me that Simmons vanished entirely without a trace. Your story tells me that all three men departed by means of the cave. In retrospect, the Captain did not confide in me the existence of such an underground passage. I knew nothing of it. It is therefore something that he created. He displeases me. Essentially, the cave is the only means available to avoid detection or capture." He drummed fingers nervously. "When I pressed him, the Captain explained to me that he was off in Niagara bargaining for a transfer of marines from the Newfoundland fisheries. Your account places him at Ontario. In all likelihood, he watched it being ravaged before abandoning the premises. This is abominable. I held certain suspicions about him over the disappearance of my sutler's stores. Now I know by what route they departed the garrison. He lied to me. No one *ever* lies to me."

James spoke: "Sir. A tunnel descended straight down. I stumbled over it in error. It was in the form of a long, cylindrical opening, great enough to admit one man comfortably."

"The route by which everyone abandoned the garrison, the natives as well," Lord Carleton submitted, falling backward in a high-back.

The commandant's man-servant returned shortly. Beside him stood the commandant's house servant. The small, bronzed native of about thirty years bowed before Lord Carleton and spoke hurriedly to the man-servant. Nodding, the man-servant approached his superior:

"Lord Carleton. I have a message of importance,"

"By all means, Carruthers."

"Sir. I place great faith in Domenico to tell the truth."

"Yes, yes! Proceed, Carruthers!!"

"On the night in question, Sir, Domenico went to the Captain's rooms to tend to his needs." He paused.

"Continue, please," an irritated Lord Carleton returned.

"Domenico was unable to find the Captain there, Sir. He looked in other rooms to no avail." He stood motionless, head lowered deferentially before the commandant.

Blushing scarlet, Lord Carleton brought the palm of a hand down strongly upon the table top. "That man! What does that man hold me out to be?"

"I am sorry, Sir."

"That is all right, Carruthers. You may go." Turning to the guests, Lord Carleton gave an explanation: "I asked my servant to make inquiries concerning the Captain after he returned from the west. It is good that I did." He stroked his chin. "He bears watching and, by your stories, I see that you speak the truth as you know it. You stand united in your convictions, so much so that I hesitate to ask Matthew his thoughts." His expression dour, the commandant summoned the fortitude to call upon Matthew.

"Matthew, lad. It is your turn. Please carry on."

"Before the incident on the St. Lawrence took place, I knew nothing of the burly man, **Black Jack,** nor of the presence of my family here on the frontier. In all truth I came to Oswego in answer to a call which the Captain made to build up the defenses of the fort. Little did I know that it was all part of a ruse which the Captain hatched to gain favor in the eyes of superiors. I now have reason to believe that, during the siege of Ontario, the Captain occupied himself by consorting with the burly man to sell off young natives. These maneuvers I knew nothing of— apart from his official duties. I thought him a hero to the degree that I begged to accompany him to Pointe Aux Bois. He told me the enemy lay hidden in an old mission, prepared to strike out in the slaughter of innocent settlers. Pointe Aux Bois to me loomed as a place of evil until I learned the truth." He smiled toward James and Caroline. "I am not the only one deceived here. It is only after my capture and discovery by my own father that I came to my senses. How strange is that?" Matthew slumped forward. Tears filled his eyes.

A candid Lord Carleton spoke: "My sutler, Van Schaack, kept a storage depot at Ontario. He housed furs there bound for market. I knew it to contain a wealth of valuables. In any event, he often reported missing pieces and Van Schaack, mind you, if anything, is a superb 'enumerator.' If he states a theft has been made, I support him to the letter. I place his 'word' next to that of the Almighty for truthfulness." He leaned wearily forward, and, facing the family, made a declaration:

"I believe that I have heard ample testimony to pursue a case against my surveyor. Matthew, I must tell you that **Black Jack** has escaped. Two of my guards have been killed in the process. I spoke to the Captain before his capture and he tried to deflect my concerns. Now that you and others have come forward, I believe that we are able to proceed further. Of course you require additional witnesses. Allow me to make some inquiries."

Matthew nodded understandably and Lord Carleton continued, although in less than buoyant form:" The pirate's escape and your account of the cavern shake me to my foundations. By process of elimination it is evident that the Captain escaped by means of this underground passage. Looking back, he has led a *double life* in my opinion, achieving success in chosen duties on the one hand and reaping great profits in his *secret* life on the other. Now that I sit here and ponder, I recall the manner in which he deceived me. When I first asked him why he absented himself from the garrison in her hour of need, the Captain convinced me that he merely responded to an earlier obligation to go to Niagara to secure reinforcements for the frontier garrisons—Ontario among them. In my mind this looked to be a strong argument, given that Niagara has long recognized a dearth of fighting men. Little did I know that the redoubtable Captain persuaded Niagara's commandant to call upon the Crown's marine reserves in Newfoundland, dispatching from that region a ship to sail to Oswego staffed with marines. In looking back, I thought the Captain's unannounced departure on the eve of the siege strange, although at a distance his efforts appeared commendable. Nevertheless, I judged him guilty of deserting his post at a critical moment, and of leaving Ontario in charge of a subordinate officer. He sought to redeem himself, I recall. He contended that Pointe Aux Bois harbored marauding aborigines and that the French gave them shelter.

He declared that the leading of a solid strike against the post would restore order and balance to the frontier. I offered him the ultimatum of making good on his claim, or being forced to forsake his commission. He accepted the challenge and set off in high spirits."

"If I may interject, Sir," the General interrupted.

"Yes. Yes. By all means."

"If it will help you sort out your thoughts, Sir, I caught a glimpse of the Captain standing with the pirate on a bright and festive occasion, during your late absence. It turned out to be a slave sale. I must stress that he knew not of my presence on the parade grounds. This tells me that prior to the siege of the garrison he absconded with all the valuables that he was able to carry: the native youth and the furs from the cavern. In my estimation, he set the fort ablaze, counting on the flames to call attention away from himself. During the heat of the assault, the tunnel and cavern provided him with the means to escape. This is the only acceptable explanation of the matter."

The General struck the table with clenched fist: "I believe that he assigned the aborigines to the pirate as a matter of course who spirited them away on a skiff or frigate. Each one of the three carried out an integral role, allowing the feat to be executed without a snag. All three have honed their skills to the accuracy of a cutting edge."

"I am hard put to assign a party to track the pirate at this point," Monsieur, Lord Carleton offered.

"I understand. Perhaps that is not necessary. Your Van Schaack has knowledge of the Great Lakes forts. There is no love lost between him and the Captain in my estimation. Perhaps Van Schaack will make inquiry of the pirate along his trade routes. Tell me. What amount of influence does he carry in the land of the lakes?"

"Henry Van Schaack (65) has traveled far and wide. He is well-received in many ports."

"Good. You say that you primarily entrusted the Captain to watch over the garrison in your absence?"

"Yes. I often go on hunting forays once a month. It is my form of diversion—a much needed respite from pouring over unending budgets. I am pledged to account for the Crown's expenses, leaving me precious little time to enjoy this great land." Tugging a starched collar, Lord Carleton smiled tentatively.

"That is it!!" the General cried. "The Captain held a slave sale to coincide with your monthly recess. I believe that on the night in question he joined with the pirate, the two of them sailing to Niagara with their charges. Currency exchanged hands. The Captain bade his partner farewell, returning here to base with a fortified defense."

"You paint a colorful portrait of events, Monsieur." Lord Carleton sat back as though a great weight had been removed from his shoulders.

"Given the events and the players, this is the one explanation for it all," the General conceded.

Nodding in agreement, Lord Carleton made several notes. Looking up, he acknowledged Caroline York.

"Sir. In my intercourse with the natives of this land, I noticed something of peculiar interest. It is the women who play the leading role in the day-to-day operations of the villages. Because of the women-folk, ancient family traditions are kept strong, laws are formed and carried out, and children are fed and clothed and schooled in the native tongue. Indeed, the home is the center of the universe, a sanctuary in which the women have established binding rules of conduct for all."

"I have heard stories to that extent. Is there a point to be made?"

Caroline bristled slightly, but remained on course. "Far more than obedient servants, the women represent the true strength of the village. Sir. It is the women who supply the central beliefs necessary to sustain a village. They pass them along by word of mouth in the maintenance of oral traditions. By their unique position within the village governing body, the women are revered by one and all. I have spent the majority of my days as a free woman at the side of the wife of a village chieftain. By example and word of mouth she taught me the truths of her People's way of life. This discovery truly amazed me. By contrast the world from which I issued, and the one in which you reside, holds women in a subservient status to men and within a rigid hierarchy. For example, women own no property, are not permitted to cast ballots, do not voice their opinions in the assembly for fear of reprisals. They are forbidden to challenge their menfolk at home, and are denied advanced schooling. All this rings of subservience.

"Sir. My point: Given this restrictive setting in which some of us struggle to survive, it is little wonder that servitude and bonded indebtedness have escaped deep scrutiny in courts of law anywhere in the western world. What are these institutions in essence? Mere substitutes for subservience, whereas the value of certain members of the human species is reduced to its simplest form and held there by the policy-makers who make the laws of the land. On the Continent abduction and human bondage are rife. They are so tightly interwoven into the community that they have become an accepted part of it. By contrast, the number of reformers that come along are few and far between. Those who survive chastisement and censure find themselves without the necessary public support to put much needed reforms into place. Sir. My point. The Captain and others of his cloth see nothing improper in carrying on these age-old practices. In their own eyes they are merely following entrenched pathways, fully aware that legislation has not caught up with the injustices which they visit upon innocent victims in their charge."

"You are saying, Madame, that the people of the forest are far advanced over the western world in terms of paying homage to women?"

"I am saying that the self-serving makers of western policy have cut women and youth out of the community mainstream, denying them the prerogative of making choices and decisions for their own welfare."

"This is a very complex matter which is not at issue here, Madame."

"Oh, but it is, Sir. The manner in which a civilization treats with its women and children reflects upon the quality, the worth, the productiveness of that civilization."

"So it does, Madame. Let us leave that to the lawmakers and press on."

"I think not, Sir. They have been reluctant to address the matter for generations. It is because of the general reluctance to act that the matter persists to this day. Our terms for peace, may I test your memory, call for equal treatment of women and children in concert with their menfolk."

Lord Carleton looked to the General for clarification of the terms.

"Madame is correct, Lord Carleton. A small section of the terms calls for the establishment of rapport, that is, amicable relations, in the treatment of women and children who are in the presence of or under the guidance or care of the male of the species, regardless of race."

"I expect you to present me that section before we adjourn, Monsieur."

"With certainty. Madame believes that this is not too much to ask of a leader as well-known as yourself in the Americas. She believes that keeping the peace extends to providing for all manner of folk without regard to their rank or standing in the general order. Implementing the plan here within your purview will carry universal ramifications. You will go down as a benevolent and knowledgeable leader. You have nothing to lose."

The soothing litany found its mark, leaving Lord Carleton to rest comfortably. "That is conceivable, Monsieur Le General. Let us move ahead. After all, I am your captive agent to the tune of two hundred of my men."

Caroline asked Lord Carleton to discuss his method of treating with women and children.

"Over the years I have instructed all of my officers to treat with native peoples as hosts in their own land, and we as guests, accordingly. I have instructed them to extend every form of accommodation to them when in their presence. Of course there are exceptions . . ."

"When the lives of your men are in danger."

"Yes. Of Course. Let me be frank, Madame. Basically, I am opposed to James Worthy's marginal conduct in the furtherance of duty. Moreover, his unsanctioned liaisons lead me to question the ability to lead. By all means I intend to delve into this matter in all haste. If I find him to have conducted himself in ways disparaging to the Crown's intents and purposes in the Americas, he will pay a severe penalty."

"Sir!! You have confined your response to the immediate disposition of the Captain without entertaining a policy respecting women and children, namely, all those under the care and supervision of an army of occupation. You must admit, were such a policy in place, replete with stringent penalties, I would not be speaking with you now. Indeed, the whole of the Captain's escapades would not have taken place as we know them."

"I must admit that your argument is compelling, Madame."

"I merely seek justice for women and children—*all* women and children. It is a way of ensuring the peace that we are about to conclude. Justice restores order to the community. Indeed, it defines a civilization."

"Human justice," a jubilant Suzanne quipped, writing in her journal.

"Thank you, dear. Yes! Human Justice! So be it. Sir. Your countryman, William Penn, practiced such a form of justice. He established a colony bearing his name where everyone, women and natives alike, held the prerogative of addressing the assembly with a list of acute needs. Indeed, Penn's *experiment* proved that people of diverse backgrounds are able to live in peace. Do you agree?"

"Yes, of course, Madame, but William Penn died and all chaos broke out among his heirs and agents."

"This is true. We both know the details. Disorder replaced order. The weak and dispossessed suffered and the community structure became torn to shreds by hordes of armies sent in by the rich and powerful."

"Something tells me that you placed me in the midst of that statement."

"Pure accident. I assure you. However, Sir, unlike Penn, you are alive and in a position to make lasting changes, perhaps even earning the final respect and admiration which history denied to Penn."

"I am sincerely at a loss to oppose your requests, Madame. Lord Amherst will send me no men without demanding an explanation and I fear that I have not been able to put a suitable one together. Besides. I do not care for this entire affair to be known beyond the confines of these rooms. I am at your mercy, Madame, yet I believe that under the circumstances we may be able to support each other's ambitions." Lord Carleton reached for some tea. Sipping it, he studied Caroline York carefully.

"Good. I request your opinion on yet another pressing concern. It is a burning matter infecting the frontier. It is another form of subservience of which we have spoken. Simply, it is the importation of cheap and servile labor."

Lord Carleton tugged at his starched cuffs." I myself do not subscribe to the subjugation of a species, nor do I condone it among my officers and staff."

"Yet until now you have not contemplated erecting a policy prohibiting such a practice."

"Madame. Let me assure you that the entire British Empire holds no written policy in that regard. The Crown has no formal stance on the matter since no binding measure treating with the aborigine species has been introduced before Parliament. All matters of governance thereby fall to the discretion of the provincial governing body and its chief administrator." He leaned forward intently.

Caroline held her ground: "But *you* are the governing body in the Lake Country."

"That I am, Madame. However, I am reluctant to set a policy where there exists no history of a criminal act."

"Recent history has given you to believe otherwise. Agreed?"

"Yes, Madame. In light of your disclosures and the testimony I have witnessed today, I confide to you that many of the travails suffered by the aborigines and other disenfranchised inhabitants of this country will dissolve with a successful conclusion of the Captain Worthy affair."

"I am agreed, Sir. It is a step in the proper direction, although we both know that neither justice nor laws are able to compel people to love each other."

"It is outstanding leaders who have brought diffident peoples together. This situation is no different, Madame."

"Caroline cocked her head to one side: "I believe that I have met at least one of them already."

Lord Carleton regarded Caroline closely, dwelling upon her words. At length he spoke:

"I am drawn by the opportunity to make a gesture toward benefitting human-kind, yet I recall that you hold imprisoned a great deal of my men. Therefore, I shall perhaps never know that what I am about to conclude is either an act of selflessness or simply the fear of incurring His Majesty's wrath. Let me ask you." He bowed his head.

"By all means, Sir."

"If I give you my support, you will henceforth dissociate my name from all correspondence, conversations, documents, and decrees having to do with the Captain. It is he, after all, who so insisted upon assuming a command, not I." His delivery made, Lord Carleton reclined in the high-back, looking straight ahead.

"You have made an excellent choice, Sir," the General returned, joining Caroline. "Your stance is well-received and we in turn will support you in defending your good name before one and all."

"Very well. Let us come to terms on the return of my men and the surrender of the Captain on the understanding that this is an agreement among gentlemen." Finishing his tea, Lord Carleton smoothed his silk vest and rising, stood facing the General. He brandished a faint smile. A full head taller than the Frenchman, the commandant looked him squarely in the eye and extended a firm handshake, after which he circulated about the table offering a hand to the remaining principals. Before Caroline he bowed and pressed her hand firmly.

"This of course will neither be documented nor repeated in provincial offices."

"As you wish, Sir." The General bowed. "I believe that we have reached an understanding."

—

Shaking with alarm, Carruthers rushed to the commandant's side. A distorted countenance announced to all that the man stumbled upon a compromising situation.

"There is a disturbance without, Sir. Your presence is called for."

A hand falling to his sword, Lord Carleton rose sharply. With a great sweep of the arm he motioned Matthew and Smythe to accompany him, whereupon the three men beat a hasty path to the porch of the mansion. Coming to rest three abreast they witnessed an altercation in progress on the front lawn. There, a section of Lord Carleton's guard and scattered members of the Le Rocher rangers engaged in taunting each other to the point of exchanging blows. Matthew York and Dana Smythe fired pistols overhead, temporarily halting the mêlée. A hand shielding his sword, Lord Carleton passed among the disputants, drawing them apart while calling for a resumption of order. At length the combatants obeyed his entreaties and the commandant invited a number of them, chiefly soldiers of the BEF, to search for a peaceful solution to the fracas.

One of the first to come forward, a short and slight of build army regular, he doffed his cap and, shaking Lord Carleton's hand, regarded the commandant entreatingly: "Sir. In my travels with the Captain we have tread hard by Death's Door on numerous occasions. That he is an apt surveyor, yeah, but a leader of men he is not. He is fit with an *evil streak* which compels him to put his own ends before those of the corpsmen."

Drawn by the man's frankness, Lord Carleton asked him to proceed: "Please go ahead, Mr. Dobbs."

Dobbs gripped the watch-cap tightly. "Early this season the Captain struck a native village. To this day I know not where it stood exactly. He drove us through the night to find it, claiming that he sought revenge for an ambush which the aborigines set for us on the preceding eve. If you ask me, there is little knowledge to support this claim. In a rage he gathered up women and children, wagon loads of furs, and set fire to the village, shooting whoever among the natives tried to stop him. The

Red Men fought back strongly. They sorely beat us, causing us many casualties.

"Taking stock of losses, the Captain went mad. He raced up and down the countryside, looting native stores, burning villages, and running off with women and children. Sir. I have thought long and hard about this incident. Whatever is that man doing with all the people he has snatched away? There is only one answer to it: He sells them on the slave market— making a tidy sum in the process."

"These are serious charges, Dobbs. Are you willing to take them before a magistrate or judge?"

Wringing the cap between his fingers, Dobbs shivered: "The Captain conducts clandestine affairs. They usually happen in the dead of night and always when you are away a'hunting. To you he is a surveyor of note, but we know his true passion." Dobbs looked about him and a low swell of voices rumbled through the crowd.

"I see, Mr. Dobbs. You do not speak alone."

"Yes!! I do not speak alone. I speak now because I know that the Captain is far and away in a place where he is not able to find me."

"Very interesting, Dobbs, yet all the while no one flying your stripes has approached me with concerns."

"The Captain purchases the loyalty of others, and with it their silence. They are sworn to secrecy under penalty of death. Many men profit from the slave trade, Sir," Dobbs conceded, lowering his head in deference to the commandant, "but I am not one of them."

"You are saying that in my command reside those who conduct prohibited maneuvers?"

"It is commonplace, Sir. I try to keep my head bent low and my eyes half-closed when on assignment."

"I am aghast, Mr. Dobbs, but thankful for your honesty."

"There are others of my kind. We have struggled to keep our distance from the Captain. We refuse to be bribed or intimidated. It is only now that I am free to speak." Quickly he ushered an associate before the commandant.

"Sir. I am Mr. Rice. I genuinely support the claims of my comrade, Mr. Dobbs, and ask permission to speak."

"Granted, Mr. Rice."

"Sir. I harken back to Dobb's story. He and I camped together during the fated campaign upon the village. On the night in concern, preparatory to assaulting the village, the Captain became convinced that we was under siege by hostile natives. In the dead of night he ordered a mass evacuation. He did not think to study the land in advance and many men plunged over an escarpment to certain death. An ambush never came. His ravaged mind invented the entire affair. When he regained his senses, he grew enraged. Striking off toward the village, he plunged into it recklessly, costing many more men their lives. His anger mounting, he set about plundering neighboring villages at will. He invented yet another tale which claimed that the natives owed him a fee or toll for his steadfast defense of them against the French—which, of course, they refused to pay. Sir. Britain's troubles with France have come to an end. A peace is in the offing, unless I miss my mark. In my mind he has no argument for conducting raids." The spare, bearded man stepped to the side. Bowing, he extended an arm to a comrade beside him: "I give you my friend, Mr. Samuels."

A short, stocky man ambled forward on a crutch, an arm bound in a sling. Before speaking, he regarded his comrades with a smile, a sign that brought them to mill about him. Approaching Lord Carleton, the man gestured toward his injured extremity. He spoke with candor and conviction: "I present you, Sir, what remains of one Mr. Samuels—battered, but not broken." With those words his comrades chanted his name.

"Sir. I lay at the bottom of a ravine. Along with other comrades, I believed myself more dead than alive. Dobbs and Rice and Hastings came to my rescue. Their intelligence in putting together a plan brought about my rescue and salvation from certain death. While the Captain deserted the grounds, my comrades saved my life. I owe them my life." He shifted his weight and began again:

"I remember seeing the Captain consult a trail watch during the rescue operations. I later learned that he fully expected to push ahead without rescuing the wounded or burying the dead. With stern pressure from the aide, Simmons, he relented. However, he sent us back home without a full escort and sufficient transport wagons. He maintained that the *enemy* must not be allowed to escape and that every able soldier and conveyance must be enlisted to pursue him. Sir. In my mind the Captain saw demons where none existed: where the demons existed solely in his mind. He saw the *enemy* under every rock and twig on the trail. Watkins tried to snatch him back to his senses, but he killed him."

Lord Carleton interrupted: *"Watkins?* Is he not the one who struck a superior officer, namely the Captain? Did he not defy an order to advance upon the belligerents and so abandoned his post?"

"Yes, Sir, but many of us are troubled over the disposal of Watkins. You see no one has *found* his body, which places into question how he met his end. I must say, Sir, that in light of present-day circumstances concerning the Captain, Watkins performed most-admirably. He is one to be honored, not chastised." Turning to his comrades, Samuels met with overwhelming approval in the form of brisk 'hurrahs.'

Lord Carleton assumed a conciliatory tone: "I confess, Mr. Samuels that from the beginning I found it disturbing to believe Watkins capable of such objectionable conduct. Moreover, given that a body has *never* been found, we must assume that he still lives. I refuse to close the book on the life and death of Watkins."

"That, Sir is the basis of our altercation here on the grounds. Some of us say that he is long since a goner. The French with Monsieur Le General maintain that he eluded the Captain's death sentence. They declare that Watkins is far too clever to be snared by one whom they term a Bungling Rogue."

Lord Carleton reflected momentarily before responding: "You must recall that we-all of us- have accepted that Watkins died from shots fired to prevent escape. The Captain told me as much and I believed him. Looking into the matter from your point of view I find that Watkins may have safely eluded pursuers and escaped into the unknown. The men chasing him merely reported a falsehood. Aware of the Captain's impudence and wrath, I am able to understand their reasoning. Mr. Samuels. Are Watkins' pursuers up and about? Are they still with us?"

"No, Sir. They perished in a subsequent skirmish with the aborigines."

"I see. I have no need to learn their names. I am drawn by the possibility that Watkins is alive and I praise you for giving me the opportunity to pursue the matter further." Gripping Samuels by the shoulder, the commandant escorted him up the porch steps, across the veranda and into the spacious mansion.

"I want to introduce you to some colorful souls very familiar with recent events in this region. If there is a Watkins, they may know of him all too well."

Lord Carleton introduced Samuels to James, Caroline and Suzanne York, who, during the disturbance out-of-doors, scattered to all points of the great hall. Once reassembled, the commandant introduced Mr. Samuels.

Samuels delivered a passionate speech, his voice a pleasant monotone: "I have a friend, a fellow soldier with whom I have spent many hours on the trail. He has always been loyal to just causes and brave beyond question. Most recently he challenged the absurd demands put upon him and the corps by a stern and unrelenting task-master. My friend has always sought the truth and worked tirelessly to find it. When his superior ordered an all-out assault on an aborigine stronghold, my friend refused to be a part of it. He even tried to prevent his superior from going through with the project, knowing full-well that his own life lay in the balance. I am told that he died at the command of his superior— murdered— but I refuse to believe it. I believe that my friend lives on to fight another day to bring to justice the scoundrel who tormented him." His voice cracking, Samuels daubed at tears. He spoke under increased labor, showing outward signs of grief and a veil of melancholy descended over the room. Suzanne spoke, if only to depart from the moribund tenor of the moment:

"Your friend. Who is this man? Pray tell?"

"He is a loyal friend. His name is *Watkins*."

Suzanne gasped, fingers darting to her lips. James and Caroline York sat impassively, yet exchanged knowing glances. Sensing these nuances, Lord Carleton came to stand behind James and touching his shoulder asked: "Tell me what you know about this *Watkins*."

James asked to speak privately with the General. He reasoned that to speak of Watkins meant speaking of the Round Tops in the same breath, the sanctuary of his friend, the Bear Chief, a tract of land unknown to the British command at Oswego, and hence free up to that point from reprisals and the ravages of the war. The General advised James to tell what he knew of Watkins, now that Lord Carleton gave a promise to set forth charges. Nodding, James took the floor:

"Sir. I am able to tell you that indeed there is a Watkins. He *is* alive and well and resides in the Lake Country. "He has been very helpful to my family in seeing them through the rigors of life in these harsh and unforgiving climes. He has always lived in pain of death from an avenging Captain and for that reason I hold his residence in secrecy.

Upon the court-martial of the Captain, Watkins will be willing to present valued testimony."

In deep thought Lord Carleton stood tall facing James, jaw straight forward, chest arched. "I understand, Mr. York. Let me tell you that from all that I have heard today there is a strong foundation for a court-martial. You may rest assured that Watkins and all witnesses will be protected from injury and bodily harm. It appears that a court-martial is the only civil way to determine what has transpired here behind my back, so to speak. Of course, Monsieur Le General, you will, upon the conclusion of a court-martial, irrespective of the results, release my men to me as a condition of my compliance with your terms."

"Of course, Sir—as a condition of your compliance," the General offered the commandant his hand.

"Very well, then. Let us get moving," Lord Carleton returned, succinctly, permitting himself a brief smile.

* * *

The early investigation completed, the Bear Chief and trusted companions. Cerf Courant and Teedyuscung, returned to the home of John Rhoades. He believed his efforts thus far a moderate success, although the name of a single assassin failed to surface. However, furnished with two more possible suspects— Simmons and Hastings— the Bear Chief believed that the incident of Charles Martin's death involved the labors of more than one man of consequence. He breathed a sigh of relief upon gaining this knowledge, for he knew that under certain forms of persuasion, whetted by incentives, allies often turned one upon the other. His task lay in applying that persuasion. Once having found these men or suspects, he intended to gain greater knowledge about the Charles Martin incident by playing off one suspect against the other. Little did he know that certain events were coming together which would make his task less onerous, and, in a certain sense, enjoyable.

John Rhoades invited the three campaigners to a sumptuous repast. He spoke about aiding his neighbor, Teedyuscung, preserve the fragile peace between the onrush of new settlers and the resident Delaware, ever-aware of William Pitt's aggressive colonial policy (66), one which favored the removal of the waning elements of French influence in the Lake Country. In a testimonial to Teedyuscung, John Rhoades extended a covenant of eternal friendship to the Delaware chieftain and his Cayuga ally, the Bear Chief. With regret he explained that the recent withdrawal of the French from the Lake Country left the Delaware and other native populations open to exploitation in matters relating to the jurisdictional sovereignty of aboriginal lands. A member of the colonial legislature, John Rhoades offered to intercede on Teedyuscung's behalf. Furthermore, in the role of church elder, John Rhoades promised to open inquiries about the Martin affair among church leaders along the Susquehanna frontier:

"Gentlemen. You are not able to be in all places at all times and yet you must keep your suspects under strict surveillance. With your permission I will contact members of the Friends in communities near and far to you. They will serve as additional eyes and ears and will report to me faithfully regarding the habits of the men you have drawn into suspicion. Let me assure you that I am about to make the name of Charles Martin a high point of my speeches when I meet with church members." Taking a sheet of parchment he transcribed the several journal entries from Charles Martin's ledger, signed his name to the Bear Chief's letter of introduction, and, folding both documents, placed them in the Bear Chief's cachet bag.

"Please present these to your commandant, Le General Rocher, gentlemen. They are proof of Charles Martin's authentic claims." He rose, offering this hand.

The Bear Chief turned to Cerf Courant: "Deyo:danohyanihdoh. Henohweis. Howayenhe:oh."— "Awesome. I like him. He is a learned man."

Grasping John Rhoades' hand, the Bear Chief spoke once again: "Ejidwadro:he"—"We will be meeting again."

—

The way back to Pointe Aux Bois found the little party in good spirits, due largely to the pleasant encounter with John Rhoades. En route they saw fit to stop over at the homes of several of the Friends where the Bear Chief proudly displayed John Rhoades' signature to all who came forward to meet him. The travelers met with cordiality and undue politeness at the hands of the Friends and entertained entreaties to sample some of the foods for which their hosts became well-known along the frontier. It is at the outskirts of Shamokin that the two campaigners took leave of Teedyuscung at the home of a Friend who invited the Delaware leader to come sit with him on his porch.

Knapsacks stuffed with comestibles, the Bear Chief and Cerf Courant resumed travel. Proceeding by foot and horseback, the men retraced the original route northward. Eager to convey their findings to Le Rocher, they chose to travel by day and night. They sought the high ground once again, cresting ridges and bridging valleys, along an Appalachian spur which would gradually descend into the vast Onondaga valley. Under a fiercely blue sky to guide them, the travelers commanded an infinitely clear and expansive view of the rolling lands which lay at their feet many leagues below. Periodically the Bear Chief surveyed the landscape with a lens or scope, a gift from Le Rocher. At one juncture he made note of the date by consulting his trail calendar: Saturday, November 11th, 1760. Marking good time, he hoped to reach Pointe Aux Bois on the next day, Sunday, in order to join in the Mass with his friends, the Yorks.

Through the lens he inadvertently discerned a billowing, white plume coursing lazily upward through the dense canopy below. 'Strange,' he thought. 'No village to my knowledge lies there.' He allowed the lens to linger, keeping all thoughts to himself for the moment; yet, at length Cerf Courant grew curious and pressed forward:

"Deho:nisagyeha?"—"What are you doing?"

"Je vois de la fumée en bas,"—"I see smoke below," the Bear Chief answered in French.

"Gatse:se"—"Let me look at it," his co-partner broke in, borrowing the lens.

"Hmmm. Te:deknohweis. Deho:de:nedwa:gye."—"I do not like it. What will we do?"

Already in motion, the Bear Chief called out: "Agatgehsehe"—"I am going there to view." Starting down from the heights he called over a shoulder: "Otowegeh:gwadih:ha:ge."—North side. I am going."

Swinging into step behind him, Cerf Courant exclaimed: "Wa:jihya:i;wi:e:kne."-Just wait. I want to go with you."

Together the master woodsmen tethered their mounts out of view, then began a laborious descent from the lofty crest. Into the thick underbrush they stole after having committed the spot of smoke to memory against the horizon. It lay a full kilometer ahead, they ascertained. Fearlessly they began picking a path through the intense forest. Pursuing a direct course, the men steadfastly conquered all obstacles in their path. In so doing they turned and twisted and vaulted over boulders and fallen limbs. They surged through thickets and clumps of nettles and hurdled over clusters of poison ivy and poison oak. Stemming from the closeness of the forest about them, a dampness filtered through the trees numbing their fingers and faces, and, when they spoke to each other, they caught sight of their words forming in tiny beads of moisture before their eyes. Alarmed, the men moved on quickly, encased in a shroud of chilling vapors in a misty realm removed from sunlight and its warmth, where the vapid odor of mold and mildew filled the nostrils and a viscous gel of a sticky liquid formed in the throat.

Presently a raw and repugnant stench rose up to assault the senses. Trapped deep within the forest canopy and fed to the men by gentle vapors, the malodorous aroma hung in perpetual suspension. The thick, pungent, yet sweet-smelling odor clung heavily to the men's clothing and exposed extremities. Bringing tears to the eyes, it tore at the lining of the throat and nostrils. Coughing and gasping for breath, the two woodsmen bent low to the earth. Progressing at a snail's pace, they struggled to maintain bearings within the bosom of the dark and damp forest. Something horrible lay ahead, the men feared, something dead or dying, the victim of recent and savage predation and they attributed the strange odor to that of burning flesh, eviscerated and charred and left to bake under hot coals. Despite a growing urge to depart the region, the men pressed wearily on, senses fully-engaged to react to the slightest alarm. In silence they crept along the forest floor, bent low at the waist, weapons drawn, disturbing not a single leaf nor twig. All the while with each step the forbidding odor bore down more heavily upon them, testing their resolve to the limit.

Up ahead a broad shaft of sunlight penetrated the forest canopy. The men stepped along briskly, eager to explore the welcomed nuance. Descending straight to earth, the beam broke over the forest floor to reveal a spacious clearing awash in sunlight and devoid of trees and forest greenery. The robust woodlands terminated abruptly where the clearing began so precipitously that the men came close to breeching the opening and stepping out into full daylight. Retracing their steps, the two woodsmen sought shelter, and, when securely hidden from view, peered out into the clearing, devouring all that fell in line before their eyes.

They spied a lone tree. Spare and truncated, it inhabited the center of the clearing. Its limbs stripped away, the tree displayed the ravages of centuries-old devastation. A great fissure cleaved the trunk of the tree, wide-open from top to bottom, exposing the interior to all manner of abuse from wind and rain to worm-infested burrows. Lichens and mosses lined the trunk's blackened core, most likely the site of multiple conflagrations down through the years. A nest of sorts rested in the bottom of the trunk, suggesting that, apart from its unsavory appearance, the trunk occasionally provided temporary lodgings for the forest's frail creatures. A blackened urn stood directly before the tree. From deep within issued the unmistakable signs of embers burning, crackling and sizzling. Fitted with green, immature boughs across the opening, the urn sent forth bales of smoke. Wide enough to contain a human, the urn glowed deep red around the upper reaches. Their gaze fixed upon the urn, the pair initially disregarded the silhouette of a figure slipping, almost gliding, over the field. A pair of tongs in hand, this shadow-figure of a man stealthily approached the urn. Halting beside it, the man applied the tongs, toppling boughs from the urn to the earth. He fastened upon one in particular. Shaking and probing it, he tossed it decisively to earth and proceeded to pick amidst its smoldering tendrils. In so doing he succeeded in releasing that deadly-sweet fragrance so reminiscent of death. In a detached manner, the shadow-figure nibbled fiercely at the bough's limbs for a short period. Grunting with satisfaction, he licked his lips, tossed the limb upon the earth and glided effortlessly away.

The Bear Chief studied these concerted movements from the shelter of the hiding-place. Together with Cerf Courant, he withdrew into the forest to confer and at length determined that he stumbled not upon a man at labor, but upon the scene of an execution. These limbs, the pair deduced, were the remains of *human bones*.

A commotion from within the clearing prompted the woodsmen to creep forward. At a safe distance they inspected the field, whereupon they spied a bedraggled crew approaching the tree. Encircling the crusty, scarred shell, the small party sat down cross-legged on command. Native youth, shackled at the waist, they expressed no outward signs of distress. Spare and gaunt from lack of nourishment, the youth sat meekly, awaiting a command or suggestion.

Presently a party of men came up beside the tree. Laughing gaily, they ranged among the youth. The men wore the earth-colors of the *forest rangers*, a tough Canadian crew noted for hand-to-hand combat, excellent fighters in close quarters, where the pistol and blade excelled over larger, more powerful weapons. Emerging from the rangers' circle, a man, dressed not like the others, obviously the chosen leader, stepped along sharply. He wore the colors common to a British officer: red tunic, leather breeches, long black patent-leather boots. The handsome and trim officer boldly faced the youth. His hair, the color of corn silk, stirred in the soft vapors. He adjusted the broad white collar of his shirt, before brandishing a sword. Flexing it slightly, he called out:

"Bring the prisoner forward!"

Pulled by soldiers on a chain secured about the wrists, an aged native man walked in lockstep. Bronzed from a lifetime of exposure to the sun, the man's frail skeleton strained against loosened flesh which hung suspended from his frame like a thin, porous sheet of parchment. He uttered gruff tones in what the Bear Chief believed to be moans of pain and anguish. Along with the youth seated nearby, he displayed the signs of advanced starvation. The man turned slightly and the Bear Chief caught a disturbing glimpse of the hollowed cheeks and the cavernous eyes about to drop from their confines. The man's sallow complexion did little to mask the sooty, dusty aspect of his countenance, which, from a distance imparted to his features a grim, deathly pallor— the image of a dead man walking. Stumbling on fragile limbs, the man recovered his footing sufficiently to come to rest before the sword-bearing officer. The guards withdrew and the wizened creature drew to full height, albeit consumed by pain. Facing his chief tormentor, he stared the officer boldly in the eye.

"I understand that you carry great influence among your followers," the officer spoke, tapping the old man's shoulder with the blade.

"If that is true, I would not find myself here with you now," the old man replied. Speaking with difficulty, he coughed and began to foam at the mouth. Several of the guards reacted by laughing, composing themselves after the officer admonished them. He continued with his quarry:

"Be that as it may; however, you have but one way of saving your spare bones the fate of a defector's death." The officer paused to allow the speech to be translated, then: "I need from your village strong and healthy youth, not more examples of these simpering skeletons." He gestured menacingly toward the solemn-faced youth.

Having established a modicum of stability, the old man replied: "The strong and fleet of foot escaped when they caught sight of your horsemen. They will never return to their village. They know your history of starving your prisoners. I envy them their freedom."

"You are telling me that you refuse to track them for me?"

"They are scattered among the winds. You will never find them. Soon they will tell their story to all the inhabitants of this country and you will have to walk with your head low to the earth and look over your shoulder with each step that you take. I am unable to assist you." He spat on the earth at the officer's feet, coughing up a thick, paste-like substance.

The officer looked about him. All eyes fastened upon him. Calmly he spoke: "So be it. I will relieve you of any further discomfort. You too shall have your freedom." Taking a step backward the officer lashed out with the sword. With the thrust of an expert he cleaved the old man's chest cleanly from a point below the throat to the pit of the stomach. A thin, red ribbon formed, then erupted into a torrent of the prisoner's life blood.

The old man staggered, but did not cry out, nor drop to the earth. With great effort he spat into the officer's face, smiling victoriously. Angered, the officer drew a trail knife. Plunging it into the man's chest, he held it firmly in place, sneering at him through clenched teeth, all the while meeting his victim's eyes head-on. Still standing, the old man refused to fall. Staggering forward, he grasped the officer about the shoulders, expelling yet more bile, whereupon his antagonist, shouting in anger, slammed the poor creature to the earth. Stooping, the officer retrieved the knife, leaving the man where he lay, inert at his feet in that indeterminate region where life ends and death begins.

The officer daubed at the lapels of the once crisp, white tunic, now mottled with traces of his victim's blood. Applying medicinal alcohol, he rubbed the fabric vigorously, achieving modest success. Cursing the stricken figure at his feet the officer called out: "Take him! Put him into the tree! Burn him!"

The guards heaved to, eager to commence the grisly assignment. Jesting among themselves, they dragged the old man to the base of the hollow tree. Four of them lifted him upright, one man for each appendage, pressing him into a standing position within the blackened cavity. The old man neither moved nor protested and no one attempted to take measure of his state of being. A soldier took several turns around the tree with a stout rope, binding the old man tightly within the crevice, the coarse fibers ripping at the pulpy flesh. In all likelihood the old man had already released his spirit. No one really knew, for the guards and the officer seized this moment to congratulate each other. Afterward they came to stand before the captive youth to make certain that they witnessed the dispatching of one of their elders—an elder who refused an officer's order.

With the flick of a match, the brush tightly packed into the base of the hollow cavity erupted into flames. Quickly encircling the ravished elder, the flames rose steadily and, intermingling with plumes of smoke, enveloped the old man. He moaned pitifully and in response a Huron confederate of the soldiers tossed heaps of dried leaves into the inferno. Other Hurons joined him in crying a chant before the whole lot danced around the tree howling in the manner of frenzied dogs.

"The old man is Delaware, Fearless One," Cerf Courant whispered.

"Yes. This is true. We must save the children. Are you ready, my friend?"

Cerf Courant nodded knowingly. Drawing an arrow from a sheaf, he notched his bow.

"Spare the officer. He will face another form of judgment."

The two woodsmen stepped from the hiding place. They fixed eyes upon targets. They chose a hide-and-run attack: firing on the soldiers from behind ground cover, shifting to a new position, and firing anew. Upon scattering the enemy they planned to capture several of them, secure the children and escape from the clearing while the remaining soldiers took flight. They believed the soldiers' numbers few, a small body, but one capable of retaliation.

Cerf Courant struck first. His arrow pierced the breast of a Huron. The Bear Chief readily dispatched another of the ignominious Hurons. Taking advantage of ground cover, the pair prepared to make selections from among the soldiers themselves. The burning of the old man afforded them the opportunity to strike while the enemy remained preoccupied with the ritual and spectacle of the burning. The woodsmen struck swiftly and silently, the arrows making not a sound. The soldiers died instantly, so quickly that not a word crossed their lips. Subsequently, several of the soldiers lay dead before their comrades became aware of their destiny. Suddenly, with the stark realization that they resided within a killing-field, a startled few shouted in alarm. The entire body fled the clearing in heated confusion. Screaming into the forest, many of them threw down arms in order to gain greater footing along the irregular terrain. In all of an instant they vanished in total, leaving in their wake, the self-assured officer— the old man's chief accuser— to his own devices.

The officer, cowering before the victors, begged for his life. He offered a credential to the Bear Chief before dropping to his knees. To that end the Bear Chief inspected the man's purse. He found him to be British and proceeded to speak aloud the man's name letter-for-letter. The man trembled, and shaking his head, uttered his name at his captor's insistence:

"It is Hastings. I am Hastings—a British officer."

The Bear Chief, in one swift motion pulled the officer upright. He bound him tightly and marched him off into the forest where he secured him to a tree. Cerf Courant severed the children's bonds, bidding them to follow him. He dispatched two youth to bring back the mounts with promise of a reward. The two woodsmen gathered those few soldiers unable to flee. They suspended operations to carve out a grave for the old man beside the smoldering tree. Fitting a mound with a cairn of stones, they bowed in reverence to the one who sacrificed his life so that others of his kind may live. They never learned of the elder's name, but vowed that his story would be told in campfires for as long as the People continued to exist.

* * *

The rains having abated, the Festival of the Ripe Corn began in earnest at the Round Tops. Servers and bearers carried trays of foods to the shelter which housed dining accommodations for the celebrants. In this, the third portion of the Festival, celebrants gathered to dine and listen to the principal speaker of the afternoon. Fawn and Watkins assisted in the preparations, he dutifully following her instructions. Fawn looked radiant in a new gown of combed deerskin. Colombe

Blanche too appeared in her finest raiment. She adorned the dining tables with seasonal blooms and herbs and the boys, also nattily attired, placed mats and bowls and eating utensils in their proper places. In a pocket Colombe Blanche rubbed the golden stones. Turning them over, she looked to the heavens and silently praised the Lord of the Forest for granting her a warm and pleasant afternoon.

With everyone comfortably seated, Oh:nehsi:yo, the guest speaker, passed among them. He bade good tidings to all before climbing a small platform facing the gathering. To his immediate right sat Fawn and Watkins, followed by Colombe Blanche and the two boys. The esteemed chieftain looked out upon the audience, rose to full height and began to speak:

"You, the residents of the Round Tops, I honor you in your new home. You have labored long and hard to create this village, a monument to your faith and dedication to the People's way of life, where families may live and grow in peace and prosperity. Your great leader, the Standing Bear, first cousin of Tah:gah:jute, has led you over a difficult trail in a courageous effort to secure your place in history. In so doing, he has delivered you from the clutches of evil on numerous occasions. His largesse reaches out far and wide, for, even now as I speak, the Standing Bear is far off in the land of our neighbors, the Delaware. He is trying to solve difficulties, which have placed the People and the peaus blancs at odds. I am confident that he will succeed in his mission.

"In his goodness the Standing Bear has offered the Round Tops as a haven for the sick, the wounded, and the oppressed. So it has come to pass that this man on my right side, Monsieur Watkins, is among the celebrants of this Festival. It is under the Standing Bear's superior guidance that Monsieur Watkins has come to develop the quality of providing for others, becoming a miniature image of the Standing Bear himself. Such is the power of the Standing Bear, who is known affectionately by several names. He has seen fit to develop within others a greater sense of strength. This is the essence of his goodness which benefits those who come close to him, those who teach others, those who lead by example.

"It is with humility therefore that I dedicate this Festival on equal terms to the Lord of the Forest, to you the villagers, and to the Standing Bear and his disciple, Monsieur Watkins. In the absence of the Standing Bear, Monsieur Watkins has become the surrogate parent of his family.

Moreover, Monsieur has faithfully discharged the duties which the Standing Bear has reserved for him. Similarly, he has executed the meticulous plans for creating the Round Tops. Furthermore, Monsieur has accepted the way of life of our People without condition and has earned their deep respect as a result. In so doing he has also earned the faithful devotion of the young flower who sits at his side. She, the Fawn, or Dewahohde:s, has approached Colombe Blanche, wife of the Standing Bear, to begin the process of adopting Monsieur into her extended family. Her request carries the approval of the clan mothers who met earlier in discussion. Before he departed on his journey, the Standing Bear made known to me his intentions. Therefore, I ask the man who has gained the universal support of the Lords of the Nation to rise."

Fawn elbowed Watkins who, having no foreknowledge of his newly-acquired status, sat passively at her side. At her insistence he rose and, bewildered, bowed from the waist, facing Oh:nehsi:yo. The chieftain spoke:

"Monsieur Watkins. Is there any reason for you to refuse adoption into the Bear Clan of the Gayono:hogo?"

With Fawn translating, Watkins uttered "no," having no knowledge of the turn of events around him.

"What name have you chosen?" Oh:nehsi:yo asked.

With Fawn's help Watkins uttered "Deyojia:n:edo:t,"—Stagdeer—"in honor of one sorely missed."

"The name is accepted upon presentation of the wampum."

Fawn produced a single strand of white shells. Handing them to an amazed Watkins, she whispered: "Walk slowly to Oh:nehsi:yo and hand them to him, palms opened."

In leaving his place, Watkins stumbled over a leg of the banquet table. Guests rushed to restore order to the table settings. Someone guided Watkins to his feet and the ceremony proceeded on course without scorn or sarcasm leveled at the unfortunate Watkins, for the guests understood the historical impact of the occasion.

Poised and unperturbed, Oh:nehsi:yo continued: "Your gift is well-received, Monsieur. Its value is beyond the ability of words to describe. You may rest assured that the People will, by your token, regard you with the respect and dignity which you justly deserve."

With arms raised aloft, Oh:nehsi:yo spoke loudly and clearly; "I now pronounce you a full member of the Bear Clan of the Gayono:hogo based at the Round Tops, your adopted village, subject to all the prerogatives and limitations thereof"(67). The esteemed chieftain permitted a thin smile to cross his lips, a gesture which set the congregation to declaring its own form of approval. They shouted praises, slapped their hands together, stomped upon the hard earth, setting into play every sort of expression of candor within the limits of established boundaries. Caught up in this outpouring of warmth, Watkins stood tentatively at attention before the throng. Throwing up his arms, he beamed a broad smile and rendered his appreciation in a few, well-chosen words. For a moment he stood apart from the crowd, absorbing the accolades of the congregation, which followed him as he returned to his place at the table. There, he wept briefly, leaving Fawn and Colombe Blanche to welcome him with open arms.

—

Oh:nehsi:yo promptly donned a *gestoweh:* the ceremonial headpiece of chieftains. He drew a long, ankle-length robe over his shoulders: a vestment of fine furs. He beckoned to Colombe Blanche, whereupon she quickly gathered the boys and urged Fawn and Watkins to join her. Fawn beamed her understanding and, taking Watkins by the hand, preceded Colombe Blanche, coming to rest a few steps before the chieftain. Reaching behind, she accepted a string of shells from Colombe Blanche. She approved of the deep blue shade of the shells, their hue the color of her eyes. She passed them to an unsuspecting Watkins. He clasped them tightly, eyes directed forward.

The sagacious chieftain raised arms on high. The ample cloak billowed in the gentle vapors, imparting to him a regal aspect. He summoned the guests forward. They obeyed, in anticipation of the imminent ceremony.

"Gao:dehse!"—Come here, all of you! The guests joined arms in a great circle around Watkins and Fawn. Colombe Blanche and the boys stood in the forefront and Oh:nehsi:yo of the Gayono:hogo began to speak:

"I am pleased to preside at this Festival. Its memory will always reside in a warm spot in my heart. This Festival is of especial importance to me for several reasons. For one, it marks the opening of a new village, the Round Tops, the crowning achievement of a People once driven to the brink of despair. Like this couple, the village is strong and resilient and will endure for ages to come. Secondly, I am proud to welcome Monsieur Watkins to the Round Tops. He is the newest member of *any* race to have that distinction. He is testimony that the White Flesh and the Red Man are able to live together under one sky in peace. Third, I am honored to stand in as surrogate for the Standing Bear in this ceremony of adoption. In the same breath I am most honored to represent the Standing Bear in the marriage of his adopted daughter, the Fawn, to the man who stands beside her. I ask that the Fawn and her Chosen One, Monsieur Watkins, come forward."

Fawn clasped Watkins' hand and, smiling softly, guided him before the chieftain. She did not provide a translation of the proceedings thus far for fear of inserting an inopportune delay into the ceremony. Blushing slightly, Watkins stood firmly at his partner's side, unmindful of his role. in the proceedings. Now, with Fawn's assistance, Watkins reached forward, passing the string of shells to Oh:nehsi:yo. He otherwise stood mute, shedding a thin smile.

Accepting the shells, Oh:nehsi:yo beckoned the couple to face each other with hands joined. He extended his arms over the betrothed, commensurate with the rhythmic beating of a drum, and began to speak:

"This humble pair before me found each other when the land around them pounded under the heavy boots of an encroaching army of invaders, when the sky rained down burning embers from the enemy's big booming engines, and when their life as they knew it lay in certain ruin. They, however, clung to each other steadfastly, defying evil's presence, so strong and unwavering their devotion, that evil fled from their doorstep, leaving them with the opportunity to form a life together, a pair bound by trust, affection, and understanding, the very qualities that drove evil away and granting it no quarter in which to take root. They stand before us today, united, two acting as one. The success of this pair serves as an example of all that is good and just in this world.

"The members of the Standing Bear's family want all of you to learn of the devotion that this man and this woman hold for each other. By means of this ceremony they hope that you will share in their devotion and labor to infuse your own lives with the trust and affection and understanding which they have manifested to each other. This ceremony carries the sanction of Colombe Blanche, wife of the Standing Bear. You are her invited guests and the foods you have brought to this Festival will become a part of the gaiety and celebration of this marriage ceremony." From among the celebrants hoops of joy rang out. Bound by oath, Oh:nehsi:yo asked the critical question:

"I ask anyone to step forward to explain why this ceremony should not take place."

Again the earth shook with chants and shouts of joy, leaving Oh:nehsi:yo the benign task of instructing the betrothed to stand fully erect and silent before him. No one came forth to protest the pending union, whereupon he lowered a hand over the crown of Fawn's head. Speaking clearly and distinctly he asked:

"Do you, Dewahohde:s, the Fawn, take this man Monsieur Watkins, the Stagdeer, as your husband, to honor and obey, to cherish and to aid all the days of your life, through all of life's passages good and evil, to comfort him when sick, to encourage him to achieve to the depths of his being all the days of your life under the sanction of the Great and Heavenly Father?"

Facing Watkins, Fawn linked his fingers with her own and whispered softly: "I do."

Stern and resolute, Oh:nehsi:yo continued: Holding a hand over Watkin's head, he repeated the declaration:

"Do you, Deyogja:edo:t, take this woman, the Fawn, as your wife, to honor and obey, to cherish and to aid all the days of your life, through all of life's passages good and evil, to comfort her when sick, to encourage her to achieve to the depths of her being all the days of your life under the sanction of the Great and Heavenly Father?"

Watkins, his gaze fixed immovably upon Fawn, uttered: "I do."

"Have the attendants brought the rings of marriage?"

"They have, great leader of the Gayogoho:no," Colombe Blanche spoke.

Raven and Little Bear broke from the circle. Bearing pillows of down covered with combed deerskin, the boys came to rest on either side of Watkins and Fawn— each placing a finger ring of blue shells in the center of his pillow. The rings, chosen and fabricated by Fawn and Colombe Blanche, consisted of blue shells sewn into deer skin, secured by a clasp around the ring finger.

Ohnehsi:yo spoke: "May the passing of the rings begin."

A drum beat softly. A young woman stepped into view. Standing beside the chieftain, she raised her voice in song. Head high, she warbled in clear and dulcet tones, her voice ringing in praise of the young pair about to unite in marriage. Her song ended upon a signal from Oh:nehsi:yo. Raven stepped forward and extended his pillow to Fawn. She deftly plucked up the ring and, grasping Watkins by the wrist, placed it upon the third finger of the right hand and broke out into a solemn litany:

"This ring is a pledge to you of my deep affection and steadfast faith in your goodness."

With Fawn's guidance Watkins repeated the oath and placed the ring which Little Bear tendered to him upon the third finger of Fawn's right hand. Speaking tenderly, he appeared a portrait of blissfulness.

"Who shall speak for this man and this woman?" Oh:nehsi:yo asked.

Colombe Blanche came to stand beside the pair, According to custom, she chose a space beside the male. She spoke demurely: "I give my permission for this man and this woman to marry. Their union will make each of them stronger and the world will become a much better place because of their union. They will be able to conquer any adversity which visits them and build a proud legacy for generations to come. Already our village is a better place now that they reside among us. I wish them peace and prosperity from this day forward."

There remained for Oh:nehsi:yo to pronounce the marriage of Watkins and Fawn; however, at this point the congregation erupted in spasms of jubilation following Colombe Blanche's declaration. Fawn clasped Watkins about the shoulders, her head coming to rest on his chest. Oh:nehsi:yo forced himself to curtail the merriment in order to perform the final ceremonial obligation, according to the Iroquois Constitution. Thrusting arms aloft, he waited a long moment for the gaiety to subside before giving with the final declaration:

"I now name you husband and wife."

Immediately the congregation burst forth with acclamations of praise. Men whooped loudly and women tossed garlands of flowers at the feet of the newly-weds. Heeding Colombe Blanche, Watkins and Fawn walked in procession around the banquet tables, pausing to receive accolades from well-wishers. Oh:nehsi:yo joined Colombe Blanche at table— surrendering the speaker's dock to vigorous, young dancers.

In a long line dancers cavorted, a splendid cavalcade of physically-adept youth. They broke into pairs, a young man and woman in each and performed a series of challenging acts often seen in competitions of games of skill. The dancers performed various feats more notably named: broad—jumping, head-over-heels turns, walking on hands, and jumping through hoops, maneuvers intended for strong and resilient youth. Meanwhile, the congregants partook of the variety of foods on display, intermixed with samples from a myriad of sweetened beverages.

Through all the excitement Watkins and Fawn sat quietly. Along with Colombe Blanche and Oh:nehsi:yo, they observed the gaiety which took place in all quarters. The boys gained their mother's permission to indulge themselves at the banquet tables and later played a game of skill in which they drove a hoop along a serpentine path with a stick with others of their age. The game tested one's alacrity and dexterity and found the boys rushing to their mother's side to report early successes. As the day lengthened, congregants broke into small clusters where they renewed old acquaintances, generally enjoying the glory of the moment with friends and siblings. Elders conversed and young men challenged each other to foot races. The new man and wife waited to be served by the congregation where by custom they chose samples from among the many foods brought to them for inspection.

"This merriment makes me sleepy," Colombe Blanche stated.

"My bones ache after standing so long," Oh:nehsi:yo offered, laughing in self-pity.

"Eat, children. Eat!" Your bowls are still full," Colombe Blanche called to the newly-weds.

"We are much too tired," Fawn answered. "May we be excused?" she asked, standing.

"Of course, child. Here! Take these with you. My gift to you both." Rising, she presented Fawn with two embroidered woolen blankets, two pairs of moccasins, and two sleeping robes of bearskin.

"You see, the animals of the forest also rejoice in your marriage," she jested. "You deserve a rest. Go to it." The newly-weds humbly thanked Colombe Blanche. Then Watkins escorted his new wife toward his cabin. Behind them the merriment continued long into the early evening.

* * *

Teedyuscung returned to Shamokin, to an insular refuge tucked away in obscurity. He registered early optimism toward the Friends whom he met in traveling with the Bear Chief. They seemed committed to a theme of 'human justice' where it came to bear upon the death of Charles Martin. Perhaps their fervor would follow him to his doorstep. He hoped that the successor to former provincial secretary James Logan, a Friend, would speak well of him in councils with the new territorial governor.

He decided against pressing for land claims. The Friends already knew of his keen interest in his ancestral lands. Moreover, he longed to demonstrate compassion for others beyond his immediate race. Perhaps his participation in solving Charles Martin's death would bring him into greater credibility among the whites whom he characteristically did not trust. At least he left a strong impression among the Friends, recalling to them how the family of Tah:gah:jute, first cousin to the Bear Chief, christened the young orator with the name of Logan in honor of James Logan, Quaker and secretary to William Penn. He, Teedyuscung, gave the Friends to understand this knowledge with the expectation that word would pass down to the *new* governor pointing out the connection between the major players. He, Teedyuscung, hoped that by the strength of this historical bond, the new governor would return his original lands to him. He wanted to summon Tah;gah;jute, but he knew him to be away in the land of the Ohio where he strove to keep the peace with the whites. He left only his wife at home, his sons having run away to the west in the wake of a strong invasion of settlers. He made inquiry concerning her and learned of developments at once disturbing to him. She occupied herself, he learned, by traveling to the colonial assembly of Pennsylvania to make known a set of grievances. There, officers denied her admittance—her gender and race mitigating factors. Returned home, she filled his ears with horror stories, upon his arrival from John Rhoades' home.

"The settlers have stripped us of our lands. They say that we do not care for them properly as true tillers of the soil. They do not honor the promises that Mr. Penn made to our fathers. They treat us with contempt and have on numerous occasions, beaten, robbed, cheated and even killed our fellow Delaware. Only last week the wife of our neighbor found him dead beside his doorstep. Mr. Penn's younger sons are no better than common thieves. They lack the honesty and fortitude of their father. Indeed, they have given in to the Iroquois, namely Seneca, who, together with the settlers, have forced us to flee our homeland. All this has taken place in force since you left" (68).

Taken aback by this knowledge, Teedyuscung retired permanently to his cabin where he remained a perpetual recluse, his thoughts beclouded by the white man's cheap whiskey. He lashed out against enemies from behind closed doors, whipping together raiding parties along the frontier, yet they soon ran their course and died out and nothing basically changed in his favor. Alone for hours on end he drank and smoked himself into a stupor, setting fire to his clothing, some claim, by design. The colonial legislature made no incursions upon the slender parcel of land containing his cabin and out-buildings, their members perhaps sensing the inevitable. Shortly, his wife, overcome by his escapades, abandoned him, and one evening, according to legend, a party of strangers gathered outside of his home. Lighting firebrands, they carelessly tossed them upon the wooden cabin. The structure went up in smoke and flames and he failed to emerge from the ashes.

(64)Taylor, Alan & Foner, Eric American Colonies: Part 2, Chapter 12: *Middle Colonies: 1600-1700,*

The Penguin Group, (2002) pgs: 268-271.

(65)Van Schaack, Henry Cruger. Memories of the Life of Henry Van Schaack. Chicago: A. C. Mc Clurg & Co., (1892) Chapter 1: pgs: 1-5.

(66)Ayling, Stanley The Elder Pitt, Chapter 17: *The War: June 1757-January 1759.* David Mc Kay Co.,

New York, NY (1976). pgs: 229-232.

(67)Callison The Iroquois Constitution: *Laws of Adoption,*(1999) pgs13-14.

(68))Taylor, Alan & Foner, Eric (2002) pgs:322-323.

CHAPTER FOURTEEN

Transitions
Black Jack on the Move.
Samuel Kirkland & Friend.
A Gathering of Principals.
Fond Farewells.

Secure in self-imposed exile at Fort Detroit, **Black Jack** enjoyed life. Originally he purloined a skiff and fled straightaway to the fort along with his small band. Keeping close to the shoreline of Lake Ontario he entered Lake Erie and thence sailed its length west to its terminus. A fording place enabled him to sail north on the St. Clair River until he came to its junction with the Detroit River. At their crossing, tucked upon a sandy peninsula, sat Fort Detroit in the shadow of Lake St. Clair. In all, he traveled some five hundred miles, aided by the fresh-water vapors which skimmed his craft over the pristine waters. He knew the route well, having made innumerable voyages over the past five years, laden with a ship's hold of young natives bound for a life of servitude in ports of call along the frontier. Fort Detroit, no different from other garrisons of the day, required strong backs, arms, and legs to perform the numerous menial tasks, which, taken together, helped to drive early engines of commerce and manufacturing.

At Fort Detroit, **Black Jack** became an entrepreneur of sorts. By oral agreement he contracted with local Huron and Erie chieftains who brought willing young men to the fort to do labor. In return, the fort's commandant furnished the chieftains with a surfeit of goods, clothing, and utensils, articles which brought comfort to the aboriginal inhabitants by satisfying basic needs. Muskets, with ball and powder, objects valued at a premium, went to native leaders, who, in turn parceled them out to subordinates. **Black Jack** earned an allowance for having recruited these hardy youth, these new supplies of labor, a tidy sum dependent upon the success of his efforts, and one to which he looked forward with anticipation. Occasionally he persuaded the locals to part with their furs in exchange for additional largesse, although the fur trade as a whole lay in decline in and about Albany. Nevertheless, the great outpouring of goods to the locals drew them ever more into the French camp, nothing less than a growing state of dependency on the French for their livelihood. Now that he abandoned the British flag, he took up with the French immediately following his escape from confinement. A survivor in a land of loosely-formed alliances, he performed the functions necessary to put food on his plate and currency in his purse, all the while distancing himself from those associations which may earn him the hangman's noose. Overall, his superiors held him in good stead, a man true to promises and **Black Jack** settled back to occupy himself with the pleasant task of whetting the commandant's appetite indefinitely.

During idle moments his mind harkened back to his association with the Captain. 'The more he thought of the man, the more he detested him. Although he, **Black Jack**, introduced the Captain into a scheme of selling natives into bondage, he himself, much to his chagrin, never profited from the venture. By agreement he supplied natives to the Captain, transporting them to distant ports on the faith of the Captain's promise to recompense him.' He vividly recalled the Captain's explanation for withholding payment, one which he rehearsed over and over in his mind's eye:

"Periodic payments for our transactions will leave behind a trail of currency and all the wealth which it engenders, so tying us together, easy prey, ripe for detection by the unscrupulous. Better that I make you a single lump-sum payment down the road." Initially, the Captain's reasoning held merit in an occupation which depended on the utmost secrecy among all the players, and the fewer the players, the more successful the operation. After much thought he acquiesced, sealing their partnership with a handshake.

Nonetheless, a persistent thought groped at his vitals. The man of mystery who tried to kill him conjured up several questions, unsolved riddles at this point: 'How did this man happen by the cell door at the moment of escape? Who provided him with a key to the cell? How did he slip past the guards? Mysteries all and made more compound in the Captain's absence. He would find the Captain and collect not only dues owed, but answers sorely needed to insure peace of mind in light of the sleepless nights he spent tossing in the bunk cursing himself, temples pounding, bombarding him with persistent headaches.'

With spies in the field, loyal members of his band gave him to understand that the Captain now resided as a prisoner in a little-known French trading-post far-removed from the usual trade routes. They volunteered to conduct a search with him. One morning at the crack of dawn, with hearty enthusiasm and many sips of whiskey, **Black Jack** and several confederates set out from Fort Detroit by canoes, accompanied by native Huron and Erie scouts, men familiar with the lands surrounding the many lakes of the Lake Country to the east. En route he mocked the Captain's predicament, his disposition to no small end fortified by rum and brandy. The sheer irony of knowing that his former partner sat under lock and key gave him a momentary sense of satisfaction. On the other hand, in captivity the Captain lay exposed to the devices of interrogators, men dedicated to bringing to light the wealth of secrets the Captain so closely guarded concerning clandestine maneuvers—*his* secrets as well. The thought of exposure struck fear into him and he ordered the little band to travel by day and night without respite.

—

Meanwhile, the Bear Chief and Cerf Courant, pressing the captives hard, entered the Onondaga valley. Pointe Aux Bois lay straightway. The woodsmen planned to deposit them in the garrison stockade, already swollen with British prisoners. Arriving without incident, the Bear Chief learned of the Le Rocher sojourn to Fort Oswego. He considered joining his French ally there, but feared leaving the prisoners in the hands of the post's youthful guards. A sour note soon came to light, for on learning that the York family accompanied the General, he anticipated spending a dull period of disengagement at Pointe Aux Bois until his friends should return. Although comfortable among the post's residents, he preferred to remain detached from them, for he considered the York family genuine friends in whom he may confide without qualification.

From the beginning the Bear Chief noted the ease with which the man Hastings communicated with the noted prisoner-in-residence— the one who walked with a stick. This awareness intrigued him, giving him to believe that the captives shared points in common. He requested the guard to circulate among all prisoners, remaining vigilant, particularly concerning the men called Hastings and the Captain, and to report to him their exchanges, however mundane. From his early years he knew that men in captivity often commiserate with each other, telling tale after tale, each one carrying a stamp of embellishment and characteristically more grandiose than its predecessor. From the badinage gathered by guards he hoped to grasp precious kernels of wisdom in quantities sufficient to point to a singular personage or event. Alone with his thoughts, he beat a steady path back and forth between his modest cabin on the concourse and the several guard stations. Conversant in French, he required no interpreter, a facile tongue earning him a bit of celebrity among the soldiers who took delight in conversing with him.

The guard dwelt upon Hastings and the Captain. Occasionally the name **Black Jack** surfaced. Although they learned few details, the guard reported to the Bear Chief the possibility of an imminent visit by one *Jacques Noir*, a name which Hastings and the Captain exchanged at will. The name itself, the French equal of **Black Jack**, led the Bear Chief to reflect about stories he heard concerning a supposed villain of late who plucked the countryside of its fertile native youth. In the end he tied the two names together and, with an eye toward caution, took steps to prepare the post for an unsolicited arrival of an unwanted guest: First, he spread word among the guard to refuse to admit all new visitors within the walls. Two, strangers must submit to questioning by the Commander of the Guard, giving in part, points of origin and final destinations. Third, the French contingent must remain within the post as a body, under no circumstances to leave it, thus abandoning the works to a possible hostile takeover.

Pacing continuously, the Bear Chief sought to dispose of the portentous gloom which followed his every step. It is perhaps for this reason that he longed for the return of the General and the York family. Their presence drew him outside of himself and his immediate concerns.

He reeled full-circle when, walking beside the gate, the Captain of the Guard announced the arrival of an emissary from afar. The Bear Chief hastened to the guard's station in order to silently observe the unknown guest.

The messenger, in the guise of an aboriginal native, announced that a hostile British corps unduly pressed in upon the main camp at Kanonwalohule, or Oneida Castle, only hours earlier. The man begged the Captain of the Guard to send a force in relief of their allies, the Oneida, the People of the Standing Stone, who feared the loss of the village to the enemy. On hearing these words, the Commander of the Guard suffered visions of a British return to the Oneida valley, the region from which French forces drove them a scant four years earlier during the sacking of Forts Bull and William (69). The messenger claimed that Skenando, Oneida chieftain, and friend of the missionary, Samuel Kirkland (70), sent him.

The Bear Chief acted with reserve: Tied to the Oneida through his grandfather, Schkellimy, father of Tah:gah:jute, he once journeyed with his own father, Moray, Schellimy, and famous cousin Tah:gah:hute to a meeting which Samuel Kirkland hosted. With Skenando in attendance, he remembered the meeting vividly: At home near Oneida Castle Samuel Kirkland revealed plans to build an elementary school for children— *all* children at no cost to families. To Tah:gah:jute this development represented the peaceful coming-together of two distinct races, a goal he labored toward during his entire life. All parties agreed to support the plan and at Kirkland's invitation, everyone smoked the pipe of peace, after which Kirkland gifted Skenando, Tah:gah:jute and the others with a miniature wooden pipe of peace on a necklace. Kirkland insisted that from that day forward emissaries must always bear the pipe and necklace when conducting affairs of binding importance to the People, or to convey the tokens to an elected surrogate upon the inability to do so.

The Bear Chief studied the envoy. The man wore *no* miniature pipe of peace and necklace, nor did he wear the customary crown cap of feathers marking him an Oneida. On closer inspection he caught sight of the formation of a full beard along the man's jaw. He knew from exposure to clan histories that the Lord of the Forest gave the aboriginal man *no* ability whatsoever to grow a facial beard, much less to care for one. Therefore, in His beneficence, the Great Spirit absented hair from the faces of *all* aboriginal men, with the result that the male of the species walked the woodlands without the additional baggage of a coarse, thick, and uncomfortable jaw full of whiskers— facial hairs which required continual maintenance with instruments such as combs, razors, a mirror and soap. On the other hand, the Great Spirit gave *all* of these instruments to the peaus blancs, the Bear Chief believed, along with the ability to cultivate a beard and remove it at will. These observations uppermost in his thoughts, he hastened to find the Commander of the Guard. He reported his thoughts in no uncertain terms, while urging him to delay any demands which the emissary may put forth. Alas, he spoke too late for, in a matter of moments a sizable body of men mustered out and made haste for Oneida Castle—the mysterious emissary leading the way.

Lamenting briefly, the Bear Chief dispatched Cerf Courant to all corners of the works to deliver word of an imminent attack— in the very least, a deceptive invasion. With dusk approaching the wise Cayuga sachem requested that the Captain of the Guard transfer Hastings and the Captain to a private and secluded shelter, a certain low-lying stone warehouse with a stone roof which customarily housed corn and grains. He himself stood guard from a distance along with two soldiers. Periodically he conducted an inspection over the concourse and outlying lands, an exercise which produced no signs of suspicion. All remained quiet—too quiet, the Bear Chief believed.

From a vantage point the Bear Chief's keen eyes bore in on the outbuildings along the rooftops, most of which were built of thatch and came within close proximity of the post's palisades. In short order he caught the scent of smoke. He moved quickly to the suspected location when one, two, three rooftops went up in flames in a single stroke. Bales of smoke billowed upward. Flames flickered after them. The thatched roofs of dried grasses erupted quickly, the intense heat coursing through the structures, chasing the occupants onto the concourse in a flurry of confusion and congestion. Bolting to the top of a guard tower, the Bear Chief sounded the fire-bell, before dashing off to form a bucket-brigade. Many residents fled the garrison outright, leaving the main gate ajar, and, save for the fire fighters, everyone rushed about shouting wildly. Thick smoke ran freely, filling the dirt lanes between structures with a thick, pungent smoke screen, making of them forbidden corridors which burned the eyes and cut one off from one's neighbor.

Flames hopped to the warehouse's roof. A modest stone structure, the roof was never seriously challenged by the conflagration. On the side of caution, Cerf Courant summoned guards to remove Hastings and the Captain, and a nameless sort found lurking nearby, and to deposit them in a neighboring building well-doused with water. To his astonishment, four soldiers came up behind him unannounced. Dashing within the warehouse, they reappeared moments later with the three captives in hand. Moving off swiftly, the pack made for the granary, a stone's throw from the front portals. Shouting an alarm, Cerf Courant gave chase. The Bear Chief, engaged in quelling the flames, withdrew from operations to join him. Accompanied by a party of fire fighters, he quit the garrison by means of a little-used side exit and dashed ahead to conceal himself beside the massive front timbers of the gate. At a given signal, he and his companions intercepted the fleeing pack in the act of making off to the heavily-invested undergrowth of coppices along the rock-strewn hillside.

The fugitives offered little resistance. Surrounded, they lay down on the hard earth at the Bear Chief's command. One of the fugitives— the unknown sort— disavowed association with the others. He rose, hurling out his presumed name, leaving the others lingering in the dust. In searching the lot, the Bear Chief and his party found loaded pistols: instruments deemed the property of the post. The Bear Chief ordered the men tied about the wrists and shoulders preparatory to installing them in yet another structure. By now all traces of the fire vanished, save for blackened rooftops and scorched palisades. One of the captives, a beefy and surly lot, hands and clothing flecked with grime, refused to be bound. He drummed up a raucous protest, followed by a rambling discourse of little intelligible substance. His outbreaks drew a crowd of onlookers, some of whom railed against him with oaths of sarcasm, and in short order a scene bordering on chaos erupted. In danger of losing command to a disorderly mob, the Bear Chief made a quick decision: A water bucket in hand, he upended the contents over the head of the unseemly character. He followed suit with a blow to the back of the knees with a war-club, a stroke which sent the malcontent sprawling on an ample stomach, a position which the Bear Chief commanded him to maintain without fail.

"Qui connait cet homme?"—Who knows this man?–the Cayuga sachem called aloud.

Marchand, dormant since the Le Rocher departure, issued forth: "He appears to be the very Son of Satan who came to life in the Slave Sale not long ago. Guillaume and I have since spoken of such a man. Monsieur Le General is due soon and may fit a name to him. In the meanwhile, confine him securely." He paused to converse with the Bear Chief— a man whom he trusted implicitly:

Meeting with the Bear Chief, the tradesman praised him for valor in capturing the wild-looking character who sat in the dust at his feet. Glancing intently upon the ruffian, the tradesman gave vent to suspicions, passing the word that the captive was none other than the nefarious **Black Jack**. He gave the Cayuga sachem reason to understand that the men whom he now held in custody formed the corps of a smuggling ring, a small, yet powerful band of thieves and renegades. Marchand sought to bring the Bear Chief abreast of recent developments:

"I glimpsed this man from afar at Ontario. He stood at the Captain's side under a black night framed in the heat of brilliant camp fires. Guillaume will know him. Of this I am certain. Come! Let us walk."

"At this moment Guillaume is at Fort Oswego. He is about to bind over our Captain for trial, putting into play the plan which Madame York first proposed to him. Your friends, the York family are at Oswego selecting witnesses. Madame York persuaded Oswego's commandant, Lord Carleton, to conduct a military trial there for an express purpose. She has bent the ear of Lord Carleton to her way of thinking. Soon the Captain and others will stand before a tribunal. All of these men will answer for their evil ways". He glanced toward **Black Jack** and Hastings.

The Bear Chief nodded in understanding and asked to speak:

"The prisoners are confined here at Pointe Aux Bois. Do you not want to judge them here and avoid the danger of removing them to Oswego?"

"Granted, mon ami. However, the prisoners are English and under the terms of the Le Rocher proposal to the commandant, the handing out of justice will take place in the English camp."

The Bear Chief restated the question: "You do not care to obtain a measure of justice for your suffering on your home soil?" His eyes bore into the shorter, man, lips tracing a thin line.

"Yes, yes, mon ami, however I must tell you that bringing the Captain to justice carries greater weight in the English camp than in the French camp." He grasped the chieftain lightly about the shoulder.

"He must be tried by both English and French, for he has erred against both," the Bear Chief maintained.

"This is good, mon ami and it shall be done. Frankly, I have searched for a neutral site, but am unable to find one. Oswego is ample enough to house the great number of participants and witnesses who are expected to gather. One other thought: Lord Carleton has pledged to carry on legitimate proceedings. It is his way of washing off the guilt he carries for having fallen prey to the Captain's schemes. After consideration, I consented to the procedure."

The Bear Chief stood mute and the tradesman continued:

"I know what you are thinking, mon ami. Yes. There is a degree of danger. However, sometimes one must put faith in the unknown and hope for the best outcome. Let me tell you a story: Throughout our American experience we French have been forced to compromise. We are few in number, but great in courage. This forces us to address challenges many of which are overwhelming. How do we survive? We give something in exchange for something. We barter. We negotiate. We make promises and deliver accordingly. We regard each day as though it is our last, but we give our total commitment to the task at hand. That is why I have survived in this wilderness."

The Bear Chief remained silent.

"There is one more thought: "If the men are brought to justice at Pointe Aux Bois, the garrison may lie in danger of an attack by partisans or friends of the villains."

"You say that Oswego is stronger than Pointe Aux Bois?"

"The structure itself, yes, but it lacks soldiers. We have them!! One day Lord Amherst will return from Montreal, and we will be hard put to resist him. Our one great hope is to try the Captain and the lot, exposing their conduct for what it is before Amherst arrives. He, a man in high standing with the Crown, will without question conduct an investigation, purging the military of all purveyors of human flesh and violators of women and children. We leave it for him to conclude that which we have begun, so to speak. It is wise to bring the Captain before an English court where we, the poor and defenseless French, may expose the evil coursing through the British ranks and fall upon the good graces of Lord Amherst to put an end to it."

He spoke further: "Reports of our success here will travel far across the great ocean. Many people will learn the extent of the evils that have taken place on the frontier. A ground-swell of popular support will call for human justice on a grand scale and our star will rise. Amherst's star will also rise. Everyone wins!!"

"Is the world ready for such a development, Monsieur?"

"That remains to be seen. At least by our efforts we have begun such a movement. Let me tell you what Guillaume has planned at Oswego. He will demand the swift judgment of the Captain and his associates. In return Guillaume will release the whole lot of the English prisoners we now hold, provided English land encroachments cease. The success of the meeting depends upon the commandant's willingness to compromise, to seek the truth, and to demand that justice be served."

"He holds the commandant hostage, you say?"

"In a manner of speaking. It is the clever plan of Madame York."

"Yes. The plan allows him to hold on to honor, an important ally.

"Ah, yes. I know about honor. It is for honor that I fought the English at Osco and built a new village at the Round Tops."

"Do not forget that you helped Monsieur York preserve honor by searching for the assassin of Madame York's uncle." The Frenchman cast an appreciative glance at the Cayuga sachem.

"Ah, yes," the Bear Chief sighed. "Honor causes men to fight for their beliefs, however worthy or foolish."

"You are an honorable man. You fought for your own honor and that of your family and friends."

"Defending one's honor pushes men to either great heights or to abysmal depths, Monsieur."

"You have conducted yourself admirably in our days together," Marchand offered.

"Enough of this small talk!!" the chieftain erupted, uncomfortable when the center of attention. He turned to the tradesman and asked:

"Am I able to go with you to the English court?"

"By all means! You will tell your story before the court in order to earn your share of justice, for justice must be spread among all those from whom it has been denied," the tradesman smiled, delighted by his choice of words.

"I understand you now, Monsieur." The two men shook hands and repaired to respective quarters in anticipation of a well-deserved rest.

* * *

The Bear Chief did not remain idle indefinitely. Before long a great rumbling from without the works brought him to his feet from a comfortable bed. Outside the cabin he encountered Cerf Courant. Both men ran headlong toward the main portals of the post. At the gatekeeper's station they witnessed the Crier shouting:

"Horsemen approach from the south!"

The two allies scrambled to the summit of the gatekeeper's tower, there to catch a glimpse of what lay beyond the periphery of the works. They spied two columns advancing. The General commanded the first, composed of an escort and the York family. Close behind rode the Pointe Aux Bois soldiers, newly returned from Oneida Castle, the village where they allegedly brought the mysterious envoy. In the forefront the two woodsmen glimpsed the legendary missionary of Oneida Castle, Samuel Kirkland, and the heralded chief of the Oneidas, Skenando.

To the Bear Chief the riders appeared careless and detached. They called jubilantly to each other. Having crested the threshold of the works, the guard on duty flung open the gates, flooding the concourse with a frolicsome and merry throng who, with few exceptions, removed themselves to the dining quarters. The Bear Chief and Cerf Courant made straight for Samuel Kirkland and Skenando, two friends of long standing. Eager to exchange stories with them, the Cayuga sachem restrained himself, the clamor of the revelers all but drowning out his words. The General came alongside and restored calmness with a few well-chosen verses, and in the same gesture called upon the Bear Chief to address the enthusiastic crowd. He, however, in all humility deferred to the General, for he considered himself a guest at Pointe Aux Bois. Facing the crowd, a beaming General Le Rocher bellowed:

"Je me trouve comblé d'aise"—I find myself overwhelmed with joy. He spoke in French.

Following a brief ripple of applause, he continued: "I am pleased to announce that Lord Carleton, commandant of Fort Oswego, has agreed to preside over a general court-martial of our infamous guest, Captain Worthy. The commandant is in the process of securing witnesses. We are to depart for Oswego on the morrow. He has pledged to bring peace and tranquility to the frontier. Madame has a discovery. Madame— s'il vous plaît."

Caroline took a deep breath and, turning to face the principals, her aspect somewhat pensive, spoke decisively, her words well-chosen: "In due course I wish to bring to light the hardships I endured when under my captor's strict regimen. No one should have to suffer those travails again anywhere across the face of this land. The extent of the injustices committed in this land have long been kept under wraps. The truth longs to break free. I will speak before the court because I long for justice for myself, to be sure, but also for the untold scores of defenseless souls who have been defiled, humiliated, chastised, and sold into bondage. My husband, James, wishes to speak:"

"I have secured a witness with whom I have spent the better part of my stay here in the Lake Country. He and I have labored so closely together that I view him as a brother. Although he originally carried the colors of the opposition, he broke away from living under a set of self-seeking standards. His life among the native residents has taught him to place the needs of others before his own. He has paid a penalty, however, for, since first we met, he has lived in fear of his very life. Now, with the recent turn of events, he will, when asked, cast his lot with us." Again, a ripple of approval passed through the assembly. "Monsieur Marchand. I give you your audience."

An ebullient Marchand adjusted his collar. A man not at a loss for words, he spoke loud and clear: "I am pleased to announce the capture of the mysterious man-in-white. He, of course, formed one-third of that infamous triumvirate that Guillaume and I witnessed first-hand at Ontario. It happens that the lingering soul captured of late is none other than Simmons—the man in white— leader of the imposters. He attempted to free our captives. He did not come forward alone. Seeking clemency, **Black Jack** came to me in all confidence. He explained to me that Simmons fired the warehouse. Dashing within, he was at the point of freeing his comrades when captured. It is Simmons —our man in white—who entered Pointe Aux Bois to restore a liaison with the Captain. This is perhaps the sole instance in which I tend to believe the pirate. He confided to me that the pair are part of a combination. At its core they share a love-hate relationship where there lies a tenseness between them borne of mistrust. I ask. Who would know this better than the pirate himself? With that, let me introduce the hero of the hour." He summoned the Bear Chief.

"This man, the Bear Chief, deserves your praises fully. Not only has he captured an outstanding thief and predator in the form of **Black Jack**, but an officer, Hastings, cut from the same cloth, fell into his grasp by happenstance. These two and a third villain. The dandy in white. This Simmons. It is Simmons, I repeat, who set afire the outer buildings to draw attention away from his comrades. This man, the Bear Chief, stomped it out and captured the villains red-handed. Yes! There will be a trial. And a tremendous trial it will be! The major players have all but waltzed into our parlor, longing to take their places before the bar of justice. And it is justice they shall receive!! Without further delay I give you my friend, the Bear Chief, the Standing Bear of the Cayugas."

Overcome by the praises heaped upon him, the Bear Chief gestured to Skenando, or Oskanondonha, to speak in his stead. He stood beside the tall, lean Oneida chieftain who, greeting his ally, took a place within the tight circle, eager to make a discovery: The elegant Oneida (Onyota'a'ka) of middle age waited for cheers to subside, then, bowing from the waist, acknowledged the audience and spoke with conviction:

"I have a story to tell. It is why I am here today. A courier from your post dashed into my village with a number of your soldiers. He urged me to gather my forces and stand fast against a body of British cavalry approaching from the west. I summoned all warriors and together we made a considerable presence on the plain. Soon the enemy showed himself. Tawdry specimens, they looked worse than a ship's spoiled cargo: riffraff cast into the hold and forgotten. Ragged and dirty, they were a far cry from the trim and unruffled British cavalry to whom I am accustomed. We drove them back with a show of force, but several of them succeeded in planting a string of small fires along our main wall. We quickly snuffed them out and captured the entire pack. Upon pain of death they confessed that one of their number induced them to attack us. They called him Jacques Noir and begged for their lives. We searched for this Jacques Noir to no avail and they refused to tell us of his location. We killed them, for their manner made them out to be pirates: in my mind, the scourges of the earth. We teased the courier with hot coals and before he gave up his spirit he swore to me that your post would fall victim to the torch under a plan laid out by this same

Jacques Noir, the villain **Black Jack,** who now rests in your hands. I sped here to warn you of the danger."

"Your presence is always welcomed here, my friend. I am forever in your debt. Your alertness saved my men–saved Pointe Aux Bois," the General replied. Quickly he called attention to Samuel Kirkland:

"Does your companion, Monsieur Marchand, care to make a discovery?" the General asked.

Samuel Kirkland entered the fold of speakers. The modest, yet successful missionary and landowner greeted everyone with a handshake before breaking out in speech: "I have kept the secret of Pointe Aux Bois, the site of the last remaining French trading post below the St. Lawrence, from those who seek to disparage her. Beginning with General Le Rocher, the residents of Pointe Aux Bois have reached out in friendship to their neighbors, the Oneida: Our two camps have opened favorable trade relations through the efforts of Monsieur Marchand. We have long exchanged vital elements of trade, necessary to sustain life on the frontier. For example, we of Oneida Castle have supplied Pointe Aux Bois with the hardy herbs so necessary to fighting the contagions which crop up in confined quarters. We have equipped the soldiers of Pointe Aux Bois with thick robes and bedding with which to fight off the cold winter's chill. We have supplied Pointe Aux Bois with foods from our gardens and with grains from our vast stores. In turn, you of Pointe Aux Bois have donated us your iron vessels for the hearth, your crockery and dining utensils for the table, your comfortable articles of daily living and, of course, the essential musket with powder and ball. These exchanges have transformed the quality of life for those of us who inhabit this patch of the forest. We, all of us, are much the better off. What is more, we are alive and prospering.

"Our two camps are two *bodies* acting as one—a marriage of neighbors. We at Oneida Castle view our intercourse with you as an illustration of family life—the extended family—where men white and brown have joined together in union within our Creator's great, earth-bound assembly. The Creator, the one above us all, has entrusted us to keep His earthly properties secure and inviolate. That is why the Creator insists that all of us, all of His creatures, labor together. When I learned of this imposter of a courier, I called upon my friend, Oskanondonha, to send warriors against those who choose to become our enemy. We beat them back. The imposter is dead and I came here to demonstrate my continued support for you, Monsieur."

"I am deeply moved by your speech, Monsieur Kirkland. I know that I may always count on you when I am imperiled. We must remain close friends especially during this troubled period," a humble General replied.

Looking about him, Marchand asked: "Has everyone spoken who wishes to speak?"

Suzanne, standing beside Matthew, raised her brother's arm in full view of the General. Matthew, discovering her scheme, brought his arm down swiftly. Too late. The General summoned Matthew to address the gathering, luring him with praises. Reluctantly, a timid Matthew took a place before the onlookers:

"My words are meaningless beside the eloquence of Monsieur Kirkland. However, I have one major thought in mind which may be of service to you. Life sometimes brings us unforeseen surprises. Some are bad. Some are good, but they seem to be connected. In the campaign against this garrison, my company suffered a disastrous defeat. This is bad, but, on the other hand, my capture reunited me with my family. This is good. We never know where life's road may lead us. We hope that the road will bode well for us so that we may fulfill our duties, our ambitions, and our dreams and live to wake up at the end of our life's journey on that final road and say: "I have traveled life's road and it is a good road and I have lived the good life and am much the better for it."

Profound applause followed. The General stepped forward to shake Matthew's hand. He whispered to him. Matthew blushed and resumed a place among the spectators.

The General then bid the principals: Skenando, Samuel Kirkland, the Bear Chief and Henri Marchand to join him atop a small promontory on the concourse. At a signal they circulated among each other, shaking hands. Marchand beckoned James York to join him. Grasping Caroline and Suzanne, James joined Marchand. Matthew elected to remain among the spectators. The crowd roared approval and on the little hillock, swelled to capacity, the principals stood in a grand line, arm-to-arm, swaying side to side, basking in a moment of triumph and glory.

"I like this very much, mother," Suzanne quipped.

"You are indeed starved for attention, my daughter," Caroline returned, winking at Suzanne.

"I have never been in the presence of so many elders before," Suzanne blushed.

"You should prepare yourself. After today your life is going to change—and change quickly."

Suzanne cast her mother a blank, although curious stare.

"Before we go our separate ways, I must meet with Monsieur Kirkland and Skenando," Caroline replied, a hint of authority in her voice.

Suzanne took a step backward.

"Do not fret. Of course you may come along," Caroline smiled.

Delighted, Suzanne squeezed her mother's hand.

—

The principals removed to the dining commons, already the scene of much liveliness. There they dined on foods largely from the gardens. Meanwhile, native residents served the soldiers, the Skenando warriors, and the omnipresent escort of rangers. No one spoke of the plot to capture the post, nor of those who launched it. Looking about her, Suzanne marveled at the harmony which prevailed among all the diverse parties at table. Moments such as these convinced her that she lived but a dream and that the setting in which she dwelled formed yet another part of that heroic fantasy.

By design, Caroline York found herself in the company of Samuel Kirkland and Skenando. She heard good stories about life in Oneida Castle and wanted to explore certain avenues first-hand. Samuel Kirkland made no secret of his successes. He indulged Caroline to her heart's content:

"I have found the Oneida eager to learn about life beyond the confines of the Confederacy. With this in mind, I established a school, rudimentary at best, on a patch of land which these good people donated to me." His eyes fell upon Skenando who sat stoically beside him.

"What brought you here from the start, if I may be so bold?" Caroline asked.

"That old missionary zeal. I am a preacher by trade. I am too weak to fell trees for a living and too honest to be a fur trader, so I allowed the Lord to choose a career for me."

"Speaking in forums suits you. That goes along with being a preacher," Caroline confided.

"Yes. I found that people listened to me. I took it one step further into the classroom and began giving lessons."

"Let me see. English lessons, to be sure," she chided.

"Yes, of course; however, I also took the trouble to learn the Oneida tongue. Skenando taught me. Later, I taught him to speak English." He looked at his dear friend affectionately.

"Are you the only teacher, Monsieur Kirkland?"

"My wife and daughter assist from time to time. Of course there are volunteers, but they are itinerant tradesmen for the most part. I need to expand my classes. Demand is high. That means I need a teacher every day— five days a week." He looked imploringly into Caroline's eyes.

"I have the suitable teacher for you." Caroline regarded Suzanne. "She has taken upon herself to give classes here at Pointe Aux Bois. She has taught reading, writing, and ciphers. Do I have it all, Suzanne?"

Blushing, Suzanne joined her mother. "It began with my introduction into the Bear Chief's family. I taught Raven and Little Bear to speak English." She spoke with a note of affection.

"Good. I need someone with compassion and dedication," Samuel Kirkland spoke, rising.

"Do not let my mother escape, Monsieur. She is a born teacher," Suzanne burst forth. "She has gifted many natives with her incomparable talents."

"How has this come about?" Samuel Kirkland asked with curiosity.

"You may find this ironic, but it is my former captor who introduced me to the natives and their children." Caroline paused, searching for words.

"Mother set up classes for the natives, especially at Kanandesaga," Suzanne intervened. "She also introduced villagers to her fine cooking." She smiled approvingly, patting Caroline's shoulder.

"Thank you, dear for rescuing me. My labors with the natives helped me to preserve my sanity, Monsieur."

"I understand full well. On that note let me welcome you both to your new duties here at Oneida Castle. You will have your own cabin—a place to sleep and eat and eager and prepared students."

Caroline wept with delight. "But, Monsieur. I am due at Oswego by Friday, November, 17th."

"That gives you two more days. I understand. Do not fret. You are a woman very much in demand. Rest assured that when your obligation is finished, your new duties will be held in reserve for you." He winked at Suzanne, who returned the gesture.

—

Friday, November 17th @ 06:00 hours: The four captives: Hastings, **Black Jack**, Simmons, and the Captain, departed Pointe Aux Bois under ranger escort. Behind them rode a French party consisting of an armed guard and primary witnesses, among them the York family, the General, and Marchand. The Bear Chief rode with Watkins, whom he summoned by courier from the Round Tops. Watkins brought Fawn, who held a fervent interest in the whereabouts of her missing brother. Although not physically in attendance, John Rhoades, by previous arrangement, remained available for questioning.

Ahead at Fort Oswego, Lord Carleton assembled a tribunal of judges. They consisted of six magistrates, three English and three French. Formal jurists resided in Albany and in Boston and Philadelphia to be sure, but mitigating circumstances, when taken together, proved them a poor choice: First, they did not handle affairs of a military bent beyond the bounds of their jurisdiction. Second, they held no knowledge of the history which preceded the up and coming trial proceedings. Third, their choice held the possibility of disclosing Lord Carleton's shortcomings to a wide audience, thus opening him to censure back home, and damaging the proceedings locally. By mutual agreement, Lord Carleton and the General vowed to adhere to an English/French tribunal in preserving the wishes of the two major parties concerned.

The magistrates ultimately chosen held military backgrounds, served in the recent struggle in North America for their respective sovereigns, possessed letters and education in the law, currently practiced law, and, most important, previously presided over military tribunals in North America. To that effect, the French magistrates came from Montreal and Quebec and the English gentlemen came from Raleigh in Virginia. Lord Carleton, laboring feverishly behind the scenes, secured their consent, and paid for their lodging and transportation to Oswego while his superior, Lord Jeffery Amherst, remained in Montreal hashing out the particulars of a British-based military government in that fallen French bastion (71). Needless to say, Lord Carleton looked to proceed quickly without having to offer explanations or undergo interruptions.

The tribunal convened within the hard, stone walls of Oswego, the sole solid structure extant for miles in either direction. The chapel became the site of the proceedings, spacious enough to accommodate all principal parties, in addition to community residents, guests, itinerants, and friends of the witnesses. These passive onlookers occupied the ample pews of the chapel. A tier of boxed seats stood along the west wall to hold witnesses and additional spectators. Directly opposite them along the east wall, sat the defendants in boxed seats framed with stern wooden sides or blinders which compelled one to sit upright with eyes facing forward. The simple procedural rules required that defendants refrain from conversing with one another, speak only when addressed by a magistrate, give a complete response to each posed question, and maintain an air of civility.

A tabernacle, unadorned and resembling a great, sturdy table, occupied a generous space at the head of the main aisle on the north side of the chapel. Here would gather the principal litigants and witnesses. Behind, a stained-glass window filled much of the wall and beneath it stood the chief magistrate's trappings: a stout bench followed by a sumptuous leather chair. To his left stood similar yet lesser trappings for the prosecution and to his right a set of furnishings for the defense. Since the French instituted the proceedings, their magistrates formed the prosecution, leaving the English magistrates with the defense. It is from within this tight battery that the direction and course of the proceedings would flow, and all decisions, great and small would be made. At that moment in history some of the most renowned legal minds to inhabit the New York colony came together in the pristine chapel to weigh evidence in a case carrying broad ramifications for all of the western world. Overall, a tone of solemnity permeated the court. All in attendance recognized, once Lord Carleton explained proceedings, that the ultimate decisions handed down carried binding weight and finality, forging a heretofore unknown precedent for what became known as 'human justice' in later years throughout judicial circles in the New York colony.

Rising from a station beside the chief magistrate, Lord Carleton called for quiet in the assembly. At once the low drone of intermingling voices ceased. Everyone sat calmly, waiting for Lord Carleton's opening statement. Speaking to everyone and to no one in particular, he began in a plodding, steadfast manner:

"My friends. We are gathered here today to witness the application of justice to a portion of our community in which it has been denied. I say 'our community,' for, in the eyes of the law, we are all of us treated with equanimity: our origins, gender, race, and beliefs notwithstanding. Brought before the court today are four men charged basically with the same offense, although in varying degrees. They are charged with the inducement of involuntary servitude into this region for the sole purpose of monetary gain. Of course this court does not restrict itself to the trying of a single offense where that offense is a component of a corresponding offense. Let it be known therefore that the accused are charged with the theft of personal property not owned by themselves, again for monetary gain. Long a practice on the Continent, indeed worldwide, involuntary servitude, or slavery, has become through the years an institution— a most unsavory one. Obscured by the most recent conflict between Great Britain and France in the Seven Years' War, slavery, and its kindred practices have been long-tolerated by law-abiding people everywhere: governmental representatives, continental and colonial alike.

"Ironically, it is that War which has brought the matter forward into the collective consciousness today. Let me explain: The two leading powers learned early-on that they needed the support of the native aborigines in order to pull victory from the jaws of defeat. At first they seduced them with gifts, each in his own way, and, lo and behold, the natives fought their wars for them. One of the powers, Great Britain, required a steady influx of cheap labor in order to carry on the war effort. It is in this manner that involuntary servitude reared its ugly head. Youth were stripped from families, never to be seen again. If that were not enough, men of high station who represented Great Britain in the new world made a sport of the matter, buying and selling youth for a profit. An institutional practice evolved into a game of opportunity. Mindful, a decision of this court may carry broad implications.

"This court has been convened at the request of men and women who have first-hand suffered the effects of involuntary servitude, either directly or indirectly. You may call them either victims or witnesses, and, indeed the court agrees to enter them as witnesses. They are here because they have been befriended by French entrepreneurs who govern a small enclave seeking to preserve cherished trading privileges with the aborigines. It is perhaps the one remaining French outpost in the Lake

Country. The French magistrates, therefore, constitute the prosecution in this matter. Their counterparts, the British, form the defense team. The French will present evidence consistent with involuntary servitude and corresponding offenses: theft, personal and material and physical abuse, as they pertain to those charged. The defense will offer counter-claims or counter-evidence. The chief magistrate will make a final decision regarding those charged based on the preponderance of evidence presented. Please stand everyone and repeat the prayer of invocation which the chaplain has prepared. Following the prayer, let proceedings begin."

Lord Carleton yielded to the chaplain who led the assembled in a prayer wrought with hope and charitableness. Following, the Chief Magistrate rose. Walking the few steps to the tabernacle, he posed large and ponderous in a black gown, the sleeves of which flowed luxuriously over its surfaces. William Bigelow by name, the judge, chosen at random by lots, came from Fort Niagara, the fortress which the British recently wrested from the French. Rotund about the waist, ample cheeks, a smaller version of his stomach, glowed red. He spoke in a booming baritone, a voice that the high-vaulted ceiling of the church greatly augmented and sent crashing down upon the attendees, prompting everyone to cast aside idle thoughts and lend an earnest ear. "The prosecution may make opening remarks. Monsieur Moulet, I believe."*

Chosen chief prosecutor, Edouard Moulet, a tall and spare man who exhibited youthful enthusiasm, rose from the dock. Crossing to the prisoners' bank, he faced the spectators, hands clutching the firm rail behind. Standing erect, he appeared much taller than his reputed 190cm. Stooped slightly, he spoke in a stern voice:

"A breach of trust has come to my attention of late, a breach of trust so ignominious and abominable that I have encountered difficulty in putting it into words. In short, gentlemen charged with honoring the dignity of human-kind have disavowed their oaths of office and forced certain segments of human-kind into subservience before them. I speak of the whole raft of prisoners behind me, but none more earnestly than the man on the extreme left— Captain James Worthy. It is he who stood at the core of the subterfuge which he allowed to take root about him. Far from expunging it, he encouraged it, turning it into a rewarding occupation. Consuming greed eventually caught up with him and that is why he sits before you today."

M. Mouton turned to face Captain Worthy. With a sweep of the arm he pointed him out to the attendees: "The co-defendants before you supported him to varying degrees. I plan to illustrate my claims with witnesses germane to this case. I call Christopher Dobbs."

Eager to speak, Dobbs made an excellent witness for the prosecution. He spoke of midnight raids against native villages, of the abduction of women and children, and of looting with abandon.

The defense, headed by Stewart Leming of Raleigh in the Virginia colony, sought to dislodge Dobb's testimony: "You witnessed first-hand these engagements of which you speak?"

"Yes Sir."

"Did you disapprove of them in any way?"

"Yes Sir."

"Did you make your reservations known to your superiors?"

"To my comrades, yes. To my superiors, no."

"Interesting. Why the disparity, Mr. Dobbs?"

"I feared for my life, Sir."

"Please explain, Mr. Dobbs."

"My immediate superior, Captain Worthy, let it be known that he entertained no deviation from his commands, unless one was willing to pay a severe penalty."

"What kind of penalty, Mr. Dobbs?"

"Lashes. Starvation. Execution."

"Did you witness any of these penalties being exacted?"

"Not exactly, Sir."

"Continue, please."

"The man in question customarily disappeared all of a sudden, or ran away of his own volition."

"You spoke with no other superior?"

"A party of us sought an audience with Lord Carleton. Either the Captain or loyal confederates saw fit to intercept our petitions." When prompted, Dobbs continued: "The commandant never received our petitions and after several attempts we abandoned our efforts to reach him."

"Here you are, in fear for your life, and you abandon attempts to make your concerns known."

"I feared for my life, Sir."

"Yet you went ahead with your labors in the BEF?"

"Yes. I tried to maintain a low profile. I tried to labor long and hard to rid my mind of the barbarities that went on about me."

"You adapted to your surroundings. May it be said that everyone must do so—especially on the frontier?"

"On the frontier, especially, Yes, Sir."

"Everyone? Regulars and officers alike?"

"Yes, Sir."

"Did you labor in an arena of comparative ease on the frontier?"

"Life on the frontier is unpredictable. Secure one moment and unforgiving the next."

"You labored under fear. Is that fair to say?"

"One must be wary. Yes."

"In your mind did the Captain labor under fear?"

"He always believed that an attack lay over the horizon."

"Is it safe to say that the Captain sought to control his surroundings by setting rigid codes of conduct for his men and subduing the occasionally aberrant aborigine wherever he may find him?"

"Hmmm. It is possible to look at it in that light—from his point of view."

"From his point of view. Thank you, Mr. Dobbs. You may step down."

—

M. Mouton sought a stronger witness than Christopher Dobbs, whom he believed played into the hands of the defense: "I call James York."

James, tall and ruddy, a pillar of silent strength, gripped Caroline's hand before ascending to the stand.

"Mr. York. I understand that you came upon the Lake Country charged with a mission. You may explain."

"Along with my daughter I came in search of my wife. Someone of stature took her by force from my household. All indicators pointed out that indeed the Captain absconded with her and set her up in his rooms here at Fort Oswego."

"How did you come to name the Captain so precisely?"

"My wife left small traces of herself along a trail of abduction for me to follow. A flower here. A blade of grass there: the same trail which the Captain followed on his trek through the Delaware country." He coughed, then continued: "If that were not enough, I know a man who recalls Caroline in the Captain's service."

"This man. He is a friend of yours?"

"Outside of my family he is the best friend that one may ever have."

"You may go on."

"We met under trying circumstances, but it turned out rewarding for me—for all of my family."

"Ah! A fortuitous event. I understand."

"He came to me a wounded soldier in the Captain's command. At the time I lived as a guest in a native village. He no sooner warned me of an attack about to take place but several columns drew into position below the village. Soldiers attacked and many people lost their lives."

"Thank you. This man. This friend. He did not attack the village, you say?"

"This is true. He ran from the Captain because he did not want to take part in the senseless sacking of an innocent village. He came to warn me and the others."

"The others?"

"The villagers. The chief in particular."

"Then what happened?"

"Thanks to my friend, the chief was able to prepare defenses and a path of retreat for his people."

"He is a hero, then. Your friend."

"Yes. A hero to many, but do not tell him that."

"I understand. He saved your life and that of your wife."

"Yes. This is true."

"Did he help you in other ways?"

"He offered to help me find the Captain . . . not directly, of course. He also feared for his life."

"I must meet your friend. Is he coming to the proceedings?"

"He is waiting to be sworn as a witness."

"And a most compelling witness he will make, I venture."

—

Mr. Leming rose. He strode casually back and forth before James York, eyes glued to the floor, hands folded behind him. Tall and blond with broad shoulders and a long, pointed nose, he resembled a man searching for something lost, a valued possession, perhaps. Stopping with a click of the heel, he faced James York:

"Have you and your wife enjoyed satisfactory relations during your marriage?"

"Relations? Of what sort?"

"The relations that bind together a man and his spouse."

"Of course. We have enjoyed each other immensely."

"Your wife. Has she ever entertained thoughts of visiting far off lands—of going off by herself for a respite: a relief from her duties?"

"I do not see how this goes anywhere."

"You will. Answer please."

"Caroline is a born adventuress. She took upon herself to come to America to assist her uncle with his farm. She and I administered it following his untimely death."

"Oh. I am sorry to hear that."

"She is also a teacher. She has schooled native children in the arts and ways of the western world."

"She has carved out a path for herself in this wilderness: a land innately foreign to her. Tell me. Did she usually finish a project once begun?"

"Why, yes. She has the strength to stay the course. Yes. She is a remarkable woman on several counts." James wiped a tear from his eye.

"She labored long and hard on that farm. Did she not?"

"Yes. We both did. There are no guaranties for success."

"How did she take the death of her uncle?"

"She went into the doldrums for a spell . . . not eating . . . not sleeping."

"She needed relief. Is that true?"

"Yes. She needed to catch her bearings."

"And soon thereafter she disappeared . . . without leaving notice? What thoughts possessed you?"

"How odd of her to vanish. Suddenly my whole life passed in front of me."

"Your life with your spouse. Little unresolved tiffs coming to the surface? Little doubts?"

"Yes. Yes. . . . but not to be unexpected under the circumstances."

"It is a pattern common to spouses who seek a remedy from the aches and pains of domestic living."

"No! No! Caroline did not run off." James started to rise in protest, but the bailiff restrained him.

"Do you have a witness to support your claim?"

"Of course. You see . . . my daughter accompanied my wife to market. She grew restive when Caroline failed to meet her for the journey home."

"Yes."

"My daughter, Suzanne, was detained by a man whom she thought a comrade of the Captain. In due course she later pointed him out to me."

"This man. Is he present now?"

"Yes. He sits at the Captain's left hand."

"Let the court be aware that the witness has identified Mr. Simmons."

Murmurs floated through the courtroom. An agitated Simmons crossed and uncrossed his feet. The Captain meanwhile sat implacable. The Chief Magistrate summoned the attendees to order and Mr. Leming, changing tact, continued:

"Mr. York . . . in your view, how did the Captain treat with Mrs. York during her stay with him?"

"At first she retained her own quarters. She was free to traverse the grounds at will. She became the Captain's chef and secretary."

"She enjoyed the comforts of home so to speak. Perhaps more, is that true?"

"She was free to move within the bounds set by her master."

"An otherwise perfect master-to-servant relationship, you say?"

"Harsh terms . . . but . . . yes . . . master-to-servant."

"Your wife. Was she beaten or bruised?

"No."

"Was she denied adequate food or drink?"

"No."

"Did she have a shelter or residence? Dry and clean clothes?"

"Yes . . . and, yes."

"To your knowledge, Mr. York, did your wife attempt to flee her surroundings or her relationship?"

"No. But there was the fierce, harsh winter and . . ."

"Thank you, Mr. York. Hmm. Tell me. Why this sudden fall from grace which led to her confinement in a holding pen?"

Growing angry, James responded in a strong baritone: "She wanted her freedom as all of God's children want their freedom."

"I say not, Mr. York. I say that she *willfully* broke the terms of her contract, so driving her master to take corrective measures."

"That is a lie!!" James shouted, standing up, fists clenched.

"That is all, Mr. York. You may step down." A thin smile apparent, Mr. Leming retired to a high-back.

—

All eyes fixed upon James. Ruffled, he took long strides to his place where Caroline and Suzanne attempted to comfort him. Edouard Mouton conferred briefly with him. He confided that Mr. Leming may have cast Caroline in a participatory role, one in which she agreed to accept a partnership with the Captain as a means of improving her lot on the frontier. He studied James closely:

"Mr. Leming wishes to show that Caroline entered a relationship willingly and broke it of her own accord when its terms no longer pleased her. He wishes to show her fickle and undecided—a poor candidate to make the claim of abduction stand."

Sighing, James hung his head. He revived himself when the prosecuting counselor made an announcement:

"I call Sgt. William Watkins," M. Mouton declared.

A wealth of commotion pervaded the rear of the church. Heads turned and necks strained to catch a glimpse of the witness. By ordinary circumstances the witness was an English officer— a man invaluable to the defense. M. Mouton, however, sought him for the prosecution. Tall, hair thick and flowing, the witness wore a trail outfit of finely-combed deerskin embroidered with tiny, colorful shells. Head erect and eyes straight forward, he appeared in full command of his bearings: one suffused with a surfeit of discoveries and revelations. A few paces from the witness stand, he paused, glimpsing momentarily into the prisoners' bay. The occupants in the first two boxes, the Captain and Simmons, stirred restlessly. The Captain, jaw agape, shrank back, pulling against restraints. An audible moan ushered from between his lips, his sole response since he first sat before the tribunal. Watkins' presence aroused unsolicited palaver among the attendees. From a distance Edouard

Mouton allowed the talking to grow in strength until a look from the Chief Magistrate forced him to step forward. With a sweep of an arm, the prosecutor motioned for silence.

"I thank you for coming, Sgt. Watkins," M. Mouton bowed, smiling. "You may be seated."

Sgt. Watkins nodded obligingly. Legs shoulder-width apart, he sat with hands folded before him in anticipation of the prosecution's queries:

"May you please tell the court in concise form of a particularly horrendous misfortune befalling you in the BEF?"

"Certainly. I found myself running for my life. Shot by a ball, fired by my own company, I hid among the brambles beside a lake. Natives found me and took me to their village. Mr. York pulled out the ball. His daughter and her dear friend brought me back to health. From there I helped the village chieftain prepare his defenses for an imminent attack."

"What prompted such a vindictive move against you?"

"I disagreed with the Captain's reconnaissance and let it be known that it smacked of sheer folly."

"The Captain took exception to your point of view?"

"To say the least. He brooks no other opinion save his own. He ordered me bound and held for court martial."

"Continue, please."

"I escaped my bonds and ran down a steep hill. Shot flew by me. A ball lodged in my shoulder. Fortunately, I hid from view. It is also fortunate that the scouts found me."

"You still reside in that village, do you not?"

"Yes. It is one I helped to build after the Captain destroyed the original village."

"Was the Captain under orders to challenge the natives? Abscond with them?"

"No. Not to my knowledge."

"Was he under orders to seize and burn villages?"

"No."

"What gain fell to the Captain in your opinion?"

"He accumulated a cargo of booty . . . as well as a select crew of young people."

"He profited thereby?"

"The spoils he believed the natives owed him for protecting the frontier for them."

"And the young people?"

"He brought some to labor in the garrison . . . in other garrisons. I heard that he sold off a great lot of them."

"You did not witness this eye-to-eye, did you?"

"No, not eye-to-eye. I heard stories from reliable sources. Always the stories. Many stories."

"How many sallies with the Captain did you take part in?"

"Only the one . . . the one in which I fled."

"Did you know what the Captain was truly about when he sacked the village?"

"We did not receive marching orders. I . . . We assumed that we were en route to a new site."

"Go ahead."

"Charting plots for development . . . opening new lands for settlement."

"I see. Then you stand unknowing of your commander's intentions?"

"Yes . . . the lot of us."

"Unlike you, your comrades did not bolt and run, did they?"

"No. They fell in line with his dictates."

"Do you have your own personal thoughts about that?"

"Yes. Some of the older men ached to engage the foe."

"The foe, you say."

"The Captain convinced the lot of us that marauding savages attacked our camp the previous evening. It was his intention to teach his errant children a well-deserved lesson."

"I see. However, you elected not to go along with his deductions?"

"No. I did not. You see . . . a bear wandered into camp. Some of the men killed it. Shortly thereafter a flight of arrows showered the grounds. Several men were hit. Chaos broke out and everyone fled into the night." Watkins paused to daub at his eyes which began to shed tears. "Pardon me," he stammered.

"Understandable. You may proceed at your leisure."

"In their haste many men plunged over a waterfall. Running in the black night they lost their discipline and with it their lives."

"A harsh lesson learned."

"To be sure." Watkins paused again to catch his breath. "In thinking back, no attack came. I knew that we were in no imminent danger from the natives. I tried to convey my thoughts to the Captain, but he would hear none of it. It is as though he decided beforehand to sack the village."

"He conducted a drama of sorts?"

"Yes. He set a spectacle into motion. I . . . We became the players and he was the grand impresario."

"And like a drama it reached a conclusion?"

"Yes. A most predictable one. Victory for the conqueror. Defeat for the upstarts."

"Let me ask you why you came forward at this point."

"I came so that justice may be served. By the same token, I want to see dignity restored to the command in which I once served . . . the British Expeditionary Forces."

"You do not fear for your life?"

"One must decide between his own needs and those of others. I came to speak on behalf of the greater good."

"You may explain, please."

"Of course. I want to attempt in my own way to bring to an end the contempt that a few have toward the native inhabitants of this vast region."

"A most noble undertaking."

"A matter of utmost importance in the scheme of things."

"Go on, please."

"You see . . . if we explorers are to cultivate the wilderness, we must labor in concert with the natives . . . else we will lose it to those who are able and willing to do so. Usurpers, if you will." He paused and, looking directly at the prisoners' box, stated: "A first step in that direction may be made here today."

"Thank you, Sgt. That is all for the present. Your witness, Mr. Leming."

—

Pacing back and forth before Watkins, hands clasped behind his back, Leming of the defense cast his eyes upward, as though drawing upon strength from the heavens. Coming to an abrupt halt, he fired off a crisp and brusque salvo:

"You disobeyed orders, did you not?"

"I acted out of conscience."

"Nonetheless, you stepped beyond your bounds. Correct?"

"In a manner of speaking."

"*In a manner of speaking.* Since when are you privileged to interpret a command? To dissect it? To inspect it? To accommodate it to your own liking? Do you believe that by your rank you have the capacity to refute your superior? To disrupt well-executed plans to build a peaceful frontier?" Barely taking a breath, the defense pushed forth in a vibrant staccato, tinged with a hint of venom.

Watkins sat momentarily stunned by the assault. He knew not how to respond, but found his tongue after the defense prodded him with an open, innocuous question:

"What have you to say for yourself?"

Looking Mr. Leming directly in the eye, Watkins replied soberly: "The natives posed no threat to us. My superior acted out of a lust for power. He did so without thinking of the human cost—the cost in lives of the brave men of the BEF. He did so out of a lust for blood— the blood of innocent natives who huddled in fear in what remained of their once-proud village. He did so out of greed—for the accrued wealth which the sale of the natives would bring him. He did so out of defiance—of thumbing his nose at his corps commander. He did so to bind his men ever-tighter to his beck and call. For these reasons and more he did these things for his own edification. He is a man dedicated to his own self-preservation. I have nothing more to say."

A collective gasp filled the great room. A low murmuring followed during which attendees stared at each other in wonderment. People awe-struck sat transfixed, numbed by the words and their implications. A faint smile crossed the lips of Caroline York and Suzanne. They, so close to the events which Watkins cited, inwardly rejoiced, but restrained themselves further. On the stand Watkins pursued a ramrod posture and exemplary comportment. His riveting declaration stuck fast in the minds of the attendees and accounted for much of the murmuring. Mr. Leming made a curt comment before dismissing him.

"The words of an ungrateful soldier who harbors preconceived beliefs. You may step down."

—

Edouard Moulet conferred with William Bigelow. The Chief Magistrate nodded affirmatively and, looking out upon the multitude, made an announcement: "Two witnesses wish to come forward. They have been delayed by a reluctance to speak before this tribunal, the trappings of which are new and foreign to them. They bring with them a friend who has offered his services to act as interpreter. On that account they agreed to convene at this tribunal. They are the Bear Chief of the Cayuga branch of the Iroquois and his adopted daughter, the Fawn, who lives with him. Speaking for them is Guillaume Le Rocher, French commandant of a little-known, yet vital trading post. Their testimony has been critically evaluated and accepted into the body of the proceedings. You are to give them your unswerving attention and respect."

With the General leading the way, the Cayuga sachem and Fawn proceeded side by side along the aisle from a point in the rear vestibule of the church. Standing behind the great doors, their presence remained unknown to all save the lone attendant who ushered them within. Upon glimpsing the stately duo from a distance, clad in their very finest livery, the spectators, packed tightly together on hard benches since mid-morning, rose and pressed heavily against the extremes of the benches lining the aisle. The great massing of flesh proved unbearable for many occupants with the result that, losing footing, a number of them tumbled upon the aisle. In no small measure spectators fell over each other in order to glimpse the two regal figures who strolled along the corridor, unaware of the mass confusion which played out in their wake.

Speaking in French, the General converted Edward Mouton's questions for the Bear Chief into French, then translated the responses into English for the benefit of the defense and the court in general. In giving testimony to M. Mouton and taking questions from the defense, the Bear Chief described the unprovoked attack upon Osco, the torching and looting of the village, the theft of valued furs and skins, and the abduction of young people.

Fawn privately told the General of the abduction of her brother from a previous year. In looking about the room, she allowed her eyes to fasten more than once upon Hastings in the prisoners' box. She spoke slowly, but made strong gestures and took short steps, walking in a tight circle. At once she broke free and, darting toward the prisoners' box, gestured wildly at Hastings.

The General came to stand beside her. She filled the General's ear with a flurry of words before he restored her to calmness. Facing the assemblage, he interpreted Fawn's remarks: "Mademoiselle Fawn has found the man who stole away with her brother."

Following the proceedings with rapt attention, Hastings turned his head away. To the General he seemed to shrink before the accusing finger of Fawn, which, like a pointed dagger, marked him for execution.

"Let the court note that a second usurper has been identified," Edouard Mouton declared.

Hastings strained in his harness, a caged beast seeking escape from its shackles. Edouard Mouton summoned him to testify on his own behalf. Rubbing his wrists, Hastings tripped lively to the witness-dock. There he faced questions which the Bear Chief channeled to the General who translated them into English for M. Mouton.

"Mr. Hastings. You are called here today to give an account of your conduct on the day that you captured many aborigine youth. How do you respond?"

"I was in the process of questioning them, Monsieur."

"You may be more definitive."

"I learned enemy forces may be nearby, waiting to pounce upon my unit."

"These youth appeared sorely neglected for want of food and clothing. Is this true?"

"They repeatedly threw off my attempts to intercede with them."

"You may continue."

"I believe that my—our uniforms startled them."

"Something tragic took place that day which the children were forced to witness. Do you recall what it was?"

"No. I know of nothing of the sort, Monsieur."

"Let me refresh your memory: A man—a wise elder of the turtle clan—the very clan to which some of the children belonged—suffered the pains of torture and death—finally burned to put him out of his misery. Tell me. Is this the manner in which you question simple and benign denizens of the forest?"

"That man. Aahh!! That man!" In the throes of recalling old memories, Hastings shook his head vigorously from side to side: "That man!! In the guise of friendship he offered tainted food to several of my men. Those who ate it grew deathly ill. We found ourselves obligated to leave them behind on the trail. Later we learned that his allies killed them all to the last man."

"And you subsequently exacted your own brand of vengeance?"

"No!! I did not."

"I have it that, while your men lounged and dined, the children sat huddled in fetters. You killed the old man because he refused to tell you where the strong young men of their clan resided. Is this not true?" Edouard Mouton spoke, his voice rising in volume.

"No!! The old man produced a knife in an attempt to slay me. We struggled for possession and he fell."

"Mortally wounded?"

"Yes. A case of self-defense."

"His charred corpse bore the markings of a grave wound—a wound so severe that his entrails poured out and the fire consumed them. A knife, you say?"

"All right! I struck him with my sword—but the life of him had since departed, so ravaged he became from insanity."

"And the burning?"

"I accorded him the last rites of his own people—rather than leave him to fester on the plain."

"How charitable of you, Mr. Hastings. That is all I have for now."

—

Mr. Leming of the defense approached: "Mr. Hastings. What exactly did you learn from the shackled youth?"

"I learned that a large band of savages-er-aborigines-planned to ambush my unit."

"Did these youth come to you of their own free will?"

"Not exactly. My men happened upon them by chance. They lashed out at us with spears and knives."

"It is because of this that you shackled them?"

"Why yes. Of course."

"Purely a measure of self-defense?"

"Yes. Certainly."

"And the incident of the old man: An unfortunate occurrence, nothing more?"

"Yes, unfortunately. I tried to reason with him, but he grew defiant and tried to slay me."

"And what did you plan for the children once you finished with them?"

"Why—to release them. They served their purpose. I wanted nothing more from them."

"Did you follow generally approved military standards in your treatment of the youth?"

"Under those conditions—yes. I did not waver in my conduct."

Nevertheless, you found yourself under attack."

"Yes."

"From a large band of aborigines?"

"No—from two—maybe three adult natives."

"Two or three. Do you recognize anyone here who attacked you?"

"Yes. That man. (He pointed to the Bear Chief)."

"Let it be known that the witness has identified his attacker in this court and that he is the same man who accused him of trafficking in human flesh. That is all, Mr. Hastings. You may step down."

—

To anyone other than Edouard Mouton, Hastings may have presented plausible testimony in his own defense. Monsieur Mouton, however, saw through the accused's convenient fabrications whereas a passerby may have affixed to them a stamp of approval and subsequent validity. Therefore, in order to garner support for the prosecution, Monsieur Mouton decided to draw a relationship between Hastings and the Captain—a relationship of association whereby each man held full knowledge of the schemes of his comrade in such a manner that the schemes of both men actually complemented each other. He conferred with the General before approaching the witness and co-defendant:

"I call upon Horatio Simmons."

Clothed in a white tunic and leggings, Simmons descended to the court room floor where he promptly took a place on the witness stand. His clothing, wrinkled and tarnished from continuous exposure, still maintained a trace of luster which bestowed upon him a bit of sophistication. Having been sworn, he leaned back comfortably in anticipation of speaking his mind, something which recent confinement denied him.

"White. The color white," Edouard Mouton began. "Over the ages the color *white* has transferred a host of virtuous traits to the owner of that tunic . . . that pair of leggings . . . that particular article of clothing which one chooses to drape over his skeleton." He began counting on his fingers: "Candor, frankness, sincerity, truth, innocence . . . all these and more traits accrue to the wearer of *white*." He smiled, pleased with his delivery.

"As you wish, Monsieur."

"Tell me, Mr. Simmons. These traits are the qualities of the officers' corps of your unit, are they not?"

"Yes . . . in a matter of speaking."

"For sure you held these thoughts when you chose your *white?*"

"That may be. I do not recall. I do not indulge in trifles."

"Of course—but going way back, you, at one interval, adopted *white* for the simple reason that it is accompanied by these glowing terms . . . these favorable traits . . . and others would tend to see you in terms of these traits."

"The thought never occurred to me . . . but . . ."

"I understand. And the officers' corps embodies these very traits— this select corps."

"They are a kind of fraternity. One for all and all for one."

"Exactly. And all knowledge: be it schemes, plots, secrets, fears, are properties of the whole. This fraternity. This family, if you will."

"That is an interesting way of putting it, Monsieur."

"Thank you, Mr. Simmons. Tell me. Your posts of aide-de-camp and Procurer of Victuals make you privy to the continuous flow of knowledge investing the corps—this fraternity—this family. Is this true?"

"My posts require me to treat with many officers."

"You share in their thoughts?"

"Yes."

"Few new developments escape your scrutiny?"

"We are a small fraternity, Monsieur."

"You are aware of the Captain's exploits—*all* of his exploits—and those of Hastings and others?"

"In the broad sense, yes. We are a family, you must know."

"How does the name Charles Martin strike you?"

"Hmmm. I have heard that name before."

"His niece, Caroline York, sits in this room as we speak. He died—murdered, many believe. I have it from a competent source that you met with him."(He did not allude to Glenn Joseph or other Friends).

"Yes. I recall hearing of the tragedy. My condolences to Madame York. I met him once. He came to our encampment in need of a service."

"Yes. He came for a smithy. You are among three men to have last seen him alive. Tell me, did you speak with Mr. Martin during his stay?"

"No. I escorted him and went my merry way."

"With whom did you leave the now-deceased?"

"In the Captain's able hands."

"I have it from reliable sources that the Captain is the *last* man to see the now-deceased alive?"

"That may very well be true, but he is not involved."

"How do you know?"

"Why, the deceased died from a blow to the head. His horse spooked and threw him. The Captain told me."

"You put no questions to the Captain?"

"No—but a single thought concerned me."

"Continue."

"The horse—the deceased's horse. It is an old and reliable mount, I am told. Nothing disturbed that horse. Martin rode it to camp on many an occasion. The sudden knowledge startled me."

"But you pressed the Captain no further?"

"No."

"What does the Captain mean for you?"

"He is the symbol of the corps."

"Would you lie for him?"

"No."

" . . . kill for him?"

"No."

"The Captain's word is inviolate?"

"In my mind.—yes."

"Reliable sources have determined that the deceased died from a blow to the head with a deadly instrument. How say you on the matter, given this knowledge?"

"There must be some mistake."

"May not the Captain be in error?"

"The Captain does not make errors."

"Did he not profit from the proceeds of a Slave Sale?'

"No. He assigned young aborigines to stations on the frontier to begin new trades."

"Did the Captain not advance against native villages?"

"How do you mean?"

"Burning them. Looting them."

"No. He merely moved against those seeking to destroy him."

"Are you willing to proceed against those who would malign the corps?"

"The corps is my life. Its principles must not be violated. The corps is sacred. It is my family."

"For you the corps and the Captain are synonymous? He is a part of your family too.—is he not?"

"If you mean— do they go together. My answer is 'yes.'"

"That fraternity. That family. They must remain whole and chaste beyond the shadow of a doubt?"

"Yes, Monsieur. Whole and chaste."

"And the Captain embodies that wholeness and chastity."

"By all means." (A collective hush fell over the assembly).

"He has never erred in your eyes."

"No. Never."

"Thank you, Mr. Simmons."

———

Mr. Leming saw himself at a crossroads. Simmons, by his statements, either wittingly or unwittingly, lent an air of legitimacy to the Captain's conduct, already drawn into question by corps witnesses. Indirectly he connected himself with Hastings and **Black Jack**, thereby casting culpability upon the lot of them. Ironically, in adhering to corps tenets, Simmons demonstrated a naive willingness to dismiss the weaknesses of others in their application of those tenets. His solid faith in others of rank blinded him from distinguishing between corps virtues and simple ambition driven by a lust for power. The prosecutor did not call Captain Worthy, hoping to build a case around him. The Captain, with allegations mounting, sat mute and brooding during proceedings. **Black Jack**, undeniably the Captain's partner in the human flesh trade, Mr. Leming preferred to excuse from the stand. To bring him forward opened him to questions from the prosecution, and Edouard

Mouton stood in the wings with a raft of eye witnesses garnered from distant frontier posts, and Matthew York himself, no less. All waited to offer irrevocable, eye-witness evidence connecting **Black Jack** and the Captain in nefarious acts of slaving all along the Great Lakes.

The Chief Magistrate reviewed the genesis of the slave trade for the court:

"Penalties for trafficking in human flesh have become severe, considering the rampant escalation in slaving. France and England, and other leading nations, needed to acquire strong backs for the hard labors associated with building towns and villages where once there stood fields and valleys. On the surface entrepreneurs acquired laborers legitimately, but the demand for solid, cheap labor rose suddenly in the New World, giving rise to a corrupt class of men who would pillage all available stock and sell these unfortunate beings at a premium to the highest bidder. Not only known criminals, but mere colonials, bought into the slave trade in such numbers that the labor pool which supplied the large, imperial nations began to dwindle across the world stage, prompting the unscrupulous to invade the Americas. In Parliament leaders have come forward to curtail slaving and its attendant evils where its presence impugns human productiveness in Crown-sanctioned outposts and colonies. Proclamations are pending."

Sensing defeat, Leming placed **Black Jack** on the stand in an effort to gain him clemency, in spite of witnesses' accounts. He maintained never having accepted wages in slaving. Like Hastings he maintained that he merely transported youth to new places of employment, that he suffered from a spurious charge of mistaken identity in a court hastily convened to find him guilty, finally that he knew the Captain through sheer coincidence. Mr. Leming gave him to understand that if he agreed to testify against his former partner he may well win acquittal from slave trafficking and be allowed to plead guilty to the lesser charges of violating the public trust and disturbing the public tranquility. Reluctantly **Black Jack** agreed, upon learning of the penalties for trafficking in humans for profit, an offense which, according to Mr. Leming, appeared all but indefensible. Therefore, with **Black Jack's** permission and the surrender of a vast share of his liquid assets applied to his defense, Mr. Leming fought in closed chambers to reduce the charges leveled at his client. Subsequently **Black Jack** pleaded guilty to the two lesser charges.

Although presented here in capsule form, the proceedings gave rise to a persistent rumor which followed them long after they ended, suggesting that **Black Jack** bought his way out of a lengthy prison term, using his wealth to tip the scales of justice in his favor. For the remainder of the proceedings he sat silent and disconsolate, awaiting his fate. Ultimately he received a sentence of seven years at hard labor. Broken, alone, and destitute, he was shipped to Montreal where he joined gang crews in rebuilding the fortifications and major structures which the British leveled in the sacking of that city.

Simmons received a comparatively light sentence. He lost his rank and returned to yeoman's status, then went to Fort Niagara to labor in the newly-planned British shipyards on Lake Erie for three years.

Hastings was assigned to return to Great Britain, there to be incarcerated in the infamous Glasgow prison for a term of five years. Before sentencing, in a plea for mercy, he revealed the whereabouts of Fawn's brother. The lad resided at Fort Detroit where he was part of a maintenance crew. The Chief Magistrate ordered Hastings to pay for the lad's return by ship to Ft. Oswego, there to join his sister. The original sentence stood firm.

The tribunal came down heavily upon the Captain. In the matter of Charles Martin, the judges found him guilty of complicity in contributing to Martin's death by failure to keep secure the surroundings in which Martin prevailed. He was spared hanging because no plausible weapon was ever found. In the matter of slaving he was found guilty of the related offense of interfering with the commerce of a sovereign nation, namely, Great Britain. He was convicted expressly of promoting the conversion of a race of people of an independent, foreign nation to a life of servile labor under miserable living conditions. He was also convicted of forceful detention of another against her will-namely, Caroline York. Convicted on multiple counts, he was stripped of his captaincy and chief surveyor positions, denied a pension, removed from the British Expeditionary Forces, fined 1000# and ordered to report to prison at Fort Niagara within a fortnight for a period of seven years. The court conferred upon him a new name, in part to protect him from predations from other prisoners and in part to spare him anguish from further prosecution at the hands of ambitious officials from both within and without the prison system. By the close of proceedings, therefore, James Worthy, the man, ceased to exist.

$* * *$

Finally, it ended. Slightly before the midnight hour of that Wednesday, the 22nd of November, the court-martial came to an end. Exhausted, the York family joined the long procession leading from the crowded church. Lord Carleton provided a brief, yet welcomed repast for all major principals of the prosecution, throwing open the doors of the officers' galley. In the process he met with the General. The two commanders shook hands, vowed to speak no longer of the infamous affair, and established a timetable for the release of the Le Rocher prisoners. They parted on amicable terms, leaving the General to seek out the York family. He found them with the Bear Chief, Cerf Courant, Watkins and Fawn enjoying an assortment of foods.

"If only Henri Marchand were here," the General jested, sampling a turkey leg. He studied his loyal comrades carefully and, standing in their midst, made a sober announcement:

"I believe that this is the proper moment to take my leave." With all eyes fixed upon him he continued: "My purpose here has ended. I leave soon with Henri Marchand. Together we join his old partner, Richard Clement. He has a post in the North Country—far from the rush of civilization."

"But what of Point Aux Bois?" an anguished Suzanne poured forth.

"It belongs to the British—to Sir William Johnson. He bought all the lands surrounding the lake not long ago. Soon the whole countryside will be English-speaking."

Caroline York observed a hint of sadness in the General's eyes. "But how has that come to pass, Monsieur?"

"The Onondagas sold out to him. He paid them a pretty penny for their salt"(72).

"*Salt*?' Caroline asked.

"This entire region is steeped in salt—underground. Crude salt. When you boil it in water it changes to fine particles—the kind that you sprinkle on your meat and other delicacies. I taught the Onondaga to boil it. When you pack meats in salt they withstand extremes in temperatures. I introduced the Onondaga to that as well. I have stored some of it. Blocks of it adorn my ice house." He laughed. "Let the British pay for what I found free of charge."

"But who will administer Pointe Aux Bois?" Caroline asked. "William Johnson is at Niagara."

"A man named Webster* has an interest in the site. With Johnson's permission he has brought one or two families to the region. He plans to manufacture salt. That means people and a town. A city perhaps."

"The end of a beautiful friendship," Suzanne mused.

"I bear the Onondaga no ill will. The British will pay an annual rent to the Onondagas in order to extract minerals. They in turn will own the finest firearms, silks and broadcloths. They will live in sturdy cabins. Johnson will see to it. He is an ambitious man and the Onondaga: They know how to drive a hard bargain." He laughed again. "Besides, I am a bit uncomfortable with a large standing army to the north of me. Who is to say that Lord Amherst will not strike out against me? He will return to Oswego soon, his ear filled with the stories that went on here—and there will be many stories."

"What of your pact of secrecy with Lord Carleton?" Caroline asked.

"I adhere to it strictly, Madame, for the simple reason that Lord Carleton is the lone Red Coat I have encountered who is a true gentleman and a man of his word. Lord Amherst will never learn of Lord Carleton's failure to take Pointe Aux Bois from my lips. If asked, I shall deny everything. Remember! It is through Lord Carleton that we were able to clear the frontier of those scoundrels in his ranks. The earth will be a better place now because of him."

"And the same may be said of you, Monsieur," Caroline spoke. She embraced the General about the shoulders.

"Because of you I am now able to walk the land free from molestation. I am free to walk the land and speak for those whose minds and bodies are held captive by their masters." Her tall and willowy form eclipsed the General by several inches.

"What do you call your movement, Madame?"

"Human justice. We saw a bit of it unfold in court." Her fair complexion turned crimson as she gripped the General's hand firmly. "I *so* wanted to speak in court, but I know that women are forbidden."

"Something tells me that we will hear much more from you, Madame."

Caroline hooked her arm around the General's elbow and walked him along a path. "Perhaps. I leave with my family for Oneida Castle. The Reverend Kirkland has invited me to teach among the native children. He is in great need of teachers. Suzanne will be at my side. She will enjoy herself immensely."

"And what of James, Madame?"

"The great builder? Do you know that he constructed an entire village out of the virgin woodlands for his friend—our friend—the Bear Chief? He too will teach . . . teach the Oneida to build homes . . . to till the soil . . . to conserve the soil without exhausting it." She gazed in the direction of the Bear Chief who sat with Watkins and Fawn.

"Watkins, of course, is James's right hand. Together they helped to save a civilization. To James's delight, Watkins will return to the Round Tops to help to preserve that civilization."

"You speak in glowing terms. I am certain that this is a defining part of your approach to human justice."

"I want to plant little seeds: new ideas among people everywhere. For that I need to teach: to reach others. I will have to travel widely and address great audiences." She stepped lively along, exuding confidence, her long tresses catching the vapors. Suddenly she stopped and reached for the General's hand.

"Thank you for rescuing me. Without you I would be locked away somewhere on the frontier."

"I know that you will accomplish great things. I believe that I have always known that, Madame."

"Mother, mother!! May we join you?" Suzanne bounced merrily along, holding fast to Matthew's hand. James trailed at a leisurely pace. "Mother!! Matthew has an announcement."

Caroline curtailed her discussion with the General, who, in turn, went to take his dinner. Turning, she met Suzanne head-on, the excitement pouring out of the spirited young woman. "Well, daughter. Let the young man speak for himself. Matthew! Do you have a message for me?"

"Why, yes, mother," a struggling Matthew stammered. With hands folded before him, he faced a curious yet stern Caroline York. Standing defiant before river pirates, capturing an entire band of brigands, rescuing young natives from certain death, these feats did little to prepare him to face his mother on those occasions when someone interrupted her in the midst of an important session. She met Matthew with hands on hips, jaw firmly set, and legs shoulder-width apart. Her toe tapping the hard earth, she voiced her unease. "What is it, Matthew?"

Struggling to find the proper words, Matthew allowed Suzanne to poke him once again in the ribs before confronting his mother face-to-face:

"We have come together for such a short period when I find that I too must be leaving." Without awaiting a response, he continued: "I have a young woman. I left her behind to come to Oswego. Distance keeps us apart, but we belong together. I must go to her and bring her back with me."

"Is she pregnant, Matthew?"

Her question startled him, but he kept his bearings. "We are very much in love. I want to live with her. I want to have a child with her."

"Do you plan to marry her?"

"Why, yes. I thought that we would wed soon after her arrival."

"By all means. Bring her. I will provide lodging for the two of you following the ceremony. Tell me about her."

His exuberance obvious, Matthew spoke rapidly: "She speaks several tongues. She speaks and reads English. She is an excellent homemaker and well-mannered."

"Indeed! Now I must meet her. "Hmmm . . . Matthew. Do you plan to return to the marines?"

"No. In some quarters I am a deserter. My place is with my family and my *new* family."

"Then she is pregnant after all."

"Nature has its ways, mother," Matthew returned, somewhat perturbed.

"Not to worry. Your father was a 'pistol' in his day—eh, James?"

"Matthew. You may be sought as a deserter. They will drag you off to be shot," James advised his son.

"How well do you know the General, mother?"

"Fairly well. What do you have in mind?"

"General Le Rocher and Lord Carleton see eye-to-eye. If you would speak to the General about interceding with the commandant on my behalf."

" . . . and the commandant declares that you came to a premature end in defense of the Crown . . ."

" . . . then I may be declared legally deceased."

"Your ship's captain would know the truth, however, Matthew. Needless to say, you are speaking nonsense."

"Aah, Smythe. A fine mate. I think he would side with me. Better not to tell him and let fate take its course. I hate disappointing him to his face."

"Good. I shall speak with the General. On the other hand, I fear that your Smythe has performed a bit of thinking on his own". She looked toward Suzanne. In due course we will know." She set off with James to find the General.

"Mother is on a mission," Suzanne chided. "Here, Matthew. I want you to meet some friends of mine." She ushered before her, Watkins and Fawn.

The two men shook hands, after which Matthew greeted Watkins most warmly. "I have heard many accounts of your bravery and prowess. I hope they are true."

"Purely a matter of interpretation," Watkins returned. Turning to Fawn, he brought her before Matthew. Matthew, on the other hand, noticed Fawn since first she entered the courtroom and thereafter often found himself glimpsing after her. Initially he did not greet her, as though trying to deny the ardor which rose up within him.

"Is she not a peach, old boy?" Watkins called, slapping Matthew playfully.

"Yes. Yes. She brings to mind my beloved," Matthew stated, with a note of melancholy.

"Has something happened to her?" a concerned Watkins asked.

"No. No. Nothing of the sort. I miss her terribly." He turned toward Fawn. "For a moment I thought she stood before me." He shook his head and rubbed his brow.

"Confound it! Bring her here! Besides myself, she has a friend waiting in Fawn."

"That is good to hear."

"What is the name of your woman?"

"Dewai. She is the world to me."

"I see it in your eyes—all thick and misty."

"Does it show, mate?"

"Yes. It really shows—but that is all right. Think nothing of it!"

"Thank you," Matthew returned, wiping his eyes. "I leave for her village at first light."

"Where, if I may be so bold, does she reside?"

"Newfoundland—in the neighborhood of."

"You need a rugged vessel."

"Yes. I have one. I found a fisherman's scow in Oswego harbor."

"For sure you are not taking on the St. Lawrence alone."

"I have not met with any willing volunteers," Matthew returned, a hint of despair in his voice.

"Hold on there, mate. Stay with Fawn. I will return soon."

Alone with Fawn, Matthew attempted to speak to her in the Iroquois tongue. She laughed and greeted him in English. They were still laughing when Watkins returned with Cerf Courant at his side. Out of the corner of his eye Matthew spied Smythe accompanied by the General and his mother.

"Matthew!!" Smythe called. "When is your enlistment ending?"

Matthew thought a moment: "Next year in April."

"Meet your new comrades." Smythe pointed to Watkins and Cerf Courant. "By the time you start for Newfoundland, the St. Lawrence will be frozen. You must wait until spring to start out. By then your enlistment will be exhausted. You will be a *free* man—free to live among your family here." Smythe shook Matthew's hand vigorously. "I will sign your discharge papers—with a commendation, of course."

Looking about him Matthew regarded his mother. Their eyes met. She winked at him approvingly as the General stepped forward to greet him. Turning to James, the General shook his hand.

"You have an outstanding son, Monsieur York. With Watkins and Cerf Courant he travels in good hands."

"Thank you one and all," Matthew replied," a smile on his lips.

"Give that girl a big hug for me," Suzanne whispered to Matthew, tugging at his sleeve.

"That I shall, dear sister. That I shall."

(69)Wikipedia: Fort Ponchartrain du Detroit, (2009) pgs: 1-3.

(70)Answers.com: Samuel Kirkland: Biography of Samuel Kirkland, (2009) pgs: 1-4.

(71)Anderson, Fred. The Crucible of War. Chapter 48: *Amherst's Dilemma* (2000) pgs: 472-475

*In the interest of brevity, only excerpts of key proceedings are presented

*Ephraim Webster: first white settler to live among the Onondaga in what became Syracuse, NY

(72)Munson, Lilian Steele (1969)Shades of Oakwood: Early History of Syracuse, Pageant press International, pgs :1-2.

CHAPTER FIFTEEN

—◆•◆•◆—

Sometimes a Great Moment
Caroline York at Albany.
She Secures Allies.
City Hall.
Afterthoughts.

In acceptance of Samuel Kirkland's invitation, the York family, save Matthew, newly departed for Newfoundland and Dewai, entered into residence at Oneida Castle. At once Caroline and Suzanne took to the teaching of the young natives. James, ever the builder, labored with the Oneida men. Under his guidance, the men constructed, not mere cabins, but homes replete with front porches and gabled roofs of slate. The Oneida men also built the school in which Caroline and Suzanne gave lessons. Connected to the school by a long corridor, a room housed a lavatory with running water generated from a well.

Caroline insisted that her school have long and wide windows opening to the east from whence the sun rose each morning. In the two grand classrooms Caroline hung illustrations of the children's drawings on two adjacent walls. A giant slate blackboard covered a third wall. Cabinets and shelves stocked with books and encyclopedias and a thesaurus rose up against the fourth wall. She ordered each wall painted in soft hues. She chose light yellow, a creamy orange, a subdued red and a pastel blue. James and the native men eagerly applied the paint to the thick plaster walls. Visitors remarked upon the abundant gay brightness throughout. With the fall of the year in full sway, the rooms took on a warm, peaceful ambiance, certain to put the most irascible observer at ease, the colors complementing the rich reds and rust browns of the thick autumnal carpet which covered the school yard beyond the great bay windows.

A fireplace stood manifest in one idle corner and a pot-bellied iron stove complete with a flue occupied a nook behind the headmistress's desk. The ceilings of the classrooms climbed to a height of twelve feet and the floors of hardwood strips pegged together glistened beneath fresh coats of varnish. In each classroom twenty hardtop desks in five rows stood before the headmistress's desk. Iron grille-work streamed down the sides. James chiseled openings in each desktop to hold an inkwell. He also built the desktops on swivels so that students may raise them and place books and valuables within the desks. The students sat on smooth, sturdy benches, broad enough to hold more than a single occupant. Here and there Caroline and Suzanne spread small, colorful carpets which delightfully accented the richly varnished and polished floors.

No unoccupied spaces remained vacant for long. A charcoal bust of Chief Skenando kept vigil beside the blackboard. Opposite, the sketch of a young Samuel Kirkland looked out upon the classroom. Beside her desk Caroline kept a copy of a portrait of the young Colonel Washington, presumably executed a short while after the Braddock campaign against Fort Duquesne. She mounted her artwork on easels supported by tripods. In her classroom Suzanne too kept artwork. They consisted of her pen and paper sketches of the Iroquois leaders whom she encountered thus far in her travels. Sketching from memory, Suzanne took care to dress her subjects in traditional attire.

Mother and daughter divided students by age, with Caroline taking the older youth and Suzanne the younger. From the very first day they enjoyed great success with their charges, who avidly embraced the new surroundings. Although teaching in French, the language approved by the Confederacy, Caroline and Suzanne devoted one period each day to instruction in English. Over all they adopted a curriculum similar to that which they themselves studied when students back home. They adapted it however to comply with current needs. Therefore, the staple subjects consisted of mathematics, the history of western civilization, geography, ethics, homemaking, an introduction to classical Greek and Roman writers, public speaking, science and architecture(woodworking), choral and instrumental music, and art, including woodcarving. By no means an inflexible curriculum, Caroline and Suzanne sought to add new disciplines during the school term: Together they completed outlines for classes in animal husbandry, pharmacology (the study of herbs and plants in disease prevention), chemistry (studying microbes under a microscope), and Euclidean geometry.

Most mornings before classes began, Caroline brought out her favorite goose-feathered duster and applied it liberally to where it did the most good: the portraits and the bookshelves. Although donated to the school, the literature and books of the period smacked of the Protestant ethos, imbued with moralistic overtones in the Calvinist spirit. To her knowledge Calvinism embraced adherents among the greater community's powerful elite, city fathers who owned vast properties and wealth. To Caroline Calvinism and its kindred denominations shunned the greater masses, those immigrants who formed the laboring backbone of the colonies. Moreover, according to her research, the elite held the prerogative of saving themselves from the perils of original sin by embracing Calvinist tenets: an exclusive set of immutable doctrines, inflexible rules, which bound one steadfastly to pre-conceived standards from birth to death. Early Calvinists, Caroline recalled, all but condemned non-believers, leaving the so-called unchaste masses to wallow in sin and everlasting damnation on earth.

A practicing Catholic, Caroline longed to expose her students to the more liberal and egalitarian teachings of her faith, a faith slowly gaining ascendancy in Protestant New England. In teaching she saw herself as a disciple of the Christ, executing good works on behalf of the poor and needy. She did not conduct blistering sermons or lead protests or pilgrimages, but simply went about her day administering to her charges, quietly practicing her faith. The truly educated, she believed, reached beyond familiar, parochial surroundings. Making intelligent choices, they sampled different points of view while challenging long-accepted traditions. She intended to make of her classroom a microcosm of the world beyond the native village so that her students may better understand the intricacies of life in this emerging era of new and complex community settings. To that extent Caroline needed to supplement her school's scantily-clad library with volumes written by the masters in literature. Many of these came from the ancient Greek and Roman civilizations. Copies all, other works drew upon Queen

Elizabeth's England and the Age of Chaucer and Spain in the era of Cervantes and his epic poem, Don Quixote. In coursing through a gazette she discovered that a reform movement which gripped France by mid-century gave rise to reformist writers and philosophers under the term: The Enlightenment. She longed to secure copies of these works.

When Caroline learned that Reverend Kirkland planned to go on a book-buying spree she eagerly begged him to take her with him. Albany lay to the east, a good six day's excursion by horse and wagon. He tried to dissuade her, citing dangers inherent in travel for a woman, but she persisted. Occasionally an Albany gazette found its way to her school and, in skimming pages, she learned of the burgeoning settlement's predilection for publishing. The names of bookshops streamed along one page on a street aptly named Market. Where bookshops abounded, authors and artists convened. The gazettes also told of commerce and manufacturing thriving in the Albany community: namely ironworks and beer breweries. These attracted artisans of many stripes. The fur trade, she found, stood at the pinnacle of commercial development, and Albany, the center of that trade, gave rise to entrepreneurs, many of whom became city fathers in politics and government. They formed the upper crust of the community at large and returned a generous portion of their wealth to the construction of Albany's early remarkable edifices, notwithstanding the elegant homes which they built to honor themselves. Reverend Kirkland rubbed shoulders with some of these leaders. Among his friends he counted the scions of some of Albany's oldest Dutch families, men who carried considerable influence in affairs political and religious. In her mind's eye, Caroline conceived of bringing her school into the public consciousness and Albany, its leaders, and its infectious spontaneity, furnished the stage upon which she may present not only her students' achievements, but to garner support for her adopted theme: erudition for all under the banner of human justice.

On that morning of Sunday, December 17th, a small entourage departed the confines of Oneida Castle. The troupe consisted of Caroline and Reverend Kirkland, a small armed guard, and Caroline's precocious native student, Thomas Steed. Suzanne longed to go in order to write in her journal, but her mother persuaded her to remain with the students and teach in her stead, promising to render her an exciting account upon returning. The party journeyed beside the Mohawk River, all scouting signs pointing to clear passage to the east. They spent a full five days on the trail, reaching Albany on Friday, December 22nd about mid-morning.

Immediately they passed through the palisades and entered Fort Frederick where the British commandant granted Reverend Kirkland a merchant's permit of welcome to enter the city. Everyone rested, bathed, and devoured turkey dinners and exchanged thoughts of the journey. The troupe unanimously complained of worn boots and sore limbs, whereupon Reverend Kirkland secured the services of a native tradesman. John Root, a Mohawk, lived in a village nearby and regularly brought caches of furs to the fort. One of a few wealthy natives, Root boasted of a frame house and a surfeit of goods on hand, to wit, soft deerskin boots and pliant moccasins. Overwhelmingly the travelers accepted an offering of footwear and fought for position at the booth where he displayed them. Drinking from a flask, John Root laughed uproariously at the hectic scene playing out before him. The footwear chosen, he appointed himself guide and took everyone on a tour of the fort's grounds.

Fort Frederick sat atop the highest point in Albany, a high hill about one mile in length which sloped sharply down to meet the Hudson River. A dirt street carved from the barren earth followed the course of the hill to the river. It seemed to bisect the hill equally into two halves, giving rise to streets running north and south of it. According to John Root, someone named this main path Jonkers. Bringing his guests to a tower in the fort, John Root pointed out the grand width of the street. From an exclusive vantage point, the visitors discerned two-storied gabled homes of wood and brick flanking Jonkers. Interspersed among the homes, artisans' shops and mercantile houses occupied all remaining spaces. The whole panorama seemed prim and proper, accentuated in no small way by the rows of shade trees and cultivated garden patches that sat before each home and many public buildings. The fort itself served a rather hollow purpose at present, John Root confessed. According to his sources it never entered into battle. The long-anticipated clash with the French and their Indian allies never came and the fort slowly declined in relevance. A small force still staffed the fort, and its hospital served as Albany's infirmary. Formerly the western-most boundary of the city, the fort now remained an island amid a sea of new developments which pushed over the hilltop and westward into the forest beyond (73).

At Caroline's urging Samuel Kirkland led her and her student, Thomas Steed, along the upper reaches of Jonkers Street. Stately structures came into view and her host described them in brief detail. Subsequently the little party passed before the manor of Sir William Johnson, Secretary of Indian Affairs, the Stadt Huys, or City Hall, the Dutch Reformed Church, the Livingston estate and many more structures, all of which devolved about Jonkers Street. At a point midway along the artery, Caroline stopped long enough to delve into her surroundings, remarking to her host how small and compact the city appeared to her. Remnants of the original palisades encircled the city from where she stood. She noted how diminutive the streets running south were in contrast to those running north. Caroline next explored the book stores of Market Street, coming away with a handful of treasured volumes. She sampled oysters in one of the open-air markets, chasing them down her throat with a mug of beer. In the waning afternoon hours Caroline stood at the foot of Jonkers straining to view the remains of the old Fort Orange, an early citadel from the Dutch period. She visited Beaver Street, that narrow passageway, home to inns and taverns strewn among the ateliers of tradesmen and laborers. She concluded that the city served as a gathering place for men of many stripes: men of the cloth, men of letters, artists, artisans, and authors, the wealthy and the humble. She looked forward to making Albany a home away from home and, drawing Samuel Kirkland apart from Thomas Steed, made these observations known to him.

Samuel Kirkland guided the party to North Pearl Street where his friend Cornelis Cuyler, the object of his visit, resided in a sector populated by most of Albany's city fathers and prominent families. Cuyler, one of several members of the CIA—Commission of Indian Affairs—came to prominence in the community by way of astute entrepreneurial abilities. Specifically, he was a leading fur trader of the day, a persuasive man who induced local natives to bring to him exclusively their prized furs and pelts (74). Early successes allowed him to purchase land tracts in and about Albany which he gifted to family members. City fathers endeared themselves to him, helping to make him mayor of colonial Albany. He belonged to the Dutch Reformed Church. Some members customarily conducted missions within neighboring Iroquois camps. Like many of his peers he kept slaves at home, but benevolently regarded them as domiciled servants. Like them he adhered to a form of hierarchy within the church which rested upon class and birthright— two outstanding qualities of an immutable system with rigid boundaries. In practice one's class and birthright marked one's station in the community, a rigid design in the conceivable shape of a pyramid. At its apex stood the community's wealthy and influential. Artists and artisans comprised the mid-section and crowding around the base flocked the day laborers, (skilled and unskilled), trade apprentices, indentured servants, slaves, soldiers of modest rank, the insane (the habitually stressed), and the dumb (uneducated). Thus, Reverend Kirkland prepared Caroline for her meeting with Cornelis Cuyler. She conveyed none of this knowledge to Thomas Steed, hoping to deter him from forming preconceived notions about the famed entrepreneur.

Although Cuyler owed his post of Indian commissioner to William Johnson and served directly under him in that capacity, he by no means universally adopted royalist leanings. He understood the dual nature of the post lay in persuading natives to trade unilaterally with the British and in renouncing ties with the French. He spent many hours on the road visiting the natives and building their loyalty by distributing gifts and other amenities. He helped them to drive off rival bands in pursuit of British trade and he struggled to diminish the devastating affect which the so-called independent traders exerted upon the fur trade, those colonials who skirted established channels and sold directly to willing customers. Cuyler performed these tasks well, tasks both unrelenting and unforgiving, for, in the absence of strict preparedness, today's friend may become tomorrow's enemy. William Johnson, like most supervisors, demanded positive results for efforts expended and it is at this juncture that the two men infrequently quarreled with each other— not so much of substance, but of method.

That afternoon found the small party in the warm library of Cornelis Cuyler. Their host invited them to tea and no sooner did they take places before the fireplace than a maid-servant ushered in the piping hot beverage along with a tray of crumpets. The library, a veritable museum to Caroline, stood swathed in rich tapestries. Thick draperies cascading to the polished oak floor billowed forth from the full-length windows. Lush chairs and sofas bestrewn with hand-embroidered coverlets beckoned to the visitor. Maple paneling framed the doorway and fireplace and from the center of the ceiling a two-tiered candelabra, elliptical in shape and fitted with candle-holders, hung suspended in bold relief. While the guests became seated, a servant holding an extended wick reached upward, effortlessly lighting the lower bank of candles. At once the room stood awash in brilliant light. Narrow fingers of light glanced from the walls. They fastened upon the solid row of bookcases behind Cuyler's ample desk, running along the entire length of the wall, coming to rest beside the fireplace. Caroline permitted herself a bit of reverie for, encased behind glass-covered doors, the books, miniature soldiers all, stood at attention, ready to jump from their confines and inundate an entire colony with page after page of accumulated knowledge.

The visitors seated before him, Cuyler, rather tall and spare, took a place behind a desk in a sumptuous recliner which allowed him to lean backward to the extreme. He did so when contemplating subjects of great importance. On this occasion he launched himself upright, eyes bearing down upon young Thomas Steed. Caroline made certain to place the young man between Reverend Kirkland and herself, undeniably making him the center of attention. She introduced him, praising his mastery of the English tongue, explaining his passion for reading, the perfect cue for her host to open conversation:

"I, too, am fond of reading," Cuyler opened, smiling appreciatively, making a passing glance toward scores of volumes. "Tell me. What have you read of late?" He knitted his brow in anticipation of a response.

Thomas looked first to Caroline, then back to his host: "My headmistress has been able to secure a number of ancient Greek works—English copies to be sure, I have been involved with the Republic by Plato."

"Yes, yes. I have the work—two copies, to be precise. Read it more than once. What are your impressions?"

Thomas spoke with conviction:

"The author makes the reader aware of life in a state befriended by honest and conscientious lawgivers. I find that interesting in that it is a condition existing only in a near-perfect universe—one removed from conflict."

"What do you know of conflict at your age, lad?" Cuyler asked soberly.

"Governments and conflict go hand-in-hand. Governments thrive on it. They *need* conflict in order to function—otherwise they dissolve, the office-holders die, and a new government takes their place."

"Are you able to provide an example of this phenomenon?"

"Of course. Look at the fur trade. It is the driving force in this colony. The Crown—the government wants to regulate the flow of furs in order to keep all rivals at bay."

"Is that not the way of any governmental body?"

"Not in the classical sense. You see, in the classical sense, governments do not take form in order to assert total authority: i. e. make a profit. They simply perform the people's will. On the other hand, the Crown wants full possession of the fur trade—over France—over all comers. even over the natives who provide the furs."

"A most profound claim. Please go ahead." Cuyler leaned forward.

Thomas Steed, not knowing of his host's background, continued: "I see a situation in which the British want Iroquois lands in order to gain unrestricted access to furs and pelts. The Iroquois want to keep their lands. However, in falling prey to ruthless government agents, the Iroquois have sold precious lands, passing unwittingly thereby under British influence. The lands are gone forever and they themselves become British vassals. Herein lies the conflict."

"I do not see a conflict here. What you have said speaks of the flow of trade."

Thomas Steed became more specific: "The British colonial government has appointed trade commissioners to direct the flow of furs into the colony at Albany. Those who administer the fur trade have become wealthy. Upon surrendering their furs, the Iroquois forever relinquish ownership of them. British merchants now own them. Deep within, the Iroquois know that the British want their lands and that buying furs is a prelude to that takeover. Sometimes the Iroquois are reluctant to sell. They seek counsel from the French, but the French are vulnerable to British incursions. In the process the Iroquois leave behind villages open to forceful takeover. Some try to sell directly to Albany residents, but Albany leaders deny them access. This is unfortunate, for the Mohawk who originally provided the British with furs are forbidden from selling within the city itself, thus losing the opportunity to be their own merchants. Again the conflict, a game of give and take where two adversaries forever weigh each other's strengths and weaknesses. Every Iroquois lives with the fear of a hostile takeover."

Cuyler leaned forward, arms leaning heavily on the desk. He remained fixed upon Thomas Steed's every word, studying him. Ruffled, but not alarmed, he spoke in defense of the trade commissioners: "The commissioners answer to Sir William Johnson and to my knowledge he has treated with the natives fairly."

"Of this I have no doubt. He has a grand home not far from here. It bespeaks of his success in winnowing away from the natives valued pieces. He and the commissioners have prospered while the natives are drawn into their service, much like a deep well with steep sides traps the poor wretch who tumbles into it when fetching water."

"You have a great way with words," Cuyler spoke softly.

"I have read that the Albany merchants have appealed to the mother country to pass laws in their favor to regulate the trade. More recently, they have banished those natives who seek to enter the trade for themselves. The government and the merchants have combined forces. They do not share the wealth. They seek advantages. They seek untold profit. They *covet*."

"They covet?" Cuyler spoke in disbelief.

"Yes. They covet that which is not theirs—the lands of the Iroquois. The furs are but an excuse to move in, set up shop, and take possession. Meanwhile, the poor native, lured with sweet assurances, agrees in the beginning. Yet when he drops back to think about it, the moment has passed. He has lost his lands—given them away with the stroke of a pen. Yes. They *covet*. To covet is a major transgression according to this colony's dominant religious establishment— an establishment which has loyal followers among the trading elite on both sides of the great ocean. They covet with a passion, openly defying their religion—their higher power. They do it out of self-interest—more plainly, greed."

The entrepreneur sat in silence. A mask of bewilderment covered the prominent features. For a long moment he sat motionless, saying nothing, leaving the precocious guest to fathom the substance of the thoughts coursing through his mind. When at last he spoke he did so in the apologetic tone of one seeking forgiveness: he, the model entrepreneur tainted with the stain of sin, sin that must be expiated. Before the visitors Cuyler spoke in terms which Caroline later described as penitent.

"I am sorry, Thomas, if I have offended you. Yes. To covet is to transgress. Then I must be guilty of it for many years for I have acted in much the same way throughout my life. I did not think in that vein until now. It has taken an innocent stranger to open my eyes. The demands that my labors put upon me— pushing back obstacles to meet the expectations of others—striving to attain lofty ends. Yes! Yes! I see your point. I have led a double life." He wrung his hands. He rubbed his wrists. Rising, he approached Thomas Steed.

"I must ask my congregation to absolve me. Thomas. Tell me. Will you address my congregation? Tell them what you have told me? Ask for forgiveness? For me?" He placed his arm over Thomas's shoulder and looked with melancholy into his eyes.

The events of the past few moments unbridled the usually retiring student, but he exerted a tight rein over visceral urges to cry out in acclamation of a small victory. Fighting to remain calm, he projected an air of reserve. He sat relaxed before his host, a handsome youth, dressed in the black suit of a Sunday worshiper, black hair parted down the middle, his texture pale in terms of native standards, coal-black eyes retentive, seeing all.

"Yes. I will speak," Thomas replied softly. Looking to Caroline, he noted her approval.

"It is set then." Cuyler breathed a sigh of relief. "There is an afternoon service tomorrow. You will stay the night. You must visit more of our town. I know that you will find it to your liking." Cuyler spoke rapidly. Running words together, he repeatedly opened and closed his hands, rubbing them against his trousers, not knowing quite what to do with them, his agitation obvious. Soon, however, he gathered himself and made an announcement. "Let us finish our tea. I want to take you all on a brief tour of my home."

Caroline too sensed relief, albeit of a different context. She stepped into place to begin the tour when a torrent of thoughts ran through her mind. Here, she learned, by means of her able student, that Thomas was able to crack into the fabric of the upper crust of the community. Solid arguments compelled Cuyler, one member of the staid and landed proprietors, to take a hard look at himself and in so doing to view how he looked in the eyes of another— an innocent cherub. For Caroline the renowned entrepreneur came face-to-face with the unadorned native who by example compelled him to evaluate himself in terms of strict religious doctrine. Slowly she realized that Thomas Steed now owned the soul of Cornelis Cuyler: free to tend to it in any fashion he deemed just. He would of course restore the man to his soul, but not until the pain of his self-centered ways manifested itself—not until Cuyler recanted openly in his church before his peers--tomorrow. 'A masterful coup', she caught herself whispering aloud. She did not immediately realize however that her student had ushered into place a chain of events destined to change the course of her life.

On the following day, December 23rd, the principals: Caroline, Samuel Kirkland, and Thomas Steed, accompanied Cuyler and his wife to the Dutch Reformed Church. Close by the home at North Pearl, the church sat at the intersection of Jonkers and Market Streets. It protruded noticeably into Jonkers, compelling all itinerants and conveyances to pass around it when negotiating the convergence of the two arteries. A single story, squared structure, topped with a pyramid-like roof, the church rose up from the dusty intersection like an intrusive monolith. Within, rows of benches ran full length on either side of a broad corridor, which terminated before the simple altar, little more than a great table. Behind the altar and built into the west wall an all-encompassing stained-glass window allowed the light of the day to fill the cavernous interior with soothing shades of color, covering all with a warm glow. Home-spun carpets lay in a semi-circle about the altar, comely signs of adornment in an otherwise modestly-appointed edifice. Tall candles, one placed in the bay of each great window, reminded one of the arrival of the Christmas season. Above the congregants' heads, the vaulted roof climbed endlessly skyward (75).

Caroline and company took places reserved for them in the first row to the right of the altar. Hewn from stout timber and polished to a high gloss, the benches or pews allowed one to sit in comfort, in as much as church services often ran over two hours in length. Ahead of her, in an alcove behind the altar, Caroline spied a flood of candles shielding a pastoral scene, La Crèche, a facsimile of the crude stall in which Jesus of Nazareth was born. A wave of melancholy enveloped her, for she must forsake being among her loved ones during the beginning of this Holy Season. In her excitement of late she confessed to herself of having forgotten that Holy Week thrust itself suddenly upon her. Christmas Eve lay but a day away and she found herself adrift from the members of her family. She watched with curiosity as congregants one by one walked to La Crèche, and with lighted candles in hand placed them in neat rows before the manger. Reverend Kirkland whispered to her that each candle represented a loved one whom the celebrant is physically unable to reach. Nodding, she rose and silently slipped into line behind the celebrants. Reaching the sextant, she asked him for three candles.

Crossing to La Crèche, she lit one for James, Suzanne, and Matthew. Placing them at the foot of La Crèche, she knelt low, shed a tear, and wearing a thin but distinct smile, slipped back to her place. Once seated, her smile broadened. She gripped the Reverend's hand and her heart skipped a lively beat once again.

The Domine approached the altar. Newly-appointed, Eilardus Westerlo* held credentials from the church leadership in Holland. Beside him an assistant Domine accompanied him, for this, according to the Reverend Kirkland, was to be an extraordinary service. Following a simple invocation, the chief Domine beckoned to Cornelis Cuyler who rose and came to stand before him. The service began the moment that the Domine acknowledged him, the petitioner.

A slight man, Eilardus Westerlo possessed a deeply-resonant voice, one which rose to the heights of the roof before descending to break over the heads and shoulders of the congregants. For this reason it was not uncommon for congregants to hold several points of view when discussing his height and weight. For many, if not all, he appeared much larger, even overbearing, when he spoke, attributes they willingly assigned to him— properties suitable to a Domine.

"I am told that you come in search of absolution from your transgressions, Brother Cuyler."

"Yes, Your Grace. I have committed a grave transgression which brings me to hang my head in shame."

"You have the congregation on your side, as well as myself and my assistant, Brother Cuyler. We will pull you through. Tell me what troubles you."

The entrepreneur spoke in a mild, soft manner. "I have become wealthy from my endeavors in the fur trade—enough to bring happiness to all of my family. My name is well known in the community. People look to me for counsel and guidance. I have tried to be worthy of the trust that people have placed in me." The congregants strained to hear his soft tones: all but lost amid the enormity of the vaulted ceiling.

"Yes, brother Cuyler?"

"In my labors to procure trade relations with the natives of these parts, I operated from a strict self-serving frame of mind. I wanted to govern the fur trade in terms of Albany's interests. This is not altogether evil, but it establishes a poor beginning: The practice makes of the native a debtor—one who is drawn into the service of another. In this case I speak about the native who conforms to the demands of his creditor: myself and others of my profession. I *covet* that which the native holds dear. This **is** evil because I give to him so little in return for his contribution to my wealth. The little that I give him suffices to bring him back to me with yet more riches, for I have deceived him into believing that I am giving him value for value. I even pay him in coin so that he may purchase the goods of other merchants; however, he knows not the worth of the coin and pays exceedingly more for the goods. Last, in my avarice, I have pitted native against native: They battle with each other to earn the prerogative of trading with me. Family foundations have been disrupted. Animosities have spread among otherwise peaceful siblings. To satisfy my own lust for wealth and the power which accompanies it, I have made ignominious strides in bringing down an entire civilization." On the point of tears, he stepped back and daubed at his eyes.

"What do you ask of us, brother Cuyler?"

"I ask for forgiveness so that I may rebuild my life. In the eyes of our Saviour. I am a selfish being. It has taken the wisdom of a young boy to make me aware of my transgressions. Through my greed, I have poisoned his elders with rum. I have outfitted them with cheap strouds and duffles (76). I have withheld full value for native goods." He turned to face Thomas Steed. Caroline gently pushed her precocious charge forward where he came to stand by the side of the penitent parishioner.

"Domine. Here is the lad who has rescued my soul from further temptation. He is the worthy exemplar of his civilization—a civilization which I have abused in countless ways for most of my life. Tell me that it is not too late to redeem my soul." With arms gripping Thomas by the shoulder, Cornelis Cuyler burst forth: "He is a Godsend. The Lord, Our Saviour, has sent him to me. He believes there is a bit of me worth saving. Tell me this is true, Domine." He gripped Thomas Steed ever-tighter.

"Let the young man speak." Facing Thomas Steed, the Domine raised his arms.

"I come in support of my host, Cornelis Cuyler. He has taken me into his home where I am his guest. He is a good man who, in quest of his dreams, believes that he has strayed from the narrow path of righteousness set forth by his faith. In my view he must be permitted to make amends. He has the courage and strength to do so. To deny him forgiveness is to cast him out of the house of his God. That alone is an unforgivable transgression in my mind. He deserves the support of this congregation. Please heed his request."

The congregants began to chant. Applauding in a steady beat, they sang in unison: "Save brother Cuyler." Beneath Caroline the oaken flooring creaked. The bright candles flickered. Meanwhile, the chorus of determined voices inundated the church, flooding the senses and turning the ears deaf to all other sounds.

Again the Domine raised arms aloft. In response the chorus subsided and the congregants, each man, woman, and child, strained at the edge of the pews in order to remain cognizant of the words of the clerical leader.

"I hear your pleas, faithful servants. You have spoken most admirably. Please bide your time and allow me to confer with my associate and other peers." The Domine vacated the altar, a small retinue in his wake.

Caroline stood in awe of the events unfolding about her—events which she set into motion stemming from a simple concern over books for her school library. Beside herself, she was alternately elated and fear-struck: elated, following the attention which Thomas Steed commanded: fear-struck, in that she knew not the depth of his newly-won celebrity. She abandoned these thoughts as soon as the Domine returned to the altar.

"Brother Cuyler. Your peers are in favor of acquitting you of your transgressions. I am inclined to follow their lead; however, I will, in my official role, absolve you provided that you demonstrate your sincerity to change. You know that this entails making a sacrifice on your part. Are you prepared to make a sacrificial offering?"

"Yes, my Domine."

"State your sacrifice, please."

Drawing a deep breath, the entrepreneur gushed forth in a flurry of words: "I propose to equip and supply the school of this dear lad, Thomas Steed, with the finest and most complete library ever to burst upon the frontier."

The congregants swooned in approval in a wave of expostulations. Motioning for quiet, Cuyler spoke again: "I propose to pay the wages of the teachers at the school which Thomas Steed attends."

Applause filled the church. The congregants rose in a body, chanting approval. The Domine allowed the flock to rejoice unabated for several minutes before calling them back to order.

"Brethren. Your enthusiasm overwhelms me. Brother Cuyler. You have at your disposal a request to make of this congregation, attendant upon your sacrifice."

"Esteemed Domine. I request that my new friend, Thomas Steed, be at will to take part in the services of this church alongside others of his population."

An otherwise buoyant expression shrunk from that of overt joy to one of consternation. Motionless, the Domine stumbled for words. "Your charge is not a church member," he stated flatly.

The statement brought sighs of disdain from the congregants. Gathering himself together, the Domine sought to mollify the congregants and remain true to church practice in a single stroke. "He is not precluded from becoming a member, certainly when he reaches the age of majority and declares residency. In the meanwhile, he is welcomed as a guest as often as he shall desire." Smiling, he backed away from the altar, chin thrust forward, a sense of proprietorship having returned.

Cornelis Cuyler conferred with his young guest, after which he summoned the Domine to his side. "Excellency. Thomas has a request to make. It appears both laudable and suitable under these circumstances."

A delighted Caroline watched as Thomas offered a hand to the Domine in friendship. The tall cleric bent low to receive Thomas's message. In short order the pastor blushed scarlet red, an unexpected turn for him. He conferred with the entrepreneur. When at last he resumed a place behind the altar, he made an announcement:

"Brother Cuyler and his young charge have conceived of a novel method for increasing church membership, principally making of the church a truly representative body. They propose to admit those members of the community who heretofore have been omitted, yeah, prevented from attending services at our beloved church."

While the congregants pondered the impact of the statement, the Domine continued: "There are those of the community who perform dear services and yet receive little recompense, yeah, respect. They are everywhere visible in our daily lives, but because we do not know them by name, they remain strangers to us. Nameless, they go about their lives paying tribute to and serving those of a higher station to whom they have become indebted. In the eyes of the Church this is an irregular construction. It is one that church leaders have not successfully addressed down through the years. Therefore, the Church must come forward and make amends. The church--our Church--that magnanimous assembly of worshipers dedicated to spreading the word of our Saviour to everyone must come forward to right this indiscretion. We must recognize changes taking place around us reflective of the greater community in which we live. We have the power!"

Arms raised to the heavens, the booming voice descended over the congregation. Tall and erect, head aloft, the Domine ardently shouted in an appeal which sent shivers along Caroline's spine. Not far from her, a congregant swooned and crumpled to the floor. An elderly man, in obvious stress, sat down abruptly, moping his brow. Eager to assess the opinion of the congregation, the Domine issued a request in no uncertain terms:

"What say thee to throwing open our doors to admit the silent ones of our community? The servants? The dock laborers? The iron makers? The brew masters? The widowed washer woman with children? The flesh and bones of our community?"

"It is a bold gesture," a congregant called.

"It is highly contrary to tradition," another added.

"Our church is strong," a man called. "We have the power."

"We are up to the task. We are the most significant institution in the community. Everyone looks to us to lead," an older congregant called.

"Then let us lead," his younger colleague returned.

With the latter's declaration the congregation began to chant support for the measure in a series of exclamations accompanied by generous foot-stomping. From the corner of her eye Caroline spied whole rows locking arms and swaying to and fro. Beside her Reverend Kirkland stood in wonder with jaw agape. Cuyler and Thomas Steed joined hands. In spite of the din rising, the Domine maintained a rigid stance, his features expressionless.

Hard pressed to gain the attention of his flock, the Domine waited until the enthusiasm appreciably diminished. Reaching for a gavel, he brought it down forcefully upon the altar. Again the strong voice rang out:

"By acclamation you have chosen to absolve Brother Cuyler. You have also by acclamation accepted his sacrifice and finally you have voiced your approval of reaching out to all who would enter the Church but for the intercession of mitigating circumstances. Your proposal carries prodigious implications. As you know, the Church council in the mother country has binding jurisdiction over measures introduced here on this soil; however, given your solid support for these measures today, I am confident that they indeed will become adopted and that as a consequence our lives will become that much more enriched."

The congregants, upon learning of the leanings of their Domine, came together once again. Rising, they applauded him and several worshipers reached out to touch Cornelis Cuyler and his young charge. The celebration showed no signs of waning until Cuyler himself stood beside the Domine and called for attention. Now in a hall suddenly silent, the Domine spoke:

"As you know we are in the Christmas Season. In the corner of our church sits La Crèche. It stands for the many virtues which you have been infused with since your youth. There is Hope—the hope for a better world. There is Birth—the birth of new ideas for a new tomorrow. There is Rebirth—the rebirth of happiness in a world wrought with pain and sorrow. There is Love—the love of stranger to stranger, of man to woman, of parent to child, of the patroon for his humblest laborer. Yeah, of nation to nation. Yeah! There is Love for one and all. In our church this is who we are. We are all of these qualities. We need to profess them, lest they die on the vine."

Pausing, the Domine allowed the words to settle among the congregants in preparation for a concluding statement, one behind which he threw the full strength of his voice, one in which by his every movement and gesture he manifested true sincerity.

"In deference to the passion of the Christmas Season, I sanction forgiveness for Cornelis Cuyler. I sanction the adoption of his sacrifices. I sanction the admission of his young companion and those of his choosing into our church. Finally, I sanction that our church embrace the broader community so that all may partake of our beneficence and the gifts of Our Saviour."

In this final address, the Domine collapsed upon the altar, exhausted. The assistant, followed by Cornelis Cuyler, ran to his side. They gave him water to drink and presently the Domine sat upright, straightened his garments, and glanced about with arms uplifted. "We have accomplished much here today," he uttered wanly. "I am privileged to be a part of history in the making." Adjusting his frock, he spoke again: "We have above all assembled here to pay homage to Our Saviour. Let the ceremony begin."

A chorus of children paraded along the great aisle between the pews. Reaching the altar they split into two spurs and proceeded to La Crèche. There, facing the congregants, they broke into song. Slowly the pews emptied, the congregants spilling into the aisle, walking shoulder to shoulder in two long rows. Coming to rest beside the children they too broke into song. From behind La Crèche a pair of trumpeters appeared. Taking places at either end of the grand organ, they awaited the organist's signal before sounding their instruments. An obeisant Caroline swept into the procession. At her side walked Reverend Kirkland, followed by Thomas Steed and Cornelis Cuyler.

Caroline's party constituted the last of the congregants to assume places before La Crèche. Turning forward, Caroline and her companions faced the church proper. They formed the front row in a thick profusion of devotees who came together to lift their voices in song. The trumpets called out, the signal for the entire congregation to lock together upon a favorite theme. At once the throng of some four hundred voices opened with "O Holy Night." The Domine stood before them, leading his flock to the accompaniment of the organist. With spine arched and head held high, he closed his eyes and with arms gesturing like soft waves rolling in the sea, he gently swayed back and forth, a man who, at that moment, resided more in heaven than on earth.

The heightened spirit of the event overwhelmed Caroline. Not a songster by choice, she threw her voice into concert with those of the congregants. The voices swelling behind her lifted her state of consciousness to a higher level. She sang ever the louder, her chin and neck straining to push out into the hall every bit of melody that she was able to summon her lungs to muster. Like the Domine, she too struck out with her arms. Tall and willowy, blonde tresses cascading over her shoulders, she became caught up in the fervor of the moment. She broke into tears, tears of joy. Sporadic at first, they soon poured generously down her cheeks. She tossed her head in a futile effort to dislodge them, but never did she break from her song. Her cheeks aglow, she joined hands with Reverend Kirkland on her right and with Thomas Steed on her left and sang on through a host of pastoral melodies far into the afternoon.

* * *

That evening, at the Cuyler mansion, Caroline thought of little else but rest. Her throat ached from singing and her sore feet pounded against her high-buttoned shoes. Obligingly she eased into a high-backed chair before a fireplace and closed her eyes. Presently a soft voice beckoned to her. She opened them to find a servant bent over her with a hot cup of tea and warm crumpet. Beside her Reverend Kirkland and Thomas Steed sipped tea while conversing lightly. Soon, Cuyler, wearing a thin but distinct smile, joined them. He sat behind an ornate desk poised to make an announcement. Her mind wandering beneath a thin veil of semi-lucidness, Caroline struggled to gain cognizance of her surroundings at the moment he broke into discourse. She bolted upright, fully awake.

"I am gratified that you chose to spend Christmas with me and my wife. I have spoken to her and she is eager to meet you in the flesh."

Turning in her chair, Caroline nodded in approval.

"Of course I am not able to replace your loved ones at home. This must be a difficult period for you."

"I have no one to blame but myself. I begged Reverend Kirkland to take me to Albany." She made a fleeting glance in the missionary's direction. Forcing herself to smile, she thrust out her chin. "If I did not arrive now you would have to wait longer to meet Thomas Steed."

"And to become absolved," her host reminded her.

"Yes, yes, of course," Caroline smiled impishly, now fully-awake.

"I am truly grateful that you arrived," Cuyler stated, in a voice marked with sincerity "Be aware that I will make good on my pledges. If there is anything more that you need."

Caroline leaned forward. "There is something I wished to discuss with you." Her eyes followed the black servant who brought out a tray of treats. Depositing them on the spacious desk, she curtsied, and left the room briskly, full skirts billowing behind her.

"Thank you, Birdie," Cuyler called over his shoulder. "That is Birdie," he mouthed, snacking. "I am at a loss without her. My second arm, next to my wife, of course." He sensed a question looming. Sipping tea, he awaited Caroline's delivery.

She began slowly. "As you know I teach the native youth in my adopted village of Oneida Castle. I have found them alert and intelligent and eager to learn. They are, I dare say, just as able as white youth. Occasionally a Thomas Steed comes along who supports a long-held theory of mine."

Cuyler bore in on her, eyes unblinking. "I believe that I know your theory, Mrs. York." He placed the tea cup down gently. "You believe that learning is not confined to the whites of the species human-kind. Am I correct?" A thin smile crossed his lips.

"In a word, yes." Laughing softly, Caroline smiled. "You may call me 'Caroline.'" Hands folded, she continued: "I know that you provide a home for your servants. Yet the thought has occurred to me concerning your investment in their erudition."

Her host grimaced. "Ah, *erudition*. I have not heard that term since my days in grade school not far from here." He rubbed his hands together vigorously, a sign to Caroline of latent nervousness. She sat calmly, awaiting a reply.

"My dear Mrs. York. Caroline. My servants are home-schooled to the extent that they have no occasion to strike out on their own."

"In all due respect, Sir, the advantages of public erudition are many. Why, in terms of tools alone . . ."

"Yes, yes. I know; however, my wife devotes a major portion of her day to administering to the servants."

"And administer to her household duties as well? I find her an incredible woman as such," Caroline returned, maintaining her ground.

"I stand corrected. She has confined her teaching to Saturdays of late."

"Well after Services, I conjecture," Caroline returned, a hand buoying up her chin.

"Not at all. *Before* Services. You see, Services require most of the afternoon's devotion."

Shifting in place, Caroline pressed home her point: "You are allowing a great opportunity to slip away. For sure you want to impart to your staff every advantage to learn and grow. By the way, do they go with you to Services?" Smiling, she sat back.

Cuyler attempted to gather himself: "No. They do not accompany me to Services. As for their erudition, their days are taken up by chores. There is very little . . ."

" . . . in the way of idle moments to devote to erudition, you say?" She smiled, her eyes never leaving him.

"In a manner of speaking. It is simply . . ."

" . . . something not warranted to have any lasting value."

Her host tensed. He searched for words. "You make me appear so negligent—so remiss." Irritated, he pushed back the chair and prepared to rise.

The Reverend Kirkland came to Caroline's rescue. "Caroline loves a good argument," he jested, elbowing his old friend playfully. For Caroline's benefit, he spoke distinctly: "Stubborn that she is, she is unable to conceive of anyone not being tested to the limits of his intelligence." He crossed to within inches of Caroline, allowing her to catch the twinkle in his eye. "She is all for public schools and dedicated teachers." The Reverend turned to face the entrepreneur—a maneuver which invited comment.

The entrepreneur sat down. He uttered a challenge to Caroline: "Perhaps you will come here to teach the servants . . . *all* servants. You may then put your theory to the test."

"And pray that I am able, Sir. For certain the thought has not escaped me. Unfortunately, I am wanted at the Reverend Kirkland's school." She snapped her fingers. "In my stead will you accept my daughter, Suzanne? She is quite able, having taken lessons from her mother."

Cuyler stole a glance after Reverend Kirkland. "As you wish. Bring her to me and I will open a school. It will be a universal school open to all." He wrung his hands, nervously.

"A remarkable way of fulfilling your pledges, Sir," Caroline nodded, holding out a hand to him.

"There is land for such a school. I have recently made a sizable purchase which I intended to donate to this fair city for want of a good reason." He thumped the desk with a broad palm: "Now I have good reason."

In the next instant Cuyler made a disclosure which thrilled Caroline to the depths of her being:

"My wife will teach at your new school with your permission." He thought momentarily, then: "It is good that you are here. You will want to meet my friend, Philip Livingston. He is a man languishing in erudition. His wife, Christina, is a teacher of the first order." So stated, the entrepreneur slapped himself upon the knee.

Caroline repeated the name 'Livingston' (77) aloud from memory.

"You may not have heard of him so far north, but Philip not long ago helped to organize the New York Public Library in that sprawling trading post on the lower Hudson."

"Yes, yes. Now I recall," Caroline demurred, eager to demonstrate agreement.

"He and Christina are due tomorrow. There will be much feasting." Rubbing palms together, Cuyler grinned in the manner of a small boy opening a gift box. "For now I have a light dinner prepared." He rang a bell and Birdie appeared with an assistant. Together they distributed an assortment of warm foods on trays to the three guests, placed on portable fold-out tables.

"I am in complete agreement with your theory of erudition, Caroline," Cuyler began, cutting a slice of ham for himself. I believe that the community as a whole must participate in the venture of building a school—mind you—*subscribe* to its construction. How do you say on the matter?"

Caroline gulped down a fork crammed with sweet potatoes long enough to give approval: "That is most generous of you, Sir." Beside her Reverent Kirkland nodded. Thomas Steed beamed.

"The number of subscriptions will determine the ultimate importance of the school to the community," her host continued. "Albany will have achieved another mark of excellence." He smiled broadly, his contentment overflowing.

"I have reason to believe that with your support it will be a smashing success, Sir," Caroline responded softly.

"Good! Good!! We need to push the project, however—bring it before the masses. Tell me, Caroline. Are you averse to speaking before an audience?" He put aside his fork and regarded her closely.

Thus challenged, Caroline sat back in stoic contemplation. Striking a pose of self-confidence, she uttered the words which her host yearned to hear:

"I have long held that well-educated youth lend to the strength of the community. Albany is made up of ten percent of Blacks (78) and another five percent of natives, so I am told. Developing these productive segments will put Albany in the forefront of growth and development here in the east for years to come. New forms of commerce for Albany are issuing forth as surely as I speak. These new students will step into new roles in furtherance of their own future and that of Albany as a whole. It is a sign of the period in which we live."

"My sentiments exactly, Caroline. That settles it. You must speak at City Hall (79)." He stretched and yawned, a movement which the guests replicated. "We will speak more of this on the morrow. The hour grows late. Birdie will see you all to your rooms." Slowly he rose, a sign that the meeting had adjourned.

"Yes. By all means," an exhausted Caroline intimated, rising. Together with her comrades, she waited for an escort. An obliging Birdie led the little party to separate rooms in the mansion. Upon leading Caroline to her quarters, she paused at the doorway with eyes aglow:

"Mister Cuyler likes you, Madame. Yes, He really *does* like you." Birdie smiled a broad and toothy grin, closing the door softly behind her. It was the last memory of the day for Caroline, for she fell promptly asleep. Outside, in the coldness of the night, strong winds blew gusts of drifting snow against the bedroom window. In a far corner of the room a fire burned low in the fireplace. Birdie came to tend to it at intervals, keeping it at a modest level. With each visit she smiled at the inert form before her on the bed and headed back merrily to her quarters, enthused at having met the winsome, pretty woman from the west.

Birdie awakened her early on the following day. Her comforting greeting soothed Caroline no less than the thick blankets in which she slept. Pleasant thoughts consumed her and she burrowed deeper into her 'nest.'

"Time to rise and greet the new day, Miss—and a joyous Sunday it is." Birdie swept back the ample curtains to allow a shaft of bright light to strike Caroline full in the face, startling her.

"You have much to do today, Miss Caroline. You will give away presents. You will dine with important guests. You will take a tour of the city." She counted off the events on her fingers. Finishing, she stood with hands on hips.

"Merry Christmas, Miss Caroline. Tonight is Christmas Eve."

Sitting up in bed, Caroline rubbed her eyes. "Oh, so it is, Birdie. Oh, Birdie. What am I to do? My family is miles away and I am playing the ambitious wife."

"I have good thoughts about you.—great thoughts," Birdie whispered, helping Caroline into a robe. "Here. Let me help you get refreshed." She led Caroline to the bathroom where she gathered articles with which to complete her toilette. Dressing quickly, Caroline followed Birdie to the kitchen where she approached a breakfast table brimming with occupants bent on curbing a hunger all the more exacerbated by the wealth of foods greeting the eye.

"The Livingstons are due momentarily," Cuyler smiled, joining everyone at table. He tucked a napkin into the shirt collar beneath his chin. "This is my wife, Adelaide."

Caroline rose to greet a short, fairly stout matron, whose stern countenance cast aside any doubt that she ranked side by side with her husband in the administration of the household. "Cornelis tells me good things about you," she whispered, lips taut and barely moving. "I look forward to hearing you speak."

Nodding, Caroline accepted the praise, but was unable to dispel the little cough which arose whenever events of significance centered about her. "I shall do my best, Madame," she uttered softly.

Birdie entered hurriedly. Crossing the room, she spoke directly into the entrepreneur's ear. "By all means, Birdie, show them in," he replied. Rising, he put aside the napkin and made for the portal behind him. Spirited voices flowed into the room from the foyer beyond, voices which Caroline recognized. She put aside a fork, and looking up, made an exclamation:

"My word! It is you! Suzanne! James! Ghosts of the past! What has brought you here?"

Dashing forward, Suzanne hugged her mother. James conferred with the entrepreneur, who brusquely ushered him to Caroline's side. An astonished Caroline embraced them, while searching for words of greeting.

"Take care, mother. No words are necessary," Suzanne declared.

"Suzanne insisted on paying a visit, now that classes are dismissed for Christmas," James York explained to the patriarch: "I tried to restrain her, but she is hard-headed," he confessed, cuffing his jaw.

"Determined, father, *not* hard-headed," Suzanne retorted.

"How did you find me, dear child?" Caroline asked, bewildered.

"The guards at the fort sent us to you straightaway," Suzanne recalled, arms around her mother's waist. "Are you enjoying yourself at Albany?" she asked, cheerfully.

Reverend Kirkland spoke in place of the overwhelmed Caroline. "Your mother has gained new friendships. She has toured the city and visited shops. You came at the opportune moment when she will be addressing the city fathers the day after Christmas—Monday, I believe." Withdrawing a timepiece, he regarded it closely.

Suzanne pressed her hands tightly together. Alone with her thoughts, she put them into words. "Let me see: You have come to gain support for the school!" Pleased with her discovery, she looked for approval.

"Yes, yes and more, child," Caroline returned, eager to agree. Careful to respect her benefactor's confidence in her, she refrained from further discussion: "Come with me to City Hall and your questions will be answered," she demurred. With eyes sparkling, she beckoned her husband and daughter to join her at table.

Birdie appeared once again. Before she was able to announce Mr. Livingston, his wife entered the kitchen. Claiming a seat for herself, she steered her husband into place beside her, manifesting that stern countenance so characteristic of her spouse. Livingston, the severely diplomatic-looking scion of a wealthy and influential Albany family, drew up next to the patriarch. To Caroline the Livingstons exemplified the deep bond that grew between husband and wife which the many years of marriage solidified, blurring the lines of distinction between man and wife, making of the one a replica of the other in appearance, word, and deed.

"There you are, Philip, always surfacing during the most important part of my day—breakfast." Cornelis Cuyler embraced Livingston and after hasty introductions, the engaging entrepreneur launched into a hearty serving of Birdie's scrambled eggs and biscuits.

"Ah! We have crossed many broad rivers in this room. Agreed, Cornelis?" Philip Livingston intoned, gazing about. He fixed upon the three visitors from the west.

"We are about to make yet another epic crossing, Philip: Meet Caroline York and her young student. Caroline will be speaking at City Hall today." Flashing a broad smile, he made ample gestures toward the pair, as though imparting to them a special blessing.

"I have not seen you so enthused, Cornelis, since you first secured trading privileges with the Mohawks. Indeed, you must have something important planned."

"That I do. Let me have Madame York explain in detail." He returned to dining with an eye to re-entering the discourse at will.

Caroline chose her words carefully, making certain to extend every courtesy to the patriarch. She knew that the name 'Livingston' turned a great many heads in the community among the gentry and commoners alike who viewed him as a public servant of impeccable credentials. Support from a member of the Livingston dynasty all but guaranteed the success of her school and perhaps much more.

"Very pleasant to meet you, Mr. Livingston. I must tell you that I have arrived here under the most circuitous and haphazard of circumstances, but that is the subject of another day. I am a teacher by profession. Native children are my students. My station is at Oneida Castle and the man beside me, Reverend Kirkland, is the man who conceived of a plan to teach the natives to study the ways of the whites in order to preserve their own way of life."

"You have my rapt attention, Madame," Philip Livingston replied, adjusting his broad girth.

"I have found that, with proper instruction, native children are avid learners. Unfortunately, when they mature, they have found themselves isolated from the community at large, and, aside from bringing trade goods to Albany, have been unable to participate in matters of community intercourse. I hope that with a community-supported school, the abilities of the native will receive just recognition with the result that he and she will be able to actively participate in the growth of this fair city."

"I applaud you, Madame," Philip Livingston returned, intrigued by the winsome woman's remarks.

Caroline became more emphatic: "I have personally witnessed abuses visited upon natives by those in His Majesty's service.—men who regarded them as little more than pawns on a chess table." Raising her voice, she continued: "This basic disregard for human life must come to an end and only a knowledgeable and full legislature has the power to remedy the situation. This is why I venture to speak at City Hall. To equality I dedicate the remainder of my days on earth."

The room fell into silence. Suzanne and her father stole glances at each other. Birdie leaned heavily upon the china cabinet, eyes upon Caroline. Reverend Kirkland gripped Thomas Steed's hand tightly. The Livingstons sat motionless, unresponsive. Cuyler broke the silence. Somewhat dismissive, he waved a hand aloft:

"I agree with you wholeheartedly, Madame; however, today is much too festive an occasion to dwell upon matters of a political bent. Let us turn to the full meaning of Christmas." He summoned Birdie. She arrived behind a pushcart teeming with wrapped gifts in assorted shapes and sizes.

"I reserve Christmas Eve and Christmas Day for the distribution of gifts to the needy of the city. It has caught on handsomely. Philip and I look forward to doing this each year." He looked to Philip Livingston who, having accepted his topcoat and gloves from Birdie, headed for the vestibule of the mansion. Moments later, however, he returned, head and shoulders downcast.

"There is a deep snowfall outside. Best to go by sleigh."

The patriarch beckoned and the guests prepared to depart the mansion, arms laden with gifts. Once out-of-doors, he brought forth a hand-drawn sleigh with wooden rails, the perfect receptacle to hold gifts. Caroline snuggled close to James, burying his gloved hand in the warmth of her fur-lined mittens.

"I need two volunteers to haul this bold contraption," the patriarch called, looking directly at Suzanne and Thomas Steed.

"Reporting for duty, Sir!" Suzanne responded gaily. Saluting her host, she tugged on Thomas Steed's arm, effectively pulling him to the head of the sleigh where two stout ropes attached to either running blade accounted for pulling the ponderous conveyance.

"Onward, soldier!" Suzanne teased her companion. "We need to move smartly, or I will reduce your rations once we return to your barracks." Her spontaneous banter excited the entire party and, as they rounded North Pearl and headed down the steep pitch of Jonkers, everyone laughed and cajoled in a merry, carefree spirit, drawn together by the festiveness germane to the Holiday season.

The party halted where Dock, Orange and Market Streets came together. An intersection of sorts arose at the juncture and at its center sat an imposing wooden gazebo with a crowned roof sheltering a porch beneath. A small troupe of bell-ringers occupied the porch chanting carols. Adults and children alike, they readily accepted the gifts of the

Cornelis Cuyler party, piling them in a great bundle. By degrees the heap of gifts in brightly-colored paper rose steadily, threatening to spill over the gazebo's railings. Soon, more pedestrians arrived and in an orderly fashion everyone began to pass the gifts amongst themselves.

"These are gifts fit for the household," Cuyler explained to the household guests. "They apply to the kitchen, the bath, and the bedroom, but in general make one's life more bearable. At any rate they are not labeled with name tags. I have found that nameless gifts add to the mystique of the occasion. They are evenly distributed. No one is omitted," he concluded, tying a muffler under his chin. "Follow me," he gestured, waving 'goodbyes'.

Departing the gazebo, now teeming with a sizable gathering of townspeople, the entrepreneur turned to the immediate west, leading the party upward on Jonkers. The heightened pitch of the snow-covered lane challenged the surefootedness of the little flock, bringing Suzanne and Thomas Steed to dig their heels in deeply. She registered visible relief when the patriarch halted before one of several inns which traditionally welcomed itinerants during Christmas Eve and Christmas Day. Passing inside, everyone remained long enough to sip hot cider, eat tender pastries and absorb the warmth of the fireplace while exchanging pleasantries with the owner and patrons. Then, plunging out into the cold evening, they headed for the next refuge of warmth and hospitality.

Steadily upward they walked to the apex of the hill that was Jonkers Street. In the distance the old fort, looking very forlorn, rose out of the darkness. Crossing broad Jonkers, everyone followed the patriarch, who began to make his descent, once he reached the shops lining the opposite side of the street. Pedestrians called out to him, he, the well-known fixture of Albany's trading elite. Some of them joined the plodding procession, following the merrymakers to Beaver Street, past the home of inn-keeper, Richard Cartwright, who kept the renowned King Arms Tavern next door to his mansion (80). Here Cuyler often ushered in the New Year in the accompaniment of many acquaintances, those tradesmen, laborers and tavern keepers who called Beaver Street and its environs their home. Tonight ale and lager flowed freely, along with hot chocolate, and Caroline made certain that Suzanne made chocolate her beverage of note. Everyone gathered around a banquet table of roasted duck and turkey and seafood, the likes of which Thomas

Steed only read about in journals, all compliments of the Cuylers and Livingstons.

Progressively Caroline found herself and Thomas Steed the center of attention among the patrons. They insisted upon learning of her agenda at City Hall. She sparked interest by inviting them to attend the session in two days, on Tuesday, December 26th, the last Tuesday of the year. She found interest in her undertaking so keen that she took upon herself to make a brief announcement to that effect. Cuyler set out chairs and stools in a space before the bar and beckoned the patrons to come forward and occupy places around Caroline. She unabashedly acknowledged those gathered before her, a role into which she stepped with ease. Taking a deep breath, she folded her hands over broad, pleated skirts:

"Word travels quickly. Yes. I will speak at City Hall. The first woman to do so, I am told. I ask all of you to join me there. I need your support. My plan needs your support. Together we will be able to cross new thresholds by scaling old barriers. I want to see all of you there."

She raised a mug to toast the spectators, almost shouting through the din that rose up around her. She gulped the ale and brought the mug heavily down upon the hard wooden table top beside her. The male-dominated crowd roared approval in recognition of Caroline's aggressiveness.

"I will follow you through a blizzard to City Hall," one drunken man called.

"Thank you, but my husband has already volunteered," Caroline jested to a round of applause. She brought forward James and Suzanne, who tugged Thomas Steed by the hand.

"My family and I are pleased to be among you," she called. "We are pleased to be so richly welcomed in this delightful post so far from our home."

"How about making Albany your *new* home?" a male patron called.

Caroline started to answer when the man interrupted: "*You* may stay as long as you like," he grinned coyly.

Sensing an impending disturbance, Philip Livingston rang out, his voice booming: "Dessert is served!!" He snapped his fingers and Richard Cartwright himself appeared, carrying the first of many dishes of cherry cobbler topped with whipped cream. Swiftly a cadre of servers circulated the popular dessert throughout the tavern. Another snap of the fingers and a new round of beverages followed, the timely maneuvers successfully diverting attention away from the aroused and drunken patron.

Caroline rounded out the evening by conversing with selected patrons, who, at the insistence of Cornelis Cuyler, were forbidden from probing into her agenda for City Hall. She referred delicate inquiries to Reverend Kirkland who clung closely beside her. At long last she summoned her retinue, James and Suzanne, and young Thomas Steed, all of whom spent the evening exchanging pleasantries with the Cuyler and Livingston wives. To all practical purposes the evening belonged to Caroline. James and Suzanne made certain not to draw her away from those with whom she sought to commiserate, the very fabric of Albany, the people whom she planned to address in two short days.

The hour came to depart for North Pearl. Cuyler begged Caroline to sever ties with her audience in order to return to the mansion and the opening of presents. An exhausted but contented Caroline took her leave to the tune of an impromptu refrain set into motion by one of the patrons. It began with "Sweet Caroline," but she did not remain to hear it through, for the hour grew late. She and her party departed the inn along a route which her host deemed free of loiterers. Descending Beaver Street, they came to Court Street at Hudson Street, There, before them stood a three-storied, rugged brick building set beneath a pitched, tile rooftop. Its austere presence drew the curious forward to study the somber yet defiant façade. The patriarch guided Caroline along a flight of well-worn granite steps to the weather-beaten oaken door. Behind it stood City Hall.

"Here it is, your battlefield, Madame," he bowed before her.

Caroline rubbed her mittens together in the cold of the evening. When she spoke, her breath escaped in thick plumes. "It is such a staunch and hardy building. I hope that I measure up to its reputation."

"You will, Caroline. You will. Much of Albany will be behind you."

Fighting the coldness, Caroline tugged at her broad skirts. On the sidewalk Suzanne stirred restlessly.

"Come. We all deserve a rest," her host spoke. Taking Caroline's elbow, he escorted her back to the little party.

* * *

On Christmas Day the home on North Pearl turned to gift-giving: "the true meaning of Christmas," to quote Cornelis Cuyler. His wife and Madame Livingston assisted Birdie in the doling out of presents, each one attractively wrapped and bearing a name tag. Intermittently the wives circulated trays of sweet treats and copious mugs of hot chocolate to the guests. The entrepreneur described the gifts in detail, often before they became opened, taking deep draughts of hot cider from a favorite mug. A keen observer, Suzanne whispered to her mother:

"It is more than cider he is sipping, I fear." Looking up, she accepted a gift from Birdie. The handsome servant wore one of her expansive smiles.

"It is beautiful," Suzanne exclaimed, displaying a white pullover of angora wool.

"The only one of its kind in town," her host the fur trader replied, teetering ever so noticeably.

James received a beaver top hat with ear guards for winter wear. For Caroline a pair of deerskin leggings replaced her full-length ankle skirts. Thomas Steed received beaver mittens and a pair of beaver ear muffs, suitable gifts for the incumbent winter season.

Cuyler challenged Philip Livingston to a game of chess, once the gift-giving came to an end. The two entrepreneurs withdrew to a remote corner of the library. Calling for cigars and claret, they prepared to spend the remainder of the afternoon pitting their wits against each other.

The ever-industrious Birdie brought out a pair of small cloth bags in the shape of a woman's purse. She pulled three miniature and naked cloth dolls from one bag and the makings of miniature clothing from the other. "Will you please help me sew these?" she beamed, thrusting a doll into the outstretched hands of Caroline and Suzanne.

"Madame Cuyler wants to present them at her sewing circle." Her large brown eyes pleading, she draped the tiny pieces of cloth over the tiny arms and legs.

"How quaint!" Suzanne laughed softly. "Shall we, mother?"

"By all means, dear daughter," an ebullient Caroline agreed.

The three women took up places around an oval-shaped hardwood maple table and proceeded to lay into the task. Birdie's gregariousness set mother and daughter at ease during this, a too infrequent moment in their lives.

Reverend Kirkland, Thomas Steed, and James perused the bookshelves of the salon. After careful deliberation, each selected a volume and retired to comfortable chairs, making certain that they sat next to an oil-burning lamp.

The Cuyler and Livingston wives disappeared into the kitchen where they put new twists on community rumors.

Within this serene setting residents and guests found comfortable niches in the great mansion into which they descended, a form of diversion, however self-serving or creative, the scene of uninterrupted Christmas pageantry for almost half a century. Over the years the players came and went, yet the overall substance of the occasion remained constant, one of close fraternity mixed with light-hearted gaiety, in an atmosphere disassociated from the oppressing weight of matters politic. While everyone took turns regaling each other, events beyond the mansion's walls took a different turn, smacking of a darker and sinister side of the human species:

—

Brig. Gen. John Forbes, commander of a British force in the Carolinas so dishonored the native Cherokees with his outwardly abusive conduct and caustic remarks toward them that he almost singlehandedly precipitated the Cherokee uprising that struck terror into neighboring farmers and settlers. Initially offering their services to Forbes' exhausted and bedraggled soldiers, the Cherokees grew angry when Forbes failed to honor current agreements guaranteeing them access to their lands in the face of white incursions. An appeal to Lyttleton, the royal governor, garnered no support, who demonstrably gave tacit approval to the mass influxes. Lyttleton went so far as to hunt the Cherokees down whenever practicable (81).

Not unlike the zealous Forbes, other British field commanders, having gained the natives' trust, proceeded to set up permanent forts within their territories, form ad hoc companies, and sell native lands to settlers at a grand profit. Charlatans all, they mollified these clandestine acts by inundating native villages with British trade goods and rum, the effects of which temporarily delayed the onset of native reprisals. Consistently, in efforts to subdue errant chiefs whose warriors fought for their very lives, commanders such as Col. John Bradstreet and Col. Henry Bouquet demanded the spoils due a conqueror. This entailed that the lands of dispossessed natives must form the basis of a peace process thence to be ceded to the conquerors who in turn would dole them out to partisans and settlers in anticipation of comfortable fees. Despite general proclamations prohibiting extended settlement along the new Ohio and Carolina frontiers, the Cherokees learned that they stood alone in the halls of justice and on the battlefield when confronting aggressors (82).

Closer to home in the vicinity of Albany, natives met with more equitable treatment from established merchants and white traders; however, the degree to which they received justice and respect depended largely on the character of the magistrates in positions of power and authority. That the Dutch and later the British establishment welcomed the nearby Iroquois to dispose of their pelts and furs within city walls is testimony to the high value these merchants placed upon the goods and the ability of the natives to deliver faithfully and to settle for little in return in the way of compensation. Both the Dutch and British held their own ulterior reasons for courting the native and his abundance of animal skins and none of them encompassed an innate fondness for him. Indeed, the Dutch sought to carve out a lucrative empire for themselves in native furs. The British, meanwhile, hoped to gain access to native lands after offering the Iroquois and others military protection against their enemies. Both Dutch and British merchants introduced the native to woolen goods, utensils, and rum, with the intention of keeping him close at hand in a subservient state of being indefinitely (83).

———

Her sewing completed, Caroline took up a copy of the *Albany Gazette,* that compact and comprehensive daily which her host brought in regularly from the market place. Many sat bound in journals. She leafed through copies: the interesting ones bearing reports of military campaigns, of Forbes and Bradstreet, of the Dutch and British and the Indians, the acid tongues of editors, and the state of affairs in the colony. For the duration of the afternoon Caroline devoured the copies avidly. More than once she learned that the names 'Cuyler' and 'Livingston' appeared in less than glowing terms. In her remote little corner she took notes and studied them. No one interrupted her, least of all James and Suzanne, who intuitively sensed that she was preparing for her presentation at City Hall. Restricting herself to a light repast, she wrote far into the evening, a flickering oil lamp her sole companion. Birdie came by once or twice and found her talking to herself and making broad gestures, but thought it unwise to disturb her. Much later, Caroline lay aside her quill, closed her journals, and, lying back in the plump chair, fell fast asleep.

She awoke to find herself in the guest-bedroom, tucked firmly into place beneath the quilts which Birdie selected with care. Stirring, she moaned, showing the first signs of hunger, telling her that a new day awaited her, and with it, a rewarding breakfast. Sweeping into the room, Birdie tossed back the window curtains, allowing the sun's bright rays to fall upon Caroline's placid countenance. She sat up. Rubbing her eyes, she heard Birdie's cheerful greeting:

"Rise and shine, Miss Caroline. This is a bright and sunny day. Good things will happen to you today."

James and Suzanne soon joined her. They waited patiently as Caroline washed and dressed before descending to the kitchen. Once settled, she met with the full complement of the mansion's residents at the breakfast table.

"Best to eat a hearty breakfast. You may have a long day," the entrepreneur stated blandly, taking his place beside his wife. Adelaide Cuyler smiled sheepishly, but otherwise said nothing.

"Who is my audience? Who will I speak to?" A curious Caroline asked.

"About half of the legislature and all of the city's residents," Philip Livingston offered in a dour voice.

"Only half?" Caroline asked, facetiously.

"They are on holiday-leave, dear," Adelaide Cuyler finally spoke, in the manner of the master to the student.

Between mouthfuls of scrambled eggs and sausage links, Reverend Kirkland and Thomas Steed sat with eyes fixed upon Caroline. Presently the missionary tapped Caroline's shoulder:

"We found you asleep late last night."

"It is good that you put me to bed, then," she thanked her headmaster.

"Oh, no! We did nothing. Birdie came to your rescue. She does not want you to be late," Thomas Steed returned, consulting his pocket watch.

"Someone thinks of me," Caroline teased. "Oh, my! What time is it?" she exclaimed, suddenly wide-awake.

"Time is wasting," Birdie chirped, and, with that outburst, everyone donned overcoats and winter boots and trouped to the foyer where an omnipresent Birdie swept open the door and one by one wished everyone in the little party well.

Suzanne brushed by Birdie's side, pausing to give her a quick buss on the cheek. "You are coming too, are you not, Birdie?"

Birdie started to object, all the while casting an entreating glance at her master, Cornelis Cuyler. He, having heard Suzanne's plea, turned peremptorily toward the pleasant servant.

"Do you have a topper hereabouts? I believe you wore it on occasion?"

"Why, yes," Birdie replied, somewhat intimidated.

"Well. Best to go put it on and join us," the entrepreneur returned, summarily.

Relieved, Birdie scampered off. She returned wearing a thick, woolen cloak complete with muffler. Without a word she grasped Suzanne's outstretched hand and the little party departed the mansion.

"The door! You locked the door, Birdie?" Mrs. Cuyler called over her shoulder.

"Without fail, Ma'am." She held out a key fastened to a delicate chain about her neck to the discriminating matron's approval. Without losing a step, she buried Suzanne's gloved hand within her thick mitten, reserving for her one of her glowing smiles. The two allies, bringing up the rear of the party, proceeded to exchange confidences with each other during the short walk to City Hall.

—

City Hall: With family and acquaintances seated before her, Caroline stood on an elevated dais in the center of the great hall and addressed a full house of some three hundred strong:

"Albanians. During my short stay in your robust community I have taken note of your several attributes. I see vigorous movement among your merchants and shopkeepers. They have much for sale and many come from distant parts to partake of your city's endless bounty. On your river front I see ships' captains directing crews with cargo bound for your warehouses. I see the small manufacturers where skilled laborers prepare a wide assemblage of goods for immediate and foreign consumption. Into this mixture of humanity pour the artisans, craftsmen, servants, deck hands, the men who bend the iron bars, the bookbinders, and indeed all those who have made your city a bright light in the forest. They are men and women of color. They are white, brown, and black. They go about daunting tasks in exactly the same manner day after day in order to reach a common goal: providing for loved ones and keeping their home larders well-stocked.

"On the surface all seems well. The community lives and grows by means of disparate sectors coming together and forming a cohesive whole. In this sense everyone is inter-related, united to bring about prosperity for one and all. From my perspective, however, a closer look throws open inequities, serious flaws, which, if unattended, will set the stage for the community's dismemberment. I propose a plan whereby this community may bring everyone together on equal terms. I propose a school open to all people of color, yes, to the white, brown, and black among us who yearn to improve their lot, who yearn to gain ascendancy within the community hierarchy.

"I do not seek to restructure the community. Nay. That is a task far beyond the ability of a mere mortal. Rather, I seek to redefine it by making available the tools necessary for achieving success for all those who avail themselves of them. I now throw this forum open to questions which I understand may be considerable. I ask that you observe decorum, since it is through the good graces of His Majesty *that we are able to congregate here today."

"You speak of 'serious flaws.' What are they?" a man asked, raising a hand.

"I find that people of color and, yes, women, have been placed aside and restricted from fully engaging in community processes. There are several examples which may have eluded you." Caroline made certain to speak dispassionately in order to mitigate confrontation.

"Servants are not taught to read or write. The same applies to the sons and daughters of laborers. Natives are restrained from congregating in the city. Women are urged to raise many children and lead a purely domestic life. Erudition is the province of a chosen few. The community as a whole suffers when its members are denied an opportunity to espouse innate abilities. In my opinion these may be nurtured through a school open to the masses— one which embraces the diversity of the community."

"It has *always* been that way!! There have always been differences." a man called from the rear of the hall.

Caroline overlooked his bombast. Prepared for conflict, she returned: "Is this the only way? I believe there is another way. It is called Erudition. It is found in a school. Erudition reaches out to everyone, in particular the young, exploring with them God-given gifts. It develops one's inner strengths, equipping one with a unique set of skills with which to master the challenges thrust upon one by an indifferent world."

"Too little too late. No one man . . . or woman . . . is able to compel changes," an elderly man offered, earning a round of applause. He stood, shaking a fist.

"You are correct my good man. That is why my school shall embrace the *total* community. It will draw upon tools from the skilled and enlightened among you."

"Why change what is traditionally accepted?" another asked.

"Let me ask you. Do you hold learning in reserve solely for the men of your community?"

"Men make the important decisions. Men are the . . ."

"Leaders of the community?"

"Why, yes. A community is only as strong as its leaders."

"Granted . . . but what school in your memory expressly teaches leadership?" Caroline posed.

"Not in a school," another man joined in. "Leadership is learned by trial and error. It is not taught."

"Exactly. It is a quality, you say? May not a school plant the seeds of that quality in our youth?" Caroline asked.

"Perhaps in a coming generation. Regardless. Some lead while others follow, Madame."

"What of the woman, I dare ask?"

"Women are expected to remain close to home," her male critic returned.

"Has anyone ever asked the woman?" Caroline's question produced a stir among the women present, chiefly among the young wives who sat beside those husbands who chose to speak. One of them, noticeably agitated, raised a hand and, not waiting to be recognized, uttered the question which Caroline waited to hear:

"Are you saying that women must become leaders?"

Caroline answered the young woman with a question of her own: "Do you exercise leadership at home?"

"I clothe and feed my children. I care for them when they are sick. I read with them from the Bible. I teach them their letters and numbers," the engaging young mother replied.

"Excellent!" Caroline retorted. "This is leadership. It may be learned in various ways. In my school the teacher is a leader and the lessons given prepare the student for leadership each in his /her own way. In my school the student exercises tasks taught by a leader. The teacher. Let us not forget that the school is an extension of the home and family, where the teacher plays the part of the significant parent. The skills learned at home will be admitted into my school where dedicated teachers will transform them into foundations for learning—each one unique to the student. This Erudition, if you will, builds trust within the student: the *stepping stone* to leadership. A trusting student is a leader in his/her own right—one who may mold his/her surroundings to meet his/her needs. The student learns by example laid down by significant elders: teachers. You may very well be such a teacher."

Speechless, the woman sat back. Several young women whispered to her, prompting her to rise again:

"I understand what you are saying, but I have no training in Erudition, and rarely do my opinions go beyond the walls of my home."

"You are not alone. Fear not. The home is where Erudition begins. My school builds upon it. I ask that the teacher begin instruction at her own level of comfort. Concerning the more advanced forms of Erudition—science and history, I will employ the services of scholars— other teachers— in the field at a fair rate of compensation."

"Where will you find the funds for everything?" an elderly man asked.

Caroline looked to the front row where the patriarch and the Livingstons sat together. "I have solicited assistance from two dear friends," she recited calmly.

"It will never come to pass," a man objected. Rising, he shook a fist and spoke in support of the traditionalists present in the hall: "You are tampering with the teachings of John Calvin. He would turn over in his grave were he to learn that you treat with servants on an equal footing with those who made this colony great." His directness brought forth a mild round of applause from among the older men in attendance.

Caroline struggled to remain on course, apart from allowing herself to be dragged into confrontation. She viewed the man's objection as an opportunity to quash old hatreds and class distinctions. She chose her words carefully:

"The teachings of John Calvin suited the period in history in which he lived. The Dutch in particular struck out to discover and populate unknown stretches of the world. These bold ventures required bold leadership of the sort that John Calvin implanted among chosen members of his flock. For him a strong elite shall bear the weight of providing for the common masses of which there are many.

"What has changed since his day? The masses, long a silent voice in affairs of state, have grown in strength and numbers. Most recently it is they who have pushed back the wooded frontiers of the Appalachians and the Ohio valley. It is they who have become the builders of a new America, an America in need of a vast array of manufactured goods, of domestic goods, and of ocean-going vessels in which to transport them. It is the masses who will inherent and shape America. They will be her new leaders. What outstanding feature marks a leader, you ask? What makes a leader stand above the crowd? In a word: Independence. You ask, how does the leader gain Independence? Let me tell you that somewhere along the line he or she has learned to read and write, to tally sums and perform measures— to do the functions required of the successful student. These fundamentals of leadership, start with the school, which, together with the home, provide one with the capacity to make sound decisions affecting not one but many lives.

"Why is all of this important, you ask? Some say: "my patron, who knows how to read and write, is able to provide me with all of the substance that I require" You say: "Why do I need this Independence"? The answer is simple, my friends. Independence guarantees that one's voice is heard in the market place. The independent man or woman becomes his or her *own* patron. He or she thus imparts a unique stamp upon his/her labors, labors which carry one's own seal of approval. The independent man and woman, however silent or outspoken, is a true leader in as much as his/her contributions to the community help to shape it for generations to come. In my school the student will help to build: yeah, shape the community. He/she will lead by example and my teachers will set *good* examples."

Caroline spoke with conviction, giving the impression that she was in full command of her subject matter. Members of the audience sat on the edges of their seats to catch the words of this glib woman, so tall and straight, so certain of her beliefs, not in a haughty way. Her family members and attendant coterie sat enthralled by Caroline's poise and by the analogies she brought forth to press her argument.

"In my school students develop independence in thought and manner from which spring the seeds of leadership. I ask you. What is a stout ship without sails? What is the mighty eagle without flight feathers? My school provides students the equipment with which to launch their fondest ambitions. They will become strong and, bending down the strong shall extend a hand and pull up the weak to join them. Together they will face the new challenges of the day in the wake of the Great War* with abundant enthusiasm. They will be as beams of bright light, beacons of hope, shining resplendently in the forest."

At the end, her manner almost evangelical, Caroline raised her arms in triumph. Bowing, she smiled and stepped backward. A roar of approval surged through the hall. Young women jumped from their places to applaud her. Older, more recalcitrant folk, rose out of respect for Caroline's steadfastness. Suzanne stomped her feet in unbridled joy. Reverend Kirkland wiped his brow feverishly and shook hands with James, who hugged Thomas Steed. Birdie, in possession of an infatuating smile, gripped Suzanne's arm tightly. The patriarch and Philip Livingston applauded mildly and summoned Caroline to join them. Passing over to them, Caroline stood among a party of legislators, one of whom broke from the pack to address her:

"We approve of your plan for the most part. It never occurred to us that Albany needed a school."

"Where to build it?" a legislator asked.

"Next to my home. I have a large tract," Cuyler quipped, half-jesting.

"Up on the hill . . . near the fort," another returned.

"Let the school masters reside in the fort until they find more permanent lodgings."

"Should the school itself survive."

"It will, gentlemen. It will," Caroline spoke soberly, hands folded over flowing skirts. Briefly she recited the tale of Thomas Steed's success at the Oneida school.

"Under controlled conditions that may be true," a doubter spoke, "but this is Albany, a frontier riddled with diverse opinions where everyone plots against his neighbor."

"All the more reason for a school to lend stability to a turbulent set of conditions," Caroline offered calmly.

Sensing an objection, she continued: "Natives already reside at the fort. Whole families call it home while they hunt in the countryside and bring furs in for exchange. The Commissioners of Indian Affairs have welcomed the Iroquois into the city for a generation—even looked the other way while the Iroquois carried on trade with selected families and merchants (84). You have only to inquire of Messieurs Cuyler and Livingston in that regard. It is well known that the Mohawk have come together to defend the city on more than one occasion. Yes, they want to establish exclusive trading privileges, but they truly enjoy a firm relationship with the residents, most of whom have befriended them.

"We all know that the Church*together with the chambers of City Hall are either too small or ill-equipped to house students—students who will grow in number as they meet with success. A larger venue is needed—one such as the fort. I know it is visited much less of late and that it may not be long among us, but, for the foreseeable future, it is a suitable site for this noble undertaking upon which I place my hopes and dreams."

"Who will come to the fort to fill places in your school?" a legislator asked.

"Sons and daughters of laborers who live along Dock and Hudson and Patroon and all the streets I have visited where new-arrivals live . . . the Black servants who reside in your homes . . . the native Mohawk and their children who come to the city to trade." With each example cited, Caroline raised a finger in full view of her audience.

"A large and contented family, you say," a man grumbled.

"I am pleased that you said that. Yes. My school will be a family . . . for many a second home . . . for others a much needed refuge . . . for all a repository of knowledge waiting to be discovered."

"I say that we give it a try," Cornelius Cuyler expounded. Approaching Caroline, he shook her hand vigorously. Behind him stood his associate, Philip Livingston. He whispered to him in passing:

"If it fails the fort still stands. If it succeeds, public outcry will demand a school dedicated solely to the upbringing of the city's youth and we will be seen as the famous architects of it. Yes!! Do it, Cornelis!"

"Good, Philip. I will bring the matter up with Sir William**. He is due back from New York to convene a session with the Commissioners later this week."

"To my knowledge Sir William has long sought a more practical outlet for the old fort. The prospect of a school will delight him," Philip Livingston offered. "Of course we will need to supply a guard to keep order on the grounds."

"Guard? We should supply it with teachers," Mrs. Cuyler added, with a hint of sarcasm.

"I will speak with the Domine, dearest," her husband returned, not at all ruffled by her impetuosity. "Ah! That reminds me. There is a certain bookseller on Market Street to whom I extended credit to open his shop. He has teaching credentials, you know. He still owes me a tidy sum. Perhaps in full realization of his debt he will volunteer his services. What do you say, dearest?"

"Fitzhugh? Yes!! William Fitzhugh?" his wife erupted. Dolefully she cast the merchant in a sad state of affairs: "The poor man—so lost and lonely among his many books. His partner died and now he is tied to the store like an ox to a stake. He will jump at the opportunity to return to his old passion of Erudition. Is that the name, Cornelis?"

"Good. It is settled. I will speak with him. I will even offer him an allowance—with more in sight should he furnish me with a slate of candidates."

"Do not become too generous, Cornelis. You do not want to be seen as a never-ending spigot of flowing wealth."

"A what?"

"Yes. This thought of a school for all classes does not sit well with everyone, you know."

"You would have me forsake my vows to the Church?" He stomped heavily on the floor. "I am fighting for my redemption and I intend to earn it."

"And you shall have it, but you must allow others to enter the fray."

"You have seen the legislators' responses, dearest," the patriarch returned, visibly annoyed.

"Yes. Yet they are but a small measure of the whole."

"I will ask Sir William to vote a stipend for teachers and books— the essentials. In the meanwhile I have a certain tract of land sitting unoccupied. A school house will fill the space handsomely. I will dedicate it not in my name but in the name of the residents of Albany. It will be *their* school and we will have become pioneers in that regard."

"You always have a curious way of stealing center stage from behind the scenes."

"Someone has to take the reins."

"Now you remind me of that Caroline woman."

"Do I detect a note of jealousy? I like her. She is devout and stalwart. You should come to like her too."

"I do believe that you *are* smitten with her."

"I intend to ask her to stay behind, supervise her first school, and teach the first class of students."

"A great task even for such a spirited woman."

"With monetary incentives the task will become more palatable."

"The lucrative bait you hold out will draw any number of greedy riffraff."

"Dearest. I have no intention of seeing this venture fail."

"Oh, yes. Your vows. I remember, Cornelis. You must know that one may have good intentions and fail nevertheless, yet *not* fail his vows in the eyes of the Church and Domine."

"I am aware of that, dearest. However, I have gone too far with the woman to withdraw my plans."

"Then you *are* smitten with her."

"I am determined that she succeed—she and her precocious student. All students. Let us look beyond ourselves. Let us act in the manner of leaders of this city—something lacking, I sense. Let us rebuild our destiny. Caroline comes from such humble beginnings. She seeks rewards not for herself, but for others. That is something I always admired in a human— man or woman— but to see it in a woman is astonishing." He gripped his wife about the shoulders, staring directly into her eyes, his gaze so intensive that she turned her head away from him. Leaving her side, he rejoined Caroline, her family, and coterie and together the little party exchanged pleasant memories of the day.

—

In January of that New Year 1761, the irrepressible Henry Van Schaack lived in Albany. A prosperous fur-trading merchant, he married one Jane Holland of that city in 1760. Visiting forts along the western Great Lakes, he acquired the pelts of the regional natives along a trade route that he established from Michilimackinack to Schenectady where he sold quantities of his harvest to local merchants.

In so doing he transgressed upon trade routes within the province of the Iroquois, beginning in the vicinity of Fort Niagara. He appreciatively cut into the native trade, much of it bound for Albany where the neighboring Mohawk conducted an active fur trade with local merchants. Not only Van Schaack,(85) but others wrested away a portion of the Mohawk clients for themselves, claiming that their goods were of superior quality. In some cases this observation rang true and the new white traders earned a handsome profit.

However, in no small measure, they earned the enmity of the native chieftains. Peacefully at first the Mohawk directed complaints to the Commissioners, who chose to study the matter at length, yet provided few solid remedies. Unable to contain pent-up emotions indefinitely, small bands of warriors roamed the countryside looking for defenseless innocents upon whom to vent their ire. They found many. Farmers in outlying regions, travelers, and itinerants, even neighboring Mohegan, lost life and limb to avenging warriors. The slaughter may have continued without intermission save that the Iroquois maintained a strong regard for Sir William Johnson. In their eyes he always addressed their grievances equitably. In this instance he demanded that city fathers tolerate the Mohawk and others who came to trade with local merchants, this at a period when Oswego more than Albany became a haven for fur traders. To sweeten his demand, he allowed merchants to placate the native with liberal offerings of spirits, rum, small arms, and powder.

Within the same time frame, Lord Amherst, fresh from victory at Montreal, the decisive battle of the Great War, began to distance himself from native allies, who, until that point, considered themselves vital to the success of his military exploits against the French. With the war won, Amherst threw off ties to the natives, leaving them to their own devices, which usually meant the denial of gifts. Conscious of the war's great expense, he consented to requests from the Crown to curtail costs. Consequently, fewer British troops garrisoned frontier forts and the old custom of purchasing native loyalties by offering an array of presents markedly declined. Amherst loathed the giving of small arms, a dangerous gesture, which may, in his opinion, set the stage for those same weapons to be turned against frontier garrisons. Therefore, he passed word through the colonial legislatures to adopt a policy of restraint when enacting measures of trade with the natives, particularly those native forces who settled grievances with the war club and musket. Already, with the coming of the New Year, stories of a native movement of unification fell upon his ears and the more he consulted his sources, the more ominous the stories grew.

Two events occurred almost simultaneously to give him cause for concern. For one, with the conclusion of the French and Indian War, the native tract, or Ohio reserve, became inundated with immigrants. For the most part settlers cast aside legislative warnings to desist from crossing the Appalachians. Secondly, with William Pitt out of power, the new ministry started pulling troops out of the Americas, in part because of a cost-saving move, but also to augment the forces of Frederick of Germany in his raging war against France in Europe. These two developments left the American frontier with an acute lack of defenses, shoddy at best, held together in segments by poorly-trained and ill-provisioned colonial militias. Into this desultory mix streamed bands of warriors from the Great Lakes region who overran forts and settlements in a wide sweep of fury in places where the colonials proved most vulnerable. One by one whole communities fell to roving war parties, culminating in the so-called Pontiac's war of 1763 (86).

In anticipation of a native uprising, new recruits took up residence at Albany's Fort Frederick, summarily preempting the conversion of the fort into a school. Moreover, the Commissioners forbade traveling parties to depart the city lest they come under attack, or worse. The mood among Caroline and her adherents grew sullen and, although she possessed her own escort, she deferred to the Commissioners' wishes and remained within the city limits, abandoning laid plans to return to Oneida Castle for the foreseeable future.

Although disappointed, Caroline was not defeated. One afternoon she studied the terrain to the north of the fort where she spied a project under way in its early stages. An interesting thought gripped her and she brought it before the patriarch, her patron:

"What is that mound of earth and stones?"

"That is the beginning of Albany's first hospital, Madame," her host chanted merrily.

"For the soldiers, I presume. Yes?"

"It will be a free hospital. The first of its kind in these regions."

"Free you say?"

"Yes. Open to all, particularly to those unable to pay for services."

"Revolutionary, Mr. Cuyler. This is your proposal?"

"Not entirely; however, city fathers have seen to intervene after I advocated for the project. It is a plan to place Albany at the forefront of growth. There is ample space for additional venues here in what may become the center of an expanding city."

"I have come to the right place then. Tell me. Is it possible to reserve a section for a school? A *free* school?"

"It will demand a vote of the legislature. Then there is the question of funding. I must say that the Crown is growing reluctant to fund overseas operations following the Great War. The War has cost the royal treasury millions of pounds. I stand behind you and since we are fast friends, I see it as a *fait accompli*." He moved close to her.

Caroline spoke: "Reports tell me that we have legislative support. The community approves for the moment. but we must act quickly lest interest wane. I say that we solicit support in the form of laborers and artisans. With the termination of the war there are rafts of craftsmen afoot itching to put a few guilders into their purses."

"Interesting, Madame. Let me speak with Sir William and the Livingstons. They have in the past extended credit to worthy projects and I know that Philip is behind you."

"Over the years the project will pay for itself with a tax levy."

"Always a ticklish subject."

"We start out with a small levy. We insist upon *two* free institutions open to all on equal terms. The community will not deny such a project, knowing that it is for the good of all. For certain the military will support it. Free medical attention and daily lessons in reading and writing, where the latter are tied to promotional opportunities. With the fort, hospital and school in tandem, there stands the makings of a growing community."

"Where *every*one regardless of status or standing may partake of services. I applaud your plan, Madame." He touched her shoulder.

"Yes, Yes. It has a certain ring to it," Caroline returned, smiling appreciatively at her host.

"It is good that you chose to remain behind, Madame. Is James returning to Oneida soon?"

"After the curfew is lifted," she laughed. "Now we are trapped here together," she cajoled.

"As long as the Mohawk is iced over, raiding parties will dart back and forth in search of prey. Do not fret. When warm weather comes, the ice will melt and they will be gone by spring," he confessed, gently placing an arm over her shoulders. "You know, I have grown accustomed to having you here as my guest."

Caroline did not withdraw. Turning to him, she spoke: "Reverend Kirkwood needs to return to Oneida. There is no one to open classes now that I am stranded."

"I will send him back with a body of the King's soldiers—enough to fight off raiders. In the interim you have the luxury of joining your family as my guest and choosing scholars and teachers."

"Perhaps this setback is not a setback after all, Monsieur."

"I am certain that Albany holds many delights for you, Madame," her host returned, holding her tighter.

"The hour grows late," Caroline feigned, pulling away gently. "This coolness makes me hungry for dinner."

"By all means, Madame. Let us go see what Birdie has prepared."

(73)Huey, Paul R.(1988) Comprehensive narrative on Fort Frederick, *Aspects of continuity and change in Colonial Dutch Material Culture at Fort Orange.* PhD Dissertation, University of Pennsylvania.

(74)Bielinski, Stefan. The New Netherland Dutch: *Settling In and Spreading Out in Colonial Albany.* Edited by Jean E. Hunter & Paul T. Mason. Pittsburgh, (1991). Pgs : 1-23

*The ninth minister of the Dutch Reformed Church: (1760-1790).

(75)Alexander, Robert S. Albany's First Church: And Its Role in the Growth of the City, 1642-1942 (1988) Albany.

(76)Norton, Thomas Elliott. The Fur Trade In Colonial New York: 1686-1776, Chapter 6, *Traders And Merchants*, The University of Wisconsin Press, Madison (1974) pgs: 83-99

(77)Livingston, Melvin P. (2008). *Descendants of the Signers of the Declaration of Independence.* 18th Century Resources, State Education Dept., Albany, NY. pgs: 1-5.

(78)The Colonial Albany Social History Project (2010): *Afro-Albanians*, State Education Dept., Albany, pgs: 1-2.

(79)The Colonial Albany Social History Project (2010): *City Hall*, State Education Dept., Albany, pgs: 1-3.

(80)The Colonial Albany Social History Project (2010). *City Streets*, The State Education Dept., Albany, pg: 3.

(81)Anderson. The Crucible of War. Chapter 47. *The Cherokee War and Amherst's Reforms in Indian Policy,*

(2000) pgs: 457-460

82) Anderson (2000) The Crucible of War. Chapter 64. *Pontiac's Progress.* (2000). pgs: 620-623.

(83) Norton, Thomas Elliott. The Fur Trade in Colonial New York, Chapter 6: *Traders and Merchants*, (1974) pgs: 83-100.

*King George III

*The French & Indian War.

*Dutch Reformed Church of Albany

**Sir William Johnson, Commissioner of Indian affairs and entrepreneur

(84)Norton Chapter 5, *Trade Regulations And Frontier Security*,(1874) pgs: 60-68.

(85)Van Schaack, Henry V. (1892), pgs: 6-8.

(86)Borneman (2006) Chapter 19: *A Matter Unresolved*, pgs: 280-296.

CHAPTER SIXTEEN

All Things Righteous and Just
Fond Ambitions.
A Conflict Resolved.
Reunion.
Clash along the Mohawk

A cold and raw winter's morning assaulted the senses of the hardy contingent that departed Fort Frederick that Wednesday, January 10th, 1761. In the cavalcade of twenty four armed men rode Reverend Kirkland, drawing a wagon-load of books and supplies, gifts of Cornelis Cuyler, his friend and collaborator. Beside him rode Thomas Steed, to some a walking thesaurus, eager to resume studies at Oneida. James York came also. He intended to await the arrival of his son, Matthew, due from Newfoundland, at Oneida, preparatory to escorting him to the Round Tops and a reunion with the Bear Chief.

From a distance below the fort Caroline and Suzanne watched the procession embark during that unsettled hour when wind-whipped gales spun the fallen snow into columns of fury, blowing the little frozen crystals into their faces, stinging the cheeks and turning them red. There, at the corner of Jonkers and North Pearl, Caroline and Suzanne stood cloaked in thick furs, paying silent tribute to James, the soft-spoken, yet stalwart patriarch of the family. Their eyes following the cavalcade, mother and daughter remained vigilant until the last rider in the troupe disappeared over the hilltop and headed west.

Turning briskly with heads bowed to fight off fierce gales, Caroline and Suzanne hurried back to the warm parlor of the Cuyler mansion. Seated before a spacious table scattered with traces of her labors, Caroline resumed the lengthy task of composing a list of candidates to fill positions in teaching. On the table lay strewn sets of cards, each bearing the name, address, and brief description of a candidate for her proposed school. Learned scholars all, the candidates hailed from as close as the diminutive New York City and as distant as grand Amsterdam in Holland. In studying the cards, she paid a silent tribute to her host, the patriarch, who supplied her with most of the references from among his vast store of entrepreneurial engagements over many years.

Across from her sat Suzanne, an eager volunteer. She enjoyed writing and, with each card that Caroline passed to her, she prepared a letter of invitation, each one unique unto itself. She shuddered at the thought of having to post the letters later that day. Some were destined for the inn just below the fort where a coach would carry them off to all points of the compass. Others must go by ship, overseas to Holland and even France and England. She viewed with displeasure the trek down slippery Jonkers to Dock Street where the intimidating merchantman lay at anchor. The closer she came to the ship the more she envisioned falling into the clutches of a ravenous pirate. Again she shuddered, yet her fears abated when out of a corner of her eye she spied the omnipresent Birdie running to join her. Together the two young ladies posted Caroline's cache of letters with the ship's master, dipping into the allowance which the baron set aside for postage.

On most mornings Suzanne and Birdie accompanied Caroline to the site of the new school. A few paces north of the fort, the makings of the basement already took shape. Cut from the hard, cold earth, the rock-like foundation descended some sixteen feet. Soon its sides would be buttressed with stone blocks, its bottom covered with rows of bricks. Destined to become a basement housing dining facilities and reading salon, an exterior stairwell would connect it with the proposed first floor above.

On this morning she came to oversee the installation of a fireplace in the basement. A chimney would ascend out-of-doors from an alcove to the rear of the fireplace to provide warmth to all floors above. By pre-arrangement with her benefactor and patron, she held sway over the school's more intimate appointments. The legislature, she noted, assuredly with Sir William Johnson's approval, awarded a separate and distinct site for the school upon a campus shared in common with the proposed hospital. In her opinion both structures would, upon completion, furnish the growing Albany with prodigious assets.

By the close of January Caroline received replies from a wealth of candidates. She prepared to conduct interviews during February and make final selections soon afterward. She tapped into her allowance once again to pay for the transportation and lodging of all promising candidates. Although longing to return to Oneida Castle, she remained true to the task at hand, and offered suggestions to the laborers daily. She took delight in seeing native men actively engaged in the project, a sign that her appearances in the city began to reap rewards.

One afternoon the baron summoned her to his study, presumably to supplement her allowance. He often asked her opinion of the construction, demonstrating faith in her observations. On this day, unlike the others, without James at her side, she saw herself alone and vulnerable. She sent for Suzanne to accompany her, and without disclosing the basis of her fears, ushered her daughter into the entrepreneur's study. Together they stood lock-step and rigid before him. Their host, bent over a stack of documents, avoided them at first, yet, when Suzanne noisily cleared her throat, he perked up in earnestness, coming to full attention.

"Conditions are poor to the west," he quipped, producing a letter. "Natives have surprised two forts on the Mohawk." Anticipating queries, he chose to respond prematurely.

"The origin is presumably Huron," he spoke, perusing the letter. "Seeking revenge on the Iroquois," he lamented. "Old wounds heal slowly." Reading on, he spoke again: "Militia turned them away." In deep thought he stroked his chin. "There will be more of it," he concluded, folding the letter.

Mother and daughter shared dour expressions. If Suzanne's presence unnerved the baron, he displayed no outward signs of it and returned to perusing documents.

"You sent for me, Sir?" Caroline asked, her stomach in a knot, following her host's foreboding disclosures.

Standing, he smiled wryly: "Yes. I have dipped into my private reserves and put together an allowance for contingencies as they may arise." Stepping forward he handed her a note for 1000lbs. "I know that it means much to you," he replied, softly.

"And to you, Sir," Caroline added. Accepting, she nodded knowingly, aware that with the payment he hoped to dispel any lingering guilt associated with former transgressions. She turned to depart, when he spoke:

"I have a letter for *you*. Judging from the label, it holds pleasant thoughts."

"Oh!! From James! James! My husband!," she returned. Caught unawares, she clutched the letter to her bosom. Again she prepared to depart. "Suzanne!"

"Hmm. Well," her host implored, expecting Caroline to share the letter with him.

An animated Caroline reached for Suzanne's hand and together mother and daughter dashed from the room. Over her shoulder Caroline called out: "Thank you, Monsieur. We need to be alone for a while."

In the seclusion of her bedroom Caroline leafed through James's letter, giving half of the six page missive to Suzanne. Avidly retaining the remainder, she chose to read aloud while pacing to and fro. Suzanne sought the comfort of a plush lounge and dived into the contents. Caroline reported her findings in fits and starts:

"He writes from Oneida Castle. Reverend Kirkland has taken my classes and patiently awaits my return. Matthew has come back from Newfoundland. He is at Oneida. He brings a wife. Cree woman. Fluent in English and French. A great homemaker. Suzanne!! I am a grandmother. That makes you an aunt." She ceased reading and gasped with joy.

"Yes, I know, mother. Mother! Which is it? Boy or girl?"

"A boy. Not named yet. Matthew is taking nominations."

Suzanne read. "There has been an incident along the way, mother. It is all right now: Matthew and his friend from the *Courageous* fought off a band of marauders with Rogers' Rangers. Who is Rogers?"

"An Indian fighter. Hates pirates with a passion."

"Mother!! Father has returned to the Round Tops. He says that Colombe Blanche and the boys are well. The boys have grown much taller. They all want us to visit when opportunity permits."

"We may be waiting for a while," Caroline sighed, looking up from her reading.

"Father says that the village is well-nigh finished. My! My! Watkins is a new father. A girl. He and Fawn are the 'perfect pair.' Watkins adores her to the bone. Fawn's brother has come back. Released from evil's clutch. Oh, mother! Now we must go to see everyone!"

"Her brother? Ah! Released from bondage. The Captain again. Shades of the Devil Incarnate. Will we ever be free of that name?"

Suzanne gasped. "Look, mother! The Bear Chief may remove to Ohio. He has much to do there in keeping the peace." She directed Caroline to her portion of the letter.

"Is he taking Colombe Blanche and the boys?" She leafed through Suzanne's letter.

"I do not see it. He is going to meet with his cousin, Tah:gah:jute."

"Mother. Is that the chief who lived . . . ."

" . . . Yes, Suzanne—at Osco for a short while. He is on a peace mission along the Ohio." Caroline explained that in support of the western Delaware, recently removed to the Ohio region, Tah:gah:jute has stepped in to replace Teedyuscung as interim chief and peacemaker, who quit his post in shame and disgrace over the sale of Delaware lands in the east.

"How do you know these matters, mother?"

"I found them among the daily journal stores along Market Street."

"But why the Bear Chief?" Suzanne complained.

"The Cayugas and Delaware are not only blood-related, but have shared hunting grounds over generations. We discussed this already, did we not?" Caroline probed, slightly irritated.

"Yes. Yes. I believe so. Oh! Everything running together has turned my head into a knot." She pressed hard on her temples, tears welling in her eyes.

"You are forgiven," Caroline condescended. "Do not cry. You will see them again." She herself fought back a lump in her throat. Changing the tone of the conversation, Caroline suggested that the two of them draft a letter to James. They pulled a table between themselves and, taking seats, started making notations.

—

Caroline began February in a flurry. Each morning, rising early, she walked the wards of Albany with Suzanne to solicit pledges for her school from among households in the populace. Dutifully, mother and daughter called at homes in sections devoted to laborers and their families. Following introductions, Caroline skillfully disclosed the purpose of her visit in an introductory statement:

"Your son/daughter has the opportunity to become a member of the first graduating class of the first public school between Albany and Boston. I have come to seek your reassurance that you will permit your child to attend." Caroline found that a few embellishments did not harm the substance of her theme and occasionally she resorted to them, for she intended to impress upon parent and child that they stood at the threshold of a historical undertaking— one made only the more sanctified by their unqualified acquiescence. With few exceptions, householders grasped at Caroline's prospect of a school, associating the tall, winsome woman with the very same woman who gained celebrity at City Hall. In general, mothers confided to her that they sought a safe refuge for their children while they went to the houses of manufacture, breweries, mills and the docks of the city to labor each day far into the afternoon.

When a householder in the Black ward asked Caroline the name of her school, she replied calmly: 'The Free School, open to all."

"We have always been tutored by Old Noah," the woman, Hannah Moses, returned. Going further, she explained that Noah Mc Veigh was an itinerant teacher who lived on the road in a covered wagon all year. In lieu of payment, modest at best, he accepted donations of food and clothing from those householders he visited to conduct lessons. A former Harvard professor, Mc Veigh, in his own words, "abandoned the cloistered halls of academia in order to reach deep down into the bowels of colonial America where the real people resided." To the amazement of colleagues he opened a school in an abandoned warehouse among the row houses of Boston's Back Bay section. There he administered to the city's poor until a mysterious fire burned him out. Removing to Albany, he never trusted another property owner and chose to travel about in a wagon and teach in the homes of those householders who invited him to tend to their children. "The children are most grateful for him," Caroline recalled Hannah Moses saying in tribute.

"Now they will have their own school, and yes, Noah may stay," Caroline assured Hannah Moses.

"You have not met him, Ma'am. He is in need of a full set of new clothes and a bath. More of the latter, I wager," she laughed, enjoying the session with the friendly young matron.

"Well within my means," Caroline declared. The two women shook hands and as Caroline turned to depart, Hannah Moses delivered a most memorable epithet. Looking up into Caroline's eyes she recited warmly: "You are the one who walks with the Lord leading you by the hand. Never stray far from the Lord."

—

Caroline committed Hannah Moses' phrase to memory, the essence of which she interpreted as an unexpected reward— a spark of encouragement. With that in mind, she rejoined Suzanne at the foot of Jonkers Street, and, overcome with enthusiasm, half-pulled her daughter up the steep hill, slowing when the venerable gates of Fort Frederick came into view.

She called over her shoulder to Suzanne: "We go to enlist the native youth. Today is a trading day when boys and young men go with their fathers to the fort to learn the ways of the traders." Ahead, the courtyard, brimming with trading tables, bustled with movement. Everywhere native men jostled for position in long lines before the tables, arms and back packs laden with furs: the stuff of trade. Some resided nearby. Others came straight from the Great Lakes country and beyond. Facing them, the tradesmen, representing many points of the northeast and Canada, doled out currency on the one hand and hard goods on the other. The native men kept the hard goods for their families and kept the currency, usually gold coin, for making purchases at the mercantile houses of the city. At any one moment a cross-section of the entire North American continent trafficked and bartered within the fort and the general comportment of the population was exceptionally well-mannered. Suzanne made note of the observation to her mother, yet another form of encouragement which gave Caroline reason to trip lightly over the grounds.

Twice a month natives entered the fort to dispose of precious cargos. Under the auspices of the principal Commissioner of Indian Affairs, Sir William Johnson, native men were allowed to shop in the city with currency earned at the tables. They may not, however, remain overnight or seek residency or asylum in the homes of residents. Nor may they bear exposed arms such as a rifle or tomahawk or smell of alcohol or seek the same from incidental providers. All things being equal, native men may not incite quarrels with residents or entice them into a quarrel. The same measure applied to the white residents, and although aggrieved parties may consult an attorney to settle old and current scores, the native usually lacked the financial resources to make good on his grievance, no matter how much he earned from the sale of his pelts and skins. Penalties ranged from banishment from the city for the native and a stiff fine and perhaps more for whites. Occasionally Sir William made contributions to a legal defense fund, but more often than not the fund stood exhausted or grossly underfunded. When all was said and done, Sir William Johnson sought to preserve peaceful relations between the two races, and, despite infrequent breakdowns in the administration of policy, white and native relations remained benign as long as Sir William held the reins of authority (87).

On this day commemorating the inauguration of new policies, Sir William himself visited the fort and wherever he walked a sizable body of native men gathered around him. They generally approved of his principles, for he made certain to establish boundaries over which they may not step and still hope to retain the gifts which he set aside for them. The sword and cape, hallmarks of his attire, he flourished conspicuously in full view of all, forms of recognition which separated him from the crowd. He enjoyed the attention almost as much as he enjoyed handing down policies with which to administer to the denizens of the colony.

Caroline and Suzanne approached a gathering of native men milling about the Commissioner. Through an interpreter Caroline learned that native fathers insisted upon receiving gifts in return for pledging their sons' attendance at her school. Immediately Caroline saw this maneuver as an extension of the gift-giving practices which Sir William employed so tactfully on the frontier. She did not care to spread gifts unilaterally, receiving nothing in return. She paused to contemplate a suitable response. Before long she found an interpreter and explained to him that she did not disavow the giving of gifts; however, they must be given to *all* students, not merely to native children, and they must be given as a *condition* of solid student performance. After some discussion, the native men agreed to these terms, leaving the matter of the nature of the gifts an open question. Caroline eagerly stepped in to fill the void. She proposed the offering of hot lunches and sundries to all students who came to school daily, with a bonus or supplement given to the students who excelled. This the native men welcomed heartily and a sizable body decidedly shifted to Caroline's side of the grounds. Forming rows, they staked out places in order to capture a glance of this newcomer. Her candidness and belief in her cause won the men's pledges and a number of them volunteered to commit additional laborers for the school's construction.

—

Every Saturday afternoon Caroline and Suzanne attended services at the Dutch Reformed Church where they became an anticipated fixture in the front pews. The baron gave Birdie permission to accompany them. On this occasion following the service, the Domine asked for volunteers to join the chorus of the young men and women of the congregation. Suzanne raised her own hand and Birdie's as well without Birdie's consent. The young servant protested mildly, giving a few congregants occasion to laugh among themselves. They fell silent, however, under the Domine's baleful gaze, whereupon he turned to the two young ladies:

"You must be able to sing well," the Domine related, in no uncertain terms.

"Birdie sings the whole day through. Her home is gay and cheerful from dawn to dusk," Suzanne quipped, a hint of mischief in her eye.

Not to be trifled with, the Domine addressed Birdie: "Is this true, Miss?" his deep voice resounding over the church's stout masonry walls. Dressed in a thick, black robe, the Domine bore an overbearing likeness to the classical, indomitable magistrate of legend, and Birdie, momentarily intimidated beyond words, hesitated to respond.

"So be it, ladies. The first rehearsal begins this evening at seven. Be prompt and bring your best voices. May I add that gaining a position with the choir is a cherished desire among the congregation, one entered into with all humility and sincerity." Finishing, he trod briskly to his rooms.

Arriving that evening for rehearsal, Suzanne and Birdie waited to be introduced to the current choral body, all of whom milled about in anticipation of the choir master. Amid the light banter, several young ladies expressed an interest driven by morbid curiosity in Suzanne and her new friend.

"You say that your friend sings at will through the day?" a young lady asked.

"Why yes. We share the same home and Birdie keeps everyone's spirits merry."

"She must sing from memory then," and before Suzanne may reply the girl interjected: "We sing from a psalm book. Much is in Latin. Do you read Latin? Do you read?" She dwelt upon Birdie.

"I read when asked to and I have an excellent teacher," the young servant returned, turning to Suzanne.

"You will be doing much of it here," her adversary replied. "Tell me. Have you sung in chorus before?"

"Why yes. In Church of the Gospel I sang every Sunday," Birdie maintained in her candid, disarming demeanor.

"Why! What? Where is that? I have not heard of it'?"

"It is in the Bahamas," Birdie intoned cheerfully.

"My! My! You are a *long* way from home. Do you intend going back one day soon?"

"No. My people have died. They are all dead. Will there be any more questions, Miss?"

Her adversary withdrew and the room grew quiet. The caustic inquisitiveness ceased and Suzanne and Birdie found themselves isolated in the center of the room. The estrangement prevailed until a generous clapping of hands from the wings signaled the choir master's approach into the room.

"Places everyone. I am Maude Brambles," rasped the frail spinster in the homespun full-length gown who, facing the choristers, ceased the fierce clapping. Audibly clearing her throat, she handed out psalm books from a rack behind her desk. She went through extreme maneuvers to distribute the manuals. Stretching forward, she reached over the heads of the choristers in the first row, peering eerily down at the cherubic faces below her through pince-nez lenses. Her cold, dark eyes bored into each member as she cavorted and twisted her spare form among them. The regular members seemed well apprised of her gyrations and stood before her undaunted. Suzanne came close to bursting out in laughter. Containing herself, she squeezed Birdie's hand and nudged her playfully in an effort to place her at ease.

"We will sing Psalm # 25 on page 36, class, otherwise known as: 'My Lord is King of the World.' There are two parts: choral and solo. Be thinking along those lines. Begin!"

With Suzanne pointing to the lyrics, Birdie sang along in unison, her voice blending in superbly with those of the chorus. Intrusively, Maude Brambles came to stand before small bodies of choristers. Tilting her head to one side, she listened for those tones that to her paid fitting homage to the melody. Once satisfied, she grimaced in stern approval and moved on. Twisting at the waist and pulling her head askew, she stopped suddenly and rammed her heel down hard on the bare oaken flooring whenever she met with tones which displeased her. Pointing out the offending party, she demanded an instant repetition of the verse, standing with arms folded and toe tapping incessantly until the correction was made. Rue to the hapless chorister who erred, for he or she must endure the scathing gaze of Maude Brambles, as well as incisive peer ridicule once the session ended.

On this day Maude Brambles demanded a repetition from no one— a rare occurrence. To the body as a whole she seemed consumed with moving ahead to select a chorister for the solo portion of the performance, a lengthy process which involved listening to candidates singing in turn a few bars of the solo itself. Perhaps still reeling from one of Maude Brambles' scene-stealing demonstrations from a previous session, none of the regular choristers volunteered to audition.

"I understand, class. Tongue-tied are we? Let me see." She walked unpretentiously along the front row of choristers. Bending and stretching, she lowered her pince-nez to the tip of her nose. Gazing intently on each member in the manner of a merchant judging livestock, she extended her lank frame most adroitly into the second row where her tiny, coal-hard eyes fastened upon each member in turn, a customary ritual which compelled more than a few choristers to shy away from her rather than meet her gaze.

"I have not met with you before, my dear," crackled Maude Brambles, coming to rest before Birdie.

"I am new, Madame. Newly-arrived," Birdie returned, her broad smile shining forth.

"I am in grave need of a soloist for the climax of our hallmark piece. Would you care to volunteer a few bars?" Her toe tapping out a staccato, Maude Brambles stretched to her full height. Crooking up her brow, she ground her teeth together audibly, thrusting her hands across her hips, a pose which insisted upon one and only one response.

"Why, yes, Madame. I am most honored to be asked," Birdie replied, showing no signs of fear.

"Excellent choice," the choir master rasped. "George will lead you on the piano. George!!" She clapped loudly and a diminutive and rotund elderly man appeared out of the wings of the hall. "At your service, Madame."

Maude Brambles gave a down-beat, a signal to George, after which she glowered at her new charge, hands pressed to her hips. A candidate of less fortitude may have demurred, but Birdie, with head high and shoulders thrust back, stood straight and brave. Having committed the solo to memory, she shunned Suzanne's offer of the psalm manual and launched into the sweet refrain in a brilliant alto, her voice effortlessly rising and falling with the strains of the music. A short piece, it nevertheless called upon one to traverse almost the entire chromatic scale in brief, vibrant bursts of punctuation. Historically, choristers all but shrank in exhaustion at the finale, but Birdie surged ahead, her voice strong and soaring. She ended as she began, full of vitality, projecting an aura of triumph.

Behind Birdie the choral body swooned. Although Maude Brambles forbade demonstrations of joy, young ladies clasped hands to hearts and moaned while young men tossed up their arms in a sign of victory. Looking to the choir master, everyone witnessed a display of uncanny behavior— an act which countermanded Maude Brambles' own stringent prohibition of outward signs of spontaneity: To wit, Maude Brambles ingenuously arched her back mightily. Stretching to full height, she cupped her hands to either cheek. Opening her mouth to its fullest extent, she shrieked at the top of her lungs: "YEOWW!!"

"I have found my soloist," she shouted. Hands clasped to her chest, she breathed heavily. "Please be advised young lady that you are now the featured singer of this heavenly church." Stepping forward, Maude Brambles extended her hand to Birdie, who accepted it appreciatively.

"Now! First things first. What is your name, dear child?"

From that day forward, Birdie, the constant fixture of the Cuyler household, unknown beyond the mansion's walls, became a celebrity in the hearts and minds of the townspeople. Strangers greeted her on the streets when she walked to market. Others stopped her to discuss important events of the day, and everyone offered words of praise which the young lady greeted with a transforming smile designed to melt the hardest heart of the most obstinate merchant.

* * *

The first wave of teacher-candidates arrived. Caroline found them of excellent quality, women and men of scholarly backgrounds who harbored no reservations about living on the frontier in colonial New York. She came away from interviews with a wealth of choices, sufficient to staff her new school and beyond. Some she planned to send to Oneida Castle, even to the Round Tops and wherever her dream took root. Staffing the Round Tops provided her with the opportunity of renewing relations with the Bear Chief, her original benefactor, and his family.

At this point Caroline believed that, in light of gross white incursions into native lands, the fate of the native lay with the ability of white settlers to accept him as a human being, rather than as an obstacle to circumvent in the omnipresent fur trade industry. For Caroline, schools spread over the frontier held the possibility of affording the two races-white and red-the opportunity to collaborate over values held in common. At the same time she predicted the demise of the fur trade to coincide with the extermination of certain fur-bearing species. Therefore, for her it became imperative to bring the two races together by building bonds of common understanding in an effort to cast off pent-up hostilities and animosities between them. What a better way than a school, she concluded. Many schools open to all!! The more she thought about the scheme, the more necessary it became. She entertained thoughts of it constantly and when she convinced herself that her plan needed to be expanded immediately, she brought her concerns before her sponsor, the baron Cuyler. In no small way, the desire to be at her husband's side played a supporting role in extending a school to the Round Tops.

"The frontier is still turbulent, Madame," her patron confessed soberly.

"I must provide teachers for the Oneidas and Cayugas—yeah, the Senecas. You say that an escort is out of the question?" She paced about her host's study anxiously.

"Yes, where the lives of innocent militia are concerned," he returned, raising his voice.

"My plan. *Our* plan must be put into motion lest it die on the vine," she stated defiantly.

"You have indeed a noble mission, but you must not invite misfortune to follow it."

"I assume all responsibility for the venture's success or failure," Caroline retorted, in no uncertain terms.

"Hah! It is I who have the responsibility. Have I not turned my purse inside out? Long after you have departed the region it is I who will be long remembered for better or worse." He turned full-center, meeting her head-on.

Approaching him, Caroline brought two chairs forward. "You need to sit while I tell you about myself."

Placing the chairs opposite each other, she invited him to sit and listen. At first he hesitated, accepting when she vowed to leave the room in a storm.

She began slowly, hoping to compel his full attention. "We never spoke of me. I know about you and your lineage, your destiny— much of it predictable and without incident." Smiling, she gazed at him intently.

"I, on the other hand, faced death at every turn since setting foot in this colony. It is through guile and good fortune that I am able to tell you my story." The baron, now fully-involved, sat on the edge of the chair.

"My husband and I used to farm lands next to the Susquehanna down near the Chesapeake. My uncle held a large spread, a gift from the neighboring Delaware. Valuable land, he needed hands to farm crops of which there were many. Together with the Delaware, James and I assisted him. The British military wanted the lands to sell to homesteaders. Charles refused to sell. One day he was found dead. I too refused to sell the properties. One day I was abducted and taken north to Fort Oswego. My abductor, a very influential officer, kept me at his side day and night. He forced me to become his servant upon pain of death to my family should I refuse to serve him. When I tried to escape, he bundled me in men's clothing and took me off to a native village where I was forced to sleep in a corn crib. Repeatedly he took me off to native villages so as to throw off pursuers. I traveled in caravans laden with young native prisoners bound for sale. At one village a kind chieftain released me in my captor's absence to tend to village children.

I instructed them in English and writing, and gradually an entire curriculum."

The baron leaned forward, features stoic, eyes set upon Caroline.

"I left small traces of myself at every turn for James to follow and often he was but a few hour's march from me. At no time did I submit to my tormentor physically and because of this he kept me confined in despicable quarters. Eventually, through the intercession of a Cayuga chieftain, a French tradesman, and his commandant—principal friends of mine, incidentally— James and Suzanne tracked me to within a few miles of Oswego. There my friends staged an ambush. A skirmish took place without a clear victor. The rogue officer threatened to kill all prisoners. These were young natives whom he often sold into a life of servitude. I was also a prisoner and when the fighting died down, I offered to go with him as a hostage to Oswego— a peace-token, if you will— in exchange for his promise not to execute the captive natives. Alas, he confined us all in a pen at Ontario, most likely bent upon employing us as 'bargaining chips' or selling us outright. Soon I gained my freedom when my astute friends rescued me from a roaring inferno in the pen which careless soldiers heedlessly touched off. They carried me to a remote post where I developed my true passion: teaching young natives to read and write. I resolved to begin my own school once my abductor became locked away and, through good fortune, this came to pass. Soon thereafter I met Reverend Kirkland. He provided me with the opportunity to open a school at Oneida Castle, One day he brought me to Albany to visit with you and I found myself your constant guest."

"You are very courageous." Her host permitted himself to smile meekly. "What is most remarkable is that you turned tragedy into triumph." Rising, he patted her shoulder sympathetically.

"I would not be here now without the support of my family and dear friends." Rising, she took a few steps, stopped and glimpsed longingly through the great bay window in the study. "I miss them," she confessed, pouting.

"There, there, Caroline," her host spoke consolingly, coming to stand behind her. "I sense that there is much more to your story, but we need not speak of it now." He spoke softly, moving closer.

"I do not want to burden you with my cares." She stepped backward, coming to rest against his chest.

He rubbed her back about the shoulders. "You are very tense here. You need to loosen up a bit." With that he massaged her back in ever-widening circles. "Now, tell me more of your story."

Pressed against the window, Caroline saw drops of her breath forming on the pane. "I find it difficult to breathe. May we sit down?" She made faint attempts to draw away from him, but not strident enough to reject him outright.

"Of course, Caroline. Forgive me my indulgences. Let me assist you," He guided her to a waiting chair. Once seated, Caroline lowered her defenses and continued:

"James and my principal friends have gained irrefutable evidence about my uncle's death." She followed quickly with her findings: "After extensive searching they concluded that my abduction and my uncle's death to have been brought about by the same man."

"Good heavens, Caroline!! And to say that this man held you at his mercy day and night all of those days."

She hurried along. "He did not learn of my knowledge of his total involvement until the day of his trial."

"Otherwise he may have killed you."

"The possibility of that crossed my mind more than once."

"By what process did he come to trial?"

Caroline tread carefully here, not wanting to disclose Lord Carleton's role in capturing her abductor, nor her own for that matter. Although she trusted the baron, she did not care to rescind her vow of secrecy originally conceived to protect the commandant's name from scandal. Subsequently, she decided to defer from the telling of the Le Rocher capture of Lord Carleton's reconnaissance force at Pointe Aux Bois. Deviating from the true course of events, she offered instead what she believed a convincing tale:

"My principal friends besieged Fort Ontario. Capturing my abductor, they removed him to the French post where they held him for ransom. Reluctantly the British commandant paid the ransom, but only on condition that the French release any imprisoned British soldiers held, and most important, only with the proviso that the French abandon their post immediately or suffer it to go up in flames."

"These friends of yours. They were struck by your strong sense of duty," He studied his hands as he spoke.

"They are honorable people. They were the difference between my living and dying. I must go to them for they are a part of my extended family."

"At Oswego you must have met with Lord Carleton."

"Ah, yes," Caroline replied, bracing herself. "My friends spoke highly of him."

"Word has it here that he put down a conspiracy from among his own soldiers."

Playing the curious ingénue, Caroline gasped: "Oh my!!"

"Apparently a band of pirates stole from his stores—furs and pelts—carrying them off to make a handsome profit. There was a leader too. Two leaders. One a pirate—captured. No one knows of the other. Does any of this ring familiar with you?"

Feigning an interest in his account, Caroline spoke: "I have heard traces of such chicanery, but I have known Lord Carleton to be nothing less than an honest and able administrator."

"He is a rich administrator these days," the baron confessed, bringing a hand down heavily upon the desk. In a moment of levity he spoke with renewed vigor: "Lord Carleton has assumed command of the fur trade at Oswego following the disruption of the conspiracy. Goods now flow from Canada and the west through Oswego to Albany and all points east. Where once Oswego was a fort, it now resembles a supply base devoted to the distribution of trade goods. Because of Oswego, Albany is no longer the center of fur trading." He leaned back in his chair, pleased with his disclosures.

"My son, Matthew, came through Oswego en route to Oneida to visit me." She took a step backward, lowering her voice. "Of course I am not there to greet him."

"The corridor between Oswego and the Mohawk is a frequent battleground." Resting his chair squarely on the floor, he uttered a comment which uprooted her: "I believe that we are sailing uncharted waters here."

Challenging her host, Caroline charged ahead boldly: "In order to protect his supplies Lord Carleton out of necessity has armed his traders and increased the men-at-arms at Oswego. There is much turmoil in that corridor, but I have yet to hear of a single coup against a trading party there, due in part to Lord Carleton's preparedness. By contrast, I ask for but a small bit of security along a secondary route little traveled by brigands."

Her host bristled, the gleam gone from his eye: "Caroline. You are asking for the impossible."

"Let Matthew lead me to Oneida!!" she erupted. "He has proven his mettle with rogues and brigands."

"Matthew? Matthew York? The same?"

"Aah! You know the name!!" She stamped her foot, hands on hips, head thrown back proudly.

"My word! The gazettes hereabouts were filled with his exploits. I have a collection of them somewhere." Her host went on to describe Matthew's mission in Newfoundland, his encounter with the St. Lawrence pirates, his subsequent rescue of native captives, his capture of the pirate leader and his promotion to aide-de-camp. In this latter role, according to gazettes, Matthew rode with the military arm of the British Expeditionary Forces which sought after enemies of the British in the Lake Country. Shortly thereafter, he dropped from the headlines and readers everywhere thought him killed in battle. Finding one such article, the baron appeared puzzled that young Matthew, believed by many to have died a hero's death, now emerged unscathed and eager to seek new challenges.

"That is indeed a story for another day," Caroline intervened, touching her host's hand ever-softly.

"A true hero, that lad," the baron expounded. "To think I have entertained his mother all the while." Striking a knee, he rose and strode to Caroline's side. "Now I see where he acquired all of his pluck and dash." Overcome in the manner of a chemist on the verge of a new discovery, the baron reared back his head and shouted in elation, then set about shadow-dancing over the carpeted study. Birdie, followed by Suzanne, and Mrs. Cuyler, responded to the commotion. Expecting the worst, they found the entrepreneur cutting small capers with Caroline, all the while holding her at arm's length. Birdie and Suzanne broke into a laugh, leaving Mrs. Cuyler, to tuck in her plump chin beneath a profound scowl.

The delighted entrepreneur approached Suzanne. Bending low, he whispered into her ear: "Now tell me about your brother, Matthew York."

Somewhat at a loss for words, Suzanne fought to calm herself, before coming forth assertively: "He is all that you say he is, and more. To say the least, he has endeared himself to Lord Carleton." Her eyes found Caroline, who nodded with approval, and Suzanne continued with words of praise:

"Matthew has fought pirates and Indians, crossed treacherous rapids, saved his flagship from disaster, braved the ice and snow, and led armies into battle. He has faced death a thousand times over, rising above it and staring it full in the face before casting it aside and returning to the fight ever-stronger. Legendary exploits all have placed him in good stead with Lord Carleton." In her presentation Suzanne stood soberly before the baron, delivering the speech that she hoped would weigh heavily in the entrepreneur's decision to grant her mother passage to travel west. She spoke as though delivering a sermon to a religious yet doubting audience, an audience wanting desperately to believe in the speaker's message and, when she finished, she stepped unabashedly to one side, eyes upon him.

"Brilliant!!" the baron roared. Turning to Caroline, he grasped her by the shoulders: "You have my full support. However, you must think of a way to conduct Matthew here safely, and more so, how to conduct your entire party safely over a tedious voyage. You are taking a land route, are you not?"

From her pocket Caroline produced a thick sheet of browned paper which she dropped into her host's hand. "Open it! I believe that it answers the second part of your concern."

Hesitantly, the baron unfolded the paper. Because of its width he placed it upon the desk and smoothed it at the seams. At first a maze of etchings caught the eye, but, upon looking closer, he found them to be components drawn to scale of a vessel or boat of some sort. Struggling with the maze of etchings, he looked up.

"It is a bateau. Fortified, I like to believe," Caroline returned. "Let me describe it to you. It has a cabin fitted with gun ports for marksmen. It has a deck circumscribing the cabin, the width of a man's shoulders and not an inch more. The foredeck is highly-arched to dissuade boarders from mounting the vessel at the bow. Below decks is space for passengers and cargo."

Her host pointed to a long-pole-like protuberance fastened to the center piece of the cabin's flat roof.

"A tiller, no less," Caroline chimed merrily. "At its lower extreme it widens to a paddle. A driver steers the vessel from atop the cabin on deck."

"Are you not forgetting something?" the entrepreneur inquired, regarding the sketch closely.

"What will pull this vessel, you ask?" Caroline rebounded. "In a word: 'horses'". She pointed to a pair of iron loopholes fastened to the curved deck near the apex of the bow. "You pass the rigging through them and double it back to the lead harness and you have completed a circuit and your team is secure. Then you are off to the races," she exclaimed, laughing.

"Horses and a tiller? My word!! I believe you have something there." The entrepreneur studied the sketch carefully, turning over its application in his mind.

"Another function for the tiller is to push the vessel away from the shallows or shoals."

"A busy chap, the tiller-man. Tell me. How does he stay removed from danger?"

"We may build a shed for him atop the roof. Of course there are the gun ports lining the craft. They will be occupied by marksmen."

"Very good. Now to the part about getting word to your son. I expect a supply of furs (88) from the west soon. John Root, the guide you met at the fort, will bring them in. He is favorably known in the territory and has pulled himself out of more than one tight pinch. He will conduct your escort with some of his trusted aides west along the Mohawk to your destination. There will be no reprise of the Saratoga massacre back in '45 (89). John Root goes to Oswego soon. He will bring your son here to Albany to lead a command. With Matthew we will have almost forty good fighting men to defend against raiders. This gives us ample opportunity to protect the horses, fortify the cabin, and watch over the tiller. Unfortunately, I am unable to offer you a company of the King's soldiers, for this venture is a private one and, although not illegal, it is not sanctioned by the Crown for any one of several reasons."

"I understand. You have proved most helpful. We have only to build our vessel at this point," Caroline replied, holding out her hand in a gesture of appreciation.

The baron shook her hand firmly. "Or *purchase* one," he returned, a gleam in his eye. "I have been thinking, Caroline. There is an old bateau down on the waterfront. It is in dry dock simply because it is too small to haul the great loads that come through the port. For a few pennies the dock master will part with it without asking embarrassing questions." He paused, thinking. "Of course we will have to make adjustments."

"It is laborers that you need. I have them." Eagerly Caroline stepped forward. "I have in mind native men—those who trade at the fort. They long to become a part of the greater community. After all, they stomped through these lands long before our arrival. A sizable crew is already committed to the school. That leaves others looking for an outlet to join their confrères. I say that we approach them with an offer of employment. A better way to keep the peace has not been conceived. They must be paid in currency, currency that they are at will to exchange for hard and soft goods in Albany's shops. And no rum is to be given them!! On this I stand resolute! In addition we have a raft of local craftsmen. Bring them along as well. A splendid method to promote understanding between the races this shall be. I am thoroughly in favor of it. Ask Sir William to bestow his blessing on the project and the native men will leap at the prospect."

Caroline spoke convincingly, in a speech tailored to arouse her host's entrepreneurial spirit. All the while the baron studied her, seeing her in a new light. He thought to himself: 'She is as an ambassador to the native inhabitants of the region, stemming from her fight for survival during the period of her captivity, an omnipresence whose enthusiasm is bound to extend the peace and tranquility between the races for as long as she remains in residence. Her good fortune with the natives will in all likelihood come to rest at my doorstep, coming at a moment when I need native allies to launch a serious challenge to the growth of the Oswego fur trade industry. Now her son, a battle-hardened leader, stands poised to join me to rid the waterways of raiders and skirmishers, giving me unrestrained access to that port.'

At that point the baron came to recognize the powerful influence that the tall, suave woman who shared his mansion brought to bear upon his fortunes. In Caroline's presence he made light of this realization with a flippant remark:

I believe that I am about to embark on a brave, new venture."

"That you are, Sir. That you are," Caroline repeated merrily. "Think of it as an investment in navigation for the greater good of the colony." Smiling, she gripped his elbow.

Lying in bed that evening, Suzanne dwelt upon the unique set of circumstances which formed the bond that linked her mother and her host, the baron, together. 'Although strong and independent in mind and body, the two formed a reciprocal relationship borne out of mutual need: Her mother's quest for capital and material support led her to the baron. On the other hand, his need for peer approval and a guarantor of safe transit for his furs brought him to her mother. The two events did not occur side by side, Suzanne confessed: Mother started the whole relationship and, before he knew it, he swallowed the bait, hook, line, and sinker, agreeing to all of mother's requests. Good!! Good for her! She survives by her wits and endurance and perhaps because of her beauty.' A bit of envy crossed her mind briefly. Alone with her thoughts, Suzanne snuggled deeply within her blankets. Soon she fell asleep, a smile gracing her lips.

* * *

"Wake up, Miss Suzanne! A new day awaits you!" Birdie playfully tugged at her friend's thick coverlet. Crossing to the bedroom windows, Birdie swept back the curtains and threw open the sash. Bright sunlight and cool morning vapors enveloped the room, bringing Suzanne to rise up precipitously.

"The perfect groundhog, hiding from the world," Birdie scolded her gleefully. Shaking Suzanne about the shoulders, she bent low and spoke strongly into her ear: "Your brother is here." Deftly she jumped back, awaiting a response.

Suzanne squealed in delight. Shaking her head vigorously, she covered her face and exclaimed: "Oh, Birdie! Where am I?" and proceeded to attach words to the stream of thoughts which occupied her dreams during the night. "I found myself out-of-doors, half-hidden in the snow, trapped under a mound of snow, and you were trying to shovel me out." Peering through sleepy eyes, Suzanne found the calendar at its familiar place on the wall next to her bed. Since arriving at the mansion, she fastidiously circled each day of the month. Reaching out, she traced the last entry with her fingertips, repeating it aloud: 'Sunday, April 1st, 1761.'

"Today is April 2nd, then. Gads! How long have I slept,?" she lamented.

Crackling with delight, her effusive ally crossed to the wash stand at the foot of the bed. Dipping a cloth into a vase of cold water, Birdie applied it to Suzanne's face and forehead. "Better now, Miss? Quite a dream you had, if you ask me."

"Well, I certainly am in fine fettle to meet with Matthew," Suzanne remarked, regaining her bearings. Looking about her, she inquired helplessly: "Birdie. Where are my clothes?"

"Not to worry, Miss. Miss Caroline has given Matthew her undivided attention." She handed Suzanne an outfit for the day. "Matthew has brought friends along. A pair of strange-looking men are in the parlor. One of them asked for you." She began to rearrange the bed clothes.

Hopping out of bed, Suzanne seized her clothing and dashed for the wash room where a hot bath awaited her.

"Entertain them for me, Birdie. I shall not be long." Her thoughts upon the new-arrivals, she stepped gingerly into the bath tub.

A refreshed Suzanne descended to the kitchen, eager to meet the visitors, particularly Matthew. Hunger put aside, she gazed about, intently seeking familiar faces. Many people flooded the capacious room, pressing into every available space. Seated or standing, everyone partook of the breakfast offerings while engaging in animated conversation. At the oven Birdie stood turning griddle cakes, having carved out a niche for herself free of congestion. Mrs. Cuyler fried eggs and bacon and the baron distributed hot beverages and little cakes and hot biscuits on a platter. Peering intensely about the room, Suzanne reflected upon a body of strangers, who, although pressed tightly together, sought each other's company. Retreating before the amorphous sea of humanity which befell her, she found refuge in a remote corner of the kitchen. There, in the shadows, she attempted to survey her surroundings. Finding herself alone in a crowded room, she struggled to subdue the haunting pangs of isolation which crept into the hollow of her stomach. To her relief all signs of distress dissipated when a familiar voice, calling her name, rose above the palpable din of the gathering.

"Suzanne!"

She reciprocated: "Matthew!" At once rushing forward, she breeched the throng, sending guests askew. Instinctively they fled to the left and right, creating an opening along which she swept into the outstretched arms of her brother. For one long moment brother and sister embraced in the center of the room. Parting, they acknowledged the applause of onlookers, which subsided as they bowed before the assembly. Brother and sister promptly retired to a vacant corner of the kitchen, arms entwined. Thereupon, Matthew, not in a small way influenced by the enormity of the occasion and gaiety of the guests, spoke first, somewhat facetiously, albeit sincerely:

"My long-lost sister," he beamed, holding her at arm's length.

"I almost forgot how you looked, Matthew," Suzanne confessed, blushing.

"You have only to fasten upon the most handsome beau in the house," Matthew returned, glowing.

"You have lost none of your self-centeredness," Suzanne cajoled.

Seizing Suzanne by the hand, Matthew pulled her into the crowd. He came to rest behind a diminutive figure with back turned and surrounded by admirers. Matthew spun the figure around. Facing him, he stepped aside, placing the little man in full view of his sister. Without warning, the little man crumpled to the floor. Moaning, he began to thrash arms and legs against the flooring. The guests accorded him a wide berth. Perplexed, they cast querulous eyes at each other. Suzanne broke into laughter. Addressing the gathering, she explained the man's comportment as a function of his current state of being: decidedly euphoric.

"That is the way of Aboyant," she admitted. Bending over the little man's prostrate form, she beckoned him to rise. Perhaps awaiting her benign request, Aboyant raised his head and opened his eyes widely and peered about him. Forming a generous smile, he thrust his hips forward, violently urging himself upward in one swift movement, coming to attention firmly on his feet. He broke out with a greeting in French:

"N'acceptez pas auncun de sucédanés. C'est moi L'Aboyant à votre service!!"

Sharing his greeting with the guests, Suzanne translated, while restraining herself from erupting into laughter:

"Accept no substitutes. It is I, Aboyant at your service!!"

Suzanne grasped his hand, exclaiming: "French. The tie that has bound us together." They embraced, the little man gripping her about the waist and she holding him about the shoulders. He, a cauldron of burning enthusiasm, began leading her in a waltz in ever-widening circles to the delight of the onlookers until Matthew intervened.

"I present you with yet another ghost from the past," he remarked, whereupon he withdrew a tall, bronzed native of noble countenance from among the visitors. Clothed in festive regalia, the man glided effortlessly over the floor. He came to rest before Suzanne where he bowed deeply, stepped back and assumed a rigid stance.

"Ah! Cerf Courant. My guide. I remember you well. When under your leadership never did I stray from the beaten path. You must guide me once again."

He stood mute, but smiled briefly, all the while maintaining a stern aspect. Nodding, he turned to join Aboyant in a line of celebrants who stood munching sweet treats.

"Bonjour, Mademoiselle," a pleasant voice called.

Whirling about, Suzanne came face to face with Henri Marchand:

"Ma foi!! Est-ce que c'est vous vraiement?"—Good heavens! Is it really you?"

"Matthew found me on the trail. Once a tradesman, always a tradesman." Marchand went on to state that he frequented Fort Oswego to gather pelts for his shop in Montreal. He gave Suzanne to understand that he had become of late a purveyor of furs for Cornelis Cuyler, bringing them down the Mohawk to Schenectady from Montreal where the baron accompanied them to Albany.

"Not long ago I met Matthew at a hostel on the Mohawk. Hearing the name of 'York' tossed about the inn, I approached a handsome and able ranger enjoying a beverage and introduced myself. The young man turned out to be Matthew York. Upon my inquiry, he gave the names of his sister and mother whom he planned to visit at Albany. I, of course, wanted to see them and gave my cargo to the safekeeping of my partner, Richard Clement, and rode east with Matthew the following day at the crack of dawn."

Suzanne stood captivated by the tradesman's refreshing manner. Never at a loss for words, Marchand took great pleasure in speaking of adventures in which he played a major role. Eyes aglow, she shared with him the days they spent on the trail filled with unpredictable turns in the road. Soon thereafter she gathered herself together and asked bluntly:

"What of Le General Le Rocher?"

"I thought that you would never ask, Mademoiselle. The last I saw of him he was off in a corner partaking of libations with John Root."

"Incredible! They are friends?" Suzanne quipped, suspended in veritable confusion.

"In a manner of speaking. John Root stumbled into him by sheer coincidence. I met him at Niagara at a conference with the Seneca. Let me explain: Since we abandoned Pointe Aux Bois, Guillaume and I struck out into the fur industry. Next to cultivating my gardens, it has always been my first attraction. We are both based in Montreal, but Guillaume treats with Niagara almost exclusively. The Seneca claim ownership to the land passage around the falls, giving them free rein to select who will carry their furs to the eastern markets. Guillaume numbers the Seneca among his friends. Through Guillaume the Seneca came to your assistance, making possible the return of your mother. In the recent past scores of white traders have sought a monopoly of the trade goods leaving Niagara (90). This angered the Seneca as well as Commissioner Johnson. Out of gratitude to Guillaume, the Seneca have named him their agent in treating with unscrupulous white merchants. Given his military credentials, Guillaume's new post is but an extension of his previous role at Pointe Aux Bois. Now, somewhat ironically, he finds himself in the employ of Commissioner Sir William Johnson, a former adversary during the Great War. Guillaume has nothing but kind words for the Commissioner who passed favorably on his nomination.

"Guillaume dispatches cargos from Niagara to Schenectady into the waiting arms of your patron Cuyler at Albany. By the same token he heads up to Fort Oswego where he receives consignments from Lord Carleton— also bound for Albany and points east. John Root is a liaison for Cuyler. He scouts the rivers for signs of unrest. He met Guillaume on the Mohawk where the name of 'York' passed between them, becoming a favorite piece of conversation. I have for you a long-standing friend whom I believe that you remember quite vividly. He is another one of the denizens of the forest who tendered you a hand in your hour of need. Here!! Let me make an inquiry."

Smiling broadly, Marchand disappeared among the visitors— leaving Suzanne in a state of elation. Hurriedly she sought out her mother in order to relate her good fortunes of the afternoon. Mother and daughter stood avidly conversing when someone, grasping her shoulder, approached Suzanne from the rear. Filled with anticipation, Suzanne gritted her teeth, and, closing her eyes, spun around. Opening them, she beheld a splendidly-attired Guillaume Le Rocher, hand shielding the hilt of a sword. He smiled in the familiar twinkle of which she grew so fond, a regal figure whose erect bearing placed him head and shoulders above the common soldier. He need not speak a word for those around him to deduce that there before them stood a man of substance.

"Enchanté une fois de plus ma chérie. Le Seigneur a repondu à mes prières."—Delighted once more my dear. The Lord has answered my prayers—spoke the commandant of Pointe aux Bois.

"You are much too kind, Monsieur, but I love every word of it," Suzanne returned, bowing from the knee. "I thought you long departed, but I am pleasantly struck that you have come to visit."

"I found myself tending my humble shop when Henri came to me with the prospect of becoming an agent based at Niagara. It brings back fond memories. Going back is similar to returning to one's home. Niagara was my first assignment in the colonies. I remained until the British reduced the fort. Hence, I opened Pointe Aux Bois. Secretly I hoped that one day I may be able to return to Niagara, the place of the grand waterfall, the gateway to the continental interior. Those two thoughts alone never cease to send chills along my spine."

"The Marchand position and yours seem very similar yet different," Suzanne remarked.

"Yes, they are. The great difference is that Henri operates as an independent tradesman: *Un voyageur.* I, however, am paid by the Commission of Indian Affairs and Commissioner Johnson is my overseer." Turning to his rear, the General brought forward a man who heretofore remained hidden from Suzanne's view. When he stood before her, the man's extraordinary costume threw Suzanne back on her heels, forcing her to struggle to identify him. The General came to her assistance.

"This is Oh:nehsi:yo, Suzanne, the Sandpiper who served you well." He stepped back to allow the chieftain a moment alone with her. The Sandpiper promptly launched into a discourse in French, for he spoke little English:

"Il me plaît beaucoup de faire ta connaissance une fois de plus. Bien entendu tu te souviens du renversement du chateau-fort à coté du lac. Sur ce jour-là nous chassâmes après les bâtardes anglaises et elles s'enfuirent la toute la première, les queues retroussées entre les jambes. C'était un jour magnifique!!"

"—I am very pleased to meet you once again. Of course you remember the overthrow of the fortification beside the lake. On that day we hunted the English dogs and they took flight with their tails tucked between their legs. It was a great day!!"

Beside herself, Suzanne hugged the slender yet sturdy man. "Always the French. It is your French that has brought us together. Without it I would forever be the timid innocent consumed by the wilderness. I thank you for speaking with me and for guiding my family over the trail."

"We have one more journey to make together soon, Mademoiselle before I go on my final journey."

"No! No! My friend. You will never be far from me and my family." A tear in her eye, Suzanne threw her arms around the Sandpiper. At that moment the ageless warrior withdrew a medallion from around his neck.

"This is a token of good fortune, Mademoiselle". Suzanne nodded and Oh:nehsi:yo fitted it about her shoulders.

"I am speechless," she exclaimed. "I shall treasure it always."

"It will keep you safe wherever you shall roam."

Caroline and Matthew joined Suzanne during the height of her exuberance over the renewal of acquaintances.

In bouncing among visitors, Suzanne's enthusiasm grew exponentially. She avidly shared stories with the principals, leaving her mother and brother temporarily abandoned. Caroline and Matthew marveled at her spontaneity, yet reminded themselves that beyond the gaiety spread roundabout, serious matters lay ahead. Reluctantly, Caroline stepped forward to summon her daughter's attention.

"Alas, dear girl. We need to prepare for tomorrow."

"You will need all of your spirit for the sojourn," Matthew remarked soberly.

"I am beside myself with joy that we are all going together," Suzanne declared, looking to both Caroline and Matthew. "Have I missed greeting anyone?" She looked about inquisitively.

"I hear that my friend, Captain Smythe may join us," Matthew conceded, "however that remains to be seen."

"Ah!! The *other* hero of the *Courageous*. I do hope that he comes along," she said softly.

Caroline gazed about the guest-filled room: "This is a most auspicious occasion, I dare say. The major players are intact, alive and well. It smacks of a strong beginning." She winked covertly at Matthew, confident that Suzanne knew nothing of her detailed labors in reuniting old friends under one roof.

"A splendid reunion," Matthew observed, shaking hands with his mother. "And a good omen at that."

"Matthew. In speaking with Monsieur Cuyler, he believed through the gazettes that you died in battle."

"That is the occasion when a vicious rumor turned to my advantage."

"I met with Lord Carleton. Fear no more. He believes you a hero."

"Thank you, mother."

"Do not thank me. Le Rocher feigned your disappearance, after heralding your exploits to Lord Carleton."

"Oh?"

"He wanted to protect you from assassination, should the pirate escape custody and come searching for you."

* * *

With the dawn of the new day, Wednesday, April 4th, the Cuyler household transformed into an efficient base of operations. The women in residence—Mrs. Cuyler, Birdie, Caroline and Suzanne—served breakfast to the thirteen candidates chosen as teachers. With a freshly-scrubbed Old Noah among them, the number rose to fourteen. Next, the women handed each teacher a full day's worth of rations packaged neatly in knapsacks. The principal guests, the likes of Marchand and Oh:nehsi:yo, took breakfast and accepted rations. Dried beef for the most part, along with fruits and powdered meal for cereal, the rations, when consumed sparingly, contained adequate nutritional value for a voyage of considerable duration.

Repairing to their rooms, everyone packed clothing for four days on the trail, along with sundries devoid of luxuries. In the interim the women took breakfast, after which those bound for the journey dropped back to prepare knapsacks with foods and clothing. In the foyer of the mansion the baron stood impatient with tablet and stylus in hand, waiting to commence the repetitive task of accounting for all those who approached his station. Save for the teachers, everyone carried a firearm, either rifle or pistol, with plenty of shot and powder, which they displayed to the discriminating entrepreneur. When Suzanne drew up beside him, the baron made certain that she retained a field-dressing unit among her possessions. Under his watchful eye she produced a knapsack of quinine water, iodine, rubbing alcohol, bromine antiseptic, saline solutions, swathing, bandages, and splints.

The main body of escorts, stood entrenched at Fort Frederick. After taking leave of Birdie, Suzanne joined her mother. Caroline longed to learn of the size and strength of the complete outfit assembled. With Suzanne at her heel, she rushed to the fort where she reviewed the contingent: Oneida warriors on loan from Skenando. They mingled freely with John Root's band of resident Mohawks. Out of the corner of her eye Caroline spied Matthew commiserating with a band of Cayugas from the Round Tops. They in turn huddled with the Oh:nehsi:yo Seneca around a fire. She acknowledged her son with a wave of the hand and tread along steeped in satisfaction. Nearby stood a body of garrison-soldiers. They spoke with someone who, from the rear, resembled the impeccably-dressed Sir William Johnson. A fair young woman stood beside him, imbibing his every word. Curious, Caroline guided Suzanne to a point opposite the attractive pair, announcing her presence with a trite bit of humor.

"We have the makings of a small army on these grounds, I truly believe," she quipped, acknowledging the various camps which met the eye.

"Madame Caroline. This marks our second fortuitous meeting. I regret not having chatted with you previously." Sir William Johnson approached her, hand extended in friendship. Together they regarded the campaigners in silence for a long moment— each waiting for the next to open discourse.

The young lady at the Commissioner's side provided him with an opportunity to shatter the impasse:

"Madame! With great pride I present my wife, Molly Brant (91). She is my constant companion since the passing of my former wife, Catherine." He patted Molly's stomach, drawing a blush from her. "She is pregnant with our first child. I pray it is a boy. I need many hands to tend to my estate on the Mohawk." He withdrew, leaving the two women free to converse.

In speaking with Molly Brant, Caroline learned that the Johnsons spent most of the year at the rambling estate on the Mohawk near the town of Canajoharie, a Mohawk village. There the Mohawk lived in common with local white settlers on lands made available to them by Sir William Johnson, perhaps the largest landowner in the colonies outside of the Van Rensselear manor north of Albany. The Johnson estate constituted a self-sufficient undertaking, a community within a community, counting a school for young natives and whites among its attributes. Molly, herself, or Konwatsi, attended the school until she found herself involved more and more with the daily operations of the estate. Her brother, Thayendanegea, also attended the school as a youth. Sir William took steps to make him a part of his extended family, having him baptized "Joseph Brant." Later he sent the youth to a boarding school in Connecticut to further his upbringing until he learned that the schoolmaster administered harsh punishments to the native youth on a regular basis. Passing into manhood, Joseph Brant, with Sir William's support, became a prominent leader of the Iroquois. His name generated either praise or fear among settlers. There was no middle ground when discussing this able, young Mohawk.

Molly explained that Joseph Brant provided his mentor with knowledge about reconnaissance in as much as Sir William demanded to learn the whereabouts of those parties posing a threat to his holdings and state of being. Sir William did not rise to the status of prominent landowner however without incurring a measure of enmity along the way. On the other hand his holdings in general grew large enough to warrant protection. At a moment's notice Joseph Brant commanded loyal followers eager to repel intrusive forces from Johnson's domain. Originally non-committal toward whites, Joseph Brant placed a firm trust in Sir William, who traditionally opened his doors to the Mohawk. He employed many of them on his estate, later increased to an additional manor, Johnson Hall, at Johnstown, a town Sir William named after his son, John. Sir William endeared himself to the Mohawk by learning their language, safeguarding their lands from exploitation, and by winning battles for the Crown at venues such as Fort Niagara and Crown Point (92). He raised a large family with Molly Brant, an additional point which endeared him to his brother-in-law, Joseph Brant.

Molly confessed that Sir William presented a contradiction in terms, if not in principle, along two fronts, both of which never seriously affected his professional career. For one, although he kept a large number of slaves in his employ, Sir William detested slave-running—the capture of young men and women for profit— and sought to stamp it out with the help of Joseph Brant. Second, Sir William became a wealthy landowner at the behest of the Mohawk, who, in displays of appreciation, bestowed upon him great tracts of land (93) which he in turn sold to settlers for suitable gains. Despite incidental shortcomings, Sir William remained the preeminent authority on Iroquois lore in the colonies and it is not by chance that whenever Sir William and native allies entered into battle against France for the Crown, the Crown inevitably won. To this extent, the Crown readily sought Sir William's counsel when planning a major campaign.

"The hour has come ladies to break company," Sir William intervened, rejoining Molly and Caroline. "Have you ever seen a more loquacious hostess?" he cajoled, in reference to Molly.

"She has been most candid, Commissioner," Caroline returned. "I hesitate to take my leave." She gazed upon her escort who moments earlier had received marching orders and began to form into ranks.

Sir William addressed Caroline in a conciliatory manner, albeit tinged with a hint of paternalism: "You have two bateaux at your service, one more than you requested. Needless to say, they are both set to your specifications. I found the move necessary in light of your tremendous baggage."

"Monsieur Cuyler has supplied me with a mountain of materials," Caroline answered, deferentially.

"I support you wholeheartedly. I must tell you that I too put together a school. It is on my principal estate. It has enjoyed great success over the years. At Johnstown there is no distinction between the races. I regard everyone with a stroke of the same brush and everyone follows suit. We all learn from each other from within and without the classroom and during my tenure not one drop of blood has been shed, red or white, in either Johnstown or Canajoharie. Of this I am most proud." He spoke softly, intending his words for Caroline alone.

"You have a noble purpose and I commend you. Your family must be proud of you. This will not be our last meeting. Unfortunately I am unable to accompany you. I must prepare for a convention in Detroit soon which may decide the fate of the western lands for years to come. I have been asked to address the Shawnee. They are growing restless and have been stirred up by a presumptive leader among them (94)." He shifted his weight in contemplating the end of the discourse.

"There will be many speakers. There is one, a native Cayuga, who will speak. He is known as an orator among certain circles and his fame precedes him. He is called Tah:gah:jute. You may have encountered him in your travels."

Caroline recoiled in amazement. At a loss for words, she thought of how intertwined with the comings and goings of Sir William her life had become of late. It was through the Bear Chief that she came to learn of his famed cousin, Tah:gah:jute, now a part of the Commissioner's lexicon. She searched for a response:

"Why, yes. I am a friend of his cousin, the Bear Chief. You bring back strong memories. The Bear Chief led my family and me through a difficult period. It is because of him that I am able to have a second thrust at life. You may very well meet with the Bear Chief at Detroit. He will be at the right hand of Tah:gah:jute. Together they will advocate for justice—for the red man as well as for the white. You will stand in good company."

Sir William studied Caroline carefully. He knew implicitly that she understood the substance of his labors yet to follow: where he must attempt to assuage Ohio natives for losses in land to incoming white settlers. Come that day, he would no longer be able to unobtrusively court her friendship. He sought to put her at ease:

"You are a staunch defender of the native people. I will try to be worthy of your trust. For now I leave you in good hands." Shaking Caroline's hand in friendship, he snapped a call to John Root. Briskly the assembly of campaigners launched into single formation behind the fort's main gate. Before passing from the fort they stopped at a station for one final inspection. Each unit commander paused to salute the Commissioner. Adhering to decorum, Caroline restrained herself from waving to Matthew when he approached at the head of a unit. Silently she berated herself for not having spoken with him before he departed. 'Such unions must be rekindled on the journey itself,' she resolved. She considered finding a suitable berth on board a bateau. She spun on her heel to point out Matthew's train to the Commissioner.

To her disappointment she caught not a glimpse of Sir William or Molly. The two simply vanished, leaving her forlorn and confused. The scene itself marked the second interval in the presence of Johnson that she envisioned herself part of a dream, or fable. She was, she believed, one of many small players on a stage: a drama which, despite a noble façade carried a portentous message of glory mixed with travail. She shuddered in an effort to divest herself of the melancholy which clung to her vitals. Suzanne found her shaking her head and speaking aloud to no one in particular. Pulling her mother by the arm, she hustled her down the steep descent of Jonkers Street to the boarding place beside the Hudson River. There they climbed in with the teachers and crew, finding places beside each other on the hard, bench-like seats of the second bateau. With baggage firmly stowed, mother and daughter spent precious moments together discussing the merits of the forthcoming excursion. They stole fleeting glances at the landscape through an open portal, yet to Suzanne her mother seemed lost in thought. An uneasy peace passed between them.

—

The Mohawk began somewhat north of Albany in a town later named Cohoes. It flowed generally northwest to Oneida Castle on the eastern shore of Oneida Lake, where, for all practical purposes it terminated. It kept its name over the course of Oneida Lake, coming to an end at Fort Brewerton on the lake's western shore. Fort Oswego, which stood watch over Oswego Bay, lay a few miles above the Mohawk. All along the course of the river lay forts in various stages of occupancy and repair, most of which were temporary in duration, their fate dependent upon the needs of the two principal belligerents of the day: Great Britain and France. With the fall of Montreal that preceding September, the forts formally passed into British hands where subsequent administrators determined their ultimate destiny. Generally, the Crown chose not to maintain all of the forts, and, when applicable, requested colonial militias and well-endowed entrepreneurs alike to volunteer the funds and physical effort necessary to maintain those structures deemed of value.

Pushing off from the boarding place, the bateaux, laden with voyagers and precious cargo, struck out for the hamlet of Cohoes, a short distance away. There, a cascading waterfall fed from mountain streams formed the basis of the Mohawk River. The tiller-men pulled the crafts into the shallows of a deep lagoon beside the swift-flowing waters. It is there that the bateaux joined with the full complement of horsemen who assumed formation along the river's southern flank. John Root broke the horsemen into segments of ten. All totaled, fifty riders escorted the bateaux, which kept to the middle of the river, nestled comfortably mid-way between the first and last segments of the command. John Root chose the southern flank because of the preponderance of fortified, well-kept garrisons along the waterway.

Schenectady, on the river's northern bank, became the first substantial community which loomed into view. Although a sizable town, John Root did not intend to stop there. To his amazement, young children red and white, shouting hurrahs, rushed to the water's edge to catch a glimpse of the passersby. Entering the river, some of the children hurled colorful blossoms into the wake of the water craft. Through an open portal Suzanne thrust out a hand in greeting. An observant Caroline, possessed of indescribable fears, questioned how the children may have learned of the voyagers' presence on the river, during this otherwise unannounced undertaking.

Once the tiller-men approached Fort Hunter, John Root called for a respite. Situated on the river's southern flank, Fort Hunter stood hard beside the Mohawk village of Lower Mohawk Castle. Directly across the river on its northern bank stood Fort Johnson, Sir William Johnson's principal estate. The three locations comprised a tight-knit community whose inhabitants in several cases shared common ancestors, some of them of mixed red and white origins. Everyone exercised amicable, neighboring relations. Sir William more than once declared that never did the two races come to serious blows during his tenure.

No sooner did the bateaux lean close to shore than an unfortunate event unfolded. A pack of dogs, apparently from the village, charged after the horses. Some of them nipped at the horses' heels, sending the temperamental beasts into a frenetic gallop, the results of which caused several riders to plummet headlong to the earth. One of the men, a soldier, drew a saber and hacked the offending cur to pieces amid a host of witnesses. No one reacted initially for another event carrying greater implications took place at approximately the same moment.

Several children, having swum out to the bateaux, made good on their objective of climbing aboard one of them. The small band of carefree native youngsters soon gained the upper deck, the exclusive province of the tiller-man. They promenaded at will and called down to friends on shore, heedless of the warnings which the tiller-man hurled at them. Infuriated, the tiller-man heaved at the nearest youngster with the butt of his tiller-shaft, catching him full on the chin and sending him headlong into the waters. The youngster dipped below the surface, failing to rise of his own volition. All the while John Root and most of the unit commanders, were nowhere to be seen, having entered Fort Hunter to seek food and refreshments. A mêlée erupted in earnest between defenders of the boy from the village and the mounted horsemen. Men from Mohawk Castle descended upon the horsemen with clubs and war hatchets.

A blood-bath lay imminent without the rapid application of bold measures. Fortunately for the horsemen, Oh:nehsi:yo chose to stay behind with the voyagers. Weighing the scene before him, he leaped into action. Drawing his famed longbow, he called upon the tiller-man to retrieve the drowning boy or suffer the pains of instant death. Speaking in the native tongue, his words required no translation to be understood. With all eyes upon him, the tiller-man took cognizance of the chieftain's rage and plunged into the river. Rising with the boy in his arms, he gained the shore where he deposited the still form at Oh:nehsi:yo's feet. Roundly castigating the tiller-man, the astute chieftain put into effect a plan he first conceived long ago: Pinching off the boy's nose, he breathed deeply into his mouth. He followed with compressions to the chest delivered with strong hands pressing slowly but firmly. He buffeted the boy about the cheeks. He repeated the procedures once-twice-three, so fully-occupied that he took no notice of the crowd gathered about him. When the boy coughed, Oh:nehsi:yo pulled him into a sitting position and thumped his back, after which he raised and lowered the boy's arms overhead in a firm, steady, motion. The boy coughed again and, unfortunately for his benefactor, spat over him generously.

Oh:nehsi:yo took no offense, On the contrary, he stripped the boy of his shirt and dressed him in his own shirt. Pulling him upright, the chieftain handed the boy off to his mother who stood nearby with outstretched arms. From his belt loop the chieftain withdrew a long cord. Seizing the tiller-man, he bound his wrists firmly together and pulled him beside one of the horseman. In no uncertain terms he commanded the horseman to secure the free ends of the cord to the pommel of his mount and to thenceforth guide the tiller-man overland in precisely a tethered state for the duration of the journey. This accomplished, the chieftain snatched away the mount of the horseman who killed the dog. He ordered him to occupy the post of the deposed tiller-man. The mount's reins secure in hand, he ambled through the assembled crowd with the steed in search of the owner of the slain dog. At length he regaled the saddened owner with a gift of the horse, a specimen of high quality, after which, accepting no praises, he returned to the river bank to assume watch.

Aboyant, who originally dashed off to Fort Hunter to notify the unit-commanders of an impending crisis, now returned to the scene of the disturbances reinforced by the presence of the General, Marchand, Matthew, and others. He found nothing out of the ordinary, the aroused villagers having dispersed following the Oh:nehsi:yo disposition of the matter with the tiller-man. The horsemen, despite the insistence of Aboyant, stood mute to his inquiries. Mounting, they prepared to move out. Subsequently, without much ado, the two bateaux maneuvered out to deeper waters and the expedition resumed course of its own accord, leaving an embarrassed Aboyant aloof to ponder how to treat with inquiries from the returning principals.

On board Suzanne wrote feverishly in her journal. Despite appealing to her mother, Caroline refused to come to the portal to absorb the colors of the season, choosing to remain disengaged and brooding on her bunk.

—

Marchand voiced concerns when the hamlet of Little Falls came within view. Straddling the southern bank of the Mohawk, Little Falls rose where a bend in the river developed into a deep and fast-flowing expanse beside which mills sprung up to grind wheat and corn. Settlers soon followed and the community grew to five hundred inhabitants. It may have grown larger, but for an inhibiting feature of the river beyond the hamlet's western flank: Great slabs of rock lay across the river, blocking transit and changing the course of the water. In place since the age of glaciers, the slabs protruded ominously at irregular shapes and sizes, too great to be ignored and too heavy to be removed. In spring the rains and snow-melt driven from the surrounding hills flowed mightily over the slabs, opening swirling eddies and miniature waterfalls among them. No boats flowed along the river at this point and the little hamlet never pushed on westward. Travelers and traders in boats were reduced to portaging the river —literally hauling the craft out of the water, dragging them over the land, and reissuing them further downstream. Well-equipped for the task of portaging, Marchand set about assigning the horsemen to hauling the two flat-bottomed bateaux ashore. The General brought out two pairs of block and tackle lines and winches, a set for each bateau. Securing a foothold in the hard river bank for each winch, he passed a line through a notch in the bow of a corresponding bateau, trailing it to shore where a party of horsemen, equally spaced, held the lines firm. At a signal, the horses dug in and, pulling forward, began the arduous struggle of hauling each bateau to shore. To assist the passengers in gaining the bank, Marchand released a pair of air-filled pontoons into the water which his charges gratefully mounted, without incident. Looking about, he spied Aboyant running along the river's edge:

"A rider comes on the northern bank!!" the little man barked.

Matthew, Cerf Courant, and others looked up to view a lone horseman approaching at a steady gait. Reaching the river's edge, he paused in review of the sojourners gathered along the bank. Presently he waved in greeting, smiling in a manner that Matthew recognized at first glance.

"Dana Smythe!! Captain Dana Smythe! We never turn away a helping hand. Cross over!!"

The dashing young officer plunged his mount into the river. He trusted the steed to carry him safely without balking. Guiding the mount over the shifting bottom and soft sands, Dana allowed the horse to find solid footing, whereupon he lurched upon the bank and rode straight for Matthew. Gripping his colleague's hand firmly, he smiled broadly, yet before he spoke a word, Matthew realized that Dana bore him discomforting tidings:

"**Black Jack** is afoot and headed this way, Matthew," he warned, his words causing heads to turn.

"Perhaps he wishes to renew old acquaintances," Matthew returned, facetiously.

"He slipped his chains while on a labor detail. Probably had a confederate on the inside. I suspect he is penniless and looking for a quick way to convert plunder into currency."

"We have only school teachers here laden with books," Matthew offered.

"Of course, but **Black Jack** does not know that. He is foolhardy enough to make a run for you, Matthew." Captain Smythe studied the passengers: Some of the women appeared particularly vulnerable to the aggressiveness attributed to the insidious river pirate.

"Ah!! I see that the slave trade is alive and well," Matthew jested, seeking to mitigate latent fears.

"He will come with a party of renegades: Iroquois and others of his cloth," Smythe confessed.

"How did you learn of our whereabouts?" Caroline asked, entering the discussion.

"Matthew and I have labored side by side rebuilding Ontario. There are no secrets between us. Before he departed for Albany, Matthew told me of joining the voyage one day soon."

"Did someone carry an official message to Matthew notifying him of his new command?" Caroline asked.

"Joe. Joe Root. Joe Root sent a messenger from the fort at Albany along with a cache of furs for Lord Carleton," Dana Smythe deliberated.

"The messenger. He spoke with Matthew directly?" Caroline asked, intensely curious.

"No. No, Madame. Matthew and I were away for a bit. Joe left a note with the secretary to the new aide, a fellow named Caldwell."

"Then Caldwell told Matthew. He took charge of the note?" Caroline persisted.

A beleaguered Captain Smythe took a deep breath. All eyes fell upon him. "Not exactly, Madame. Oddly I found a note addressed to Matthew in my quarters. After a bit I summoned Matthew and presented it to him."

Caroline looked about her. Sympathetic voyagers leaned forward, longing to learn more. "Well, Captain. It appears that this note has passed through a maze of hands before reaching yours. Anyone may have revealed its contents to the brigand who is running rampant through the countryside. Does that surprise you at all?" Falling short of taking an accusatorial stance, her incisive retort weighed heavily upon the young marine.

"I am at a loss for words. I ask your forgiveness. I believe that I am in error for failing to recognize the urgency of making prompt delivery. That is how it has been done since I joined with the marines."

"A kind of implicit trust, you say?"

"Yes. Yes, for lack of a better term, Madame."

"That kind of trust will get you killed, and those around you whom you love and respect." Caroline regarded her audience, seeking approval. She found it as the crowd moved closer to her.

"We shall have to capture this brigand and offer him his life in exchange for what he knows, provided we are still alive," she conceded.

"I pray that I may be able to do so, Madame," Captain Smythe offered, chafing over the matter.

"See that you do. At any rate, take Matthew with you. You two are unstoppable together." She began to walk away, leaving poor Smythe stoop-shouldered with hat in hand.

Caroline consulted with Suzanne. To soothe Smythe, Suzanne spoke to him softly: "We thank you for coming to our defense." The precocious young woman fastened upon the gallant marine for a long moment, the first instance in which the two of them sincerely noticed each other.

Portaging required the participation of all able-bodied men. Each horseman seized a section of the lengthy block and tackle, and, pulling in concert with comrades, urged the mounts to dig in along the river bank. Once ashore, the able horsemen beached the bateau and repeated the performance with the second craft. Following, there remained only to haul both vessels beyond the forbidding boulders and stones and reissue them downstream into the river, an engaging exercise even for a team of stout steeds. Unfortunately, the total-commitment of all the principals left the expedition open to attack or ambush around its periphery. No one seized upon this gross breech in security more keenly than Aboyant. He trod the shore back and forth surveying operations, eyes devouring the horizon. He was not the last to sound an alarm, however.

The portaging having begun in earnest, Fox Tail, Cerf Courant's brother, walked a short distance downstream to study the river beyond the stretch of perilous rocks. The waters pooled and to the right the river bank stood thick with patches of rushes and wild grasses. Tall enough to conceal an approaching band of marauders, the foliage attracted the wise scout's attention. His bow fitted with an arrow, Fox Tail crept into the first patch to cross his path. He kept low to the earth, looking for footfalls. He found a profusion of them heading back into the interior. He knew the folly of going further alone. Rising, he poised to turn on his heel when he came face-to-face with a pair of tall, haggard-looking natives bent upon subduing him. He knew not their origins. They uttered not a word, but began to flank him, grimacing in the manner of the devil incarnate. Momentarily his mind darted back to stories of the devil's death mask, tales which his uncle used to relate to him from the People's collection of ancient mythologies. The ruffians before him bore an uncanny resemblance to the horrendous etchings on the death masks which his uncle used to illustrate in vivid detail. Such stories struck fear into him during his youth. Now a warrior, he was not about to adopt those fears, nor become a victim to the endemic evil which the death masks evinced.

Instinctively he drew back the bow. An arrow bore into the chest of the aggressor nearest him, bringing him down. He withdrew a trail knife, the blade tapering into a fine point. He plunged it between the ribs of the next marauder who was almost upon him. The tall grasses stirred whereupon a raft of marauders charged forth to intercept him. He released another arrow, killing one man instantly. The pistol in his belt held two shots, far too few to disperse the entire band which he estimated at thirty blood-thirsty souls. Fearlessly he discharged both barrels into the faceless throng bearing down on him, claiming two more coups. Turning on a heel, he kept low in the grasses and made a dash for his comrades gathered beside the river. Footsteps closed in behind him. Exhausted, he surged upright and made a dead run along the sands. At this point his comrades discerned the full strength of the storm about to descend. Shouting the patented alarm YEOWWAY, Fox Tail fell forward when a ball ripped into his shoulder. The missile sent him reeling into heavy brush, where he fought to conceal himself from certain death.

Caught unawares, the voyagers and soldiers-in-escort thrust themselves into a skirmish line along the river bank. The horsemen, having retired their mounts behind a prodigious dune, formed a second skirmish line before the first in a maneuver to shield them from frontal assault. The action opened a thin corridor in the sand between the two lines stretched out along the river's edge. Captain Smythe ordered all those on hand without arms to flee to the pontoons by means of the man-made corridor. The defenseless teachers obeyed, leaving a fighting force of thirty hearty souls to face the enemy. All able fighters now melded into one skirmish line and, gathering ample shot and ball, faced the marauders head-on. The besiegers came screaming across the sands, the evacuation of the innocents having aroused their anger to a fever pitch. They halted, however, before a withering broadside. Stepping back out of rifle range, a number of them burrowed trenches into the slippery sands into which they flung themselves. Opening fire en masse, the besiegers presented small targets. The defenders, on the other hand, erect and vulnerable, presented bold targets which played into the marauders' hands. Captain Smythe, sensing impending disaster, ordered the skirmishers to break into two squads, whereas the first squad to fire dropped to one knee to reload while the second squad rose to open fire, each squad alternately standing and kneeling. The Smythe method allowed the skirmishers to fire selectively at chosen targets, thus conserving shot and powder and maintaining discipline within the ranks.

The firing between the two camps continued unabated with neither camp gaining appreciable ground over his adversary. Eager to spread consternation within the skirmishers' ranks, the besiegers flanked archers out to the left and right. Equipped with flame-tipped arrows, and effectively concealed, the archers released a concerted flight of missiles. Each thrust spun the defenders into disarray, nevertheless they fought off all impulses to bolt and run. Unfortunately, for them, the enemy crept a few paces closer to them with each burst of the fire-arrows, forcing them to divert attention away from the front line of defense. To compound the defenders' plight, a number of the horsemen abandoned the fight in order to fetter their mounts at the dune. They returned in short order, but not before the marauders crept closer to the line of defense.

The line itself wavered, standing at the point of disintegration. Moreover, the likes of the General and Marchand were nowhere to be seen, leaving the expedition in dire need of senior leadership. It is here that Smythe and Matthew York hatched a plan to both carry the day and save the horsemen's valued steeds in a single coup. They decided to mount a cavalry charge, once the horsemen stole back to the fold. The skirmishers' robust fire allowed the horsemen to return to the dune where they unfettered their mounts and prepared to deploy. During this interlude the horsemen adopted the name of 'cavalry,' sending a runner back to Captain Smythe with the announcement. Smythe believed the enemy consisted of a loose assortment of Hurons, Abenakis, river pirates, and criminals, who may eventually 'cut and run,' given a good fight. From his position among the skirmishers, Smythe sent word to the sequestered horsemen to form a cavalry out of twenty of their number. He and

Matthew York joined them, running behind the backs of their comrades who, in full approval of the plan, opened a withering fire over the sands.

Each cavalryman carried a full complement of weapons. In measured movements each one untethered and saddled his mount, leading the steed to a staging grounds behind the grassy dune. There the men mounted five abreast in four rows, twenty able equestrians on the sandy terrain. All the while the skirmishers along the shore fully engaged the enemy, the heavy fire preventing him from advancing. Smythe gave a crisp hand gesture and in the lengthening shadows of the afternoon, joined by Matthew York, he led the gallant cavalry from behind the dune.

Over the silent sands the horses cantered. Neither man nor beast emitted a single sound. Cutting a wide berth from behind the grassy dune, the cavalrymen tracked forward—implacable agents of war bent on wreaking destruction. Creeping slowly, they came to rest directly behind the backs of the marauders, who stood engaged in battle some twenty meters before them. Consumed with directing the fight, the marauders knew not of the cavalrymen's presence, attributable in no small part to the sandy texture of the terrain and the discreet stealth which Smythe insisted upon. Soon the gap narrowed between hunter and hunted. With each step forward the horses' paces quickened by degrees. Neither beast nor rider uttered a cry. In utmost silence the cavalrymen swung into position behind the unsuspecting foe. Exercising a prerogative, Captain Smythe signaled to Matthew York. Matthew promptly cut away from the main body with twenty cavalrymen. Moving forward, they branched off, drawing swords. Smythe, to Matthew's rear, remained behind in single file with ten cavalrymen. Less than eighteen meters from the enemy, they fixed bayonets.

Smythe thrust out an arm. The force broke into a gallop. The sands shifted audibly under the horses' weight. A lone archer who turned away to release a mouthful of tobacco reeled backward in horror. He sounded an alarm, the only alarm his comrades ever received, but it was too late. Smythe's men galloped directly into the marauders' ranks. Who they did not trample to death, they pierced with bayonets. Following orders, the men dismounted and fired point-blank into the screaming mass. Those who did not perish outright attempted to flee the grounds. The flight brought Matthew's force into the fray. His cavalrymen, not content to sit adrift on the fringe of battle, charged forward. The steeds tore into the marauders. The cavalrymen separated them one from the other and set about employing a number of methods in disposing of them: Many marauders fell to the sword. Others were trampled to death, shot head-on, or bayoneted. Smythe and Matthew, save for a few wounded, suffered not a single loss to man or beast.

Despite great losses, a body of marauders fled to the river bank where they came together downstream from the fight. One of them shouted a command and they ran screaming into the shallow waters of the river, bound straight for the pontoons housing the unarmed voyagers. Meanwhile, the once-persistent archers, fell one by one, once the tide of battle turned favorably in favor of the skirmishers. In desperation these last of the surviving marauders boarded the pontoons where they held a number of men and women at knife point, slashing them, and threatening them with death. Belatedly the General entered the fray. Joining the skirmishers, he wracked his brain for a plan to save the innocents without costing precious lives. Beside him Aboyant vehemently berated the marauders in the river. One of their number drew his sights upon the little man. Firing a ball, he killed him instantly.

—

Among the first to flee the river bank, Suzanne and her mother witnessed the onrush of the besiegers and the death of Aboyant from the stern of a pontoon. Suzanne screamed when her little friend slumped to the earth and began to grieve openly. Caroline, however, realized that she and her daughter must remain calm in light of the bizarre chain of events which befell them. She put into effect a hasty plan— its objective: to save the teachers on board her pontoon. Turning to Suzanne, Caroline persuaded her to stand behind her. The sobbing young woman reluctantly complied. In the next instant Caroline retrieved a pistol from beneath her skirts. Suzanne, attempting to foil what she believed an act of self-destruction, lashed out, her hand reaching for the weapon. Swiftly Caroline pushed her daughter into the arms of a voyager with the command to hold her fast. At that point three marauders stormed the pontoon, their eyes cold and hard and blood-red. Caroline calmly stepped out to meet them. Extending her arm fully, she waited until the first of the marauders came within five paces before discharging the piece full into his shrieking visage. Howling, the man crumpled to the deck of the pontoon, whereupon a second marauder bounded into view. With a snarl he leaped over his fallen comrade, coming face-to-face with Caroline, knife drawn back. He never gained the opportunity to strike, for Caroline fired the second ball into his chest, dispatching him forthwith. Behind him a third sneering marauder lunged forward, convinced that his prey had spent her allotted rounds. Unruffled, Caroline brought out a second pistol. The assailant, knife in hand, leaped toward her, bounding over the corpses of his comrades. To a cowering Suzanne he seemed to have sprouted wings. Caroline, unshaken, taking steady arm, struck the assassin between the eyes while in full flight. He dropped in a lump, sending the pontoon to reeling side to side. Someone from within the amassed innocents passed Caroline a pistol. Holding her ground, she waved the two pieces menacingly at still another wave of assassins. Looking to the shore, she spied Matthew and Dana Smythe leading a small party of soldiers through the shallow waters. Fixing upon two ruffians, she called out to Matthew in words which stood out in Suzanne's memory for years to come:

"Matthew!! Come here! I need you!!" She fired twice, felling two of the bandits; however, at this juncture, Matthew's party overtook the pontoons, driving off and dispatching the enemy with swords and bayonets. Fellow soldiers dragged to shore those few assassins who survived the encounter. The two young marines inspected them closely, when at length Captain Smythe let out a hoop of elation.

"Here he is!! The **Black Jack**, come to pay his respects. Welcome back," Dana barked facetiously. He pulled the grizzled-faced man's head from the sand into which he attempted to burrow. Sitting him upright, he held him at the point of his rapier.

"My, my! I see you have removed your flowing moustaches. One question I have for you!!"

"I have the answer in exchange for my life," the large, disheveled man returned.

"Who sent you?" Dana Smythe shouted in anger.

"First our bargain," the man belched.

"What bargain? There is no bargain!"

"What are you going to do? Put me in prison? Again?" The pirate sneered.

Dana Smythe drew back his sword. At that moment Matthew approached and he relented.

"All right. You win. Your life for a name," Matthew began.

"Finally I earn a kernel of respect," **Black Jack** retorted. Coughing, he spat into the sand. "The name you want is Caldwell, aide to Lord Carleton."

"He told you directly?" Matthew leaned forward in interest.

"Not exactly," the burly pirate returned. "I listened over his shoulder while in the trading depot."

"What?" Dana Smythe struck his forehead in disbelief.

Turning from Dana Smythe, **Black Jack** addressed Matthew. "I learned that you made journeys inland as an agent of Lord Carleton, the fur trader. When I heard of the bateaux coming, I figured that they carried a great cache ripe for the taking, that with my forces of persuasion, the voyagers would gladly part ways with their treasure." He laughed vociferously in the manner of one who had scored a major coup.

"In other words, you dressed in disguise and entered the fort as a peaceful tradesman. Is that it?" Matthew asked.

"Almost," the pirate mumbled. "I came seeking asylum, feigning I survived an attack by hostile warriors."

"Of course. Of course. How clever of you," Matthew smiled.

"You are mocking me," the big man protested.

"On the contrary. I am placing you on a tight leash. You are an invaluable source of knowledge and I do not want you to slip away." Turning to a disapproving Dana Smythe, Matthew winked at him, in so doing, sending him one of their many rehearsed signals of mutual understanding.

"Captain! See that our acquaintance rides undisturbed atop a bateau with the tiller-man once we get under way. Oh, yes. Remember to tie him down lest he roll off and drown."

A confused, yet grateful **Black Jack** ranted under heavy breathing, but otherwise showed no further opposition.

"By all means, Matthew. By all means," Dana Smythe replied. "Always pleased to take part in the taming of the wilderness. On your feet, Mr. **Jack**. The day is growing short."

—

The senior principals, occupied with portaging the bateaux, never joined in the main fight. They held nothing but lavish praise for Smythe and Matthew York. "Think not of me," Matthew addressed Marchand. "It is my mother who turned the tide of battle in our favor. Mother. Do not tarry. Come forward to receive your laurels!!"

"Matthew. You will never know the fear running through my veins on the pontoon." Caroline asked for a cloth to wipe herself dry. Behind her Suzanne clung to her shoulder. After a moment of silence she asked:

"Mother. I would like to take Aboyant with us to be buried at the Round Tops."

"Yes. Of course, dear." Thrusting out her jaw, Caroline fastened upon a thought to share with her daughter: "He must be tightly-wrapped first and fitted out with ice. There is a block of it in our foot locker." Looking about, she spied Dana Smythe. "Perhaps the good Captain will lend you a hand." She stepped aside to allow the two young people to come together.

Marchand reported light losses among the total contingent. Both he and the General reiterated that the quick thinking of Matthew and Captain Smythe saved the expedition from doom.

"The combat units proved too immobile, Henri. The horseman carried the day," the General confessed.

"That is why there is a need for seasoned fighters, Guillaume— something that may evolve long after we are gone."

"You are departing the campaign trail, I assume."

"We are merchants now, Guillaume. The trail has grown cold for us. Our days on it are numbered. We spent too much time with the bateaux."

Overhearing them, Oh:nehsi:yo stepped into the discussion: "With age comes wisdom and infirmities. You two have much of the former. You will be able to call upon that wisdom in your new vocations. You are going to a better place." He bowed and shook each man's hand.

"Well said, my old friend," Marchand spoke. Together they walked off to assist in the stowing-away of the block and tackle lines, leaving the General together with Caroline York.

"Will you be staying at Oneida Castle long, Madame?"

"I will leave three teachers with Reverend Kirkland and push on to the Round Tops. I owe myself some moments with my husband. I want to see the village and Colombe Blanche and Watkins and Fawn." With each name spoken she daubed at her eyes.

"I take it that you will be moving along from there."

"Yes. I will leave teachers at the Round Tops, at Kanandesaga, at the Oh:nehsi:yo village, at Cayuga Castle and at a Seneca village near the Genesee." She counted the locations on her fingertips. Looking up at the General, she smiled broadly, but her eyes betrayed a hint of uncertainty.

"Where will you stay? Where will be your home?"

"My principal home continues to be the Round Tops. I will stay as long as conditions permit. Of course I have a home on the Susquehanna. I have yet to decide about it. Then again, I am needed where my labors take me. Life is not simple, Monsieur," she confessed, head bowed in contemplation.

"Are you not afraid of spreading yourself too thin?"

"Always the thought upsets me. I have a strong family though, all of whom support me in what I try to achieve."

"You have won important allies along the way, Madame— all because of your dedication and zeal."

"For sure you flatter me, but I enjoy it. I must move quickly, for there will come the day that I am unable to move at all." Giving a faint sigh, she threw up her hands and glimpsed at the heavens.

"Who will keep my efforts going after I am gone?" she sighed, watching Suzanne and Dana Smythe converse.

"The younger generation. The younger generation, Madame."

(87) Norton (1974) pgs: 69-82.

(88)Norton 1974) pg. 200-201.

(89)Norton (1974) pg. 184.

(90)Norton (1974) pgs: 203-204.

(91)Falkner, Julie Molly Brant: Mohawk Loyalist. *History's Women. Com.* (2011) pgs: 1-3.

(92)Hamilton, Milton W. *Sir William Johnson: Colonial American, 1715-1763* Kennikat Press, Port Washington,

NY (1976) pg: 165.

(93)Hamilton (1976), pg: 299

(94)Hamilton (1976) pgs: 283-296.

CHAPTER SEVENTEEN

In The Company of Heroes
Tragedy at the Round Tops.
Oswego Revisited.
A Display of Unity.
Defining Moments.
Caroline Is Anointed.

Caroline's entourage headed slowly, yet steadfastly westward. Henri Marchand, self-appointed chronicler of events, estimated reaching Oneida Castle on or about Friday, April 20th, barring contingencies. The spring season in full bloom, the voyagers took delight in stealing glances at the flora and fauna which greeted them through the cabin-portholes. Confined on board for great lengths, everyone ate, slept, and conversed the whole day, every day, coming ashore infrequently to take short promenades. On board, limited yet fulfilling exercises devolved around reciting psalms, singing hymns, and reading literary excerpts.

When patches of wild strawberries presented themselves to her, Suzanne fondly recalled the days she spent with the boys, Raven and Little Bear, gathering berries and roots along the slopes of the Round Tops. She longed to return to the serene and intensely pastoral setting of that place. Harkening back to her days as a student and avid reader, the mythical kingdom of King Arthur came to mind whenever she dwelt upon the Round Tops. She assigned strong similarities to the two venues. In retrospect, neither yielded to internal strife. Moreover, each devised ways to repel danger from without. What is more, the two scenarios shared an impermeable veil of mystery cloaked in idyllic tranquility which set them apart from other inhabited regions. In her mind's eye, the recurrent pitch and roll of the bateau pulled Suzanne beyond the confining cabin, thrusting her back to the Round Tops, that domain in which she cumulatively developed a sense of attachment to the land and its indigenous inhabitants.

Attaining Oneida Castle without incident, the voyagers disembarked to take a well-deserved leisurely stroll in the verdant shade of a wooded glen. While their comrades enjoyed idle moments, Caroline and Suzanne and the principal commanders sought after Samuel Kirkland. They found him speaking with Skenando, his firm ally:

"I see that you have arrived in one piece, Caroline," the missionary stated, trying his best to be humorous.

"I am so grateful to be here. Look! All of your books arrived unscathed." Already young natives began the onerous task of unloading the precious cargo— gifts of the renowned baron.

"Trouble followed you," Skenando observed, catching a glimpse of **Black Jack** swathed in fetters.

Treading in shackles between Cerf Courant and the wounded Fox Tail, the pirate grumbled nonsensically.

"You see the source of our trouble being led away," Caroline sighed in relief. "Do you consent to his staying here with you? Confined, of course." Samuel Kirkland contemplated. "It is part of a plan of mine to put him at hard labor under the supervision of young natives—the very ones he relished abusing. Perhaps he will strive to redeem himself under your tutelage."

"Ah, Caroline. Ever the evangelist. Duty-bound to save the world," the missionary teased.

"Not the world, Reverend. Only a few within it who are a danger to others and themselves."

"I understand, Caroline. Let me think on it. Who knows? You may have another miracle in the making to add to your list of accomplishments." Before his words took root, Reverend Kirkland asked the inevitable question:

"Will you stay with us awhile? Your classroom remains the same."

"Suzanne will stay to help the new teachers settle in. She so adored the school. May I see it?"

"A most fitting request. Let us be off."

The pair walked the short distance to the school which her husband and a team of hardy Oneidas fashioned from the forest's timbers that previous fall. Caroline tread lightly over the hard earth, her spirits lifted.

"The newness of it. I still smell the resin from the trees in this room." She moved gracefully about, taking in all of the furnishings. The solid oak floor sparkled. Desks and chairs stood at rigid attention side by side. Not a corner of the room lacked for functional adornment of some kind. Her pot-bellied stove, dormant since the past winter, stood polished and defiant and prepared to meet the coming change of seasons.

"I shall be moving on to the Round Tops. I will open a school there." She laughed lightly. "I have made initial selections of students with many more to come," she called, sweeping her skirts behind her. "Let me see: There are Raven and Little Bear, Suzanne's new friends, and Watkins, a dear man, and his wife, Fawn. She already has a commanding lead in speech and cursive. Oh!! I am so excited." She threw her arms around the missionary's neck.

"We missed you during your leave," Samuel Kirkland confessed. "Thomas Steed missed you immensely."

"Ah!! Thomas! My worthy assistant and co-conspirator. I missed all of you. Tell me. What plans do you have for *your* school? I believe we broached that subject when last we met."

Here Caroline approached a favorite theme, leaving the missionary to dwell upon his entry into the land of the Oneidas. "I had been installed here a mere week doing the Lord's bidding and graciously the natives flocked to my cabin to hear me. They willingly offered me land and brought me food to eat and wanted to learn much of my strange speech and origins. I gratefully acquiesced and have remained steadfastly at the helm. Your school I plan to enlarge, along with the subject-matter. One day it will climb to a higher plane to draw in acolytes from far off places—the whole of the colony and beyond."

"You are speaking of a university, I presume."

"Yes. My church will provide some of the early funds and later, when these territories become formed into self-governing bodies, I will be able to seek funding from subscriptions."

"Hmmm. Where will these governing bodies be based?"

"Most likely at Albany. It is the only substantial settlement north of New York City with a diverse population that avidly seeks new residents from all corners of the colonies."

"Do you speak for the Lake Country as well?"

"Yes. As long as tradesmen frequent the Indian trails and bring their bounty to Albany, developers and land agents will have an interest in coming to the Lake Country to found settlements. Some of them may even rival Albany in significance. I envision sizable communities rising in places where whites and natives commune peacefully. That is why I open my school to whites and natives alike. To build the peace and understanding are the twin goals of my plan of education."

"You say "Education?"

"Yes. Yes. It is no longer Erudition or Pedagogy. Too narrow in scope. Education has a broader meaning. It reaches beyond the classroom to disseminate the many seeds of knowledge which a community has to offer."

"Then, he or she who teaches . . ."

" . . . Is an Educator, Madame."

"I like that. I truly like that," Caroline repeated, blushing with excitement.

"For yourself, your schools will succeed once they have proper support. You already have some of it from among your new acquaintances in Albany."

"Indeed I am grateful, but I am about to move well beyond Albany's shadow."

"Tell me. Who tends to your holdings on the Susquehanna?"

"Why, the Friends. Trustworthy one and all. They employ the Delaware to assist them."

"There you have it. A great example of Education in motion. You see, Madame. Education teaches the toleration of one people for another, their attributes and differences, combining them into a functioning whole. You will want to gain additional support by knowing the Friends."

"Do they not restrict themselves to the Pennsylvania colony?"

"Not at all. They are forever searching for fertile fields to plow. You will find them along the route of your proposed schools."

"I understand them to be masterful tillers of the soil, apart from pioneers in Education."

"That they are. They have schools as well. Self-contained in close-knit communities. They teach all that is necessary to succeed in life: The essentials. Cultivate the Friends. They will show you how to make your students self-sufficient beyond the classroom." He laughed. "Soon you will have too many students."

"I am grateful for the lessons you have taught me."

"I know that you will take them to heart. Please be disposed to keep me abreast of your achievements."

"I will visit from time to time. Meanwhile, I will correspond with you."

"On that account you will be pleased to learn that your letters will travel by coach. A new route has opened at Oswego. Following the growth of the fur trade there, a community sprouted about the fort. Lord Carleton, a major player, sanctioned the installation of a stage line in anticipation of westward migration."

"How far does it travel?"

"It logs doggedly all the way to Kanandesaga. It is the largest community beyond Albany and Oswego to the west. The stage benefits tradesmen who used to hack paths through the forest." He sighed, kicking the earth beneath his feet: "In a little bit Caroline, this country will be awash with settlers and all of them will be in need of schools for their youngsters. Of course, they may not recognize the need, but that is where *you* enter the scene."

He smiled at her approvingly: "You know Caroline, that in your own way you are promoting the growth of this country. Once your teachers take note of the splendid vistas, clear streams, deep lakes, and rich soil, they will be reluctant to depart these lands. Lo! They will take quill in hand and write to friends and family in eloquent praise of what they have found beyond their doorstep. They will come. Yes. Family and friends will come from the east where the cities are cramped and dirty and the soil is hard and rocky. Yes! You have started a movement, Caroline. It is one that may have no equal and exceeds your expectations. That is why I tell you to build your schools *now*. You alone may one day be held accountable for having planted the seeds of knowledge within the young pioneer who will go on to build a great nation. To me the thought of that is earth-shaking". He shuddered. "Oh!! The thought of it makes me quake. To think that *I*—that *you*—that we came along at this point in history to literally mold our surroundings for generations to come."

Caroline stood in awe of the missionary's delivery, her eyes sparkling with enthusiasm.

"I know that we spoke earlier of women. You are devoted to bringing them within the mainstream of the community. Look about you, Caroline. By and large your teachers are women. They are scholars in the main. They are women who manifest the high standards you have established. Once you install them in schools of your design, these mirror images of yourself will carry forth as exemplars of your standards. This process called Education will take root beside other core disciplines of the day— law and theology— and that infant scion of science: medicine. Women will have at long last attained a foothold in the community by means of their prowess in the classroom. The days of the itinerant horse-bound master are a *fait passé*. You and your women have something unique: dedication and fortitude. You are among the silent heroes of the frontier." Exhausted, he stooped to mop his brow.

Caroline studied the missionary: 'Here stood a man fully devoted to his convictions, clothing them in speech so powerful that projects of his design invariably succeeded outright.' She recalled that in the brief period following his arrival in the Lake Country, Reverend Kirkland had opened the Oneidas to the ways of western civilization. One day a greater school would follow, she knew, one approaching a university— his will and drive guaranteeing it. She hoped to live to see that day arrive and that a fraction of his resolve and ingenuity may pass to her by association.

"Caroline. Please take Suzanne with you. She needs to be with her father and loved ones at the Round Tops. All things considered, it is your home base. My wife and I will tend to the new teachers."

"Oh! I did not know that you remarried after your wife passed on," Caroline blushed, changing the subject.

"That is understandable. You were away. I took an Oneida woman to wife. It is one of the best decisions that I have ever made."

"You are still newly-weds. Wait a few years down the road," Caroline teased.

"I look forward to a long and pleasant journey. The Iroquois do not divorce, you know."

"Yes. Colombe Blanche told me. The woman merely puts the man's belongings outside of the lodge."

"Knowing that, I would do well to wear clean underwear at all times," the missionary jested. They joined hands and laughed together and when Suzanne found her, Caroline invited her to come with her to the Round Tops.

The party rested for three days in deference to their host. Caroline and Suzanne passed friendly sessions with Skenando and his wife. Less the teachers who remained with Reverend Kirkland, everyone rose early on Monday, April 23rd and prepared to begin the next leg of the journey. The Marchand maps gave the party to understand that no navigable waterway linked Oneida Castle with the Seneca River to the west. No one posed objections to go by foot, for all stood relieved to have escaped the cramped confines of the bateaux-cabins. After bidding pleasant farewells to the missionary and Skenando, the voyagers set forth along a forested trail.

—

Aside from Caroline and Suzanne and Marchand, who knew of the Round Tops intimately, the picturesque village tucked among grassy slopes remained but a myth to the voyagers. Mother and daughter sought to introduce the curious in the party to the village in terms of its short-lived, yet uncommon history. They told stories in which they themselves played roles in bringing the village to the threshold of becoming a vibrant community. In general, the travelers stood in awe of the stories told on their behalf. Privately, however, they strived to qualify the narrative, but at length decided to reserve final judgment until journey's end. To that end the voyagers kept close to mother and daughter, relishing the scenes that their hosts played out for them like so many spectators beholding a theatrical revue.

Adhering to a course known well to Cerf Courant, the voyagers crept along the southern bank of the Seneca River, beside which lay a major footpath long-frequented by Iroquois hunters and warriors. Most recently, travelers of several stripes followed the path, by far the straightest line between any two points east and west in the Lake Country. In single file they tread, fighting back the mounting monotony of the march, when Cerf Courant bid everyone to turn sharply south where the path met with yet another. He departed briefly, where he searched the marshy grasses near the river. Soon he returned with a welcomed announcement: He had discovered sleds hidden in the rushes— planking fitted to runners capable of carrying great loads. The Iroquois employed sleds, he stated, when moving precious belongings to new campsites and always kept them in reserve for others in need. At that point the principals doled out the sleds to eager voyagers who eagerly loaded them with stockpiles of goods which Caroline brought from Albany. Her books and supplies thus found safe haven, earning for the exhausted bearers a well-deserved reprieve.

Walking south, the party maintained a strict linear defile over hills and down valleys which seemed to rise instantaneously from the earth. Heads turned frequently to marvel at the remarkable terrain: rolling hills thickly lined with trees of multiple origins: the rising and falling of the land beside bogs and marshes. A meandering waterway perpetually accompanied the voyagers. Caroline and Suzanne brought Matthew and Captain Smythe to walk with them, imparting to them brief histories of the region from memory. The waterway, Suzanne revealed, was the 'Osco,' the very stream she and her father navigated before reaching the Bear Chief's village on a day wrought with summer storms. A chill in her voice, Suzanne explained that she almost drowned in the swollen waters while searching for her mother, a day that culminated with her rescue.

One more hill to climb— one more bog to circumvent. Then, abruptly the land leveled off into a treeless plain over which ran a wide path east and west: the so-called Western Trail. Rushing forward, Marchand, who maintained a home next to it, beckoned the voyagers to look directly south into a thick glade capped by lofty drumlins. All eyes discerned nothing but the fastness of the primeval forest, lending support to the shroud of mystery which surrounded the Round Tops. A gleam in his eye, the tradesman assembled the party along a path which disappeared into the trees. Caroline and Suzanne conversed lightly, whereupon, taking a cue from the tradesman, everyone plunged into the black grove, suffering through limbs and branches that blotted out all vestiges of sunlight. Cerf Courant and Fox Tail pushed forward to clear away obstructions from the path. By degrees the party emerged from the thickness into a clearing bestrewn with four great mounds rising mightily before them. Majestic sentinels all, the mounds rose to an imposing height, casting a giant shadow over the adjoining plain.

The voyagers paused in awe of these great earth forms, prompting some to make inquiries of each other. All came away with the thought that the mounds were unique to the region and may have been man-made. A wooden palisades ran before them, encircling them on either flank before vanishing into the distance. Eager to canvass what appeared to be a village, the voyagers granted Marchand the prerogative of leading them forward. He, however, to everyone's surprise, elected the General to enter the village proper so that he may be the first of the voyagers to greet his ally and friend, the Bear Chief.

The General found the palisades unattended, the usual guards absent. Entering the village concourse, he struck off toward the Bear Chief's quarters. Drawing from memory, he recalled the description of a sturdy cabin which Watkins and James York, the principal architects, once related to him. He counted on Colombe Blanche to provide him with a tour of the village. The Bear Chief's cabin, according to legend, sat in the center of the village within a cluster of lesser mounds, a meeting place where young and old congregated. He listened for the sound of children's voices, and half-expected to be surrounded by a rash of warriors. Looking upward toward the ramparts, he found them devoid of guardsmen. Curious, he wound his way toward the cabin, only to find the portal wide-open. No one issued forth to greet him. On all sides the village proper stood barren of inhabitants. A lone dog, disheveled and gaunt, ambled to his side. Curling about his legs, it whined pitifully.

From deep within his bosom a pain of dread struck him. Of its own accord it branched out, sending tremors into his fingers and toes. The General knew this sensation from days gone by. It always surfaced with the onset of an overwhelming event, an impending calamity about to cast the lives of many into chaos. With trepidation he walked on, lingering to watch for signs of life. He almost doubled over with cramps, the pain intensifying with each step. The discomfort unrelenting, the General located the Bear Chief's cabin. He knew that he must find a single living soul in order to quell the persistent agony coursing through his limbs. Imploringly he called at the doorway the names of the Bear Chief and his family. Not a sound broke through the stark, eerie silence. Alerted, he entered the cabin. Before him, lying in the darkness in a frame bed heaped with blankets, lay an immobile Colombe Blanche. Approaching, he saw that the dimness did little to mask her pallid features. He lay an ear to her bosom in anticipation of a heartbeat. She breathed ever so weakly, and when he opened her eyelids, he found her eyes rimmed in redness, the forehead hot to the touch, lips swollen and parched. He gazed intently upon her two sons, stumbling into them where they lay pressed into a corner tightly together. Unlike their mother, the boys moaned and shivered when he touched them. Placing a hand to their forehead, he found the flesh hot.

He turned to find Marchand and Caroline and Suzanne behind him. Saddened, he faced them, full of grief with eyes swollen, hard put to form words:

"They have the *fever*, Guillaume," the tradesman whispered.

"The camp is stricken," Caroline lamented.

He heard himself ask: "Has anyone died?"

"The horsemen are searching the camp, Guillaume. We will learn more at length, but I must tell you this: We need to treat everyone immediately. I have seen this kind of malady before. It arrives during the season of mosquito-breeding. Is there a standing pool of water nearby?" He looked about querulously.

"There *is* a source of water nearby," Caroline confessed. "We all drank from it at one point, but the cabins have their own sources of water now from the wells," she added, shaking her head wearily.

"This source. Does it lie in a quiet pool surrounded by marshes?" the tradesman asked, interest mounting.

"Yes! Yes!" Caroline returned. "However, it is largely abandoned, so I am told."

"That may be, yet mosquitoes carry the fever with them." The tradesman allowed his words to settle, then: "When one bites you it spreads the fever to you and anything it has touched or eaten impregnates your body with the maladies of these foreign bodies." Speaking in whispers, eyes bugging, the rotund tradesman suddenly pinched his forearm. Wincing, he jumped backward, sending his companions into retreat.

"Ah!! Now I have your attention. Mosquitoes congregate over standing water. Such an incident once befell Pointe Aux Bois long before Guillaume arrived on the scene. Our friends here may well live through this, but we must act now." He proceeded to unveil a recipe for treating with the mosquito-borne contagion. "Bring me blankets. Wrap the infirm securely. They need to drink a mash of honey, beer, sugar, (95) and willow bark. That reduces the fever and replenishes the body. Find some quinine salts and mix with hot tea. That also reduces the fever. The fever must be reduced or the internal organs will burn away. When that happens, you are as good as dead."

Frantically the tradesman looked about: "Are there any fruits on hand? Peaches? Berries?"

"The Round Tops is well-stocked with peaches and berries," Suzanne offered, at the point of tears.

"We have quinine," Caroline interjected. "I brought sacks of it for the voyagers."

"Good! Quickly! Bring out all of the blankets that you packed, Madame."

"We have beer, Henri, from my collection," the General replied, approaching his colleague.

Through the remainder of the day the principals found and relocated the victims around a central fire pit which they stoked and kept burning brightly. Caroline, Suzanne, and Matthew adhered to the tradesman's procedures: They administered honey mash. They doled out cups of hot tea with quinine salts. They reduced peaches and berries to a kind of soup and circulated them in wooden bowls. All able-bodied voyagers and many of the horsemen volunteered to assist, freeing the principals to make the required rounds of visitation. Among the victims sporadic episodes of vomiting and diarrhea periodically erupted. Beyond suffering from the 'chills', the infirm became disposed to throwing off their blankets and refusing to recline by the warm fire. The tradesman posed a solution: First, he demonstrated the art of transferring the infirm from a soiled to a clean wrapper. Next, he assigned a care-giver to each victim, one who by earning the victim's trust may conditionally enforce agreed-upon care procedures. With few exceptions, the tradesman's plan met with success, his adherents forming an *ad hoc* collection of dedicated servants driven by a strong sense of duty.

Presently Matthew and Dana Smythe went off with the horsemen in search of casualties and runaways. Later in the afternoon, Matthew returned to Marchand and the General, his countenance a mask of bewilderment:

"They have gone. Simply gone."

"Is that why you abandoned your search?" a concerned Marchand asked.

"No! No! We searched the entire camp and beyond. There are no traces of villagers anywhere." Matthew looked about. Perplexed, he asked: "How many missing have we?"

"About thirty," Le Rocher replied. "Ah! I see your point. We know not whether they live or have perished."

"I have a thought", Matthew sighed. "They left to seek relief, my father among them. Strange. Watkins is not to be found." He whirled about, trying to make sense of the situation.

Marchand set Matthew at ease. "Good attempt, Matthew." He stroked his chin. "I believe that your father and others departed the village to secure medicines once the contagion broke out. I deem it unlikely that the village held the necessary applications."

"But where would he go?" Matthew asked, growing tense.

"Kanandesaga, most likely. Many traders go there. It is a source of many remedies. Some good. Some bad. One may find all that falls within the realm of possibilities. Do not worry! Kanandesaga is reliable. It is in the hands of the Cornplanter. He is a firm ally of the Bear Chief."

Stepping forward, Matthew pumped the tradesman's arm vigorously. "For my sake, I pray you are correct."

"You will need to burn that marsh, Matthew. You must kill all of the 'skeeters' before they lay eggs for the following year." He spoke in a paternal, yet convincing manner. "I did the same when at Pointe Aux Bois."

Acknowledging the tradesman, Matthew consulted his trusted comrade, Dana Smythe.

"No need to do it now, Matthew. The damage has been done."

"Follow me," Marchand gestured, making strides toward the great camp fire.

"We are fortunate to have Marchand with us," Matthew averred to Smythe, having gained an appreciation of the tragedy into which he stumbled.

"This is the first of your travails with contagion, Matthew. Chin up! You are doing well."

"We must bear down upon this blight as strongly as it descended upon the village and we will rout it. We are a *team*, my good man. Nothing is able to defeat us." Marchand slapped Matthew affably about the shoulders. Maintaining an affirmative stance in the midst of widespread grief and sadness, he made a sudden announcement: "Come! Let us go to the Bear Chief's wife and children. They may have need of us. Our tour is well-nigh due."

Once within Colombe Blanche's cabin the two marines found Caroline and Suzanne preoccupied with the stricken members of the Bear Chief's family. They studied the somber scene, longing to provide assistance.

"They must have water—clean water to drink and bathe in," Caroline looked up, imploringly.

Unfamiliar with the region in general, the two men looked helplessly at each other. Caroline sensed their growing discomfort. Passing her duties to Suzanne, she detailed aspects of the near-surroundings to the two marines:

"Not far north of here the Osco takes a wide turn to the left. Where it narrows there is a fording place. To reach it, follow the trail to the immediate left of the Marchand mansion. It lies through the trees behind us. Take a number of leather pouches and fill them and hurry back. At the fording place you will see a modest waterfall. The water there is cool and clean.* Take horses if you will, but hurry." Caroline's eyes burned brightly.

The two young marines lunged into the new task. They brought with them Cerf Courant and a number of horsemen from Caroline's original escort. Not long thereafter the triumphant party returned with many pouches of water destined for a variety of purposes: preparing hot-mashed corn cereals for the sick, washing soiled garments and bedding, for drinking, for bathing, and for cooking hot foods. With Caroline's insistence on clean water ringing in their ears, Matthew and Dana Smythe rested easily that evening as they stretched out beneath the stars.

The following day Matthew's command burned the thick forestation girding the choking marsh. They filled in adjoining bogs and lowlands. They diverted the original fast-flowing mountain stream to the west of the village where it joined with another yielding fresh water. Caroline observed most events from a distance. During idle moments she inspected medical devices for cleanliness, retaining most. Despite her attentiveness, several of the victims died during treatment— primarily elder residents. In response Caroline solicited assistance from Le Rocher and Marchand in selecting suitable sites for burial in light of the widespread contagion. With forethought she selected the long grassy slope in the southwest corner of the village. It is there that twelve hardy souls came to rest for eternity. They, along with Chien Aboyant, lay in rich alluvial soil, facing east in the direction of the rising sun.

* * *

The treatments continued. Over the course of a fortnight younger victims demonstrated strong signs of recovery. They clamored for more hearty foods. They responded well to hot liquid broths, the properties of which cleansed the bowel of poisonous wastes. Suzanne more and more confined her efforts to the boys' recovery. Once she reduced the boys' fever, their alertness and responsiveness improved markedly. Caroline, meanwhile, injected a pattern of exercise into her daily ministrations. She wrapped victims warmly and walked them over the grounds in an effort to curtail the joint-stiffness attendant upon those who must lie idle.

She noted that a good deal of the victims of medium age merited the services of a visiting physician. Thereafter, Caroline began to address Colombe Blanche's needs more attentively. Slowly Colombe Blanche renewed a dialogue with her. She began to ask for complete meals. At one point she disclosed that many villagers had moved off following the contagion and that James and Watkins had made repeated romps through the countryside in search of an able physician. At last they settled upon Fort Oswego, although to go there meant divulging the Round Tops' location to an alleged enemy. In a passing gesture, Colombe Blanche related that Fawn administered to the boys when they took sick. Weakening with signs of the contagion, Watkins forbid her from continuing with them, setting her apart from the village on a hillside and seeing to her needs.

Thankful for this round of knowledge, Caroline summoned Matthew and Dana Smythe away from duty. She dispatched them to Fort Oswego and Lord Carleton, there to make good the case of the afflicted and to return with a competent physician and medical supplies. In all haste the two marines borrowed a pair of steeds from the horsemen and fled into the wind. The pair followed the most direct route to the fort: the well-worn pathway running beside the Seneca River. Reaching its junction with the Oswego River, they bent to the north along another familiar land route, intent on entering the fort before nightfall. Consumed by a singular purpose, oblivious to all extraneous events, the young men urged their mounts to the utmost. Making haste, they came within inches of colliding with a pair of riders bearing down on them headlong. When Smythe sharply pulled Matthew's mount to one side, Matthew caught a glimpse of his father and another in full stride. Crying out, Matthew leaped to the ground. Running to James York's side, he leaped up to embrace him.

Father and son spent precious moments renewing acquaintances, whereupon Watkins introduced himself to the young marines. Without further delay, James told of his failed efforts to procure a physician at Fort Oswego, having been denied an audience with Lord Carleton. According to James, the new aide, one Caldwell, insisted that his rank of junior officer prohibited him from making major decisions in lieu of the commandant, who apparently was not in residence. Caldwell also refused to bunk him and Watkins overnight in advance of the commandant's return. Thoroughly rebuffed, James related that he spun off to render a report of his unpleasant encounter to the General at the Round Tops. He cautioned Matthew and Smythe, yet the two marines plunged ahead, leaving James and Watkins to return to the village.

Meeting with the General, James gave a full accounting of his treatment. The General met with other principals to plan a course of intervention. A council no sooner convened when Matthew and Smythe galloped into the village. Dispirited, they poured out Caldwell's repeated refusals to grant them assistance, much less address their concerns. Word of the looming impasse reached Caroline before nightfall. Angered, she excused herself from care-giving, and, drawing her son and Smythe to her side, spoke to them in riveting terms:

"Of course he refused you. He knows you are asking on behalf of the stricken natives. The natives of this land are to him mere grist beneath his feet." Her countenance reddened. Her eyes narrowed in the manner of a catamount about to pounce upon its prey. Caroline tossed aside her apron and turned to the young marines:

"Gentlemen. Come with me. We are about to pay our neighbor Caldwell a visit." Seizing her skirts, she summoned a mount. Clambering aboard unassisted, she issued a flurry of instructions: "James and Watkins!! You are my escort. We go to Oswego. Follow me." To a teacher she called out: "Take over for me on my rounds. I shall not be long." Mounted, she turned the great, swift steed toward the narrow path departing the village. Reaching the Genesee Road, she sprung across it, glided past the Marchand mansion and headed in the direction of the fording place— Matthew, Smythe, James, and Watkins hard upon her heels.

Pausing at the fording place of the Osco,* Caroline awaited her escort at the precise location where Matthew earlier filled the water skins. She made note of the event upon his approach, which Matthew promptly acknowledged with satisfaction, a welcomed departure from the tenseness of affairs back at the village. Reluctantly she consented to bring along Suzanne when her daughter joined the little party. They reached Oswego ahead of expectations, foregoing respites. Smythe furnished credentials to admit everyone without qualification. The grounds stood relatively empty of soldiers, and, Caroline, no stranger to the great hall, strode briskly over the oaken flooring with heels clattering, coming to rest before a lone desk at its terminus. A new and foreign figure occupied the desk, who, despite the cacophonous resonance of her footwear, remained fixed upon a stack of documents strewn before him. Hands on hips, Caroline dispensed with making formal introductions and confronted the occupant brusquely:

"You are Caldwell, I presume," her manner insistent.

"That is correct," the officer returned, hands probing through papers on his desk.

"I require the services of your post's physician. Time is of the essence."

Caldwell, unmoved by Caroline's sense of urgency, continued at task, yet attempted to disarm her request:

"I do not envision that wrinkled old sot doing much of anything."

"Perhaps you are in need of a new physician," Caroline returned, harmlessly. "In the meanwhile I shall speak with him irrespective of his condition."

Perturbed, Caldwell looked up, sliding his spectacles down the bridge of his nose. "Dr. Bradley Morris is in no condition to speak with anyone." Standing, he approached Caroline: "You must understand that he has consumed during my watch exceedingly more pain-killer tonic than he has administered to patients."

"By your words I am amazed that the usually proper Lord Carleton chooses to keep a man of such limited ability on the payroll." (Caroline hoped to convey that she collaborated at will with the commandant).

"He wants to shelter the old fool from a court-martial," Caldwell postured." Besides. From where are we going to acquire another doctor? The young ones do not come here. The wages leave a stench in one's nostrils."

"Then, why are *you* here?" Caroline insisted, sensing blatant callousness. She walked past him and turned: "A love for adventure is it? Are you on probation until your outstanding warrants are excused?"

"Stop!! Where are you going?" Caldwell started after her, arms laden with papers.

"The physician's quarters are next to the commandant's suite," Caroline replied, nonchalantly. Do not concern yourself. I shall make introductions."

Caldwell overtook her. A hand on her shoulder, he spun her around to face him, whereupon Caroline coiled a fist and struck him squarely on the jaw. The blow staggered him, knocking him backward.

"The next time I shall not be so gentle," Caroline admonished, hands on hips. "Now, out of my sight!!"

The commotion drew Matthew and Smythe into the hall. Together they followed Caroline into an adjoining room where a man lay prostrate on a bed, lashed to the headboard with sturdy twine. A noticeable red gash lingered on his cheek.

"He has bouts of wandering, wandering aimlessly," Caldwell called from without the room. The portly, robust officer stormed into the room to find Caroline tending to the physician's wound.

"I must keep him confined. He may injure himself," he asserted.

"I grant that, bent on destroying himself, he stumbled out of bed and struck his head," Caroline snapped.

"I found him face down on the floor passed out," Caldwell claimed, defending himself.

Caroline examined the doctor closely. "A blow from falling produces a lump and discoloration. This man has none of that." Standing, she accosted the aide: "This man has been beaten with a sharp tool—a letter opener per chance—like this one, for example."

Approaching the bed stand, Caroline delicately removed a sharp knife-like instrument with a heavy grip from a pile of letters lying opened—letters addressed to Dr. Bradley Morris. All bore dates running back several weeks and months. Caroline brought water for the doctor to drink. The two young marines dressed and bandaged his wound and set him into a comfortable chair. The doctor gulped the water and asked for more, along with a hot plate from the kitchen. He rubbed at his wrists where the bonds left the flesh reddened. Entreatingly he looked up at Caroline, a signal that he wished to speak:

"Please keep that man away from me," Dr. Morris whispered hoarsely, pointing to Caldwell.

Caldwell stood aghast. James and Watkins entered the room. Seizing him, they led him to a high-backed chair in the great hall where they forced him to sit idle while they took places beside him at arm's length.

Caroline procured additional food and drink for Dr. Morris. In feeding him by hand, she found him all the more spontaneous the more he consumed. At length she covered him with a thick robe and allowed him to speak as he lay in bed on fluffed pillows. Presently, Matthew and Smythe joined James and Watkins in the vigil over Caldwell. He, however, spoke not a word, choosing to contemplate the floor with a frozen gaze. Soon Caroline emerged from the bedroom to address the little party:

"Dr. Morris has been held against his will by Caldwell for a fortnight. He has subsisted on the barest of rations. He is the lone physician hereabouts and is called upon to serve a broad population. Now that Lord Carleton has employed young native men to labor in the fur industry, he has designated the doctor to tend to their needs. Natives tend to catch the same maladies as we, but are slower to recover, if at all. It is not extraordinary for the doctor to travel to Oneida Castle, Kanandesaga, even Fort Johnson and Canajoharie where Sir William Johnson maintains a sizable lot of native laborers. The letters? They are requests for the doctor's services—highly sought after. His letters come from reputable men and are genuine. The doctor made a point of telling me that Caldwell is reluctant to allow him to serve the general populace, for that involves natives. Caldwell told him that his services are needed *here* before they may be taken elsewhere. The main point of contention is that the doctor has never been granted leave where native populations reside since Caldwell assumed watch."

Exhausted, she sat on a divan: "Dr. Morris told me that Caldwell locked him in his rooms, denying him food and drink, shutting him off from all obligations. He did this whenever Lord Carleton sallied forth into the hinterland. Lord Carleton suspects nothing awry. The gash to the cheek came from a blow which Caldwell delivered to silence the doctor's pleas for mercy." Sighing, Caroline slipped backward, leaving Suzanne to console her.

"When is Lord Carleton due to return?" an intense Matthew asked his mother.

"In a day or two. Dr. Morris chose to speak with the hope that we may confront the commandant."

"In order to draw light upon his plight," Smythe returned, fighting to contain a smoldering rage.

"Yes. You have it, lad," Caroline replied, forcing a weak smile.

"Understood. Matthew and I will tend to matters," Smythe concluded. He immediately released Caldwell to James and Watkins who placed him in a retaining cell to the rear of the great hall over which they kept guard. Meanwhile, Matthew and Smythe withdrew to prepare a written report for the commandant's eyes only.

—

Lord Carleton returned to the fort the following morning. The two young marines greeted him with report in hand. After reviewing the document, he sought corroboration of details from Caroline herself. Calling at her rooms, he absorbed Caroline's account of the grim report, reading from it as she quoted its contents from memory. Finding a chair, he sat beside her a long moment in silence, his hand upon her shoulder, a man searching his soul, searching for the proper words:

"Apparently I am unable to find anyone to mind the store in my absence." Digressing, he moved back to the disastrous period in which the former Captain and aide-de-camp Simmons abandoned Ontario to assault. "I am surrounded by self-serving traitors who cast the Crown and myself under an evil spell." Gripping Caroline's hand, he gazed at her, as though seeking the strength to make a pronouncement. At length he assumed a deliberative posture:

"I may be stretching my neck out a bit, but the services of a good doctor are as vital to me as they are to you. With this in mind, I propose that the rendering of medical services to functionaries who labor for the Crown shall extend unequivocally to them and to all members of their primary unit and extended families wherever they reside within the boundaries of the Oswego trade route."

"By this you say that an entire village may receive medical treatment, Sir?"

"That I do, Madame. After all, without the dedication of the natives of Iroquoia, I stand helpless to haul my furs to market, thereby leaving Oswego to flounder and to cease to grow."

The remark caught Caroline unawares and she tried to subdue her elation by changing the subject:

"Whatever happened with your sutler . . . Van . . . Van..?"

"Van Schaack? He has his own operation on Lake Michigan. I stepped in when he took leave and here I am, still at it. En route I have always sought to solicit the efforts of a few good men. He looked benevolently toward Matthew and Smythe who entered unannounced.

"Yes. Matthew. Your son. A lad of inestimable worth. He first visited me with his new wife before joining you at your home-base. Smythe highly recommended him and we formed an alliance over a handshake. How is that sweet woman of yours, Matthew?" the commandant asked, turning to him.

"She ran. She ran when the fever struck. There is a party searching for her," Matthew offered, head hung low.

"She will make it, lad. She is hale and hearty. Unfortunately, the fever burrows into the very young and old," the commandant returned, in a conciliatory manner. Changing the subject, he regaled the budding community which he helped to found: "Look about you! Oswego is no longer a fortress. It is a settlement. It is growing—largely through a renewable labor force of young natives who prepare my skins for market, among other duties. And how do my laborers remain in such fine fettle? Why, Dr. Morris. None other."

Caroline smiled approvingly. "I have been thinking, Sir. Many of my teachers come from erudite backgrounds. I have drawn upon a small section of that community. Among them are physicians. They are young and eager to begin a career of service in venues where their best efforts may be put to the test. They, like my teachers, are in search of new frontiers in which to hone their skills. With proper encouragement, a goodly number may be persuaded to come west."

"And that encouragement is wages, most likely. Am I correct, Madame?"

"That you are." Sensing opposition, Caroline presented her argument: "A yeoman physician does not demand a king's ransom. To a greater extent, one is drawn to a region by the sense of community already residing there where there are friends and relatives and fellow comrades."(She hoped to induce the commandant to adopt a plan she long held dear).

Lord Carleton nodded in the affirmative. "That is a colossal thought worth exploring. Let us establish a supplementary fund to bring them here."

"The fur industry is alive and well, I take it, Monsieur," Caroline remarked, making her plan his own.

"By all means!" He slapped a thigh. "Sir William would like to be a part of this undertaking. He is soon to become Superintendent of Indian Affairs of the entire colony (96). Most likely he will impose a tax on furs. Disguised as a fee, it will evoke no consternation among the frugal. Sir William will see your proposal as a boon, for the improved disposition of the native translates into his prolonged and loyal service to the Crown."

"To the Crown. Of course, Sir."

"Yes. Yes. To the Crown," Lord Carleton winked.

Sensing victory, Caroline spoke: "Allow me to speak to my teachers and my patron at Albany."

"Patron?"

"Monsieur Cuyler. The fur baron. You have heard of him, no less?" she demurred.

"My, my!! You have touched shoulders with the high gentry in your travels. I am amazed at your success in reaching the crafty old skinflint."

"Monsieur Cuyler is a dear and engaging man once one reaches his soft side."

"Yet a mite stingy with the guineas, judging from my intercourse with him."

"Let me say that I gave him to understand features of himself that he never knew existed." She smiled impishly.

"Heavens!! To do that, one would have to put the wrath of God upon him."

"Something of that sort," Caroline chortled, eyes aglow.

———

During the course of her audience with Lord Carleton, Caroline noted the commandant's intercession on her behalf on at least four fronts: For one, he drafted a letter to Sir William Johnson seeking impending medical attention applicable to all friendly natives of the

Confederacy laboring in the service of the Crown. He followed with a second letter requesting the recruitment and deployment of young physicians to the Lake Country under the auspices of Superintendent of Indian Affairs. Next, Lord Carleton wrote to Sir William requesting him to allow qualified young women to serve under young physicians for wages upon completing an approved, supervised program. He also wrote the entrepreneur, asking him to adopt his proposal of drafting young physicians through a modest tax on furs. Finally, Lord Carleton wrote Sir William Johnson once again imploring him to remove the abusive Caldwell from service by the most expedient means possible.

Caroline realized that the foregoing points which Lord Carleton framed in accordance with her wishes would not have come to pass had she allowed him to fall from grace following the sack of Fort Ontario. That, and the battle for Pointe Aux Bois posed two sound defeats for him, marking him for failure and disgrace in the eyes of the hierarchy. Her gambit: convincing him to try her abductor at Oswego in exchange for sparing Matthew a prison term for deserting, played well for the both of them. To wit, since the court-martial, Lord Carleton's superiors believed him incorruptible in the face of temptation. She, in turn, welcomed an undefiled Matthew back into the family fold.

She studied Lord Carleton, now a prosperous entrepreneur in the fur trade, a man prepared to honor her requests beyond question. She asked herself: 'How much of Lord Carleton's beneficence owed itself to a genuine sincerity of purpose or to a latent fear that she may divulge his shortcomings to would-be tormentors?' She may never know, she reasoned. On that account, there may be no need to know. Gracefully she thanked the commandant for his indulgence, and prepared to return to duty at the Round Tops.

"I must go to my adopted village to bring it back to the land of the living," she spoke solemnly.

"What will you do thereafter, Madame?" Lord Carleton asked with interest.

"I shall open my school for natives and newcomers alike in the house that Henri Marchand built."

"Ah, yes. The tradesman of whom you have told me plenty."

"His manservant maintains it. By agreement the students will lend him a hand. It is spacious and only lacks for the clatter of little feet along the corridors."

"May I keep Matthew for a while? He is so good with the young native men."

"Of course he is. He is *my* son. Matthew and Captain Smythe belong together. They are fast friends."

"All is settled. I shall send these dispatches on the morrow. Changes are coming to this land and you stand in the forefront of them. Perhaps you will think kindly of me." Shaking her hand, the commandant broke into a smile.

"Changes long overdue. Incidentally, I see no soldiers here. Where are they?"

"They are out scouting new lands. Now that my aide-de-camp has suddenly retired from service, they are currently without a leader." He winked knowingly: "Yes. Changes are overdue, Madame." Caroline prepared to depart. Matthew and Captain Smythe saluted her as she descended the steps of the grand porch. Tall and erect, she returned the gesture, repeating when Lord Carleton came to bid her farewell. Mounting, she waited for her little party to draw into position beside her, and, tipping the brim of her trail hat, set off at a gentle trot.

* * *

Returned to the Round Tops, Caroline accepted the Le Rocher summary of the convalescents' status with a cautious eye. Finding the report favorable, she briefed him on the turn of events past at Oswego. Delighted with Caroline's successes, the General launched into an expanded discourse concerning the disposition of the care-givers: they having risen from a state of gloom to one of hope. For many of the stricken the fever peaked and dissipated, due to strict adherence to the Marchand method of treatment. An encouraged Suzanne ran headlong to Colombe Blanche's cabin where she threw herself between Raven and Little Bear. The boys, though weak, reached out to her with limbs still warm to the touch. She procured more blankets and fed them hot turkey broth, long a favorite. An aide fed the boys blackberries by request. At length Suzanne chose to release them from the strictures of the malady by testing their sense of humor.

"How are my dear urchins? Are you playing possum in order to weasel treats from the nanny?"

"Oh no, Mademoiselle Suzanne. A fox came and ate my food while I slept and I awoke to an empty and grinding stomach," Raven whispered playfully, despite obvious stress.

"What on earth did you do?" Suzanne teased.

"Little Bear killed it with a sling," Raven murmured, though parched lips.

"I have the pelt, Suzanne. Look where it is pegged," Little Bear returned, stirring restlessly in his blankets.

(True. A fox pelt clung to the wall. Suzanne recognized that it bore a strong resemblance to one that the Bear Chief himself placed there several months past). "A handsome pelt it is, boys. A testimony to your valor," she declared, allowing herself to be duped.

"We are simply *supreme* hunters," Raven reminded her. "We will take you hunting with us one day."

"That pleases me, boys. I look forward to it," Suzanne returned, brushing a tear from her eye. Rising, she tore to the window where she glimpsed a disturbance on the grounds. "Pardon me," she whispered, fleeing outside.

—

In the clearing between two cabins a congregation of villagers milled about a figure who spoke loudly while making lavish gestures. A mixed gathering, it consisted of the voyagers, the horse-cavalry, returning villagers, Henri Marchand, Oh:nehsi:yo, the General, and a foreign body of native men. The lone figure appeared poised to direct a tirade upon the tradesman and venerable chieftain. Suzanne retired to the rear of the assembly. When the General spied her, he broke away to join her. Drawn by the commotion, James and Caroline York entered the fold.

"He is an emissary from the western Delaware," the General explained. "He has come to warn us of a great native uprising in the Ohio country near Fort Detroit. A prophet has convinced several nations to take up the war hatchet in retaliation for what has been taken from them." Turning to Caroline, he quoted: "their lands and their dignity."

Oh:nehsi:yo spoke: "I have heard of this prophet. He is Neolin (97) of the Ottawas. Other prophets have joined him. Hard behind him, the fire-brand Pontiac and a fierce band have captured lesser forts in Ohio and along Lake Michigan."

"They are all British installations?" James asked.

"Oui, Monsieur York. Neolin and Pontiac hold the British at fault for building many settlements in native country without providing just compensation. Most recently, Neolin has moved ahead to Illinois where he seeks to persuade the remaining French forces to unite with him."

Marchand coughed: "That will never happen."

A confused James York regarded the tradesman enigmatically, prompting him to elucidate:

"The French are still reeling from the loss of Fort Duquesne. You must bear in mind that any French reprisals stall for lack of fighting men. British numbers exceed French numbers by four-to-one. In desperation, to strike a counterbalance, the French strive to preserve their preferential standing among the western natives as opposed to sparking a confrontation they may well lose."

"Who are the leading contenders among the western natives?" Caroline asked.

"The Delaware and Ottawas, Madame. These Delaware comprise the remainder of the Teedyuscung eastern federation betrayed by the Penn family and other conspirators."

"They are looking to make a final stand," the tradesman returned, pensively.

"That is where the Bear Chief has gone, mother!" Suzanne exclaimed, tugging Caroline's skirts.

"I understand, dear. As a Cayuga chieftain, he is fulfilling the terms of a treaty compact with the Delaware."

"How will he do that, mother?" a puzzled Suzanne asked.

"Peace councils," came a subdued voice from the background. Everyone turned to find Colombe Blanche, wrapped in blankets, approaching slowly. "He is camped in a small village south of Fort Detroit opposite Pontiac's camp. He will remain until he persuades all warring factions to cease hostilities. You must know that he is not alone. Tah:gah:jute is with him. Together they will do what others before them have failed to do. Both present a history of building friendly relations between the red man and white man."

From all quarters people gathered around Colombe Blanche, for she uttered words which rang true and incisive.

Spying her, the uninvited speaker thrust himself into the crowd. Mounting a hogshead,* he shouted:

"Pontiac needs recruits to strike a blow against the treacherous whites who have invaded our lands and refuse to depart." He spoke in passable French. Confident, he locked his gaze upon Colombe Blanche.

"The men you see before you are survivors of the *fever*, Monsieur," the General declared. "They are needed here to bring this village back to prosperity." He caught a trace of rum on the speaker's breath and recoiled.

"Are you not kin to the Delaware?" the speaker demanded, addressing the whole body.

Colombe Blanche came forward. Waving the General aside, she faced the interloper: "I speak for my husband in his absence. I am the wife of the Bear Chief. He is a friend to all who seek to live in peace. You and he are direct opposites, for you are a man of war. At this very moment my husband is in the Ohio country addressing a native assembly representing the entire Ohio basin."

"You are but a woman!! I do not speak with women," the speaker shouted, full into Colombe Blanche's face. Matthew, arriving moments earlier with a wagon of furs, pressed forward to shield her, a maneuver which everyone present took to heart. A grateful Colombe Blanche spoke to her adversary:

"You may speak with my husband's chosen representative," she stated firmly, nodding to Oh:nehsi:yo. "He and I are of the same mind, although he is more stubborn than me. Therefore, I urge you to treat with me exclusively." Her boldness drew the intruder's attention. Dismissing his entourage, he invited her to speak. Her ploy successful, Colombe Blanche won the opportunity to confront the speaker on her own terms:

"Your demand for warriors violates the pact of trust which the ancient Delaware and Cayugas forged in the days of Hiawatha. That bond brought together two distant peoples for the purpose of sharing hunting grounds when food ran scarce and to defend common interests from raiding warriors. Your proposal requires universal agreement by Delaware and Cayuga leaders. I see that you have not honored sacred agreements. Going further, under the pact, no *one* Delaware or Cayuga may impose his will upon another without his consent and understanding." She shook her finger in disgust at the speaker. "These are truths which every male member of the Confederacy has learned from an early age. I am galled that you did not learn them. This alone tells me that you are a fraud and are doing this for a reward." Her case stated, she stepped into the open arms of Suzanne and Matthew.

The speaker's followers encircled him. Together they shouted into the gathering. They called for every able-bodied warrior to join them in one final battle of vindication. Ranting, they chastised the populace. The harangue, too vehement for the usually quiescent Cerf Courant and Fox Tail, prompted them to erupt. Pushing through the gathering, they cast men to left and right before coming to rest before the speaker himself. Speaking in French, Cerf Courant, the otherwise taciturn ally of the Bear Chief, vent his spleen in an oration which declared in no uncertain terms where his allegiances lay:

"I stand with Colombe Blanche. All of you are about to sell your souls to the devil. Look around you. These white men and women with whom I stand are strong examples of the goodness of human kind. Each has labored without rest to improve the lot of the humble multitudes who walk these lands. He spoke of Watkins: "There stands the man who built this village not for his own glory, but for your humble residents." He spoke of Caroline: "This woman by her own hand has saved from servitude and execution your blood brothers and sisters." Of Matthew and Captain Smythe he spoke: "They have saved a great number of children from entering into servitude by stomping out evil before it took root. I may speak more, but I want to make known the contributions of these peaus blancs to the resurrection of our People. It is their selfless desire to help those in need that I come to praise. The orations of this charlatan lead only to the demise of our way of life. I stand against him."

Rumblings of rancor flowed among the speaker's adherents. Stepping forward, Fox Tail spoke in an effort to winnow undecided villagers away from the speaker's point of view. He shouted above the rising din of the crowd. Standing tall, he spoke: "My brother is the fierce ally of the Bear Chief who is now in the Ohio country pleading for our civilization. We need the whites in order to save ourselves. Those whom I have met are good. When red renegades wounded me on the Mohawk, leaving me for dead, the white horsemen of my party came to my rescue. They pulled me to safety. They cleaned and dressed my wound. They sheltered me behind the lines. That is why I am here today. I stand here with some of these same benefactors. To them I give my heartfelt gratitude. I do not forget them now for their kindness."

An audible hush settled over the village. Residents chose to stand beside the two brothers. The brash speaker's followers gathered at his side. A confrontation loomed imminent. Each camp railed against the other. With the daylight waning, the speaker's supporters vacated the grounds by degrees. By early evening he stood isolated: a voice without an audience. He hurled weak epithets upon the on-looking residents. Garnering no response, he mounted and abandoned the village altogether. Upon his departure a clan mother issued forth. She gave Colombe Blanche to understand that, during the speaker's tirades, she circulated a petition among the residents. Returns revealed that overwhelmingly the villagers favored supporting the western Delaware by diplomatic, not warlike measures, in the manner of Tah:gah:jute.

* * *

By mid-May all vestiges of the *fever* having dissipated, the village assumed a calm and peaceful ambiance. Fawn rejoined Watkins from her hillside retreat. Dewai, Matthew's wife, returned from self-imposed quarantine, finding in Fawn a spirited and loyal companion. Raven and Little Bear knocked about the village's fringes, incessantly testing their mother's endurance. Colombe Blanche recovered sufficiently to resume a domestic posture. Matthew and Dana Smythe continued in Lord Carleton's service, becoming scouts for his overland fur-trading caravans. Marchand and the General lingered at the Round Tops, taking rooms in the mansion before returning to Canada and Richard Clement, his prosperous trading post demanding more staffing. Suzanne became preoccupied writing in her journal. She dated her first entry Saturday, May 19th, 1761, the same day that she wrote the first of a long line of letters to Birdie, her beloved friend in Albany. Caroline opened a school in the Marchand mansion after James and scores of villagers arranged school books on shelves and tables in the spacious library. She gave a banquet on the lawn for the inaugural class to the delight of students and teachers alike.

The spring planting season arrived. Watkins and James enjoyed the out-of-doors immensely. Together with the horsemen and their steeds and plows, they cut row upon row of furrows. Women and children followed, depositing the seeds of corn, squash, green beans, sweet potatoes, and more: the kernels of the coming year's harvest. Water. Rather, the lack of it, posed a problem. The once-reliable mountain stream, recently diverted to a fast-flowing branch, slowed to a trickle during the drought that arrived that first spring. To recoup water, villagers walked the two kilometers north to the familiar fording place where the Osco always ran fast and deep. There they filled-deerskin pouches with water, bringing them back by wagon.

One day Watkins and James put their heads together. They constructed a water tower on the northern slope near the plowed fields. Cylindrical, the drum-like wooden tower opened at the top to admit rainwater through a funneled aperture. It stood on four wooden legs, reaching some ten meters in height. The men found that the tower filled quickly during rapid midday downpours. A faucet at the base allowed bearers to fill water bags and carry them the short distance to the fields. The men built a second and third tower, the latter reserved solely for the residents themselves. They soon discovered that the village lacked a continuous water supply for daily needs during the persistent dry season. Marchand suggested that they search for underground springs and dig wells accordingly. He reminded them to dig near newly-opened wells which currently supplied the village's homes. Watkins and James leaped headlong into this newest of challenges. They had no difficulty recruiting volunteer-laborers and soon opened four fully-functioning wells: two each on the eastern and southern slopes amid the fertile fields. They lined each well-shaft with small stones, which both fortified the well proper and cleansed the water coursing among the stones. Heeding Marchand's instructions, the men inserted an iron pipe topped off by a faucet into each well-shaft. When the season's drought arrived, the men eagerly raced to the wells to tap each faucet. Initially no water flowed and the men lamented their fate and refused to speak with each other.

Then, one day in June water gushed from two pipes at once. A third and fourth pipe responded the following day, giving the men to embrace and run into the village to proclaim the success of the operation. Jubilant residents paraded Watkins and James on their shoulders and many flocked to the sites to see first-hand the results of the men's noble experiment. Children drank from the faucets and women served picnic lunches to families in the fields. An entire week of celebration sprung up with residents choosing to sleep under the stars at night. On the final day of gaiety, Watkins and James attached hoses to the faucets and admitted bearers to fill deerskin bags with water. In a competition of sorts, bearers streamed over the fields to water the furrows laden with the seeds for the fall crop.

—

By the end of May the first of Birdie's letters arrived at the Round Tops by means of the new stage line running between Albany and the Niagara frontier. The Genesee Road swung directly before the mansion, Caroline's school. The letters came wrapped in a ponderous bundle, explaining why Suzanne waited several weeks for them. The coachman deposited them at the mansion's doorstep, between the two lion sentinels. Caroline delivered them unceremoniously to her brooding daughter whom she often found pining away in her room for her new-found friend. Reading them in a flurry, Suzanne dashed downstairs to render a spirited report to whomever stood within range of her voice:

"Birdie is the leading songstress of her congregation," Suzanne announced breathlessly, leafing through the pages. "She sings at every service and is sought after for community performances."

"She wants to come for a visit soon, mother," the delighted young woman warbled. She read on:

"Mr. Cuyler says that your school in Albany is doing well. The Mohawk like it. They found that some of the teachers you chose speak their language. Very good, mother." She patted Caroline's shoulder affectionately.

"Mother! Listen to this: Thanks to the Cuylers and Livingstons, many servants in Albany have been allotted living quarters on South Pearl Street and Hudson Street" (98). She punctuated her disclosure with a 'Whoop.'

Suzanne's revelations brought Caroline to her side. "Look, mother! That scruffy McVeigh has been forced to bathe and shave in order to keep his teaching post." When she reached a piece concerning Mrs. Livingston, Suzanne arched her chin high, and, pursing her lips profoundly, spoke in clipped, precise syllables. "Mrs. Livingston teaches Ethics and Rhetoric in your school, mother."

Playfully pleased with all that she read, Suzanne tossed the letters upon the thick carpet at her feet and lay down among them laughing with glee. Caroline bent to retrieve them and at once mother and daughter found themselves intertwined in a jumble of arms and legs. They broke out laughing, more over the embarrassing configuration they struck than from Suzanne's reference to the staid and redoubtable Mrs. Livingston. For a long moment they lingered interwoven, enjoying each other's company before Caroline broke loose. Sitting up quickly, she announced soberly:

"I am pushing ahead to Kanandesaga. I have one more school to open, dear daughter," she stated bluntly, patting Suzanne's leg. Rising to the occasion, Suzanne asked her mother to take her along.

"Not now, dear heart. Raven and Little Bear have need of you. With their loyalty assured, the entire village will come to the mansion for lessons. Our school will be filled to the rafters." Her eyes swept the spacious library which rose voluminously behind them.

"You will need an escort mother. Is Captain Smythe about?" Suzanne asked light-heartedly.

Caroline's opportunity to tease her daughter arrived: "My! My! I see that you have an interest in the military."

Rapidly digressing, she interjected: "Birdie is a dear girl. Write her and ask her to come at first liberty." Calmly Caroline rose. Patting Suzanne's head softly, she slipped on a pair of kid gloves and glided from the room.

—

That very afternoon Caroline and Matthew departed for Kanandesaga. Oh:nehsi:yo and a party of stalwart horse-cavalry escorted the four teachers chosen for the new school. The teachers, in turn, brought the 'lock and stock' of earthly belongings with them. With great effort, bearers loaded box after box into four high-back wagons with stout axles. From among the steeds taken at the fierce Osco fight, Fox Tail chose eight draft horses to pull the wagons. Privately he hoped that both horses and wagons survived the rigors of the sometimes corrugated roadway.

The journey furnished Caroline with the opportunity to reminisce. In retrospect, events of the year past seemed remote to her, as though the property of a different woman. Not her. Not the Caroline she became since the turn of the New Year when her life raced in a new direction. 'Where once she feared for her life, she now found herself sought after for her counsel. Strong leaders paid homage to her designs of educating the colony, endorsing her upon reviewing her latest achievements.'

She communed less and less with James in all respects. While he labored in the fields and devised methods of curbing the vagaries associated with the seasons, she maintained a vigorous correspondence with well-known luminaries. Furthermore, her sojourns into the interior demanded thorough preparations. To begin, she required and demanded an armed escort when on the trail, given the recurrent volatility in certain regions. Before striking out, she habitually pursued a report of the political climate of her host's camp. Moreover, she requested of her host a detailed scenario of the avenues of escape in the event of enemy attack. In constant concern for her security on the trail, she ate her meals sparingly. When at home she kept to a solitary bed, half awake, half asleep, poised to take flight. Rising early each morning, she went about her duties and obligations with almost militaristic precision. Returning directly to her room at dusk, she crouched beneath candlelight to read, to write, and to plan.

She regarded Matthew riding beside her. 'In him she witnessed a younger version of James. The resolve, the determination, the innocent humor of her husband stood out in Matthew.' She looked forward to witnessing situations in which Matthew gave forth with these qualities. Steeped in thought, she gave a start when Matthew interrupted her reverie:

"Dewai is with child."

"Oh, Matthew! So soon after the *fever*?"

"Strange, mother. She never fell ill with the fever. Her pain simply came from . . ."

"The new life in her womb?"

"Yes. I believe so. Others better versed in the matter of motherhood have told me."

"She will turn out well. Tell me. Have you ever met with the Cornplanter?" she asked, changing the subject.

"No, but I have the suspicion that you are about to tell me about him," Matthew countered, somewhat defeated.

"During my captivity, he released me at random to tend to the Seneca children. I taught them reading, writing, spelling, and the like, when he easily may have kept me locked in a pen. I carry those memories with me to this day whenever the talk of children enters into the conversation. I open my school in his village to repay him for his kindness." She looked straight ahead, her voice betraying no emotion.

"You say that your mission began with the Cornplanter, mother?"

"Most likely, although all sorts of images flew through my head for a while."

"Rumor has it that he plays favorites."

"He wants what is best for his flock. This requires him to bargain with powerful strangers."

"Such as the British command?"

"Exactly, Matthew."

"Do you fear there will be more uprisings?"

"Among the Seneca? Yes! The General tells me that bands of Seneca have joined with bands of Ohio natives to chase the British out of the entire country. By the same token they have risen against the French out west, hoping to goad them into restoring the beneficence of Onontio."

"Onontio is too weak to confront the British. Do they know that? Also, the British offer shoddy gifts of late."

"I believe that the thought of this is taking root. If so, it makes their anger that much more intense, Matthew."

"What stand will the Cornplanter take?"

"He is a leader among very few who recognized that once the Iroquois began to accept British favors they gave permission to see their lands occupied prematurely—all in one stroke. I believe that he will try to bargain with the colonials."

"Failing that, there will be war, mother."

"Unless Onontio makes a decisive return—but Onontio is waiting to learn how Pontiac performs in his stead."

"The games of war, mother."

—

The party held fast to the Seneca River road. A southern branch led them to Skoyase, the Oh:nehsi:yo homeland, from whence in the fall of 1760 he led a band of warriors to take part in the September campaign against Fort Ontario. The thought of the confrontation there which set her free consumed her immediate thoughts. Reaching the village, she released a body of teachers to the chieftain's care. Departing shortly, she allowed her fond memories of Oh:nehsi:yo to linger en route to Kanandesaga, her next stop, and the Cornplanter or Gayanthawageh. She found him in the cornfields, inspecting the spring planting:

"This is by far the greatest stretch of crops I have ever seen." She spoke in French.

"A hungry village needs the bounties of a beneficent deity, Madame." He offered a hand.

"I have brought you teachers for your school. I know how much you value the upbringing of your youth."

"If one lives among aliens, one must learn their language," the Cornplanter replied, invoking a barb intended for his white neighbors. He walked with her a bit. Halting, he extended an arm. "Over there will rise the new school." He pointed to a pile of logs about to be planed and shaped into rudimentary walls.

"Do not forget the hearth and flue," Caroline jested.

Passing over the remark, the Cornplanter broke into discourse: "The school will be opened for all four seasons. Its doors will never be locked. It is akin to a sanctuary." Satisfied with his delivery, he gazed at her.

"I see few men hereabouts. Is there cause for concern?"

"Many warriors have gone out west to the Ohio country. They go to find Onontio and bring him back to the Confederacy. Onontio is our one true friend among the peaus blancs."

"Onontio has been severely wounded, mon ami. He may never rise again in this region."

"Yes. Yes. I have heard those stories, but my warriors are carving out a path for him to follow."

"I have heard that your warriors make war against their former friends the French in the west. By joining with the British I understand that they intend to threaten Onontio to return to the Confederacy."

Her host crushed a lump of earth beneath his boot before fixing a stern gaze upon Caroline "And he *will* return one day. I do not know when that day will come. Because of that I worry. We all worry."

"I worry no less than you," Caroline confessed.

"Tonight our sachems hold a seance. They want to look into the future to see what lies in store for us. We do that when we worry. What do you do when you worry," he asked bluntly.

"I go to my church with my family and talk to the Lord."

"Ah, yes. We go to the church that the Long Robes built for us. They preach there and we sing in an effort to awaken the Lord to our problems." He dug into the soil with the toe of a boot. "So far the Lord has given us bountiful harvests, but a lasting peace has become too elusive to capture."

"You need to bring your warriors home. Let the Bear Chief and Tah:gah:jute search for peace. They have a special talent for bringing dissenters to the table."

"Indeed they have, Madame. It is the young ones, however, who thirst for war. Look about you. The elderly are building the school. They have built our church. The women young and old tend to the fields."

"The further that the warriors stray from home, the more they open themselves to predatory attacks, Monsieur."

"This I have told them: They must not string themselves out so thinly over our vast domain. They will return for the autumn hunting and when their powder horns run dry. They always return then." He rubbed his hands nervously.

"Who will guard your towns and rich fields with your warriors gone?"

"I have sent emissaries to the Bear Chief and Tah:gah:jute to send the warriors home. A reply is forthcoming."

"This is good, Gayathawahgeh. Nothing less than their presence will conserve your lands". She thought for a long moment: "Do not enter into any binding alliances with strangers. They may well be your enemies and the decision you make may one day come back to haunt you."

"This is wise counsel, Madame. You think like a sage. I am glad that you visited me today." Caroline's host conducted her and the entourage on a tour of the village. Inevitably she met with former students, those whom she taught while officially a prisoner of her nefarious abductor. She called the period her 'Dark Moments' and discussed them with no one but her ultimate savior, the Cornplanter, that evening during a roast in her honor. Accepting an invitation, she stayed the night.

Rising with the dawn, she and Matthew struck out on the next leg of the journey. Adhering to the wishes of the Cornplanter, she vowed to install the remaining teachers in selected villages of the Seneca domain in the Genesee valley, home to the Allegheny Seneca. The trek overland consumed three days and on Friday, June 15th, an exhausted Caroline reached the first of her destinations. At the final settlement she lay the cornerstone for a school to be built beside the solitary church and hostelry overlooking lush forests and fertile fields (99). The village sachem regaled her with gifts of beads and clothing. The colorful orator Red Jacket gave a brief speech. In parting, he gave Caroline to understand that the Bear Chief and Tah:gah:jute were at that moment making passage back to the Round Tops. She collapsed with delight. Following a much-needed respite, she, along with her escort, cut a straight path back to her adopted village.

—

Returning in good form to the Round Tops, Caroline discovered a village in transition. Where formerly the sick and dying held sway, able-bodied men and women bustled ceaselessly to and fro, cleansing away traces of the contagion and replacing old accouterments with new ones. The mood turned festive. Young and old broke into song. Suzanne and her friend, Birdie, loaned their voices to the effervescent display of conviviality. The central hearth overflowed with roasted meats. Maidens trod the pathways carrying trays of fruits and edible gourds. By early evening rumor presaged the coming of the Bear Chief and Tah:gah:jute to the Summit. In twos and threes villagers followed the two esteemed leaders at a comfortable distance, taking places around the base of the Summit. Taking to the mound, Suzanne spied Colombe Blanche and the boys struggling to catch a glimpse of her husband's famous cousin. The sight of the two leaders together suggested the onset of a prodigious event in the making, prompting all in attendance to listen and look with rapt attention.

The Bear Chief opened: "I am pleased to return to my homeland and to this village of peace and serenity. I have spent many months on the frontier with my esteemed cousin in search of the same peace and serenity which all of you enjoy here. Tah:gah:jute and I have learned that peace carries a price—a high price in lives and property. The native inhabitants of the Ohio valley are desirous of such peace, and are prepared to make reasonable concessions to preserve it. Sharp divisions exist between the red and the white camps—each driven by opposing forces; yet, my cousin and I labor without cease to join these warring camps together to form an agreement based on trust and understanding. Such a task is not beyond us, but opportunities are growing less common. Tah:gah:jute will speak."

Cheers flooded the camp as the famed orator rose. Tall and rugged of aspect in a buckskin suit, Tah:gah:jute exuded a regal bearing coupled with homespun wholesomeness. He spoke slowly and distinctly, his words suspended in the cool, misty vapors:

"We men and women of native origin face major challenges brought upon us by a changing universe. They have come so swiftly that we find ourselves sorely unprepared for them. Yet, we do not shy away from them. That is not the way of the Iroquois. It is not the way of the People of the Swamp.* The Seneca, Keepers of the western Gate, and, we, the Cayuga, are joining forces with our allies in Ohio. We intend to restrict the British to the environs of Niagara—that fortress which they wrested from the French and presented to His Majesty, George II, ripe for occupancy—a feat accomplished with great support from our Seneca and Cayuga brothers. The Bear Chief and I have learned that the British, despite denials to the contrary, have made consistent inroads upon Iroquoia. Exercising chicanery and deceit, they have purchased for a pittance great land tracts from agents claiming to represent our best interests. They have taken the lands outright. We regret these losses and we regret that Onontio has been vanquished. My cousin and I see ourselves at a crossroads. One path, the more convenient, the path of war, leads to irretrievable losses of life, losses too repugnant for us to fathom. We avoid this path. The other, the unknown path, is wide, clear, and bright and lined with handsome trees and flowers. It offers a ray of hope. We have decided to follow it, though we know not where it leads. We believe that we must follow it, or go to our graves without learning what rewards we may have reaped.

"This new path is one of negotiation. It comprehends meeting with our antagonist, the British command, and gaining from him small concessions of land—indeed, our very own from the beginning—which altogether, over an extended period, will amount to great gains. It comprehends striking a bargain with him whereby we pledge ourselves to assist him in his hour of need in exchange for his hard and soft goods, and, yes, one more bit of land. We must follow this stratagem with an eye toward the aggressor remaining confined to the Niagara frontier under the watch of a host of able warriors. Once the aggressor grows accustomed to occupying Niagara, he will grow secure in his trappings and desist from sallying forth to make war. He will fear that we who surround him on all sides will rush in to grab Niagara for ourselves.

Given this construction, we must treat with the aggressor as we treat with a rival-in-trade, not as with an enemy in war. In this manner we will earn his respect, as opposed to his ire and thirst for revenge. With the passing seasons he will tire of us and move away forever.

"During the Moon of the Harvest Corn, that which the whites call September, Sir William Johnson will call a meeting of many natives at Fort Detroit. It is important that the Six Nations be well-represented in order to press forward with claims to lands falling between Niagara on the west to the Slim Fingers** and beyond on the east. This may be the first of many more meetings to come, all the more reason for dedicated supporters to attend in full force. I ask you to choose from this council two representatives to accompany the Bear Chief and myself to Fort Detroit to support the positions we assume without exception."

Stepping back, Tah:gah:jute bowed to the gathering. With arms raised overhead, he gazed heavenward, striking a long pose. The villagers followed his gaze and all remained quiet with eyes bent upon the legendary peacemaker. For a long moment the assembly remained locked in suspension, in wonder of the one whom many deified and entrusted with the fate of their species.

The Bear Chief set about seeking two representatives to serve. By tradition the clan mothers transferred the process of selection to older and wiser men. Unfortunately, the village held no eligible older men, they having fallen to sickness, injuries incurred in battle, or the excesses of old age. Confederation laws prohibited the Bear Chief and Tah:gah:jute from serving for they already occupied distinct offices. The matter perplexed the gathering and some began to openly bemoan the brewing impasse.

Caroline met privately with the two principals. Prompted by her solicitous daughter, Suzanne, she intercepted them as they abandoned the mound, once Tah:gah:jute concluded his delivery.

"I want very much to go with you, "she declared unabashedly.

"You have not introduced me to your friend," Tah:gah:jute spoke, turning to the Bear Chief.

"My humble regrets. Madame York is a dear friend whom I adopted once I learned of the particular gifts she possessed." The Bear Chief spoke softly, urging Caroline forward.

"Is this *the* Madame York of whom you have recounted to me endless passages? I am honored to meet with her under these humble circumstances. You have kept her far too long in the shadows, Fearless One." He faced his companion squarely, gauging the strength of his words upon him.

"Forgive my intolerance. We of the Round Tops have survived a host of misfortunes, many of which have pulled me in different directions at once. I need to gather my strength."

The gallant peacemaker graciously accepted the Bear Chief's apology. Placing an arm about his shoulders, he spoke: "Understandable. Tell me. What do you say of this woman?"

"In my view she has the guile and wit of the ablest of leaders. Above all, she shares our beliefs and passions."

"Your deeds and exploits precede you, Madame," the peacemaker replied. "For many nights on the trail the Bear Chief's stories of your endeavors kept me refreshed long after our camp fire died. He kindled my interest in you and I longed to meet you face-to-face. I am grateful that our meeting has come to pass." His eyes aglow, the famed orator returned to the matter at hand:

"You are not a native resident nor a voting man. You are treading upon uncharted waters. Tell me. What is your success in accomplishing what you have set out to do?"

Caroline spoke carefully, hoping to gain a needed ally in the peacemaker. "I have met with Sir William Johnson on at least two occasions. From the beginning we struck an accord. He assisted my patron at Albany with the selection of teachers for my schools. By the same token, he supported the building of my first school at Albany on a hilltop above his home. When I came west with my teachers, Sir William furnished me with boats, built in part by his own laborers. My tillers, porters, and bearers all received Sir William's approval before my boats set forth." Smiling, she rose to her full height: "The success of my venture falls upon an understanding I have reached with Sir William Johnson."

"A very honorable venture it is, Madame," Tah:gah:jute returned, bowing from the waist. "The Bear Chief tells me of your efforts to teach his children in the words and ways of the whites. The Cornplanter too has confided in me. Is there any truth to this claim?"

Again, Caroline chose to speak carefully. Reaching deep within her memory, she withdrew a patterned-response, conceived during the days of her captivity:

"From the beginning of my days in this country I found that a pronounced gulf reigned between two different sets of people: the Iroquois whom you represent, and the whites. They stand divided over the treasures which the land releases in varied, yet limited amounts. The two camps are reluctant to share these treasures with each other: the streams and forests, the animals and fertile fields. Each in his own way tends to convert for his own exploitation these treasures to such extremes that they approach exhaustion, if not extinction. Each camp is guilty in its own way: The Iroquois deplete the soil by sustained planting on the same plots over generations. The whites strip the forests and kill great numbers of animals, namely the beaver— the engineer of the woodlands.

"In my school I shall not dwell upon the differences in our two camps. I do not wish to establish rigid boundaries between them. I will not compel your native children to mimic my white students. Nay. I call on *all* children to develop mastery of their surroundings, however great or small. In doing so, I will teach the children to share the treasures that Nature has provided, with an eye to conserving them and keeping them whole." She brought out a cloth-bound text.

"The gathering of knowledge is a form of art. One learns by accumulating knowledge and applying it to everyday sets of circumstances. In my school the written word will be merely one means to acquire knowledge. My teachers also bring accumulated knowledge to the classroom. I have selected them with care. They are skilled in surviving on the frontier, demonstrating mastery of their surroundings. In my schools my teachers challenge students to both apply and conserve the precious treasures: resources. True. My students speak the peau blanc tongue. Do not be alarmed. It is but a tool for acquiring knowledge—not an end in itself. Language, all language, distributes knowledge. Knowledge confined or held hostage unto itself, defeats the process of learning. It must be disseminated, sown as though little kernels of wisdom over the fair vapors. My schools are open to all. They spread knowledge afar, making of the student a true scion of the universe."

Tah:gah:jute nodded appreciatively, indicating a willingness to learn more.

"The day is upon us when men and women of all stripes must put aside differences and labor together in the stream of life. In short this entails the appreciation, application, and conservation of resources, some of which I have given. Increasingly the lands around us shrink before the onrush of new settlers. This development intensifies the conflict between the Iroquois and peaus blancs. In my school students will learn to understand the whites as neighbors, co-inhabitants of Mother Earth, those who have the same basic needs as your People—yeah, those who make use of the treasures, yes, resources held in common with the People."

"I sense that 'resources' are much more than what meets the eye. Is this true?"

"Yes. The word 'resource' has a broad meaning. People are wont to speak of 'resource' as something visible— open to the touch. This is its 'external' aspect. A 'resource' may also be 'internal': those images which we create in our brain. We shape them into items or objects within our brain and churn them out into the finished product, so to speak. For example, my friend Watkins built the Round Tops. First, he formed an image of what he wanted to build. From whence came this image? It came from others engaged in building. He made inquiries. He observed men at labor, visiting locales which supported the image. When he began building, he shaped the surroundings to fit the image—thus joining the internal and external aspects of our term 'resources' together— in effect, yielding the Round Tops."

"I believe that I follow you, Madame. Your school does not limit the student to books and the classroom. It goes beyond books and the classroom into the greater community."

"Yes. You have it." Caroline pumped her host's hand. In my schools one exercises all available means to bring about mastery. Essentially the student develops a plan, then draws from the surroundings the tools needed to fulfill the plan. The student, therefore, is instructed to master a task by studying the parts or components composing the whole or entirety."

"Hmmm. Students choose tools from among resources which help form a plan to accomplish a task."

"Excellent! You make a superb student. All of this is called Education," Caroline concluded. Tah:gah:jute paused a long moment then: "When I was a boy, we spread seeds in the field by hand after we dug the rows. My back ached for hours. Now there are horses to pull plows that dig the rows. A clever sort came along with a better plan after examining the resources open to him."

"Yes. He delved into his surroundings long before the classroom and books emerged. In passing, a great deal of human kind's creativeness has been conceived of apart from the classroom."

"I understand. In my own way I have gone about your process for many years. Now you have put words to it and books have come along to bring this knowledge before everyone. Of this knowledge I am grateful. Our People have a creed which explains what you call 'Education.' I shall recite for you from memory, for my traditional school does not have books or a classroom. Our creed places 'Education' in the hands of the predominant village Lord:

"It shall be the duty of all five Nations' Confederate Lords to act as mentors

And spiritual guides of their People and remind them of their Creator's will and words.

They shall say: United People, let not evil find lodging in your minds, for the great Creator Has spoken and the cause of peace shall not become old. It shall not die if you remember the Great Creator. All Lords of the five nations must be honest in all things. They must not idle or gossip.

It shall be a serious wrong for anyone to lead a Lord into trivial affairs. The heart of each Lord shall Be filled with peace and goodwill and his mind filled with a yearning for the welfare of his People.

Look and listen for the welfare of the whole People and have always in view not only the present but also the coming generations, even those whose faces are yet beneath the surface of the ground."(100).

A this point Tah:gah:jute turned to face Caroline:

"Your success, Madame York, has been considerable in a land wracked by unending tragedies. You have emerged victorious and have moved on to lend sustenance to the less fortunate for whom you care deeply. In your labors you have vindicated those deceived or humiliated by a stronger opponent. In your travels you have given a face to hidden dangers about to strike the innocent. By your hand you have made the afflicted whole again so that they may enjoy the life which the Creator has reserved for them. By your zeal and fighting spirit you have made these lands a better place in which to live and raise children. Your story of 'Education' is to my liking. It tells me that you are worthy of my trust. Therefore, without further delay, I honor your request to become village representative-in-conference. With that, I invite you to join me on my voyage to the west."

In a curt, simple bow Caroline accepted the nomination. She accepted praises from the Bear Chief and his family. Soon Watkins and Fawn joined the circle of well-wishers which swelled to include Matthew and Dewai, Suzanne, Birdie, and James York, content to remain in the background. The Clan Mothers met to select Cerf Courant as representative, owing to his military prowess. The Bear Chief and Tah:gah:jute agreed and by afternoon's end Caroline and Cerf Courant became guests of honor at a feast given to commemorate their selection to that unique and austere post which severed traditional expectations.

—

During the summer months the villagers' concerns followed two courses: planting crops for the fall harvest and preparing for contingencies. Women and youth played major roles in the planting. Early each morning they rose, ate a light breakfast, and breaking off into teams of threes and fours to conquer the fields. Laden with bags of seeds often carried in carts, team members exercised a strict division of labor. Therefore, for each team there evolved a Digger, a Planter, A Waterer, and a Tamper—the one who stomped the soil tightly into place over the seeds. Raven and Little Bear insisted upon joining the ranks of planters. Together they formed one half of a team. Their eagerness heightened the level of participation among the two older team members. The boys loaned a youthful spirit to operations, one that everyone welcomed from the beginning. For their part, the boys adhered strictly to procedures for fear of facing reprimand or dismissal.

In preparing the village, the Bear Chief and Tah:gah:jute supervised first-hand the new construction projects. Laborers fortified the palisades with dried-mud plaster. They fitted the underground tunnels with supporting beams. The stock of horses and swine moved to newly-built pens with pitched roofs. A shop to house the forge, a gift from Marchand, stood beside the stockade— a repository for all firearms and shot and gunpowder. A new granary of sorts held legumes and fruits in air-tight casks. Wild animals were slaughtered and stored in an ice house lined with sawdust. Iron tools lay labeled in a tool house.

At midday the laborers took a respite whereby they ate foods which family and friends brought to them. James ate with the laborers, eating food which Suzanne prepared. He slept long and hard by night, alone in a bedroom apart from Caroline. Husband and wife rarely saw each other by day and Suzanne forgot when last they conversed with each other. Outwardly she showed no distress, but her concerns found their way into her journal where she dutifully made entries.

One morning in mid-July Raven and Little Bear looked up from their labors in the field to catch a glimpse of two Onondagas winding toward them. They recognized the Onondagas by the peculiar twist of goose feathers in their headbands. The two strangers communicated with hand gestures, reserving speech for the elders. In deference to the visitors' wishes, the boys led them to the Bear Chief, their father, who stood conferring with subordinates over the building of stables. Thanking the boys, the Bear Chief summarily sent them away to gather honey before turning to the two Onondagas.

"Ewado:geh:dajihah:dego:ni:goha:e?"—May I bother you a little while?—the taller of the two asked in the Cayuga tongue.

"D'accord. Il me reste un peu de temps,"—All right. I have a little time—the Bear Chief spoke, in French.

The shorter man chose French in keeping with the Bear Chief's prerogative: "During the Moon of the Harvest Corn you will need to keep your fields in condition for next year. We have stumbled upon something that aided us greatly in preserving our foods. We want to share it with you." He stepped back, awaiting a reply.

"Of course. What have you brought me?" an inquisitive Bear Chief asked.

The Onondaga released a bag from his shoulder. Opening it, he scooped out a handful of granular, glittering crystals rough to the touch. "Salt," he exclaimed. "Pour it over your stored foods. They will endure for many months over the winter."

"I have heard of such a substance. The French made it known to us and brought some last year."

"A long while ago, my friend. You need to increase your supply. We have plenty at our village."

A cautious Bear Chief asked a poignant question: "Do you give it to us or offer it for sale?"

"Neither, my friend. We offer it in trade," the man smiled, turning to his partner. "You have a great forest here. Everywhere there are trees. We have few trees. The lands around our village are bare. We need to boil the salt in kettles. This consumes much firewood. Boiling breaks the salt into small pieces. From there we cool it and strain it and soon it is ready for hearth and home. We offer you salt at no cost to you in exchange for your trees. We will cut the trees here and carry them by bateaux to Onondaga. How say you on this?" He grinned in satisfaction, pleased with his delivery.

Fox Tail and Cerf Courant happened upon the scene. The Bear Chief drew them aside for a conference. Shortly he returned to the Onondagas with a decision. Tall and straight, he presented himself as a leader of deep convictions:

"All of us enjoy our forests: They furnish us with animals to hunt. Their falling leaves nourish our rich soil. Most important, our forests gives us wood to burn in our homes. We have warmth in the winter and warm hearths in which our women prepare meals." Looking about, he continued: "I must not forget the chain of defenses our trees have provided us. Look! You see how every dwelling stands next to a tree? This is no accident." He stretched an arm toward the palisades: "How many trees went into making this great wooden wall? I do not know. I know, however, that without the palisades, our villagers would sleep less soundly at night. Regarding the Lord of the Forest, our laborers harvested His trees with care and reverence. We shall not impugn His beneficence by giving away His greatest treasures. Therefore, in all humility, I must refuse your offer."

The Onondaga turned away in contemplation of making another offer. Soon he made a presentation to the Bear Chief: "If you would but send us some of your laborers to produce the salt, we will grant them an ample portion at no cost to you."

"I have heard of the hardships that men endure when producing the salt. The hours are long. The heat of the fires is overbearing. Men are burned from flying embers and scalded by the hot water in the kettles. A man of thirty years reaches fifty years before the end of a single season. I see little wisdom in committing my laborers to such dangers."

"Tell me. How do you care for your foods, once harvested," the visitor inquired, sensing defeat.

"My father's father discovered a cave leading underground along the shore of Lake Tiohero*. He dug deeply into the soil in pursuit of the cave's end. He brought others with him and everyone dug. Before spring became summer, the men stumbled upon a stone slab dripping with gray-looking water. Tasting it, they found it salty. Our People learned how to remove the salt from the water. When dried, it improved the taste of our foods. After moving to our new village, we often sent young men back to the cave to break off more chunks of it. We store the chunks in our ice house until they are needed. We have plenty of it, so I am told." The Bear Chief stood tight-lipped and resolute, a sign that all further discussion was pointless.

Soundly defeated, the Onondagas attempted to snatch a small victory for themselves. The taller one asked for seeds with which to restore his empty forests. A compassionate Bear Chief sent bearers to bring forth four substantial sacks of seeds: oak, maple, ash, and birch. Eager to return to his labors, the Bear Chief dismissed the two visitors without inviting them to dine with him, according to custom. Thankful nonetheless, the Onondagas departed, uttering a flurry of terse acknowledgments.

The Bear Chief called a village meeting on the Summit following the Onondagas' departure. A strict devotee to the tenets of the Iroquois Constitution, he often looked for opportunities to rekindle the People's interest in what he held to be a sacred document. Citing one particular clause, he spoke from memory: "It is written that no one nation's members shall tempt those of another nation with hollow promises they are unable to fulfill. Thus, no one nation shall be self-serving to the detriment of its neighbor, or seek to place that nation at a disadvantage in the scheme of things. Moreover, a nation having an abundance of property shall share it on request with the nation which has not. Looking at the Onondagas you will see where I stand on these matters". Adjourning the meeting, he returned to his labors in the field, leaving the villagers to talk among themselves.

* * *

Early the following day, Tah:gah:jute set out for Fort Detroit with the two chosen representatives: Caroline and Cerf Courant. Upon recommendation from the Clan Mothers, Tah:gah:jute settled upon the swift and loyal warrior. The Bear Chief noted the day and date on a trail calendar: Wednesday, July 16th, 1761. He elected to remain in the village to attend to the planting. Fox Tail accompanied his brother and Suzanne begged her mother to take her along. The little party visited Seneca country to invite Oh:nehsi:yo before moving on to invite the Cornplanter. At full strength the sojourners walked due west along the Lake Ontario shore, keeping to the high bluffs when feasible. In short order they found themselves on a grassy peninsula leading into Irondequoit Bay. There they solicited two canoes and departed for Lake Erie. By coincidence, they found themselves over the ruins of the fort built by the Marquis de Denonville, who, a century earlier, attacked the Seneca village of Ganondaga (101) with a large force of Canadians, Lake Country warriors and French troops. The assault soured relations between the Iroquois and French for many years, stirring winds of revenge among the western Seneca, culminating, some say, in the eventual Seneca-aided British conquest of Niagara. On Lake Erie the sojourners headed due north, keeping close to the shallows in the event of a sudden summer shower or strong cross-winds fronting the lake. Save for two drenching rainstorms which sent them inland to seek cover, the sojourners maintained course without incident and pulled into the straits of Detroit on Thursday, July 31st, one day prior to the beginning of the conference.

Once landed, the sojourners addressed the first priority: securing a campsite on the outskirts of Fort Detroit. They soon learned that, because of the great number of delegates in attendance, unoccupied sites came few and far between. A guide of Sir William Johnson solved the dilemma for them. Drawing forth a map showing assigned plots, he expertly penned in a new plot for the six sojourners between two spacious ones presently occupied. Satisfied with his handiwork, he gratefully accepted the two guineas which Caroline handed him.

Well-situated, the sojourners roamed the open grounds. They partook of foods and beverages. They listened to the fifes play marches. They watched actors in medieval garb toss and catch wooden hoops. The men of the party casually sipped stout ale, refusing rum when offered. Caroline and Suzanne reclined upon embroidered blankets, lounging at the campsite. They fought off the cool vapors by covering themselves with mats of woven rushes. Intermittently mother and daughter sampled the almost unlimited offerings of food which bearers brought to them. They inspected garments for sale by natives of the western territories. At day's end they lay back comfortably in blankets beneath the stars, tired, yet content. They contemplated the temperament of the convention to follow, hoping that it may run quickly and smoothly, much like the first few hours on the grounds. Neither one slept soundly that first night, not while spinning fanciful and humorous tales of delegates whom they encountered earlier that day.

Caroline and Suzanne awoke early the following morning to the aroma of roasted swine and fowl over an open hearth, compliments of the Sir William Johnson food detail. Dashing to the dining tables, they indulged themselves. Presently a chaplain summoned all delegates to an invocation. A military escort stood near the chaplain, and, upon completing recitations, he disappeared among the members who closed ranks around him. In an instant the escort split into two columns and Sir William Johnson himself stepped into full view. The delegates pressed forward and he acknowledged them ceremoniously. Regally attired in a scarlet tunic offset by black breeches and knee-length boots, he wore the familiar flowing cape of legend which cascaded over his shoulder. The tricorn, cocked to one side, gave the impression that he perpetually stood on the brink of extending a hearty greeting to whomever crossed his path. This morning he walked along briskly, having taken leave of well-wishers, his thoughts occupied with Caroline. Coming to rest before mother and daughter, Johnson held out a hand in greeting:

"We meet again, my fair Madame. This has the appearance of a secret tryst." He bussed Caroline's fingertips and bowed deeply.

"Mind you. There is a ready audience on hand," Caroline quipped, making light of the situation.

"I am elated that you chose to attend this conference," Sir William returned, speaking softly. "We are about ready to begin. Come hear the speakers."

Caroline led Suzanne to an open space on the grounds sheltered by a great canvas tent. At Sir William's invitation, the three sat in a semi-circle of delegates, seemingly stuffed within the enclosure. Ahead, standing on a raised platform, a robust young native with fiery eyes addressed the crowd, many of whom were Ottawas, the band he represented.

"Brothers! Look about you! You gather in the shadow of Fort Detroit, that great trading place where you bring your furs to market. The tradesmen reward you in wondrous ways: For the first time in your lives you prepare your venison in iron kettles. You see your image in the looking glass. You straighten your hair with combs and you clean your bodies with fragrant soaps and wash your faces with smooth cloths. You wear trappings made in distant lands. Strangers pay tribute to you and you are exalted and believe yourselves invincible. Life is good for you and keeps getting better, measured by the surplus of your possessions. Your wants are negligible. You have forsaken the older, original comforts, replacing them with gifts which the tradesmen lay before you as they beat a broad path to your villages."

Leaping straight upward, this firebrand, this Pontiac, landed with a shout: "Aieee!! You are deceived, my brothers!! While you quarrel among yourselves to receive gifts, the tradesmen usher in scores of settlers. They come from across the great ocean. More so, they come from east of the Alleghenies. They produce young faster than we kill mosquitoes and are untouched by the mysterious maladies which decimate us. They will live when you will die. These lands--our land--will one day belong to them and those of you still alive will crawl to them to beg for a day's worth of rations in order to scratch out one more miserable day in your miserable lives. And what will happen then? Your new neighbors will not have to kill you because you will already be dead. They will let you lie where you fall and soon you will become a part of the earth from which our ancestors sprung many centuries ago. Over your remains will sprout the settlers' new towns, symbols of their prosperity at your expense. Your rotting flesh will nourish their fields and you will be forgotten forever, a mere speck upon the land you have forsaken."

Pontiac leaped into the crowd. He called upon fellow Ottawas to rise in protest against free settlement. They joined with other bands: Ojibwa, Potawatomi, Menominee, Saux Fox, and Shawnee. They marched in an unbroken queue within the tented enclosure. Reaching the dining tables, they paused to dine and drink and make speeches, but maintained a peaceful decorum overall. Sir William Johnson gave no signs of alarm. He summoned another speaker, one of more conciliatory comportment— one Tah:gah:jute—who mounted the platform in measured steps.

"Pontiac speaks of making war. It is a decision certain to cost lives that we are unable to sacrifice, my brothers. I propose the way of negotiation. I ask: What do we have that the white traders cherish? Furs and skins! I propose that we, namely the Seneca, govern the distribution of these materials at the principal point of trade: Niagara. To do so places the lands surrounding the great cataract, and the cataract itself, within Seneca hands. Under the terms of a treaty with the colonial governor, the Seneca shall charge a fee for the passage of all goods to all points east. The Seneca shall also have the authority to name the parties to be granted passage. This course I have determined holds several advantages for the native Seneca: For one, the regulation of trade will pass from Albany's tight grasp to the western frontier where it will be shared with Albany. Therefore, native bearers at Niagara will no longer be subject to Albany's practice of restraining trade. Second, native bearers at Niagara will be able to purchase either French or British goods with revenue earned from fees. In this manner they will acquire greater freedom of choice in making purchases. Next, inspectors based at Niagara will select only the freshest and most luxuriant furs and skins to place into trade, thus keeping standards in the trade high and open to scrutiny. I propose that forthcoming inspectors be jointly appointed by the colonial governor acting alone and by a Seneca council of sachems acting together. Fourth, and most important, the prices at which materials are placed into trade will be governed by supply and quality of the specimens, not by governmental decree. By these steps, all quarreling over price and quality will come to an end with all parties subject to a level playing field."

"All well and good, but the Seneca want war," a native shouted, rising. "Many have joined the Ottawas."

"There are two bands of Seneca," Tah:gah:jute reminded the speaker. "You speak of the western band. The eastern band is more docile. Their lands border the Cayuga who are also docile and have a strong influence over their strong western neighbor. We, the Cayuga, hold council with many Confederacy leaders. There are Red Jacket, Cornplanter, Handsome Lake Chief Blacksnake, and Fish Carrier, to begin. They all choose peaceful solutions to pressing matters. The alternative is war and the extermination of our species. The whites are able to replenish themselves much faster than we. Therefore, we as a People must learn to live within self-imposed boundaries of restraint.

"We have always sought coexistence with the whites," a chief rose to state. "They choose to confound our pleas for peace. They take our furs, give us a few articles for our villages, then go on to capture our lands, sending agents among us who deceive us into signing away our properties for a pittance. We long for Onontio's return."

"I know line and verse of these calumnies, dear brother. Unfortunately the face of Onontio in the visage of King Louis will never return. The British will have you believe that King George is your *new* Onontio. Meanwhile, King Louis has committed what remains of Onontio to fight new wars for him in a place called Europe.* I tell you this to give you the strength to unite behind my plan. All inhabitants to the north, south, east, and west must commit to it, to form a league to protect our interests. Remember!! A show of strength opens the door to negotiation." His voice hoarse, Tah:gah:jute deferred to Sir William Johnson.

Rising, the Superintendent of Indian Affairs strode leisurely to the speaker's platform. With the aid of an interpreter, he addressed the agitated crowd: "I wholeheartedly support our noble speaker, Tah:gah:jute. His words ring true. He has found a simple and direct path to peace in the Niagara proposals. We all know the principal combatants on the frontier who seem at eternal loggerheads. From this day forward I am willing to do my part to secure the peace. I have a proposal of my own design: I will empower British soldiers and cruisers to build protective trade corridors surrounding Forts Michilimackinac, Detroit, Niagara, and Oswego. They will guarantee the free and unobstructed flow of goods from the interior of this land through Niagara and to all points east. You, my brothers, will reap the benefits of this maneuver, for most of the lands are within your domain. Yes! You must unite behind Tah:gah:jute. Throw down the hatchet. Shake the hand of your enemy and you will know prosperity during your lifetime." Satisfied with his delivery, the Superintendent resumed his place beside Caroline and Suzanne.

A Huron chief rose. "For this design to succeed, a leader must be drawn from among the many nations present. He must be a chief and one held in high regard by all parties, red and white. He will sit in a central place where he will receive knowledge from all nations who bring forward goods-in-trade. He must insist upon strict adherence to the terms of distribution and sale agreed upon in the manner of Tah:gah:jute and hand out punishment when it is justified. This is a great task demanding a great and wise leader, selflessly devoted to his charge. I ask where such a leader may be found. If found, will he serve?"

Caroline stirred restlessly on her bed of reeds. Suddenly, as though propelled by fierce vapors, she jumped upright, casting aside her comforting blankets: "I have such a man!" she called to the chief.

All eyes fell upon her. A steady buzz of voices melding together erupted. Through the din the speaker called upon Caroline to name her candidate. Suzanne twisted with delight. Sir William sat impassively, knowing what must follow. Caroline stepped forward. Pausing, she waited for the voices to subside:

"I am proud to announce my choice of Hnyagwai-Hahsenowa:neh. He is the Bear Chief of the Gayogoho:no, known by several appellations, among them The Standing Bear and Fearless One." The assembled stirred.

"Some of you may have met him when he came west last fall with his more well-known cousin, Tah:gah:jute. Together they dwelt upon bringing peace to the middle regions. They held councils in villages from the land of the Iroquois to the plains of Illinois. He encouraged natives to resettle near Fort Detroit (102) in order to find shelter from attacks by the warlike western Seneca. This selfless act alone saved many natives from slaughter and their women and children from enslavement. He did this out of love for the human species.

The Bear Chief saved my life: He saved me from an evil predator lurking amid the British rank and file. He saved me from an evil officer seeking easy prey for the flesh markets so common along the Great Lakes. Yes! He exposed him and others of his cloth who purloined fair women and innocent children. He brought this predator before the proper authorities, removing him and his evil deeds from the frontier in a single coup. I am one of the survivors who escaped the predator's talons. Without the Bear Chief at my side, my labors on behalf of the women and children of Iroquoia must wait until the dawn of a new century to become fulfilled.

"A quiet man. A decisive man. A brave and selfless man, one who holds no rancor toward others. He is unknown to many— save for his family and loved ones. Yes! He is all of these qualities at once. Think of it! How rare! These qualities alone mark him a leader of men. He chooses not to speak of his accomplishments. In all humility I speak for him. By my oath I place the name of the Bear Chief in nomination for Inspector General of Trade Relations for the Middle Region." Her speech delivered, Caroline sat down, not knowing that she in effect created a post where none of its kind existed.

She hugged her daughter. A smile on her lips, Caroline waited for the translation to be given. During the interval, chiefs and warriors rose by twos and threes. At first sporadic applause greeted her. When the full translation became known, all seats in the assembly emptied at once. Applause broke out in a feverish pitch, leaving Caroline to shield her ears. Tah:gah:jute bid Caroline to acknowledge the crowd. Standing, blushing red, she waved and bowed before stealing back to Suzanne's side. In the next instant Superintendent Johnson rose. Stoically he approached the speaker's platform where he announced a brief respite in the proceedings. In the next breath he invited everyone to partake of the feast he prepared in the courtyard. Reeling about, following the spirited testimonial of the pale white woman, the delegates heaved onto the grounds where they dined and spoke with great animation. Caroline stood alone with Suzanne in observance of events. Superintendent Johnson stole beside her, wearing a smile of contentment.

"We find ourselves together once again, Madame," he spoke softly.

Nervously Caroline pulled at her skirts, convinced that something of consequence lay imminent. Suzanne drew apart from her. Dropping a weak excuse, she left her mother alone to face the Commissioner.

Sir William Johnson invited Caroline to walk with him as he spoke. "You know, Madame, that my labors take me to the far reaches of the colony—this land of lakes and extremes in hills and valleys. This comes as no surprise to you. I enjoy what I do. There are occasions when I literally see myself coming and going—when there are not enough hours in the day. I enlist the aid of assistants. Livingston and others are of great value, yet he and they are compromised by obligations closer to home, leaving me burdened once again with pressing matters demanding immediate attention. Of course, they have served without compensation. This may affect their tenure, yet all of them lack for want of intense dedication and zeal." Caroline met his eyes directly, delving into his thoughts.

"According to my sources, the people of the Confederacy are enamored of you. You have spent a year among them. During that period you have learned how to survive in the wilderness. You have formed lasting relationships and fought off detractors. You have established safe havens for the less fortunate. You do this with a tireless passion that knows no boundaries. You came from an arena of neglect and abuse—nameless, out of the shadows—to a position in which your counsel is sought by men of wealth and prominence. You have attained heights that I have yet to reach over my entire career." He pulled her chin up to meet his eyes.

"I need you to become my Deputy Commissioner of Indian Affairs. I have created it especially with you in mind. Its range is the length and breadth of the New York colony. There is no post of its kind in the Americas. It shall become as significant as you yourself are willing to make it. Your service is at my leisure, of course, but given our strong rapprochement, you may serve indefinitely. I have set aside funds for the post. Therefore, you will be amply compensated." He paused, waiting for his words to take root.

"This post has been expressly created for one of your dimensions. It is tailor-made to accommodate your person. Men will report to you. The Bear Chief, Tah:gah:jute, Cornelis Cuyler, they and more, will bear you knowledge of conditions in their respective bailiwicks. You, in turn, will make all necessary adaptations to improve their lot in the eyes of the Crown, for the greater good of the colony, of course. You have a keen ear and keen sense of your surroundings: the two most basic qualifications. You also need no introduction to your constituency. The post begs of you to take it. With these words, I beg of you to take it." Gripping Caroline's hand, the Superintendent dropped to one knee before her.

"How much of me do you know, Mi'Lord?" Caroline asked reservedly.

"I know much. It is in keeping with my duties on the frontier."

"It appears you have been tracking me."

"I first caught notice of you during the courts-martial at Oswego. I admire how you saved the career of Lord Carleton—absolving him of all blame in the capture of his soldiers at your Pointe Aux Bois. Very astute." Eyes sparkling, he smiled.

"Lord Carleton always conducted himself admirably. I offered him an acceptable solution."

"I say somewhat differently. You offered him a solution that he was unable to refuse. You recall that you used as security his own soldiers in bringing about the trial of your abductor."

"I will accept your version of the story at your leisure," Caroline returned, alert and self-assured.

"Your appropriation of a patron in the name of Cornelis Cuyler is a coup d'état. My neighbor, no less. Again, brilliant."

"Thank you," Caroline returned, in all humility.

"I must tell you that the singer—that little girl."

"Birdie?"

"Yes. Birdie. She is all-the-rage in Albany. The voice of an angel. I saw her sing in New York. Church enrollment has tripled." He tugged at her waistcoat. "Tell me. What became of that learned lad—Thomas?"

"Thomas Steed?" Smiling, Caroline tossed back her head. "He is studying to become a teacher. He is waiting for the day when Reverend Kirkland charters a university. He shall not wait long. For the present he is completing missionary studies with the Reverend, his mentor and tutor."

"Your laurels are many. Of course I may go on and on, but . . ."

"What of my schools? My family? "Caroline exclaimed, grasping the magnitude of her host's proposal.

"No cause for alarm. I am providing additional teachers where needs arise. I have also placed your schools within the purview of your new post and you are free to commiserate with your loved-ones at will."

"Provided that I am not beating a stubborn path through the forests," Caroline added, playfully sarcastic.

"I recalled that you enjoy travel. Do you have a sudden change of heart?"

"No. Not at all. The enormity of your proposal is almost overwhelming."

"You are not about to be cast adrift. Your supporters are everywhere. Fortunately, you have already cultivated strong ties in the region. I expect you to do well. Decided? Do you accept?"

"This is so unexpected. So breathtaking." Caroline summoned Suzanne to her side.

"Mother. Please take it. Then I will be able to visit with Birdie in Albany."

Caroline patted Suzanne's head. "Where shall I live? Somewhere? Everywhere?"

"A fair question. When in Albany, you have the run of my mansion. I am seldom in residence. In the central region there is the Round Tops of which you are fond. In the west there is Niagara. It has a staffed officers' quarters and full commissary since the British occupation."

"It is settled, then," Caroline merrily returned, half-believing her ears. "When shall I begin?"

"From the moment you reach Niagara. Allow me to brief you on developments afoot there."

—

The Commissioner directed Caroline to a remote corner of the grounds removed from human intercourse. Beside a spacious maple he halted and, facing her soberly, began a dour litany: "There is a great deal of smuggling taking place in and about Niagara. Traders and renegade natives are exporting rum, molasses, and more at inflated prices. This casts British commerce in a dim light and prepares the stage for the French to move in and undercut us. To add insult to injury, the slave trade prospers there. Youth taken from former French islands in the Caribbean are finding their way to Niagara and hence to Great Lakes forts and beyond. This surge in undocumented laborers undercuts the labors of current settlers engaged in the manufacturing and service trades. All of this must stop!!" He slapped a thigh in anger.

"Your trust is to scrupulously inspect Niagara—particularly the books of account. You will interview operations officers. You will walk among staff exercising your powers of observation. You will make periodic reports to my trusted aides. Tah:gah:jute is one of them. He will go later to Niagara, but you will remain apart from him. Your reports will flow to Albany where I will compare them with those of my own. Do not arrest corruption when you see it. You may be injured, or worse. Transfer to me all pertinent findings. Agreed?"

"So be it, Mi'Lord. The post is at once intriguing and honorable. Tell me. Do I have my own bureau? Do I wear a uniform?"

"Nothing of the sort. You will pass among the populace maintaining a discreet profile. You will be known as the administrative assistant to the governor. Do shades from the past come to light?"

"Why, yes. My past has prepared me for the present and beyond.'"

"I hoped to hear you make such a citation. Knowing this, the post is yours."

"I stand prepared, Commissioner."

"Settled. You may begin when you reach Niagara. Stay a fortnight, then go to your home at the Round Tops. Tah:gah:jute and your daughter will join you there. I too will receive the first of your reports there. Become reunited with your family. Your husband. You remember him, do you not?"

"Poor James. By now he has forsaken me."

"You will find that one's success often depends on the strength of one's family life. Do visit without fail."

—

Early the next morning Caroline departed Detroit with Tah:gah:jute, Fox Tail, and Cerf Courant: the little party bound for Niagara. Suzanne lingered with the Commissioner as his guest. Canoeing by day and night over calm waters, the sojourners reached the environs of Niagara on Saturday morning, August 9th. Caroline presented Sir William's letter of introduction to the forts' commandant. Short and concise, the letter gave her position as that of assistant to the governor without remuneration. She repaired immediately to her quarters for a much-deserved respite, rising later to attend the first of two dinners held for newcomers of stature. In the late afternoon she toured the buildings and grounds, not the least of which was the out-of-doors compound reserved for prisoners. Standing orders prohibited her from visiting the general lockup or cells.

She viewed in passing bands of prisoners congregating—all of them keeping a respectable distance from her. None dwelt upon her presence, save for one who incessantly pursued her with his eyes. The man appeared indistinguishable from his companions, yet when he walked, he leaned on a walking stick while limping on the right foot. Caroline pondered these features of the man and when she retired for the evening she lay restlessly in bed turning. At one moment she jumped upright, frozen in fear. Dripping in sweat, her lips pursed to utter a name long expunged from her lexicon: "My God! It is James Worthy."

Early the next morning Caroline set about her first day of duties. She visited storehouses, warehouses, granaries, the forge, and the counting house in which all books of account lay on shelves in tidy rows. She asked for and received the tallies from these sources, after which she made a manual count of all stores and provisions. Both sets of tallies agreed with each other and she breathed a breath of relief. The following day she adhered to the same regimen. Meeting with pertinent officers, she garnered results which corresponded with her own findings. A reservation, however, gnawed at her senses, and on the fifth day she varied her approach. Returning to the venues, she made note of the changes in quantities of hard and soft goods, well after the close of the official day. The books of account did not reflect these changes during her next review—nor for the remainder of the week. Truly, depletions in goods-on-hand had not been noted, the original tallies remaining artificially inflated. Caroline made a note in her log.

She spent a restless night without sleep. Her quarters lay below a spacious and vacant room above her, framed by a series of great bay windows fronting the Niagara River. On a clear night with the naked eye, one may capture the opposite bank and a good portion of the lake where it broke away from the beach and the postern wall of the fort. The coolness of the evening enthralled her. She entered the room, dimly aglow in tendrils of moonlight. She tarried indefinitely at the great windows. Gazing without, she spied silhouettes in motion stirring about the postern wall. Lightly they moved, gray shadows in the shimmering moonlight, living specters twisting and turning. They climbed atop each other, and, jumping and reaching and vaulting, they assumed human proportions, when suddenly a number of them mounted the wall and dropped over, leaving no sound nor trace. Other shapes emerged to ferret still other forms over the wall. Rushing below, Caroline wrote in her log, the visions of the bizarre events distressing her. Making detailed notes, she dashed into bed, falling asleep immediately. On the following evening she witnessed the same exercises. She told no one, relying on the moonlight to guide her, and wrote in her log. On the third evening, she grew disappointed upon seeing nothing of substance.

She confided in no one during her tour the following day. She visited the prisoners' compound where she made inquiry of the man with the stern gaze. She learned after persistent questioning that the man himself, together with a host of young native men, bolted the wall that previous evening—some willingly, some under duress. She longed to report her observations to the commandant, but desisted, for she knew not whom to trust. (It was the former commandant, she recalled, who secretly collaborated with her abductor to fabricate an excuse for his absence from duty at Oswego). By month's end, her little log held a wealth of knowledge for the fastidious Commissioner. She made a copy of it, and, secreting the original in her bosom, sent Cerf Courant off to the Round Tops to present it first hand to Sir William Johnson.

Later that morning Caroline took leave of the fort, citing the need to attend an urgent meeting with the Commissioner. Her departure aroused no suspicions among officers, knowledgeable as they were of the mercurial nature of her post. She thanked the commandant for his generosity, accepting a ride by stage as a parting measure of his appreciation. Fox Tail accompanied her, the remaining members of her retinue traveling by other means.

About midday of Saturday, August 30th, she arrived at the Round Tops to find a village at the height of celebration. The Corn Festival in full sway, Caroline walked the grounds of the village constantly bouncing from one pocket of congestion to the next. Originally she sought after Sir William Johnson with whom she longed to review her observation of events at Niagara. She crossed paths, however, with many of the principal players who comprised a small, select body of close friends. Shunning the spectacle of the games and the many sumptuous foods, she kept to herself. Repelling invitations to speak of her appointment, she seemed to be looking for solace amid a sea of gaiety.

From afar she spied the Bear Chief communing with Tah:gh:jute. The peacemaker bowed to her, yet she walked on. Colombe Blanche approached her. The Bear Chief's wife enticed her to hold the two glittering stones long a part of her regimen. Caroline gripped them, waiting until her hostess recited an oath of praise in her name, before moving on. She found Watkins and Fawn cuddling their newborn in a shady grove. They begged her to join them, but she walked on, driven by an innermost compulsion. She almost stumbled over Suzanne in an adjoining grove, deeply engrossed in conversation with Dana Smythe. Smiling, she rushed on ahead, turning to face Matthew and his wife, Dewai, who traveled a great distance to attend the festival. At her inquiry, Matthew pointed out the Commissioner's last known whereabouts, leaving Caroline to wind her way over a narrow, pebble-strewn path. Ahead, bent over a table beside one of Watkins' water towers, stood Sir William Johnson, pouring over pieces of correspondence and depositing them into every conceivable corner of the table. Looking up at Caroline's approach, he quoted most perfunctorily:

"Thank you for your messages. I see that we have much to occupy us in the coming months."

"Yes. You certainly do," she replied tersely, not pausing to elaborate.

She said nothing more. Picking up her skirts, she went whirling over the drumlins at a frenzied pace—the protective mother in search of her brood of offspring. She spun through packs of celebrants woven tightly together, voices lifted in song. She skirted the crowds gathered to watch the mock war dances. She passed by men and women dining at the banquet tables, paying little heed to those calling her by name. Revelers paraded before her, beckoning to her. She walked on, her pace accelerated. At length she came to rest before a lone elm, standing in the shadow of a drumlin overlooking her cabin. A tall, lithe figure stood next to the cabin whittling, a man, with his back to her. Seizing him by the shoulders, she spun him around, exclaiming in full voice:

"James! James! I am home to stay. We are a family again."

(95) Centolanzo, Brandy. Treating Disease: Colonists Relied On Natural Remedies to Cure Ailments. The Health Journal, 4808 Courthouse St., Suite 204, Williamsburg, VA (2008), pgs: 1-2

*The Owasco River where it crosses State Street in Auburn, NY

*State Street in Auburn, NY, where the Owasco River crosses beside the Auburn Correctional Facility

(96) Drew, Raymond Paul. Sir William Johnson, Indian Superintendent: Colonial Development and Expansionism: An Essay. The Early American Review, fall '96 (1996). vol 1. No. 2

(97)Anderson. *Amherst's Reforms and Pontiac's War* Chapter 56(2000), pgs: 535-541

*a large cask or barrel

(98) Streets of Early Albany: *City Streets*: New York State Department of Education, Albany, NY (2010), pgs:1-2

(99)Parker Area Tourism Committee: *General Eli Parker*, 1217 California Avenue, Parker AZ (2001) pgs: 1-4

*The Cayugas

**The Finger Lakes

(100)The Iroquois Constitution: *Rights, Duties and Qualifications of Lords* (2005) pg: 6

*Cayuga Lake

(101)Mohawk, John. War against the Seneca: The French Expedition of 1687. Published for the Ganondagan State Historic Site by the New York State Dept. of Parks, Recreation, and Historic Preservation. (2001) pgs: 1-16

*Referring to the alliance between Louis XV and Frederick William of Prussia in the Seven Years War.

(102)Taylor, Alan American Colonies: French America, 1650-1750. Chapter 16: *The Upper Country* pgs 376-381

EPILOGUE

Caroline spent the remainder of summer at the Round Tops surrounded by friends and loved-ones. The swift pace she set over the preceding year gave her reason to pause in order to refresh herself in mind and body. She longed to disassociate herself from the main stream of events long enough to interact with family members, most of whom communed with her up to this point only in passing. She regaled in her appointment under Sir William Johnson: To her it represented an opportunity to thrust before the colonial stratum the leadership qualities of women. She planned to expand upon that theme as long as Sir William exuded faith in her.

Her return to the Round Tops marked, among other matters, the betrothal of her daughter, Suzanne, with the dashing Captain Dana Smythe. They vowed to wed at the Round Tops, which held for Suzanne special memories, a place where her true home lay, she averred. Caroline too, in responding to her daughter, regarded the village as her home, but for a different reason. For her the village formed the basis for literally reaching out into the wilderness to lend a hand to those in search of a better quality of life.

She made preparations for the wedding: from setting aside a cabin for the newly-weds to having the last word on the list of invited guests. The young couple desired to reside initially at Fort Oswego where Dana expected to be elevated in rank following his valor in the *Courageous* affair. Matthew York, his steady friend and ally, although resigned from the British forces, divided his days between the Round Tops, where he drew closer to his father, and the family farm down on the

Susquehanna. There with Dewai, he set up permanent quarters in Charles Martin's main house, and administered to the lands in concert with a team of Friends and a delegation of Delaware.

Over the next several seasons the Round Tops prospered: Owing to Watkins' method of introducing crop rotation, the fertile slopes remained viable and refreshed with each planting season. Corn, known to deplete the soil, he removed to the far slopes, alternating it with members of the gourd family, such as pumpkins and squashes. The population of the village grew and James and Watkins found themselves building new cabins to the south and east, beyond the protective palisades. From a distance the Bear Chief kept a careful watch over these two developments. Speaking little, he harbored private thoughts, much a function of his character.

Caroline's school at the former Marchand mansion hummed with the patter of little feet as she welcomed native children to classes each day. Suzanne taught alongside her mother on those occasions when her husband James visited the village. Her visits usually coincided with the arrival of the Corn Festivals, of which there were several during the year. She took special interest in administering to Little Bear and Raven, along with Fawn. By the close of 1761 all three of her charges professed an above-average proficiency in English: reading, writing, and speaking, and looked for ways to demonstrate their new-found skills. Early-on English-speaking visitors to the village found themselves inundated with a swarm of words and expressions as the boys sought to engage all whom they met in conversation. Colombe Blanche stood delighted with the transition, which, for her proved her children's ability to adapt to new challenges. Her husband, the Bear Chief, reserved commenting publicly, yet insisted to his wife that the boys adhere to the native tongue when in formal settings.

Birdie wrote Suzanne frequently from Albany where early in 1762 she gained a permanent box in the Cuyler section of the Reformed Church at Saturday services. She sang regularly with the choir, becoming Maude Brambles' featured soloist. Maude brought the choristers to New York and Boston during Yuletide in a program designed to usher neonates into the Church. A success, two chapters opened in either city by year's end. Thomas Steed formed a strong correspondence with Birdie and visited her at the Cuyler mansion when Samuel Kirkland left Oneida to go book-purchasing in Albany. He departed often during any given year, prompted no less by his sagacious student. Thomas and Birdie, full of dash and spirit, made a fetching pair to passers-by on Albany streets. Some regarded them more as brother and sister, given the uniform character of their dress perhaps.

Early in 1763 word reached the Bear Chief of Pontiac's uprising in the Ohio country. Where earlier clashes with settlers turned inconsequential, this renewed series of attacks waxed prodigious with the sacking of a chain of British-held forts along the Great Lakes. Seneca emissaries beckoned to the Bear Chief to join Seneca war parties out west, but he respectfully declined to commit warriors, a reprise of his earlier stance. Sir William Johnson called Caroline back into the service of the Crown. They met at the mansion house and Caroline agreed to present the Commissioner's plans to the western Seneca at Kanandesaga, a town well-known to her, presided over by her friend, the Cornplanter. In Pennsylvania angry Seneca already destroyed several colonial forts and showed no signs of ceasing hostilities. Only a concerted British offensive in the Ohio country quelled the disturbances temporarily, but the natives remained restless in general. Sir William sought to evade all further conflicts by purchasing a north-to-south strip of Seneca lands near the Niagara cataract for the Crown.

Despite Johnson's proposal of lavish gifts to the natives, Caroline opposed Johnson's plan overall on the grounds that it would inflict irretrievable hardships upon the Confederacy to the extent of unauthorized inroads by settlers upon native lands. Nonetheless, she met with the Cornplanter, gaining his promise to defer sending warriors to Pontiac in return for her forestalling Johnson's plans until peace returned to the volatile regions. Reluctantly Johnson agreed to withdraw his offer until a more propitious moment arose, yet the two parted amicably, each wary of the demands of the other, and never again did Caroline trust Johnson implicitly.

Caroline presented the results of her meeting with Johnson to the Bear Chief where she still maintained residence. She never forgot the Bear Chief's hospitality in her time of need and believed that she owed him full disclosure. For the first time he confided in her that recent events prompted him to move the village to a different site: The burgeoning population, periodic bouts with drought, the prohibitive distance from a fast-moving stream, and now foreign entreaties, all weighed upon his thoughts. Caroline brought to his attention the vast tract near the Osco crossing about one and a half leagues due north of the village.* Bordered by two major Iroquois trails, it is there that bearers filled water pouches when the mosquito malady descended upon the Round Tops. She recalled to him when Cerf Courant reported favorably on the lay of the terrain, and how the swift-flowing Osco ran cool and clear. His aspect taciturn, the Bear Chief promised to consider the location following an inspection. The boys overheard him speaking and, eager for adventure, clamored that he take them and go soon. He yielded to their plaints, for he saw them as miniature images of himself at the same age and on the morrow father and sons and Cerf Courant and Fox Tail set out to reconnoiter the land at the Osco crossing.

Henri Marchand and his partner, Richard Clement paid an unexpected visit to the Round Tops late in 1763. Following the Treaty of Paris ending the French & Indian War, the two entrepreneurs saw the fur trade of Montreal pick up where it left off. They outfitted hunters and traders at their post who ventured off into Iroquoia in search of furs and skins, taking a share for themselves and turning a profit. Essentially they came to make inquiries of Iroquois chiefs concerning the status of fur-bearing animals along the St. Lawrence-Lake Ontario watershed. They met with mixed reviews along the way, but learned, in speaking with the Bear Chief, that beaver and deer thrived in abundance in the lands of the Cayuga and Seneca, but much to the contrary in the lands to the east. Where white settlements proliferated, beaver and deer populations appreciably declined, specifically where settlers regarded the species essential to both their diet and as a means to creating wealth. He suffered no such decline at the Round Tops he declared, for he practiced wildlife conservation, a procedure introduced by Watkins, the refugee whom he adopted into his extended family some years before.

Watkins, the Bear Chief recounted, established an animal sanctuary south of the Round Top's periphery shortly after arriving. There, laboring with James York and able native volunteers, he diverted a fresh-flowing stream into a lowland after clearing the surrounding land of swamp water and congestion. Animals visited the enclosure, shielded by trees and lush greenery and residents temporarily drew water from the clear lagoon which formed. Prized animals, such as beaver and deer, visited the sanctuary and astute village hunters took their fill periodically, never disturbing the overall natural balance. Other nations have need to follow the example set, the Bear Chief resolved, lest they acquire shortages, even stock depletions, in the long run.

Caroline and James met with Marchand and Clement, two friends and allies of note to whom she owed her very existence. She disclosed her special assignment at the behest of Sir William Johnson to the men, who paid her homage, invoking in the same breath the name of her late nemesis, Captain Worthy. The two merchants spewed forth effusively upon hearing the name of 'Worthy,' launching into an account which kindled Caroline's interest:

A *certain* outfitter, they noted, set up shop recently on the boulevard of commerce in Montreal, a stone's throw from their works. At first his stockpiles stood meager in comparison to their own; however, owing in part to the expanding market in furs in and about Montreal, the newcomer grew to rival them in trade.

They kept him under close scrutiny, comparing notes at day's end. The man exhibited familiar features in both manner and presence, and, although they never met with him, they delved into his history: He surfaced shortly after the prisoner breakout at Fort Niagara where coins placed in the proper hands effected the escape of several ne'er-do-wells. This they garnered from native fur-bearers who brought them stock from the western nations twice a year while trading at Niagara. Following the breakout, Commissioner Johnson removed the commandant and jailed two officers, leaning in part upon Caroline's reconnaissance. The guard doubled in force around the prisoners' block, leaving the matter to pass into oblivion until Marchand and Clement at Montreal did a bit of investigating: They sent a spy into the newcomer's shop in the guise of a tradesman. While making purchases, he keenly observed the newcomer, who called himself Damien La Chance. The man, slender, almost gaunt, spoke English and French, and flaunted a thick mane of blond hair tied in back. He boasted of out-of-doors adventures, yet presented a sallow, jaundiced complexion, indicative of one bereft of sunlight, such as befits one held in confinement. He walked with a noticeable, yet subdued limp, aided by a walking stick. The latter observation all but convinced Marchand of the man's true namesake. He hired an artist to sketch a likeness of the man on parchment, drawing from the spy's account. Unfolding it before Caroline, he displayed it with care.

Caroline studied the sketch, turning it from side to side. At length her eye caught the button loop high on the collar of the starched white shirt: 'Worthy faithfully wore the family's coat of arms in his lapel: a lion brandishing a cache of arrows in one paw. He wore it passionately wherever he went. He always wore the crest close to the flesh as though imbibing the lion's strength and ferocity.' The artist labored well, Caroline resolved. There, beneath the stern chin of the irascible Captain, sat the undeniable crest. She gave a start, catching her breath. In the next instant she laid plans to capture him in a single coup, beginning with sending a messenger off to Commissioner Johnson in Albany.

Capturing fugitives held a high priority for Commissioner Johnson. He longed to reduce the incidences of bribery in frontier prisons, having recently installed new and competent principal keepers throughout the penal system. He set up a snare for the newcomer, the subject of clandestine observation: A creature of habit, the newcomer took meals in a dining salon near his shop. One afternoon a cordon of the Crown's city guard surrounded him as he departed the eatery. Whisking him aboard a cruiser, they spirited him over the St. Lawrence, hence down Ontario's eastern flank to Fort Oswego where he found himself summarily incarcerated for an indefinite term. Not content with that locale, Caroline implored the Commissioner for a change of venue to the new compound at Albany. He acquiesced wholeheartedly, in as much as the institution lay on Jonkers Street, halfway between his mansion-house and Caroline's new two-story school. A stone's throw from the fort at Albany, the Captain found himself well-supervised on all sides.

In the spring of 1764 Caroline, James, and Suzanne paid a visit to the Reverend Kirkland at Oneida Castle. She came in part to learn of the progress of her school there. The young Steed taught side by side with his mentor and their combined efforts brought additional students forward from among the Oneida themselves and the small, white-populated hamlets of the countryside. For a considerable period the nation's school remained the sole establishment of higher learning in the region. Reverend Kirkland reiterated his passion for building a university. With a Skenando gift of additional lands, the Reverend began to clear away forest for primary construction—the first structure to be deemed the president's home. Caroline's hand-chosen teachers still applied themselves vigorously and she went about them soliciting the names of new prospects to staff the proposed university.

With few exceptions, Reverend Kirkland allowed Caroline a free hand in recruiting staff from among requests she made to prestigious allies in Albany and Boston and Providence. The entire process demanded much travel. Caroline wholeheartedly assumed the new role with gusto, often bringing James and Suzanne with her. In the wake of her recent successes on the frontier, the Commissioner looked with favor upon her and granted her a leave of six months with compensation.

While in Albany, the family met with Caroline's outstanding patron, the baron. He took the family on a tour of her new school and they observed classes in full swing, after which Caroline disclosed the nature of her visit. To her astonishment the fur baron anticipated her need and rendered her the names of a qualified list of new candidates which he and his wife assembled and set in reserve for her. Suzanne romped with Birdie who invited her to a concert in New York City in the fall of the year where she planned to give a solo surrounded by the choristers. Disappearing from view briefly, Birdie returned with two tickets for the event which she entrusted to her friend's safe keeping, extracting her promise to attend. In return Suzanne handed Birdie two embroidered cards bearing wedding invitations, leaving her friend speechless, yet buoyant at Suzanne's good fortune. Birdie blushed when she opened the second card containing Thomas Steed's name, for she believed until then that her prolific correspondence with the astute young man remained known only to the two of them.

In Boston and again in Providence, Caroline secured pledges from among several prominent Quaker families to deliver teachers to her schools. She enjoyed a special bond with the Friends, dating back to the days when she administered her uncle's farm. Several Friends' families lived bordering the holdings, and it is they who took over the reins of tending to the farm during her protracted absence. They offered to teach for mere food and clothing and insisted upon constructing their own residences on school grounds. The thought of nascent communities springing up around her schools delighted Caroline immensely and on her return to the Round Tops a burning thought literally kept her awake most nights.

Caroline met with the Bear Chief, reinforcing his original plan to move the village. She proposed that the swift and clear waters of the Osco on that same tract north of the Round Tops offered the most suitable grounds for a larger, more expansive village, owing to an observable truth: The land permitted unlimited growth in all directions. In due course the site may become the focal point of a village or town, a town open to all, wherein the intrinsic diversity of newcomers may lend to the growth and stability of the region. In her mind's eye Caroline envisioned a great transformation about to take place along the frontier, one in which she and others of her persuasion played a major role. The thought alone excited her to no end and her general enthusiasm spilled out upon everyone with whom she associated. The Bear Chief too shared in her vision, yet not without reservation. His greatest fear lay in becoming absorbed by a wave of immigration, bringing into play the loss of land and national integrity. She and the Bear Chief recognized that immigration brought for some natives advantages to the quality of life, but sowed the seeds of disintegration for others. They resolved to pay close heed to unfolding events about them and to maintain strong communications with each other in the coming months.

Beginning about 1765, the baron's grip upon the fur trade began to loosen. Albany no longer enjoyed the position of leading trade depot in the New York colony. Albany traders reluctantly yielded to competitors entering the scene in Montreal and the newly-arrived Oswego. There, tradesmen procured furs at lesser cost from Canada, transporting them cheaply over inland New York waterways. At the same time the fur industry witnessed a slow, yet certain decline: For one, consumer tastes changed in Europe. Connoisseurs turned to items made of broadcloth and felt, a new, composite fabric, particularly when the price of purchasing fur apparel rose dramatically. Broadcloth and felt cost less to prepare for sale, and this point alone opened a new market to factors who appealed to day laborers and their families, whose level of wages placed genuine furs beyond reach. Second, the decimation of beaver populations along the Great Lakes and Mississippi drove up the prices of those furs finding their way to Albany. Third, in the wake of Pontiac's rebellion, tradesmen and native hunters quarreled over establishing stable routes from the west to the east, resulting in delays of product delivery and higher prices for factors. Cuyler lamented his losses to Commissioner Johnson, seeking a hand in alleviating his plight. Sir William in turn summoned Caroline York.

The Commissioner knew well of Caroline's proximity to Lord Carleton: Her son, Matthew, stood high in the commandant's hierarchy of praise, chiefly because of demonstrated valor and ingenuity during the *Courageous* affair. Also, Matthew's bringing to bay the nefarious pirate **Black Jack**, thus precipitating the disintegration of a slave-ring involving some of his high command, championed a cause which pulled mightily at the commandant's heart strings. Lord Carleton's firm prosecution of the Captain on his home grounds further convinced Sir William that he sought to make of the frontier a civilized, if not revered place. This change in Lord Carleton's temperament, from one of palpable indifference to one of unbridled indulgence, came about after his association with Caroline began. Whatever powers Caroline wielded over the commandant in the scheme of things came as a mystery to Sir William, but he did not waste precious moments pondering it. He charged her to convince Lord Carleton to rescue the baron, and, indirectly the government in Albany as well, in as much as municipal coffers lay pitifully bare of the revenues needed to finance administrative operations.

The thought of meeting with Lord Carleton intrigued Caroline. At long last she may approach the opportunity to test the strength of her secret agreement with him. She planned to ask Lord Carleton to arrange for the transfer of furs to Albany by means of three significant waterways: the Oswego River, the Seneca River, and the Mohawk River— the routes which his own cargoes traveled— thus sparing fur barons such as Cornelis Cuyler the additional expense of going overland by coach. Caroline regarded her charge seriously: To be sure, the growth of her schools became possible through Cuyler donations. To come away from the meeting with anything less than Lord Carleton's blessing signaled the end to a noble experiment in education, opening her to chastisement from the Commissioner himself, who also invested heavily in her educational scheme.

Lord Carleton greeted her admirably. In the same breath he brought to her attention that whenever they chanced to meet something portentous lay in the wings. Caroline set forth her argument, prepared for her by none less than the Commissioner himself. Lord Carleton sat back to ponder: 'Granting the transfer meant sharing trading lanes with a competitor. To deny meant incurring the wrath of the Commissioner who carried great weight among the landed gentry driving Albany commerce.' In his mind's eye he feared losing his hard-won corner of the trade. He also feared alienating Caroline, who, in retaliation, may disclose their closely-kept secret to the Commissioner. (Yes, that Pointe Aux Bois debacle loomed omnipresent, in which he inadvertently allowed an obscure French force to rout and capture his contingent, led no less by an insidious, self-serving officer whose evil ways consistently eluded him). No! He sought to keep the peace. Not to ruffle feathers! Yield to the Commissioner's request. Drawing himself together, he composed a letter to Commissioner Johnson pledging full compliance. After inviting Caroline to dine with him and his wife, he sent her off merrily, the dispatch sealed in a case about her waist.

Carolyn conveyed the good tidings to Commissioner Johnson, meeting with him in his mansion on Albany's Jonkers Street. Meanwhile, she took the opportunity to welcome observations of conditions in her school, that tall, stoic edifice at the top of the hill. The Mohawk sent their children to the school, these same elders who constructed it and came to trust the pretty blonde woman with the winsome smile. Caroline in turn admitted both boys and girls to classes, drawing no distinction between the races. In some classes Mohawk children predominated.

When some white families complained about class composition, Caroline took immediate steps to alleviate the outbreak of conflict: She divided the classes racially, assigning teachers fluent in the Mohawk tongue to classes holding Mohawk children. The curriculum remained unmodified, however, the children of either race receiving the same rich and detailed instruction. The students came together during respites, lunches, and recreation, making of the total program a school within a school. Friendships formed and prospered, despite the separation of the races, and gradually a sizable body spoke openly of wanting to come together again, whereupon Caroline brought an equal number of white and native children together, rebuilding classes along a fifty-fifty split. The children sounded their satisfaction and the tedious and copious complaints ceased altogether.

The Mohawk rejoiced. Having scored what they deemed a victory, they soon sought to score again: Since the days of the Dutch occupation, the neighboring Mohawk sent traders into Albany to bargain with resident merchants. There the natives offered furs and skins which they extracted from surrounding forests, receiving goods and utensils in return and the occasional Dutch guilder honored in local shops and eateries. Albany lawmakers, fearful of native raids in the years leading up to the American Revolution, favored restricting all trading to daylight hours and balked at treating with the Mohawk's insistence of trading directly with local merchants. The Mohawk, accustomed to receiving the most value for their valued pelts by means of trading directly at merchant venues, stood outraged, and threatened to seek new avenues of intercourse further east. Moreover, the opening of the inland waterway route from Montreal to Albany threatened to kill the trade which local native tradesmen enjoyed with the likes of Cornelis Cuyler and other entrepreneurs.

Caroline viewed these latest developments as a threat to the funding of her network of schools, which not only drew sustenance from the fur trade but enrolled many Mohawk children. In several cases the native children composed the majority of students in attendance. She met with Commissioner Johnson and the baron, voicing the Mohawk's firm stand. Together, the three principals met with a multitude of residents at old Fort Frederick, the legislative rooms too limited to contain a great gathering. There, they hammered out an agreement in concert with active participants. The meeting lasted for hours and in the end all parties departed in satisfaction:

Resolved that the Mohawk may trade during daylight hours with selected merchants at selected venues in the city. They must enter free of arms and the influence of alcohol. They must restrict themselves to small parties and not linger idly by the wayside of shops and homes. They must not ask for quarter in homes nor occupy them. In return for following all rules of conduct, the Mohawk are to be fed wholesome foods at the discretion of the participating merchants and receive payment in either hard goods, coin, or both, the latter to be spent on additional hard goods. Finally, the Mohawk may not bargain for whiskey, and merchants are bound to offer quality-made items for trade.

This agreement went into effect almost immediately and continued intact up until the sudden demise of the Commissioner in 1774 during the early stages of the Revolutionary War. Until a new Commissioner may be found, Caroline insisted upon strict adherence to the passages of the Mohawk agreement, spending the final days of her waning career in Albany where she boarded with the Cuylers.

While affairs went along peacefully in the eastern Confederacy, the situation in the near west became strained. Following the Fort Stanwix Treaty of 1768, called by Sir William Johnson in which Caroline served as his delegate, the invasion of white settlers into lands reserved for the Shawnee and Delaware continued unabated. Moreover, certain Iroquois factions, western Seneca and Cayuga, refused to abandon the

Ohio country to which they fled, seeking shelter from white predations. Wherever lines of demarcation were crossed, clashes between incoming settlers and resident natives broke out. Caroline believed that, although well-intentioned, the treaty lacked the power of enforcement: She advocated the circulation of Crown soldiers in regions of tension, but many native leaders looked upon the British with enmity. Meanwhile, colonial militias refused to retaliate against fellow neighbors and nothing short of building a string of heavily-armed forts may have prevailed against white aggression. Financially, the latter route was out of the question and profound attacks on native encampments proliferated. Already in the Ohio country, Tah:gah:jute traveled to scenes of conflict, often bringing family members, in an effort to effect peace. On one such occasion in 1774, revenge-seeking soldiers of questionable virtue goaded several of Tah:jah:hute's clan with offers of food and drink, and, upon drawing them near, shot and killed most of them, leaving the remainder to perish. Tah:gah:jute went into a rage, and, despite the efforts of the Bear Chief and others to calm him, conducted a series of short-lived, yet brutal campaigns upon the aggressors where blood flowed freely.

The year 1774 marked a turning point in the history of the Haudenosaunee, torn as they became in choosing sides between the British and American colonials in the early battles which comprised the American Revolution. An active British command plied the stronger members of the Confederacy with gifts, provisions, and whiskey, while giving assurances of protecting them from greedy colonial land-grabbers. While a few Cayuga remained neutral, owing to the efforts of the Bear Chief, the more western-looking Cayuga joined with the warlike western Seneca who linked arms with the British. Eventually the Mohawk, long-allied with the late Commissioner, supported the British early in the fighting. The Oneida and Tuscarora, however, stood with the colonials, due in no small measure to Reverend Kirkland's success in bringing the native flock within the influence of the Presbyterian Church, where, during services they sat side by side with white colonials. The Cornplanter, on the other hand, allowed himself to be swayed by leading chiefs of the Confederacy and gradually fell into league with them, allowing British soldiers to occupy hallowed lands in return for offering protection against white inroads. Caroline took exception to his reasoning: She saw the rising conflict in terms of a clash of wills between a stated power: the British, and a rising voice in the wilderness: the colonials. The Cornplanter, she declared, saw the conflict in terms of a bargaining chip, i.e. exacting more lucrative trading privileges with the British who, he claimed, were more than a match for the clumsy colonials on the battle field. In village after village Caroline presented her point of view, but the die had already been cast among the chiefs and she spoke principally to deaf ears. With the Commissioner now deceased and the destiny of her auxiliary position cloudy under the young Guy Johnson, Caroline repaired in haste to the Round Tops where major events lay in the making.

Once arrived, she learned that the Bear Chief all but completed plans to move to the flats north of the village where the Osco ran cold and deep. The setting sat at the crossroads of two native trails* and a vast hunting range lay to the north interspersed with forests yielding multiple varieties of wild fruits, roots, and greens.** Laborers already constructed a row of palisades and plans lay imminent for a water tower under Watkins' guidance. In conferring with the Bear Chief, Cerf Courant offered that the inexhaustible water course at the site provided an irreplaceable opportunity to the villagers that must not be overlooked. This latter feature may have been the decisive factor in the Bear Chief's decision, although to Caroline he seemed most eager to forsake the Round Tops after learning of Tah:gah:jute's personal loss and own tragic death.

Reuniting with Colombe Blanche, Caroline learned that the boys, Raven and Little Bear, now young men, intended to enter the growing conflict between the British and colonials. Each brother chose to fight under a different banner: The more docile Raven joined with the British and his headstrong brother, Little Bear, supported the colonials. Colombe Blanche openly lamented losing her sons in battle. Caroline and Suzanne doggedly pursued her in an effort to soothe her qualms. The Bear Chief did not step forward to dissuade his sons. He respected their points of view and welcomed them to join him in the new village on the flats, rapidly taking shape.

When the battle at Saratoga erupted to begin the War of the Revolution, the boys found themselves facing each other on the field of battle. In the fight which took place over grassy fields and wooded terrain, the colonials routed the British in fierce fighting. They suffered significant losses to musket and ball. Raven came away alive, but wounded in the thigh. In the absence of a field medical team, he extricated the ball in much the same manner that James York treated with the wounded Watkins several years earlier— a maneuver he witnessed first-hand and committed to memory. With little loss of blood, he administered faithfully to the wound in camp, applying antiseptic and fresh wrappings daily. When the colonials dispersed following the engagement, he requested leave and received a short holiday, a not uncommon action, given the extent of the colonials' victory. He immediately departed for the flats and the open arms of his mother amid a host of welcoming villagers. Still a volunteer army at that point, the colonial forces depended upon willful enlistments, leaving a great deal of choice to the men themselves. This status changed with the growing intensity of the conflict, leaving many men, Raven among them, to lick their lips in eagerness to rejoin the ever-expanding fight.

Matthew York, meanwhile, formed a colonial militia. Headquartered at the York homestead along the Susquehanna, he received and drilled volunteers from among the neighboring populace. His success in recruitment and training led to a commission as a brigadier. He preferred the garb of the trail-blazer, shunning an ostentatious uniform, and led his men into engagements against Tory strongholds along the lower Hudson River valley. He learned of General Washington's plight at Valley Forge, where soldiers literally froze to death for want of blankets and provisions. In response he detailed a convoy from his home, that cold, forbidding winter of 1776, laden with supplies for the indomitable Washington, among them, snowshoes, mittens, and woolen caps and stockings. Little Bear's contingent traveled with the supply train and the two friends exchanged greetings before attending to more urgent matters. They did not meet again until arriving at the main camp at Valley Forge where they fortuitously encountered Washington himself administering to the sick and wounded. They spent but a short interval with Washington who asked for their points of origin and thanked them for intervening. Upon Matthew's insistence, Little Bear conferred upon the General his name and lineage, who, before moving on, grasped the young Cayuga's hand and vowed to remember him to the end of his days.

Closer to home, the tentacles of war spread to the environs of Fort Stanwix, where colonial defenders learned of a British plan to capture, if not burn it. Possession of the fort all but assured a British sweep of the lands in the heart of Iroquoia inhabited of late by enterprising colonials. Seneca and Mohawk warriors, assured of a British victory ripe with spoils, marched with them. Some of the more aggressive Cayuga marched also, despite the Bear Chief's pleas to the contrary. In a bold gesture, he dispatched Cerf Courant and Fox Tail to slip through the enemy camp and warn the fort's sentries. The mission successful, the colonials stepped up recruitment and handed the leadership of their force to one Nicholas Herkimer, gentleman farmer, whom the Tryon County lawmakers named 'General.' Cerf Courant and Fox Tail elected to march with the colonials and on a hot late summer's morning, General Herkimer's swelled ranks struck out due west from his homestead along the rolling hills beside the Mohawk to replenish the fort's manpower and to engage the enemy where threatened.

The British and their allies headed due east, investing the forest in the highlands along the Mohawk. Led by General Barry St. Leger, they anticipated attempts by the colonials to confront them and came prepared to employ stealth in order to precipitate an ambush in a venue yet to be determined. The colonials, young and undisciplined for the most part, new to warfare, much less a skirmish, marched blindly, yet fearlessly, into the unknown. St. Leger counted on them to bolt the fight and run away, following a robust broadside. The Bear Chief's two scouts, however, knew well of the landscape, and struggled ceaselessly to keep the force together in a compact defile, avoiding low-lying ravines strung with thick underbrush in which men may become divorced from the main body.

They almost succeeded, save for a surge of colonials from the rear who ran forward, pushing the main column needlessly together, propelling it into a ravine. The narrow passageway restricted the men's progress, while one-by-one more colonials poured into it from the rear with the objective of surfacing en masse some one hundred meters beyond. They never made it. A flood of screaming savages swooped down upon them, trapping the colonials within the ravine, into which they poured musket shot and flights of arrows. Gaining the upper hand early, the savages descended into the ravine, subjecting the panic-stricken colonials to deadly thrusts from the bayonet and war hatchet. General Herkimer, ever vigilant, succeeded in allaying the annihilation of his force: He stationed a newly-arrived cadre of volunteers on a gentle rise at the ravine's outlet, allowing the trapped colonials to exit. The natives and Tories, aware of the maneuver, attacked in a rush from the woodlands. Surrounding their quarry, they bore into them mercilessly and the slope shone red with blood. For one brief moment the colonials broke loose and, assuming higher ground, set up a defensive corridor where they engaged the enemy in mortal hand-to-hand combat. Many on both sides fell— General Herkimer and Fox Tail among them. For those at Osco flats, Fox Tail's death came as a harsh blow: During heavy fighting, he turned to lead a fallen Cayuga warrior to safety, only to see him rise up against him, call him traitorous oaths and stab him in the chest. Counting their losses, the hostile natives abandoned the field, fleeing into the forest, granting the tattered volunteers a Pyrrhic victory. Beaten, but not broken, the colonials repaired to Fort Stanwix, which remained in colonial hands over the duration of the American Revolution, the British never making another attempt to capture the heartland of the New York colony.

The growing intensity of the conflict, now termed a war, began to weigh heavily upon Suzanne. Although she longed to wed her beloved Smythe, she knew that he remained true to the British standard: making her the wife of a British officer who owed his livelihood to serving his king wherever George III may send him. Nonetheless, she hoped to live with her husband at the family homestead along the Susquehanna, sharing the grounds with Matthew and his wife, Dewai, in anticipation of building a home there near the principal mansion. Events often do not conform to one's plans however, and while Dana spent endless weeks in the Crown's service patrolling the St. Lawrence where it joined with Lake Ontario, Matthew transformed the mansion and outbuildings into staffed mercantile posts, supplying the material needs of Washington's army along the lower Hudson.

With Dana more at home leading an officer's life at Fort Oswego, Suzanne, grew steadily apart from him and also from the members of her family, scattered as they had become throughout the colony. In Dana's absence, she filled her days teaching alongside her mother in the new wooden school* Caroline opened on a hill directly across from the flats— the new Osco. During idle moments, she penned letters to Dana, reaffirming her love and fidelity. Posting them at the school, the letters traveled by stage directly overland to Fort Oswego over a broad, dusty lane,* formerly the native trail over which she and her father walked when first seeking the Bear Chief's village those several years ago.

For the most part her letters went unanswered. She refused to heed her mother's counsel that the consuming war had molded a great breech into her relationship with Dana, bringing to the fore the inherent differences between her sense of values and those of the military. Where Suzanne savored family and a tightly-knit home and community, Dana sought honor in the form of male camaraderie, sustained by exploits of valor, Caroline explained.

Deeply saddened by Dana's indifference, Suzanne wrote to Lord Carleton, the former commandant, now a successful landowner in the blossoming Oswego community. Although a state of war existed between Great Britain and the colonials, Lord Carleton agreed to seek after her letters. He found them in the new commandant's anteroom, trussed into a tight bond and awaiting dispatch, provided that Dana establish a residence near a postal route. This condition did not come to pass, for Dana, entrusted with reconnaissance on Lakes Ontario and Erie, rarely set foot on shore. The war wore on and Suzanne cast him out of her heart, but not out of her mind, awaking many mornings in her cabin at the Osco flats with his image burning brightly before her eyes, immaculate in the sterling white tunic of a fleet commander— the day before he walked out of her life forever.

Little Bear, fighting for the colonials, survived several close brushes with death. Binding his wounds, he came to the Osco flats to convalesce whenever he received formal leave. On those occasions he sought Suzanne's company, confiding to her innermost thoughts on the conduct of the war. She changed his wrappings and cleaned his wounds. Tending to him reverently, she served him proper nourishment and sent him off again in a clean change of clothing. Colombe Blanche labored diligently beside her, the two of them making of his visits a subsequent homecoming to which he eagerly looked forward. He and Suzanne went for walks together. They visited her mother's new school in which Little Bear for a short period became a student once again. He reveled over the beef stews she prepared whenever he came to the village. They drew close, spiritually and physically, relaxing in each other's light embrace. She read to him evenings by candlelight. They reminisced about the days of their youth at the former Osco where he unveiled to her the myriad wonders of the forest mere steps from her lodgings: he, the wily junior woodsman, and she, the curious maiden.

One morning in school Little Bear stood before the class to conduct the daily reading session. He chose Hannibal's march on Rome, taken from an ancient text and translated into English. He no sooner began when the class door opened to admit a young man who secured a position in the rear of the room. Standing tall in a white tunic, with arms folded before him, he emitted an air of confidence mixed with arrogance. Standing beside Little Bear, Suzanne gave a shriek and swooned, falling into his arms. Regaining her bearings, Suzanne met the stranger's gaze directly. Suspending the lecture, she guided the young man to a corner where they conversed briefly, after which Suzanne pulled violently at her finger from which she dislodged a golden ring. In the next instant she held the stranger's palm open into which she deposited it, before tossing back her head and resuming her place at Little Bear's side. The young officer betrayed no emotion. Pocketing the bauble, he turned crisply on his heel and departed the classroom. Suzanne never brought the incident to the attention of others, nor did she dwell upon it with Little Bear who did not press her for details.

With the conflict winding down with respect to the New York colony, Suzanne accepted Little Bear's proposal of marriage. They wed in the small chapel to the rear of Caroline's schoolhouse one sunny day in April, 1782, a ceremony attended by Caroline and James York, the Bear Chief and Colombe Blanche and all principal members of their extended families. Following the ceremony, the proud couple repaired to a new cabin which Watkins had prepared and furnished for them— his method of paying homage to the newlyweds. When Matthew York and Dewai arrived two weeks later, in defiance of Washington's ban on traveling, Suzanne and her spouse promptly conducted the ceremony once again, in this instance throwing a celebration lasting well into the evening.

Caroline's string of schools across the colony survived the war, yet with the Treaty of Paris signed in 1783, formally ending the great conflict, the face of the lands surrounding Osco flats changed appreciably. In sum, the victorious colonials accepted rewards of land across the breadth of the New York colony, sites vacated by the British-seeking Iroquois, particularly Seneca and Cayuga. These latter members of the once-indomitable Confederacy fled in 1779, offering little resistance, before a yearling army of farmers which Washington assembled to punish them for having conducted murderous raids on white homesteads. All around the former Round Tops and the current Osco flats, native communities were put to the torch and countless stores of provisions destroyed, yet the Round Tops and Osco flats were spared Washington's wrath, some say, due to a *certain* Cayuga presence at Valley Forge one wintry day in 1776.

The Bear Chief, once at liberty to visit neighboring villages at will, began to chafe within the small pocket of isolation in which Osco flats lay. To the east his closest ally remained Skenando at Oneida. To the west he needed to travel the considerable distance to Niagara to commiserate with those Seneca and Cayuga who camped about the fort, guests of the British, and living lives of subsistence. On a broad hill east of the flats, the first of Dutch settlers came to claim lands promised as a result of the spoils of war. He withdrew inwardly, just as Caroline reached out to the newcomers. She took the Dutch children into her school, also white children and black servants alike, teaching them grammar, mathematics, penmanship, and ciphering— all the rudiments of a free, not-for-hire education. About 1793, where the Osco took a great turn below the flats, a Dutchman built a grist mill, where, for a fee, he ground the grains of wheat-growing farmers. A community began to take root,* It spread down a great hill, skirted the swamp at its base, and struck directly north, dotting the landscape along the northern trail with homes and shops and surrounding Caroline's school— all within sight of the new Osco.

In council after council the Bear Chief urged village members to welcome the influx of new arrivals, but during an extraordinary session, he lost his position of leadership to a committee of upstarts, young men who chose to join fellow Cayuga and Seneca at Niagara. While his village dissolved before his eyes, he sought refuge with Caroline, who resided nearby with James and Suzanne and her husband, Little Bear, in the house which Watkins built for Suzanne's wedding. When a great conclave of chiefs met at Canandaigua in 1794 to petition delegates of the newly-founded United States to return Iroquois lands, Caroline agreed to represent the Bear Chief's interests, he being too stressed to attend. Proudly Caroline went to the conference, meeting among others, two old friends, Mary Jemison and the Cornplanter. On the surface the chiefs and the delegates from Washington practiced strict decorum, but behind the scenes the chiefs fought among themselves, settling for small parcels of land and selling off great portions for mere pennies on the dollar. Caroline and Mary Jemison, although women, railed at the chiefs, but the tacit leader, the Cornplanter, proved of lesser stature, his role having diminished among peers. In the end, many Cayuga moved to Ontario. Others settled on a parcel encapsulating the head of Cayuga Lake, only to sell it to the new State of New York a few years later. A saddened Bear Chief moved to the village of Canoga where he boarded with the Cayuga chief Fish Carrier until the latter's death. Caroline, although saddened by the loss of her staunch ally, embraced the new community which formed around the abandoned Osco, and, standing tall with James at her side, became the premier hostess in the region, whose door stood open to all.

Caroline turned over the reins of her school to a headmaster in 1804, a Mr. Phelps**, appointed by the new Cayuga county legislature. She continued to teach in the old mansion, offering classes to young women, one of the first institutions of its kind for women in New York State. Through its portals young graduates went out to choose from among the budding professions open to women. A spry age 74, Caroline kept the school until James died suddenly from progressive respiratory failure. She sold the mansion and school to a ministerial body—one that vowed to preserve her methodologies. Watkins, distraught over James's loss, departed the vicinity. Settling in the hamlet of Cayuga, he joined a firm building fishing boats for residents on Lake Cayuga and helped Fawn raise their five children. Caroline departed the region to live with Matthew and other family members on the former Charles Martin farm along the Susquehanna. Raven went with her in order to be with his brother, Little Bear, Suzanne's husband. There she proudly performed the duties of 'sitter' for Matthew's three children, sharing responsibilities with Dewai whom she adored.

Caroline passed away in 1814 at the age of 84, of infirmities associated with advanced age. Shortly before her demise, she attended a celebration at Fort Oswego in celebration of the end of the War of 1812 in which one of her grandsons fought. It was her final public function. Matthew brought her to the former Charles Martin estate by coach, now under his name. There she lay beside James, her husband, in a single grave marked by a simple stone in accordance with her wishes.

Looking back on her life, Caroline counted her schools as her greatest achievement. The little seeds of knowledge that she planted those years ago blossomed into vibrant communities, each of them holding a school nestled amid fertile pockets of manufacturing and farming along a river corridor running east and west in upper New York State. Opportunities abounded for young men and women of 'letters.' Many of them in future generations became nationally recognized for contributions to law, medicine, science, and theology. Not all progress moved smoothly. Women and other segments of the new, multi-faceted culture still faced inherent obstructionism, yet, as epochs came and went, even these barriers began to melt away. Caroline did not live long enough to see the long-terms effects of her labors upon the American scene. Coming generations would know little of her, yet the effects of her achievements lived on. Present in spirit in the hearts of latter-day descendants, she would be most proud to learn that she played a major role in what de Tocqueville and 19th century scholars came to call: the American Experiment.

01/17/14

*site of Auburn State Prison

*State & Wall Streets, Auburn, NY

**the region bounded by York Street, going north in Auburn, NY

*One of the first schoolhouses in what became Auburn, NY near the grounds of Holy Family Church

*North Street, Auburn, NY, one of the principal roads of a village later to develop into Auburn, NY.

*the beginnings of Auburn, NY, then called Hardenbergh Corners

**Reportedly the first schoolmaster in Cayuga County.

BIBLIOGRAPHY

Books

Abler, Thomas.(2007) Cornplanter: *Chief Warrior of the Allegheny Senecas*. Syracuse University Press. Syracuse, NY.

Anderson, Fred(2000) *The Crucible of War*. Vintage Books: Random House, New York.

Anderson, Fred & Stephenson, Scott R. (2005) *The War That Made America* Viking-Penguin Group, New York.

Ayling, Stanley. (1976) *The Elder Pitt*. David Me Kay Co., New York.

Borneman, Walter R. (2000) *The French & Indian War*. Harper/Collins Publishers. 10 East 53rd St., New York,.

Brasseau, Carl A. (1987) *The Founding of New Acadia: The Beginnings of Acadian Life in Louisiana*, Louisiana State University Press, Baton Rouge.

Cooper, Leo (1995) *Seneca Indian Stories*. The Greenfield Review Press. Greenfield Center, NY

Daniel, Angela L. "Silver Star" (2007) *The True Story of Pocahontas: The Other Side Of History*. Fulcrum, Golden, CO.

Grant, Mc Vicar Annie(1846) *Memoirs of an American Lady: Arrival At Oswego.* D. Appleton & Co. New York,.

Hamilton, Milton W. (1976) *Sir William Johnson: Colonial American, 1715-1786* Kennikat Press. Port Washington, NY.

Kent, Timothy J. (2004) *Rendezvous at the Straits: Slavery During The Fur Trade Years.* Silver Fox Industries. Wayne State University, Detroit, MI.

Kimm. S.C.(l900) *The Iroquois: A History of the Six Nations of New York.* Press of Pierre W. Danforth., The Home. Middleburg, NY

Merrill, Arch (1951) *Slim Fingers Beckon.* Heart of the Finger Lakes Publishing. Interlaken, NY

Moses, W. 1.(1853) *Handbook of Fort Hill Cemetery.* Fort Hill Association Board of Trustees. Auburn, NY.

Norton, Thomas Elliott (1974) *The Fur Trade In Colonial New York: 1686-1776.* The University of Wisconsin Press. Madison.

Parker, Arthur C. (1926) *An Analytical History of the Seneca Indians.* The Time Presses. Canandaigua, NY..

Parkman, Francis (1880) Count Frontenac and New France Under Louis XIV. Little Brown & Co., Boston & New York.

Tanner, Helen H. (1987) *Atlas of Great Lakes Indian History: Inter-Colonial Warfare.* University of Oklahoma Press, Norman.

Taylor, Alan & Foner, Eric (2012) *American Colonies: French America, 1650-1750.* The Penguin Group. New York

Taylor, Colon F. & Strutevanr, William C.(2002) *The Native Americans: The Indigenous People of North America* Salamander Books. London.

Tebbell, John(1948). *The Battle for North America*: From The Works of Francis Parkman. Doubleday & Company, Garden City, NY

Van Schaack, Henry (1892) *Memoirs of the Life of Henry Van Schaack.* Mc Clurg & Co., Chicago.

Van Sickle-Wait Mary & Heidt, Jr., William (1966) *The Story of the Cayugas: 1609-1809.* De Witt Historical Society of Tompkins County, Inc., Ithaca, NY

Wait, Mary Van Sickle (1967) *The Story of the Cayugas.* De Witt Historical Society of Tompkins County, Ithaca, NY.

Williams, C. L.(1955) *Topical Review of World History.* Topical Review Book Co., 131 North St., Auburn, NY.

Articles & Essays

Alexander, Robert 8.(1988) Albany's First Church: And Its Role in the Growth of the City: 1642-1942. *New York History, January, 1999, 5-28.*

Bielinski, Stefan (1991). The New Netherland Dutch: Settling In and Spreading Out in Colonial Albany. (Edited by Jean E. Hunter & Paul T. Mason,) Pittsburg.. *The American Family: Historical Perspectives* 23 pgs.

Bielinski, Stefan (2010) *From Outpost to Entrepot: The Birth of Urban Albany,* 1686-1776. New York State Education Department.

Callison, James P. (1999) *The Iroquois Constitution: The Great Binding Law.* The University of Oklahoma. Norman.

Centolanzo, Brandy (2008) Treating Diseases: Colonists Relied On Natural Remedies To Cure Ailments. *The Health Journal.* 4808 Courthouse St., Suite 204, Williamsburg, VA.

Chase, Franklin H. (1903) Chronological Index of Onondaga History in the Documentary History of the State of New York. March 2, 1903. *Syracuse Journal*

Clark, Joshua (1849) Onondaga, Or, Reminiscences of Later and Older Times. Stoddard & Babcock, Syracuse., NY.

Drew, Raymond Paul(1996) Sir William Johnson, Indian Superintendent. Colonial Development and Expansionism. An Essay. *The Early American Review* (Fall Issue).

Falkner. Julie (2011). Molly Brant, Loyalist-Mohawk. *History's Women.* A Division of PC Publications, 22 Williams St., Batavia, NY 14020

Huey, Paul R. (1988) comprehensive narrative on Fort Frederick. Aspects of continuity and change in colonial Dutch material culture at fort orange. University of Pennsylvania. *PhD Dissertation ...*

Lamb, Martha (2007) *The Magazine of American History With Notes & Queries.* Kessinger Publishing Company

Livingston, Melvin (2009)Descendants of the Signers of the Declaration of Independence. *State Education Department*, Albany, NY..

Mohawk, John (2001) War Against The Seneca: The French Expedition of 1687. Published for the Ganondagan State Historical Site by the *New York State Department of Parks and Recreation*

Munson, Lilian Steele(1969) *Shades of Oakwood. Early. History of Syracuse.* Pageant Press International, pgs: 1-8.

Selkreg, John H. (1894) Landmarks of Tompkins County, New York. D. Mason & Co., Ithaca, NY.

Taft, Grace E. (1913) *Cayuga Notes. Chapter I.* Antiquarian Publishing Co., Benton Harbor, MI

On-Line Sources

Albany City Hall (2010). New York State Education Department. *www. nysm.nysed.gov/albany*

Cayuga Indian Tribe History (2005) *www.accessgenealogy.com/native/tribes/cayugahist*

City Hall (2010) New York State Museum. *State Education Department.* Albany, NY

City Streets (2010) New York State Museum. *State Education Department.* Albany, NY

Chief Logan (2009) *Friends of the Frontier.org.* Pgs: 1-9.

Clinton Historical Society (2009) *Samuel Kirkland (1741-1898) Missionary to the Iroquois.*

Fort Ponchartrain du Detroit (2009) *Wikipedia.com*

General Eli Samuel Parker (2011) *Parker Area Tourism Committee,* Parker, AZ.

Goiogouen (2005). Wikipedia: The Free Encyclopedia. *The Wikimedia Foundation.*

History of the French and Indian War. Part IV. (2006) *http://web.svr.edu.*

Liverpool History (2009) Liverpool Public Library. *www.lpl.org.*

Livingston., P. (201 0) Descendants of the Signers of the Declaration of Independence. *www.DSDI1776.com/Signers*

Samuel Kirkland: (2009) Biography of Samuel Kirkland.. *Answers.com*

Streets of Early Albany: City Streets (2010). *New York State Department of Education.* Albany, NY

The Colonial Albany Social History Project (2010) The People of Colonial Albany: A Community History Project ... *State Education Department.* Albany, NY

The Commissioners of Indian Affairs (2010) New York State Museum. *State Education Department.* Albany, NY

The First Church in Albany (2010). New York State Museum. *State Education Department*, Albany, NY.

William Penn, Proprietor (2009) *xroads.virginia.edu/CAP/PENN*